GREAT
GHOST
STORIES

GREAT GHOST STORIES

Selected by the Editors of Reader's Digest

The Reader's Digest Association Limited
LONDON SYDNEY AUCKLAND MONTREAL CAPE TOWN HONG KONG

FIRST EDITION 1997
Reprinted 1998, 1999, 2000

Published by The Reader's Digest Association Limited
11 Westferry Circus, Canary Wharf, London E14 4HE.

The stories in this volume are used by permission of and
special arrangement with the holders of the respective copyrights.
(For further information see pages 527–8.)

Cover image: © Robert Wheeler/Tony Stone Images.

© 1997 by The Reader's Digest Association Limited
© 1997 by Reader's Digest (Australia) Pty Limited
© 1997 by Reader's Digest (New Zealand) Limited
© 1997 by The Reader's Digest Association (Canada) Limited
© 1997 by The Reader's Digest Association South Africa (Pty) Limited
© 1997 by The Reader's Digest Association Far East Limited

ISBN 0-276-42330-5

Reader's Digest, The Digest and the Pegasus logo
are registered trademarks of The Reader's Digest Association, Inc.

Origination by Rodney Howe Limited
Printed and bound by
The Bath Press, Bath

Contents

Introduction

There's something about a good ghost story that gives it almost universal appeal. There's nothing quite like the delicious shudder, the raising of the hair on the back of the neck, the tiny adrenaline-surge that a really terrifying tale provokes. For some people it's simply the pleasure of reading an engrossing story well told, while for others it's the vicarious thrill of enjoying a frightening experience safe in the knowledge that it is, after all, only a story. If you do enjoy a ghostly tale, then this is the volume for you. It's bursting with ghosts of every sort: evil ghosts, pathetic ghosts, ravening ghosts, sighing ghosts that speak in half-heard whispers; corner-of-the eye ghosts that you never quite see, and ghosts that you see all too clearly . . .

Ghosts, evil spirits and mysterious presences have cropped up in myths and legends around the world since time immemorial. However it wasn't until the nineteenth century that fictional ghost stories became popular. The heyday of the genre was probably the mid-Victorian era, when the repeal of the newspaper tax in 1855 and the spread of literacy had helped to create a boom in magazine publishing. Shilling monthlies came along, with special Christmas numbers in which ghost stories had pride of place. Charles Dickens edited several periodical magazines, and through the success of the Christmas editions of his magazines he was, to a great extent, responsible for popularising the festive connection with the supernatural—one Christmas number of a magazine Dickens launched in 1859 sold an amazing quarter of a million copies. Needless to say he also wrote a few ghost stories himself, such as *No. 1 Branch Line, The Signalman*, the fine example chosen for this anthology.

Many of the great nineteenth-century writers tried their hands at ghost stories, even those who were triumphantly successful in other fields. The brilliant American writer Henry James, renowned for novels that examine the psychological subtleties of relationships, put those same skills to good use in several excellent tales of the macabre. This is particularly true of the one chosen for this collection, *The*

9

Romance of Certain Old Clothes, a chilling look at sibling rivalry that extends to beyond the grave. Edith Nesbit, who is popular today for her charming classic *The Railway Children*, wrote several sinister tales including the thoroughly bone-chilling *Man-Size in Marble*. Rudyard Kipling, who made his name in the late nineteenth and early twentieth centuries with novels, poems and short stories about life in colonial India, wrote several sinister tales. We have selected *The Phantom Rickshaw*, a bitter-sweet tale of unrequited love.

We have also tracked down a number of fine stories by authors who were very popular during the late nineteenth century, but who are less well known now. Such authors include Rhoda Broughton, whose story, *The Truth, the Whole Truth and Nothing but the Truth* manages to be both chilling and witty; Bithia Mary Croker, who strays into Kipling's territory with her tale of a haunted house in India; and Tom Hood with his unforgettably creepy tale *The Shadow of a Shade*. One find from the Edwardian era is William Hope Hodgson, whose highly popular psychic investigator, Carnacki, tries to trap ghosts through scientific methods.

Most of the stories chosen for this collection are by authors writing in English, but we also have a few translated stories such as Emile Zola's only known ghost story, *Angeline, or the Haunted House*, and Alexander Pushkin's classic *The Queen of Spades*. This was first published in 1834 and is the earliest story selected for this volume.

Several of the authors included saw writing ghost stories as an interesting test of their talent—could they succeed with such a difficult and elusive genre? Writers such as Robert Louis Stevenson and Bram Stoker were more interested in the supernatural as a subject in itself, but for others the exploration of the dark corners of the mind became an obsession. This was especially the case with Edgar Allan Poe, whose fictional horrors were obviously real to him, but were in fact terrifying products of his drug-crazed imagination. Similarly, when the famous French author Guy de Maupassant described a haunting, he was surely describing a real presence in his mind as well as his obsessive fear of the encroaching madness that eventually would destroy him.

Many of the stories in this volume were written by authors who specialised in the genre, and it was these writers who firmly established ghost stories in the public's imagination. A typical example is Joseph Sheridan le Fanu, one of *the* great ghost-story writers, whose work did much to popularise the form. His story *Schalken the Painter* was first published back in 1839 and has continued to terrify readers ever since. Later on came the American writer Ambrose Bierce and also the incomparable M. R. James, whose collection *Ghost Stories of an Antiquary*, published in 1904, firmly established him as one of the master storytellers.

The early twentieth century was rich in ghost-story writers, and we feel we have selected the best: Algernon Blackwood, H. Russell Wakefield, A. M. Burrage, Holloway Horn and the distinguished ghost-story anthologist and writer Cynthia Asquith. The novelist and poet Walter de la Mare also wrote a number of powerful ghost stories during this period including his nightmarish *Seaton's Aunt*—about a young boy terrorised by an evil presence—which forms part of this collection.

The Second World War, like the First, provided the inspiration for a number of powerful ghost stories, many of which now have a slightly dated feel because of their strongly patriotic fervour. However, in the post-war period the ghost story seems to be enjoying a revival. There was a time, soon after the war, when our society showed signs of becoming so sensible and scientific that interest in the supernatural was in danger of simply withering away. But it never happened. The universal interest in life after death continues whether it is seen in films, television, plays or books and both ghost and horror stories still hold a fascination. Stories involving ghosts are like dreams: they take their authors and their readers beyond the safe boundaries of ordinary existence. They feed on deep-buried memories and they open secret doors to the imagination.

The ghost stories written after the war are set against the familiar background of the modern age, and it is this familiarity that makes them all the more plausible and frightening. There are ghosts linked to car accidents in stories by Ray Bradbury and Elizabeth Walter, to a piece of furniture in one by Alison Lurie, and even to a cruising holiday on Britain's canals, surely the most innocent of pastimes, in a tale by Elizabeth Jane Howard. Marghanita Laski subjects us to a mysterious and sinister attack of vertigo, and the lift in L. P. Hartley's building has a thoroughly unexpected passenger. Fay Weldon's poltergeist is clearly a feminist at heart and A. S. Byatt's ghost in a London summer garden moves us less to terror than to tears. There's even a chilling story by Frederick Forsyth, an author who few people associate with ghost stories, which springs from his days as a National Service pilot.

On the whole it is the darker side of human existence that prevails in this collection, and rightly so, for that is where the great tradition of ghost-story writing is at its richest. Not all the stories are so dark, however, for the Canadian author Robertson Davies brings us refreshing touches of humour, as does Oscar Wilde in his charming story *The Canterville Ghost*. Lord Dunsany offers a gently nostalgic cricketing tale and Ann Bridge tells a wry, tragi-comic story of a diplomat's wife and a less than diplomatic assignation.

This collection has been put together during the course of many months by a number of editors—all ghost-story enthusiasts. We read hundreds of stories and carefully weighed up their individual merits. Inevitably we had our differences of opinion but, in the end, we settled on this final selection with surprising unanimity. The result, we believe, is a volume of highly original and extremely readable supernatural tales. We hope you will think so too.

The Editors

Robert Aickman

1914–1981

Winner of a World Fantasy Award for short fiction in the decade before his death, Robert Aickman was a master ghost-story writer and an editor of great distinction. Much of his work, however, has gone surprisingly unrecognised by the general reading public, so we are particularly pleased to be able to offer this story, a gem of creepily atmospheric writing.

RINGING THE CHANGES

H E HAD NEVER BEEN AMONG those many who deeply dislike church bells, but the ringing that evening at Holihaven changed his view. Bells could certainly get on one's nerves, he felt, although he had only just arrived in the town.

He had been too well aware of the perils attendant upon marrying a girl twenty-four years younger than himself to add to them by a conventional honeymoon. The strange force of Phrynne's love had borne both of them away from their previous selves: in him a formerly haphazard and easy-going approach to life had been replaced by much deep planning to wall in happiness; and she, though once thought cold and choosy, would now agree to anything as long as she was with him. He had said that if they were to marry in June, it would be at the cost of not being able to honeymoon until October. Had they been courting longer, he had explained, gravely smiling, special arrangements could have been made; but, as it was, business claimed him. This, indeed, was true, because his business position was less influential than he had led Phrynne to believe. Finally, it would have been impossible for them to have courted longer, because they had courted from the day they met, which was less than six weeks before the day they married.

"'A village',' he had quoted as they entered the branch-line train at the junction (itself sufficiently remote), "'from which (it was said) persons of sufficient longevity might hope to reach Liverpool Street.'" By now he was able to make jokes about age, although perhaps he did so rather too often.

'Who said that?'

'Bertrand Russell.'

She had looked at him with her big eyes in her tiny face.

'Really.' He had smiled confirmation.

'I'm not arguing.' She had still been looking at him. The romantic gaslight in the charming period compartment had left him uncertain whether she was smiling back or not. He had given himself the benefit of the doubt, and kissed her.

The guard had blown his whistle and they had rumbled out into the darkness. The branch line swung so sharply away from the main line that Phrynne had been almost toppled from her seat.

'Why do we go so slowly when it's so flat?'

'Because the engineer laid the line up and down the hills and valleys such as they are, instead of cutting through and embanking over them.' He liked being able to inform her.

'How do you know? Gerald! You said you hadn't been to Holihaven before.'

'It applies to most of the railways in East Anglia.'

'So that even though it's flatter, it's slower?'

'Time matters less.'

'I should have hated going to a place where time mattered or that you'd been to before. You'd have had nothing to remember me by.'

He hadn't been quite sure that her words exactly expressed her thoughts, but the thought had lightened his heart.

HOLIHAVEN STATION could hardly have been built in the days of the town's magnificence, for they were in the Middle Ages; but it still implied grander functions than came its way now. The platforms were long enough for visiting London expresses, which had since gone elsewhere; and the architecture of the waiting rooms would have been not insufficient for occasional use by Foreign Royalty. Oil lamps, on perches like those occupied by macaws, lighted the uniformed staff, who numbered two and, together with every native of Holihaven, looked like storm-habituated mariners.

The stationmaster and porter, as Gerald took them to be, watched him approach down the platform, with a heavy suitcase in each hand and Phrynne walking deliciously by his side. He saw one of them address a remark to the other, but neither offered to help. Gerald had to put down the cases in order to give up their tickets. The other passengers had already disappeared.

'Where's the Bell?'

Gerald had found the hotel in a reference book. It was the only one allotted to Holihaven. But as Gerald spoke, and before the ticket collector could answer, the sudden deep note of an actual bell rang through the darkness. Phrynne caught hold of Gerald's sleeve.

Ignoring Gerald, the stationmaster, if such he was, turned to his colleague. 'They're starting early.'

'Every reason to be in good time,' said the other man. The stationmaster nodded, and put Gerald's tickets indifferently in his jacket pocket.

'Can you please tell me how I get to the Bell Hotel?'

The stationmaster's attention returned to him. 'Have you a room booked?'

'Certainly.'

'Tonight?' The stationmaster looked inappropriately suspicious.

'Of course.'

Again the stationmaster looked at the other man.

'It's them Pascoes.'

'Yes,' said Gerald. 'That's the name. Pascoe.'

'We don't use the Bell,' explained the stationmaster. 'But you'll find it in Wrack Street.' He gesticulated vaguely and unhelpfully. 'Straight ahead. Down Station Road. Then down Wrack Street. You can't miss it.'

'Thank you.'

As soon as they entered the town, the big bell began to boom regularly.

'What narrow streets!' said Phrynne.

'They follow the lines of the medieval city. Before the river silted up, Holihaven was one of the most important seaports in Great Britain.'

'Where's everybody got to?'

Although it was only six o'clock, the place certainly seemed deserted.

'Where's the hotel got to?' rejoined Gerald.

'Poor Gerald! Let me help.' She laid her hand beside his on the handle of the suitcase nearest to her, but as she was about fifteen inches shorter than he, she could be of little assistance. They must already have gone more than a quarter of a mile. 'Do you think we're in the right street?'

'Most unlikely, I should say. But there's no one to ask.'

'Must be early-closing day.'

The single deep notes of the bell were now coming more frequently.

'Why are they ringing that bell? Is it a funeral?'

'Bit late for a funeral.'

She looked at him a little anxiously.

'Anyway, it's not cold.'

'Considering we're on the east coast it's quite astonishingly warm.'

'Not that I care.'

'I hope that bell isn't going to ring all night.'

She pulled on the suitcase. His arms were in any case almost parting from his body. 'Look! We've passed it.'

They stopped, and he looked back. 'How could we have done that?'

'Well, we have.'

She was right. He could see a big ornamental bell hanging from a bracket attached to a house about a hundred yards behind them.

They retraced their steps and entered the hotel. A woman dressed in a navy blue coat and skirt, with a good figure but dyed red hair and a face ridged with make-up, advanced upon them.

'Mr and Mrs Banstead? I'm Hilda Pascoe. Don, my husband, isn't very well.'

Gerald felt full of doubts. His arrangements were not going as they should. Never rely on guidebook recommendations. The trouble lay partly in Phrynne's insistence that they go somewhere he did not know. 'I'm sorry to hear that,' he said.

'You know what men are like when they're ill?' Mrs Pascoe, spoke understandingly to Phrynne.

'Impossible,' said Phrynne. 'Or very difficult.'

'Talk about "Woman in our hours of ease".'

'Yes,' said Phrynne. 'What's the trouble?'

'It's always been the same trouble with Don,' said Mrs Pascoe, then checked herself. 'It's his stomach,' she said. 'Ever since he was a kid, Don's had trouble with the lining of his stomach.'

Gerald interrupted. 'I wonder if we could see our rooms?'

'So sorry,' said Mrs Pascoe. 'Will you register first?' She produced a battered volume bound in peeling imitation leather. 'Just the name and address.' She spoke as if Gerald might contribute a résumé of his life.

It was the first time he and Phrynne had ever registered in a hotel; but his confidence in the place was not increased by the long period which had passed since the registration above.

'We're always quiet in October,' remarked Mrs Pascoe, her eyes upon him. Gerald noticed that her eyes were slightly bloodshot. 'Except sometimes for the bars, of course.'

'We wanted to come out of the season,' said Phrynne soothingly.

'Quite,' said Mrs Pascoe.

'Are we alone in the house?' enquired Gerald. After all, the woman was probably doing her best.

'Except for Commandant Shotcroft. You won't mind him, will you? He's a regular.'

'I'm sure we shan't,' said Phrynne.

'People say the house wouldn't be the same without Commandant Shotcroft.'

'I see.'

'What's that bell?' asked Gerald. Apart from anything else, it really was much too near.

Mrs Pascoe looked away. He thought she looked shifty under her entrenched make-up. But she only said, 'Practice.'

'Do you mean there will be more of them later?'

She nodded. 'But never mind,' she said encouragingly. 'Let me show you to your room. Sorry there's no porter.'

Before they had reached the bedroom, the whole peal had commenced.

'Is this the quietest room you have?' enquired Gerald. 'What about the other side of the house?'

'This *is* the other side of the house. Saint Guthlac's is over there.' She pointed out through the bedroom door.

'Darling,' said Phrynne, her hand on Gerald's arm, 'they'll soon stop. They're only practising.'

Mrs Pascoe said nothing. Her expression indicated that she was one of those people whose friendliness has a precise and never exceeded limit.

'If *you* don't mind,' said Gerald to Phrynne, hesitating.

'They have ways of their own in Holihaven,' said Mrs Pascoe. Her undertone of militancy implied, among other things, that if Gerald and Phrynne chose to leave, they were at liberty to do so. Gerald did not care for that either: her attitude would have been different, he felt, had there been anywhere else for them to go. The bells were making him touchy and irritable.

'It's a very pretty room,' said Phrynne. 'I adore four-posters.'

'Thank you,' said Gerald to Mrs Pascoe. 'What time's dinner?'

'Seven thirty. You've time for a drink in the bar first.'

She went.

'We certainly have,' said Gerald when the door was shut. 'It's only just six.'

'Actually,' said Phrynne, who was standing by the window looking down into the street, 'I *like* church bells.'

'All very well,' said Gerald, 'but on one's honeymoon they distract the attention.'

'Not mine,' said Phrynne simply. Then she added, 'There's still no one about.'

'I expect they're all in the bar.'

'I don't want a drink. I want to explore the town.'

'As you wish. But hadn't you better unpack?'

'I ought to, but I'm not going to. Not until after I've seen the sea.' Such small shows of independence in her enchanted Gerald.

Mrs Pascoe was not about when they passed through the lounge, nor was there any sound of activity in the establishment.

Outside, the bells seemed to be booming and bounding over their heads.

'It's like warriors fighting in the sky,' shouted Phrynne. 'Do you think the sea's down there?' She indicated the direction from which they had previously retraced their steps.

'I imagine so. The street seems to end in nothing. That would be the sea.'

'Come on. Let's run.' She was off, before he could even think about it. Then there was nothing to do but run after her. He hoped there were not eyes behind blinds.

She stopped, and held wide her arms to catch him. The top of her head hardly came up to his chin. He knew she was silently indicating that his failure to keep up with her was not a matter for self-consciousness.

'Isn't it beautiful?'

'The sea?' There was no moon; and little was discernible beyond the end of the street.

'Not only.'

'Everything but the sea. The sea's invisible.'

'You can smell it.'

'I certainly can't hear it.'

She slackened her embrace and cocked her head away from him.

'The bells echo so much, it's as if there were two churches.'

'I'm sure there are more than that. There always are in old towns like this.' Suddenly he was struck by the significance of his words in relation to what she had said. He shrank into himself, tautly listening.

'Yes,' cried Phrynne delightedly. 'It *is* another church.'

'Impossible,' said Gerald. 'Two churches wouldn't have practice ringing on the same night.'

'I'm quite sure. I can hear one lot of bells with my left ear, and another lot with my right.'

They had still seen no one. The sparse gaslights fell on the furnishings of a stone quay, small but plainly in regular use.

'The whole population must be ringing the bells.' His own remark discomfited Gerald.

'Good for them,' she took his hand. 'Let's go down on the beach and look for the sea.'

They descended a flight of stone steps at which the sea had sucked and bitten. The beach was as stony as the steps, but lumpier.

'We'll just go straight on,' said Phrynne. 'Until we find it.'

Left to himself, Gerald would have been less keen. The stones were very large and very slippery, and his eyes did not seem to be becoming accustomed to the dark.

'You're right, Phrynne, about the smell.'

'Honest sea smell.'

'Just as you say.' He took it rather to be the smell of dense rotting weed; across which he supposed they must be slithering. It was not a smell he had previously encountered in such strength.

Energy could hardly be spared for thinking, and advancing hand in hand was impossible.

After various random remarks on both sides and the lapse of what seemed a very long time, Phrynne spoke again. 'Gerald, where is it? What sort of seaport is it that has no sea?'

She continued onwards, but Gerald stopped and looked back. He had thought the distance they had gone overlong, but was startled to see how great it was. The darkness was doubtless deceitful, but the few lights on the quay appeared as on a distant horizon.

The far glimmering specks still in his eyes, he turned and looked after

Phrynne. He could barely see her. Perhaps she was progressing faster without him.

'Phrynne! Darling!'

Unexpectedly she gave a sharp cry.

'Phrynne!'

She did not answer.

'Phrynne!'

Then she spoke more or less calmly. 'Panic over. Sorry, darling. I stood on something.'

He realised that a panic it had indeed been; at least in him.

'You're all right?'

'Think so.'

He struggled up to her. 'The smell's worse than ever.' It was overpowering.

'I think it's coming from what I stepped on. My foot went right in, and then there was the smell.'

'I've never known anything like it.'

'Sorry, darling,' she said, gently mocking him. 'Let's go away.'

'Let's go back. Don't you think?'

'Yes,' said Phrynne. 'But I must warn you I'm very disappointed. I think that seaside attractions should include the sea.'

He noticed that as they retreated, she was scraping the sides of one shoe against the stones, as if trying to clean it.

'I think the whole place is a disappointment,' he said. 'I really must apologise. We'll go somewhere else.'

'I like the bells,' she replied, making a careful reservation.

Gerald said nothing.

'I don't want to go somewhere where you've been before.'

The bells rang out over the desolate unattractive beach. Now the sound seemed to be coming from every point along the shore.

'I suppose all the churches practise on the same night in order to get it over with,' said Gerald.

'They do it in order to see which can ring the loudest,' said Phrynne.

'Take care you don't twist your ankle.'

The din as they reached the rough little quay was such as to suggest that Phrynne's idea was literally true.

THE COFFEE ROOM was so low that Gerald had to dip beneath a sequence of thick beams.

'Why "Coffee Room"?' asked Phrynne, looking at the words on the door. 'I saw a notice that coffee will only be served in the lounge.'

'It's the *lucus a non lucendo* principle.'

'That explains everything. I wonder where we sit.' A single electric lantern, mass-produced in an antique pattern, had been turned on. The bulb was of that limited wattage which is peculiar to hotels. It did little to penetrate the shadows.

'The *lucus a non lucendo* principle is the principle of calling white black.'

'Not at all,' said a voice from the darkness. 'On the contrary. The word black comes from an ancient root which means "to bleach".'

They had thought themselves alone, but now saw a small man seated by himself at an unlighted corner table. In the darkness he looked like a monkey. 'I stand corrected,' said Gerald. They sat at the table under the lantern.

The man in the corner spoke again. 'Why are you here at all?'

Phrynne looked frightened, but Gerald replied quietly, 'We're on holiday. We prefer it out of the season. I presume you are Commandant Shotcroft?'

'No need to presume.' Unexpectedly the Commandant switched on the antique lantern which was nearest to him. His table was littered with a finished meal. It struck Gerald that he must have switched off the light when he heard them approach the Coffee Room. 'I'm going anyway.'

'Are we late?' asked Phrynne, always the assuager of situations.

'No, you're not late,' called the Commandant in a deep, moody voice. 'My meals are prepared half an hour before the time the rest come in. I don't like eating in company.' He had risen to his feet. 'So perhaps you'll excuse me.'

Without troubling about an answer, he stepped quickly out of the Coffee Room. He had cropped white hair; tragic, heavy-lidded eyes; and a round face which was yellow and lined.

A second later his head reappeared round the door.

'Ring,' he said; and again withdrew.

'Too many other people ringing,' said Gerald. 'But I don't see what else we can do.'

The Coffee Room bell, however, made a noise like a fire alarm.

Mrs Pascoe appeared. She looked considerably the worse for drink.

'Didn't see you in the bar.'

'Must have missed us in the crowd,' said Gerald amiably.

'Crowd?' enquired Mrs Pascoe drunkenly. Then, after a difficult pause, she offered them a handwritten menu.

They ordered; and Mrs Pascoe served them throughout. Gerald was apprehensive lest her indisposition increase during the course of the meal; but her insobriety, like her affability, seemed to have an exact and definite limit.

'All things considered, the food might be worse,' remarked Gerald, towards the end. It was a relief that something was going reasonably well. 'Not much of it, but at least the dishes are hot.'

When Phrynne translated this into a compliment to the cook, Mrs Pascoe said, 'I cooked it all myself, although I shouldn't be the one to say so.'

Gerald felt really surprised that she was in a condition to have accomplished this. Possibly, he reflected with alarm, she had had much practice under similar conditions.

'Coffee is served in the lounge,' said Mrs Pascoe.

They withdrew. In a corner of the lounge was a screen decorated with winning Elizabethan ladies in ruffs and hoops. From behind it, projected a pair of small black boots. Phrynne nudged Gerald and pointed to them. Gerald nodded. They felt themselves constrained to talk about things which bored them.

The hotel was old and its walls thick. In the empty lounge the noise of the bells would not prevent conversation being overheard, but still came from all around, as if the hotel were a fortress beleaguered by surrounding artillery.

After their second cups of coffee, Gerald suddenly said he couldn't stand it.

'Darling, it's not doing us any harm. I think it's rather cosy.' Phrynne subsided into the wooden chair with its sloping back and long mud-coloured mock-velvet cushions; and opened her pretty legs to the fire.

'Every church in the town must be ringing its bells. It's been going on for two and a half hours and they never seem to take the usual breathers.'

'We wouldn't hear. Because of all the other bells ringing. I think it's nice of them to ring the bells for us.'

Nothing further was said for several minutes. Gerald was beginning to realise that they had yet to evolve a holiday routine.

'I'll get you a drink. What shall it be?'

'Anything you like. Whatever *you* have.' Phrynne was immersed in female enjoyment of the fire's radiance on her body.

Gerald missed this, and said, 'I don't quite see why they have to keep the place like a hothouse. When I come back, we'll sit somewhere else.'

'Men wear too many clothes, darling,' said Phrynne drowsily.

Contrary to his assumptions, Gerald found the lounge bar as empty as everywhere else in the hotel and the town. There was not even a person to dispense.

Somewhat irritably Gerald struck a brass bell which stood on the counter. It rang out sharply as a pistol shot.

Mrs Pascoe appeared at a door among the shelves. She had taken off her jacket, and her make-up had begun to run.

'A cognac, please. Double. And a Kummel.'

Mrs Pascoe's hands were shaking so much that she could not get the cork out of the brandy bottle.

'Allow me.' Gerald stretched his arm across the bar.

Mrs Pascoe stared at him blearily. 'OK. But I must pour it.'

Gerald extracted the cork and returned the bottle. Mrs Pascoe slopped a far from precise dose into a balloon.

Catastrophe followed. Unable to return the bottle to the high shelf where it resided, Mrs Pascoe placed it on a waist-level ledge. Reaching for the alembic of Kummel, she swept the three-quarters-full brandy bottle on to the tiled floor. The stuffy air became fogged with the fumes of brandy from behind the bar.

At the door from which Mrs Pascoe had emerged appeared a man from the inner room. Though still youngish, he was puce and puffy, and in his braces, with no collar. Streaks of sandy hair laced his vast red scalp. Liquor oozed all over him, as if from a perished gourd. Gerald took it that this was Don.

The man was too drunk to articulate. He stood in the doorway, clinging with each red hand to the ledge, and savagely struggling to flay his wife with imprecations.

'How much?' said Gerald to Mrs Pascoe. It seemed useless to try for the Kummel. The hotel must have another bar.

'Three and six,' said Mrs Pascoe, quite lucidly; but Gerald saw that she was about to weep.

He had the exact sum. She turned her back on him and flicked the cash register. As she returned from it, he heard the fragmentation of glass as she stepped on a piece of the broken bottle. Gerald looked at her husband out of the corner of his eye. The sagging, loose-mouthed figure made him shudder. Something moved him.

'I'm sorry about the accident,' he said to Mrs Pascoe. He held the balloon in one hand, and was just going.

Mrs Pascoe looked at him. The slow tears of desperation were edging down her face, but she now seemed quite sober. 'Mr Banstead,' she said in a flat, hurried voice. 'May I come and sit with you and your wife in the lounge? Just for a few minutes.'

'Of course.' It was certainly not what he wanted, and he wondered what would become of the bar, but he felt unexpectedly sorry for her, and it was impossible to say No.

To reach the flap of the bar, she had to pass her husband. Gerald saw her hesitate for a second; then she advanced resolutely and steadily, and looking straight before her. If the man had let go with his hands, he would have fallen; but as she passed him, he released a great gob of spit. He was far too incapable to aim, and it fell on the side of his own trousers. Gerald lifted the flap for Mrs Pascoe and stood back to let her precede him from the bar. As he followed her, he heard her husband maundering off into unintelligible inward searchings.

'The Kummel!' said Mrs Pascoe, remembering in the doorway.

'Never mind,' said Gerald. 'Perhaps I could try one of the other bars?'

'Not tonight. They're shut. I'd better go back.'

'No. We'll think of something else.' It was not yet nine o'clock, and Gerald wondered about the Licensing Justices.

But in the lounge was another unexpected scene. Mrs Pascoe stopped as soon as they entered, and Gerald, caught between two imitation-leather armchairs, looked over her shoulder.

Phrynne had fallen asleep. Her head was slightly on one side, but her mouth was shut, and her body no more than gracefully relaxed, so that she looked most beautiful, and, Gerald thought, a trifle unearthly, like a dead girl in an early picture by Millais.

The quality of her beauty seemed also to have impressed Commandant

Shotcroft; for he was standing silently behind her and looking down at her, his sad face transfigured. Gerald noticed that a leaf of the pseudo-Elizabethan screen had been folded back, revealing a small cretonne-covered chair, with an open tome face downward in its seat.

'Won't you join us?' said Gerald boldly. There was that in the Commandant's face which boded no hurt. 'Can I get you a drink?'

The Commandant did not turn his head, and for a moment seemed unable to speak. Then in a low voice he said, 'For a moment only.'

'Good,' said Gerald. ' Sit down. And you, Mrs Pascoe.' Mrs Pascoe was dabbing at her face. Gerald addressed the Commandant. 'What shall it be?'

'Nothing to drink,' said the Commandant in the same low mutter. It occurred to Gerald that if Phrynne awoke, the Commandant would go.

'What about you?' Gerald looked at Mrs Pascoe, earnestly hoping she would decline.

'No, thanks.' She was glancing at the Commandant. Clearly she had not expected him to be there.

Phrynne being asleep, Gerald sat down too. He sipped his brandy. It was impossible to romanticise the action with a toast.

The events in the bar had made him forget about the bells. Now, as they sat silently round the sleeping Phrynne, the tide of sound swept over him once more.

'You mustn't think,' said Mrs Pascoe, 'that he's always like that.' They all spoke in hushed voices. All of them seemed to have reason to do so. The Commandant was again gazing sombrely at Phrynne's beauty.

'Of course not.' But it was hard to believe.

'The licensed business puts temptations in a man's way.'

'It must be very difficult.'

'We ought never to have come here. We were happy in South Norwood.'

'You must do good business during the season.'

'Two months,' said Mrs Pascoe bitterly, but still softly. 'Two and a half at the very most. The people who come during the season have no idea what goes on out of it.'

'What made you leave South Norwood?'

'Don's stomach. The doctor said the air would do him good.'

'Speaking of that, doesn't the sea go too far out? We went down on the beach before dinner, but couldn't see it anywhere.'

On the other side of the fire, the Commandant turned his eyes from Phrynne and looked at Gerald.

'I wouldn't know,' said Mrs Pascoe. 'I never have time to look from one year's end to the other.' It was a customary enough answer, but Gerald felt that it did not disclose the whole truth. He noticed that Mrs Pascoe glanced uneasily at the Commandant, who by now was staring neither at Phrynne nor at Gerald but at the toppling citadels in the fire.

'And now I must get on with my work,' continued Mrs Pascoe. 'I only came in for a minute.' She looked Gerald in the face. 'Thank you,' she said, and rose.

'Please stay a little longer,' said Gerald. 'Wait till my wife wakes up.' As he spoke, Phrynne slightly shifted.

'Can't be done,' said Mrs Pascoe, her lips smiling. Gerald noticed that all the time she was watching the Commandant from under her lids, and knew that, were he not there, she would have stayed.

As it was, she went. 'I'll probably see you later to say good night. Sorry the water's not very hot. It's having no porter.'

The bells showed no sign of flagging.

When Mrs Pascoe had closed the door, the Commandant spoke.

'He was a fine man once. Don't think otherwise.'

'You mean Pascoe?'

The Commandant nodded seriously.

'Not my type,' said Gerald.

'DSO and bar. DFC and bar.'

'And now bar only. Why?'

'You heard what she said. It was a lie. They didn't leave South Norwood for the sea air.'

'So I supposed.'

'He got into trouble. He was fixed. He wasn't the kind of man to know about human nature and all its rottenness.'

'A pity,' said Gerald. 'But perhaps, even so, this isn't the best place for him?'

'It's the worst,' said the Commandant, a dark flame in his eyes. 'For him or anyone else.'

Again Phrynne shifted in her sleep, this time more convulsively, so that she nearly woke. For some reason the two men remained speechless and motionless until she was again breathing steadily. Against the silence within, the bells sounded louder than ever. It was as if the tumult were tearing holes in the roof.

'It's certainly a very noisy place,' said Gerald, still in an undertone.

'Why did you have to come tonight of all nights?' The Commandant spoke in the same undertone, but his vehemence was extreme.

'This doesn't happen often?'

'Once every year.'

'They should have told us.'

'They don't usually accept bookings. They've no right to accept them. When Pascoe was in charge they never did.'

'I expect that Mrs Pascoe felt they were in no position to turn away business.'

'It's not a matter that should be left to a woman.'

'Not much alternative surely?'

'At heart, women are creatures of darkness all the time.' The Commandant's seriousness and bitterness left Gerald without a reply.

'My wife doesn't mind the bells,' he said after a moment. 'In fact she rather likes them.' The Commandant really was converting a nuisance, though an acute one, into a melodrama.

The Commandant turned and gazed at him. It struck Gerald that what he had just said in some way, for the Commandant, placed Phrynne also into a category of the lost.

'Take her away, man,' said the Commandant, with scornful ferocity.

'In a day or two perhaps,' said Gerald, patiently polite. 'I admit that we are disappointed with Holihaven.'

'Now. While there's still time. This *instant*.'

There was an intensity of conviction about the Commandant which was alarming.

Gerald considered. Even the empty lounge, with its dreary decorations and commonplace furniture, seemed inimical. 'They can hardly go on practising all night,' he said. But now it was fear that hushed his voice.

'Practising!' The Commandant's scorn flickered coldly through the over-heated room.

'What else?'

'They're ringing to wake the dead.'

A tremor of wind in the flue momentarily drew on the already roaring fire. Gerald had turned very pale.

'That's a figure of speech,' he said, hardly to be heard.

'Not in Holihaven.' The Commandant's gaze had returned to the fire.

Gerald looked at Phrynne. She was breathing less heavily. His voice dropped to a whisper. 'What happens?'

The Commandant also was nearly whispering. 'No one can tell how long they have to go on ringing. It varies from year to year. I don't know why. You should be all right up to midnight. Probably for some while after. In the end the dead awake. First one or two, then all of them. Tonight even the sea draws back. You have seen that for yourself. In a place like this there are always several drowned each year. This year there've been more than several. But even so that's only a few. Most of them come not from the water but from the earth. It is not a pretty sight.'

'Where do they go?'

'I've never followed them to see. I'm not stark staring mad.' The red of the fire reflected in the Commandant's eyes. There was a long pause.

'I don't believe in the resurrection of the body,' said Gerald. As the hour grew later, the bells grew louder. 'Not of the body.'

'What other kind of resurrection is possible? Everything else is only theory. You can't even imagine it. No one can.'

Gerald had not argued such a thing for twenty years. 'So,' he said, 'you advise me to go. Where?'

'Where doesn't matter.'

'I have no car.'

'Then you'd better walk.'

'With her?' He indicated Phrynne only with his eyes.

'She's young and strong.' A forlorn tenderness lay within the Commandant's words. 'She's twenty years younger than you and therefore twenty years more important.'

'Yes,' said Gerald. 'I agree . . . What about you? What will you do?'

'I've lived here some time now. I know what to do.'

'And the Pascoes?'

'He's drunk. There is nothing in the world to fear if you're thoroughly drunk. DSO and bar. DFC and bar.'

'But you're not drinking yourself?'

'Not since I came to Holihaven. I lost the knack.'

Suddenly Phrynne sat up. 'Hello,' she said to the Commandant, not yet fully awake. Then she said, 'What fun! The bells are still ringing.'

The Commandant rose, his eyes averted. 'I don't think there's anything more to say,' he remarked, addressing Gerald. 'You've still got time.' He nodded slightly to Phrynne, and walked out of the lounge.

'What have you still got time for?' asked Phrynne, stretching. 'Was he trying to convert you? I'm sure he's an Anabaptist.'

'Something like that,' said Gerald, trying to think.

'Shall we go to bed? Sorry, I'm so sleepy.'

'Nothing to be sorry about.'

'Or shall we go for another walk? That would wake me up. Besides the tide might have come in.'

Gerald, although he half-despised himself for it, found it impossible to explain to her that they should leave at once; without transport or a destination; walk all night if necessary. He said to himself that probably he would not go even were he alone.

'If you're sleepy, it's probably a *good* thing.'

'Darling!'

'I mean with these bells. God knows when they will stop.' Instantly he felt a new pang of fear at what he had said.

Mrs Pascoe had appeared at the door leading to the bar, and opposite to that from which the Commandant had departed. She bore two steaming glasses on a tray. She looked about, possibly to confirm that the Commandant had really gone.

'I thought you might both like a nightcap. Ovaltine, with something in it.'

'Thank you,' said Phrynne. 'I can't think of anything nicer.'

Gerald set the glasses on a wicker table, and quickly finished his cognac.

Mrs Pascoe began to move chairs and slap cushions. She looked very haggard.

'Is the Commandant an Anabaptist?' asked Phrynne over her shoulder. She was proud of her ability to outdistance Gerald in beginning to consume a hot drink.

Mrs Pascoe stopped slapping for a moment. 'I don't know what that is,' she said. 'He's left his book,' said Phrynne, on a new tack.

'I wonder what he's reading,' continued Phrynne. 'Foxe's *Lives of the Martyrs*, I expect.' A small unusual devil seemed to have entered into her.

But Mrs Pascoe knew the answer. 'It's always the same,' she said contemptuously. 'He only reads one. It's called *Fifteen Decisive Battles of the World*. He's been reading it ever since he came here. When he gets to the end, he starts again.'

'Should I take it up to him?' asked Gerald. It was neither courtesy nor inclination, but rather a fear lest the Commandant return to the lounge: a desire, after those few minutes of reflection, to cross-examine.

'Thanks very much,' said Mrs Pascoe, as if relieved of a similar apprehension. 'Room One. Next to the suit of Japanese armour.' She went on tipping and banging. To Gerald's inflamed nerves, her behaviour seemed too consciously normal.

He collected the book and made his way upstairs. The volume was bound in real leather, and the tops of its pages were gilded: apparently a presentation copy. Outside the lounge, Gerald looked at the flyleaf: in a very large hand was written 'To my dear Son, Raglan, on his being honoured by the Queen. From his proud Father, B. Shotcroft, Major General.' Beneath the inscription a very ugly military crest had been appended by a stamper of primitive type.

The suit of Japanese armour lurked in a dark corner as the Commandant himself had done when Gerald had first encountered him. The wide brim of the helmet concealed the black eyeholes in the headpiece; the moustache bristled realistically. It was exactly as if the figure stood guard over the door behind it. On this door was no number, but, there being no other in sight, Gerald took it to be the door of Number One. A short way down the dim empty passage was a window, the ancient sashes of which shook in the din and blast of the bells. Gerald knocked sharply.

If there was a reply, the bells drowned it; and he knocked again. When to the third knocking there was still no answer, he gently opened the door. He really had to know whether all would or could be well if Phrynne, and doubtless he also, were at all costs to remain in their room until it was dawn. He looked into the room and caught his breath.

There was no artificial light, but the curtains, if there were any, had been drawn back from the single window, and the bottom sash forced up as far as it would go. On the floor by the dusky void, a maelstrom of sound, knelt the Commandant, his cropped white hair faintly catching the moonless glimmer, as his head lay on the sill, like that of a man about to be guillotined. His face was in his hands, but slightly sideways, so that Gerald received a shadowy distorted idea of his expression. Some might have called it ecstatic, but Gerald found it agonised. It frightened him more than anything which had yet happened. Inside the room the bells were like plunging roaring lions.

He stood for some considerable time quite unable to move. He could not determine whether or not the Commandant knew he was there. The Commandant gave no direct sign of it, but more than once he writhed and shuddered in Gerald's direction, like an unquiet sleeper made more unquiet by an interloper. It was a matter of doubt whether Gerald should leave the book; and he decided to do so mainly because the thought of further contact with it displeased him. He crept into the room and softly laid it on a hardly visible wooden trunk at the foot of the plain metal bedstead. There seemed no other furniture in the room. Outside the door, the hanging mailed fingers of the Japanese figure touched his wrist.

He had not been away from the lounge for long, but it was long enough for Mrs Pascoe to have begun to drink again. She had left the tidying up half-completed, or rather the room half-disarranged; and was leaning against the overmantel, drawing heavily on a dark tumbler of whisky. Phrynne had not yet finished her Ovaltine.

'How long before the bells stop?' asked Gerald as soon as he opened the lounge door. Now he was resolved that, come what might, they must go. The impossibility of sleep should serve as an excuse.

'I don't expect Mrs Pascoe can know any more than we can,' said Phrynne.

'You should have told us about this—this annual event before accepting our booking.'

Mrs Pascoe drank some more whisky. Gerald suspected that it was neat. 'It's not always the same night,' she said throatily, looking at the floor.

'We're not staying,' said Gerald wildly.

'Darling!' Phrynne caught him by the arm.

'Leave this to me, Phrynne.' He addressed Mrs Pascoe. 'We'll pay for the room, of course. Please order me a car.'

Mrs Pascoe was now regarding him stonily. When he asked for a car, she gave a very short laugh. Then her face changed, she made an effort, and she said, 'You mustn't take the Commandant so seriously, you know.'

Phrynne glanced quickly at her husband.

The whisky was finished. Mrs Pascoe placed the empty glass on the plastic overmantel with too much of a thud. 'No one takes Commandant Shotcroft seriously,' she said. 'Not even his nearest and dearest.'

'Has he any?' asked Phrynne. 'He seemed so lonely and pathetic.'

'He's Don and I's mascot,' she said, the drink interfering with her grammar. But not even the drink could leave any doubt about her rancour.

'I thought he had personality,' said Phrynne.

'That and a lot more no doubt,' said Mrs Pascoe. 'But they pushed him out, all the same.'

'Out of what?'

'Cashiered, court-martialled, badges of rank stripped off, sword broken in half, muffled drums, the works.'

'Poor old man. I'm sure it was a miscarriage of justice.'

'That's because you don't know him.'

Mrs Pascoe looked as if she were waiting for Gerald to offer her another whisky.

'It's a thing he could never live down,' said Phrynne, brooding to herself, and tucking her legs beneath her. 'No wonder he's so queer if all the time it was a mistake.'

'I just told you it was not a mistake,' said Mrs Pascoe insolently.

'How can we possibly know?'

'*You* can't. *I* can. No one better.' She was at once aggressive and tearful.

'If you want to be paid,' cried Gerald, forcing himself in, 'make out your bill. Phrynne, come upstairs and pack.' If only he hadn't made her unpack between their walk and dinner.

Slowly Phrynne uncoiled and rose to her feet. She had no intention of either packing or departing, but nor was she going to argue. 'I shall need your help,' she said, softly. 'If I'm going to pack.'

In Mrs Pascoe there was another change. Now she looked terrified. 'Don't go. Please don't go. Not now. It's too late.'

Gerald confronted her. 'Too late for what?' he asked harshly.

Mrs Pascoe looked paler than ever. 'You said you wanted a car,' she faltered. 'You're too late.' Her voice trailed away.

Gerald took Phrynne by the arm. 'Come on up.'

Before they reached the door, Mrs Pascoe made a further attempt. 'You'll be all right if you stay. Really you will.' Her voice, normally somewhat strident, was so feeble that the bells obliterated it. Gerald observed that from somewhere she had produced the whisky bottle and was refilling her tumbler.

With Phrynne on his arm he went first to the stout front door. To his surprise it was neither locked nor bolted, but opened at a half-turn of the handle. Outside the building the whole sky was full of bells, the air an inferno of ringing.

He thought that for the first time Phrynne's face also seemed strained and crestfallen. 'They've been ringing too long,' she said, drawing close to him. 'I wish they'd stop.'

'We're packing and going. I needed to know whether we could get out this way. We must shut the door quietly.'

It creaked a bit on its hinges, and he hesitated with it half-shut, uncertain whether to rush the creak or to ease it. Suddenly, something dark and shapeless, with its arm seeming to hold a black vesture over its head, flitted, all sharp angles, like a bat, down the narrow ill-lighted street, the sound of its passage audible to none. It was the first being that either of them had seen in the streets of Holihaven; and Gerald was acutely relieved that he alone had set eyes upon it. With his hand trembling, he shut the door much too sharply.

But no one could possibly have heard, although he stopped for a second outside the lounge. He could hear Mrs Pascoe now weeping hysterically; and again was glad that Phrynne was a step or two ahead of him. Upstairs the

Commandant's door lay straight before them: they had to pass close beside the Japanese figure, in order to take the passage to the left of it.

But soon they were in their room, with the key turned in the big rim lock.

'Oh God,' cried Gerald, sinking on the double bed. 'It's pandemonium.' Not for the first time that evening he was instantly more frightened than ever by the unintended appositeness of his own words.

'It's pandemonium all right,' said Phrynne, almost calmly. 'And we're not going out in it.'

He was at a loss to divine how much she knew, guessed, or imagined; and any word of enlightenment from him might be inconceivably dangerous. But he was conscious of the strength of her resistance, and lacked the reserves to battle with it.

She was looking out of the window into the main street. 'We might *will* them to stop,' she suggested wearily.

Gerald was now far less frightened of the bells continuing than of their ceasing. But that they should go on ringing until day broke seemed hopelessly impossible.

Then one peel stopped. There could be no other explanation for the obvious diminution in sound.

'You see!' said Phrynne.

Gerald sat up straight on the side of the bed.

Almost at once further sections of sound subsided, quickly one after the other, until only a single peal was left, that which had begun the ringing. Then the single peal tapered off into a single bell. The single bell tolled on its own, disjointedly, five or six or seven times. Then it stopped, and there was nothing.

Gerald's head was a cave of echoes, mountingly muffled by the noisy current of his blood.

'Oh goodness,' said Phrynne, turning from the window and stretching her arms above her head. 'Let's go somewhere else tomorrow.' She began to take off her dress.

Sooner than usual they were in bed, and in one another's arms. Gerald had carefully not looked out of the window, and neither of them suggested that it should be opened, as they usually did.

'As it's a four-poster, shouldn't we draw the curtains?' asked Phrynne. 'And be really snug? After those damned bells?'

'We should suffocate.'

'They only drew the curtains when people were likely to pass through the room.'

'Darling, you're shivering. I think we *should* draw them.'

'Lie still instead, and love me.'

But all his nerves were straining out into the silence. There was no sound of any kind, beyond the hotel or within it; not a creaking floorboard or a prowling cat or a distant owl. He had been afraid to look at his watch when the bells stopped, or since: the number of the dark hours before they could leave Holihaven weighed on him. The vision of the Commandant kneeling in the dark window was clear before his eyes, as if the intervening panelled walls were made of stage gauze; and the thing he had seen in the street darted on its angular way back and forth through memory.

Then passion began to open its petals within him, layer upon slow layer; like an illusionist's red flower which, without soil or sun or sap, grows as it is watched. The languor of tenderness began to fill the musty room with its texture and perfume. The transparent walls became again opaque, the old man's vaticinations mere obsession. The street must have been empty, as it was now; the eye deceived.

But perhaps rather it was the boundless sequacity of love that deceived, and most of all in the matter of the time which had passed since the bells stopped ringing; for suddenly Phrynne drew very close to him, and he heard steps in the thoroughfare outside, and a voice calling. These were loud steps, audible from afar even through the shut window; and the voice had the possessed stridency of the street evangelist.

'The dead are awake!'

Not even the thick bucolic accent, the guttural vibrato of emotion, could twist or mask the meaning. At first Gerald lay listening with all his body, and concentrating the more as the noise grew; then he sprang from the bed and ran to the window.

A burly, long-limbed man in a seaman's jersey was running down the street, coming clearly into view for a second at each lamp, and between them lapsing into a swaying lumpy wraith. As he shouted his joyous message, he crossed from side to side and waved his arms like a negro. By flashes, Gerald could see that his weatherworn face was transfigured.

'The dead are awake!'

Already, behind him, people were coming out of their houses, and descending from the rooms above shops. There were men, women, and children. Most of them were fully dressed, and must have been waiting in silence and darkness for the call; but a few were dishevelled, in night attire or the first garments which had come to hand. Some formed themselves into groups, and advanced arm in arm, as if towards the conclusion of a Blackpool beano. More came singly, ecstatic and waving their arms above their heads, as the first man had done. All cried out, again and again, with no cohesion or harmony. 'The dead are awake! The dead are awake!'

Gerald became aware that Phrynne was standing behind him.

'The Commandant warned me,' he said brokenly. 'We should have gone.'

Phrynne shook her head and took his arm. 'Nowhere to go,' she said. But her voice was soft with fear, and her eyes blank. 'I don't expect they'll trouble *us*.'

Swiftly Gerald drew the thick plush curtains, leaving them in complete darkness. 'We'll sit it out,' he said, slightly histrionic in his fear. 'No matter what happens.'

He scrambled across to the switch. But when he pressed it, light did not come. 'The current's gone. We must get back into bed.'

'Gerald! Come and help me.' He remembered that she was curiously vulnerable in the dark. He found his way to her, and guided her to the bed.

'No more love,' she said ruefully and affectionately, her teeth chattering.

He kissed her lips with what gentleness the total night made possible.

'They were going towards the sea,' she said timidly.

'We must think of something else.'

But the noise was still growing. The whole community seemed to be passing down the street, yelling the same dreadful words again and again.

'Do you think we can?'

'Yes,' said Gerald. 'It's only until tomorrow.'

'They can't be actually dangerous,' said Phrynne. 'Or it would be stopped.'

'Yes, of course.'

By now, as always happens, the crowd had amalgamated their utterances and were beginning to shout in unison. They were like agitators bawling a slogan, or massed troublemakers at a football match. But at the same time the noise was beginning to draw away. Gerald suspected that the entire population of the place was on the march.

Soon it was apparent that a processional route was being followed. The tumult could be heard winding about from quarter to quarter; sometimes drawing near, so that Gerald and Phrynne were once more seized by the first chill of panic, then again almost fading away. It was possibly this great variability in the volume of the sound which led Gerald to believe that there were distinct pauses in the massed shouting; periods when it was superseded by far, disorderly cheering. Certainly it began also to seem that the thing shouted had changed; but he could not make out the new cry, although unwillingly he strained to do so.

'It's extraordinary how frightened one can be,' said Phrynne, 'even when one is not directly menaced. It must prove that we all belong to one another, or whatever it is, after all.'

In many similar remarks they discussed the thing at one remove. Experience showed that this was better than not discussing it at all.

In the end there could be no doubt that the shouting had stopped, and that now the crowd was singing. It was no song that Gerald had ever heard, but something about the way it was sung convinced him that it was a hymn or psalm set to an out-of-date popular tune. Once more the crowd was approaching; this time steadily, but with strange, interminable slowness.

'What the hell are they doing now?' asked Gerald out of the blackness, his nerves wound so tight that the foolish question was forced out of them.

Palpably the crowd had completed its peregrination, and was returning up the main street from the sea. The singers seemed to gasp and fluctuate, as if worn out with gay exercise, like children at a party. There was a steady undertow of scraping and scuffling. Time passed and more time.

Phrynne spoke. 'I believe they're *dancing*.'

She moved slightly, as if she thought of going to see.

'No, no,' said Gerald, and clutched her fiercely.

There was a tremendous concussion on the ground floor below them. The front door had been violently thrown back They could hear the hotel filling with a stamping, singing mob.

Doors banged everywhere, and furniture was overturned, as the beatific throng surged and stumbled through the involved darkness of the old building. Glasses went and china and Birmingham brass warming pans. In a moment, Gerald heard the Japanese armour crash to the boards. Phrynne screamed. Then a mighty shoulder, made strong by the sea's assault, rammed at the panelling and their door was down.

'The living and the dead dance together.

Now's the time. Now's the place. Now's the weather.'

At last Gerald could make out the words.

The stresses in the song were heavily beaten down by much repetition.

Hand in hand, through the dim grey gap of the doorway, the dancers lumbered and shambled in, singing frenziedly and brokenly; ecstatic but exhausted. Through the stuffy blackness they swayed and shambled, more and more of them, until the room must have been packed tight with them.

Phrynne screamed again. 'The smell. Oh, God, the smell.'

It was the smell they had encountered on the beach; in the congested room, no longer merely offensive, but obscene, unspeakable.

Phrynne was hysterical. All self-control gone, she was scratching and tearing, and screaming again and again. Gerald tried to hold her, but one of the dancers struck him so hard in the darkness that she was jolted out of his arms. Instantly it seemed that she was no longer there at all.

The dancers were thronging everywhere, their limbs whirling, their lungs bursting with the rhythm of the song. It was difficult for Gerald even to call out. He tried to struggle after Phrynne, but immediately a blow from a massive elbow knocked him to the floor, an abyss of invisible trampling feet.

But soon the dancers were going again: not only from the room, but, it seemed, from the building also. Crushed and tormented though he was, Gerald could hear the song being resumed in the street, as the various frenzied groups debouched and reunited. Within, before long there was nothing but the chaos, the darkness, and the putrescent odour. Gerald felt so sick that he had to battle with unconsciousness. He could not think or move, despite the desperate need.

Then he struggled into a sitting position, and sank his head on the torn sheets of the bed. For an uncertain period he was insensible to everything: but in the end he heard steps approaching down the dark passage. His door was pushed back, and the Commandant entered gripping a lighted candle. He seemed to disregard the flow of hot wax which had already congealed on much of his knotted hand.

'She's safe. Small thanks to you.'

The Commandant stared icily at Gerald's undignified figure. Gerald tried to stand. He was terribly bruised, and so giddy that he wondered if this could be concussion. But relief rallied him.

'Is it thanks to *you?*'

'She was caught up in it. Dancing with the rest.' The Commandant's eyes glowed in the candlelight. The singing and the dancing had almost died away.

Still Gerald could do no more than sit upon the bed. His voice was low and indistinct, as if coming from outside his body. 'Were they . . . were some of them . . .'

The Commandant replied, more scornful than ever of his weakness, 'She was between two of them. Each had one of her hands.'

Gerald could not look at him. 'What did you do?' he asked in that same remote voice.

'I did what had to be done. I hope I was in time.' After the slightest possible pause he continued. 'You'll find her downstairs.'

'I'm grateful. Such a silly thing to say, but what else is there?'

'Can you walk?'

'I think so.'

'I'll light you down.' The Commandant's tone was uncompromising as always.

There were two more candles in the lounge, and Phrynne, wearing a woman's belted overcoat which was not hers, sat between them, drinking. Mrs Pascoe, fully dressed but with eyes averted, pottered about the wreckage. It seemed hardly more than as if she were completing the task which earlier she had left unfinished.

'Darling, look at you!' Phrynne's words were still hysterical, but her voice was as gentle as it usually was.

Gerald, bruises and thoughts of concussion forgotten, dragged her into his arms. They embraced silently for a long time; then he looked into her eyes.

'Here I am,' she said, and looked away. 'Not to worry.'

Silently and unnoticed, the Commandant had already retreated.

Without returning his gaze, Phrynne finished her drink as she stood there. Gerald supposed that it was one of Mrs Pascoe's concoctions.

It was so dark where Mrs Pascoe was working that her labours could have been achieving little; but she said nothing to her visitors, nor they to her. At the door Phrynne unexpectedly stripped off the overcoat and threw it on a chair. Her nightdress was so torn that she stood almost naked. Dark though it was, Gerald saw Mrs Pascoe regarding Phrynne's pretty body with a stare of animosity.

'May we take one of the candles?' he said, normal standards reasserting themselves in him.

But Mrs Pascoe continued to stand silently staring; and they lighted themselves through the wilderness of broken furniture to the ruins of their bedroom. The Japanese figure was still prostrate, and the Commandant's door shut. And the smell had almost gone.

EVEN BY SEVEN O'CLOCK the next morning surprisingly much had been done to restore order. But no one seemed to be about, and Gerald and Phrynne departed without a word.

In Wrack Street a milkman was delivering, but Gerald noticed that his cart bore the name of another town. A minute boy whom they encountered later on an obscure purposeful errand might, however, have been indigenous; and when they reached Station Road, they saw a small plot of land on which already men were silently at work with spades in their hands. They were as thick as flies on a wound, and as black. In the darkness of the previous evening, Gerald and Phrynne had missed the place. A board named it the New Municipal Cemetery.

In the mild light of an autumn morning the sight of the black and silent toilers was horrible; but Phrynne did not seem to find it so. On the contrary, her cheeks reddened and her soft mouth became fleetingly more voluptuous still.

She seemed to have forgotten Gerald, so that he was able to examine her closely for a moment. It was the first time he had done so since the night before. Then, once more, she became herself. In those previous seconds Gerald had become aware of something dividing them which neither of them would ever mention or ever forget.

———————

Cynthia Asquith
1887–1960

A notable society beauty and a close friend of D. H. Lawrence,
Lady Cynthia Asquith became secretary to the playwright James
Barrie in 1918. Fascinated by tales of the uncanny, she edited a
number of ghost-story anthologies during the 1920s and 1930s,
and wrote several stories of her own. These were issued in a
single volume, *What Dreams May Come*, in 1951.

THE CORNER SHOP

PETER WOOD'S EXECUTORS found their task a very easy one. He had left his
affairs in perfect order. The only surprise yielded by his tidy writing table
was a sealed envelope on which was written, 'Not wishing to be bothered
by well-meaning Research Societies, I have never shown the enclosed to anyone,
but after my death all are welcome to read what is, to the best of my knowledge,
a true story.'

The manuscript bears a date three years previous to the death of the writer,
and is as follows:

I HAVE LONG WISHED to write down an experience of my youth. I shall not
attempt any diagnosis as to its nature. I draw no conclusions. I merely record
certain facts. At least, as such these incidents presented themselves to my
consciousness.

One evening, shortly after I had been called to the Bar, I was rather dejectedly
returning to my lodgings, wishing I could afford a theatre ticket, when my
attention was drawn to the brightly lit window of a shop. Having an uneducated
love of bric-à-brac, and remembering an unavoidable wedding present, I
grasped the handle of the door which, opening with one of those cheerful clanking bells, admitted me into large rambling premises thickly crowded with all the
traditional litter of a curiosity shop. Fragments of armour, pewter pots, dark,
distorting mirrors, church vestments, flower pictures, brass kettles, chairs,

tables, chests, chandeliers—all were here! But in spite of the heterogeneous confusion, there was none of the dingy, dusty gloom one associates with such collections. The room was brightly lit and a crackling fire leapt up the chimney. The atmosphere was warm and cheerful. Very agreeable I found it after the cold dank fog outside.

At my entrance a young woman and a child—by their resemblance obviously sisters—had risen from two armchairs. Bright, bustling, gaily dressed, they were curiously unlike the type of person who usually presides over that particular sort of wares. A flower shop would have seemed a more appropriate setting.

How wonderful of them to keep their premises so clean, I thought, as I wished them good evening.

Their smiling faces made a very pleasing impression on me; one of comfortable, serene well-being, and, though the grown-up sister was most courteous in showing me the crowded treasures and displayed knowledge and appreciation, she struck me as quite indifferent as to whether I made any purchase or not. Her manner was really more that of a custodian than of a saleswoman.

Finding a beautiful piece of Sheffield plate very moderately priced, I decided that here was the very present for my friend. The child deftly converted my purchase into a brown-paper parcel. Explaining to her elder sister that I was without sufficient cash, I asked if she would take a cheque.

'Certainly,' she answered, briskly producing pen and ink. 'Will you please make it out to the "Corner Curio Shop"?'

It was with conscious reluctance that I set out into the saffron fog.

'Good evening, sir. Always pleased to see you at any time,' rang out the girl's pleasant voice, a voice so agreeable that I left almost with a sense of having made a friend.

I suppose it must have been about a week later, that, as I walked home one very cold evening—fine powdery snow brushing against my face, and a cutting wind tearing down the streets, I remembered the welcoming warmth of the cheerful Corner Curio Shop, and determined to revisit it. I found myself to be in the very street, and there—yes—there was the very corner. It was with a sense of disappointment, out of all proportion to the event, that I found the shop to be wearing that baffling—so to speak—shut-eyed appearance, and saw that a piece of cardboard, on which was printed the word 'Closed', hung from the handle.

A bitter gust of wind whistled round the corner, and my wet trousers flapped dismally against my chapped ankles. I longed for the warmth and glow within, and felt annoyingly thwarted. Rather childishly—for I was certain the door was locked, I grasped the handle and shook it. To my surprise the handle turned in my hand, but not in answer to its pressure. The door was pulled open from inside, and I found myself peering into the dimly lit countenance of a very old and frail-looking little man.

'Please to come in, sir,' said a gentle, rather tremulous voice, and soft footsteps shuffled away in front of me.

It is impossible to describe the altered aspect of the place. I assumed that the electric light had fused, for the darkness of the large room was only thinned by two guttering candles, and in the dim wavering light, the jumble of furniture, formerly brightly lit, now loomed towering and mysterious, and cast weird, almost menacing shadows. The fire was out, only one faintly glowering ember told that any had lately been alive. Other evidence there was none, for the grim cold of the atmosphere was such as I had never experienced. The phrase 'it struck chill' is laughably inadequate. In retrospect the street seemed almost agreeable; in its biting cold there had at least been something exhilarating. The atmosphere was now as gloomy as it had previously been genial. I felt a strong impulse to leave immediately, but the surrounding darkness thinned, and I saw that the old man was busily lighting candles here and there.

'Anything I can show you, sir?' he quavered, as he spoke approaching me with a lighted taper in his hand. I now saw him comparatively distinctly, and his appearance made an indescribable impression on me. Rembrandt flitted through my mind. Who else could have suggested the strange shadows on that time-worn face? Tired is a word we lightly use. Never had I known what the word might mean, till I stared at that exhausted countenance. The ineffable, patient weariness of the withered face, the eyes—which seemed as extinct as the fire, save for a feeble glow as of some purpose. And the wan frailty of the figure!

The words 'dust and ashes, dust and ashes' strayed through my brain.

On my first visit, you may remember that I had been impressed by the incongruous cleanliness of the place. The queer fancy now struck me that this old man was like an accumulation of all the dust one might have expected to see scattered over such precincts. In truth, he looked scarcely more solid than a mere conglomeration of dust that might be dispersed at a breath or a touch.

What a queer old creature to be employed by those healthy, well-to-do-looking girls! He must, I thought, be some old retainer kept on out of charity.

'Anything I can show you, sir?' repeated the old man.

His voice had little more body than the tearing of a cobweb, and yet there was a curious, almost pleading, insistence in it, and his eyes were fixed on me in a wan yet devouring stare. I wanted to leave. Definitely I wanted to go. The proximity of this pitiable old man depressed me; I felt wretchedly dispirited, but, involuntarily murmuring, 'Thank you, I'll look round,' I found myself following his frail form and absent-mindedly inspecting various objects temporarily illuminated by his trembling taper.

The chill silence only broken by the tired shuffle of his carpet slippers got on my nerves. 'Very cold night, isn't it?' I hazarded.

'Cold is it? Cold, cold, yes, I dare say.' In his grey voice was the apathy of extreme initiation.

'Been at this job long?' I asked, dully peering at an old four-poster bed.

'A long, long time.' The answer came softly as a sigh, and as he spoke Time seemed no longer a matter of days, weeks, months, years, but something that stretched immeasurably. I resented the old man's exhaustion and melancholy, the infection of which was so unaccountably weighing down my own spirits.

'How long, O Lord, how long?' I said as jauntily as possible—adding, with odious jocularity—'Old age pension about due, what?' No response.

In silence we moved across to the other side of the room.

'Quaint piece that,' said my guide, picking up a little grotesque frog that was lying on a shelf amongst numerous other small objects. It seemed to be made of some substance similar to jade and, rather struck by its uncouth appearance, I took it from the old man's hand. It was strikingly cold.

'I think it's rather fun,' I said. 'How much?'

'Half-a-crown, sir,' whispered the old man, glancing up at my face. His voice had no more body than the sliding of dust, but in his eyes there was an unmistakable gleam of eagerness.

'Is that all? I'll have it,' said I. 'Don't bother to pack up old Anthony Roland. I'll put him in my pocket. Half-a-crown, did you say? Here it is.'

In giving the old man the coin, I inadvertently touched his extended palm. I could scarcely suppress a start. I have said the frog struck cold, but its substance was tepid compared to that desiccated skin. I cannot describe the chill sensation received in that second's contact. Poor old fellow, I thought. He's not fit to be about in this cold, lonely place. I wonder at those kind-looking girls allowing such an old wreck to struggle on. 'Good night,' I said.

'Good night, sir; thank you, sir,' quavered the feeble old voice. He closed the door behind me.

Turning my head as I breasted the driving snow, I saw his form, scarcely more solid than shadow, outlined against the candlelight. His face was pressed against the big glass pane. I imagined his tired, patient eyes peering after his vanishing customer.

Somehow I was unable to dismiss the thought of that old man from my mind. Long, long after I was in bed and courting sleep I saw that maze of wrinkles, his ravaged face and his great initiated eyes like lifeless planets, staring, staring at me, and in their steady stare there seemed a sort of question. Yes, I was unaccountably perturbed by his personality, and even after I achieved sleep my dreams were full of my strange acquaintance.

Haunted, I suppose, by a sense of his infinite tiredness, in my dream I was trying to force him to rest—to lie down. But no sooner did I succeed in laying his frail form on the four-poster bed I had noticed in the shop (only now it seemed more like a grave than a bed, and the brocade coverlet had turned into sods of turf)—than he would slip from my grasp and totteringly set forth on his rambles around the shop. On and on I chased him, down endless avenues of weird furniture, but still he eluded me, and now the dim shop seemed to stretch on and on immeasurably—to merge into an infinity of sunless, airless space until at length I myself sank breathless and exhausted on to the four-poster grave.

The next morning I received an urgent summons to my mother's sickbed, and in the anxiety of the ensuing week the episode of the Corner Curio Shop was banished from my mind. As soon as the invalid was declared out of danger, I returned to my dreary lodging. Dejectedly engaged in adding up my petty household accounts and wondering where on earth I was to find the money to pay next quarter's rent, I was agreeably surprised by a visit from an old schoolfellow—at that time practically the only friend I possessed in London. He was employed by one of the best-known firms of fine art dealers and auctioneers.

After a few minutes' conversation, he rose in search of a light. My back was turned to him. I heard the sharp scratch of a match, followed by propitiating noises to his pipe. These were suddenly broken off by an exclamation.

'Good God, man!' he shouted. 'Where did you get this?'

Turning round, I saw that he had snatched up my purchase of the other night, the funny little frog, whose presence on my mantelpiece I had practically forgotten.

He was holding it under the gas jet, closely scrutinising it through a small magnifying glass, and his hands were shaking with excitement. 'Where did you get this?' he repeated. 'Have you any idea what it is?'

Briefly I told him that, rather than leave a shop empty-handed, I had bought the frog for half-a-crown.

'For half-a-crown?' he echoed. 'My dear fellow, I can't swear to it, but I believe you've had one of those amazing pieces of luck one hears about. Unless I'm very much mistaken, this is a piece of jade of the Hsia Dynasty.'

To my ignorance these words conveyed little. 'Do you mean it's worth money?'

'Worth money? Phew!' he ejaculated. 'Look here. Will you leave this business to me? Let me have the thing for my firm to do the best they can by you. Today's Monday. I shall be able to get it into Thursday's auction.'

Knowing I could implicitly trust my friend, I readily agreed to his proposal. Carefully enwrapping the frog in cotton wool, he departed.

Friday morning I received the shock of my life. Shock does not necessarily imply bad news, and I can assure you that for some seconds after opening the one envelope lying on my dingy breakfast tray, the room spun round and round me. The envelope contained an invoice from Messrs Spunk, fine art dealers and auctioneers:

To SALE OF HSIA JADE, £2,000, LESS 10 PER CENT COMMISSION —£1,800

and there, neatly folded, made out to Peter Wood, Esq., was Messrs Spunk's cheque for £1,800. For some time I was completely bewildered. My friend's words had raised hopes; hopes that my chance purchase might facilitate the payment of next quarter's rent—might even provide for a whole year's rent—but that so large a sum was involved had never even crossed my mind. Could it be true, or was it some hideous joke? Surely it was—in the trite phrase—much, much too good to be true! It was not the sort of thing that happened to oneself.

Still feeling physically dizzy, I rang up my friend. The normality of his voice and the heartiness of his congratulations convinced me as to the truth of my astounding fortune. It was no joke—no dream. I, Peter Wood, whose bank account was at present £20 overdrawn, and who possessed no securities save shares to the extent of £150, by a sheer fluke, now held in my hand a piece of paper convertible into 1,800 golden sovereigns. I sat down to think—to try to realise—to readjust. From a jumble of plans, problems, and emotions one fact emerged crystal clear. Obviously, I could not take advantage of the girl's ignorance or of her poor old caretaker's incompetence. I could not accept this amazing gift from Fate, simply because I had bought a treasure for half-a-crown.

Clearly I must return at least half of the sum to my unconscious benefactors. Otherwise I should feel I had robbed them almost as much as though I had broken into their shop like a thief in the night. I remembered their pleasant open countenances. What fun to astonish them with the wonderful news! I felt a strong impulse to rush to the shop, but having for once a case in court, I was obliged to go to the Temple. Endorsing Messrs Spunk's cheque, I addressed it to my bankers, and, consulting the flyleaf of my chequebook, made out one to the Corner Curio Shop for £900. This I placed in my pocket, determined to call at the Corner Shop on my way home.

It was late before I was free to leave the Law Courts, and on arriving at the shop, though somewhat disappointed, I was not greatly surprised to find that it was again shut, with the notice 'Closed' slung over the handle. Even supposing the old caretaker to be on duty, there was no particular point in seeing him. My business was with his mistress. So, deciding to postpone my visit to the following day, I was just on the point of hurrying home, when—as though I were expected—the door opened, and there on the threshold stood the old man peering out into the darkness.

'Anything I can do for you, sir?'

His voice was even queerer than before. I now realised that I had dreaded re-encountering him, but I felt irresistibly compelled to enter. The atmosphere was as grimly cold as on my last visit. I found myself actually shivering. Several candles, obviously only just lit, were burning, and by their glimmering light I saw the old man's grey gaze questioningly fixed upon me. What a face! I had not exaggerated its weirdness. Never had I seen so singular, so striking a being. No wonder I had dreamt of him. I wished he had not opened the door.

'Anything I can show you tonight, sir?' he rather tremulously enquired.

'No, thanks. I have come about that thing you sold me the other day. I find it's of great value. Please tell your mistress that I will pay her a proper price for it tomorrow.'

As I spoke there spread over the old man's face the most wonderful smile. 'Smile' I use for lack of a better word; but how convey any idea of the beauty of the indefinable expression that now transfigured that timeworn face? Tender triumph, gentle rapture! It was frost yielding to sunshine. Never before have I witnessed the thawing of thickly frozen grief—the dawn radiance of attainment. For the first time I had some inkling of the meaning of the word 'beatitude'. Impossible to describe the impression made on me by that transfigured face. The moment, as it were, brimmed over. Time ceased, and I became conscious of infinite things. The silence of the shop was now broken by that gathering sound of an old clock about to break into speech. I turned my head towards one of those wonderful pieces of medieval workmanship—a Nuremberg grandfather clock. From a recess beneath its exquisitely painted face, quaint figures emerged, and while one struck a bell, others daintily stepped through a minuet. My attention was riveted by the pretty spectacle, and not till the last sounds had trembled into silence did I turn my head.

I found myself alone.

The old man had disappeared. Surprised at his leaving me, I looked all round the large room. Oddly enough, the fire, which I had supposed to be dead, had flared into unexpected life, and was now casting a cheerful glow. But neither fire nor candlelight showed any trace of the old caretaker. He had vanished.

'Hello! Hello!' I called interrogatively.

No answer. No sound, save the loud ticking of clocks and the busy crackling of the fire. I walked all round the room. I even looked into the four-poster bed of which I had dreamt. I then saw that there was a smaller adjoining room, and, seizing a candle, I resolved to explore it. At the far end I discerned a small staircase obviously leading up to a sort of gallery that surrounded the room. The old man must have withdrawn into some upstairs lair. I would follow him. I groped my way to the foot of the stairs, and began to ascend, but the steps creaked beneath my feet, I had a feeling of crumbling woodwork, my candle went out: cobwebs brushed against my face. To continue was most uninviting. I desisted.

After all, what did it matter? Let the old man hide himself. I had given my message. Best be gone. But the main room to which I had returned had now become quite warm and cheerful. How could I ever have thought it sinister? And it was with a distinct sense of regret that I left the shop. I felt baulked. I would have liked to see more of that irradiating smile. Dear, strange, old man! How could I ever have fancied that I feared him?

The next Saturday I was free to go straight to the shop. On the way there my mind was agreeably occupied in anticipating the cordial welcome the grateful sisters were sure to give me. As the clank of the bell announced my opening of the door, the two girls, who were busily dusting their treasures, turned their heads to see who came at so unusually early an hour. Recognising me, to my surprise they bowed pleasantly, but quite casually, as though to a mere acquaintance.

With the fairy-tale bond between us, I had expected quite a different sort of greeting. I at once guessed that they had not yet heard the astounding news, and when I said, 'I've brought the cheque!' I saw that my surmise was correct. Their faces expressed blank uncomprehension.

'Cheque?' echoed the grown-up sister. 'What cheque?'

'For the frog I bought the other day.'

'The frog? What frog? I only remember you buying a piece of Sheffield plate.'

I saw they knew nothing, not even of my second visit to their shop! By degrees I told them the whole story. They were bewildered with astonishment. The elder sister seemed quite dazed.

'But I can't understand it! I can't understand it!' she repeated. 'Holmes isn't even supposed to admit anyone in our absence—far less to sell things. He just comes here as caretaker on the evenings when we leave early, and he's only supposed to stay till the night policeman comes on to his beat. I can't believe he let you in and never even told us he'd sold you something. It's too extraordinary! What time was it?'

'Round about seven, I should think,' I answered.

'He generally leaves about half past six,' said the girl. 'But I suppose the policeman must have been late.'

'It was later when I came yesterday.'

'Did you come again yesterday?' she asked.

Briefly I told her of my visit and the message I had left with the caretaker.

'What an incredible thing!' she exclaimed. 'I can't begin to understand it; but we shall soon hear his explanation. I'm expecting him in at any moment now. He comes in every morning to sweep the floors.'

At the prospect of meeting the remarkable old man again, I felt an appreciable thrill of excitement. How would he look in the strong daylight? Would he smile again?

'He's very old, isn't he?' I hazarded.

'Old? Yes, I suppose he is getting rather old; but it's a very easy job. He's a good, honest fellow. I can't understand his doing this sort of thing on the sly. I'm afraid we've been rather slack in our cataloguing lately. I wonder if he's been selling odds and ends for himself? Oh no, I can't bear to think it! By the way, can you remember whereabouts this frog was?'

I pointed to the shelf from which the caretaker had picked up the piece of jade.

'Oh, from that assortment? It's a lot I bought the other day for next to nothing, and I haven't sorted or priced them yet. I can't remember seeing a frog. Oh, what an incredible thing to happen!'

At this moment the telephone rang. She raised the receiver to her ear, and spoke down the instrument.

'Hello! Hello!' I heard her voice. 'Yes, it's Miss Wilton speaking. Yes, Mrs Holmes, what do you want?' There was a few seconds' pause, and then in startled tones her voice went on: '*Dead*? Dead? But how? Why? Oh, I *am* sorry!'

After a few more words she replaced the receiver and turned to us, her eyes full of tears.

'Fancy,' she said. 'Poor old Holmes, the caretaker, is dead. When he got home yesterday evening he complained of pain, and he died in the middle of the night. Heart failure. No one had any idea there was anything the matter with him. Oh, poor Mrs Holmes! What will she do? We must go round and see her at once!'

Both girls were very much upset and, saying that I would soon return, I thought it best to leave. That hauntingly singular old man had made so vivid an impression upon me that I felt deeply moved by the news of his sudden death. How strange that I should have been, except for his wife, the last person to speak with him. No doubt the fatal pain had seized him in my very presence, and that was why he had left me so abruptly and without a word. Had Death already brushed against his consciousness? That ineffable irradiating smile? Was that the beginning of the peace that passes all understanding?

I returned to the Corner Curio Shop the next day. I told them all the details of the sale of the fabulous frog, and presented the cheque I had drawn out. Here I met with unexpected opposition. The sisters showed great unwillingness to accept the money. It was—they said—all mine, and they had no need of it.

'You see,' explained Miss Wilton, 'my father had a flare for this business amounting to a sort of genius, and made quite a large fortune. When he became too old to carry on the shop, we kept it open out of sentiment and for the sake of occupation; but we don't need to make any profit out of it.'

At last I prevailed upon them to accept the money, if only to spend it on the various charities in which they were interested. It was a relief to my mind when the matter was thus settled.

The strange coincidence of the frog was a bond between us, and in the course of our amicable arguments we had become very friendly. I got into the way of dropping in quite often. In fact, I grew rather to rely on the sympathetic companionship of those two bright girls and became quite at my ease with them. I never forgot the impression made on me by the old man, and often questioned the girls about their poor caretaker, but they had nothing of much interest to tell me. They just described him as an 'old dear' who had been in their father's service as long as they could remember. No further light was thrown on his sale of the frog. Naturally, they didn't like to question his widow.

One evening, when I had been having tea in the inner room with the elder sister, I picked up an album of photographs. Turning over its pages, I came on a remarkably fine likeness of the old man. There, before me, was this strange, striking countenance; but, obviously, this photograph had been taken many years before I saw him. The face was much fuller and had not yet acquired the wearied, fragile look I so vividly remembered. But what magnificent eyes he had! Certainly there was something extraordinarily impressive about the man. I stared at the faded photograph.

'What a splendid photograph of poor old Holmes!' I said.

'Photograph of Holmes? I'd no idea there was one,' she answered. 'Let's see.'

As I approached with the open book the younger sister looked in through the open door.

'I'm off to the movies now,' she called out. 'Father's just rung up to say he'll be round in about a quarter of an hour to have a look at that Sheraton sideboard.'

'All right. I'll be here, and very glad to have his opinion,' said Miss Wilton, taking the album from my hand. There were several photographs on the page at which I had opened the book.

'I don't see anything of old Holmes,' she said.

I pointed out the photograph.

'*That!*' she exclaimed. 'Why, that's my dear father!'

'Your *father?*' I gasped.

'Yes, I can't imagine two people much more unlike. It must have been very dark in the shop when you saw Holmes!'

'Yes, yes; it was very dark,' I quickly said to gain time in which to think; for I felt quite bewildered with surprise. No degree of darkness could account for any such mistake. I had no moment's doubt as to the identity of him I had taken for the caretaker with the man whose photograph I now held in my hand. But what an amazing, unaccountable affair!

Her *father?* Why on earth should he have been in the shop unknown to his daughters, and for what possible purpose had he concealed his sale of the frog? And when he heard of its fabulous value, why leave the girls under the impression that it was Holmes, the dead caretaker, who had sold it?

Had he been ashamed to confess his own inadvertence? Or was it possible that the girls had never told him, wishing perhaps to keep their sudden wealth a secret? What strange family intrigue was this into which I had stumbled? If the father had determined thus to keep his actions in the dark, I had better not precipitate any exposure. Instinct bade me hold my tongue. The younger sister had announced his approaching visit. Would he recognise me?

'It's a splendid face,' I said, resolving on reserve.

'Isn't it?' she said with pleased eagerness. 'Isn't it clever and strong? Yes, I remember when that photograph was taken. It was just before he got religion.' The girl spoke as though she regarded 'religion' as a regrettable indisposition.

'Did he suddenly become very religious?'

'Yes,' she said reluctantly. 'Poor father! He made friends with a priest, and he became so changed. He was never the same again.'

From the sort of break in the girl's voice, I guessed she thought her father's reason had been affected. Did not this explain the whole affair? On the two occasions when I saw him, was he not wandering in mind as well as in body?

'Did his religion make him unhappy?' I ventured to ask, for I was anxious to get more light on the strange being before I re-encountered him.

'Yes, dreadfully.' The girl's eyes were full of tears. 'You see . . . it was . . .' She hesitated, and after a glance at me went on: 'There's really no reason why I shouldn't tell you. I've come to regard you as a real friend. Poor father got to think he had done very wrong. He couldn't quiet his conscience. You remember my telling you of his extraordinary flare? Well, his fortune was really founded on three marvellous strokes of business. He had the same sort of luck you had here the other day—that's why I'm telling you. It seems such an odd coincidence.' She paused.

'Please go on,' I urged.

'Well, you see, on three separate occasions he bought, for a few shillings, objects that were of immense value. Only—unlike you—he knew what he was about. The money he realised on their sale came as no surprise to him ... Unlike you, he did not then see any obligation to make it up to the ignorant people who had thrown away fortunes. After all, most dealers wouldn't, would they?' she almost angrily asked.

'Well, father grew richer and richer. Years after, he met this priest, and then he seemed to go all sort of morbid. He came to think that our wealth was founded on what was really no better than theft. Bitterly he reproached himself for having taken advantage of those three men's ignorance and allowed them to chuck away their fortunes. Unfortunately, in each case he succeeded in discovering what had ultimately happened to those he called his "victims". Most unfortunately, all three men had died in destitution. This discovery made him incurably miserable. Two of these men had died without leaving any children, and no relations could be found.

'He traced the son of the third to America; but there he had died, leaving no family. So poor father could find no means of making reparation. That was what he longed for—to make reparation. This preyed and preyed on him, until—in my opinion—his poor dear mind became unhinged. As religion took stronger and stronger hold on him, he got a queer sort of notion into his head—a regular obsession—a "complex" they would call it now. "The next best thing to doing a good action," he would say, "*is to provide someone else with the opportunity for doing one*. To give him his cue, so to speak. 'In our sins Christ is crucified afresh.' I must be the cause of three good actions corresponding to my own bad ones. In no other way can I expiate my crimes against Christ, for crimes they were—" In vain we argued with him, saying he had only done as nearly all men would have done. It had no effect. "Other men must judge for themselves. I have done what I know to be wrong," he would mournfully repeat. He got more and more fixed in his idea. Real religious mania it became!

'Being determined to find three human beings who would, by their good actions, as it were, *cancel* the pain caused to Divinity by what he considered his three crimes, he now busied himself in finding insignificant-looking treasures which he would offer to the public for a few shillings. Poor old father! Never shall I forget his joy when one day a man returned a piece of porcelain he had bought for five shillings and discovered to be worth £500, saying: "I think you must have made a mistake." Just as *you* did, bless you!

'Five years later a similar thing occurred, and he was, oh, so radiant! "Two of Humanity's crimes cancelled," he felt. Then came years and years of weary disappointment. "I shall never rest until I find the third," was what he always said.'

Here the girl began to cry, hiding her face behind her hands and murmuring something about, 'Too late, too late!'

I heard the doorbell ring.

'How he must have suffered!' I said. 'I'm so glad I had the luck to be the third.'

She withdrew her hands from her face and stared at me.

'And I'm so glad I'm going to meet him again,' I said, as I heard footsteps approaching.

'Meet him!' she echoed in amazement, as the footsteps drew near.

'Yes, I may stay, mayn't I? I heard your sister say he was coming round now.'

'Oh, I see!' she ejaculated. '*Her* father. We are only stepsisters. My dear father died seven years ago.'

THE WHITE HAND

A. L. Barker

b. 1916

Winner of the Somerset Maugham Award in 1947 for *Innocents*,
her very first collection of short stories, A. L. Barker subsequently
wrote a further eight acclaimed short-story collections and ten
novels. Over the years, her shorter fiction has been featured in
many anthologies, particularly those encompassing the
supernatural and the macabre.

THE WHIP HAND

IRENE HAS LEFT THIS ROOM on edge. As if a high, crowded chord had been struck and the air were still singing. It was the same, I remember, when she came here before. But that's because I have never been able to like Irene.

If it had been anyone else I could have spoken. I tried. 'A long while ago—' I said, but I didn't know how to put it and I was frightened. Irene jumped up and began pacing about the room. She gave me to understand that everything that had happened was my fault, if not mine personally it was the fault of my generation. After a while I stopped listening. I sat there waiting to speak. She must have asked a question because suddenly it was quiet and she was frowning at me. I said at once, 'It's rather odd—' I was going to put it as matter-of-factly as I could—but Irene cried, 'Odd? It's sheer incompetence! Muddle-headed panic. Oh, one would expect it from a clerk who had cooked the accounts'—she began to rage in her cold equable manner—'or a shopboy who'd been at the till. But not from the founder of a business, the owner of a shipping line, the managing director of an international freight company!'

Irene was frightened too, though not of the same thing, nor for the same reason. And as she talked of big impersonal affairs, of shipping companies and directorates, I felt this little piece of private information that I have taking root, and growing, and filling every corner of my mind. And now I don't think I shall ever be without it.

Irene has gone and I haven't told her and perhaps I shall never tell anyone. 'There are more things 'twixt Heaven and earth—' But I'm an old woman, I don't want to think of those things.

Irene will go to the police. When anyone is missing, that is the thing to do.

Arthur has not been heard of for three days, but I don't think Irene is afraid for him. She is afraid for his business. She talks about repercussions and loss of confidence. She calls Arthur an 'executive'. An executive cannot afford to be human, he must cover up his weaknesses. All he is allowed to admit to is a little dyspepsia. Unless Arthur returns with a very good reason—a business reason—to account for his absence, Irene says his credit will be undermined and his reputation—his business reputation—inevitably suspect.

Today, tomorrow, in a week's time, Irene will have to go to the police. They will start an investigation, question people who knew Arthur. They will question me. And I shall tell them—I shall try—what I know.

How shall I put it? I must think of that, I must be ready. It's not an easy story to tell.

How shall I begin? 'A long time ago—' No, I must begin at the beginning.

Arthur Paget is my nephew. I have known him since childhood. Perhaps the policeman won't think that has much bearing on the matter. I shall tell him it is, in fact, the crux of it. I shall also say that Arthur is neither an ordinary nor a simple man. It is only to Irene, his wife, that he seems an open book, and not a very readable one.

I REMEMBER THE FIRST inkling I had of Arthur's extraordinariness. He was six years old and in circumstances which were, to say the least, not as happy as most children's. His father ignored him; his mother—my only sister—had died at his birth. When my brother-in-law engaged a housekeeper he listed Arthur among her duties—poor child, he went with the house.

I did what I could. Sometimes I took him to the circus or the zoo or for a bus ride.

Each Saturday afternoon I would go and sit with him. I felt his need of company more than he did. He played silent, assiduous games, trotting urgently about, frowning over his toys, fetching and carrying, arranging and rearranging. He played, you might say, for dear life.

One afternoon I watched him set out his model farm. He picked up each lead animal in turn and peered at it. Already he needed glasses. When all the brown and white cows were in one corner and the black and white in another, he set a tin haystack between them. Then he brought out the bright blue farm cart, drawing the horse carefully this way and that as if to skirt the outbuildings and follow a devious track. For him, there were immutable woods and fields on the table-top.

'Lumley's have such pretty little wooden sheep, Arthur,' I said. 'Would you like some for your farm?'

He turned, squinting a little as he tried to focus on my face. 'Not sheep, thank you. The ground's too low.' He pointed to the middle of the table. 'There's a patch of marsh there and another here. It's rather damp, and that's bad for sheep. They get foot-rot, you know.'

'I didn't know. But of course I'm not a farmer.'

'Neither am I really. I'm learning.' I was about to ask him how, when he said, frowning deeply, 'We have a lot of trouble in the spring, the ground's too heavy for the plough. Sometimes I think we ought never to have bought this place.'

'It's all experience, isn't it?' I thought I was entering into the spirit of the thing. 'Why don't you look round for another farm, on the downs, perhaps?'

'We've put our money into this one.'

'I see.' Obviously one had to accept the obstacles before one overcame them. 'And I suppose you employ a lot of men?'

'No. There's only Brewer and me.'

'Brewer?'

'He's just gone into the barn to fork down some hay.'

'Is he your foreman?'

He shook his head.

'Tell me about him. Who is he?'

'He knows about farming.'

'And he teaches you?'

'I pick it up as we go along.'

'Oh well,' I said brightly, with no thought of deeper water, 'that's the best way to learn. And perhaps one day you'll have a real farm of your own.'

'This is a real farm.'

Perhaps I should have tried to make him understand about the tenuous line between the real and the imaginary and the advisability of keeping on the right side of it. Mind you, I don't know that it would have done any good.

'You haven't told me much about your Mr Brewer. Couldn't we be introduced?' I thought it was a simple matter of joining the child in his world.

'He's too busy.'

'Then you must tell me what he looks like, and where he comes from, and why he's called Brewer.'

'He's called Brewer because that's his name. I don't know where he comes from. Any more than I know where you come from.'

'I don't like rude little boys.'

There was a long pause. He seemed to be measuring me because he said, 'He's much taller than you—and big, bigger than anyone I ever saw. He has a red face and his hair's white.'

'He sounds rather nice—like Father Christmas.'

Arthur's shortsighted blinking suddenly focused in a steady stare. 'He isn't like Father Christmas.'

'Of course, farmers have red faces too, haven't they?'

'He isn't a farmer. He's old and he knows about everything.'

'How very useful. How old is Mr Brewer?'

'Fifty-five if he's a day.' He was so serious I dared not smile. 'He doesn't like people. He just doesn't like anyone looking at him.'

'Poor Mr Brewer.'

'He doesn't like pity, either.'

THAT WAS THE FIRST I heard of Brewer—forty years ago. It began a curious, one-sided acquaintanceship. I shall call it that, although the policeman will probably ask how could I be acquainted with someone I never met. I have often wondered myself.

Looking back, I understand my ready acceptance of the situation. I was a young woman of the world, a businesswoman, moving with times which were already moving too fast. But perhaps that was the trouble. In those days a woman who meant to make her own way needed almost belligerent good sense, and that was a quality I had never naturally possessed. My visits to Arthur were my one relaxation and when I went to see him I was only too glad to be neither belligerent nor particularly sensible. Indeed, had I chosen to fight it would have been a losing battle. My defeat would have done Arthur no good—perhaps not much harm, either. Most of that was done already.

I still believe Brewer got some of himself from a picture which hung in Arthur's room. It was a chalk drawing of Santa Claus, burly and benign, with a turkey-red face, a brimming sack at his feet, and hood flung back from a shock of frosty white hair. There was something a little sinister in the resemblance.

Such character as emerged, via Arthur, was unattractive. Brewer had no sense of humour and he was always right. If it hadn't been for a sort of reserve of power, as yet undeclared for good or ill, he would have been a prig. He was dreadfully lacking in human warmths or frailties, but of course that was Arthur's doing. No child, no man, for that matter, can accept frailty from his gods or devils.

My imagination has been enough for my comfort. To those small mysteries which have come into my life I have managed to find an explanation, however flimsy. The greater ones I have been content not to understand.

After the initial surprise, I didn't think there was much mystery about Brewer. Arthur had made him up out of odds and ends, like a Guy Fawkes with a paper face. Only he had taken rather less trouble with Brewer and there was nothing to show.

In agricultural matters, Brewer had a practical bent, which was why I supposed him to be confined to the toy farm, along with the invisible wood and fields. Since Arthur could not yet read and had no contact with the rare visitors to the house, I was curious to know the source of his information.

He told me, for instance, that although sheep would be a liability on his farm, pigs were a proposition. Thus instructed, I went to Lumley's and bought six, highly coloured and shiny, each wrapped in brown tissue paper.

Arthur was delighted with them. 'Aren't they *pink*! Pinker than ice-cake.'

That, of course, was only Arthur speaking. On my next visit he was waiting for me in the hall. He thrust the box into my hand before I had time to take off my hat. 'They're not the right kind.'

I looked at the little bits of shiny lead. 'I thought you liked the pink ones.'

He said scornfully, 'You don't buy a pig for its colour. It's the breed that matters. Brewer won't have anything but Wessex Saddlebacks.'

'Indeed?' I drew the long pin out of my hat. 'How do you know these aren't—what d'you call them—Saddlebacks?'

'Anyone can see they're not. Wessex Saddlebacks are black with white front legs and a white bit like a saddle. These—' Arthur shrugged. 'I don't expect the breeder even knew what he was crossing.'

'I'd be interested,' I said, 'to know how *you* know.'

'Brewer told me.'

It was high time to bring him down to earth. 'I'm sorry, Arthur, but these are the only kind they have in the shop.' He went scarlet with dismay when I took off my hat. I really believe he meant me to take those ridiculous toys back to Lumley's then and there. 'You'll just have to pretend they're something else.'

'Pretend?' said this child who had talked of Wessex Saddlebacks and hinted at a knowledge of genetics. 'What's pretend?'

'You'd better ask Brewer.'

IF I SAY ARTHUR REALLY WORKED that toy farm, the policeman will write me off as a cranky old woman. Yet I swear the lead animals and the tin haystack were to him what small stock and uncertain crops are to any struggling farmer. They were just as vulnerable, bright paint could not keep a cow from sickening nor could a lead stomach keep it from dying.

One day, Mrs Thurlow, the housekeeper, came in with something in the palm of her hand. 'What are these doing in the boiler fire?'

Arthur turned his head away. 'They're dead.'

'Why,' I said in surprise, 'two of your brown and white cows, Arthur, the ones you call Jerseys—'

He wouldn't look. 'They had a disease. If you don't burn them, it spreads.'

'What nonsense.' Mrs Thurlow made as if to put them back with the rest of the farm. 'Throwing away perfectly good toys.'

'They're dead!' Arthur sprang at her, screaming. 'Can't you see they're dead!' Rage and fear gathered in a knot on his forehead. 'Can't you see the worms crawling out of them? And the flies! They're black with flies!'

'Arthur!'

He hid his face in his hands. 'I can't see them for flies—'

Mrs Thurlow's lips tightened like a thread.

'Please,' I said hastily, 'I really think it would be best if you put them in the dustbin and said no more about it.'

She gave me a bitter look and swept out of the room without a word.

What was I to say? That he was too young for such thoughts? That death wasn't like that? That the line had been drawn between fact and fancy and he must keep on the right side of it?

'Aunt Ethne, couldn't we go for a walk?' He took away his hands—his face had a greenish tinge. 'I can still smell those cows.'

FACT AND FANCY—in those days I believed in watertight compartments for each. I was too young to wonder if the fact which looked so clear and salient to me might be distorted at the source of my own mind's eye.

Arthur used to come to me, his brow all furrowed with worry. 'We must have a new plough. Brewer says the old one won't hold together any more.' And if I, to jockey him over to the right side of the line, answered, 'But you haven't got a plough, not even an old one,' he would produce a piece of bent wire and show me where the heavy soil had queered the blade and where the sockets had dissolved into rust. Or it was a float they must have, to take the milk to the station. 'Brewer needs the cart now, you see, to get the roots in from the top field.' Or it was a pond they lacked. Brewer said they must sink a pond over by the barn. 'Look,' he'd point to the table-top, 'isn't that the first farm you ever saw without a pond in the yard?'

I'd give him sixpence, or lend him the mirror out of my handbag, and he'd set two ducks on it and his troubles would be over—until the next time.

'You really want to be a farmer, don't you?'

'No.' He sounded faintly surprised. 'Not really.'

'Then it must be Brewer who wants it.'

'Oh no.' He picked up a horse and squinted carefully at it. 'He says we could use oxen for ploughing—'

'But I thought you were so very keen on farming?'

'No, I'm not. Neither is he.'

'Then on something connected with farming?'

'He isn't keen on anything.' Arthur put the horse to drink at the looking-glass pond. 'It's failure he's afraid of.'

It was an odd thing for a child to say. Odd enough to make me do something I really disliked. I went to his father.

My brother-in-law had a smooth unimpeachable manner which made me feel like a gauche and not too attractive schoolgirl. His work took him to Paris and Rome for long periods and when he came home he seldom stayed more than a day or two. When I saw him he was already on the point of leaving again. I wondered if he had so much as set eyes on Arthur for the past six months.

'You must excuse me,' he pointed to his travelling coat. 'I have to be away again in a few moments.'

I stated my business at once. 'Something must be done about Arthur.' He raised his eyebrows without undue surprise. The subject was not one which interested him. 'Arthur is alone too much.'

'Indeed? Is he becoming dull?'

'Not at all. He has a lively imagination—too lively.'

'By what standard?'

'By mine,' I said boldly. 'I've always considered it pretty normal.'

'For a child?'

I could feel my temper rising.

'If I appear to meddle it is at least out of concern and affection for the boy.'

'Very creditable.' He went to the window and waved to the cab which had just arrived. 'You can set your mind at rest. I have arranged for Arthur to go to boarding school in the autumn.'

IT WAS A GREY SEPTEMBER morning when I saw Arthur off at the station. He looked small and owlish in his new spectacles. To me there was something barbarous in putting a child in a stiff collar and throwing him on the world. I looked at the hordes of boys, shrill and quick as monkeys, who were swarming over the train, and shuddered to think of the treatment a small recluse could expect from them. Arthur himself appeared calm and even hopeful. He did not cry or cling—who was there to cry or cling to? I was only an occasional aunt and Brewer—Brewer wasn't built for clinging. In any case, he was packed away at home with the toy farm. But not so well packed, I felt, that he would not be subject to evaporation.

During Arthur's schooldays I saw little of him. Between terms he went to stay with a family at Aldeburgh. I don't think my brother-in-law was being mindful of the dangers of solitude—he simply found it more convenient to sell his house in London and buy a villa in Italy. There was, it seemed, no place for Arthur there.

One wet evening I was alone in my flat, waiting for some friends. There wasn't much motor traffic in those days, I could hear a broken guttering steadily spilling on the other side of the Square.

The doorbell rang. My friends were early, I thought, but when I opened the door a boy, hatless and coatless, was stooping to pull his draggled socks over his knees.

'Arthur!'

He blinked at me. Beads of rain dropped from his glasses on to his cheek. He brushed them off with the flat of his hand. 'Hello, Aunt Ethne. I hope I'm not disturbing you—'

'Of course not! It's lovely to see you—but you're soaking! Come in and take off your wet things—'

I fussed round him, took his jacket and shoes and made him sit by the fire. He had had no supper, so I heated some milk and cut a plate of sandwiches. He ate hungrily and in silence, watching with pleasure the faint steam that curled off his wet clothes.

'Now tell me, what are you doing here?'

His pleasure faded at once. He took up his glass of milk and went to the window.

'It's nice here. Is that Hyde Park you can see between the houses?'

'Arthur—I asked you a question.'

'I came by train.'

It was curious, the sense of disadvantage I had, akin in a small way to the feeling his father provoked in me.

He finished his milk and turned the clouded glass between his fingers. 'I got on the train at Savernake all right. But at this end they found me out. I had to get away through a siding.'

'Found you out?'

'I hadn't a ticket.'

'Are you trying to tell me you've run away from school?' But he wasn't trying to tell me anything. It was I who was trying. 'You're old enough to have reasons for what you do and of course I'll help in any way I can. But if you've left school without permission I'm bound to send you back.'

'I know.'

'Then why—are you unhappy at school?'

'Not particularly. School's dull, of course, but you've got to grow up.'

'Were you in some sort of trouble?'

'No. I ran away because I thought I could.' He shrugged. 'I'm going back because I know I can't.'

'You couldn't get any farther than London—is that what you mean?'

'There was a goods train in the siding. Going to Bristol. I only had to climb in. And at Bristol I'd have got on a ship. I'd have worked a passage somewhere—anywhere. It wouldn't have mattered. And if they wouldn't let me work, I'd have stowed away.' I was puzzled—Arthur had never struck me as the adventurous kind. 'It wouldn't have been any use.'

'No?'

His eyes, which looked so watery behind the thick glasses, suddenly sharpened. 'I wasn't on my own any more.'

'What do you mean?'

'I had been—all day. That's why I thought it was going to work.' He added, with a kind of played-out bitterness, 'That's all *I* knew.'

'But if you weren't on your own—who was with you?'

'Who?' He gave me a wry look, like someone turning aside the precocious questions of a child.

'I can't help if you won't tell me the truth—'

'There was no one. No one to speak of.' From his pocket he took a stub of pencil. 'Shall I write an IOU for my fare back, Aunt Ethne?'

IT MUST BE YEARS since I thought of Brewer. Until Irene came today I'd forgotten—that he ever existed, I was going to say. Arthur, certainly, hasn't reminded me. After he packed up his toys and went away to school he never mentioned the name again. Yet now I wonder how often he spoke to me of Brewer without my knowing.

My brother-in-law died while Arthur was at Cambridge. In death, as in life, he ignored his son. There was enough money to see the boy through college, nothing more.

Arthur took a practical view.

'It only means I shall have to stand on my own feet. That's not a bad thing, surely?'

'Indeed no, but it was in your father's power to give you a start in life and I think you had a right to it.'

'It was his money, he may have thought he had a right to spend it.'

Knowing how and where most of it was spent, I must have been looking prim because Arthur burst out laughing.

'Cheer up, Aunt Ethne, I shan't starve. As a matter of fact, I'm going into business.'

'I'd hoped you'd choose one of the professions. There are grants and scholar-ships—'

'Not for me. My place is in the commercial world, and it's time I was carving it out.' He began to tramp to and fro with long scissoring strides. 'I shall leave college at the end of term and start looking for an opening. There'll be enough money to tide me over till I find what I want.'

'But what about your degree?'

'A degree cuts no ice in business. And there's no one to disappoint if I don't take it.'

'I shall be disappointed.'

He looked surprised. 'I'm sorry, Aunt Ethne. But you do agree it's sound common sense?'

'If I didn't, it wouldn't make the slightest difference, would it?'

'No. But that's—what d'you call it—the courage of my convictions.'

'Have you talked it over with anyone else?'

'Yes.'

'With whom? Was it someone knowledgeable?'

He smiled. 'You may take it I'm acting on the best possible advice.'

IT SEEMED AS IF HE WAS. His business career has been a brilliant one. Irene, his wife, knows far more about it than I do. It is his business she loves; I think it was his business she married. Perhaps she knows great happiness only when she walks into his office and sees the typists at their desks, the clerks, the telephon-ists, the secretaries, the departmental managers, the pebbled glass doors of the Board of Directors—all that monstrous humming hive. But it's more like a top than a hive because there's no honey, no sweetness, only a shrill fanatical hum.

Arthur comes one or two evenings a week for half an hour. He sits in that chair and I make him China tea. I can show them the tray—I set it every day at five in case he comes—and on the table I put a little Burmese brass dish for his cigarette. Arthur is what they call a chain smoker.

We don't say very much. He sips his tea and his face grows a little smoother. But he can't keep his hands still. They twitch and jump and tap and flutter, and sometimes the fingers rub the ball of the thumb as if they were trying to rub off something tacky. He told me once that it was the only time he could rest—here, in this chair. I said, 'Success hasn't made you very happy,' and he answered, 'That's something I never expected, but I always thought there'd be an end to it.' I don't know what he meant.

It's a week since he was here. Irene came tonight, and that in itself was an event. The only other time she visited me was before her marriage.

She asked if Arthur had been to see me and I said not for several days. I don't think she realises how often he came.

'Did he come here on Monday or Tuesday—or today?'

'I haven't seen him this week.'

'Neither has anyone.'

'What do you mean?'

She began to walk about the room. 'He seems to be missing.'

'Missing?' I couldn't think while she was picking up and putting down, one after the other, all my little bits of china and porcelain on the mantelshelf. I wanted to say, 'You won't find him there.'

'I haven't seen him since Sunday evening. He didn't go to his office on Monday, or Tuesday, and he hasn't been there today. He hasn't been to his club or to any of his friends—at least, not to those I know.' She opened a tortoiseshell musical box and flicked it shut at the first chime. 'He's simply vanished.'

'But—surely he must have gone away on business?'

'I know of no business,' she said slowly, stressing the word, 'to take him away so suddenly. Even if something new had come up, there's the telephone—he could have sent a wire.'

'Then, do you think—an accident?'

'I don't think he's been run over, if that's what you mean.' She drew on her gloves, smoothing them at each finger like a second skin.

'He may have been overworking'—'overdriven', I would have called it—'and had a lapse of memory. These things do happen. Oh, but I'm sure there's some perfectly ordinary explanation—'

'Arthur's such a fool.' She cried, in a gust of rage, 'I shall never forgive him for that.'

'I don't agree, and I've known him all his life.' Her shrug was offensive, as she meant it to be. 'If you can't assess him by any other standard, take him at his face value. No fool could build up and command a business as he has.'

'*He* build up? *He* command?' There was derision in her voice. 'I thought so too, when I married him. True, he was honest. He told me his were not the brains behind the business. He said he was only a glorified clerk who did as he was told. He was anxious that I should marry him for his own sake.' She smiled bitterly. 'I took that for modesty.'

'What nonsense! If Arthur doesn't control the business, who does?'

'His partner.'

'I didn't know he had one.'

'Does he never talk to you?'

'Not about business.' I said pointedly, 'He seems glad to be allowed to forget it once in a while.'

That seemed to amuse her. 'I dare say. Brewer never rests and doesn't expect anyone else to.'

'Brewer?'

'Arthur's partner. The man who holds the reins. He's smart with the whip, too.'

Strange how that name had waited under the surface of my mind. I didn't even have to dig for it. Forty years—'It isn't possible!'

Irene's brows lifted. 'What isn't?'

'You said the partner's name was Brewer?'

'What do you know about him?'

'Years ago, when he was a little boy, Arthur used to talk about someone—of that name.'

'Well it could hardly be the same man, could it?'

'No, of course not.' My laugh sounded shaky. 'That was stupid. But it is a coincidence—'

'Why? There must be hundreds of Brewers—thousands.' Her impatience suddenly flickered out. 'In a sense, of course, there aren't. There's the man himself'—she stroked her gloved fingers, smiling with private pleasure—'one of the giants who keep other men in their pockets. Arthur's afraid of him.'

'Why should he be?'

'Brewer's too big, Arthur can't keep up. The business is too big—Arthur never dreamed of, nor wanted, such power. He's afraid of it. He really is only a glorified clerk, you know.'

'This man Brewer—do you know him well?'

'If you mean socially, no I don't. Neither does anyone. He never accepts invitations and as far as I can make out, no one at the office has set eyes on him. He goes there occasionally, after the staff has gone. Arthur won't even say where he lives—sometimes I wonder if he knows himself.'

I could feel a heavy fluttering, almost a floundering, under my ribs. The room seemed to waver as if it were filling with water. I tried to speak, but I couldn't find words, and Irene stood there frowning.

'That's what makes it so difficult.' Her voice came from a long way off. 'Brewer knows where Arthur is. He must know. He saw him last.'

'Brewer? Brewer saw him?'

'On Sunday night. I went to dinner with some friends and when I came home I found that Brewer had been to the house. There was a quarrel, a pretty violent one by all accounts. They shut themselves in the library, but apparently Arthur shouted like a maniac. I was half expecting something of the sort. They've been at loggerheads for weeks over some Mexican venture of Brewer's. Arthur seemed to think it was shady.' She said scornfully, 'Sometimes he acts more like a choirboy than a businessman.'

'But Brewer was in the library, with Arthur?'

'And made himself felt. A man like that isn't lightly crossed. When I got home it was all over. Arthur had locked himself in, to lick his wounds, I imagine.'

'But no one saw Brewer!'

'I did. All these years I wanted to meet him, and on Sunday night I did. For the first time.'

'You *met* him?'

She was too full of her own thoughts to notice my agitation. 'One could hardly call it a meeting—he was in rather a hurry and we weren't introduced, but I hope it's broken the ice.'

'He was—flesh and blood?'

'Flesh and blood? What an extraordinary thing to say! As a matter of fact, my impression was of a very virile man. It's true I had only a brief glimpse. He strode past me and out of the door as I crossed the hall. But—flesh and blood—yes.'

'What did he look like?'

'Like a man'—why, I thought, she's half in love with him—'in the prime of life, big, bluff, and very solid. White hair—oh, not an old man's wispy yellow— a strong stiff thatch of pure white, standing up from his forehead. And a big, ruddy face, as if he spent a lot of time out-of-doors.'

'He used to be a farmer.'

'What?'

She was getting impatient again. If she was going to be impatient, I couldn't tell her. What was there to tell? There was something, a great deal, in a manner of speaking. If I could only find the manner. 'A long while ago—'

But Irene wouldn't listen. 'Arthur's a fool'—her anger was turned on me— 'and weak. It's a dangerous combination. He has spasms of courage and spasms of intuition, but they never coincide. Also,' she added calmly, 'he has a gun.'

'A gun!' Was there something to laugh at? I could feel laughter coming loud and shrill. 'And you're afraid for Brewer?'

'No. I'm rather afraid for Arthur.'

She touched my cheek with her gloved fingers—Irene never kisses her relatives—and went away. I heard her car start up, I listened while it swung round the Square and hooted smartly at the High Road. Irene is going home to see if any news has come through in her absence. News of Arthur. Or Brewer.

Today, tomorrow, in a week's time, she will have to go to the police. I hope she goes today. I hope she doesn't leave it later than tomorrow, because the police will be able to explain what has happened.

Of course, there's a very simple explanation. The policeman will say, 'This is what happened—'

I hope he will come soon. I wish he would. I wish he would come and explain.

Ambrose Bierce

1842–1914?

A native of Ohio, Ambrose Bierce fought bravely in the
American Civil War before becoming a journalist and writer in
San Francisco. He never quite settled down to a steady life, and in
1913 he went to Mexico, intending to report on the war that was
then raging there. He wrote one letter home and then
disappeared. Nobody knows how he died, or exactly when.

A TOUGH TUSSLE

ONE NIGHT IN THE AUTUMN of 1861 a man sat alone in the heart of a forest in western Virginia. The region was one of the wildest on the continent—the Cheat Mountain country. There was no lack of people close at hand, however; within a mile of where the man sat was the now silent camp of a whole Federal brigade. Somewhere about—it might be still nearer—was a force of the enemy, the numbers unknown. It was this uncertainty as to its numbers and position that accounted for the man's presence in that lonely spot; he was a young officer of a Federal infantry regiment and his business there was to guard his sleeping comrades in the camp against a surprise. He was in command of a detachment of men constituting a picket guard. These men he had stationed just at nightfall in an irregular line, determined by the nature of the ground, several hundred yards in front of where he now sat. The line ran through the forest, among the rocks and laurel thickets, the men fifteen or twenty paces apart, all in concealment and under injunction of strict silence and unremitting vigilance. In four hours, if nothing occurred, they would be relieved by a fresh detachment from the reserve now resting in care of its captain some distance away to the left and rear. Before stationing his men the young officer of whom we are writing had pointed out to his two sergeants the spot at which he would be found if it should be necessary to consult him, or if his presence at the front line should be required.

It was a quiet enough spot—the fork of an old wood-road, on the two branches of which, prolonging themselves deviously forward in the dim moonlight, the sergeants were themselves stationed, a few paces in rear of the line. If driven sharply back by a sudden onset of the enemy—and pickets are not expected to make a stand after firing—the men would come into the converging roads and naturally following them to their point of intersection could be rallied and 'formed'. In his small way the author of these dispositions was something of a strategist; if Napoleon had planned as intelligently at Waterloo he would have won that memorable battle and been overthrown later.

Second Lieutenant Brainerd Byring was a brave and efficient officer, young and comparatively inexperienced as he was in the business of killing his fellow men. He had enlisted in the very first days of the war as a private, with no military knowledge whatever, had been made first sergeant of his company on account of his education and engaging manner, and had been lucky enough to lose his captain by a Confederate bullet; in the resulting promotions he had gained a commission. He had been in several engagements, such as they were—at Philippi, Rich Mountain, Carrick's Ford and Greenbrier—and had borne himself with such gallantry as not to attract the attention of his superior officers. The exhilaration of battle was agreeable to him, but the sight of the dead, with their clay faces, blank eyes and stiff bodies, which when not unnaturally shrunken were unnaturally swollen, had always intolerably affected him. He felt toward them a kind of reasonless antipathy that was something more than the physical and spiritual repugnance common to us all. Doubtless this feeling was due to his unusually acute sensibilities—his keen sense of the beautiful, which these hideous things outraged. Whatever may have been the cause, he could not look upon a dead body without a loathing which had in it an element of resentment. What others have respected as the dignity of death had to him no existence—was altogether unthinkable. Death was a thing to be hated. It was not picturesque, it had no tender and solemn side—a dismal thing, hideous in all its manifestations and suggestions. Lieutenant Byring was a braver man than anybody knew, for nobody knew his horror of that which he was ever ready to incur.

Having posted his men, instructed his sergeants and retired to his station, he seated himself on a log, and with senses all alert began his vigil. For greater ease he loosened his sword belt and taking his heavy revolver from his holster laid it on the log beside him. He felt very comfortable, though he hardly gave the fact a thought, so intently did he listen for any sound from the front which might have a menacing significance—a shout, a shot, or the footfall of one of his sergeants coming to apprise him of something worth knowing. From the vast, invisible ocean of moonlight overhead fell, here and there, a slender, broken stream that seemed to plash against the intercepting branches and trickle to earth, forming small white pools among the clumps of laurel. But these leaks were few and served only to accentuate the blackness of his environment, which his imagination found it easy to people with all manner of unfamiliar shapes, menacing, uncanny, or merely grotesque.

He to whom the portentous conspiracy of night and solitude and silence in the heart of a great forest is not an unknown experience needs not to be told what another world it all is—how even the most commonplace and familiar objects take on another character. The trees group themselves differently; they draw closer together, as if in fear. The very silence has another quality than the silence of the day. And it is full of half-heard whispers—whispers that startle—ghosts of sounds long dead. There are living sounds, too, such as are never heard under other conditions: notes of strange night birds, the cries of small animals in sudden encounters with stealthy foes or in their dreams, a rustling in the dead leaves—it may be the leap of a wood-rat, it may be the footfall of a panther. What caused the breaking of that twig?—what the low, alarmed twittering in that bushful of birds? There are sounds without a name, forms without substance, translations in space of objects which have not been seen to move, movements wherein nothing is observed to change its place. Ah, children of the sunlight and the gaslight, how little you know of the world in which you live!

Surrounded at a little distance by armed and watchful friends, Byring felt utterly alone. Yielding himself to the solemn and mysterious spirit of the time and place, he had forgotten the nature of his connection with the visible and audible aspects and phases of the night. The forest was boundless; men and the habitations of men did not exist. The universe was one primeval mystery of darkness, without form and void, himself the sole, dumb questioner of its eternal secret. Absorbed in thoughts born of this mood, he suffered the time to slip away unnoted. Meantime the infrequent patches of white light lying amongst the tree trunks had undergone changes of size, form and place. In one of them near by, just at the roadside, his eye fell upon an object that he had not previously observed. It was almost before his face as he sat; he could have sworn that it had not before been there. It was partly covered in shadow, but he could see that it was a human figure. Instinctively he adjusted the clasp of his sword belt and laid hold of his pistol—again he was in a world of war, by occupation an assassin.

The figure did not move. Rising, pistol in hand, he approached. The figure lay upon its back, its upper part in shadow, but standing above it and looking down upon the face, he saw that it was a dead body. He shuddered and turned from it with a feeling of sickness and disgust, resumed his seat upon the log, and forgetting military prudence struck a match and lit a cigar. In the sudden blackness that followed the extinction of the flame he felt a sense of relief; he could no longer see the object of his aversion. Nevertheless, he kept his eyes set in that direction until it appeared again with growing distinctness. It seemed to have moved a trifle nearer.

'Damn the thing!' he muttered. 'What does it want?'

It did not appear to be in need of anything but a soul.

Byring turned away his eyes and began humming a tune, but he broke off in the middle of a bar and looked at the dead body. Its presence annoyed him, though he could hardly have had a quieter neighbour. He was conscious, too, of a vague, indefinable feeling that was new to him. It was not fear, but rather a sense of the supernatural—in which he did not at all believe.

'I have inherited it,' he said to himself. 'I suppose it will require a thousand ages—perhaps ten thousand—for humanity to outgrow this feeling. Where and when did it originate? Away back, probably, in what is called the cradle of the human race—the plains of Central Asia. What we inherit as a superstition our barbarous ancestors must have held as a reasonable conviction. Doubtless they believed themselves justified by facts whose nature we cannot even conjecture in thinking a dead body a malign thing endowed with some strange power of mischief, with perhaps a will and a purpose to exert it. Possibly they had some awful form of religion of which that was one of the chief doctrines, sedulously taught by their priesthood, as ours teach the immortality of the soul. As the Aryans moved slowly on, to and through the Caucasus passes, and spread over Europe, new conditions of life must have resulted in the formulation of new religions. The old belief in the malevolence of the dead body was lost from the creeds and even perished from tradition, but it left its heritage of terror, which is transmitted from generation to generation—is as much a part of us as are our blood and bones.'

In following out his thought he had forgotten that which suggested it; but now his eye fell again upon the corpse. The shadow had now altogether uncovered it. He saw the sharp profile, the chin in the air, the whole face, ghastly white in the moonlight. The clothing was grey, the uniform of a Confederate soldier. The coat and waistcoat, unbuttoned, had fallen away on each side, exposing the white shirt. The chest seemed unnaturally prominent, but the abdomen had sunk in, leaving a sharp projection at the line of the lower ribs. The arms were extended, the left knee was thrust upward. The whole posture impressed Byring as having been studied with a view to the horrible.

'Bah!' he exclaimed; 'he was an actor—he knows how to be dead.'

He drew away his eyes, directing them resolutely along one of the roads leading to the front, and resumed his philosophising where he had left off.

'It may be that our Central Asian ancestors had not the custom of burial. In that case it is easy to understand their fear of the dead, who really were a menace and an evil. They bred pestilences. Children were taught to avoid the places where they lay, and to run away if by inadvertence they came near a corpse. I think, indeed, I'd better go away from this chap.'

He half rose to do so, then remembered that he had told his men in front and the officer in the rear who was to relieve him that he could at any time be found at that spot. It was a matter of pride, too. If he abandoned his post he feared they would think he feared the corpse. He was no coward and he was unwilling to incur anybody's ridicule. So he again seated himself, and to prove his courage looked boldly at the body. The right arm—the one farthest from him—was now in shadow. He could barely see the hand which, he had before observed, lay at the root of a clump of laurel. There had been no change, a fact which gave him a certain comfort, he could not have said why. He did not at once remove his eyes; that which we do not wish to see has a strange fascination, sometimes irresistible. Of the woman who covers her eyes with her hands and looks between the fingers let it be said that the wits have dealt with her not altogether justly.

Byring suddenly became conscious of a pain in his right hand. He withdrew his eyes from his enemy and looked at it. He was grasping the hilt of his drawn sword so tightly that it hurt him. He observed, too, that he was leaning forward in a strained attitude—crouching like a gladiator ready to spring at the throat of an antagonist. His teeth were clenched and he was breathing hard. This matter was soon set right, and as his muscles relaxed and he drew a long breath he felt keenly enough the ludicrousness of the incident. It affected him to laughter. Heavens! what sound was that? what mindless devil was uttering an unholy glee in mockery of human merriment? He sprang to his feet and looked about him, not recognising his own laugh.

He could no longer conceal from himself the horrible fact of his cowardice; he was thoroughly frightened! He would have run from the spot, but his legs refused their office; they gave way beneath him and he sat again upon the log, violently trembling. His face was wet, his whole body bathed in a chill perspiration. He could not even cry out. Distinctly he heard behind him a stealthy tread, as of some wild animal, and dared not look over his shoulder. Had the soulless living joined forces with the soulless dead?—was it an animal? Ah, if he could but be assured of that! But by no effort of will could he now unfix his gaze from the face of the dead man.

I repeat that Lieutenant Byring was a brave and intelligent man. But what would you have? Shall a man cope, single-handed, with so monstrous an alliance as that of night and solitude and silence and the dead—while an incalculable host of his own ancestors shriek into the ear of his spirit their coward counsel, sing their doleful death-songs in his heart, and disarm his very blood of all its iron? The odds are too great—courage was not made for so rough use as that.

One sole conviction now had the man in possession: that the body had moved. It lay nearer to the edge of its plot of light—there could be no doubt of it. It had also moved its arms, for, look, they are both in the shadow! A breath of cold air struck Byring full in the face; the boughs of trees above him stirred and moaned. A strongly defined shadow passed across the face of the dead, left it luminous, passed back upon it and left it half obscured. The horrible thing was visibly moving! At that moment a single shot rang out upon the picket line—a lonelier and louder, though more distant, shot than ever had been heard by mortal ear! It broke the spell of that enchanted man; it slew the silence and the solitude, dispersed the hindering host from Central Asia and released his modern manhood. With a cry like that of some great bird pouncing upon its prey he sprang forward, hot-hearted for action!

Shot after shot now came from the front. There were shoutings and confusion, hoof-beats and desultory cheers. Away to the rear, in the sleeping camp, were a singing of bugles and grumble of drums. Pushing through the thickets on either side the roads came the Federal pickets, in full retreat, firing backward at random as they ran. A straggling group that had followed back one of the roads, as instructed, suddenly sprang away into the bushes as half a hundred horsemen thundered by them, striking wildly with their sabres as they passed. At headlong speed these mounted madmen shot past the spot where Byring had sat, and vanished round an angle of the road, shouting and firing their pistols. A moment later there was a roar of musketry, followed by dropping shots—they had encountered the reserve guard in line; and back they came in dire confusion, with here and there an empty saddle and many a maddened horse, bullet-stung, snorting and plunging with pain. It was all over—'an affair of outposts'.

The line was re-established with fresh men, the roll called, the stragglers were re-formed. The Federal commander with a part of his staff, imperfectly clad, appeared upon the scene, asked a few questions, looked exceedingly wise and retired. After standing at arms for an hour the brigade in camp 'swore a prayer or two' and went to bed.

Early the next morning a fatigue party, commanded by a captain and accompanied by a surgeon, searched the ground for dead and wounded. At the fork of the road, a little to one side, they found two bodies lying close together—that of a Federal officer and that of a Confederate private. The officer had died of a sword-thrust through the heart, but not, apparently, until he had inflicted upon his enemy no fewer than five dreadful wounds. The dead officer lay on his face in a pool of blood, the weapon still in his breast. They turned him on his back and the surgeon removed it.

'Gad!' said the captain—'It is Byring!'—adding, with a glance at the other, 'They had a tough tussle.'

The surgeon was examining the sword. It was that of a line officer of Federal infantry—exactly like the one worn by the captain. It was, in fact, Byring's own. The only other weapon discovered was an undischarged revolver in the dead officer's belt.

The surgeon laid down the sword and approached the other body. It was frightfully gashed and stabbed, but there was no blood. He took hold of the left foot and tried to straighten the leg. In the effort the body was displaced. The dead do not wish to be moved—it protested with a faint, sickening odour. Where it had lain were a few maggots, manifesting an imbecile activity.

The surgeon looked at the captain. The captain looked at the surgeon.

Algernon Blackwood

1869–1951

One of the greatest ghost-story writers, British-born Algernon
Blackwood tried farming and gold prospecting in Canada before
embarking on a literary career. Fascinated by the supernatural, he
was very successful at creating an atmosphere of terror. From the
mid-1930s, as a result of his BBC radio broadcasts, he became
nationally famous as 'The Ghost Man'.

TRANSITION

JOHN MUDBURY WAS ON HIS WAY home from the shops, his arms full of
Christmas Presents. It was after six o'clock and the streets were very
crowded. He was an ordinary man, lived in an ordinary suburban flat, with
an ordinary wife and ordinary children. *He* did not think them ordinary, but
everybody else did. He had ordinary presents for each one, a cheap blotter for his
wife, a cheap air gun for the boy, and so forth. He was over fifty, bald, in an
office, decent in mind and habits, of uncertain opinions, uncertain politics, and
uncertain religion. Yet he considered himself a decided, positive gentleman,
quite unaware that the morning newspaper determined his opinions for the day.
He just lived—from day to day. Physically, he was fit enough, except for a weak
heart (which never troubled him); and his summer holiday was bad golf, while
the children bathed and his wife read Garvice on the sands. Like the majority of
men, he dreamed idly of the past, muddled away the present, and guessed
vaguely—after imaginative reading on occasions—at the future.

'I'd like to survive all right,' he said, 'provided it's better than this,' surveying
his wife and children, and thinking of his daily toil. 'Otherwise—!' and he
shrugged his shoulders as a brave man should.

He went to church regularly. But nothing in church convinced him that he
did survive, just as nothing in church enticed him into hoping that he would. On
the other hand, nothing in life persuaded him that he didn't, wouldn't, couldn't.
'I'm an Evolutionist,' he loved to say to thoughtful cronies (over a glass), having
never heard that Darwinism had been questioned.

And so he came home gaily, happily, with his bunch of Christmas Presents
'for the wife and little ones', stroking himself upon their keen enjoyment and

excitement. The night before he had taken 'the wife' to see *Magic* at a select London theatre where the Intellectuals went—and had been extraordinarily stirred. He had gone questioningly, yet expecting something out of the common. 'It's *not* musical,' he warned her, 'nor farce, nor comedy, so to speak', and in answer to her question as to what the critics had said, he had wriggled, sighed, and put his gaudy necktie straight four times in quick succession. For no Man in the Street, with any claim to self-respect, could be expected to understand what the critics had said, even if he understood the Play. And John had answered truthfully: 'Oh, they just said things. But the theatre's always full—and that's the only test.'

And just now, as he crossed the crowded Circus to catch his bus, it chanced that his mind (having glimpsed an advertisement) was full of this particular Play, or, rather, of the effect it had produced upon him at the time. For it had thrilled him—inexplicably: with its marvellous speculative hint, its big audacity, its alert and spiritual beauty . . . Thought plunged to find something—plunged after this bizarre suggestion of a bigger universe, after this quasi-jocular suggestion that man is not the only—then dashed full-tilt against a sentence that memory thrust beneath his nose: 'Science does *not* exhaust the Universe'—and at the same time dashed full-tilt against destruction of another kind as well . . . !

How it happened he never exactly knew. He saw a Monster glaring at him with eyes of blazing fire. It was horrible! It rushed upon him. He dodged . . . Another monster met him round the corner. Both came at him simultaneously. He dodged again—a leap that might have cleared a hurdle easily, but was too late. Between the pair of them—his heart literally in his gullet—he was mercilessly caught. Bones crunched . . . There was a soft sensation, icy cold and hot as fire. Horns and voices roared. Battering-rams he saw, and a carapace of iron . . . Then dazzling light . . . 'Always *face* the traffic!' he remembered with a frantic yell—and, by some extraordinary luck, escaped miraculously on to the opposite pavement.

There was no doubt about it. By the skin of his teeth he had dodged a rather ugly death. First . . . he felt for his Presents—all were safe. And then, instead of congratulating himself and taking breath, he hurried homewards—on foot, which proved that his mind had lost control a bit!—thinking only how disappointed the wife and children would have been if—well, if anything had happened. Another thing he realised, oddly enough, was that he no longer really loved his wife, but had only great affection for her. What made him think of that, Heaven only knows, but he *did* think of it. He was an honest man without pretence. This came as a discovery somehow. He turned a moment, and saw the crowd gathered about the entangled taxicabs, policemen's helmets gleaming in the lights of the shop windows . . . then hurried on again, his thoughts full of the joy his Presents would give . . . of the scampering children . . . and of his wife—bless her silly heart!—eyeing the mysterious parcels . . .

And, though he never could explain how, he presently stood at the door of the jail-like building that contained his flat, having walked the whole three miles. His thoughts had been so busy and absorbed that he had hardly noticed the length of weary trudge. 'Besides,' he reflected, thinking of the narrow escape, 'I've had a nasty shock. It was a damned near thing, now I come to think of it . . .' He still felt a bit shaky and bewildered. Yet, at the same time, he felt extraordinarily jolly and light-hearted.

He counted his Christmas parcels . . . hugged himself in anticipatory joy—and let himself in swiftly with his latchkey. 'I'm late,' he realised, 'but when she sees the brown-paper parcels, she'll forget to say a word. God bless the old faithful soul.' And he softly used the key a second time and entered his flat on tiptoe . . . In his mind was the master impulse of that afternoon—the pleasure these Christmas Presents would give his wife and children.

He heard a noise. He hung up hat and coat in the poky vestibule (they never called it 'hall') and moved softly towards the parlour door, holding the packages behind him. Only of them he thought, not of himself—of his family, that is, not of the packages. Pushing the door cunningly ajar, he peeped in shyly. To his amazement the room was full of people. He withdrew quickly, wondering what it meant. A party? And without his knowing about it? Extraordinary! . . . Keen disappointment came over him. But as he stepped back, the vestibule, he saw, was full of people too.

He was uncommonly surprised, yet somehow not surprised at all. People were congratulating him. There was a perfect mob of them. Moreover, he knew them all—vaguely remembered them, at least. And they all knew him.

'Isn't it a game?' laughed someone, patting him on the back. '*They* haven't the least idea . . . !'

And the speaker, it was old John Palmer, the bookkeeper at the office—emphasised the 'they'.

'Not the least idea,' he answered with a smile, saying something he didn't understand, yet knew was right.

His face, apparently, showed the utter bewilderment he felt. The shock of the collision had been greater than he realised evidently. His mind was wandering . . . Possibly! Only the odd thing was—he had never felt so clear-headed in his life. Ten thousand things grew simple suddenly. But, how thickly these people pressed about him, and how—familiarly!

'My parcels,' he said, joyously pushing his way across the throng. 'These are Christmas Presents I've bought for them.' He nodded towards the room. 'I've saved for weeks—stopped cigars and billiards and—and several other good things—to buy them.'

'Good man!' said Palmer with a happy laugh. 'It's the heart that counts.'

Mudbury looked at him. Palmer had said an amazing truth, only—people would hardly understand and believe him . . . Would they?

'Eh?' he asked, feeling stuffed and stupid, muddled somewhere between two meanings, one of which was gorgeous and the other stupid beyond belief.

'If you *please,* Mr Mudbury, step inside. They are expecting you,' said a kindly, pompous voice. And, turning sharply, he met the gentle, foolish eyes of Sir James Epiphany, a director of the Bank where he worked.

The effect of the voice was instantaneous from long habit.

'They are,' he smiled from his heart, and advanced as from the custom of many years. Oh, how happy and gay he felt! His affection for his wife was real. Romance, indeed, had gone, but he needed her—and she needed him. And the children—Milly, Bill, and Jean—he deeply loved them. Life was worth living indeed!

In the room was a crowd, but—an astounding silence. John Mudbury looked round him. He advanced towards his wife, who sat in the corner armchair with Milly on her knee. A lot of people talked and moved about. Momentarily the crowd increased. He stood in front of them—in front of Milly and his wife. And he spoke—holding out his packages. 'It's Christmas Eve,' he whispered shyly, 'and I've brought you something—something for everybody. Look!' He held the packages before their eyes.

'Of course, of course,' said a voice behind him, 'but you may hold them out like that for a century. They'll *never* see them!'

'Of course they won't. But I love to do the old, sweet thing,' replied John Mudbury—then wondered with a gasp of stark amazement why he said it.

'I think—' whispered Milly, staring round her.

'Well what do you think?' her mother asked sharply. 'You're always thinking something odd.'

'I think,' the girl continued dreamily, 'that Daddy's already here.' She paused, then added with a child's impossible conviction, 'I'm sure he is. I *feel* him.'

There was an extraordinary laugh. Sir James Epiphany laughed. The others—the whole crowd of them—also turned their heads and smiled. But the mother, thrusting the child away from her, rose up suddenly with a violent start. Her face had turned to chalk. She stretched her arms out into the air before her. She gasped and shivered. There was anguish in her eyes.

'Look!' repeated John, 'these are the Presents that I brought.'

But his voice apparently was soundless. And, with a spasm of icy pain, he remembered that Palmer and Sir James—some years ago had died.

'It's magic,' he cried, 'but—I love you, Jinny—I love you—and—and I have always been true to you—as true as steel. We need each other—oh, can't you see—we go on together—you and I—for ever and ever—'

'*Think,*' interrupted an exquisitely tender voice, 'don't shout! They can't *hear* you—now.' And, turning, John Mudbury met the eyes of Everard Minturn, their President of the year before. Minturn had gone down with the *Titanic.*

He dropped his parcels then. His heart gave an enormous leap of joy.

He saw her face—the face of his wife—look through him.

But the child gazed straight into his eyes. She *saw* him.

The next thing he knew was that he heard something tinkling . . . far, far away. It sounded miles below him—inside him—he was sounding himself—all utterly bewildering—like a bell. It *was* a bell.

Milly stooped down and picked the parcels up. Her face shone with happiness and laughter . . .

But a man came in soon after, a man with a ridiculous, solemn face, a pencil and a notebook. He wore a dark blue helmet. Behind him came a string of other men. They carried something . . . something . . . he could not see exactly what it was. But, when he pressed forward through the laughing throng to gaze upon it, he dimly made out two eyes, a nose, a chin, a deep red smear, and a pair of folded hands upon an overcoat. A woman's form fell down upon them then, and he heard soft sounds of children weeping strangely . . . and other sounds . . . as of familiar voices laughing . . . laughing gaily.

'They'll join us presently. It goes like a flash . . .'

And, turning with great happiness in his heart, he saw that Sir James had said it, holding Palmer by the arm as with some natural yet unexpected love of sympathetic friendship.

'Come on,' said Palmer, smiling like a man who accepts a gift in universal fellowship, 'let's help 'em. They'll never understand . . . Still, we can always try.'

The entire throng moved up with laughter and amusement. It was a moment of hearty, genuine life at last. Delight and Joy and Peace were everywhere.

Then John Mudbury realised the truth—that he was dead.

———————————

Ray Bradbury

b. 1920

Famous as one of North America's most distinguished fantasy
writers, Ray Bradbury's mysterious stories are nevertheless firmly
rooted in the material world of science and technology. The
author of many novels, stories and plays, his best-known work is
Fahrenheit 451, which tells the chilling tale of a totalitarian state
that has banned the ownership of books.

THE CROWD

Mᴿ Sᴘᴀʟʟɴᴇʀ ᴘᴜᴛ ʜɪs ʜᴀɴᴅs over his face.
There was the feeling of movement in space, the beautifully tortured
scream, the impact and tumbling of the car with wall, through wall,
over and down like a toy, and him hurled out of it. Then—silence.

The crowd came running. Faintly, where he lay, he heard them running.
He could tell their ages and their sizes by the sound of their numerous feet
over the summer grass and on the lined pavement, and over the asphalt street,
and picking through the cluttered bricks to where his car hung half into the
night sky, still spinning its wheels with a senseless centrifuge.

Where the crowd came from he didn't know. He struggled to remain aware
and then the crowd faces hemmed in upon him, hung over him like the large
glowing leaves of down-bent trees. They were a ring of shifting, compressing,
changing faces over him, looking down, looking down, reading the time of his
life or death by his face, making his face into a moon-dial, where the moon cast a
shadow from his nose out upon his cheek to tell the time of breathing or not
breathing any more ever.

How swiftly a crowd comes, he thought, like the iris of an eye compressing in
out of nowhere.

A siren. A police voice. Movement. Blood trickled from his lips and he was
being moved into an ambulance. Someone said, 'Is he dead?' And someone else
said, 'No, he's not dead.' And a third person said, 'He won't die, he's not going to
die.' And he saw the faces of the crowd beyond him in the night, and he knew by
their expressions that he wouldn't die. And that was strange. He saw a man's
face, thin, bright, pale; the man swallowed and bit his lips, very sick. There was a

small woman, too, with red hair and too much red on her cheeks and lips. And a little boy with a freckled face. Others' faces. An old man with a wrinkled upper lip, an old woman, with a mole upon her chin. They had all come from—where? Houses, cars, alleys, from the immediate and the accident-shocked world. Out of alleys and out of hotels and out of streetcars and seemingly out of nothing they came.

The crowd looked at him and he looked back at them and did not like them at all. There was a vast wrongness to them. He couldn't put his finger on it. They were far worse than this machine-made thing that happened to him now.

The ambulance doors slammed. Through the windows he saw the crowd looking in, looking in. That crowd that always came so fast, so strangely fast, to form a circle, to peer down, to probe, to gawk, to question, to point, to disturb, to spoil the privacy of a man's agony by their frank curiosity.

The ambulance drove off. He sank back and their faces still stared into his face, even with his eyes shut.

THE CAR WHEELS SPUN in his mind for days. One wheel, four wheels, spinning, spinning, and whirring, around and around.

He knew it was wrong. Something wrong with the wheels and the whole accident and the running of feet and the curiosity. The crowd faces mixed and spun into the wild rotation of the wheels.

He awoke.

Sunlight, a hospital room, a hand taking his pulse.

'How do you feel?' asked the doctor.

The wheels faded away. Mr Spallner looked around.

'Fine—I guess.'

He tried to find words. About the accident. 'Doctor?'

'Yes?'

'That crowd—was it last night?'

'Two days ago. You've been here since Thursday. You're all right, though. You're doing fine. Don't try and get up.'

'That crowd. Something about wheels, too. Do accidents make people, well, a—little off?'

'Temporarily, sometimes.'

He lay staring up at the doctor. 'Does it hurt your time sense?'

'Panic sometimes does.'

'Makes a minute seem like an hour, or maybe an hour seem like a minute?'

'Yes.'

'Let me tell you then.' He felt the bed under him, the sunlight on his face. 'You'll think I'm crazy. I was driving too fast, I know. I'm sorry now. I jumped the kerb and hit that wall. I was hurt and numb, I know, but I still remember things. Mostly—the crowd.' He waited a moment and then decided to go on, for he suddenly knew what it was that bothered him. 'The crowd got there too quickly. Thirty seconds after the smash they were all standing over me and staring at me . . . it's not right they should run that fast, so late at night . . .'

'You only think it was thirty seconds,' said the doctor. 'It was probably three or four minutes. Your senses—'

'Yeah, I know—my senses, the accident. But I was conscious! I remember one thing that puts it all together and makes it funny. God, so damned funny. The wheels of my car, upside down. The wheels were still spinning when the crowd got there!'

The doctor smiled.

The man in bed went on. 'I'm positive! The wheels were spinning and spinning fast—the front wheels! Wheels don't spin very long, friction cuts them down. And these were really spinning!'

'You're confused,' said the doctor.

'I'm not confused. That street was empty. Not a soul in sight. And then the accident and the wheels still spinning and all those faces over me, quick, in no time. And the way they looked at me, I *knew* I wouldn't die . . .'

'Simple shock,' said the doctor, walking away into the sunlight.

THEY RELEASED HIM from the hospital two weeks later. He rode home in a taxi. People had come to visit him during his two weeks on his back, and to all of them he had told his story, the accident, the spinning wheels, the crowd. They had all laughed with him concerning it, and passed it off.

He leaned forward and tapped on the taxi window.

'What's wrong?'

The cabbie looked back. 'Sorry, boss. This is one helluva town to drive in. Got an accident up ahead. Want me to detour?'

'Yes. No. No! Wait. Go ahead. Let's—let's take a look.'

The cab moved forward, honking.

'Funny damn thing,' said the cabbie. 'Hey, *you*! Get that flea-trap out the way!' Quieter, 'Funny thing—more damn people. Nosy people.'

Mr Spallner looked down and watched his fingers tremble on his knee. 'You noticed that, too?'

'Sure,' said the cabbie. 'All the time. There's always a crowd. You'd think it was their mother got killed.'

'They come running awfully fast,' said the man in the back of the cab.

'Same way with a fire or an explosion. Nobody around. Boom. Lotsa people around. I dunno.'

'Ever seen an accident—at night?'

The cabbie nodded. 'Sure. Don't make no difference. There's always a crowd.'

The wreck came in view. A body lay on the pavement. You knew there was a body even if you couldn't see it. Because of the crowd. The crowd with its back toward him as he sat in the rear of the cab. With its back toward him. He opened the window and almost started to yell. But he didn't have the nerve. If he yelled they might turn around.

And he was afraid to see their faces.

'I SEEM TO HAVE a penchant for accidents,' he said, in his office. It was late afternoon. His friend sat across the desk from him, listening. 'I got out of the hospital this morning and first thing on the way home, we detoured around a wreck.'

'Things run in cycles,' said Morgan.

'Let me tell you about my accident.'

'I've heard it. Heard it all.'

'But it was funny, you must admit.'

'I must admit. Now how about a drink?'

They talked on for half an hour or more. All the while they talked, at the back of Spallner's brain a small watch ticked, a watch that never needed winding. It was the memory of a few little things. Wheels and faces.

At about five thirty there was a hard metal noise in the street. Morgan nodded and looked out and down. 'What'd I tell you? Cycles. A truck and a cream-coloured Cadillac. Yes, yes.'

Spallner walked to the window. He was very cold and as he stood there, he looked at his watch, at the small minute hand. One two three four five seconds—people running—eight nine ten eleven twelve—from all over, people came running—fifteen sixteen seventeen eighteen seconds—more people, more cars, more horns blowing. Curiously distant, Spallner looked upon the scene as an explosion in reverse, the fragments of the detonation sucked back to the point of impulsion. Nineteen, twenty, twenty-one seconds and the crowd was there. Spallner made a gesture down at them, wordless.

The crowd had gathered so fast.

He saw a woman's body a moment before the crowd swallowed it up.

Morgan said, 'You look lousy. Here. Finish your drink.'

'I'm all right, I'm all right. Let me alone. I'm all right. Can you see those people? Can you see any of them? I wish we could see them closer.'

Morgan cried out, 'Where in hell are you going?'

Spallner was out the door, Morgan after him, and down the stairs, as rapidly as possible. 'Come along, and hurry.'

'Take it easy, you're not a well man!'

They walked out on to the street. Spallner pushed his way forward. He thought he saw a red-haired woman with too much red colour on her cheeks and lips.

'There!' He turned wildly to Morgan. 'Did you see her?'

'See who?'

'Damn it; she's gone. The crowd closed in!'

The crowd was all around, breathing and looking and shuffling and mixing and mumbling and getting in the way when he tried to shove through. Evidently the red-haired woman had seen him coming and run off.

He saw another familiar face! A little freckled boy. But there are many freckled boys in the world. And, anyway, it was no use; before Spallner reached him, this little boy ran away and vanished among the people.

'Is she dead?' a voice asked. 'Is she dead?'

'She's dying,' someone else replied. 'She'll be dead before the ambulance arrives. They shouldn't have moved her. They shouldn't have moved her.'

All the crowd faces—familiar, yet unfamiliar, bending over, looking down, looking down.

'Hey, mister, stop pushing.'

'Who you shovin', buddy?'

Spallner came back out, and Morgan caught hold of him before he fell. 'You damned fool. You're still sick. Why in hell'd you have to come down here?' Morgan demanded.

'I don't know, I really don't. They moved her, Morgan, someone moved her. You should never move a traffic victim. It kills them. It kills them.'

'Yeah. That's the way with people. The idiots.'

Spallner arranged the newspaper clippings carefully.

Morgan looked at them. 'What's the idea? Ever since your accident you think every traffic scramble is part of you. What are these?'

'Clippings of motor-car crackups, and photos. Look at them. Not at the cars,' said Spallner, 'but at the crowds around the cars.' He pointed. 'Here. Compare this photo of a wreck in the Wilshire District with one in Westwood. No resemblance. But now take this Westwood picture and align it with one taken in the Westwood District ten days ago.' Again he motioned. 'This woman is in both pictures.'

'Coincidence. The woman happened to be there once in 1936, again in 1946.'

'A coincidence once, maybe. But twelve times over a period of ten years, when the accidents occurred as much as three miles from one another, no. Here.' He dealt out a dozen photographs. 'She's in *all* of these!'

'Maybe she's perverted.'

'She's more than that. How does she *happen* to be there so quickly after each accident? And why does she wear the same clothes in pictures taken over a period of a decade?'

'I'll be damned, so she does.'

'And, last of all, why was she standing over *me* the night of my accident, two weeks ago!'

They had a drink. Morgan went over the files. 'What'd you do, hire a clipping service while you were in the hospital to go back through the newspapers for you?' Spallner nodded. Morgan sipped his drink. It was getting late. The streetlights were coming on in the streets below the office. 'What does all this add up to?'

'I don't know,' said Spallner, 'except that there's a universal law about accidents. *Crowds gather.* They always gather. And like you and me, people have wondered year after year, why they gathered so quickly, and how? I know the answer. Here it is!'

He flung the clippings down. 'It frightens me.'

'These people—mightn't they be thrill-hunters, perverted sensationalists with a carnal lust for blood and morbidity?'

Spallner shrugged. 'Does that explain their being at all the accidents? Notice, they stick to certain territories. A Brentwood accident will bring out one group. A Huntington Park another. But there's a norm for faces, a certain percentage appear at each wreck.'

Morgan said, 'They're not *all* the same faces, are they?'

'Naturally not. Accidents draw normal people, too, in the course of time. But these, I find, are always the *first* ones there.'

'Who are they? What do they want? You keep hinting and never telling. Good Lord, you must have some idea. You've scared yourself and now you've got me jumping.'

'I've tried getting to them, but someone always trips me up, I'm always too late. They slip into the crowd and vanish. The crowd seems to offer protection to some of its members. They see me coming.'

'Sounds like some sort of clique.'

'They have one thing in common, they always show up together. At a fire or an explosion or on the sidelines of a war, at any public demonstration of this thing called death. Vultures, hyenas or saints, I don't know which they are, I just don't know. But I'm going to the police with it, this evening. It's gone on long enough. One of them shifted that woman's body today. They shouldn't have touched her. It killed her.'

He placed the clippings in a briefcase. Morgan got up and slipped into his coat. Spallner clicked the briefcase shut. 'Or, I just happened to think . . .'

'What?'

'Maybe they *wanted* her dead.'

'Why?'

'Who knows. Come along?'

'Sorry. It's late. See you tomorrow. Luck.' They went out together. 'Give my regards to the cops. Think they'll believe you?'

'Oh, they'll believe me all right. Good night.'

SPALLNER TOOK IT slow driving downtown.

'I want to get there,' he told himself, 'alive.'

He was rather shocked, but not surprised, somehow, when the truck came rolling out of an alley straight at him. He was just congratulating himself on his keen sense of observation and talking out what he would say to the police in his mind, when the truck smashed into his car. It wasn't really his car, that was the disheartening thing about it. In a preoccupied mood he was tossed first this way and then that way, while he thought, what a shame, Morgan has gone and lent me his extra car for a few days until my other car is fixed, and now here I go again. The windshield hammered back into his face. He was forced back and forth in several lightning jerks. Then all motion stopped and all noise stopped and only pain filled him up.

He heard their feet running and running and running. He fumbled with the car door. It clicked. He fell out upon the pavement drunkenly and lay, ear to the asphalt, listening to them coming. It was like a great rainstorm, with many drops, heavy and light and medium, touching the earth. He waited a few seconds and listened to their coming and their arrival. Then, weakly, expectantly, he rolled his head up and looked.

The crowd was there.

He could smell their breaths, the mingled odours of many people sucking and sucking on the air a man needs to live by. They crowded and jostled and sucked and sucked all the air up from around his gasping face until he tried to tell them to move back, they were making him live in a vacuum. His head was bleeding very badly. He tried to move and he realised something was wrong with his spine. He hadn't felt much at the impact, but his spine was hurt. He didn't dare move.

He couldn't speak. Opening his mouth, nothing came out but a gagging.

Someone said, 'Give me a hand. We'll roll him over and lift him into a more comfortable position.'

Spallner's brain burst apart.

No! Don't move me!

'We'll move him,' said the voice, casually.

You idiots, you'll kill me, don't!

But he could not say any of this out loud. He could only think it.

Hands took hold of him. They started to lift him. He cried out and nausea choked him up. They straightened him out into a ramrod of agony. Two men did it. One of them was thin, bright, pale, alert, a young man. The other man was very old and had a wrinkled upper lip.

He had seen their faces before.

A familiar voice said, 'Is—is he dead?'

Another voice, a memorable voice, responded, 'No. Not yet. But he will be dead before the ambulance arrives.'

It was all a very silly, mad plot. Like every accident. He squealed hysterically at the solid wall of faces. They were all around him, these judges and jurors with the faces he had seen before. Through his pain he counted their faces.

The freckled boy. The old man with the wrinkled upper lip.

The red-haired, red-cheeked woman. An old woman with a mole on her chin.

I know what you're here for, he thought. You're here just as you're at all accidents. To make certain the right ones live and the right ones die. That's why you lifted me. You knew it would kill. You knew I'd live if you left me alone.

And that's the way it's been since time began, when crowds gather. You murder much easier, this way. Your alibi is very simple; you didn't know it was dangerous to move a hurt man. You didn't mean to hurt him.

He looked at them, above him, and he was curious as a man under deep water looking up at people on a bridge. Who are you? Where do you come from and how do you get here so soon? You're the crowd that's always in the way, using up good air that a dying man's lungs are in need of, using up space he should be using to lie in, alone. Tramping on people to make sure they die, that's you. I know *all* of you.

It was like a polite monologue. They said nothing. Faces. The old man. The red-haired woman.

Someone picked up his briefcase. 'Whose is this?' they asked.

It's mine! It's evidence against all of you!

Eyes, inverted over him. Shiny eyes under tousled hair or under hats.

Faces.

Somewhere—a siren. The ambulance was coming.

But, looking at the faces, the construction, the cast, the form of the faces, Spallner saw it was too late. He read it in their faces. They *knew*.

He tried to speak. A little bit got out:

'It—looks like I'll—be joining up with you. I—guess I'll be a member of your—group—now.'

He closed his eyes then, and waited for the coroner.

Ann Bridge

1891–1974

As the wife of a British diplomat, Ann Bridge (the pseudonym of
Mary Dolling Sanders, later Lady O'Malley) travelled the world.
She wrote an impressive number of novels and short stories, and
her husband's postings to countries such as Turkey and China
provided her with unusual backgrounds, which—as the
following story shows—she was able to use very effectively in
her writing.

THE BUICK
SALOON

To Mrs James St George Bernard Bowlby it seemed almost providential
that she should recover from the series of illnesses which had perforce
kept her in England, at the precise moment when Bowlby was promoted
from being No. 2 to being No. 1 in the Grand Oriental Bank in Peking. Her
improved health and his improved circumstances made it obvious that now at
last she should join him, and she wrote to suggest it. Bowlby of course agreed,
and out she came. He went down to meet her in Shanghai, but business having
called him further still, to Hong Kong, Mrs Bowlby proceeded to Peking alone,
and took up her quarters in the big, ugly grey-brick house behind the Bank in
Legation Street. She tried, as many managers' wives had tried before her, to do
her best with the solid mahogany and green leather furniture provided by the
Bank, wondering the while how Bowlby, so dependent always on the feminine
touch on his life and surroundings, had endured the lesser solidities of the
sub-manager's house alone for so long. She bought silks and blackwood and
scroll paintings. She also bought a car. 'You'll need a car, and you'd better have a
saloon, because of the dust,' Bowlby had said.

People who come to Peking without motors of their own seldom buy new
ones. There are always secondhand cars going, from many sources: the leavings
of transferred diplomatists, the jetsam of financial ventures, the sediment of con-
ferences. So one morning Mrs Bowlby went down with Thompson, the new
No. 2 in the Bank, to Maxon's garage in the Nan Shih Tzu to choose her car.

After much conversation with the Canadian manager they pitched on a Buick saloon. It was a Buick of the type which is practically standard in the Far East, and had been entirely repainted outside, a respectable dark blue; the inside had been newly done up, in a pleasant soft grey which appealed to Mrs Bowlby. The manager was loud in its praises. The suspension was excellent ('You want that on these roads, Mrs Bowlby')—the driver and his colleague sat outside ('Much better, Mr Thompson. If these fellows have been eating garlic—they shouldn't, but they do—'). Thompson knew they did, and agreed heartily. Mrs Bowlby, new to such transactions, wanted to know who the car had belonged to. The manager was firmly vague. This was not a commission sale—he had bought the car when the owners left. Very good people—'from the Quarter'. This fully satisfied Thompson, who knew that only Europeans live (above the rose, anyhow) in the Legation Quarter of Peking.

So the Buick saloon was bought. Thompson, having heard at the Club that the late Grand Oriental chauffeur drank petrol, did not re-engage him with the rest of the servants according to custom, but secured instead for Mrs Bowlby the chauffeur of a departing manager of the Banque Franco-Belge. By the time Bowlby returned from Hong Kong the chauffeur and his colleague had been fitted out with khaki livery for winter, with white for summer—in either case with trim gold cuff- and hat-bands—and Mrs Bowlby, in her blue saloon, had settled down to pay her calls.

In Peking the newcomer calls first: a curious and discouraging system. It is an ordeal even to the hardened. Mrs Bowlby was not hardened; she was a small, shy, frail woman, who wore grey by preference, and looked grey—eyes, hair, and skin. She had no idea of asserting herself; if she had things in her—subtleties, delicacies—she did not wear them outside; she did not impose herself. She hated the calls. But as she was also extremely conscientious, day after day, trying to fortify herself by the sight of the two khaki-and-gold figures in front of her, exhaling their possible garlic to the outer air beyond the glass partition, she called. She called on the diplomats' wives in the Quarter; she called on 'the Salt' (officials of the Salt Gabelle); she called on the Customs—English, Italian, American, and French; she called on the Posts—French, Italian, American, and English. The annual displacement of pasteboard in Peking must amount to many tons, and in this useful work Mrs Bowlby, alone in the grey interior of her car, faithfully took her share. She carried with her a little list on which, with the help of her Number One boy (as much a permanent fixture in the Bank house, almost, as the doors and windows), she had written out the styles, titles, and addresses of the ladies she wished to visit. The late chauffeur of the Banque Franco-Belge spoke excellent French; so did Mrs Bowlby—it was one of her few accomplishments; but as no Chinese can or will master European names, the European needs must learn and use the peculiar versions current among them. 'Ta Ch'in chai T'ai-t'ai, Turkuofu,' read out Mrs Bowlby when she wished to call on the wife of the German Minister. 'Oui, Madame!' said Shwang. 'Pei

T'ai-t'-ai, Kung Hsien Hutung,' read out Mrs Bowlby when visiting Mrs Bray, the Doctor's wife; but when she wished to call on Mrs Bennett, the wife of the Commandant of the English Guard, and Mrs Baines, the Chaplain's wife, she found that they were both *Pei T'ai-t'ai* too—which led to confusion.

It began towards the end of the first week. Possibly it was her absorption in the lists and the Chinese names that prevented her from noticing it sooner, but at the end of that week Mrs Bowlby would have sworn that she heard French spoken beside her as she drove about. Once, a little later, as she was driving down the Rue Marco Polo to fetch her husband from the Club, a voice said 'C'est lui!' in an underbreath, eagerly—or so she thought. The windows were lowered, and Mrs Bowlby put it down to the servants in front. But it persisted. More than once she thought she heard a soft sigh. 'Nerves!' thought Mrs Bowlby—her nerves were always a menace to her, and Peking, she knew, was bad for them.

She went on saying 'Nerves' for two or three more days; then, one afternoon, she changed her mind. She was driving along the Ta Chiang an Chieh, the great thoroughfare running east and west outside the Legation Quarter, where the trams ring and clang past the scarlet walls and golden roofs of the Forbidden City, and long lines of camels, coming in with coal from the country as they have come for centuries, cross the road between the Dodges and Daimlers of the new China. It was a soft brilliant afternoon in April, and the cinder track along the glacis of the Quarter was thronged with riders; polo had begun, and as the car neared Hatamen Street she caught a glimpse of the white-and-scarlet figures through the drifting dust on her right. At the corner of the Hatamen the car stopped; a string of camels was passing up to the great gateway, and she had to wait. She sat back in the car, glad of the pause; she was unusually moved by the loveliness of the day, by the beauty and strangeness of the scene, by the whole magic of spring in Peking. She was going later to watch the polo, a terrifying game; she wished Jim didn't play. Suddenly, across her idle thoughts, a voice beside her spoke clearly. 'Au revoir!' it said, 'mon très-cher! Ne tombe pas, je t'en prie.' And as the car moved forward behind the last of the camels, soft and unmistakable there came a sigh, and the words, 'Ce polo! Quel sport affreux! Dieu, que je le déteste!' in a passionate undertone.

'That *wasn't* the chauffeur!' was what Mrs Bowlby found herself saying. The front windows were up. And that low, rather husky voice, the cultivated and clear accent, could not be confounded for a moment with Shwang's guttural French. Besides, what chauffeur would talk like that? The thing was ridiculous. 'And it *wasn't* nerves, this time,' said Mrs Bowlby, her thoughts running this way and that round the phenomenon. 'She did say it.' 'Then it was she who said "C'est lui!" before,' she said almost triumphantly, a moment later.

Curiously, though she was puzzled and startled, she realised presently that she was not in the least frightened. That someone with a beautiful voice should speak French in her car was absurd and impossible, but it wasn't alarming. In her timid way Mrs Bowlby rather prided herself on her common sense, and as she shopped and called she considered this extraordinary occurrence from all the common-sense points of view that she could think of, but it remained a baffling and obstinate fact. Before her drive was over she found herself wishing simply to hear the voice again. It was ridiculous, but she did. And she had her wish. As the car turned into Legation Street an hour later she saw that it was too late to go to the polo; the last chukker was over, and the players were leaving the ground, over which dust still hung in the low brilliant light, in cars and rickshaws. As she passed the gate the voice spoke again—almost in front of her, this time, as though the speaker were leaning forward to the window. 'Le voilà!' it said—and then, quite loudly, 'Jacques!' Mrs Bowlby almost leaned out of the window herself, to look for whoever was being summoned—as she sat back, conscious of her folly, she heard again beside her, quite low, 'Il ne m'a pas vue.'

There was no mistake about it. It was broad daylight; there she was in her car, bowling along Legation Street—past the Belgian Bank, past the German Legation; rickshaws skimming in front of her, Mme de Réan bowing to her. And just as clear and certain as all these things had been this woman's voice, calling to 'Jacques', whoever he was—terrified lest he should fall at polo, hating the game for his sake. What a lovely voice it was! Who was she, Mrs Bowlby wondered, and what and who was Jacques? 'Mon très-cher!' she had called him—a delicious expression. It belonged to the day and the place—it was near to her own mood as she had sat at the corner of the Hatamen and noticed the spring, and hated the polo too for Jim's sake. She would have liked to call Jim 'mon très-cher', only he would have been so surprised.

The thought of Bowlby brought her up with a round turn. What would he say to this affair? Instantly, though she prolonged the discussion with herself for form's sake, she knew that she was not going to tell him. Not yet, anyhow. Bowlby had not been very satisfied with her choice of a car as it was—he said it was too big and too expensive to run. Besides, there was the question of her nerves. If he failed to hear the voice too she would be in a terribly difficult position. But there was more to it than that. She had a faint sense that she had been eavesdropping, however involuntarily. She had no right to give away even a voice which said 'mon très-cher' in that tone.

This feeling grew upon her in the days that followed. The voice that haunted the Buick became of almost daily occurrence, furnishing a curious secret background to her social routine of calls and 'At Homes'. It spoke always in French, always to or about 'Jacques'—a person, whoever he was, greatly loved. Sometimes it was clear to Mrs Bowlby that she was hearing only half of a conversation between the two, as one does at the telephone. The man's voice she never heard, but, as at the telephone, she could often guess at what he said. Much of the speech was trivial enough: arrangements for meetings at lunches, at the polo; for weekend parties at Pao-ma-chang in the temple of this person or that. This was more eerie than anything else to Mrs Bowlby—the hearing of plans concerned with people she knew. 'Alors, dimanche prochain, chez les Milne.' Meeting 'les Milne' soon after, she would stare at them uneasily, as though by looking long enough she might find about them some trace of the presence which was more familiar to her than their own. Her voice was making ghosts of the living. But whether plans, or snatches of talk about people or ponies, there came always, sooner or later, the undernote of tenderness, now hesitant, now frank—the close concern, the monopolising happiness of a woman in love.

It puzzled Mrs Bowlby that the car should only register, as it were, the woman's voice. But then the whole affair bristled with puzzles. Why did Bowlby hear nothing? For he did not—she would have realised her worst fears if she *had* told him. She remembered always the first time that the voice spoke when he was with her. They were going to a *Thé Dansant* at the Peking Hotel, a farewell party for some Minister. As the car swung out of the Jade Canal Road, past the policemen who stand with fixed bayonets at the edge of the glacis, the voice began suddenly, as it so often did, in French—'Then I leave thee now—thou wilt send back the car?' And as they lurched across the tramlines towards the huge European building and pulled up, it went on, 'But tonight, one will dance, n'est ce pas?'

'Goodness, what a crowd!' said Bowlby. 'This is going to be simply awful. Don't let's stay long. Will half an hour be enough, do you think?'

Mrs Bowlby stared at him without answering. Was it possible? She nearly gave herself away in the shock of her astonishment.

'What's the matter?' said Bowlby. 'What are you looking at?'

Bowlby had not heard a word!

She noticed other things. There were certain places where the voice 'came through', so to speak, more clearly and regularly than elsewhere. Intermittent fragments, sometimes unintelligible, occurred anywhere. But she came to know where to expect to hear most. Near the polo ground, for instance, which she hardly ever passed without hearing some expression of anxiety or pride. She often went to the polo, for Jim was a keen and brilliant player; but it was a horror to her while he played, and this feeling was a sort of link, it seemed to her, between her and her unseen companion. More and more, too, she heard it near the Hatamen and in the *hu-t'ungs* or alleys to the east of it. Mrs Bowlby liked the East City. It lies rather in a backwater, between the crowded noisy thoroughfare of Hatamen Street, with its trams, dust, cars, and camels, and the silent angle of the Tartar Wall, rising above the low one-storey houses. A good many Europeans live there, and she was always glad when a call took her that way, through the narrow *hu-t'ungs* where the car lurched over heaps of rubbish or skidded in the deep dust, and rickshaws pulled aside into gateways to let her pass. Many of these lanes end vaguely in big open spaces, where pigs root among the refuse and little boys wander about, singing long monotonous songs with a curious jerky rhythm in their high nasal voices. Sometimes, as she waited before a scarlet door, a flute-player out of sight would begin to play, and the thin sweet melody filled the sunny air between the blank grey walls. Flowering trees showed here and there above them; coppersmiths plied their trade on the steps of carved marble gateways; dogs and beggars sunned themselves under the white and scarlet walls of temple courtyards. Here, more than anywhere else, the voice spoke clearly, freely, continuously, the rapid rounded French syllables falling on the air from nowhere, now high, light, and merry, with teasing words and inflection, now sinking into low murmurs of rapturous happiness. At such times Mrs Bowlby sat wholly absorbed in listening, drawn by the lovely voice into a life not her own and held fascinated by the spell of this passionate adventure. Happy as she was with Bowlby, her life with him had never known anything like this. He had never wanted, and she had never dared to use, the endearments lavished by the late owner of the Buick saloon on her Jacques.

She heard enough to follow the course of the affair pretty closely. They met where they could in public, but somewhere in the Chinese City there was clearly a meeting place of their own—'notre petit asile'. And gradually this haven began to take shape in Mrs Bowlby's mind. Joyous references were made to various features of it. Tomorrow they would drink tea on the stone table under 'our great white pine'. There was the fishpond shaped like a shamrock, where one of the goldfish died—'pourtant en Irelande celà porte bonheur, le trèfle, n'est-ce pas?' The parapet of this pond broke away and had to be repaired, and 'Jacques' made some sort of inscription in the damp mortar, for the voice thrilled softly one day as it murmured—'Maintenant il se lit là pour toujours, ton amour!' And all through that enchanted spring, first the lilac bushes perfumed the hours spent beneath the pine, and then the acacias that stood in a square round the shamrock pond. Still more that life and hers seemed to Mrs Bowlby strangely mingled; her own lilacs bloomed and scented the courtyard behind the grey Bank building, and one day, as they drove to lunch in the British Legation, she drew Jim's attention to the scent of the acacias, which drowned the whole compound in perfume. But Bowlby said, with a sort of shiver, that he hated the smell; and he swore at the chauffeur in French, which he spoke even better than his wife.

The desire grew on Mrs Bowlby to know more of her pair, who and what they were and how their story ended. But it seemed wholly impossible to find out. Her reticences made her quite unequal to setting anyone on to question the people at the garage again. And then one day, accidentally, the clue was given her. She had been calling at one of the houses in the French Legation; the two house servants, in blue-and-silver gowns, stood respectfully on the steps; her footman held open the door of the car for her. As she seated herself the voice said in a clear tone of command, '230, Por Hua Shan Hu-t'ung!' Acting on an impulse which surprised her, Mrs Bowlby repeated the order— 'Deux cent trente, Por Hua Shan Hu-t'ung,' she said. Shwang's colleague bowed and shut the door. But she caught sight, as she spoke, of the faces of the two servants on the steps. Was it imagination? Surely not. She would have sworn that a flicker of some emotion—surprise, and recollection—had appeared for a moment on their sealed and impassive countenances. In Peking the servants in Legation houses are commonly handed on from employer to employer, like the furniture; and the fact struck on her with sudden conviction—they had heard those words before!

Her heart rose with excitement as the car swung out of the compound into Legation Street. Where was it going? She had no idea where the Por Hua Shan Hu-t'ung was. Was she about to get a stage nearer to the solution of the mystery at last? At the Hatamen the Buick turned south along the glacis. So far so good. They left the Hatamen, bumped into the Suchow Hu-t'ung, followed on down the Tung Tsung Pu Hu-t'ung, right into the heart of the East City. Her breath came fast. It must be right. Now they were skirting the edge of one of the rubbish-strewn open spaces, and the East Wall rose close ahead of them. They turned left, parallel with it; turned right again towards it; stopped. Shwang beckoned to a pancake-seller who was rolling out his wares in a doorway, and a colloquy in Chinese ensued. They went on, slowly, then, down a lane between high walls which ended at the Wall's very foot, and pulled up some hundred yards off it before a high scarlet door, whose rows of golden knobs in fives betokened the former dwelling of some Chinese of rank.

It was only when Liu came to open the door and held out his cotton-gloved hand for her cards that Mrs Bowlby realised that she had no idea what she was going to do. She could not call on a voice! She summoned Shwang; Liu's French was not his strong point. 'Ask,' she said to Shwang, 'who lives here—the T'ai-t'ai's name.' Shwang rang the bell. There was a long pause. Shwang rang again. There came a sound of shuffling feet inside; creaking on its hinges the door opened, and the head of an old Chinaman, thinly bearded and topped with a little black cap, appeared in the crack. A conversation followed, and then Shwang returned to the car. 'The house is empty,' he said. 'Ask him who lived there last,' said Mrs Bowlby. Another and longer conversation followed, but at last Shwang came to the window with the information that a foreign *T'ai-t'ai*, '*Fa-kuo T'ai-t'ai*' (French lady), he thought, had lived there, but she had gone away. With that Mrs Bowlby had to be content. It was something. It might be much. The car had moved on towards the Wall, seeking a place to turn, when an idea struck her. Telling Shwang to wait, she got out, and glanced along the foot of the Wall in both directions. Yes! Some two hundred yards from where she stood one of those huge ramps, used in former times to ride or drive up on to the summit of the Wall, descended into the dusty strip of wasteland at its foot. She hurried towards it, nervously, picking her way between the rough fallen lumps of stone and heaps of rubbish; she was afraid that the servants would regard her action as strange, and that when she reached the foot of the ramp she might not be able to get up it. Since Boxer times the top of the Tartar Wall is forbidden as a promenade, save for a short strip just above the Legation Quarter, and the ramps are stoutly closed at the foot, theoretically. But in China theory and practice do not always correspond, Mrs Bowlby knew; and as she hurried, she hoped.

Her hope was justified. Though a solid wooden barrier closed the foot of the ramp, a few feet higher up a little bolt hole, large enough to admit a goat or a small man, had been picked away in the masonry of the parapet. Mrs Bowlby scrambled through and found herself on the cobbled slope of the ramp; panting a little, she walked up it on to the Wall. The great flagged top, broad enough for two motor lorries to drive abreast, stretched away to left and right; a thick undergrowth of thorny bushes had sprung up between the flagstones, and through them wound a little path, manifestly used by goats and goatherds. Below her Peking lay spread out—a city turned by the trees which grow in every courtyard into the semblance of a green wood, out of which rose the immense golden roofs of the Forbidden City; beyond it, far away, the faint mauve line of the Western Hills hung on the sky. But Mrs Bowlby had no eyes for the unparalleled view. Peeping cautiously through the battlements she located the Buick saloon, shining incongruously neat and modern in its squalid and deserted surroundings; by it she took her bearings, and moved with a beating heart along the little path between the thorns. Hoopoes flew out in front of her, calling their sweet note, and perched again, raising and lowering their crests; she never heeded them, nor her torn silk stockings. Now she was above the car: yes, there was the lane up which they had come, and the wall beyond it was the wall of that house! She could see the doorkeeper, doll-like below her, still standing in his scarlet doorway, watching the car curiously. The garden wall stretched up close to the foot of the City Wall itself so that, as she came abreast of it, the whole compound—the house, with its manifold courtyards, and the formal garden—lay spread out at her feet with the minute perfection of a child's toy farm on the floor.

Mrs Bowlby stood looking down at it. A dreamlike sense of unreality came over her, greater than any yet caused even by her impossible voice. A magnificent white pine, trunk and branches gleaming as if whitewashed among its dark needles, rose out of the garden, and below it stood a round stone table among groups of lilacs. Just as the voice had described it! Close by, separated from the pine garden by a wall pierced with a fan-shaped doorway was another, with a goldfish pond shaped like a shamrock, and round it stood a square pleached alley of acacias. Flowers in great tubs bloomed everywhere. Here was the very setting of her lovers' secret idyll; silent, sunny, sweet, it lay under the brooding protection of the Tartar Wall. Here she was indeed near to the heart of her mystery, Mrs Bowlby felt, as she leaned on the stone parapet, looking down at the deserted garden. A strange fancy came to her that she would have liked to bring Jim here and people it once again. But she and Jim, she reflected with a little sigh, were staid married people—with no need of a secret haven hidden away in the East City. And with the thought of Jim the claims of everyday life reasserted themselves. She must go—and with a last glance at the garden she hastened back to the car.

During the next day or so Mrs Bowlby brooded over her new discovery and all that had led to it. Everything—the place where the address had been given by the voice, the flicker of recognition on the faces of the servants at the house in the French Legation, the fact of the doorkeeper in the East City having mentioned a *Fa-kuo T'ai-t'ai* as his late employer, pointed to one thing—that the former owner of the Buick saloon had lived in the house where she had first called on that momentous afternoon. More than ever, now, the thing took hold of her—having penetrated the secret of the voice so far, she felt that she must follow it further yet. Timid or not, she must brace herself to ask some questions.

At a dinner a few nights later she found herself seated next to Mr van Adam. Mr van Adam was an elderly American, the *doyen* of Peking society, who had seen everything and known everyone since before Boxer days—a walking memory and a mine of social information. Mrs Bowlby determined to apply to him. She displayed unwonted craft. She spoke of Legation compounds in general, and of the French compound in particular; she praised the garden of the house where she had called. And then, 'Who lived there before the Vernets came?' she asked, and waited eagerly for the answer. Mr van Adam eyed her a little curiously, she thought, but replied that it was a certain Count d'Ardennes. 'Was he married?' Mrs Bowlby next enquired. Oh yes, he was married right enough—but the usual reminiscent flow of anecdote seemed to fail Mr van Adam in this case. Struggling against a vague sense of difficulty, of a hitch somewhere, Mrs Bowlby pushed on nevertheless to an enquiry as to what the Comtesse d'Ardennes was like. 'A siren!' Mr van Adam replied briefly—adding, 'Lovely creature, though, as ever stepped.' He edged away rather from the subject, or so it seemed to Mrs Bowlby, but she nerved herself to another question—'Had they a car?' Mr van Adam fairly stared, at that; then he broke into a laugh. 'Car? Why yes—she went everywhere in a yellow Buick—we used to call it "the canary".' The talk drifted off on to cars in general, and Mrs Bowlby let it drift; she was revolving in her mind the form of her last question. Her curiosity must look odd, she reflected nervously; it was all more difficult, somehow, than she had expected. Her craft was failing her—she could not think of a good excuse for further questions that would not run the risk of betraying her secret. There must have been a scandal—there *would* have been, of course; but Mrs Bowlby was not of the order of women who in Peking ask coolly at the dinner table, 'And what was *her* scandal?' At dessert, in desperation, she put it hurriedly, baldly, 'When did the d'Ardennes leave?' Mr van Adam paused before he answered, 'Oh, going on for a year ago, now. She was ill, they said—looked it, anyway—and went back to France. He was transferred to Bangkok soon after, but I don't know if she's gone out to him again. The East didn't suit her.' 'Oh, poor thing!' murmured Mrs Bowlby, softly and sincerely, her heart full of pity for the woman with the lovely voice and the lovely name, whose failing health had severed her from her Jacques. Not even love such as hers could control this wretched feeble body, reflected Mrs Bowlby, whom few places suited. The ladies rose, and too absorbed in her reflections to pay any further attention to Mr van Adam, she rose and went with them.

At this stage Mrs Bowlby went to Pei-t'ai-ho for the summer. Peking, with a temperature of over 100 degrees in the shade, is no place for delicate women in July and August. Cars are not allowed on the sandy roads of the pleasant straggling seaside resort, and missionaries and diplomatists alike are obliged to fall back on rickshaws and donkeys as means of locomotion. So the Buick saloon was left in Peking with Jim, who came down for long weekends as often as he could. Thus separated from her car, and in changed surroundings, Mrs Bowlby endeavoured to take stock of the whole affair dispassionately. Get away from it she could not. Bathing, idling on the hot sunny beach, walking through the green paths bordered with maize and *kaoliang*, sitting out in the blessedly cool dark after dinner, she found herself as much absorbed as ever in this personality whose secret life she so strangely shared. Curiously enough, she felt no wish to ask any more questions of anyone. With her knowledge of Mme d'Ardennes' name the sense of eavesdropping had returned in full force. One thing struck her as a little odd: that if there *had* been a scandal she should not have heard of it—in Peking, where scandals were innumerable, and treated with startling openness and frank disregard. Perhaps she *had* been mistaken, though, in Mr van Adam's attitude, and there had not been one. Or—the illumination came to her belated and suddenly—hadn't Mr van Adam's son in the Customs, who went home last year, been called Jack? He had! and Mrs Bowlby shuddered at the thought of her clumsiness. She could not have chosen a worse person for her enquiries.

Another thing, at Pei-t'ai-ho, she realised with a certain astonishment—that she had not been perceptibly shocked by this intrigue. Mrs Bowlby had always believed herself to hold thoroughly conventional British views on marriage; the late owner of the Buick saloon clearly had not, yet Mrs Bowlby had never thought of censuring her. She had even been a little resentful of Mr van Adam's calling her a 'siren'. Sirens were cold-hearted creatures, who lured men frivolously to their doom; her voice was not the voice of a siren. Mrs Bowlby was all on the side of her voice. Didn't such love justify itself, argued Mrs Bowlby, awake at last to her own moral failure to condemn another, or very nearly? Perhaps, she caught herself thinking, if people knew as much about all love affairs as she knew about this one, they would be less censorious.

Mrs Bowlby stayed late at Pei-t'ai-ho, well on into September, till the breezes blew chilly off the sea, the green paths had faded to a dusty yellow, and the maize and *kaoliang* were being cut. When she returned to Peking she was at once very busy—calling begins all over again after the seaside holiday, and she spent hours in the Buick saloon leaving cards. The voice was with her again, as before. But something had overshadowed the blissful happiness of the spring days; there was an undertone of distress, of foreboding often, in the conversations. What exactly caused it she could not make out. But it increased, and one day halfway through October, driving in the East City, the voice dropped away into a burst of passionate sobbing. This distressed Mrs Bowlby extraordinarily. It was a strange and terrible thing to sit in the car with those low, heartbroken sounds at her side. She almost put out her arms to take and comfort the lovely unhappy creature—but there was only empty air, and the empty seat, with her bag, her book, and her little calling list. Obeying one of those sudden impulses which the voice alone seemed to call out in her, she abandoned her calls and told Shwang to drive to the Por Hua Shan Hut'ung. As they neared it the sobs beside her ceased, and murmured apologies for being *un peu énervée* followed.

When she reached the house Mrs Bowlby got out, and again climbed the ramp on to the Tartar Wall. The thorns and bushes between the battlements were brown and sere now, and no hoopoes flew and fluted among them. She reached the spot where she could look down into the garden. The lilacs were bare too, as her own were; the tubs of flowers were gone, and heaps of leaves had drifted round the feet of the acacias—only the white pine stood up, stately and untouched amid the general decay. A deep melancholy took hold of Mrs Bowlby; already shaken by the sobs in the car, the desolation of this deserted autumn garden weighed with an intense oppression on her spirit. She turned away slowly, and slowly descended to the Buick. The sense of impending misfortune had seized on her too; something, she vaguely felt, had come to an end in that garden.

As she was about to get into the car another impulse moved her. She felt an overmastering desire to enter the garden and see its features from close at hand. The oppression still hung over her, and she felt that a visit to the garden might in some way resolve it. She looked in her purse and found a five-dollar note. Handing it to the startled Shwang—'Give that,' said Mrs Bowlby, 'to the *k'ai-men-ti*, and tell him I wish to walk in the garden of that house.' Shwang bowed; rang the bell; conversed; Mrs Bowlby waited, trembling with impatience, till the clinching argument of the note was at last produced, and the old man whom she had seen before beckoned to her to enter.

She followed him through several courtyards. It was a rambling Chinese house, little modernised; the blind paper lattices of the windows looked blankly on to the miniature lakes and rocky landscapes in the open courts. Finally they passed through a round doorway into the garden below the Tartar Wall, and bowing, the old custodian stood aside to let her walk alone.

Before her rose the white pine, and she strolled towards it, and sitting down on a marble bench beside the round stone table, gazed about her. Beautiful even in its decay, melancholy, serene, the garden lay under the battlements which cut the pale autumn sky behind her. And here the owner of the voice had sat, hidden and secure, her lover beside her! A sudden burst of tears surprised Mrs Bowlby. Cruel Life, she thought, which parts dear lovers. Had *she* too sat here alone? A sharp unexpected sense of her own solitude drove Mrs Bowlby up from her seat. This visit was a mistake; her oppression was not lightened; to have sat in this place seemed somehow to have involved herself in the disaster and misery of that parted pair. She wandered on, through the fan-shaped doorway, and came to a halt beside the goldfish pond. Staring at it through her tears, she noticed the repair to the coping of which the voice had spoken, where 'Jacques' had made an inscription in the damp mortar. She moved round to the place where it still showed white against the grey surface, murmuring, 'Maintenant il se lit là pour toujours, ton amour!'—the phrase of the voice had stayed rooted in her mind. Stooping down, she read the inscription, scratched out neatly and carefully with a penknife in the fine plaster:

Douce sépulture, mon coeur dans ton coeur
Doux Paradis, mon âme dans ton âme.

And below two sets of initials:

A. DE A.

de

J. ST G. B. B.

The verse touched Mrs Bowlby to fresh tears, and it was actually a moment or two before she focused her attention on the initials. When she did, she started back, as though a serpent had stung her, and shut her eyes, and stood still. Then with a curious blind movement she opened her bag and took out one of her own cards, and laid it on the coping beside the inscription, as if to compare them. 'Mrs J. St G. B. Bowlby'—the fine black letters stared up at her, uncompromising and clear, from the white oblong, beside the capitals cut in the plaster. There could be no mistake. Her mystery was solved at last, but it seemed as if she could not take it in. 'Jim?' murmured Mrs Bowlby to herself, as if puzzled—and then 'Jacques?' Slowly, while she stood there, all the connections and verifications unrolled themselves backwards in her mind with devastating certainty and force. Her sentiment, her intuition on the Wall had been terribly right—something *had* come to an end in that garden that day. Standing by the shamrock pond, with the first waves of an engulfing desolation sweeping over her, hardly conscious of her words, she whispered, 'Pourtant celà porte bonheur, le trèfle, n'est-ce pas?'

And with that second quotation from the voice she seemed at last to wake from the sort of stupor in which she had stood. Intolerable! She must hear no more. Passing back, almost running, into the pine garden, she beckoned to the old *k'ai-men-ti* to take her out. He led her again, bowing, through the courtyards to the great gateway. Through the open red-and-gold doors she saw the Buick saloon, dark and shiny, standing as she had so often, and with what pleasure, seen it stand before how many doors? She stopped and looked round her almost wildly—behind her the garden, before her the Buick. Liu caught sight of her, and flew to hold open the door. But Mrs Bowlby did not get in. She made Shwang call a rickshaw, and when it came ordered him to direct the coolie to take her to the Bank. Shwang, exercising the respectful supervision which Chinese servants are wont to bestow on their employers, reminded her that she was to go to the polo to pick up the *lao-yé*, Bowlby. Before his astonished eyes his mistress shuddered visibly from head to foot. 'The Bank! The Bank!' she repeated, with a sort of desperate impatience.

Standing before his scarlet door, lighting his little black-and-silver pipe, the old *k'ai-men-ti* watched them go. First the rickshaw, with a small drooping grey figure in it, lurched down the dusty *hu-t'ung*, and after it, empty, bumped the Buick saloon.

Rhoda Broughton

1840–1920

Rhoda Broughton was the niece of ghost-story writer, Sheridan
Le Fanu, and when she was young she read him a few chapters
from her early novel. Afterwards he said, 'You will succeed, and
when you do, remember that I prophesied it.' She went on to
write many successful novels and stories, including the volume,
Twilight Tales, from which this unnerving tale has been taken.

THE TRUTH,
THE WHOLE TRUTH,
AND NOTHING
BUT THE TRUTH

Mrs De Wynt to Mrs Montresor

18 Eccleston Square
May 5th

My Dearest Cecilia,

Talk of the friendships of Orestes and Pylades, of Julie and Claire; what are
they to ours? Did Pylades ever go *ventre à terre*, half over London on a day more
broiling than any but an *âme damnée* could even imagine, in order that Orestes
might be comfortably housed for the season? Did Claire ever hold sweet con-
verse with from fifty to one hundred house agents, in order that Julie might have
three windows to her drawing room and a pretty *portière*? You see I am determined not to be done out of my full meed of gratitude.

Well, my friend, I had no idea till yesterday how closely we were packed in
this great smoky beehive, as tightly as herrings in a barrel. Don't be frightened,
however. By dint of squeezing and crowding, we have managed to make room
for two more herrings in our barrel, and those two are yourself and your
other self, i.e. your husband. Let me begin at the beginning. After having

looked over, I verily believe, every undesirable residence in West London; after having seen nothing intermediate between what was suited to the means of a duke, and what was suited to the needs of a chimney sweep; after having felt bed-ticking, and explored kitchen ranges till my brain reeled under my accumulated experience, I arrived at about half past five yesterday afternoon at 32, — Street, May Fair.

'Failure No. 253, I don't doubt,' I said to myself, as I toiled up the steps with my soul athirst for afternoon tea, and feeling as ill-tempered as you please. So much for my spirit of prophecy. Fate, I have noticed, is often fond of contradicting us flat, and giving the lie to our little predictions. Once inside, I thought I had got into a small compartment of Heaven by mistake. Fresh as a daisy, clean as a cherry, bright as a Seraph's face, it is all these, and a hundred more, only that my limited stock of similes is exhausted. Two drawing rooms as pretty as ever woman crammed with people she did not care two straws about; white curtains with rose-coloured ones underneath, festooned in the sweetest way; marvellously, *immorally* becoming, my dear, as I ascertained entirely for your benefit, in the mirrors, of which there are about a dozen and a half; Persian mats, easy chairs, and lounges suited to every possible physical conformation, from the Apollo Belvedere to Miss Biffin; and a thousand of the important little trivialities that make up the sum of a woman's life: ormolu garden gates, handleless cups, naked boys and *décolleté* shepherdesses; not to speak of a family of china pugs, with blue ribbons round their necks, which ought of themselves to have added fifty pounds a year to the rent. Apropos, I asked, in fear and trembling, what the rent might be—'three hundred pounds a year'. A feather would have knocked me down. I could hardly believe my ears, and made the woman repeat it several times, that there might be no mistake. To this hour it is a mystery to me.

With that suspiciousness, which is so characteristic of you, you will immediately begin to hint that there must be some terrible unaccountable smell, or some odious inexplicable noise haunting the reception rooms. Nothing of the kind, the woman assured me, and she did not look as if she were telling stories. You will next suggest—remembering the rose-coloured curtains—that its last occupant was a member of the demimonde. Wrong again. Its last occupant was an elderly and unexceptionable Indian officer, without a liver, and with a most lawful wife. They did not stay long, it is true, but then, as the housekeeper told me, he was a deplorable old hypochondriac, who never could bear to stay a fortnight in any one place. So lay aside that scepticism, which is your besetting sin, and give unfeigned thanks to St Brigitta, or St Gengulpha, or St Catherine of Sienna, or whoever is your tutelar saint, for having provided you with a palace at the cost of a hovel, and for having sent you such an invaluable friend as

Your attached,
ELIZABETH DE WYNT

P.S. I am so sorry I shall not be in town to witness your first raptures, but dear Artie looks so pale and thin and tall after the whooping cough, that I am sending him off at once to the sea, and as I cannot bear the child out of my sight, I am going into banishment likewise.

MRS MONTRESOR TO MRS DE WYNT

32, —— Street, May Fair
May 14th

Dearest Bessy,

Why did not dear little Artie defer his whooping-cough convalescence, etc., till August? It is very odd, to me, the perverse way in which children always fix upon the most inconvenient times and seasons for their diseases. Here we are installed in our Paradise, and have searched high and low, in every hole and corner, for the serpent, without succeeding in catching a glimpse of his spotted tail. Most things in this world are disappointing, but 32, — Street, May Fair, is not. The mystery of the rent is still a mystery. I have been for my first ride in the Row this morning: my horse was a little fidgety; I am half afraid that my nerve is not what it was. I saw heaps of people I knew. Do you recollect Florence Watson? What a wealth of red hair she had last year! Well, that same wealth is black as the raven's wing this year! I wonder how people can make such walking impositions of themselves, don't you? Adela comes to us next week; I am so glad. It is dull driving by oneself of an afternoon; and I always think that one young woman alone in a brougham, or with only a dog beside her, does not look *good*. We sent round our cards a fortnight before we came up, and have been already deluged with callers. Considering that we have been two years exiled from civilised life, and that London memories are not generally of the longest, we shall do pretty well, I think. Ralph Gordon came to see me on Sunday; he is in the —th Hussars now. He has grown up such a *dear* fellow, and *so* good-looking! Just my style, large and fair and whiskerless! Most men nowadays make themselves as like monkeys, or Scotch terriers, as they possibly can. I intend to be quite a *mother* to him. Dresses are gored to as *indecent* an extent as ever; short skirts are rampant. I am so sorry; I hate them. They make tall women look *lank*, and short ones insignificant. A knock! Peace is a word that might as well be expunged from one's London dictionary.

Yours affectionately,
CECILIA MONTRESOR

MRS DE WYNT TO MRS MONTRESOR

The Lord Warden, Dover
May 18th

Dearest Cecilia,

You will perceive that I am about to devote only one small sheet of note-paper to you. This is from no dearth of time, Heaven knows! time is a drug in the market here, but from a total dearth of ideas. Any ideas that I ever have, come to me from without, from external objects; I am not clever enough to generate any within myself. My life here is not an eminently suggestive one. It is spent in digging with a wooden spade, and eating prawns. Those are my employments, at least; my relaxation is going down to the Pier, to see the Calais boat come in. When one is miserable oneself, it is decidedly consolatory to see someone more miserable still, and wretched, and bored, and reluctant vegetable as I am, I am not *seasick*. I always feel my spirits rise after having seen that peevish, draggled procession of blue, green and yellow fellow Christians file past me. There is a wind here *always*, in comparison of which the wind that behaved so violently to the corners of Job's house was a mere zephyr. There are heights to climb which require more daring perseverance than ever Wolfe displayed, with his paltry heights of Abraham. There are glaring white houses, glaring white roads, glaring white cliffs. If anyone knew how unpatriotically I detest the chalk cliffs of Albion! Having grumbled through my two little pages—I have actually been reduced to writing very large in order to fill even them—I will send off my dreary little billet. How I wish I could get into the envelope myself too, and whirl up with it to dear, beautiful, filthy London. Not more heavily could Madame de Staël have sighed for Paris from among the shades of Coppet.

Your disconsolate, BESSY

MRS MONTRESOR TO MRS DE WYNT

32, — Street, May Fair
May 27th

Oh, my dearest Bessy, how I wish we were out of this dreadful, dreadful house! Please don't think me very ungrateful for saying this, after your taking such pains to provide us with a Heaven upon earth, as you thought.

What has happened could, of course, have been neither foretold, nor guarded against, by any human being. About ten days ago, Benson (my maid) came to me with a very long face, and said, 'If you please, 'm, did you know that

95

this house was *haunted*?' I was *so* startled: you know what a coward I am. I said, 'Good Heavens! No! is it?' 'Well, 'm, I'm pretty nigh sure it is,' she said, and the expression of her countenance was about as lively as an undertaker's; and then she told me that cook had been that morning to order in groceries from a shop in the neighbourhood, and on her giving the man the direction where to send the things to, he had said, with a very peculiar smile, 'No. 32, — Street, eh? h'm! I wonder how long *you*'ll stand it; last lot held out just a fortnight.' He looked so odd that she asked him what he meant, but he only said 'Oh! nothing; only that parties never *did* stay long at 32. He had known parties go in one day, and out the next, and during the last four years he had never known any remain over the month.' Feeling a good deal alarmed by this information, she naturally enquired the reason; but he declined to give it, saying that if she had not found it out for herself, she had much better leave it alone, as it would only frighten her out of her wits; and on her insisting and urging him, she could only extract from him that the house had such a villainously bad name, that the owners were glad to let it for a mere song. You know how firmly I believe in apparitions, and what an unutterable fear I have of them; anything material, tangible, that I can lay hold of—anything of the same fibre, blood and bone as myself, I could, I think, confront bravely enough; but the mere thought of being brought face to face with the 'bodiless dead' makes my brain unsteady. The moment Henry came in, I ran to him, and told him; but he pooh-poohed the whole story, laughed at me, and asked whether we should turn out of the prettiest house in London, at the very height of the season, because a grocer said it had a bad name. Most good things that had ever been in the world had had a bad name in their day; and, moreover, the man had probably a motive for taking away the house's character, some friend for whom he coveted the charming situation and the low rent. He derided my 'babyish fears', as he called them, to such an extent that I felt half ashamed, and yet not quite comfortable, either; and then came the usual rush of London engagements, during which one has no time to think of anything but how to speak, and act, and look for the moment then present. Adela was to arrive yesterday, and in the morning our weekly hamper of flowers, fruit and vegetables arrived from home. I always dress the flower vases myself, servants are so tasteless; and as I was arranging them, it occurred to me—you know Adela's passion for flowers—to carry up one particular cornucopia of roses and mignonette and set it on her toilet table, as a pleasant surprise for her. As I came downstairs, I had seen the housemaid—a fresh round-faced country girl—go into the room, which was being prepared for Adela, with a pair of sheets that she had been airing over her arm. I went upstairs very slowly, as my cornucopia was full of water, and I was afraid of spilling some. I turned the handle of the bedroom door and entered, keeping my eyes fixed on my flowers, to see how they bore the transit, and whether any of them had fallen out. Suddenly a sort of shiver passed over me; and feeling frightened—I did not know why—I looked up quickly. The girl was standing by the bed, leaning forward a little with her hands clenched in each other, rigid, every nerve tense; her eyes, wide open, starting out of her head, and a look of unutterable stony horror in them; her cheeks and mouth not pale, but livid as those of one that died a while ago in mortal pain. As I looked at her, her lips moved a little, and an awful hoarse voice, not like hers in the least, said, 'Oh! my God, I have seen it!' and then she fell down suddenly, like a log, with a heavy noise. Hearing the noise, loudly audible all through the thin walls and floors of a London house, Benson came running in, and between us we managed to lift her on to the bed, and tried to bring her to herself by rubbing her feet and hands, and holding strong salts to her nostrils. And all the while we kept glancing over our shoulders, in a vague cold terror of seeing some awful, shapeless apparition. Two long hours she lay in a state of utter unconsciousness. Meanwhile Harry, who had been down to his club, returned. At the end of the two hours we succeeded in bringing her back to sensation and life, but only to make the awful discovery that she was raving mad. She became so violent that it required all the combined strength of Harry and Phillips (our butler) to hold her down in the bed. Of course, we sent off instantly for a doctor, who, on her growing a little calmer towards evening, removed her in a cab to his own house. He has just been here to tell me that she is now pretty quiet, not from any return to sanity, but from sheer exhaustion. We are, of course, utterly in the dark as to *what* she saw, and her ravings are far too disconnected and unintelligible to afford us the slightest clue. I feel so completely shattered and upset by this awful occurrence, that you will excuse me, dear, I'm sure, if I write incoherently. One thing, I need hardly tell you, and that is, that no earthly consideration would induce me to allow Adela to occupy that terrible room. I shudder and run by quickly as I pass the door.

Yours, in great agitation,
CECILIA

MRS DE WYNT TO MRS MONTRESOR

The Lord Warden, Dover
May 28th

Dearest Cecilia,

Yours just come; how very dreadful! But I am still unconvinced as to the house being in fault. You know I feel a sort of godmother to it, and responsible for its good behaviour. Don't you think that what the girl had might have been a fit? Why not? I myself have a cousin who is subject to seizures of the kind, and immediately on being attacked his whole body becomes rigid, his eyes glassy and staring, his complexion livid, exactly as in the case you describe. Or, if not a fit, are you sure that she has not been subject to fits of madness? *Please* be sure and ascertain whether there is not insanity in her family. It is so common nowadays, and so much on the increase, that nothing is more likely. You know my utter disbelief in ghosts. I am convinced that most of them, if run to earth, would turn out about as genuine as the famed Cock Lane one. But even allowing the possibility, nay, the actual unquestioned existence of ghosts in the abstract, is it likely that there should be anything to be seen so horribly fear-inspiring, as to send a perfectly sane person *in one instant* raving mad, which you, after three weeks' residence in the house, have never caught a glimpse of? According to your hypothesis, your whole household ought, by this time, to be stark, staring mad. Let me implore you not to give way to a panic which may, possibly, probably prove utterly groundless. Oh, how I wish I were with you, to make you listen to reason! Artie ought to be the best prop ever woman's old age was furnished with, to indemnify me, for all he and his whooping cough have made me suffer. Write immediately, please, and tell me how the poor patient progresses. Oh, had I the wings of a dove! I shall be on wires till I hear again.

Yours, BESSY

MRS MONTRESOR TO MRS DE WYNT

No. 5, Bolton Street, Piccadilly
June 12th

Dearest Bessy,

You will see that we have left that terrible, hateful, fatal house. How I wish we had escaped from it sooner! Oh, my dear Bessy, I shall never be the same woman again if I live to be a hundred. Let me try to be coherent, and to tell you connectedly what has happened. And first, as to the housemaid, she has been removed to a lunatic asylum, where she remains in much the same state. She has had several lucid intervals, and during them has been closely, pressingly questioned as to what it was she saw; but she has maintained an absolute, hopeless silence, and only shudders, moans and hides her face in her hands when the subject is broached. Three days ago I went to see her, and on my return was sitting resting in the drawing room, before going to dress for dinner, talking to Adela about my visit, when Ralph Gordon walked in. He has always been walking in the last ten days, and Adela has always flushed up and looked happy, poor little cat, whenever he made his appearance. He looked very handsome, dear fellow, just come in from the park in a coat that fitted like a second skin, lavender gloves, and a gardenia. He seemed in tremendous spirits, and was as sceptical as even you could be, as to the ghostly origin of Sarah's seizure. 'Let me come here tonight and sleep in that room; *do*, Mrs Montresor,' he said, looking very eager and excited, 'with the gas lit and a poker, I'll engage to exorcise every demon that shows his ugly nose; even if I should find

> Seven white ghostisses
> Sitting on seven white postisses.'

'You don't mean really?' I asked, incredulously. 'Don't I? that's all,' he answered, emphatically. 'I should like nothing better. Well, is it a bargain?' Adela turned quite pale. 'Oh, don't,' she said, hurriedly. '*Please*, don't; why should you run such a risk? How do you know that you might not be sent mad too?' He laughed very heartily, and coloured a little with pleasure at seeing the interest she took in his safety. 'Never fear,' he said, 'it would take more than a whole squadron of departed ones, with the old gentleman at their head, to send me crazy.' He was so eager, so persistent, so thoroughly in earnest, that I yielded at last, though with a certain strong reluctance, to his entreaties. Adela's blue eyes filled with tears, and she walked away hastily to the conservatory, and stood picking bits of heliotrope to hide them. Nevertheless, Ralph got his own way; it was so difficult to refuse him anything. We gave up all our engagements for the evening, and he did the same with his. At about ten o'clock he arrived, accompanied by a friend and brother officer, Captain Burton, who was anxious to see the result of the experiment. 'Let me go up at once,' he said, looking very happy and animated. 'I don't know when I have felt in such good tune; a new sensation is a luxury not to be had every day of one's life; turn the gas up as high as it will go; provide a good stout poker, and leave the issue to Providence and me.' We did as he bid. 'It's all ready now,' Henry said, coming downstairs after having obeyed his orders; 'the room is nearly as light as day. Well, good luck to you, old fellow!' 'Goodbye, Miss Bruce,' Ralph said, going over to Adela, and taking her hand with a look, half laughing, half sentimental—

> 'Fare thee well, and if for ever,
> Then for ever, fare thee well,

that is my last dying speech and confession.' 'Now mind,' he went on, standing by the table, and addressing us all; 'if I ring once, *don't* come. I may be flurried, and lay hold of the bell without thinking; if I ring twice, *come*.' Then he went, jumping up the stairs three steps at a time, and humming a tune. As for us, we sat in different attitudes of expectation and listening about the drawing room. At first we tried to talk a little, but it would not do; our whole souls seemed to have passed into our ears. The clock's ticking sounded as loud as a great church bell close to one's ear. Addy lay on the sofa, with her dear little white face hidden in the cushions. So we sat for exactly an hour; but it seemed like two years, and just as the clock began to strike eleven, a sharp ting, ting, ting rang clear and shrill through the house. 'Let us go,' said Addy, starting up, and running to the door. 'Let us go,' I cried too, following her. But Captain Burton stood in the way, and interrupted our progress. 'No,' he said, decisively, 'you must not go; remember Gordon told us distinctly, if he rang once *not* to come. I know the sort of fellow he is, and that nothing would annoy him more than having his directions disregarded.'

'Oh, nonsense!' Addy cried, passionately, 'he would never have rung if he had not seen something dreadful; do, *do* let us go!' she ended, clasping her hands. But she was overruled, and we all went back to our seats. Ten minutes more of suspense, next door to unendurable, I felt a lump in my throat, a gasping for breath—ten minutes on the clock, but a thousand centuries on our hearts. Then again, loud, sudden, violent the bell rang! We made a simultaneous rush to the door. I don't think we were one second flying upstairs. Addy was first. Almost simultaneously she and I burst into the room. There he was, standing in the middle of the floor, rigid, petrified, with that same look—that look that is burnt into my heart in letters of fire—of awful, unspeakable, stony fear on his brave young face. For one instant he stood thus; then stretching out his arms stiffly before him, he groaned in a terrible husky voice, 'Oh, my God, I have seen it!' and fell down *dead*. Yes, *dead*. Not in a swoon or in a fit, but *dead*. Vainly we tried to bring back the life to that strong young heart; it will never come back again till that day when the earth and the sea give up the dead that are therein. I cannot see the page for the tears that are blinding me; he was such a dear fellow! I can't write any more today.

Your broken-hearted
CECILIA

This is a true story.

───────────

A. M. Burrage

1889–1956

When he was seventeen, faced with the need to support his
family, following the death of his father, Alfred McLelland
Burrage turned to writing fiction to earn a living. Over the next
forty years or so, he produced a stream of successful novels and
short stories. Some of his early work, influenced by his
experiences in the First World War, was published under the
pseudonym Ex-Private-X.

SMEE

'No,' said Jackson, with a deprecatory smile, 'I'm sorry. I don't want to
upset your game. I shan't be doing that because you'll have plenty without me. But I'm not playing any games of hide-and-seek.'

It was Christmas Eve, and we were a party of fourteen with just the proper
leavening of youth. We had dined well; it was the season for childish games, and
we were all in the mood for playing them—all, that is, except Jackson. When
somebody suggested hide-and-seek there was rapturous and almost unanimous
approval. His was the one dissentient voice.

It was not like Jackson to spoil sport or refuse to do as others wanted.
Somebody asked him if he were feeling seedy.

'No,' he answered, 'I feel perfectly fit, thanks. But,' he added with a smile
which softened without retracting the flat refusal, 'I'm not playing hide-and-
seek.'

One of us asked him why not. He hesitated for some seconds before replying.

'I sometimes go and stay at a house where a girl was killed through playing
hide-and-seek in the dark. She didn't know the house very well. There was a
servants' staircase with a door to it. When she was pursued she opened the door
and jumped into what she must have thought was one of the bedrooms—and
she broke her neck at the bottom of the stairs.'

We all looked concerned, and Mrs Fernley said:

'How awful! And you were there when it happened?'

Jackson shook his head very gravely. 'No,' he said, 'but I was there when
something else happened. Something worse.'

'I shouldn't have thought anything could be worse.'

'This was,' said Jackson, and shuddered visibly. 'Or so it seemed to me.'

I think he wanted to tell the story and was angling for encouragement. A few requests, which may have seemed to him to lack urgency, he affected to ignore and went off at a tangent.

'I wonder if any of you have played a game called "Smee". It's a great improvement on the ordinary game of hide-and-seek. The name derives from the ungrammatical colloquialism, "It's me." You might care to play if you're going to play a game of that sort. Let me tell you the rules.

'Every player is presented with a sheet of paper. All the sheets are blank except one, on which is written "Smee". Nobody knows who is "Smee" except "Smee" himself—or herself, as the case may be. The lights are then turned out and "Smee" slips from the room and goes off to hide, and after an interval the other players go off in search, without knowing whom they are actually in search of. One player meeting another challenges with the word "Smee" and the other player, if not the one concerned, answers "Smee".

'The real "Smee" makes no answer when challenged, and the second player remains quietly by him. Presently they will be discovered by a third player, who, having challenged and received no answer, will link up with the first two. This goes on until all the players have formed a chain and the last to join is marked down for a forfeit. It's a good noisy, romping game, and in a big house it often takes a long time to complete the chain. You might care to try it; and I'll pay my forfeit and smoke one of Tim's excellent cigars here by the fire until you get tired of it.'

I remarked that it sounded a good game and asked Jackson if he had played it himself.

'Yes,' he answered; 'I played it in the house I was telling you about.'

'And *she* was there? The girl who broke—'

'No, no,' Mrs Fernley interrupted. 'He told us he wasn't there when it happened.'

Jackson considered. 'I don't know if she was there or not. I'm afraid she was. I know that there were thirteen of us and there ought only to have been twelve. And I'll swear that I didn't know her name, or I think I should have gone clean off my head when I heard that whisper in the dark. No, you don't catch me playing that game, or any other like it, any more. It spoiled my nerve quite a while, and I can't afford to take long holidays. Besides, it saves a lot of trouble and inconvenience to own up at once to being a coward.'

Tim Vouce, the best of hosts, smiled around at us, and in that smile there was a meaning which is sometimes vulgarly expressed by the slow closing of an eye. 'There's a story coming,' he announced.

'There's certainly a story of sorts,' said Jackson, 'but whether it's coming or not—' He paused and shrugged his shoulders.

'Well, you're going to pay a forfeit instead of playing?'

'Please. But have a heart and let me down lightly. It's not just a sheer cussedness on my part.'

'Payment in advance,' said Tim, 'ensures honesty and promotes good feeling. You are therefore sentenced to tell the story here and now.'

And here follows Jackson's story, unrevised by me and passed on without comment to a wider public:

SOME OF YOU, I know, have run across the Sangstons. Christopher Sangston and his wife, I mean. They're distant connections of mine—at least, Violet Sangston is. About eight years ago they bought a house between the North and South Downs on the Surrey and Sussex border, and five years ago they invited me to come and spend Christmas with them.

It was a fairly old house—I couldn't say exactly of what period—and it certainly deserved the epithet 'rambling'. It wasn't a particularly big house, but the original architect, whoever he may have been, had not concerned himself with economising in space, and at first you could get lost in it quite easily.

Well, I went down for that Christmas, assured by Violet's letter that I knew most of my fellow guests and that the two or three who might be strangers to me were all 'lambs'. Unfortunately, I'm one of the world's workers, and I couldn't get away until Christmas Eve, although the other members of the party had assembled on the preceding day. Even then I had to cut it rather fine to be there for dinner on my first night. They were all dressing when I arrived and I had to go straight to my room and waste no time. I may even have kept dinner waiting a bit, for I was last down, and it was announced within a minute of my entering the drawing room. There was just time to say 'hello' to everybody I knew, to be briefly introduced to the two or three I didn't know, and then I had to give my arm to Mrs Gorman.

I mention this as the reason why I didn't catch the name of a tall, dark, handsome girl I hadn't met before. Everything was rather hurried and I am always bad at catching people's names. She looked cold and clever and rather forbidding, the sort of girl who gives the impression of knowing all about men and the more she knows of them the less she likes them. I felt that I wasn't going to hit it off with this particular 'lamb' of Violet's, but she looked interesting all the same, and I wondered who she was. I didn't ask, because I was pretty sure of hearing somebody address her by name before very long.

Unluckily, though, I was a long way off her at table, and as Mrs Gorman was at the top of her form that night I soon forgot to worry about who she might be. Mrs Gorman is one of the most amusing women I know, an outrageous but quite innocent flirt, with a very sprightly wit which isn't always unkind. She can think half a dozen moves ahead in conversation just as an expert can in a game of chess. We were soon sparring, or, rather, I was 'covering' against the ropes, and I quite forgot to ask her in an undertone the name of the cold, proud beauty. The lady on the other side of me was a stranger, or had been until a few minutes since, and I didn't think of seeking information in that quarter.

There was a round dozen of us, including the Sangstons themselves, and we were all young or trying to be. The Sangstons were the oldest members of the party and their son Reggie, in his last year at Marlborough, must have been the youngest. When there was talk of playing games after dinner it was he who suggested 'Smee'. He told us how to play it just as I've described it to you.

His father chipped in as soon as we all understood what was going to be required of us. 'If there are any games of that sort going on in the house,' he said, 'for goodness' sake be careful of the back stairs on the first-floor landing. There's a door to them and I've often meant to take it down. In the dark anybody who doesn't know the house very well might think they were walking into a room. A girl actually did break her neck on those stairs about ten years ago when the Ainsties lived here.'

I asked how it happened.

'Oh,' said Sangston, 'there was a party here one Christmas time and they were playing hide-and-seek as you propose doing. This girl was one of the hiders. She heard somebody coming, ran along the passage to get away, and opened the door of what she thought was a bedroom, evidently with the intention of hiding behind it while her pursuer went past. Unfortunately it was the door leading to the back stairs, and that staircase is as straight and almost as steep as the shaft of a pit. She was dead when they picked her up.'

We all promised for our own sakes to be careful. Mrs Gorman said that she was sure nothing could happen to her, since she was insured by three different firms, and her next of kin was a brother whose consistent ill luck was a byword in the family. You see, none of us had known the unfortunate girl, and as the tragedy was ten years old there was no need to pull long faces about it.

Well, we started the game almost immediately after dinner. The men allowed themselves only five minutes before joining the ladies, and then young Reggie Sangston went round and assured himself that the lights were out all over the house except in the servants' quarters and in the drawing room where we were assembled. We then got busy with twelve sheets of paper which he twisted into pellets and shook up between his hands before passing them round. Eleven of them were blank, and 'Smee' was written on the twelfth. The person drawing the latter was the one who had to hide. I looked and saw that mine was a blank. A moment later out went the electric lights, and in the darkness I heard somebody get up and creep to the door.

After a minute or so somebody gave a signal and we made a rush for the door. I for one hadn't the least idea which of the party was 'Smee'. For five or ten minutes we were all rushing up and down passages and in and out rooms challenging one another and answering, 'Smee?—Smee!'

After a bit the alarums and excursions died down, and I guessed that 'Smee' was found. Eventually I found a chain of people all sitting still and holding their breath on some narrow stairs leading up to a row of attics. I hastily joined it, having challenged and been answered with silence, and presently two more stragglers arrived, each racing the other to avoid being last. Sangston was one of them, indeed it was he who was marked down for a forfeit, and after a little while he remarked in an undertone, 'I think we're all here now, aren't we?'

He struck a match, looked up the shaft of the staircase, and began to count. It wasn't hard, although we just about filled the staircase, for we were sitting each a step or two above the next, and all our heads were visible.

' . . . nine, ten, eleven, twelve—*thirteen*,' he concluded, and then laughed. 'Dash it all, that's one too many!'

The match had burned out and he struck another and began to count. He got as far as twelve, and then uttered an exclamation.

'There are thirteen people here!' he exclaimed. 'I haven't counted myself yet.'

'Oh, nonsense!' I laughed. 'You probably began with yourself, and now you want to count yourself twice.'

Out came his son's electric torch, giving a brighter and steadier light, and we all began to count. Of course we numbered twelve.

Sangston laughed.

'Well,' he said, 'I could have sworn I counted thirteen twice.'

From halfway up the stairs came Violet Sangston's voice with a little nervous trill in it. 'I thought there was somebody sitting two steps above me. Have you moved up, Captain Ransome?'

Ransome said that he hadn't: he also said that he thought there was somebody sitting between Violet and himself. Just for a moment there was an uncomfortable Something in the air, a little cold ripple which touched us all. For that little moment it seemed to all of us, I think, that something odd and unpleasant had happened and was liable to happen again. Then we laughed at ourselves and at one another and were comfortable once more. There *were* only twelve of us, and there *could* only have been twelve of us, and there was no argument about it. Still laughing we trooped back to the drawing room to begin again.

This time I was 'Smee', and Violet Sangston ran me to earth while I was still looking for a hiding place. That round didn't last long, and we were a chain of twelve within two or three minutes. Afterwards there was a short interval. Violet wanted a wrap fetched for her, and her husband went up to get it from her room. He was no sooner gone than Reggie pulled me by the sleeve. I saw that he was looking pale and sick.

'Quick!' he whispered, 'while father's out of the way. Take me into the smoke room and give me a brandy or a whisky or something.'

Outside the room I asked him what was the matter, but he didn't answer at first, and I thought it better to dose him first and question him afterwards. So I mixed him a pretty dark-complexioned brandy and soda which he drank at a gulp and then began to puff as if he had been running.

'I've had rather a turn,' he said to me with a sheepish grin.

'What's the matter?'

'I don't know. You were "Smee" just now, weren't you? Well, of course I didn't know who "Smee" was, and while mother and the others ran into the west wing and found you, I turned east. There's a deep clothes cupboard in my bedroom—I'd marked it down as a good place to hide when it was my turn, and I had an idea that "Smee" might be there. I opened the door in the dark, felt round, and touched somebody's hand. "Smee?" I whispered, and not getting any answer I thought I had found "Smee".

'Well, I don't know how it was, but an odd creepy feeling came over me, I can't describe it, but I felt that something was wrong. So I turned on my electric torch and there was nobody there. Now, I swear I touched a hand, and I was filling up the doorway of the cupboard at the time, so nobody could get out and past me.' He puffed again. 'What do you make of it?' he asked.

'You imagined that you had touched a hand,' I answered, naturally enough.

He uttered a short laugh. 'Of course I knew you were going to say that,' he said. 'I must have imagined it, mustn't I?' He paused and swallowed. 'I mean, it couldn't have been anything else *but* imagination, could it?'

I assured him that it couldn't, meaning what I said, and he accepted this, but rather with the philosophy of one who knows he is right but doesn't expect to be believed. We returned together to the drawing room where, by that time, they were all waiting for us and ready to start again.

It may have been my imagination—although I'm almost sure it wasn't—but it seemed to me that all enthusiasm for the game had suddenly melted like a white frost in strong sunlight. If anybody had suggested another game I'm sure we should all have been grateful and abandoned 'Smee'. Only nobody did. Nobody seemed to like to. I for one, and I can speak for some of the others too, was oppressed with the feeling that there was something wrong. I couldn't have said what I thought was wrong, indeed I didn't think about it at all, but somehow all the sparkle had gone out of the fun, and hovering over my mind like a shadow was the warning of some sixth sense which told me that there was an influence in the house which was neither sane, sound nor healthy. Why did I feel like that? Because Sangston had counted thirteen of us instead of twelve, and his son had thought he had touched somebody in an empty cupboard. No, there was more in it than just that. One would have laughed at such things in the ordinary way, and it was just that feeling of something being wrong which stopped me from laughing.

Well, we started again, and when we went in pursuit of the unknown 'Smee', we were as noisy as ever, but it seemed to me that most of us were acting. Frankly, for no reason other than the one I've given you, we'd stopped enjoying the game. I had an instinct to hunt with the main pack, but after a few minutes, during which no 'Smee' had been found, my instinct to play winning games and be first if possible, set me searching on my own account. And on the first floor of the west wing following the wall which was actually the shell of the house, I blundered against a pair of human knees.

I put out my hand and touched a soft, heavy curtain. Then I knew where I was. There were tall, deeply recessed windows with seats along the landing, and curtains over the recesses to the ground. Somebody was sitting in a corner of this window seat behind the curtain. Aha, I had caught 'Smee'! So I drew the curtain aside, stepped in, and touched the bare arm of a woman.

It was a dark night outside, and, moreover, the window was not only curtained but a blind hung down to where the bottom panes joined up with the frame. Between the curtain and the window it was as dark as the plague of Egypt. I could not have seen my hand held six inches before my face, much less the woman sitting in the corner.

'Smee?' I whispered.

I had no answer. 'Smee' when challenged does not answer. So I sat down beside her, first in the field, to await the others. Then, having settled myself I leaned over to her and whispered:

'Who is it? What's your name, "Smee"?'

And out of the darkness beside me the whisper came back: 'Brenda Ford.'

I didn't know the name, but because I didn't know it I guessed at once who she was. The tall, pale, dark girl was the only person in the house I didn't know by name. Ergo my companion was the tall, pale, dark girl. It seemed rather intriguing to be there with her, shut in between a heavy curtain and a window, and I rather wondered whether she was enjoying the game we were all playing. Somehow she hadn't seemed to me to be one of the romping sort. I muttered one or two commonplace questions to her and had no answer.

'Smee' is a game of silence. 'Smee' and the person or persons who have found 'Smee' are supposed to keep quiet to make it hard for the others. But there was nobody else about, and it occurred to me that she was playing the game a little too much to the letter. I spoke again and got no answer, and then I began to be annoyed. She was of that cold, 'superior' type which affects to despise men; she didn't like me; and she was sheltering behind the rules of a game for children to be discourteous. Well, if she didn't like sitting there with me, I certainly didn't want to be sitting there with her! I half turned from her and began to hope that we should both be discovered without much more delay.

Having discovered that I didn't like being there alone with her, it was queer how soon I found myself hating it, and that for a reason very different from the one which had at first whetted my annoyance. The girl I had met for the first time before dinner, and seen diagonally across the table, had a sort of cold charm about her which had attracted while it had half angered me. For the girl who was with me, imprisoned in the opaque darkness between the curtain and the window, I felt no attraction at all. It was so very much the reverse that I should have wondered at myself if, after the first shock of the discovery that she had suddenly become repellent to me, I had had room in my mind for anything besides the consciousness that her close presence was an increasing horror to me.

It came upon me just as quickly as I've uttered the words. My flesh suddenly shrank from her as you see a strip of gelatine shrink and wither before the heat of a fire. That feeling of something being wrong had come back to me, but multiplied to an extent which turned foreboding into actual terror. I firmly believe that I should have got up and run if I had not felt that at my first movement she would have divined my intention and compelled me to stay, by some means of which I could not bear to think. The memory of having touched her bare arm made me wince and draw in my lips. I prayed that somebody else would come along soon.

My prayer was answered. Light footfalls sounded on the landing. Somebody on the other side of the curtain brushed again my knees. The curtain was drawn aside and a woman's hand, fumbling in the darkness, presently rested on my shoulder. 'Smee?' whispered a voice which I instantly recognised as Mrs Gorman's.

Of course she received no answer. She came and settled down beside me with a rustle, and I can't describe the sense of relief she brought me.

'It's Tony, isn't it?' she whispered.

'Yes,' I whispered back.

'You're not "Smee", are you?'

'No, she's on my other side.'

She reached a hand across me, and I heard one of her nails scratch the surface of a woman's silk gown.

'Hello, "Smee"! How are you? *Who* are you? Oh, is it against the rules to talk? Never mind, Tony, we'll break the rules. Do you know, Tony, this game is beginning to irk me a little. I hope they're not going to run it to death by playing it all the evening. I'd like to play some game where we can all be together in the same room with a nice bright fire.'

'Same here,' I agreed fervently.

'Can't you suggest something when we go down? There's something rather uncanny in this particular amusement. I can't quite shed the delusion that there's somebody in this game who oughtn't to be in at all.'

That was just how I had been feeling, but I didn't say so. But for my part the worst of my qualms were now gone; the arrival of Mrs Gorman had dissipated them. We sat on talking, wondering from time to time when the rest of the party would arrive.

I don't know how long elapsed before we heard a clatter of feet on the landing and young Reggie's voice shouting, 'Hello! Hello, there! Anybody there?'

'Yes,' I answered.

'Mrs Gorman with you?'

'Yes.'

'Well, you're a nice pair! You're both forfeited. We've all been waiting for you for hours.'

'Why, you haven't found "Smee" yet,' I objected.

'*You* haven't, you mean. I happen to have been "Smee" myself.'

'But "Smee"'s here with us,' I cried.

'Yes,' agreed Mrs Gorman.

The curtain was stripped aside and in a moment we were blinking into the eye of Reggie's electric torch. I looked at Mrs Gorman and then on my other side. Between me and the wall there was an empty space on the window seat. I stood up at once and wished I hadn't, for I found myself sick and dizzy.

'There *was* somebody there,' I maintained, 'because I touched her.'

'So did I,' said Mrs Gorman in a voice which had lost its steadiness. 'And I don't see how she could have got up and gone without our knowing it.'

Reggie uttered a queer, shaken laugh. He, too, had had an unpleasant experience that evening. 'Somebody's been playing the goat,' he remarked. 'Coming down?'

We were not very popular when we arrived in the drawing room. Reggie rather tactlessly gave it out that he had found us sitting on a window seat behind the curtain. I taxed the tall, dark girl with having pretended to be 'Smee' and afterwards slipping away. She denied it. After which we settled down and played other games. 'Smee' was done with for the evening, and I for one was glad of it.

Some long while later, during an interval, Sangston told me, if I wanted a drink, to go into the smoke room and help myself. I went, and he presently followed me. I could see that he was rather peeved with me, and the reason came out during the following minute or two. It seemed that, in his opinion, if I must sit out and flirt with Mrs Gorman—in circumstances which would have been considered highly compromising in his young days—I needn't do it during a round game and keep everybody waiting for us.

'But there was somebody else there,' I protested, 'somebody pretending to be "Smee". I believe it was that tall, dark girl, Miss Ford, although she denied it. She even whispered her name to me.'

Sangston stared at me and nearly dropped his glass.

'Miss *Who*?' he shouted.

'Brenda Ford—she told me her name was.'

Sangston put down his glass and laid a hand on my shoulder.

'Look here, old man,' he said, 'I don't mind a joke, but don't let it go too far. We don't want all the women in the house getting hysterical. Brenda Ford is the name of the girl who broke her neck on the stairs playing hide-and-seek here ten years ago.'

A. S. Byatt

b. 1936

For many years, Antonia Susan Byatt combined lecturing at an
art school with writing several novels and short-story collections.
In 1990 she won the Booker Prize for her novel *Possession* and
was awarded the CBE. Her work is thoughtful and understated
but has an underlying power—qualities that are superbly
displayed in this poignant story.

THE JULY GHOST

'I THINK I MUST MOVE out of where I'm living,' he said. 'I have this problem
with my landlady.'

He picked a long, bright hair off the back of her dress, so deftly that the
act seemed simply considerate. He had been skilful at balancing glass, plate and
cutlery, too. He had a look of dignified misery, like a dejected hawk. She was
interested.

'What sort of problem? Amatory, financial or domestic?'

'None of those, really. Well, not financial.'

He turned the hair on his finger, examining it intently, not meeting her eye.

'Not financial. Can you tell me? I might know somewhere you could stay. I
know a lot of people.'

'You would.' He smiled shyly. 'It's not an easy problem to describe. There's
just the two of us. I occupy the attics. Mostly.'

He came to a stop. He was obviously reserved and secretive. But he was telling
her something. This is usually attractive.

'Mostly?' Encouraging him.

'Oh, it's not like *that*. Well, not . . . Shall we sit down?'

THEY MOVED ACROSS THE PARTY, which was a big party, on a hot day. He stopped
and found a bottle and filled her glass. He had not needed to ask what she was
drinking. They sat side by side on a sofa: he admired the brilliant poppies bold
on her emerald dress, and her pretty sandals. She had come to London for the
summer to work in the British Museum. She could really have managed with
microfilm in Tucson for what little manuscript research was needed, but there

was a dragging love affair to end. There is an age at which, however desperately happy one is in stolen moments, days or weekends with one's married professor, one either prises him loose or cuts and runs. She had had a stab at both, and now considered she had successfully cut and run. So it was nice to be immediately appreciated. Problems are capable of solution. She said as much to him, turning her soft face to his ravaged one, swinging the long bright hair. It had begun a year ago, he told her in a rush, at another party actually; he had met this woman, the landlady in question, and had made, not immediately, a kind of *faux pas*, he now saw, and she had been very decent, all things considered, and so . . .

He had said, 'I think I must move out of where I'm living.' He had been quite wild, had nearly not come to the party, but could not go on drinking alone. The woman had considered him coolly and asked, 'Why?' One could not, he said, go on in a place where one had once been blissfully happy, and was now miserable, however convenient the place. Convenient, that was, for work, and friends, and things that seemed, as he mentioned them, ashy and insubstantial compared to the memory and the hope of opening the door and finding Anne outside it, laughing and breathless, waiting to be told what he had read, or thought, or eaten, or felt that day. Someone I loved left, he told the woman. Reticent on that occasion too, he bit back the flurry of sentences about the total unexpectedness of it, the arriving back and finding only an envelope on a clean table, and spaces in the bookshelves, the record stack, the kitchen cupboard. It must have been planned for weeks, she must have been thinking it out while he rolled on her, while she poured wine for him, while . . . No, no. Vituperation is undignified and in this case what he felt was lower and worse than rage: just pure, childlike loss. 'One ought not to mind places,' he said to the woman. 'But one does,' she had said. 'I know.'

She had suggested to him that he could come and be her lodger, then; she had, she said, a lot of spare space going to waste, and her husband wasn't there much. 'We've not had a lot to say to each other, lately.' He could be quite self-contained, there was a kitchen and a bathroom in the attics: she wouldn't bother him. There was a large garden. It was possibly this that decided him: it was very hot, central London, the time of year when a man feels he would give anything to live in a room opening on to grass and trees, not a high flat in a dusty street. And if Anne came back, the door would be locked and mortise-locked. He could stop thinking about Anne coming back. That was a decisive move: Anne thought he wasn't decisive. He would live without Anne.

FOR SOME WEEKS after he moved in he had seen very little of the woman. They met on the stairs, and once she came up, on a hot Sunday, to tell him he must feel free to use the garden. He had offered to do some weeding and mowing and she had accepted. That was the weekend her husband came back, driving furiously up to the front door, running in, and calling in the empty hall, 'Imogen, Imogen!' To which she had replied, uncharacteristically, by screaming hysterically. There was nothing in her husband Noel's appearance to warrant this reaction; their lodger, peering over the banister at the sound, had seen their upturned faces in the stairwell and watched hers settle into its usual prim and placid expression as he did so. Seeing Noel, a balding, fluffy-templed, stooping thirty-five or so, shabby corduroy suit, cotton polo neck, he realised he was now able to guess her age, as he had not been. She was a very neat woman, faded blonde, her hair in a knot on the back of her head, her legs long and slender, her eyes downcast. Mild was not quite the right word for her, though. She explained then that she had screamed because Noel had come home unexpectedly and startled her: she was sorry. It seemed a reasonable explanation. The extraordinary vehemence of the screaming was probably an echo in the stairwell. Noel seemed wholly downcast by it, all the same.

He had kept out of the way, that weekend, taking the stairs two at a time and lightly, feeling a little aggrieved, looking out of his kitchen window into the lovely, overgrown garden, that they were lurking indoors, wasting all the summer sun. At Sunday lunch time he had heard the husband, Noel, shouting on the stairs.

'I can't go on, if you go on like that. I've done my best, I've tried to get through. Nothing will shift you, will it, you won't *try*, will you, you just go on and on. Well, I have my life to live, you can't throw a life away . . . can you?'

He had crept out again on to the dark upper landing and seen her standing, halfway down the stairs, quite still, watching Noel wave his arms and roar, or almost roar, with a look of impassive patience, as though this nuisance must pass off. Noel swallowed and gasped; he turned his face up to her and said plaintively,

'You do see I can't stand it? I'll be in touch, shall I? You must want . . . you must need . . . you must . . .'

She didn't speak.

'If you need anything, you know where to get me.'

'Yes.'

'Oh, well . . .' said Noel, and went to the door. She watched him, from the stairs, until it was shut, and then came up again, step by step, as though it was an effort, a little, and went on coming, past her bedroom, to his landing, to come in and ask him, entirely naturally, please to use the garden if he wanted to, and please not to mind marital rows. She was sure he understood . . . things were difficult . . . Noel wouldn't be back for some time. He was a journalist: his work took him away a lot. Just as well. She committed herself to that 'just as well'. She was a very economical speaker.

So he took to sitting in the garden. It was a lovely place: a huge, hidden, walled south London garden, with old fruit trees at the end, a wildly waving disorderly buddleia, curving beds full of old roses, and a lawn of overgrown, dense rye grass. Over the wall at the foot was the Common, with a footpath running behind all the gardens. She came out to the shed and helped him to assemble and oil the lawn mower, standing on the little path under the apple branches while he cut an experimental serpentine across her hay. Over the wall came the high sound of children's voices, and the thunk and thud of a football. He asked her how to raise the blades: he was not mechanically minded.

'The children get quite noisy,' she said. 'And dogs. I hope they don't bother you. There aren't many safe places for children, round here.'

He replied truthfully that he never heard sounds that didn't concern him, when he was concentrating. When he'd got the lawn into shape, he was going to sit on it and do a lot of reading, try to get his mind in trim again, to write a paper on Hardy's poems, on their curiously archaic vocabulary.

'It isn't very far to the road on the other side, really,' she said. 'It just seems to be. The Common is an illusion of space, really. Just a spur of brambles and gorse bushes and bits of football pitch between two fast four-laned main roads. I hate London commons.'

'There's a lovely smell, though, from the gorse and the wet grass. It's a pleasant illusion.'

'No illusions are pleasant,' she said, decisively, and went in. He wondered what she did with her time: apart from little shopping expeditions she seemed to be always in the house. He was sure that when he'd met her she'd been introduced as having some profession: vaguely literary, vaguely academic, like everyone he knew. Perhaps she wrote poetry in her north-facing living room. He had no idea what it would be like. Women generally wrote emotional poetry, much nicer than men, as Kingsley Amis has stated, but she seemed, despite her placid stillness, too spare and too fierce—grim?—for that. He remembered the screaming. Perhaps she wrote Plath-like chants of violence. He didn't think that quite fitted the bill, either. Perhaps she was a freelance radio journalist. He didn't bother to ask anyone who might be a common acquaintance. During the whole year, he explained to the American at the party, he hadn't actually *discussed* her with anyone. Of course he wouldn't, she agreed vaguely and warmly. She knew he wouldn't. He didn't see why he shouldn't, in fact, but went on, for the time, with his narrative.

THEY HAD GOT TO KNOW each other a little better over the next few weeks, at least on the level of borrowing tea, or even sharing pots of it. The weather had got hotter. He had found an old-fashioned deck chair, with faded striped canvas, in the shed, and had brushed it over and brought it out on to his mown lawn, where he sat writing a little, reading a little, getting up and pulling up a tuft of couch grass. He had been wrong about the children not bothering him: there was a succession of incursions by all sizes of children looking for all sizes of balls, which bounced to his feet, or crashed in the shrubs, or vanished in the herbaceous border, black and white footballs, beach balls with concentric circles of primary colours, acid-yellow tennis balls. The children came over the wall: black faces, brown faces, floppy long hair, shaven heads, respectable dotted sunhats and camouflaged cotton army hats from Milletts. They came over easily, as though they were used to it, sandals, training shoes, a few bare toes, grubby sunburned legs, cotton skirts, jeans, football shorts. Sometimes, perched on the top, they saw him and gestured at the balls; one or two asked permission. Sometimes he threw a ball back, but was apt to knock down a few knobby little unripe apples or pears. There was a gate in the wall, under the fringing trees, which he once tried to open, spending time on rusty bolts only to discover that the lock was new and secure, and the key not in it.

The boy sitting in the tree did not seem to be looking for a ball. He was in a fork of the tree nearest the gate, swinging his legs, doing something to a knot in a frayed end of rope that was attached to the branch he sat on. He wore blue jeans and training shoes, and a brilliant T-shirt, striped in the colours of the spectrum, arranged in the right order, which the man on the grass found visually pleasing. He had rather long blond hair, falling over his eyes, so that his face was obscured.

'Hey, you. Do you think you ought to be up there? It might not be safe.'

The boy looked up, grinned, and vanished monkey-like over the wall. He had a nice, frank grin, friendly, not cheeky.

He was there again, the next day, leaning back in the crook of the tree, arms crossed. He had on the same shirt and jeans. The man watched him, expecting him to move again, but he sat, immobile, smiling down pleasantly, and then staring up at the sky. The man read a little, looked up, saw him still there, and said, 'Have you lost anything?'

The child did not reply: after a moment he climbed down a little, swung along the branch hand over hand, dropped to the ground, raised an arm in salute, and was up over the usual route over the wall.

Two days later he was lying on his stomach on the edge of the lawn, out of the shade, this time in a white T-shirt with a pattern of blue ships and water lines on it, his bare feet and legs stretched in the sun. He was chewing a grass stem, and studying the earth, as though watching for insects. The man said, 'Hi, there,' and the boy looked up, met his look with intensely blue eyes under long lashes, smiled with the same complete warmth and openness, and returned his look to the earth.

He felt reluctant to inform on the boy, who seemed so harmless and considerate: but when he met him walking out of the kitchen door, spoke to him, and got no answer but the gentle smile before the boy ran off towards the wall, he wondered if he should speak to his landlady. So he asked her, did she mind the children coming in the garden. She said no, children must look for balls, that was part of being children. He persisted—they sat there, too, and he had met one coming out of the house. He hadn't seemed to be doing any harm, the boy, but you couldn't tell. He thought she should know.

He was probably a friend of her son's, she said. She looked at him kindly and explained. Her son had run off the Common with some other children, two years ago, in the summer, in July, and had been killed on the road. More or less instantly, she had added drily, as though calculating that just *enough* information would preclude the need for further questions. He said he was sorry, very sorry, feeling to blame, which was ridiculous, and a little injured, because he had not known about her son, and might inadvertently have made a fool of himself with some casual reference whose ignorance would be embarrassing.

What was the boy like, she said. The one in the house? 'I don't—talk to his friends. I find it painful. It could be Timmy, or Martin. They might have lost something, or want . . .'

He described the boy. Blond, about ten at a guess, he was not very good at children's ages, very blue eyes, slightly built, with a rainbow-striped T-shirt and blue jeans, mostly though not always—oh, and those football practice shoes, black and green. And the other T-shirt, with the ships and wavy lines. And an extraordinarily nice smile. A really *warm* smile. A nice-looking boy.

He was used to her being silent. But this silence went on and on and on. She was just staring into the garden. After a time, she said, in her precise conversational tone,

'The only thing I want, the only thing I want at all in this world, is to see that boy.'

She stared at the garden and he stared with her, until the grass began to dance with empty light, and the edges of the shrubbery wavered. For a brief moment he shared the strain of not seeing the boy. Then she gave a little sigh, sat down, neatly as always, and passed out at his feet.

After this she became, for her, voluble. He didn't move her after she fainted, but sat patiently by her, until she stirred and sat up; then he fetched her some water, and would have gone away, but she talked.

'I'm too rational to see ghosts, I'm not someone who would see anything there was to see, I don't believe in an afterlife, I don't see how anyone can, I always found a kind of satisfaction for myself in the idea that one just came to an end, to a sliced-off stop. But that was myself; I didn't think *he*—not *he*—I thought ghosts were—what people *wanted* to see, or were afraid to see . . . and after he died, the best hope I had, it sounds silly, was that I would go mad enough so that instead of waiting every day for him to come home from school and rattle the letterbox I might actually have the illusion of seeing or hearing him come in. Because I can't stop my body and mind waiting, every day, every day, I can't let go. And his bedroom, sometimes at night I go in, I think I might just for a moment forget he *wasn't* in there sleeping, I think I would pay almost anything—anything at all—for a moment of seeing him like I used to. In his pyjamas, with his—his—his hair . . . ruffled, and, his . . . you said, his . . . that *smile*.

'When it happened, they got Noel, and Noel came in and shouted my name, like he did the other day, that's why I screamed, because it—seemed the same— and then they said, he is dead, and I thought coolly, *is* dead, that will go on and on and on till the end of time, it's a continuous present tense, one thinks the most ridiculous things, there I was thinking about grammar, the verb to be, when it ends to be dead . . . And then I came out into the garden, and I half saw, in my mind's eye, a kind of ghost of his face, just the eyes and hair, coming towards me— like every day waiting for him to come home, the way you think of your son, with such pleasure, when he's—not there—and I—I thought—no, I won't *see* him, because he is dead, and I won't dream about him because he is dead, I'll be rational and practical and continue to live because one must, and there was Noel . . .

'I got it wrong, you see, I was so *sensible*, and then I was so shocked because I couldn't get to want anything—I couldn't *talk* to Noel—I—I—made Noel take away, destroy, all the photos, I—didn't dream, you can will not to dream, I didn't . . . visit a grave, flowers, there isn't any point. I was so sensible. Only my body wouldn't stop waiting and all it wants is to—to see that boy. *That* boy. That boy you—saw.'

HE DID NOT SAY that he might have seen another boy, maybe even a boy who had been given the T-shirts and jeans afterwards. He did not say, though the idea crossed his mind, that maybe what he had seen was some kind of impression from her terrible desire to see a boy where nothing was. The boy had had nothing terrible, no aura of pain about him: he had been, his memory insisted, such a pleasant, courteous, self-contained boy, with his own purposes. And in fact the woman herself almost immediately raised the possibility that what he had seen was what she desired to see, a kind of mix-up of radio waves, like when you overheard police messages on the radio, or got BBC 1 on a switch that said ITV. She was thinking fast, and went on almost immediately to say that perhaps his sense of loss, his loss of Anne, which was what had led her to feel she could bear his presence in her house, was what had brought them—dare she say—near enough, for their wavelengths to mingle, perhaps, had made him susceptible . . . You mean, he had said, we are a kind of emotional vacuum, between us, that must be filled. Something like that, she had said, and had added, 'But I don't believe in ghosts.'

Anne, he thought, could not be a ghost, because she was elsewhere, with someone else, doing for someone else those little things she had done so gaily for him, tasty little suppers, bits of research, a sudden vase of unusual flowers, a new bold shirt, unlike his own cautious taste, but suiting him, suiting him. In a sense, Anne was worse lost because voluntarily absent, an absence that could not be loved because love was at an end, for Anne.

'I don't suppose you will, now,' the woman was saying. 'I think talking would probably stop any—mixing of messages, if that's what it is, don't you? But— if—*if* he comes again'—and here for the first time her eyes were full of tears—'if—you must promise, you will *tell* me, you must promise.'

HE HAD PROMISED, easily enough, because he was fairly sure she was right, the boy would not be seen again. But the next day he was on the lawn, nearer than ever, sitting on the grass beside the deck chair, his arms clasping his bent, warm brown knees, the thick, pale hair glittering in the sun. He was wearing a football shirt, this time, Chelsea's colours. Sitting down in the deck chair, the man could have put out a hand and touched him, but did not: it was not, it seemed, a possible gesture to make. But the boy looked up and smiled, with a pleasant complicity, as though they now understood each other very well. The man tried speech: he said, 'It's nice to see you again,' and the boy nodded acknowledgment of this remark, without speaking himself. This was the beginning of communication between them, or what the man supposed to be communication. He did not think of fetching the woman. He became aware that he was in some strange way *enjoying the boy's company*. His pleasant stillness—and he sat there all morning, occasionally lying back on the grass, occasionally staring thoughtfully at the house—was calming and comfortable. The man did quite a lot of work—wrote about three reasonable pages on Hardy's original air-blue gown—and looked up now and then to make sure the boy was still there and happy.

HE WENT TO REPORT to the woman—as he had after all promised to do—that evening. She had obviously been waiting and hoping—her unnatural calm had given way to agitated pacing, and her eyes were dark and deeper in. At this point in the story he found in himself a necessity to bowdlerise for the sympathetic American, as he had indeed already begun to do. He had mentioned only a child who had 'seemed like' the woman's lost son, and he now ceased to mention the child at all, as an actor in the story, with the result that what the American woman heard was a tale of how he, the man, had become increasingly involved in the woman's solitary grief, how their two losses had become a kind of *folie à deux* from which he could not extricate himself. What follows is not what he told the American girl, though it may be clear at which points the bowdlerised version coincided with what he really believed to have happened. There was a sense he could not at first analyse that it was improper to talk about the boy—not because he might not be believed; that did not come into it; but because something dreadful might happen.

'He sat on the lawn all morning. In a football shirt.'

'Chelsea?'

'Chelsea.'

'What did he do? Does he look happy? Did he speak?' Her desire to know was terrible.

'He doesn't speak. He didn't move much. He seemed—very calm. He stayed a long time.'

'This is terrible. This is ludicrous. There *is no boy*.'

'No. But I saw him.'

'Why you?'

'I don't know.' A pause. 'I do *like* him.'

'He is—was—a most likeable boy.'

SOME DAYS LATER he saw the boy running along the landing in the evening, wearing what might have been pyjamas, in peacock towelling, or might have been a track suit. Pyjamas, the woman stated confidently, when he told her: his new pyjamas. With white ribbed cuffs, weren't they? and a white polo neck? He corroborated this, watching her cry—she cried more easily now finding her anxiety and disturbance very hard to bear. But it never occurred to him that it was possible to break his promise to tell her when he saw the boy. That was another curious imperative from some undefined authority.

They discussed clothes. If there were ghosts, how could they appear in clothes long burned, or rotted, or worn away by other people? You could imagine, they agreed, that something of a person might linger—as the Tibetans and others believe the soul lingers near the body before setting out on its long journey. But clothes? And in this case so many clothes? I must be seeing your memories, he told her, and she nodded fiercely, compressing her lips, agreeing that this was likely, adding, 'I am too rational to go mad, so I seem to be putting it on you.'

He tried a joke. 'That isn't very kind to me, to imply that madness comes more easily to me.'

'No, sensitivity. I am insensible. I was always a bit like that, and this made it worse. I am the *last* person to see any ghost that was trying to haunt me.'

'We agreed it was your memories I saw.'

'Yes. We agreed. That's rational. As rational as we can be, considering.'

ALL THE SAME, the brilliance of the boy's blue regard, his gravely smiling salutation in the garden next morning, did not seem like anyone's tortured memories of earlier happiness. The man spoke to him directly then:

'Is there anything I can *do* for you? Anything you want? Can I help you?'

The boy seemed to puzzle about this for a while, inclining his head as though hearing was difficult. Then he nodded, quickly and perhaps urgently, turned, and ran into the house, looking back to make sure he was followed. The man entered the living room through the French windows, behind the running boy, who stopped for a moment in the centre of the room, with the man blinking behind him at the sudden transition from sunlight to comparative dark. The woman was sitting in an armchair, looking at nothing there. She often sat like that. She looked up, across the boy, at the man; and the boy, his face for the first time anxious, met the man's eyes again, asking, before he went out of the house.

'What is it? What is it? Have you seen him again? Why are you...?'

'He came in here. He went—out through the door.'

'I didn't see him.'

'No.'

'Did he—oh, this is so *silly*—did he see me?'

He could not remember. He told the only truth he knew.

'He brought me in here.'

'Oh, what can I do, what am I going to *do*? If I killed myself—I have thought of that—but the idea that I should be with him is an illusion I . . . this silly situation is the nearest I shall ever get. To him. He was *in here with me?*'

'Yes.'

And she was crying again. Out in the garden he could see the boy, swinging agile on the apple branch.

HE WAS NOT QUITE SURE, looking back, when he had thought he had realised what the boy had wanted him to do. This was also, at the party, his worst piece of what he called bowdlerisation, though in some sense it was clearly the opposite of bowdlerisation. He told the American girl that he had come to the conclusion that it was the woman herself who had wanted it, though there was in fact, throughout, no sign of her wanting anything except to see the boy, as she said. The boy, bolder and more frequent, had appeared several nights running on the landing, wandering in and out of bathrooms and bedrooms, restlessly, a little agitated, questing almost, until it had 'come to' the man that what he required was to be re-engendered, for him, the man, to give to his mother another child, into which he could peacefully vanish. The idea was so clear that it was like another imperative, though he did not have the courage to ask the child to confirm it. Possibly this was out of delicacy—the child was too young to be talked to about sex. Possibly there were other reasons. Possibly he was mistaken: the situation was making him hysterical, he felt action of some kind was required and must be possible. He could not spend the rest of the summer, the rest of his life, describing nonexistent T-shirts and blond smiles.

HE COULD THINK of no sensible way of embarking on his venture, so in the end simply walked into her bedroom one night. She was lying there, reading; when she saw him her instinctive gesture was to hide, not her bare arms and throat, but her book. She seemed, in fact, quite unsurprised to see his pyjamaed figure, and, after she had recovered her coolness, brought out the book definitely and laid it on the bedspread.

'My new taste in illegitimate literature. I keep them in a box under the bed.'

Ena Twigg, Medium. The Infinite Hive. The Spirit World. Is There Life After Death?

'Pathetic,' she proffered.

He sat down delicately on the bed.

'Please, don't grieve so. Please, let yourself be comforted. Please . . .'

He put an arm round her. She shuddered. He pulled her closer. He asked why she had had only the one son, and she seemed to understand the purport of his question, for she tried, angular and chilly, to lean on him a little, she became apparently compliant. 'No real reason,' she assured him, no material reason. Just her husband's profession and lack of inclination: that covered it.

'Perhaps,' he suggested, 'if she would be comforted a little, perhaps she could hope, perhaps . . .'

For comfort then, she said, dolefully, and lay back, pushing *Ena Twigg* off the bed with one fierce gesture, then lying placidly. He got in beside her, put his arms round her, kissed her cold cheek, thought of Anne, of what was never to be again. Come on, he said to the woman, you must live, you must try to live, let us hold each other for comfort.

She hissed at him 'Don't *talk*' between clenched teeth, so he stroked her lightly, over her nightdress, breasts and buttocks and long stiff legs, composed like an effigy on an Elizabethan tomb. She allowed this, trembling slightly, and then trembling violently: he took this to be a sign of some mixture of pleasure and pain, of the return of life to stone. He put a hand between her legs and she moved them heavily apart; he heaved himself over her and pushed, unsuccessfully. She was contorted and locked tight: frigid, he thought grimly, was not the word. *Rigor mortis*, his mind said to him, before she began to scream.

He was ridiculously cross about this. He jumped away and said quite rudely, 'Shut up,' and then ungraciously, 'I'm sorry.' She stopped screaming as suddenly as she had begun and made one of her painstaking economical explanations.

'Sex and death don't go. I can't afford to let go of my grip on myself. I hoped. What you hoped. It was a bad idea. I apologise.'

'Oh, never mind,' he said and rushed out again on to the landing, feeling foolish and almost in tears for warm, lovely Anne.

THE CHILD WAS on the landing, waiting. When the man saw him, he looked questioning, and then turned his face against the wall and leaned there, rigid, his shoulders hunched, his hair hiding his expression. There was a similarity between woman and child. The man felt, for the first time, almost uncharitable towards the boy, and then felt something else.

'Look, I'm sorry. I tried. I did try. Please turn round.'

Uncompromising, rigid, clenched back view.

'Oh well,' said the man, and went into his bedroom.

So NOW, HE SAID to the American woman at the party, I feel a fool, I feel embarrassed, I feel we are hurting, not helping each other, I feel it isn't a refuge. Of course you feel that, she said, of course you're right—it was temporarily necessary, it helped both of you, but you've got to live your life. Yes, he said, I've done my best, I've tried to get through, I have my life to live. Look, she said, I want to help, I really do, I have these wonderful friends I'm renting this flat from, why don't you come, just for a few days, just for a break, why don't you? They're real sympathetic people, you'd like them, I like them, you could get your emotions kind of straightened out. She'd probably be glad to see the back of you, she must feel as bad as you do, she's got to relate to her situation in her own way in the end. We all have.

He said he would think about it. He knew he had elected to tell the sympathetic American because he had sensed she would be— would offer—a way out. He had to get out. He took her home from the party and went back to his house and landlady without seeing her into her flat. They both knew that this reticence was promising—that he hadn't come in then, because he meant to come later. Her warmth and readiness were like sunshine, she was open. He did not know what to say to the woman.

IN FACT, SHE MADE it easy for him: she asked, briskly, if he now found it perhaps uncomfortable to stay, and he replied that he had felt he should move on, he was of so little use ... Very well, she had agreed, and had added crisply that it had to be better for everyone if 'all this' came to an end. He remembered the firmness with which she had told him that no illusions were pleasant. She was strong: too strong for her own good. It would take years to wear away that stony, closed, simply surviving insensibility. It was not his job. He would go. All the same, he felt bad.

HE GOT OUT his suitcases and put some things in them. He went down to the garden, nervously, and put away the deck chair. The garden was empty. There were no voices over the wall. The silence was thick and deadening. He wondered, knowing he would not see the boy again, if anyone else would do so, or if, now he was gone, no one would describe a T-shirt, a sandal, a smile, seen, remembered, or desired. He went slowly up to his room again.

THE BOY WAS SITTING on his suitcase, arms crossed, face frowning and serious. He held the man's look for a long moment, and then the man went and sat on his bed. The boy continued to sit. The man found himself speaking.

'You do see I have to go? I've tried to get through. I can't get through. I'm no use to you, am I?'

The boy remained immobile, his head on one side, considering. The man stood up and walked towards him.

'Please. Let me go. What are we, in this house? A man and a woman and a child, and none of us can get through. You can't want that?'

He went as close as he dared. He had, he thought, the intention of putting his hand on or through the child. But could not bring himself to feel there was no boy. So he stood, and repeated,

'I can't get through. Do you want me to stay?'

Upon which, as he stood helplessly there, the boy turned on him again the brilliant, open, confiding, beautiful desired smile.

B. M. Croker

1849–1920

The latter years of Queen Victoria's reign were a good time for
women writers in Britain, and Bithia Mary Croker became a very
successful best-selling author. Her novels have not stood the test
of time, but her shorter fiction is as enjoyable today as when it
was first written. The story included in this collection provides a
vivid insight into the day-to-day lives of the British in India.

'TO LET'

SOME YEARS AGO, when I was a slim young spin, I came out to India to live
with my brother Tom: he and I were members of a large and somewhat
impecunious family, and I do not think my mother was sorry to have one of
her four grown-up daughters thus taken off her hands. Tom's wife, Aggie, had
been at school with my eldest sister; we had known and liked her all our lives.
She was quite one of ourselves, and as she and the children were at home when
Tom's letter was received, and his offer accepted, she helped me to choose my
slender outfit with judgment, zeal and taste; endowed me with several pretty
additions to my wardrobe; superintended the fitting of my gowns and the trying
on of my hats, with most sympathetic interest, and finally escorted me out to
Lucknow, under her own wing, and installed me in the only spare room in her
comfortable bungalow in Dilkongha.

My sister-in-law is a pretty little brunette, rather pale, with dark hair, brilliant
black eyes, a resolute mouth and a bright, intelligent expression. She is orderly,
trim and feverishly energetic, and seems to live every moment of her life. Her
children, her wardrobe, her house, her servants, and last, not least, her husband,
are all models in their way; and yet she has plenty of time for tennis and dancing,
and talking and walking. She is, undoubtedly, a remarkably talented little creature, and especially prides herself on her nerve and her power of will, or will-
power. I suppose they are the same thing? and I am sure they are all the same to
Tom, who worships the sole of her small slipper. Strictly between ourselves she is
the ruling member of the family, and turns her lord and master round her little
finger. Tom is big and fair, of course, the opposite to his wife, quiet, rather
easy-going and inclined to be indolent, but Aggie rouses him up, and pushes

him to the front, and keeps him there. She knows all about his department, his prospects of promotion, his prospects of furlough, of getting acting appointments, and so on, even better than he does himself. The chief of Tom's department—have I said that Tom is in the Irritation Office?—has placed it solemnly on record that he considers little Mrs Shandon a surprisingly clever woman. The two children, Bob and Tor, are merry, oppressively active monkeys, aged three and five years respectively. As for myself I am tall and fair, and I wish I could add pretty; but this is a true story. My eyes are blue, my teeth are white, my hair is red—alas, a blazing red; and I was, at this period, nineteen years of age; and now I think I have given a sufficient outline of the whole family.

We arrived at Lucknow in November, when the cold weather is delightful, and everything was delightful to me. The bustle and life of a great Indian station, the novelty of my surroundings, the early-morning rides, picnics down the river, and dances at the 'Chutter Munzil', made me look upon Lucknow as a paradise on earth; and in this light I still regarded it, until a great change came over the temperature, and the month of April introduced me to red-hot winds, sleepless nights, and the intolerable 'brain fever' bird. Aggie had made up her mind definitely on one subject: we were not to go away to the hills until the rains. Tom could only get two months' leave (July and August), and she did not intend to leave him to grill on the plains alone. As for herself and the children—not to speak of me—we had all come out from home so recently we did not require a change. The trip to Europe had made a vast hole in the family stocking, and she wished to economise; and who can economise with two establishments in full swing? Tell me this, ye Anglo-Indian matrons. With a large, cool bungalow, plenty of punkas, khuskhus tatties, ice, and a thermantidote, surely we could manage to brave May and June—at any rate the attempt was made. Gradually the hills drained Lucknow week by week; family after family packed up, warned us of our folly in remaining on the plains, offered to look for houses for us, and left by the night mail. By the middle of May, the place was figuratively empty. Nothing can be more dreary than a large station in the hot weather, unless it is an equally forsaken hill station in the depths of winter, when the mountains are covered with snow: the mall no longer resounds with gay voices and the tramp of Jampanies, but is visited by bears and panthers, and the houses are closed, and, as it were, put to bed in straw! As for Lucknow in the summer, it was a melancholy spot; the public gardens were deserted, the chairs at the Chutter Munzil stood empty, the very bands had gone to the hills!, the shops were shut, the baked white roads, no longer thronged with carriages and bamboo carts, gave ample room to the humble ekka, or a Dhobie's meagre donkey shuffling along in the dust.

Of course we were not the *only* people remaining in the place, grumbling at the heat and dust and life in general; but there can be no sociability with the thermometer above 100 in the shade. Through the long, long Indian day we sat and gasped, in darkened rooms, and consumed quantities of 'Nimbo pegs', i.e.

limes and soda water, and listened to the fierce hot wind roaring along the road and driving the roasted leaves before it; and in the evening, when the sun had set, we went for a melancholy drive through the Wingfield Park, or round by Martiniere College, and met our friends at the library and compared sensations and thermometers. The season was exceptionally bad, but people say that every year, and presently Bobby and Tor began to fade: their little white faces and listless eyes appealed to Aggie as Tom's anxious expostulations had never done. Yes, they must go to the hills with *me*. But this idea I repudiated at once; I refused to undertake the responsibility—I, who could scarcely speak a word to the servants—who had no experience! Then Bobby had a bad go of fever—intermittent fever; the beginning of the end to his alarmed mother; the end being represented by a large gravestone! She now became as firmly determined to go as she had previously been resolved to stay; but it was so late in the season to take a house. Alas, alas, for the beautiful tempting advertisements in the *Pioneer*, which we had seen and scorned! Aggie wrote to a friend in a certain hill station, called for this occasion only 'Kantia', and Tom wired to a house agent, who triumphantly replied by letter that there was not *one* unlet bungalow on his books. This missive threw us into the depths of despair; there seemed no alternative but a hill hotel, and the usual quarters that await the last comers, and the proverbial welcome for children and dogs (we had only three); but the next day brought us good news from Aggie's friend Mrs Chalmers.

Dear Mrs Shandon—she said—

I received your letter, and went at once to Cursitjee, the agent. Every hole and corner up here seems full, and he had not a single house to let. Today I had a note from him, saying that Briarwood is vacant; the people who took it are not coming up, they have gone to Naini Tal. You *are* in luck. I have just been out to see the house, and have secured it for you. It is a mile and a half from the club, but I know that you and your sister are capital walkers. I envy you. Such a charming place—two sitting rooms, four bedrooms, four bathrooms, a hall, servants' godowns, stabling, and a splendid view from a very pretty garden, and only Rs. 800 for the season! Why, I am paying Rs. 1,000 for a *very* inferior house, with scarcely a stick of furniture and no view. I feel so proud of myself, and I am longing to show you my treasure trove. Telegraph when you start, and I shall have a milk man in waiting and fires in all the rooms.

Yours sincerely,
Edith Chalmers

We now looked upon Mrs Chalmers as our best and dearest friend, and began to get under way at once. A long journey in India is a serious business when the party comprises two ladies, two children, two ayahs and five other servants, three fox terriers, a mongoose and a Persian cat—all these animals going to the hills for the benefit of their health—not to speak of a ton of luggage, including crockery and lamps, a cottage piano, a goat and a pony. Aggie and I, the children, one ayah, two terriers, the cat and mongoose, our bedding and pillows, the tiffin basket and ice basket, were all stowed into one compartment, and I must confess that the journey was truly miserable. The heat was stifling, despite the water tatties. One of the terriers had a violent dispute with the cat, and the cat had a difference with the mongoose, and Bob and Tor had a pitched battle more than once. I actually wished myself back in Lucknow. I was most truly thankful to wake one morning to find myself under the shadow of the Himalayas—not a mighty, snow-clad range of everlasting hills, but merely the spurs—the moderate slopes, covered with scrub and loose shale and jungle, and deceitful little trickling watercourses. We sent the servants on ahead, whilst we rested at the Dak bungalow near the railway station, and then followed them at our leisure. We accomplished the ascent in dandies—open kind of boxes, half box half chair, carried on the shoulders of four men. This was an entirely novel sensation to me, and at first an agreeable one, so long as the slopes were moderate and the paths wide; but the higher we went, the narrower became the path, the steeper the naked precipice; and as my coolies would walk at the extreme edge, with the utmost indifference to my frantic appeals to 'Bector! Bector!'—and would change poles at the most agonising corners—my feelings were very mixed, especially when droves of loose pack ponies came thundering downhill, with no respect for the rights of the road. Late at night we passed through Kantia, and arrived at Briarwood far too weary to be critical. Fires were blazing, supper was prepared, and we dispatched it in haste, and most thankfully went to bed and slept soundly, as anyone would do who had spent thirty-six hours in a crowded compartment and ten in a cramped wooden case.

The next morning, rested and invigorated, we set out on a tour of inspection; and it is almost worth while to undergo a certain amount of baking on the sweltering heat of the plains, in order to enjoy those deep first draughts of cool hill air, instead of a stifling, dust-laden atmosphere, and to appreciate the green valleys and blue hills by force of contrast to the far-stretching, eye-smarting, white glaring roads that intersect the burnt-up plains—roads and plains that even the pariah abandons, salamander though he be!

To our delight and surprise, Mrs Chalmers had by no means overdrawn the advantages of our new abode. The bungalow was solidly built of stone, two-storeyed, and ample in size. It stood on a kind of shelf, cut out of the hillside, and was surrounded by a pretty flower garden, full of roses, fuchsias, carnations. The highroad passed the gate, from which the avenue descended direct to the entrance door, which was at the end of the house, and from whence ran a long passage. Off this passage three rooms opened to the right, all looking south, and all looking into a deep, delightful, flagged verandah. The stairs were very steep. At the head of them, the passage and rooms were repeated. There were small nooks, and dressing rooms, and convenient outhouses, and plenty of good water; but the glory of Briarwood was undoubtedly its verandah: it was fully twelve feet wide, roofed with zinc, and overhung a precipice of a thousand feet—not a startlingly sheer khud, but a tolerably straight descent of grey-blue shale rocks and low jungle. From it there was a glorious view, across a valley, far away, to the snowy range. It opened at one end into the avenue, and was not enclosed; but at the side next the precipice there was a stout wooden railing, with netting at the bottom, for the safety of too-enterprising dogs or children. A charming spot, despite its rather bold situation; and as Aggie and I sat in it, surveying the scenery and inhaling the pure hill air, and watching Bob and Tor tearing up and down playing horses, we said to one another that 'the verandah alone was worth half the rent'.

'It's absurdly cheap,' exclaimed my sister-in-law complacently. 'I wish you saw the hovel *I* had, at Simla, for the same rent. I wonder if it is feverish, or badly drained, or what?'

'Perhaps it has a ghost,' I suggested facetiously; and at such an absurd idea we both went into peals of laughter.

At this moment Mrs Chalmers appeared, brisk, rosy, and breathlessly benevolent, having walked over from Kantia.

'So you have found it,' she said as we shook hands. 'I said nothing about this delicious verandah! I thought I would keep it as a surprise. I did not say a word too much for Briarwood, did I?'

'Not half enough,' we returned rapturously; and presently we went in a body, armed with a list from the agent, and proceeded to go over the house and take stock of its contents.

'It's not a bit like a *hill* furnished house,' boasted Mrs Chalmers, with a glow of pride, as she looked round the drawing room; 'carpets, curtains, solid, *very* solid chairs, and Berlin wool-worked screens, a card table, and any quantity of pictures.'

'Yes, don't they look like family portraits?' I suggested, as we gazed at them. There was one of an officer in faded watercolours, another of his wife, two of a previous generation in oils and amply gilded frames, two sketches of an English country house, and some framed photographs, groups of grinning cricketers or wedding guests. All the rooms were well, almost handsomely, furnished in an old-fashioned style. There was no scarcity of wardrobes, looking glasses, or even armchairs, in the bedrooms, and the pantry was fitted out—a most singular circumstance—with a large supply of handsome glass and china, lamps, old moderators, coffee- and teapots, plated side dishes and candlesticks, cooking utensils and spoons and forks, wine coasters, and a cake basket. These articles were all let with the house, much to our amazement, provided we were responsible for the same. The china was Spode, the plate old family heirlooms, with a crest—a winged horse—on everything, down to the very mustard spoons.

'The people who own this house must be lunatics,' remarked Aggie as she peered round the pantry; 'fancy hiring out one's best family plate and good old china! And I saw some ancient music books in the drawing room, and there is a sidesaddle in the bottle khana.'

'My dear, the people who owned this house are dead,' explained Mrs Chalmers. 'I heard all about them last evening from Mrs Starkey.'

'Oh, is *she* up there?' exclaimed Aggie somewhat fretfully.

'Yes, her husband is cantonment magistrate. This house belonged to an old retired colonel and his wife. They and his niece lived here. These were all their belongings. They died within a short time of one another, and the old man left a queer will, to say that the house was to remain precisely as they left it for twenty years, and at the end of that time it was to be sold and all the property dispersed. Mrs Starkey says she is sure that he never intended it to be *let*, but the heir-at-law insists on that, and is furious at the terms of the will.'

'Well, it is a very good thing for us,' remarked Aggie; 'we are as comfortable here as if we were in our own house: there is a stove in the kitchen; there are nice boxes for firewood in every room, clocks, real hair mattresses—in short, it is as you said, a treasure trove.'

We set to work to modernise the drawing room with phoolkaries, Madras muslin curtains, photograph screens and frames, and suchlike portable articles. We placed the piano across a corner, arranged flowers in some handsome Dresden china vases, and entirely altered and improved the character of the room. When Aggie had dispatched a most glowing description of our new quarters to Tom, and we had had tiffin, we set off to walk into Kantia to put our names down at the library and to enquire for letters at the post office. Aggie met a good many acquaintances—who does not who has lived five years in India in the same district?

Among them Mrs Starkey, an elderly lady with a prominent nose and goggle eyes, who greeted her loudly across the reading-room table in this agreeable fashion: 'And so you have come up after *all*, Mrs Shandon. Someone told me that you meant to remain below, but I knew you never could be so wicked as to keep your poor little children in that heat.' Then coming round and dropping into a chair beside her she said, 'And I suppose this young lady is your sister-in-law?'

Mrs Starkey eyed me critically, evidently appraising my chances in the great marriage market. She herself had settled her own two daughters most satisfactorily, and had now nothing to do but interest herself in these people's affairs.

'Yes,' acquiesced Aggie, 'Miss Shandon—Mrs Starkey.'

'And so you have taken Briarwood?'

'Yes, we have been most lucky to get it.'

'I hope you will think so at the end of three months,' observed Mrs Starkey with a significant pursing of her lips. 'Mrs Chalmers is a stranger up here, or she would not have been in such a hurry to jump at it.'

'Why, what is the matter with it?' enquired Aggie. 'It is well built, well furnished, well situated, and very cheap.'

'That's just it—suspiciously cheap. Why, my dear Mrs Shandon, if there was not something against it, it would let for two hundred rupees a month.'

'And what is against it?'

'It's haunted! There you have the reason in two words.'

'Is that all? I was afraid it was the drains. I don't believe in ghosts and haunted houses. What are we supposed to see?'

'Nothing,' retorted Mrs Starkey, who seemed a good deal nettled at our smiling incredulity.

'Nothing!' with an exasperating laugh.

'No, but you will make up for it in hearing. Not now—you are all right for the next six weeks—but after the monsoon breaks I give you a week at Briarwood. No one would stand it longer, and indeed you might as well bespeak your rooms at Cooper's Hotel *now*. There is always a rush up here in July by the two-months'-leave people, and you will be poked into some wretched godown.'

Aggie laughed rather a careless ironical little laugh and said, 'Thank you, Mrs Starkey; but I think we will stay on where we are; at any rate for the present.'

'Of course it will be as *you* please. What do you think of the verandah?' she enquired with a curious smile.

'I think, as I was saying to Susan, that it is worth half the rent of the house.'

'And in *my* opinion the house is worth double rent without it,' and with this enigmatic remark she rose and sailed away.

'Horrid old frump,' exclaimed Aggie as we walked home in the starlight. 'She is jealous and angry that she did not get Briarwood *herself*—I know her so well. She is always hinting and repeating stories about the nicest people—always decrying your prettiest dress or your best servant.'

We soon forgot all about Mrs Starkey and her dismal prophecy, being too gay and too busy to give her, or it, a thought. We had so many engagements—tennis parties and tournaments, picnics, concerts, dances and little dinners. We ourselves gave occasional afternoon teas in the verandah, using the best Spode cups and saucers and the old silver cake basket, and were warmly complimented on our good fortune in securing such a charming house and garden. One day the children discovered to their great joy that the old chowkidar belonging to the bungalow possessed an African grey parrot—a rare bird indeed in India; he had a battered Europe cage, doubtless a remnant of better days, and swung on his ring, looking up at us enquiringly out of his impudent little black eyes.

The parrot had been the property of the former inmates of Briarwood, and as it was a long-lived creature, had survived its master and mistress, and was boarded out with the chowkidar, at one rupee per month.

The chowkidar willingly carried the cage into the verandah, where the bird seemed perfectly at home.

We got a little table for its cage, and the children were delighted with him, as he swung to and fro, with a bit of cake in his wrinkled claw.

Presently he startled us all by suddenly calling 'Lucy', in a voice that was as distinct as if it had come from a human throat. 'Pretty Lucy—Lu—cy.'

'That must have been the niece,' said Aggie. 'I expect she was the original of that picture over the chimneypiece in your room; she looks like a Lucy.'

It was a large framed half-length photograph of a very pretty girl, in a white dress, with gigantic open sleeves. The ancient parrot talked incessantly now that he had been restored to society; he whistled for the dogs, and brought them flying to his summons, to his great satisfaction and their equally great indignation. He called '*Qui hye*' so naturally, in a lady's shrill soprano, or a gruff male bellow, that I have no doubt our servants would have liked to have wrung his neck. He coughed and expectorated like an old gentleman, and whined like a puppy, and mewed like a cat, and I am sorry to add, sometimes swore like a trooper; but his most constant cry was, 'Lucy, where are you, pretty Lucy— Lucy—Lu—cy?'

AGGIE AND I WENT to various picnics, but at that given by the Chalmers (in honour of Mr Chalmers's brother Charlie, a captain in a Gurkha regiment, just come up to Kantia on leave) Aggie was unavoidably absent. Tor had a little touch of fever, and she did not like to leave him; but I went under my hostess's care, and expected to enjoy myself immensely. Alas! on that selfsame afternoon the long expected monsoon broke, and we were nearly drowned! We rode to the selected spot, five miles from Kantia, laughing and chattering, indifferent to the big blue-black clouds that came slowly, but surely, sailing up from below; it was a way they had had for days and nothing had come of it. We spread the table-cloth, boiled the kettle, unpacked the hampers, in spite of sharp gusts of wind and warning rumbling thunder. Just as we had commenced to reap the reward of our exertions, there fell a few huge drops, followed by a vivid flash, and then a tremendous crash of thunder, like a whole park of artillery, that seemed to shake the mountains, and after this the deluge. In less than a minute we were soaked through; we hastily gathered up the tablecloth by its four ends, gave it to the coolies and fled. It was all I could do to stand against the wind; only for Captain Chalmers I believe I would have been blown away; as it was I lost my hat, it was whirled into space. Mrs Chalmers lost her boa, and Mrs Starkey, not merely her bonnet, but some portion of her hair. We were truly in a wretched plight, the water streaming down our faces and squelching in our boots; the little trickling mountain rivulets were now like racing seas of turbid water; the lightning was almost blinding; the trees rocked dangerously and lashed one another with their quivering branches. I had never been out in such a storm before, and I hope I never may again. We reached Kantia more dead than alive, and Mrs Chalmers sent an express to Aggie, and kept me till the next day. After raining as it only *can* rain in the Himalayas, the weather cleared, the sun shone, and I rode home in borrowed plumes, full of my adventures and in the highest spirits. I found Aggie sitting over the fire in the drawing room, looking ghastly white: that was nothing uncommon; but terribly depressed, which was most unusual. 'I am afraid you have neuralgia?' I said as I kissed her; she nodded and made no reply.

'How is Tor?' I enquired as I drew a chair up to the fire.

'Better—quite well.'

'Any news—any letter?'

'Not a word—not a line.'

'Has anything happened to Pip'—Pip was a fox terrier, renowned for having the shortest tail and being the most impertinent dog in Lucknow—'or the mongoose?'

'No, you silly girl! Why do you ask such questions?'

'I was afraid something was amiss; you seem rather down on your luck.' Aggie shrugged her shoulders and then said:

'What put such an absurd idea into your head? Tell me all about the picnic,' and she began to talk rapidly and to ask me various questions; but I observed that once she had set me going—no difficult task—her attention flagged, her eyes wandered from my face to the fire. She was not listening to half I said, and my most thrilling descriptions were utterly lost on this indifferent, abstracted little creature! I noticed from this time that she had become strangely nervous for her. She invited herself to the share of half my bed; she was restless, *distrait*, and even irritable; and when I was asked out to spend the day, dispensed with my company with an alacrity that was by no means flattering. Formerly, of an evening she used to herd the children home at sundown, and tear me away from the delights of the reading room at seven o'clock; now she hung about the library until almost the last moment, until it was time to put out the lamps, and kept the children with her, making transparent pretexts for their company. Often we did not arrive at home till half past eight o'clock. I made no objections to these late hours, neither did Charlie Chalmers, who often walked back with us and remained to dinner. I was amazed to notice that Aggie seemed delighted to have his company, for she had always expressed a rooted aversion to what she called 'tame young men', and here was this new acquaintance dining with us at least thrice a week! About a month after the picnic we had a spell of dreadful weather—thunderstorms accompanied by torrents. One pouring afternoon, Aggie and I were sitting over the drawing-room fire, whilst the rain came fizzing down among the logs and ran in rivers off the roof and out of the spouts. There had been no going out that day, and we were feeling rather flat and dull, as we sat in a kind of ghostly twilight, with all outdoor objects swallowed up in mist, listening to the violent battering of the rain on the zinc verandah, and the storm which was growling round the hills. 'Oh, for a visitor!' I exclaimed; 'but no one but a fish or a lunatic would be out on such an evening.'

'No one, indeed,' echoed Aggie in a melancholy tone. 'We may as well draw the curtains and have in the lamp and tea to cheer us up.'

She had scarcely finished speaking when I heard the brisk trot of a horse along the road. It stopped at the gate and came rapidly down our avenue. I heard the wet gravel crunching under his hoofs and—yes—a man's cheery whistle.

My heart jumped, and I half rose from my chair. It must be Charlie Chalmers braving the elements to see *me*!—such, I must confess, was my incredible vanity! He did not stop at the front door as usual, but rode straight into the verandah, which afforded ample room and shelter for half a dozen mounted men.

'Aggie,' I said eagerly, 'do you hear? It must be—'

I paused—my tongue silenced by the awful pallor of her face and the expression of her eyes as she sat with her little hands clutching the arms of her chair, and her whole figure bent forward in an attitude of listening—an attitude of terror.

'What is it, Aggie?' I said. 'Are you ill?'

As I spoke the horse's hoofs made a loud clattering noise on the stone-paved verandah outside and a man's voice—a young man's eager voice—called, 'Lucy.'

Instantly a chair near the writing table was pushed back and someone went quickly to the window—a French one—and bungled for a moment with the fastening—I always had a difficulty with that window *myself*. Aggie and I were within the bright circle of the firelight, but the rest of the room was dim, and outside the streaming grey sky was spasmodically illuminated by occasional vivid flashes that lit up the surrounding hills as if it were daylight. The trampling of impatient hoofs and the rattling of a door handle were the only sounds that were audible for a few breathless seconds; but during those seconds Pip, bristling like a porcupine and trembling violently in every joint, had sprung off my lap and crawled abjectly under Aggie's chair, seemingly in a transport of fear. The door was opened audibly, and a cold, icy blast swept in, that seemed to freeze my very heart and made me shiver from head to foot. At this moment there came with a sinister blue glare the most vivid flash of lightning I ever saw. It lit up the whole room, which was empty save for ourselves, and was instantly followed by a clap of thunder that caused my knees to knock together and that terrified me and filled me with horror. It evidently terrified the horse too; there was a violent plunge, a clattering of hoofs on the stones, a sudden loud crash of smashing timber, a woman's long, loud, piercing shriek, which stopped the very beating of my heart, and then a frenzied struggle in the cruel, crumbling, treacherous shale, the rattle of loose stones and the hollow roar of something sliding down the precipice.

I rushed to the door and tore it open, with that awful despairing cry still ringing in my ears. The verandah was empty; there was not a soul to be seen or a sound to be heard, save the rain on the roof.

'Aggie,' I screamed, 'come here! Someone has gone over the verandah and down the khud! You heard him.'

'Yes,' she said, following me out; 'but come in—come in.'

'I believe it was Charlie Chalmers'—shaking her as I spoke. 'He has been killed—killed—killed! And you stand and do nothing. Send people! Let us go ourselves! Bearer! Ayah! *Khidmutgar!*' I cried, raising my voice.

'Hush! It was *not* Charlie Chalmers,' she said, vainly endeavouring to draw me into the drawing room. 'Come in—come in.'

'No, no!'—pushing her away and wringing my hands. 'How cruel you are! How inhuman! There is a path. Let us go at once—at once!'

'You need not trouble yourself, Susan,' she interrupted; 'and you need not cry and tremble—*they* will bring him up. What you heard was supernatural; it was not real.'

'No—no—no! It was all real. Oh! that scream is in my ears still.'

'I will convince you,' said Aggie, taking my hand as she spoke. 'Feel all along the verandah. Are the railings broken?'

I did as she bade me. No, though very wet and clammy, the railing was intact.

'Where is the broken place?' she asked.

Where, indeed?

'Now,' she continued, 'since you will not come in, look over, and you will see something more presently.'

Shivering with fear and cold, drifting rain, I gazed down as she bade me, and there far below I saw lights moving rapidly to and fro, evidently in search of something. After a little delay they congregated in one place. There was a low, booming murmur—they had found him—and presently they commenced to ascend the hill, with the 'hum-hum' of coolies carrying a burden. Nearer and nearer the lights and sounds came up to the very brink of the khud, past the end of the verandah. Many steps and many torches—faint blue torches held by invisible hands—invisible but heavy-footed bearers carried their burden slowly upstairs and along the passage, and deposited it with a dump in Aggie's bedroom! As we stood clasped in one another's arms and shaking all over, the steps descended, the ghostly lights passed up the avenue and disappeared in the gathering darkness. The repetition of the tragedy was over for that day.

'Have you heard it before?' I asked with chattering teeth, as I bolted the drawing-room window.

'Yes, the evening of the picnic and twice since. That is the reason I have always tried to stay out till late and to keep you out. I was hoping and praying you might never hear it. It always happens just before dark. I am afraid you have thought me very queer of late. I have told no end of stories to keep you and the children from harm—I have—'

'I think you have been very kind,' I interrupted. 'Oh, Aggie, shall you ever get that crash and that awful cry out of your head?'

'*Never!*' hastily lighting the candles as she spoke.

'Is there anything more?' I asked tremulously.

'Yes; sometimes at night the most terrible weeping and sobbing in my bedroom,' and she shuddered at the mere recollection.

'Do the servants know?' I asked anxiously.

'The ayah Mumà has heard it, and the *khánsámáh* says his mother is sick and he must go, and the bearer wants to attend his brother's wedding. They will *all* leave.'

'I suppose most people know too?' I suggested dejectedly.

'Yes, don't you remember Mrs Starkey's warnings and her saying that without the verandah the house was worth double rent? We understand that dark speech of hers *now*, and we have not come to Cooper's Hotel yet.'

'No, not *yet*. I wish we *had*. I wonder what Tom will say? He will be here in another fortnight. Oh, I wish he was here now.'

In spite of our heart-shaking experience, we managed to eat and drink and sleep, yea, to play tennis—somewhat solemnly, it is true—and go to the club, where we remained to the very *last* moment; needless to mention that I now entered into Aggie's manoeuvre *con amore*. Mrs Starkey evidently divined the reason of our loitering in Kantia, and said in her most truculent manner, as she squared up to us:

'You keep your children out very late, Mrs Shandon.'

'Yes, but we like to have them with us,' rejoined Aggie in a meek apologetic voice.

'Then why don't you go home earlier?'

'Because it is so stupid and lonely,' was the mendacious answer.

'Lonely is not the word *I* should use. I wonder if you are as wise as your neighbours now? Come now, Mrs Shandon.'

'About what?' said Aggie with ill-feigned innocence.

'About Briarwood. Haven't you heard it yet? The ghastly precipice-and-horse affair?'

'Yes, I suppose we may as well confess that we *have*.'

'Humph! you are a brave couple to stay on. The Tombs tried it last year for three weeks. The Paxtons took it the year before, and then sublet it, not that *they* believed in ghosts—oh, dear no,' and she laughed ironically.

'And what is the story?' I enquired eagerly.

'Well, the story is this. An old retired officer and his wife and their pretty niece lived at Briarwood a good many years ago. The girl was engaged to be married to a fine young fellow in the Guides. The day before the wedding what you know of happened, and has happened every monsoon ever since. The poor girl went out of her mind and destroyed herself, and the old colonel and his wife did not long survive her. The house is uninhabitable in the monsoon, and there seems nothing for it but to auction off the furniture and pull it down; it will always be the same as long as it stands. Take my advice and come into Cooper's Hotel. I believe you can have that small set of rooms at the back. The sitting room smokes, but beggars can't be choosers.'

'That will only be our very last resource,' said Aggie hotly.

'It's not very grand, I grant you, but any port in a storm.'

Tom arrived, was doubly welcome, and was charmed with Briarwood. Chaffed us unmercifully and derided our fears until *he* himself had a similar experience, and he heard the phantom horse plunging in the verandah and that wild, unearthly and utterly appalling shriek. No, he could not laugh *that* away, and seeing that we had now a mortal abhorrence of the place, that the children had to be kept abroad in the damp till long after dark, that Aggie was a mere hollow-eyed spectre, and that we had scarcely a servant left, that—in short, one day we packed up precipitately and fled in a body to Cooper's Hotel. But we did not basely endeavour to sublet, nor advertise Briarwood as 'a delightfully situated pukka built house, containing all the requirements of a gentleman's family'. No, no. Tom bore the loss of the rent and—a more difficult feat—Aggie bore Mrs Starkey's insufferable, 'I told you so.'

Aggie was at Kantia again last season. She walked out early one morning to see our former abode. The chowkidar and parrot are still in possession, and are likely to remain the sole tenants on the premises. The parrot suns and dusts his ancient feathers in the empty verandah, which re-echoes with his cry of 'Lucy, where are you, pretty Lucy?' The chowkidar inhabits a secluded godown at the back, where he passes most of the day in sleeping, or smoking the soothing '*huka*'. The place has a forlorn, uncared-for appearance now. The flowers are nearly all gone; the paint has peeled off the doors and windows; the avenue is grass-grown. Briarwood appears to have resigned itself to emptiness, neglect and decay, although outside the gate there still hangs a battered board on which, if you look very closely, you can decipher the words '*To Let*'.

Robertson Davies

1913–1995

Described by the *Washington Post* as 'the most distinguished and
original Canadian writer of his generation', (William) Robertson
Davies wrote a prolific number of novels, plays, short stories and
essays. As well as writing, his career also encompassed working as
as actor, a newspaper editor and a Toronto university professor.
This story shows him at his witty and original best.

THE GHOST
WHO VANISHED
BY DEGREES

SOME OF YOU MAY HAVE wondered what became of our College Ghost.
Because we had a ghost, and there are people in this room who saw him. He
appeared briefly last year at the College Dance on the stairs up to this Hall,
and at the Gaudy he was seen to come and go through that door, while I was
reading an account of another strange experience of mine. I did not see him
then, but several people did so. What became of him?

I know. I am responsible for his disappearance. I think I may say without
unwarrantable spiritual pride that I laid him. And, as is always the case in these
psychic experiences, it was not without great cost to myself.

When first the Ghost was reported to me, I assumed that we had a practical
joker within the College. Yet—the nature of the joke was against any such
conclusion. We had had plenty of jokes—socks in the pool, fish in the pool,
funny notices beside the pool, pumpkins on the roofs, ringing the bell at
strange hours—all the wild exuberance, the bubbling, ungovernable high
spirits and gossamer fantasy one associates with the Graduate School of the
University of Toronto. The wit of a graduate student is like champagne—
Canadian champagne—but this joke had a different flavour, a dash of
wormwood, in its nature.

You see, the Ghost was so unlike a joker. He did not appear in a white sheet and shout 'Boo!' He spoke to no one, though a Junior Fellow—the one who met him on the stairs—told me that the Ghost passed him, softly laying a finger on its lips to caution him to silence. On its lips, did I say? Now this is of first importance: it laid its finger where its lips doubtless were, but its lips could not be seen, nor any of its features. Everybody who saw it said that the Ghost had a head, and a place where its face ought to be—but no face that anybody could see or recognise or remember. Of course there are scores of people like that around the university, but they are not silent; they are clamouring to establish some sort of identity; the Ghost cherished his anonymity, his facelessness. So, perversely, I determined to find out who he was.

The first time I spotted him was in the Common Room. I went in from my study after midnight to turn out the lights, and he was just to be seen going along the short passage to the Upper Library. I gave chase, but when I reached the Upper Library he had gone, and when I ran into the entry, he was not to be seen. But at last I was on his trail, and I kept my eyes open from that time.

All of this took place, you should know, last Christmas, between the Gaudy and New Year. Our Gaudy last year was on December the seventeenth; I first saw the Ghost, and lost him, on the twenty-first. He came again on the twenty-third. I woke in the night with an odd sensation that someone was watching me, and as this was in my own bedroom I was very angry; if indeed it were a joker he lacked all discretion. I heard a stirring and—I know this sounds like the shabbiest kind of nineteenth-century romance, but I swear it is true—I heard a sigh, and then on the landing outside my door, a soft explosion, and a thud, as though something had fallen. I ran out of my room, but there was nothing to be seen. Over Christmas Day and Boxing Day I had no news of the Ghost, but on the twenty-eighth of December matters came to a head.

December the twenty-eighth, as some of you may know, is the Feast of the Holy Innocents, traditionally the day on which King Herod slaughtered the children of Bethlehem. In the Italian shops in this city you can buy very pretty little babies, made of sugar, and eat them, in grisly commemoration of Herod's whimsical act.

I was sitting in my study at about eleven o'clock that night, reflectively nibbling at the head of a sugarbaby and thinking about money, when I noticed that the lights were on in the Round Room. It troubles me to see electric current wasted, so I set out for the Round Room in a bad humour. As I walked across the quad, it seemed that the glow from the skylight in the Round Room was more blue and cold than it should be, and seemed to waver. I thought it must be a trick of the snow, which was falling softly, and the moonlight which played so prettily upon it.

I unlocked the doors, walked into the Round Room, and there he was, standing under the middle of the skylight.

He bowed courteously. 'So you have come at last,' said he.

'I have come to turn out the lights,' said I, and realised at once that the lights were not on. The room glowed with a fitful bluish light, not disagreeable but inexpressibly sad. And the stranger spoke in a voice which was sad, yet beautiful.

It was his voice which first told me who he was. It had a compelling, cello-like note which was unlike anything I was accustomed to hear inside the College, though our range is from the dispirited quack of Ontario to the reverberant splendours of Nigeria. The magnificent voice came from the part of his head where a face should be—but there was no face there, only a shadow, which seemed to change a little in density as I looked at it. It was unquestionably the Ghost!

This was no joker, no disguised Junior Fellow. He was our Ghost, and like every proper ghost he was transporting and otherworldly, rather than merely alarming. I felt no fear as I looked at him, but I was deeply uneasy.

'You have come at last,' said the Ghost. 'I have waited for you long—but of course you are busy. Every professor in this university is busy. He is talking, or he is pursuing, or he is on a journey, or peradventure he sleepeth. But none has time for an act of mercy.'

It pleased me to hear the Ghost quote Scripture; if we must have apparitions, by all means let them be literate.

'You have come here for mercy?' said I.

'I have come for the ordeal, which is also the ultimate mercy,' he replied.

'But we don't go in for ordeals,' said I. 'Perhaps you can tell me a little more plainly what it is you want?'

'Is this not the Graduate School?' said he.

'No, indeed,' said I; 'this is a graduate college, but the offices of the Graduate School are elsewhere.'

'Don't trifle with me,' said the Ghost sternly. 'Many things are growing very dim to me, but I have not wholly lost my sense of place; this is the Graduate School; this is the Examination Room. And yet'—the voice faltered—'it seemed to me that it used to be much higher in the air, much less handsome than this. I remember stairs—very many stairs . . .'

'You had been climbing stairs when you came to me in my bedroom,' said I.

'Yes,' he said eagerly. 'I climbed the stairs—right to the top—and went into the Examination Room—and there you lay in bed, and I knew I had missed it again. And so there was nothing for it but to kill myself again.'

That settled it. Now I knew who he was, and I had a pretty shrewd idea where, so far as he was concerned, we both were.

Every university has its secrets—things which are nobody's fault, but which are open to serious misunderstanding. Thirty or more years ago a graduate student was ploughed on his PhD oral; he must have expected something of the kind because when he had been called before his examiners and given the bad news he stepped out on the landing and shot himself through the head. It is said, whether truly or not I cannot tell, that since that time nobody is allowed to proceed to the presentation and defence of his thesis unless there is a probability amounting to a certainty that he will get his degree.

Here, obviously, was that unfortunate young man, standing with me in the Round Room. Why here? Because, before Massey College was built, the Graduate School was housed in an old dwelling on this land, and the Examination Room was at the top of the house, as nearly as possible where my bedroom is now. Before that time the place had been the home of one of the Greek-letter fraternities—the Mu Kau Mu, I believe it was called.

'The Examination Room you knew has gone,' said I. 'If you are looking for it, I fear you must go to Teperman's wrecking yard, for whatever remains of it is there.'

'But is this not an Examination Room?' said the Ghost. I nodded. 'Then I beg you, by all that is merciful, to examine me,' he cried, and to my embarrassed astonishment, threw himself at my feet.

'Examine you for what?' I said.

'For my PhD,' wailed the Ghost, and the eerie, agonised tone in which it uttered those commonplace letters made me, for the first time, afraid. 'I must have it. I knew no rest when I was in the world of men, because I was seeking it; I know no rest now, as I linger on the threshold of another life, because I lack it. I shall never be at peace without it.'

I have often heard it said that the PhD is a vastly overvalued degree, but I had not previously thought that it might stand between a man and his eternal rest. I was becoming as agitated as the Ghost.

'My good creature,' said I, rather emotionally, 'if I can be of any assistance—'

'You can,' cried the Ghost, clawing at the knees of my trousers with its transparent hands; 'examine me, I beg of you. Examine me now and set me free. I'm quite ready.'

'But, just a moment,' said I; 'the papers—the copies of your thesis—'

'All ready,' said the Ghost, in triumph. And, though I swear that they were not there before, I now saw that all the circle of tables in the Round Room was piled high with those dismal, unappetising volumes—great wads of typewritten octavo paper—which are PhD theses.

'Be reasonable,' said I. 'I don't suppose for a minute I can examine you. What is your field?'

'What's yours?' said the Ghost, and if a ghost can speak cunningly, that is exactly what this one did now.

'English literature,' I said; 'more precisely, the drama of the nineteenth century, with special emphasis on the popular drama of the transpontine London theatres between 1800 and 1850.'

Most people find that discouraging, and change the subject. But the Ghost positively frisked to one of the heaps, drew out an especially thick thesis, and handed it to me.

'Shall I sit here?' he asked, pointing to the red chair, which, as you know, has a place of special prominence in that room.

'By no means,' said I, shocked by such an idea.

'Oh, I had so hoped I might,' said the Ghost.

'My dear fellow, you have been listening to University gossip,' said I. 'There are people who pretend that we put the examinee in that chair and sit around the room in a ring, baiting him till he bursts into tears. It is the sort of legend in which scientists and other mythomaniacs take delight. No, no; if you will go away for a few hours—say until tomorrow at ten o'clock—I shall have the room set up for an examination. You shall have a soft chair, cheek by jowl with your examiners, with lots of cigarettes, unlimited water to drink, a fan, and a trained nurse in attendance to take you to the Examinees' WC and bring you back again, should the need occur. We are very well aware here that PhD candidates are delicate creatures, subject to unaccountable metaphysical ills—'

The Ghost broke in, impatiently. 'Rubbish,' he said; 'I'm quite ready. Let's get to work. You sit in the red chair. I'm perfectly happy to stand. I think I'm pretty well prepared'—and as he said this I swear that something like a leer passed over the shadow that should have been a face—'and I'm ready as soon as you are.'

There was nothing for it. The Ghost had taken command. I sat down in the red chair—my chair—and opened the thesis. *Prologomena to the Study of the Christ Symbol in the Plays of Thomas Egerton Wilks*, I read, and my heart, which had been sinking for the last few moments, now plunged so suddenly that I almost lost consciousness. I have heard of Wilks—it is my job to have heard of him—but of his fifty-odd melodramas, farces and burlesque extravaganzas I have not read a line. However, I have my modest store of professor-craft. I opened the thesis, riffled through the pages, hummed and hawed a little, made a small mark in the margin of one page, and said—'Well, suppose for a beginning, you give me a general outline of your argument.'

He did.

Forty-five minutes later, when I could get a word in, I asked him just where he thought the Christ symbol made its first appearance in *My Wife's Dentist, or The Balcony Beau*, which is one of Wilks's dreary farces.

He told me.

Before he had finished he had also given me more knowledge than I really wanted about the Christ symbol in *Woman's Love, or Kate Wynsley the Cottage Girl, Raffaelle the Reprobate, or The Secret Mission and the Signet Ring, The Ruby Ring, or The Murder at Sadlers Wells*, and another farce named, more simply, *Bamboozling*.

By this time I felt that I had been sufficiently bamboozled myself, so I asked him to retire, while the examination board—me, me, and only me, as the old song puts it—considered his case. When I was alone I sought to calm myself with a drink of water, and after a decent interval I called him back.

'There are a few minor errors in this thesis which you will undoubtedly notice during a calm rereading, and a certain opaqueness of style which might profitably be amended. I am surprised that you have made so little use of the great Variorum Edition of Wilks published by Professors Fawcett and Pale, of the University of Bitter End, Idaho. Nevertheless I find it to be a piece of research of real, if limited value, which, if published, might be—yes, I shall go so far as to say, will be—seminal in the field of nineteenth-century drama studies,' said I. 'I congratulate you, and it will be a pleasure to recommend that you receive your degree.'

I don't know what I expected then. Perhaps I hoped that he would disappear, with a seraphic smile. True enough, there was an atmosphere as of a smile, but it was the smile of a giant refreshed. 'Good,' he said; 'now we can get on to my other subjects.'

'Do you mean to say that nineteenth-century drama isn't your real subject?' I cried, and when I say 'I cried', I really mean it; my voice came out in a loud, horrified croak.

'Sir,' said he; 'it is so long ago since my unfortunate experience at my first examination that I have utterly forgotten what my subject was. But I have had time since then to prepare myself for any eventuality. I have written theses on everything. 'Shall we go on now to History?'

I was too astonished, and horrified, and by this time afraid, to say anything. We went on to History.

My knowledge of History is that of a layman. Academically, there is nothing worse, of course, that can be said. But professor-craft did not wholly desert me. The first principle, when you don't know anything about the subject of a thesis, is to let the candidate talk, nodding now and then with an ambiguous smile. He thinks you know, and are counting his mistakes, and it unnerves him. The Ghost was an excellent examinee; that is to say, he fell for it, and I think I shook his confidence once with a little laugh, when he was talking about Canada's encouragement of the arts under the premiership of W. L. Mackenzie King. But finally the two hours was up, and I graciously gave him his PhD in History.

Next came classics. His thesis was on *The Concept of Pure Existence in Plotinus.* You don't want to hear about it, but I must pause long enough to say that I scored rather heavily by my application of the second principle of conducting an oral, which is to pretend ignorance, and ask for explanations of very simple points. Of course your ignorance is real, but the examinee thinks you are being subtle, and that he is making an ass of himself, and this rattles him.

And so, laboriously, we toiled through the Liberal Arts, and some of the Arts which are not so liberal. I examined him in Computer Science, and Astronomy, and Medieval Studies, and I rather enjoyed examining him in Fine Art. One of my best examinations was in Mathematics, though personally my knowledge stops short at the twelve-times table.

Every examination took two hours, but my watch did not record them. The night seemed endless. As it wore on I remembered that at cockcrow all ghosts must disappear, and I cudgelled my brain trying to remember whether the kosher butchers on Spadina keep live cocks, and if so what chance we had of hearing one in the Round Room. I was wilting under my ordeal, but the Ghost was as fresh as a daisy.

'Science, now!' he positively shouted, as a whole new mountain of theses appeared from—I suppose from Hell. Now I know nothing whatever of Science, in any of its forms. If Sir Charles Snow wants a prime example of the ignorant Arts man, who has not even heard of that wretched law of thermo-dynamics, which is supposed to be as fine as Shakespeare, he is at liberty to make free with my name. I don't know and I don't care. When the Ghost moved into Science I thought my reason would desert me.

I needn't have worried. The Ghost was as full of himself as a Ghost can possi-bly be, and he hectored and bullied and badgered me about things I had never heard of, while my head swam. But little by little—it was when the Ghost was chattering animatedly about his work on the rate of decay of cosmic rays when they are brought in contact with mesons—I realised the truth. The Ghost did not care whether I knew what he was talking about or not. The Ghost was a typical examinee, and he wanted two things and two things only—an ear into which he could pour what he believed to be unique and valuable knowledge, and a licence to go elsewhere and pour it into the ears of students. Once I grasped this principle, my spirits rose. I began to nod, to smile, to murmur appreciatively. When the Ghost said something especially spirited about the meiosis function in the formation of germ cells, I even allowed myself to say 'Bravo'—as if he had come upon something splendid that I had always sus-pected myself but had never had time to prove in my laboratory. It was a great success; I knew that dawn could not be far away, for as each examination was passed, the Ghost seemed to become a little less substantial. I could see through him, now, and I was happily confident that he could not, and never would, see through me. As he completed his last defence of a doctoral dissertation, I was moved to be generous.

'A distinguished showing,' I said. 'With a candidate of such unusual versatil-ity I am tempted to go a little beyond the usual congratulations. Is there anything else you fancy—a Diploma in Public Health, for instance, or perhaps something advanced in Household Science?'

But the Ghost shook his head. 'I want a PhD and that only,' said he. 'I want a PhD in everything.'

'Consider it yours,' said I.

'You mean that I may present myself at the next Convocation?'

'Yes; when the Registrar kneels to take upon him the degrees granted to those who are forced by circumstance—to be absent, I suggest that you momentarily invest him with your ectoplasm—or whatever it is that people in your situation do,' said I.

'I shall; oh, I shall,' he cried, ecstatically, and as he faded before my eyes I heard his voice from above the skylight in the Round Room, saying, 'I go to a better place than this, confident that as a PhD I shall have it in my power to make it better still.'

So at last, as dawn stole over the College, I was alone in the Round Room. The night of the Holy Innocents had passed. Musing, my hand stole to my pocket and, pulling out the sugarbaby, I crunched off its head. Was it those blessed children, I wondered, who had hovered over me, protecting me from being found out? Or had it perhaps been the spirit of King Herod, notoriously the patron of examiners?

All things considered, I think it was both great spiritual forces, watching over me during the long night. Happy in the thought that I was so variously protected, I stepped out into the first light, the last crumbs of the sugarbaby still sweet upon my lips.

Walter de la Mare

1873–1956

An acclaimed ghost-story writer, Walter de la Mare was also a
poet and novelist. He had a special empathy with children, and
many of his most intriguing stories, in particular the one included
here, are told from a child's viewpoint—with sharp observation
but uncertain understanding—so that readers have to make up
their own minds about what is really happening.

SEATON'S AUNT

I HAD HEARD RUMOURS of Seaton's aunt long before I actually encountered her.
Seaton, in the hush of confidence, or at any little show of toleration on our
part, would remark, 'My aunt', or 'My old aunt, you know', as if his relative
might be a kind of cement to an *entente cordiale*.

He had an unusual quantity of pocket money; or, at any rate, it was bestowed
on him in unusually large amounts; and he spent it freely, though none of us
would have described him as an 'awfully generous chap'. 'Hello, Seaton,' we
would say, 'the old Begum?' At the beginning of term, too, he used to bring back
surprising and exotic dainties in a box with a trick padlock that accompanied
him from his first appearance at Gummidge's in a billycock hat to the rather
abrupt conclusion of his schooldays.

From a boy's point of view he looked distastefully foreign with his yellowish
skin, slow chocolate-coloured eyes, and lean weak figure. Merely for his looks he
was treated by most of us true-blue Englishmen with condescension, hostility, or
contempt. We used to call him 'Pongo', but without any much better excuse for
the nickname than his skin. He was, that is, in one sense of the term, what he
assuredly was not in the other sense, a sport.

Seaton and I, as I may say, were never in any sense intimate at school; our orbits
only intersected in class. I kept deliberately aloof from him. I felt vaguely he was a
sneak, and remained quite unmollified by advances on his side, which, in a boy's
barbarous fashion, unless it suited me to be magnanimous, I haughtily ignored.

We were both of us quick-footed, and at Prisoner's Base used occasionally
to hide together. And so I best remember Seaton—his narrow watchful face
in the dusk of a summer evening; his peculiar crouch, and his inarticulate

whisperings and mumblings. Otherwise he played all games slackly and limply; used to stand and feed at his locker with a crony or two until his 'tuck' gave out; or waste his money on some outlandish fancy or other. He bought, for instance, a silver bangle, which he wore above his left elbow, until some of the fellows showed their masterly contempt of the practice by dropping it nearly red-hot down his neck.

It needed, therefore, a rather peculiar taste, and a rather rare kind of school-boy courage and indifference to criticism, to be much associated with him. And I had neither the taste nor, probably, the courage. None the less, he did make advances, and on one memorable occasion went to the length of bestowing on me a whole pot of some outlandish mulberry-coloured jelly that had been dupli-cated in his term's supplies. In the exuberance of my gratitude I promised to spend the next half-term holiday with him at his aunt's house.

I had clean forgotten my promise when, two or three days before the holiday, he came up and triumphantly reminded me of it.

'Well, to tell you the honest truth, Seaton, old chap—' I began graciously: but he cut me short.

'My aunt expects you,' he said; 'she is very glad you are coming. She's sure to be quite decent to *you*, Withers.'

I looked at him in sheer astonishment; the emphasis was so uncalled for. It seemed to suggest an aunt not hitherto hinted at, and a friendly feeling on Seaton's side that was far more disconcerting than welcome.

WE REACHED HIS AUNT'S HOUSE partly by train, partly by a lift in an empty farm cart, and partly by walking. It was a whole-day holiday, and we were to sleep the night; he lent me extraordinary night-gear, I remember. The village street was unusually wide, and was fed from a green by two converging roads, with an inn, and a high green sign at the corner. About a hundred yards down the street was a chemist's shop—a Mr Tanner's. We descended the two steps into his dusky and odorous interior to buy, I remember, some rat poison. A little beyond the chemist's was the forge. You then walked along a very narrow path, under a fairly high wall, nodding here and there with weeds and tufts of grass, and so came to the iron garden gates, and saw the high flat house behind its huge sycamore. A coach house stood on the left of the house, and on the right a gate led into a kind of rambling orchard. The lawn lay away over to the left again, and at the bottom (for the whole garden sloped gently to a sluggish and rushy pond-like stream) was a meadow.

We arrived at noon, and entered the gates out of the hot dust beneath the glit-ter of the dark-curtained windows. Seaton led me at once through the little garden gate to show me his tadpole pond, swarming with what (being myself not in the least interested in low life) seemed to me the most horrible crea-tures—of all shapes, consistencies, and sizes, but with which Seaton was obviously on the most intimate of terms. I can see his absorbed face now as, squatting on his heels, he fished the slimy things out in his sallow palms. Wearying at last of these pets, we loitered about awhile in an aimless fashion. Seaton seemed to be listening, or at any rate waiting, for something to happen or for someone to come. But nothing did happen and no one came.

That was just like Seaton. Anyhow, the first view I got of his aunt was when, at the summons of a distant gong, we turned from the garden, very hungry and thirsty, to go into luncheon. We were approaching the house, when Seaton suddenly came to a standstill. Indeed, I have always had the impression that he plucked at my sleeve. Something, at least, seemed to catch me back, as it were, as he cried, 'Look out, there she is!'

She was standing at an upper window which opened wide on a hinge, and at first sight she looked an excessively tall and overwhelming figure. This, however, was mainly because the window reached all but to the floor of her bedroom. She was in reality rather an undersized woman, in spite of her long face and big head. She must have stood, I think, unusually still, with eyes fixed on us, though this impression may be due to Seaton's sudden warning and to my consciousness of the cautious and subdued air that had fallen on him at sight of her. I know that without the least reason in the world I felt a kind of guiltiness, as if I had been 'caught'. There was a silvery star pattern sprinkled on her black silk dress, and even from the ground I could see the immense coils of her hair and the rings on her left hand which was held fingering the small jet buttons of her bodice. She watched our united advance without stirring, until, imperceptibly, her eyes raised and lost themselves in the distance, so that it was out of an assumed reverie that she appeared suddenly to awaken to our presence beneath her when we drew close to the house.

'So this is your friend, Mr Smithers, I suppose?' she said, bobbing to me.

'Withers, aunt,' said Seaton.

'It's much the same,' she said, with eyes fixed on me. 'Come in, Mr Withers, and bring him along with you.'

She continued to gaze at me—at least, I think she did so. I know that the fixity of her scrutiny and her ironical 'Mr' made me feel peculiarly uncomfortable. None the less she was extremely kind and attentive to me, though, no doubt, her kindness and attention showed up more vividly against her complete neglect of Seaton. Only one remark that I have any recollection of she made to him: 'When I look on my nephew, Mr Smithers, I realise that dust we are, and dust shall become. You are hot, dirty, and incorrigible, Arthur.'

She sat at the head of the table, Seaton at the foot, and I, before a wide waste of damask tablecloth, between them. It was an old and rather close dining room, with windows thrown wide to the green garden and a wonderful cascade of fading roses. Miss Seaton's great chair faced this window, so that its rose-reflected light shone full on her yellowish face, and on just such chocolate eyes as my schoolfellow's, except that hers were more than half covered by unusually long and heavy lids.

There she sat, steadily eating, with those sluggish eyes fixed for the most part on my face; above them stood the deep-lined fork between her eyebrows; and above that the wide expanse of a remarkable brow beneath its strange steep bank of hair. The lunch was copious, and consisted, I remember, of all such dishes as are generally considered too rich and too good for the schoolboy digestion—lobster mayonnaise, cold game sausages, an immense veal and ham pie farced with eggs, truffles, and numberless delicious flavours; besides kickshaws, creams, and sweetmeats. We even had a wine, a half-glass of old darkish sherry each.

Miss Seaton enjoyed and indulged an enormous appetite. Her example and a natural schoolboy voracity soon overcame my nervousness of her, even to the extent of allowing me to enjoy to the best of my bent so rare a spread. Seaton was singularly modest; the greater part of his meal consisted of almonds and raisins, which he nibbled surreptitiously and as if he found difficulty in swallowing them.

I don't mean that Miss Seaton 'conversed' with me. She merely scattered trenchant remarks and now and then twinkled a baited question over my head. But her face was like a dense and involved accompaniment to her talk. She presently dropped the 'Mr', to my intense relief, and called me now Withers, or Wither, now Smithers, and even once towards the close of the meal distinctly Johnson, though how on earth my name suggested it, or whose face mine had reanimated in memory, I cannot conceive.

'And is Arthur a good boy at school, Mr Wither?' was one of her many questions. 'Does he please his masters? Is he first in his class? What does the reverend Dr Gummidge think of him, eh?'

I knew she was jeering at him, but his face was adamant against the least flicker of sarcasm or facetiousness. I gazed fixedly at a blushing crescent of lobster.

'I think you're eighth, aren't you, Seaton?'

Seaton moved his small pupils towards his aunt. But she continued to gaze with a kind of concentrated detachment at me.

'Arthur will never make a brilliant scholar, I fear,' she said, lifting a dexterously burdened fork to her wide mouth . . .

After luncheon she preceded me up to my bedroom. It was a jolly little bedroom, with a brass fender and rugs and a polished floor, on which it was possible, I afterwards found, to play 'snowshoes'. Over the washstand was a little black-framed watercolour drawing, depicting a large eye with an extremely fishlike intensity in the spark of light on the dark pupil; and in 'illuminated' lettering beneath was printed very minutely, 'Thou God Seest ME', followed by a long looped monogram, 'S. S.', in the corner. The other pictures were all of the sea: brigs on blue water; a schooner overtopping chalk cliffs; a rocky island of prodigious steepness, with two tiny sailors dragging a monstrous boat up a shelf of beach.

'This is the room, Withers, my poor dear brother William died in when a boy. Admire the view!'

I looked out of the window across the tree-tops. It was a day hot with sunshine over the green fields, and the cattle were standing swishing their tails in the shallow water. But the view at the moment was no doubt made more vividly impressive by the apprehension that she would presently enquire after my luggage, and I had brought not even a toothbrush. I need have had no fear. Hers was not that highly civilised type of mind that is stuffed with sharp, material details. Nor could her ample presence be described as in the least motherly.

'I would never consent to question a schoolfellow behind my nephew's back,' she said, standing in the middle of the room, 'but tell me, Smithers, why is Arthur so unpopular? You, I understand, are his only close friend.' She stood in a dazzle of sun, and out of it her eyes regarded me with such leaden penetration beneath their thick lids that I doubt if my face concealed the least thought from her. 'But there, there,' she added very suavely, stooping her head a little, 'don't trouble to answer me. I never extort an answer. Boys are queer fish. Brains might perhaps have suggested his washing his hands before luncheon; but—not my choice, Smithers. God forbid! And now, perhaps, you would like to go into the garden again. I cannot actually see from here, but I should not be surprised if Arthur is now skulking behind that hedge.'

He was. I saw his head come out and take a rapid glance at the windows.

'Join him, Mr Smithers; we shall meet again, I hope, at the tea table. The afternoon I spend in retirement.'

Whether or not, Seaton and I had not been long engaged with the aid of two green switches in riding round and round a lumbering old grey horse we found in the meadow, before a rather bunched-up figure appeared, walking along the field-path on the other side of the water, with a magenta parasol studiously lowered in our direction throughout her slow progress, as if that were the magnetic needle and we the fixed Pole. Seaton at once lost all nerve and interest. At the next lurch of the old mare's heels he toppled over into the grass, and I slid off the sleek broad back to join him where he stood, rubbing his shoulder and sourly watching the rather pompous figure till it was out of sight.

'Was that your aunt, Seaton?' I enquired; but not till then.

He nodded.

'Why didn't she take any notice of us, then?'

'She never does.'

'Why not?'

'Oh, she knows all right, without; that's the dam' awful part of it.' Seaton was one of the very few fellows at Gummidge's who had the ostentation to use bad language. He had suffered for it too. But it wasn't, I think, bravado. I believe he really felt certain things more intensely than most of the other fellows, and they were generally things that fortunate and average people do not feel at all—the peculiar quality, for instance, of the British schoolboy's imagination.

'I tell you, Withers,' he went on moodily, slinking across the meadow with his hands covered up in his pockets, 'she sees everything. And what she doesn't see she knows without.'

'But how?' I said, not because I was much interested, but because the afternoon was so hot and tiresome and purposeless, and it seemed more of a bore to remain silent. Seaton turned gloomily and spoke in a very low voice.

'Don't appear to be talking of her, if you wouldn't mind. It's—because she's in league with the Devil.' He nodded his head and stooped to pick up a round flat pebble. 'I tell you,' he said, still stooping, 'you fellows don't realise what it is. I know I'm a bit close and all that. But so would you be if you had that old hag listening to every thought you think.'

I looked at him, then turned and surveyed one by one the windows of the house.

'Where's your *pater*?' I said awkwardly.

'Dead, ages and ages ago, and my mother too. She's not my aunt even by rights.'

'What is she, then?'

'I mean she's not my mother's sister, because my grandmother married twice; and she's one of the first lot. I don't know what you call her, but anyhow she's not my real aunt.'

'She gives you plenty of pocket money.'

Seaton looked steadfastly at me out of his flat eyes. 'She can't give me what's mine. When I come of age half of the whole lot will be mine; and what's more'—he turned his back on the house—'I'll make her hand over every blessed shilling of it.'

I put my hands in my pockets and stared at Seaton; 'Is it much?'

He nodded.

'Who told you?' He got suddenly very angry; a darkish red came into his cheeks, his eyes glistened, but he made no answer, and we loitered listlessly about the garden until it was time for tea . . .

SEATON'S AUNT was wearing an extraordinary kind of lace jacket when we sidled sheepishly into the drawing room together. She greeted me with a heavy and protracted smile, and bade me bring a chair close to the little table.

'I hope Arthur has made you feel at home,' she said as she handed me my cup in her crooked hand. 'He don't talk much to me; but then I'm an old woman. You must come again, Wither, and draw him out of his shell. You old snail!' She wagged her head at Seaton, who sat munching cake and watching her intently.

'And we must correspond, perhaps.' She nearly shut her eyes at me. 'You must write and tell me everything behind the creature's back.' I confess I found her rather disquieting company. The evening drew on. Lamps were brought in by a man with a nondescript face and very quiet footsteps. Seaton was told to bring out the chessmen. And we played a game, she and I, with her big chin

thrust over the board at every move as she gloated over the pieces and occasionally croaked 'Check!'—after which she would sit back inscrutably staring at me.
But the game was never finished. She simply hemmed me in with a gathering
cloud of pieces that held me impotent, and yet one and all refused to administer
to my poor flustered old king a merciful *coup de grâce*.

'There,' she said, as the clock struck ten—'a drawn game, Withers. We are
very evenly matched. A very creditable defence, Withers. You know your room.
There's supper on a tray in the dining room. Don't let the creature overeat him-
self. The gong will sound three-quarters of an hour *before* a punctual breakfast.'
She held out her cheek to Seaton, and he kissed it with obvious perfunctoriness.
With me she shook hands.

'An excellent game,' she said cordially, 'but my memory is poor, and'—she
swept the pieces helter-skelter into the box—'the result will never be known.'
She raised her great head far back. 'Eh?'

It was a kind of challenge, and I could only murmur: 'Oh I was absolutely in a
hole, you know!' when she burst out laughing and waved us both out of the room.

Seaton and I stood and ate our supper, with one candlestick to light us, in a
corner of the dining room. 'Well, and how would you like it?' he said very softly,
after cautiously poking his head round the doorway.

'Like what?'

'Being spied on—every blessed thing you do and think?'

'I shouldn't like it at all,' I said, 'if she does.'

'And yet you let her smash you up at chess!'

'I didn't let her!' I said indignantly.

'Well, you funked it, then.'

'And I didn't funk it either,' I said; 'she's so jolly clever with her knights.'
Seaton stared at the candle. 'Knights,' he said slowly. 'You wait, that's all.' And
we went upstairs to bed.

I had not been long in bed, I think, when I was cautiously awakened by a
touch on my shoulder. And there was Seaton's face in the candlelight—and his
eyes looking into mine.

'What's up?' I said, lurching on to my elbow.

'*Ssh!* Don't scurry,' he whispered. 'She'll hear. I'm sorry for waking you, but I
didn't think you'd be asleep so soon.'

'Why, what's the time, then?' Seaton wore, what was then rather unusual, a
night-suit, and he hauled his big silver watch out of the pocket in his jacket.

'It's a quarter to twelve. I never get to sleep before twelve—not here.'

'What do you do, then?'

'Oh, I read; and listen.'

'Listen?'

Seaton stared into his candle flame as if he were listening even then. 'You can't
guess what it is. All you read in ghost stories, that's all rot. You can't see much,
Withers, but you know all the same.'

'Know what?'

'Why, that they're there.'

'Who's there?' I asked fretfully, glancing at the door.

'Why, in the house. It swarms with 'em. Just you stand still and listen outside my bedroom door in the middle of the night. I have, dozens of times; they're all over the place.'

'Look here, Seaton,' I said, 'you asked me to come here, and I didn't mind chucking up a leave just to oblige you and because I'd promised; but don't get talking a lot of rot, that's all, or you'll know the difference when we get back.'

'Don't fret,' he said coldly, turning away. 'I shan't be at school long. And what's more, you're here now, and there isn't anybody else to talk to. I'll chance the other.'

'Look here, Seaton,' I said, 'you may think you're going to scare me with a lot of stuff about voices and all that. But I'll just thank you to clear out; and you may please yourself about pottering about all night.'

He made no answer; he was standing by the dressing table looking across his candle into the looking glass; he turned and stared slowly round the walls.

'Even this room's nothing more than a coffin. I suppose she told you—"It's all exactly the same as when my brother William died"—trust her for that! And good luck to him, say I. Look at that.' He raised his candle close to the little watercolour I have mentioned. 'There's hundreds of eyes like that in this house; and even if God does see you, He takes precious good care you don't see Him. And it's just the same with them. I tell you what, Withers, I'm getting sick of all this. I shan't stand it much longer.'

The house was silent within and without, and even in the yellowish radiance of the candle a faint silver showed through the open window on my blind. I slipped off the bedclothes, wide awake, and sat irresolute on the bedside.

'I know you're only guying me,' I said angrily, 'but why is the house full of—what you say? Why do you hear—what you *do* hear? Tell me that, you silly fool!'

Seaton sat down on a chair and rested his candlestick on his knee. He blinked at me calmly. 'She brings them,' he said, with lifted eyebrows.

'Who? Your aunt?'

He nodded.

'How?'

'I told you,' he answered pettishly. 'She's in league. You don't know. She as good as killed my mother; I know that. But it's not only her by a long chalk. She just sucks you dry. I know. And that's what she'll do for me; because I'm like her —like my mother, I mean. She simply hates to see me alive. I wouldn't be like that old she-wolf for a million pounds. And so'—he broke off, with a comprehensive wave of his candlestick—'they're always here. Ah, my boy, wait till she's dead! She'll hear something then, I can tell you. It's all very well now, but wait till then! I wouldn't be in her shoes when she has to clear out—for something.

Don't you go and believe I care for ghosts, or whatever you like to call them. We're all in the same box. We're all under her thumb.'

He was looking almost nonchalantly at the ceiling at the moment, when I saw his face change, saw his eyes suddenly drop like shot birds and fix themselves on the cranny of the door he had left just ajar. Even from where I sat I could see his cheek change colour; it went greenish. He crouched without stirring, like an animal. And I, scarcely daring to breathe, sat with creeping skin, sourly watching him. His hands relaxed, and he gave a kind of sigh.

'Was *that* one?' I whispered, with a timid show of jauntiness. He looked round, opened his mouth, and nodded. 'What?' I said. He jerked his thumb with meaningful eyes, and I knew that he meant that his aunt had been there listening at our door cranny.

'Look here, Seaton,' I said once more, wriggling to my feet. 'You may think I'm a jolly noodle; just as you please. But your aunt has been civil to me and all that, and I don't believe a word you say about her, that's all, and never did. Every fellow's a bit off his pluck at night, and you may think it a fine sport to try your rubbish on me. I heard your aunt come upstairs before I fell asleep. And I'll bet you a level tanner she's in bed now. What's more, you can keep your blessed ghosts to yourself. It's a guilty conscience, I should think.'

Seaton looked at me intently, without answering for a moment. 'I'm not a liar, Withers; but I'm not going to quarrel either. You're the only chap I care a button for; or, at any rate, you're the only chap that's ever come here; and it's something to tell a fellow what you feel. I don't care a fig for fifty thousand ghosts, although I swear on my solemn oath that I know they're here. But she'—he turned deliberately—'you laid a tanner she's in bed, Withers; well, I know different. She's never in bed much of the night, and I'll prove it, too, just to show you I'm not such a nolly as you think I am. Come on!'

'Come on where?'

'Why, to see.'

I hesitated. He opened a large cupboard and took out a small dark dressing gown and a kind of shawl jacket. He threw the jacket on the bed and put on the gown. His dusky face was colourless, and I could see by the way he fumbled at the sleeves he was shivering. But it was no good showing the white feather now. So I threw the tasselled shawl over my shoulders and, leaving our candle brightly burning on the chair, we went out together and stood in the corridor.

'Now then, listen!' Seaton whispered.

We stood leaning over the staircase. It was like leaning over a well, so still and chill the air was all around us. But presently, as I suppose happens in most old houses, began to echo and answer in my ears a medley of infinite small stirrings and whisperings. Now out of the distance an old timber would relax its fibres, or a scurry die away behind the perishing wainscot. But amid and behind such sounds as these I seemed to begin to be conscious, as it were, of the lightest of footfalls, sounds as faint as the vanishing remembrance of voices in a dream.

Seaton was all in obscurity except his face; out of that his eyes gleamed darkly, watching me.

'You'd hear, too, in time, my fine soldier,' he muttered. 'Come on!'

He descended the stairs, slipping his lean fingers lightly along the balusters. He turned to the right at the loop, and I followed him barefooted along a thickly carpeted corridor. At the end stood a door ajar. And from here we very stealthily and in complete blackness ascended five narrow stairs. Seaton, with immense caution, slowly pushed open a door, and we stood together, looking into a great pool of duskiness, out of which, lit by the feeble clearness of a nightlight, rose a vast bed. A heap of clothes lay on the floor; beside them two slippers dozed, with noses each to each, a foot or two apart. Somewhere a little clock ticked huskily. There was a close smell; lavender and eau de cologne, mingled with the fragrance of ancient sachets, soap, and drugs. Yet it was a scent even more peculiarly compounded than that.

And the bed! I stared warily in; it was mounded gigantically, and it was empty.

Seaton turned a vague pale face, all shadows: 'What did I say?' he muttered. 'Who's—who's the fool now, I say? How are we going to get back without meeting her, I say? Answer me that! Oh, I wish to God you hadn't come here, Withers.'

He stood audibly shivering in his skimpy gown, and could hardly speak for his teeth chattering. And very distinctly, in the hush that followed his whisper, I heard approaching a faint unhurried voluminous rustle. Seaton clutched my arm, dragged me to the right across the room to a large cupboard, and drew the door close to on us. And, presently, as with bursting lungs I peeped out into the long, low, curtained bedroom, waddled in that wonderful great head and body. I can see her now, all patched and lined with shadow, her tied-up hair (she must have had enormous quantities of it for so old a woman), her heavy lids above those flat, slow, vigilant eyes. She just passed across my ken in the vague dusk; but the bed was out of sight.

We waited on and on, listening to the clock's muffled ticking. Not the ghost of a sound rose up from the great bed. Either she lay archly listening or slept a sleep serener than an infant's. And when, it seemed, we had been hours in hiding and were cramped, chilled, and half suffocated, we crept out on all fours, with terror knocking at our ribs, and so down the five narrow stairs and back to the little candlelit blue-and-gold bedroom.

Once there, Seaton gave in. He sat livid on a chair with closed eyes.

'Here,' I said, shaking his arm, 'I'm going to bed; I've had enough of this foolery; I'm going to bed.' His lips quivered, but he made no answer. I poured out some water into my basin and, with that cold pictured azure eye fixed on us, bespattered Seaton's sallow face and forehead and dabbled his hair. He presently sighed and opened fishlike eyes.

'Come on!' I said. 'Don't get shamming, there's a good chap. Get on my back, if you like, and I'll carry you into your bedroom.'

He waved me away and stood up. So, with my candle in one hand, I took him under the arm and walked him along according to his direction down the corridor. His was a much dingier room than mine, and littered with boxes, paper, cages, and clothes. I huddled him into bed and turned to go. And suddenly, I can hardly explain it now, a kind of cold and deadly terror swept over me. I almost ran out of the room, with eyes fixed rigidly in front of me, blew out my candle, and buried my head under the bedclothes.

When I awoke, roused not by a gong but by a long-continued tapping at my door, sunlight was raying in on cornice and bedpost, and birds were singing in the garden. I got up, ashamed of the night's folly, dressed quickly, and went downstairs. The breakfast room was sweet with flowers and fruit and honey. Seaton's aunt was standing in the garden beside the open French window, feeding a great flutter of birds. I watched her for a moment, unseen. Her face was set in a deep reverie beneath the shadow of a big loose sunhat. It was deeply lined, crooked, and, in a way I can't describe, fixedly vacant and strange. I coughed politely, and she turned with a prodigious smiling grimace to ask how I had slept. And in that mysterious fashion by which we learn each other's secret thoughts without a syllable said, I knew that she had followed every word and movement of the night before, and was triumphing over my affected innocence and ridiculing my friendly and too easy advances.

WE RETURNED TO SCHOOL, Seaton and I, lavishly laden, and by rail all the way. I made no reference to the obscure talk we had had, and resolutely refused to meet his eyes or to take up the hints he let fall. I was relieved—and yet I was sorry—to be going back, and strode on as fast as I could from the station, with Seaton almost trotting at my heels. But he insisted on buying more fruit and sweets—my share of which I accepted with a very bad grace. It was uncomfortably like a bribe; and, after all, I had no quarrel with his rum old aunt, and hadn't really believed half the stuff he had told me.

I saw as little of him as I could after that. He never referred to our visit or resumed his confidences, though in class I would sometimes catch his eye fixed on mine, full of a mute understanding, which I easily affected not to understand. He left Gummidge's, as I have said, rather abruptly, though I never heard of anything to his discredit. And I did not see him or have any news of him again till by chance we met one summer afternoon in the Strand.

He was dressed rather oddly in a coat too large for him and bright silky tie. But we instantly recognised one another under the awning of a cheap jeweller's shop. He immediately attached himself to me and dragged me off, not too cheerfully, to lunch with him at an Italian restaurant near by. He chattered about our old school, which he remembered only with dislike and disgust; told me cold-bloodedly of the disastrous fate of one or two of the older fellows who had been among his chief tormentors; insisted on an expensive wine and the whole gamut of the foreign menu; and finally informed me, with a good deal of niggling, that he had come up to town to buy an engagement ring.

And of course: 'How is your aunt?' I enquired at last.

He seemed to have been awaiting the question. It fell like a stone into a deep pool, so many expressions flitted across his long, sad, sallow, un-English face.

'She's aged a good deal,' he said softly, and broke off.

'She's been very decent,' he continued presently after, and paused again. 'In a way.' He eyed me fleetingly. 'I dare say you heard that—she—that is, that we—had lost a good deal of money.'

'No,' I said.

'Oh, yes!' said Seaton, and paused again.

And somehow, poor fellow, I knew in the clink and clatter of glass and voices that he had lied to me; that he did not possess, and never had possessed, a penny beyond what his aunt had squandered on his too ample allowance of pocket money.

'And the ghosts?' I enquired quizzically.

He grew instantly solemn, and, though it may have been my fancy, slightly yellowed. But 'You are making game of me, Withers,' was all he said.

He asked for my address, and I rather reluctantly gave him my card.

'Look here, Withers,' he said, as we stood together in the sunlight on the kerb, saying goodbye, 'here I am, and—and it's all very well. I'm not perhaps as fanciful as I was. But you are practically the only friend I have on earth—except Alice . . . And there—to make a clean breast of it, I'm not sure that my aunt cares much about my getting married. She doesn't say so, of course. You know her well enough for that.' He looked sidelong at the rattling gaudy traffic.

'What I was going to say is this: Would you mind coming down? You needn't stay the night unless you please, though, of course, you know you would be awfully welcome. But I should like you to meet my—to meet Alice; and then, perhaps, you might tell me your honest opinion of—of the other too.'

I vaguely demurred. He pressed me. And we parted with a half promise that I would come. He waved his ball-topped cane at me and ran off in his long jacket after a bus.

A letter arrived soon after, in his small weak handwriting, giving me full particulars regarding route and trains. And without the least curiosity, even perhaps with some little annoyance that chance should have thrown us together again, I accepted his invitation and arrived one hazy midday at his out-of-the-way station to find him sitting on a low seat under a clump of 'double' hollyhocks, awaiting me.

He looked preoccupied and singularly listless; but seemed, none the less, to be pleased to see me.

We walked up the village street, past the little dingy apothecary's and the empty forge, and, as on my first visit, skirted the house together, and, instead of entering by the front door, made our way down the green path into the garden at the back. A pale haze of cloud muffled the sun; the garden lay in a grey shimmer—its old trees, its snapdragoned faintly glittering walls. But now there was an air of slovenliness where before all had been neat and methodical. In a patch of shallowly dug soil stood a worn-down spade leaning against a tree. There was an old decayed wheelbarrow. The roses had run to leaf and briar; the fruit trees were unpruned. The goddess of neglect had made it her secret resort.

'You ain't much of a gardener, Seaton,' I said at last, with a sigh of relief.

'I think, do you know, I like it best like this,' said Seaton. 'We haven't any man now, of course. Can't afford it.' He stood staring at his little dark oblong of freshly turned earth. 'And it always seems to me,' he went on ruminatingly, 'that, after all, we are all nothing better than interlopers on the earth, disfiguring and staining wherever we go. It may sound shocking blasphemy to say so; but then it's different here, you see. We are further away.'

'To tell you the truth, Seaton, I *don't* quite see,' I said; 'but it isn't a new philosophy, is it? Anyhow, it's a precious beastly one.'

'It's only what I think,' he replied, with all his odd old stubborn meekness. 'And one thinks as one *is*.'

We wandered on together, talking little, and still with that expression of uneasy vigilance on Seaton's face. He pulled out his watch as we stood gazing idly over the green meadows and the dark motionless bulrushes.

'I think, perhaps, it's nearly time for lunch,' he said. 'Would you like to come in?'

We turned and walked slowly towards the house, across whose windows I confess my own eyes, too, went restlessly meandering in search of its rather disconcerting inmate. There was a pathetic look of bedraggledness, of want of means and care, rust and overgrowth and faded paint. Seaton's aunt, a little to my relief, did not share our meal. So he carved the cold meat, and dispatched a heaped-up plate by an elderly servant for his aunt's private consumption. We talked little and in half-suppressed tones, and sipped some Madeira which Seaton after listening for a moment or two fetched out of the great mahogany sideboard.

I played him a dull and effortless game of chess, yawning between the moves he himself made almost at haphazard, and with attention elsewhere engaged. Towards five o'clock came the sound of a distant ring, and Seaton jumped up, overturning the board, and so ended a game that else might have fatuously continued to this day. He effusively excused himself, and after some little while returned with a slim, dark, pale-faced girl of about nineteen, in a white gown and hat, to whom I was presented with some little nervousness as his 'dear old friend and schoolfellow'.

We talked on in the golden afternoon light, still, as it seemed to me, and even in spite of our efforts to be lively and gay, in a half-suppressed, lacklustre fashion. We all seemed, if it were not my fancy, to be expectant, to be almost anxiously awaiting an arrival, the appearance of someone whose image filled our collective consciousness. Seaton talked least of all, and in a restless interjectory way, as he continually fidgeted from chair to chair. At last he proposed a stroll in the garden before the sun should have quite gone down.

Alice walked between us. Her hair and eyes were conspicuously dark against the whiteness of her gown. She carried herself not ungracefully, and yet with peculiarly little movement of her arms and body, and answered us both without turning her head. There was a curious provocative reserve in that impassive melancholy face. It seemed to be haunted by some tragic influence of which she herself was unaware.

And yet somehow I knew—I believe we all knew—that this walk, this discussion of their future plans was a futility. I had nothing to base such scepticism on, except only a vague sense of oppression, a foreboding consciousness of some inert invincible power in the background, to whom optimistic plans and love-making and youth are as chaff and thistledown. We came back, silent, in the last light. Seaton's aunt was there—under an old brass lamp. Her hair was as barbarously massed and curled as ever. Her eyelids, I think, hung even a little heavier in age over their slow-moving inscrutable pupils. We filed in softly out of the evening, and I made my bow.

'In this short interval, Mr Withers,' she remarked amiably, 'you have put off youth, put on the man. Dear me, how sad it is to see the young days vanishing! Sit down. My nephew tells me you met by chance—or act of Providence, shall we call it?—and in my beloved Strand! You, I understand, are to be best man—yes, best man! Or am I divulging secrets?' She surveyed Arthur and Alice with overwhelming graciousness. They sat apart on two low chairs and smiled in return.

'And Arthur—how do you think Arthur is looking?'

'I think he looks very much in need of a change,' I said.

'A change! Indeed?' She all but shut her eyes at me and with an exaggerated sentimentality shook her head. 'My dear Mr Withers! Are we not *all* in need of a change in this fleeting, fleeting world?' She mused over the remark like a connoisseur. 'And you,' she continued, turning abruptly to Alice, 'I hope you pointed out to Mr Withers all my pretty bits?'

'We only walked round the garden,' the girl replied; then, glancing at Seaton, added almost inaudibly, 'it's a very beautiful evening.'

'*Is* it?' said the old lady, starting up violently. 'Then on this very beautiful evening we will go in to supper. Mr Withers, your arm; Arthur, bring your bride.'

We were a queer quartet, I thought to myself, as I solemnly led the way into the faded, chilly dining room, with this indefinable old creature leaning wooingly on my arm—the large flat bracelet on the yellow-laced wrist. She fumed a little, breathing heavily, but as if with an effort of the mind rather than of the body; for she had grown much stouter and yet little more proportionate. And to talk into that great white face, so close to mine, was a queer experience in the dim light of the corridor, and even in the twinkling crystal of the candles. She was naive—appallingly naive; she was crafty and challenging; she was even arch; and all these in the brief, rather puffy passage from one room to the other, with these two tongue-tied children bringing up the rear. The meal was tremendous. I have never seen such a monstrous salad. But the dishes were greasy and overspiced, and were indifferently cooked. One thing only was quite unchanged—my hostess's appetite was as Gargantuan as ever. The heavy silver candelabra that lighted us stood before her high-backed chair. Seaton sat a little removed, his plate almost in darkness.

And throughout this prodigious meal his aunt talked, mainly to me, mainly *at* him, but with an occasional satirical sally at Alice and muttered explosions of reprimand to the servant. She had aged, and yet, if it be not nonsense to say so, seemed no older. I suppose to the Pyramids a decade is but as the rustling down of a handful of dust. And she reminded me of some such unshakable prehistoricism. She certainly was an amazing talker—rapid, egregious, with a delivery that was perfectly overwhelming. As for Seaton—her flashes of silence were for him. On her enormous volubility would suddenly fall a hush: acid sarcasm would be left implied; and she would sit softly moving her great head, with eyes fixed full in a dreamy smile; but with her whole attention, one could see, slowly, joyously absorbing his mute discomfiture.

She confided in us her views on a theme vaguely occupying at the moment, I suppose, all our minds. 'We have barbarous institutions, and so must put up, I suppose, with a never-ending procession of fools—of fools *ad infinitum*. Marriage, Mr Withers, was instituted in the privacy of a garden; *sub rosa*, as it were. Civilisation flaunts it in the glare of day. The dull marry the poor; the rich the effete; and so our New Jerusalem is peopled with naturals, plain and coloured, at either end. I detest folly; I detest still more (if I must be frank, dear Arthur) mere cleverness. Mankind has simply become a tailless host of uninstinctive animals. We should never have taken to Evolution, Mr Withers. "Natural Selection!"—little gods and fishes!—the deaf for the dumb. We should have used our brains—intellectual pride, the ecclesiastics call it. And by brains I mean—what do I mean, Alice?—I mean, my dear child,' and she laid two gross fingers on Alice's narrow sleeve, 'I mean courage. Consider it, Arthur. I read that the scientific world is once more beginning to be afraid of spiritual agencies. Spiritual agencies that tap, and actually float, bless their hearts! I think just one more of those mulberries—thank you.

'They talk about "blind Love",' she ran on derisively as she helped herself, her eyes roving over the dish, 'but why blind? I think, Mr Withers, from weeping over its rickets. After all, it is we plain women that triumph, is it not so—beyond the mockery of time. Alice, now! Fleeting, fleeting is youth, my child. What's that you were confiding to your plate, Arthur? Satirical boy. He laughs at his old aunt: nay, but thou didst laugh. He detests all sentiment. He whispers the most acid asides. Come, my love, we will leave these cynics; we will go and commiserate with each other on our sex. The choice of two evils, Mr Smithers!' I opened the door, and she swept out as if borne on a torrent of unintelligible indignation; and Arthur and I were left in the clear four-flamed light alone.

For a while we sat in silence. He shook his head at my cigarette case, and I lit a cigarette. Presently he fidgeted in his chair and poked his head forward into the light. He paused to rise, and shut again the shut door.

'How long will you be?' he asked me.

I laughed.

'Oh, it's not that!' he said, in some confusion. 'Of course, I like to be with her. But it's not that. The truth is, Withers, I don't care about leaving her too long with my aunt.'

I hesitated. He looked at me questioningly.

'Look here, Seaton,' I said, 'you know well enough that I don't want to interfere in your affairs, or to offer advice where it is not wanted. But don't you think perhaps you may not treat your aunt quite in the right way? As one gets old, you know, a little give and take. I have an old godmother, or something of the kind. She's a bit queer, too . . . A little allowance; it does no harm. But hang it all, I'm no preacher.'

He sat down with his hands in his pockets and still with his eyes fixed almost incredulously on mine. 'How?' he said.

'Well, my dear fellow, if I'm any judge—mind, I don't say that I am—but I can't help thinking she thinks you don't care for her; and perhaps takes your silence for—for bad temper. She has been very decent to you, hasn't she?'

'"Decent"? My God!' said Seaton.

I smoked on in silence; but he continued to look at me with that peculiar concentration I remembered of old.

'I don't think, perhaps, Withers,' he began presently, 'I don't think you quite understand. Perhaps you are not quite our kind. You always did, just like the other fellows, guy me at school. You laughed at me that night you came to stay here—about the voices and all that. But I don't mind being laughed at—because I know.'

'Know what?' It was the same old system of dull question and evasive answer.

'I mean I know that what we see and hear is only the smallest fraction of what is. I know she lives quite out of this. She *talks* to you; but it's all make-believe. It's all a "parlour game". She's not really with you; only pitting her outside wits against yours and enjoying the fooling. She's living on inside on what you're rotten without. That's what it is—a cannibal feast. She's a spider. It doesn't much matter what you call it. It means the same kind of thing. I tell you, Withers, she hates me; and you can scarcely dream what that hatred means. I used to think I had an inkling of the reason. It's oceans deeper than that. It just lies behind: herself against myself. Why, after all, how much do we really understand of anything? We don't even know our own histories, and not a tenth, not a tenth of the reasons. What has life been to me?—nothing but a trap. And when one sets oneself free for a while, it only begins again.'

I thought you might understand; but you are on a different level: that's all.'

'What on earth are you talking about?' I said contemptuously, in spite of myself.

'I mean what I say,' he said gutturally. 'All this outside's only make-believe—but there! what's the good of talking? So far as this is concerned I'm as good as done. You wait.'

Seaton blew out three of the candles and, leaving the vacant room in semi-darkness, we groped our way along the corridor to the drawing room. There a full moon stood shining in at the long garden windows. Alice sat stooping at the door, with her hands clasped in her lap, looking out, alone.

'Where is she?' Seaton asked in a low tone.

She looked up; and their eyes met in a glance of instantaneous understanding and the door immediately afterwards opened behind us.

'*Such* a moon!' said a voice, that once heard, remained unforgettably on the ear. 'A night for lovers, Mr Withers, if ever there was one. Get a shawl, my dear Arthur, and take Alice for a little promenade. I dare say we old cronies will manage to keep awake. Hasten, hasten, Romeo! My poor, poor Alice, how laggard a lover!'

Seaton returned with a shawl. They drifted out into the moonlight. My companion gazed after them till they were out of hearing, turned to me gravely, and suddenly twisted her white face into such a convulsion of contemptuous amusement that I could only stare blankly in reply.

'Dear innocent children!' she said, with inimitable unctuousness. 'Well, well, Mr Withers, we poor seasoned old creatures must move with the times. Do you sing?'

I scouted the idea.

'Then you must listen to my playing. Chess'—she clasped her forehead with both cramped hands—'chess is now completely beyond my poor wits.'

She sat down at the piano and ran her fingers in a flourish over the keys. 'What shall it be? How shall we capture them, those passionate hearts? That first fine careless rapture? Poetry itself.' She gazed softly into the garden a moment, and presently, with a shake of her body, began to play the opening bars of Beethoven's 'Moonlight' Sonata. The piano was old and woolly. She played without music. The lamplight was rather dim. The moonbeams from the window lay across the keys. Her head was in shadow. And whether it was simply due to her personality or to some really occult skill in her playing I cannot say; I only know that she gravely and deliberately set herself to satirise the beautiful music. It brooded on the air, disillusioned, charged with mockery and bitterness. I stood at the window; far down the path I could see the white figure glimmering in that pool of colourless light. A few faint stars shone, and still that amazing woman behind me dragged out of the unwilling keys her wonderful grotesquerie of youth and love and beauty. It came to an end. I knew the player was watching me. 'Please, please, go on!' I murmured, without turning. '*Please* go on playing, Miss Seaton.'

No answer was returned to this honeyed sarcasm, but I realised in some vague fashion that I was being acutely scrutinised, when suddenly there followed a procession of quiet, plaintive chords which broke at last softly into the hymn, 'A Few More Years Shall Roll'.

I confess it held me spellbound. There is a wistful, strained plangent pathos in the tune; but beneath those masterly old hands it cried softly and bitterly the solitude and desperate estrangement of the world. Arthur and his ladylove vanished from my thoughts. No one could put into so hackneyed an old hymn tune such an appeal who had never known the meaning of the words. Their meaning, anyhow, isn't commonplace.

I turned a fraction of an inch to glance at the musician. She was leaning forward a little over the keys, so that at the approach of my silent scrutiny she had but to turn her face into the thin flood of moonlight for every feature to become distinctly visible. And so, with the tune abruptly terminated, we steadfastly regarded one another; and she broke into a prolonged chuckle of laughter.

'Not quite so seasoned as I supposed, Mr Withers. I see you are a real lover of music. To me it is too painful. It evokes too much thought . . .'

I could scarcely see her little glittering eyes under their penthouse lids.

'And now,' she broke off crisply, 'tell me, as a man of the world, what do you think of my new niece?'

I was not a man of the world, nor was I much flattered in my stiff and dullish way of looking at things by being called one; and I could answer her without the least hesitation.

'I don't think, Miss Seaton, I'm much of a judge of character. She's very charming.'

'A brunette?'

'I think I prefer dark women.'

'And why? Consider, Mr Withers; dark hair, dark eyes, dark cloud, dark night, dark vision, dark death, dark grave, dark DARK!'

Perhaps the climax would have rather thrilled Seaton, but I was too thick-skinned. 'I don't know much about all that,' I answered rather pompously. 'Broad daylight's difficult enough for most of us.'

'Ah,' she said, with a sly inward burst of satirical laughter.

'And I suppose,' I went on, perhaps a little nettled, 'it isn't the actual darkness one admires, it's the contrast of the skin, and the colour of the eyes, and—and their shining. Just as,' I went blundering on, too late to turn back, 'just as you only see the stars in the dark. It would be a long day without any evening. As for death and the grave, I don't suppose we shall much notice that.' Arthur and his sweetheart were slowly returning along the dewy path. 'I believe in making the best of things.'

'How very interesting!' came the smooth answer. 'I see you are a philosopher, Mr Withers. Hm! "As for death and the grave, I don't suppose we shall much notice that." Very interesting . . . And I'm sure,' she added in a particularly suave voice, 'I profoundly hope so.' She rose slowly from her stool. 'You will take pity on me again, I hope. You and I would get on famously—kindred spirits—elective affinities. And, of course, now that my nephew's going to leave me, now that his affections are centred on another, I shall be a very lonely old woman . . . Shall I not, Arthur?'

Seaton blinked stupidly. 'I didn't hear what you said, Aunt.'

'I was telling our old friend, Arthur, that when you are gone I shall be a very lonely old woman.'

'Oh, I don't think so,' he said in a strange voice.

'He means, Mr Withers, he means, my dear child,' she said, sweeping her eyes over Alice, 'he means that I shall have memory for company—heavenly memory—the ghosts of other days. Sentimental boy! And did you enjoy our music, Alice? Did I really stir that youthful heart? . . . O, O, O,' continued the horrible old creature, 'you billers and cooers, I have been listening to such flatteries, such confessions! Beware, beware, Arthur, there's many a slip.' She rolled her little eyes at me, she shrugged her shoulders at Alice, and gazed an instant stonily into her nephew's face.

I held out my hand. 'Good night, good night!' she cried. 'He that fights and runs away. Ah, good night, Mr Withers; come again soon!' She thrust out her cheek at Alice, and we all three filed slowly out of the room.

Black shadow darkened the porch and half the spreading sycamore. We walked without speaking up the dusty village street. Here and there a crimson window glowed. At the fork of the highroad I said goodbye. But I had taken hardly more than a dozen paces when a sudden impulse seized me.

'Seaton!' I called.

He turned in the cool stealth of the moonlight.

'You have my address; if by any chance, you know, you should care to spend a week or two in town between this and the—the Day, we should be delighted to see you.'

'Thank you, Withers, thank you,' he said in a low voice.

'I dare say'—I waved my stick gallantly at Alice—'I dare say you will be doing some shopping; we could all meet,' I added, laughing.

'Thank you, thank you, Withers—immensely,' he repeated.

And so we parted.

BUT THEY WERE OUT of the jog trot of my prosaic life. And being of a stolid and incurious nature, I left Seaton and his marriage, and even his aunt, to themselves in my memory, and scarcely gave a thought to them until one day I was walking up the Strand again, and passed the flashing gloaming of the second-rate jeweller's shop where I had accidentally encountered my old schoolfellow in the summer. It was one of those stagnant autumnal days after a night of rain. I cannot say why, but a vivid recollection returned to my mind of our meeting and of how suppressed Seaton had seemed, and of how vainly he had endeavoured to appear assured and eager. He must be married by now, and had doubtless returned from his honeymoon. And I had clean forgotten my manners, had sent not a word of congratulation, nor—as I might very well have done, and as I knew he would have been pleased at my doing—even the ghost of a wedding present. It was just as of old.

On the other hand, I pleaded with myself, I had had no invitation. I paused at the corner of Trafalgar Square, and at the bidding of one of those caprices that seize occasionally on even an unimaginative mind, I found myself pelting after a green bus, and actually bound on a visit I had not in the least intended or foreseen.

The colours of autumn were over the village when I arrived. A beautiful late-afternoon sunlight bathed thatch and meadow. But it was close and hot. A child, two dogs, a very old woman with a heavy basket I encountered. One or two incurious tradesmen looked idly up as I passed by. It was all so rural and remote, my whimsical impulse had so much flagged, that for a while I hesitated to venture under the shadow of the sycamore tree to enquire after the happy pair. Indeed I first passed by the faint-blue gates and continued my walk under the high, green and tufted wall. Hollyhocks had attained their topmost bud and seeded in the little cottage gardens beyond; the Michaelmas daisies were in flower; a sweet warm aromatic smell of fading leaves was in the air. Beyond the cottages lay a field where cattle were grazing, and beyond that I came to a little churchyard. Then the road wound on, pathless and houseless, among gorse and bracken. I turned impatiently and walked quickly back to the house and rang the bell.

The rather colourless elderly woman who answered my enquiry informed me that Miss Seaton was at home, as if only taciturnity forbade her adding, 'But she doesn't want to see *you*.'

'Might I, do you think, have Mr Arthur's address?' I said.

She looked at me with quiet astonishment, as if waiting for an explanation. Not the faintest of smiles came into her thin face.

'I will tell Miss Seaton,' she said after a pause. 'Please walk in.'

She showed me into the dingy undusted drawing room, filled with evening sunshine and with the green-dyed light that penetrated the leaves overhanging the long French windows. I sat down and waited on and on, occasionally aware of a creaking footfall overhead. At last the door opened a little, and the great face I had once known peered round at me. For it was enormously changed; mainly, I think, because the aged eyes had rather suddenly failed, and so a kind of stillness and darkness lay over its calm and wrinkled pallor.

'Who is it?' she asked.

I explained myself and told her the occasion of my visit.

She came in, shut the door carefully after her, and, though the fumbling was scarcely perceptible, groped her way to a chair. She had on an old dressing gown, like a cassock, of a patterned cinnamon colour.

'What is it you want?' she said, seating herself and lifting her blank face to mine.

'Might I just have Arthur's address?' I said deferentially. 'I am so sorry to have disturbed you.'

'Hm. You have come to see my nephew?'

'Not necessarily to see him, only to hear how he is, and, of course, Mrs Seaton, too. I am afraid my silence must have appeared . . .'

'He hasn't noticed your silence,' croaked the old voice out of the great mask; 'besides, there isn't any Mrs Seaton.'

'Ah, then,' I answered, after a momentary pause, 'I have not seemed so black as I painted myself! And how is Miss Outram?'

'She's gone into Yorkshire,' answered Seaton's aunt.

'And Arthur too?'

She did not reply, but simply sat blinking at me with lifted chin, as if listening, but certainly not for what I might have to say. I began to feel rather at a loss.

'You were no close friend of my nephew's, Mr Smithers?' she said presently.

'No,' I answered, welcoming the cue, 'and yet, do you know, Miss Seaton, he is one of the very few of my old schoolfellows I have come across in the last few years, and I suppose as one gets older one begins to value old associations . . .' My voice seemed to trail off into a vacuum. 'I thought Miss Outram', I hastily began again, 'a particularly charming girl. I hope they are both quite well.'

Still the old face solemnly blinked at me in silence.

'You must find it very lonely, Miss Seaton, with Arthur away?'

'I was never lonely in my life,' she said sourly. 'I don't look to flesh and blood for my company. When you've got to be my age, Mr Smithers (which God forbid), you'll find life a very different affair from what you seem to think it is now. You won't seek company then, I'll be bound. It's thrust on you.' Her face edged round into the clear green light, and her eyes groped, as it were, over my vacant, disconcerted face. 'I dare say, now,' she said, composing her mouth, 'I dare say my nephew told you a good many tarradiddles in his time. Oh, yes, a good many, eh? He was always a liar. What, now, did he say of me? Tell me, now.' She leant forward as far as she could, trembling, with an ingratiating smile.

'I think he is rather superstitious,' I said coldly, 'but, honestly, I have a very poor memory, Miss Seaton.'

'Why?' she said. 'I haven't.'

'The engagement hasn't been broken off, I hope.'

'Well, between you and me,' she said, shrinking up and with an immensely confidential grimace, 'it has.'

'I'm sure I'm very sorry to hear it. And where is Arthur?'

'Eh?'

'Where is Arthur?'

We faced each other mutely among the dead old bygone furniture. Past all my analysis was that large, flat, grey, cryptic countenance. And then, suddenly, our eyes for the first time really met. In some indescribable way out of that thick-lidded obscurity a far, small something stooped and looked out at me for a mere instant of time that seemed of almost intolerable protraction. Involuntarily I blinked and shook my head. She muttered something with great rapidity, but quite inarticulately; rose and hobbled to the door. I thought I heard, mingled in broken mutterings, something about tea.

'Please, please, don't trouble,' I began, but could say no more, for the door was already shut between us. I stood and looked out on the long-neglected garden. I could just see the bright weedy greenness of Seaton's tadpole pond. I wandered about the room. Dusk began to gather, the last birds in that dense shadowiness of trees had ceased to sing. And not a sound was to be heard in the house. I waited on and on, vainly speculating. I even attempted to ring the bell; but the wire was broken, and only jangled loosely at my efforts.

I hesitated, unwilling to call or to venture out, and yet more unwilling to linger on, waiting for a tea that promised to be an exceedingly comfortless supper. And as darkness drew down, a feeling of the utmost unease and disquietude came over me. All my talks with Seaton returned on me with a suddenly enriched meaning. I recalled again his face as we had stood hanging over the staircase, listening in the small hours to the inexplicable stirrings of the night. There were no candles in the room; every minute the autumnal darkness deepened. I cautiously opened the door and listened, and with some little dismay withdrew, for I was uncertain of my way out. I even tried the garden, but was confronted under a veritable thicket of foliage by a padlocked gate. It would be a little too ignominious to be caught scaling a friend's garden fence!

Cautiously returning into the still and musty drawing room, I took out my watch, and gave the incredible old woman ten minutes in which to reappear. And when that tedious ten minutes had ticked by I could scarcely distinguish its hands. I determined to wait no longer, drew open the door and, trusting to my sense of direction, groped my way through the corridor that I vaguely remembered led to the front of the house.

I mounted three or four stairs and, lifting a heavy curtain, found myself facing the starry fanlight of the porch. From here I glanced into the gloom of the dining room. My fingers were on the latch of the outer door when I heard a faint stirring in the darkness above the hall. I looked up and became conscious of, rather than saw, the huddled old figure looking down on me.

There was an immense hushed pause. Then, 'Arthur, Arthur,' whispered an inexpressibly peevish rasping voice, 'is that you? Is that you, Arthur?'

I can scarcely say why, but the question horribly startled me. No conceivable answer occurred to me. With head craned back, hand clenched on my umbrella, I continued to stare up into the gloom, in this fatuous confrontation.

'Oh, oh,' the voice croaked. 'It is *you*, is it? *That* disgusting man! . . . Go away out. Go away out.'

At this dismissal, I wrenched open the door and, rudely slamming it behind me, ran out into the garden, under the gigantic old sycamore, and so out at the open gate.

I found myself half up the village street before I stopped running. The local butcher was sitting in his shop reading a piece of newspaper by the light of a small oil lamp. I crossed the road and enquired the way to the station. And after he had with minute and needless care directed me, I asked casually if Mr Arthur Seaton still lived with his aunt at the big house just beyond the village. He poked his head in at the little parlour door.

'Here's a gentleman enquiring after young Mr Seaton, Millie,' he said. 'He's dead, ain't he?'

'Why, yes, bless you,' replied a cheerful voice from within. 'Dead and buried these three months or more—young Mr Seaton. And just before he was to be married, don't you remember, Bob?'

I saw a fair young woman's face peer over the muslin of the little door at me.

'Thank you,' I replied, 'then I go straight on?'

'That's it, sir; past the pond, bear up the hill a bit to the left, and then there's the station lights before your eyes.'

We looked intelligently into each other's faces in the beam of the smoky lamp. But not one of the many questions in my mind could I put into words.

And again I paused irresolutely a few paces further on. It was not, I fancy, merely a foolish apprehension of what the raw-boned butcher might 'think' that prevented my going back to see if I could find Seaton's grave in the benighted churchyard. There was precious little use in pottering about in the muddy dark merely to discover where he was buried. And yet I felt a little uneasy. My rather horrible thought was that, so far as I was concerned—one of his extremely few friends—he had never been much better than 'buried' in my mind.

———————————

Charles Dickens

1812–1870

Much loved for his big sprawling novels of Victorian life, such as *Oliver Twist* and *Nicholas Nickleby*, Charles Dickens was also a ghost-story enthusiast. He wrote some chilling short stories, and supernatural themes also appear in some of his longer works of fiction. As editor of *Household Words* and *All the Year Round*, he regularly commissioned ghost stories from popular writers.

NO. 1 BRANCH LINE, THE SIGNALMAN

'HALLOA! BELOW THERE!'

When he heard a voice thus calling to him, he was standing at the door of his box, with a flag in his hand, furled round its short pole. One would have thought, considering the nature of the ground, that he could not have doubted from what quarter the voice came; but, instead of looking up to where I stood on the top of the steep cutting nearly over his head, he turned himself about and looked down the Line. There was something remarkable in his manner of doing so, though I could not have said, for my life, what. But, I know it was remarkable enough to attract my notice, even though his figure was foreshortened and shadowed, down in the deep trench, and mine was high above him, so steeped in the glow of an angry sunset that I had shaded my eyes with my hand before I saw him at all.

'Halloa! Below!'

From looking down the Line, he turned himself about again, and, raising his eyes, saw my figure high above him.

'Is there any path by which I can come down and speak to you?'

He looked up at me without replying, and I looked down at him without pressing him too soon with a repetition of my idle question. Just then, there came a vague vibration in the earth and air, quickly changing into a violent pulsation, and an oncoming rush that caused me to start back, as though it had force to draw me down. When such vapour as rose to my height from this rapid train had passed me and was skimming away over the landscape, I looked down again, and saw him re-furling the flag he had shown while the train went by.

I repeated my enquiry. After a pause, during which he seemed to regard me with fixed attention, he motioned with his rolled-up flag towards a point on my level, some two or three hundred yards distant. I called down to him, 'All right!' and made for that point. There, by dint of looking closely about me, I found a rough zigzag descending path notched out: which I followed.

The cutting was extremely deep, and unusually precipitate. It was made through a clammy stone that became oozier and wetter as I went down. For these reasons, I found the way long enough to give me time to recall a singular air of reluctance or compulsion with which he had pointed out the path.

When I came down low enough upon the zigzag descent, to see him again, I saw that he was standing between the rails on the way by which the train had lately passed, in an attitude as if he were waiting for me to appear. He had his left hand at his chin, and that left elbow rested on his right hand crossed over his breast. His attitude was one of such expectation and watchfulness, that I stopped a moment, wondering at it.

I resumed my downward way, and, stepping out upon the level of the railroad and drawing nearer to him, saw that he was a dark sallow man, with a dark beard and rather heavy eyebrows. His post was in as solitary and dismal a place as ever I saw. On either side, a dripping-wet wall of jagged stone, excluding all view but a strip of sky; the perspective one way, only a crooked prolongation of this great dungeon; the shorter perspective in the other direction, terminating in a gloomy red light, and the gloomier entrance to a black tunnel, in whose massive architecture there was a barbarous, depressing, and forbidding air. So little sunlight ever found its way to this spot, that it had an earthy deadly smell; and so much cold wind rushed through it, that it struck chill to me, as if I had left the natural world.

Before he stirred, I was near enough to him to have touched him. Not even then removing his eyes from mine, he stepped back one step, and lifted his hand.

This was a lonesome post to occupy (I said), and it had riveted my attention when I looked down from up yonder. A visitor was a rarity, I should suppose; not an unwelcome rarity, I hoped? In me, he merely saw a man who had been shut up within narrow limits all his life, and who, being at last set free, had a newly awakened interest in these great works. To such purpose I spoke to him; but I am far from sure of the terms I used, for, besides that I am not happy in opening any conversation, there was something in the man that daunted me.

He directed a most curious look towards the red light near the tunnel's mouth, and looked all about it, as if something were missing from it, and then looked at me.

That light was part of his charge? Was it not?

He answered in a low voice: 'Don't you know it is?'

The monstrous thought came into my mind as I perused the fixed eyes and the saturnine face, that this was a spirit, not a man. I have speculated since, whether there may have been infection in his mind.

In my turn, I stepped back. But in making the action, I detected in his eyes some latent fear of me. This put the monstrous thought to flight.

'You look at me,' I said, forcing a smile, 'as if you had a dread of me.'

'I was doubtful,' he returned, 'whether I had seen you before.'

'Where?'

He pointed to the red light he had looked at.

'There?' I said.

Intently watchful of me, he replied (but without sound), Yes.

'My good fellow, what should I do there? However, be that as it may, I never was there, you may swear.'

'I think I may,' he rejoined. 'Yes. I am sure I may.'

His manner cleared, like my own. He replied to my remarks with readiness, and in well-chosen words. Had he much to do there? Yes; that was to say, he had enough responsibility to bear—but exactness and watchfulness were what was required of him, and of actual work—manual labour—he had next to none. To change that signal, to trim those lights, and to turn this iron handle now and then, was all he had to do under that head. Regarding those many long and lonely hours of which I seemed to make so much, he could only say that the routine of his life had shaped itself into that form, and he had grown used to it. He had taught himself a language down here—if only to know it by sight, and to have formed his own crude ideas of its pronunciation, could be called learning it. He had also worked at fractions and decimals and tried a little algebra; but he was, and had been as a boy, a poor hand at figures. Was it necessary for him when on duty, always to remain in that channel of damp air, and could he never rise into the sunshine from between those high stone walls? Why, that depended upon times and circumstances. Under some conditions there would be less upon the Line than under others, and the same held good as to certain hours of the day and night. In bright weather, he did choose occasions for getting a little above these lower shadows; but, being at all times liable to be called by his electric bell, and at such times listening for it with redoubled anxiety, the relief was less than I would suppose.

He took me into his box, where there was a fire, a desk for an official book in which he had to make certain entries, a telegraphic instrument with its dial face and needles, and the little bell of which he had spoken. On my trusting that he would excuse the remark that he had been well educated, and (I hoped I might say without offence), perhaps educated above that station, he observed that instances of slight incongruity in such-wise would rarely be found wanting among large bodies of men; that he had heard it was so in workhouses, in the police force, even in that last desperate resource, the army; and that he knew it was so, more or less, in any great railway staff. He had been, when young (if I could believe it, sitting in that hut; he scarcely could), a student of natural philosophy, and had attended lectures; but he had run wild, misused his opportunities, gone down, and never risen again. He had no complaint to offer about that. He had made his bed, and he lay upon it. It was far too late to make another.

All that I have here condensed, he said in a quiet manner, with his grave dark regards divided between me and the fire. He threw in the word 'Sir', from time to time, and especially when he referred to his youth: as though to request me to understand that he claimed to be nothing but what I found him. He was several times interrupted by the little bell, and had to read off messages, and send replies. Once, he had to stand without the door, and display a flag as a train passed, and make some verbal communication to the driver. In the discharge of his duties I observed him to be remarkably exact and vigilant, breaking off his discourse at a syllable, and remaining silent until what he had to do was done.

In a word, I should have set this man down as one of the safest of men to be employed in that capacity, but for the circumstance that while he was speaking to me he twice broke off with a fallen colour, turned his face towards the little bell when it did NOT ring, opened the door of the hut (which was kept shut to exclude the unhealthy damp), and looked out towards the red light near the mouth of the tunnel. On both of those occasions, he came back to the fire with the inexplicable air upon him which I had remarked, without being able to define, when we were so far asunder.

Said I when I rose to leave him: 'You almost make me think that I have met with a contented man.'

(I am afraid I must acknowledge that I said it to lead him on.)

'I believe I used to be so,' he rejoined, in the low voice in which he had first spoken; 'but I am troubled, sir, I am troubled.'

He would have recalled the words if he could. He had said them, however, and I took them up quickly.

'With what? What is your trouble?'

'It is very difficult to impart, sir. It is very, very difficult to speak of. If ever you make me another visit, I will try to tell you.'

'But I expressly intend to make you another visit. Say, when shall it be?'

'I go off early in the morning, and I shall be on again at ten tomorrow night, sir.'

'I will come at eleven.'

He thanked me, and went out at the door with me. 'I'll show my white light, sir,' he said, in his peculiar low voice, 'till you have found the way up. When you have found it, don't call out! And when you are at the top, don't call out!'

His manner seemed to make the place strike colder to me, but I said no more than 'Very well.'

'And when you come down tomorrow night, don't call out! Let me ask you a parting question. What made you cry "Halloa! Below there!" tonight?'

'Heaven knows,' said I. 'I cried something to that effect—'

'Not to that effect, sir. Those were the very words. I know them well.'

'Admit those were the very words. I said them, no doubt, because I saw you below.'

'For no other reason?'

'What other reason could I possibly have!'

'You had no feeling that they were conveyed to you in any supernatural way?'

'No.'

He wished me good night, and held up his light. I walked by the side of the down Line of rails (with a very disagreeable sensation of a train coming behind me), until I found the path. It was easier to mount than to descend, and I got back to my inn without any adventure.

Punctual to my appointment, I placed my foot on the first notch of the zigzag next night, as the distant clocks were striking eleven. He was waiting for me at the bottom, with his white light on. 'I have not called out,' I said, when we came close together; 'may I speak now?' 'By all means, sir.' 'Good night then, and here's my hand.' 'Good night, sir, and here's mine.' With that, we walked side by side to his box, entered it, closed the door, and sat down by the fire.

'I have made up my mind, sir,' he began, bending forward as soon as we were seated, and speaking in a tone but a little above a whisper, 'that you shall not have to ask me twice what troubles me. I took you for someone else yesterday evening. That troubles me.'

'That mistake?'

'No. That someone else.'

'Who is it?'

'I don't know.'

'Like me?'

'I don't know. I never saw the face. The left arm is across the face and the right arm is waved. Violently waved. This way.'

I followed his action with my eyes, and it was the action of an arm gesticulating with the utmost passion and vehemence: 'For God's sake clear the way!'

'One moonlight night,' said the man, 'I was sitting here, when I heard a voice cry "Halloa! Below there!" I started up, looked from that door, and saw this someone else standing by the red light near the tunnel, waving as I just now showed you. The voice seemed hoarse with shouting, and it cried, "Look out! Look out!" And then again "Halloa! Below there! Look out!" I caught up my lamp, turned it on red, and ran towards the figure calling, "What's wrong? What has happened? Where?" It stood just outside the blackness of the tunnel. I advanced so close upon it that I wondered at its keeping the sleeve across its eyes. I ran right up at it, and had my hand stretched out to pull the sleeve away, when it was gone.'

'Into the tunnel,' said I.

'No. I ran on into the tunnel, five hundred yards. I stopped and held my lamp above my head and saw the figures of the measured distance, and saw the wet stains stealing down the walls and trickling through the arch. I ran out again, faster than I had run in (for I had a mortal abhorrence of the place upon me), and I looked all round the red light with my own red light, and I went up the iron ladder to the gallery atop of it, and I came down again, and ran back here. I telegraphed both ways: "An alarm has been given. Is anything wrong?" The answer came back, both ways: "All well."'

Resisting the slow touch of a frozen finger tracing out my spine, I showed him how that this figure must be a deception of his sense of sight, and how that figures, originating in disease of the delicate nerves that minister to the functions of the eye, were known to have often troubled patients, some of whom had become conscious of the nature of their affliction, and had even proved it by experiments upon themselves. 'As to an imaginary cry,' said I, 'do but listen for a moment to the wind in this unnatural valley while we speak so low, and to the wild harp it makes of the telegraph wires!'

That was all very well, he returned, after we had sat listening for a while, and he ought to know something of the wind and the wires, he who so often passed long winter nights there, alone and watching. But he would beg to remark that he had not finished.

I asked his pardon, and he slowly added these words, touching my arm:

'Within six hours after the Appearance, the memorable accident on this Line happened, and within ten hours the dead and wounded were brought along through the tunnel over the spot where the figure had stood.'

A disagreeable shudder crept over me, but I did my best against it. It was not to be denied, I rejoined, that this was a remarkable coincidence, calculated deeply to impress his mind. But, it was unquestionable that remarkable coincidences did continually occur, and they must be taken into account in dealing with such a subject. Though to be sure I must admit, I added (for I thought I saw that he was going to bring the objection to bear upon me), men of common sense did not allow much for coincidences in making the ordinary calculations of life.

He again begged to remark that he had not finished.

I again begged his pardon for being betrayed into interruptions.

'This,' he said, again laying his hand upon my arm, and glancing over his shoulder with hollow eyes, 'was just a year ago. Six or seven months passed, and I had recovered from the surprise and shock, when one morning, as the day was breaking, I, standing at that door, looked towards the red light, and saw the spectre again.' He stopped, with a fixed look at me.

'Did it cry out?'

'No. It was silent.'

'Did it wave its arm?'

'No. It leaned against the shaft of the light, with both hands before the face. Like this.'

Once more, I followed his action with my eyes. It was an action of mourning. I have seen such an attitude in stone figures on tombs.

'Did you go up to it?'

'I came in and sat down, partly to collect my thoughts, partly because it had turned me faint. When I went to the door again, daylight was above me, and the ghost was gone.'

'But nothing followed? Nothing came of this?'

He touched me on the arm with his forefinger twice or thrice, giving a ghastly nod each time: 'That very day, as a train came out of the tunnel, I noticed at a carriage window on my side, what looked like a confusion of hands and heads, and something waved. I saw it, just in time to signal the driver, Stop! He shut off, and put his brake on, but the train drifted past here a hundred and fifty yards or more. I ran after it, and, as I went along, heard terrible screams and cries. A beautiful young lady had died instantaneously in one of the compartments, and was brought in here, and laid down on this floor between us.'

Involuntarily, I pushed my chair back, as I looked from the boards at which he pointed, to himself.

'True, sir. True. Precisely as it happened, so I tell it you.'

I could think of nothing to say, to any purpose, and my mouth was very dry. The wind and the wires took up the story with a long lamenting wail.

He resumed. 'Now, sir, mark this, and judge how my mind is troubled. The spectre came back, a week ago. Ever since, it has been there, now and again, by fits and starts.'

'At the light?'

'At the Danger light.'

'What does it seem to do?'

He repeated, if possible with increased passion and vehemence, that former gesticulation of 'For God's sake clear the way!'

Then, he went on. 'I have no peace or rest for it. It calls to me, for many minutes together, in an agonised manner, "Below there! Look out! Look out!" It stands waving to me. It rings my little bell.'

I caught at that. 'Did it ring your bell yesterday evening when I was here, and you went to the door?'

'Twice.'

'Why, see,' said I, 'how your imagination misleads you. My eyes were on the bell, and my ears were open to the bell, and if I am a living man, it did *not* ring at those times. No, nor at any other time, except when it was rung in the natural course of physical things by the station communicating with you.'

He shook his head. 'I have never made a mistake as to that, yet, sir. I have never confused the spectre's ring with the man's. The ghost's ring is a strange vibration in the bell that it derives from nothing else, and I have not asserted that the bell stirs to the eye. I don't wonder that you failed to hear it. But I heard it.'

'And did the spectre seem to be there, when you looked out?'

'It *was* there.'

'Both times?'

He repeated firmly: 'Both times.'

'Will you come to the door with me, and look for it now?'

He bit his under-lip as though he were somewhat unwilling, but arose. I opened the door, and stood on the step, while he stood in the doorway. There, was the Danger light. There, was the dismal mouth of the tunnel. There, were the high wet stone walls of the cutting. There, were the stars above them.

'Do you see it?' I asked him, taking particular note of his face. His eyes were prominent and strained; but not very much more so, perhaps, than my own had been when I had directed them earnestly towards the same spot.

'No,' he answered. 'It is not there.'

'Agreed,' said I.

We went in again, shut the door, and resumed our seats. I was thinking how best to improve this advantage, if it might be called one, when he took up the conversation in such a matter-of-course way, so assuming that there could be no serious question of fact between us, that I felt myself placed in the weakest of positions.

'By this time you will fully understand, sir,' he said, 'that what troubles me so dreadfully, is the question, What does the spectre mean?'

I was not sure, I told him, that I did fully understand.

'What is its warning against?' he said, ruminating, with his eyes on the fire, and only by times turning them on me. 'What is the danger? Where is the danger? There is danger overhanging, somewhere on the Line. Some dreadful calamity will happen. It is not to be doubted this third time, after what has gone before. But surely this is a cruel haunting of *me*. What can *I* do!'

He pulled out his handkerchief, and wiped the drops from his heated forehead.

'If I telegraph Danger, on either side of me, or on both, I can give no reason for it,' he went on, wiping the palms of his hands. 'I should get into trouble, and do no good. They would think I was mad. This is the way it would work: Message: "Danger! Take care!" Answer: "What Danger? Where?" Message: "Don't know. But for God's sake take care!" They would displace me. What else could they do?'

His pain of mind was most pitiable to see. It was the mental torture of a conscientious man, oppressed beyond endurance by unintelligible responsibility involving life.

'When it first stood under the Danger light,' he went on, putting his dark hair back from his head, and drawing his hands outward across and across his temples in an extremity of feverish distress, 'why not tell me where that accident was to happen—if it must happen? Why not tell me how it could be averted—if it could have been averted? When on its second coming it hid its face, why not tell me instead: "She is going to die. Let them keep her at home"? If it came, on those two occasions, only to show me that its warnings were true, and so to prepare me for the third, why not warn me plainly now? And I, Lord help me! A mere poor signalman on this solitary station! Why not go to somebody with credit to be believed, and power to act!'

When I saw him in this state, I saw that for the poor man's sake, as well as for the public safety, what I had to do for the time was to compose his mind. Therefore, setting aside all question of reality or unreality between us, I represented to him that whoever thoroughly discharged his duty must do well, and that at least it was his comfort that he understood his duty, though he did not understand these confounding Appearances. In this effort I succeeded far better than in the attempt to reason him out of his conviction. He became calm—the occupations incidental to his post as the night advanced, began to make larger demands on his attention; and I left him at two in the morning. I had offered to stay through the night, but he would not hear of it.

That I more than once looked back at the red light as I ascended the pathway, that I did not like the red light, and that I should have slept but poorly if my bed had been under it, I see no reason to conceal. Nor did I like the two sequences of the accident and the dead girl. I see no reason to conceal that, either.

But, what ran most in my thoughts was the consideration how ought I to act, having become the recipient of this disclosure? I had proved the man to be intelligent, vigilant, painstaking, and exact; but how long might he remain so, in his state of mind? Though in a subordinate position, still he held a most important trust, and would I (for instance) like to stake my own life on the chances of his continuing to execute it with precision?

Unable to overcome a feeling that there would be something treacherous in my communicating what he had told me to his superiors in the Company, without first being plain with himself and proposing a middle course to him, I ultimately resolved to offer to accompany him (otherwise keeping his secret for the present) to the wisest medical practitioner we could hear of in those parts, and to take his opinion. A change in his time of duty would come round next night, he had apprised me, and he would be off an hour or two after sunrise, and on again soon after sunset. I had appointed to return accordingly.

Next evening was a lovely evening, and I walked out early to enjoy it. The sun was not yet quite down when I traversed the field-path near the top of the deep cutting. I would extend my walk for an hour, I said to myself, half an hour on and half an hour back, and it would then be time to go to my signalman's box.

Before pursuing my stroll, I stepped to the brink, and mechanically looked down, from the point from which I had first seen him. I cannot describe the thrill that seized upon me, when, close at the mouth of the tunnel, I saw the appearance of a man, with his left sleeve across his eyes, passionately waving his right arm.

The nameless horror that oppressed me, passed in a moment, for in a moment I saw that this appearance of a man was a man indeed, and that there was a little group of other men standing at a short distance, to whom he seemed to be rehearsing the gesture he made. The Danger light was not yet lighted. Against its shaft, a little low hut, entirely new to me, had been made of some wooden supports and tarpaulin. It looked no bigger than a bed.

With an irresistible sense that something was wrong—with a flashing self-reproachful fear that fatal mischief had come of my leaving the man there, and causing no one to be sent to overlook or correct what he did—I descended the notched path with all the speed I could make.

'What is the matter?' I asked the men.

'Signalman killed this morning, sir.'

'Not the man belonging to that box?'

'Yes, sir.'

'Not the man I know?'

'You will recognise him, sir, if you knew him,' said the man who spoke for the others, solemnly uncovering his own head and raising an end of the tarpaulin, 'for his face is quite composed.'

'O! how did this happen, how did this happen?' I asked, turning from one to another as the hut closed in again.

'He was cut down by an engine, sir. No man in England knew his work better. But somehow he was not clear of the outer rail. It was just at broad day. He had struck the light, and had the lamp in his hand. As the engine came out of the tunnel, his back was towards her, and she cut him down. That man drove her, and was showing how it happened. Show the gentleman, Tom.'

The man, who wore a rough dark dress, stepped back to his former place at the mouth of the tunnel:

'Coming round the curve in the tunnel, sir,' he said, 'I saw him at the end, like as if I saw him down a perspective glass. There was no time to check speed, and I knew him to be very careful. As he didn't seem to take heed of the whistle, I shut it off when we were running down upon him, and called to him as loud as I could call.'

'What did you say?'

'I said, "Below there! Look out! Look out! For God's sake clear the way!"'

I started.

'Ah! it was a dreadful time, sir, I never left off calling to him. I put this arm before my eyes, not to see, and I waved this arm to the last; but it was no use.'

WITHOUT PROLONGING the narrative to dwell on any one of its curious circumstances more than on any other, I may, in closing it, point out the coincidence that the warning of the engine driver included, not only the words which the unfortunate signalman had repeated to me as haunting him, but also the words which I myself—not he—had attached, and that only in my own mind, to the gesticulation he had imitated.

Lord Dunsany

1878–1957

The talented Irish writer, Lord Dunsany, was a man of many
interests: a soldier who served in two wars, an enthusiastic fox
hunter, and a keen cricketer. He once calculated that only three
per cent of his time was actually devoted to writing, but that
small contribution gave the world some of the most charming and
original plays, poems and stories to the English language.

AUTUMN CRICKET

O N ONE OF THOSE SHORT journeys by car that one sometimes takes nowadays
I happened to pass after nightfall the once-famous cricket field of Long
Barrow. They play there still in the summer, though not so much as they
used to do; but this was autumn, when it would be deserted by day, and at night
there was nothing there but grey mists that had strayed from a neighbouring
stream that winds along under the willows at one end of the ground. Perhaps it
was the contrasts between the activity for which that field had been famous and
the loneliness of it in that autumn night that made me feel for a moment a sense
of desolation. And then my headlights flashed on the face of an old man sitting
on a wooden bench by the side of the field and gazing out into the mists whose
shapes floated up from the stream and rose every now and then in little wraiths,
as a breeze in the cold night played with them for a while and soon dropped
them again. Somehow this solitary figure there seemed to increase the loneliness.
Then just before the light left him, to sweep on and illuminate hedges and
branches of trees, the old man began to clap. Sitting all alone on that wooden
bench, looking over an empty field, he was unmistakably applauding something. I went on in the car, and that was all the story I had to tell, a field at night
covered with mist, nothing else there, and a man beside it clapping; and not a
very likely story either. But I told it, such as it was, to a friend next day who
knew Long Barrow, living nearer to it than I do, and this is what he told me.

'O, that would have been old Modgers,' he said. 'He used to be groundsman
there, but retired on account of age long ago, and has a cottage almost beside it.'

'What was he doing there at that hour?' I asked.

'Well, that's the trouble,' he said. 'It's not good for him at that age to be out in

176

the cold like that, and we can't stop him, unless we have him legally restrained.'

'But surely you can't shut a man up,' I said, 'merely to prevent him from going out in the cold.'

'It's more than that,' he said. 'The old man thinks there's a cricket match going on there every night, and he goes out to look at it.'

'Who does he think is playing?' I asked.

'W. G. Grace,' he replied, 'and Gunn, and a lot of other famous players, all of them men he has seen on that ground and all of them dead. We are trying to have him certified. And then they'll be able to keep him in at night.'

'Will he like that?' I said rather lamely.

'No,' he said. 'He wants to go and see ghosts playing cricket. But it's the only way to stop him. His wife can't do it.'

'Can you do it on that?' I asked.

'His doctor says so,' said Meadly. That was my friend's name. 'He says he has given him very detailed accounts of the games that he watches, even to the score of each ghost.'

So I imagined that I was never likely to see any more of old Modgers.

And then one day only a week or so later, when autumn was a little colder and mistier, I was passing that way after nightfall again, and there was the same old man sitting on his old wooden bench that was still by the side of the ground, and gazing steadily, just as he had before, at the wisps of mist that breezes lifted over the rest and let fall again into the greyness that went all the way to the stream. So they had not certified the old man, and he was still out there of a night in the cold.

Next day I decided to go to Meadly's house to ask him more of the story, the beginnings of which he had told me. I rang his bell—and he came to the door himself, and I apologised for disturbing him, and told him that old Modgers was still there at night.

'Come in,' he said cheerily, 'and have some tea, and I'll tell you about him.'

And I went into his smoking room with him and sat down in a comfortable chair, and he said: 'The trouble was that one doctor cannot certify a man, it takes two. That is the law. And the old fellow found out that he was going to be certified, and when the second doctor turned up he wouldn't say a word about ghosts. So, in spite of the evidence of his own doctor, we have been unable to get him into an asylum.'

'Well, I suppose we'd all try to escape that if we could,' I said.

'It isn't the asylum that he jibs at,' said Meadly, 'but he won't leave his ghosts. You see, he's somewhere in his late eighties, and kept that ground for nearly fifty years and played on it before that; and to give up cricket is to him what giving up much more important things would be to others, and he thinks he's still watching it. Of course, if we could prove that, we could get him certified. But we can't. His doctor had the whole story from him; but that is not enough. We've asked his wife to wrap him up as much as possible. And she does that, but we can't stop him.'

'Perhaps it would be possible to reason with him,' I said as tea was brought in by a maid.

'I don't think so,' he said.

'I'd like to try,' I told him. 'He can't want to be frozen to death.'

'Men don't like to be killed by any of their follies,' said Meadly, 'but they don't like to give them up. And I suppose more good advice is wasted on asking them if they wouldn't like to do so than on anything in the world.'

'Still, I'd like to try,' I said.

And so I added myself to the number of those who ask men to give up the harmful things they like most in life, one in every hundred thousand of whom succeed. So why shouldn't I? I went over by bus next night to Long Barrow an hour or two after sunset and walked alone to the cricket ground. And sure enough he was on his usual bench, looking out over the famous ground at the first thin wisps of mist that were coming up from the stream and nearing the lonely pitch. I went up to the wooden bench and sat down beside him. He hastily looked all round, evidently to satisfy himself that two men were not within hearing, and not till he had thoroughly scrutinised the misty darkness did he say anything to me. But then he spoke. 'They are just coming in to bat,' he said. 'That's Gunn, and that's W. G.'

'So I see,' I replied.

'You know them, then?' he asked.

'By sight,' I said.

'They often play here,' he told me.

'Do you watch them often?' I asked.

'Whenever they play,' he said.

'Is it a good thing to be out so late with all this mist rising?' I asked him.

'They never play by day,' he said.

'But are you sure you are warm enough?' I asked.

'I wrap up well,' he said. 'And I never stay more than two hours, unless it's a very exciting game. And I go to bed as soon as I get home.'

He stopped to clap then, gazing over the ground towards the approaching mist. And I thought over what he had said and it seemed to me that if he was really well wrapped up under the good greatcoat that he wore, and if he did not stay more than two hours, it might not be so serious as Meadly and others feared, at any rate not till the winter. And so I told Meadly next day. I sat there beside the old fellow for nearly half an hour and heard an excellent summary of a very exciting game, something I suppose that had remained in his memory, which was still fresh and vivid, whatever had happened to the rest of his mind, perhaps overweighted and upset by the sheer power of that part of the brain that stores and preserves past days. It was really a very exciting match. I remember it yet. W. G. won, though that proves nothing, because he nearly always did. I saw Modgers home hale and hearty, and I went to Meadly next day and urged him to leave the old man alone, at least till winter came, and told him that I felt sure he would be all right. And I think I persuaded Meadly. But long before winter was here the old man died.

What happened, as we afterwards heard from his wife, was, only a fortnight later, being a bit older than Meadly had thought, he reached his ninetieth birthday. And old Mrs Modgers told us that on that very evening, while they were having a bit of supper and a glass of wine with which to celebrate the occasion, the mist having risen, as it always did in the autumn, but no higher than one of their windows, old Modgers had glanced out of the window and suddenly said they had made him an honorary member, an honorary member of the ghosts who used to play at Long Barrow, because he was ninety. And Modgers had said that this was a great honour, because he was the only living man that had been invited to play at night on that ground. And they were going to play that night, Modgers had said; and the Doctor himself, that is Dr Grace, had invited Modgers to play for him. So Modgers had gone; she couldn't stop him. And this time he wouldn't even dress up warm.

'Well,' she said, 'he went out there with his bat, for he had an old bat that he still kept in a cupboard, and he said he wouldn't want pads, because the ball they were using wasn't as hard as all that, and he went out to the pitch and bent down like as if he was batting, and began hitting about.'

'But surely,' Meadly said to her, 'he didn't run.'

'He seemed to be hitting boundaries,' said Mrs Modgers.

'I stayed and watched the whole time, but he wouldn't allow me to bring him home. He seemed to be hitting boundaries, and so did the gentleman opposite to him, whoever that may have been, or perhaps I should say *whatever*, seeing they was all ghosts, but for him. But after he had hit about twenty of them he seemed to get tired and not to be able to hit so far, and then he had to run. I couldn't stop him. And after a while he took off his hat two or three times and looked round about him, seemingly very pleased. And I think he had got his century. And that was when it happened. Of course a man of his age couldn't run like he did, and he dropped dead. I could do nothing.'

We both made those vain attempts that people sometimes make with words, trying to comfort Mrs Modgers. But, though we knew we could bring her no comfort whatever, we both of us saw a gleam on her face that seemed, faint though it was, to shine from a hidden smile, as she said, 'They were never able to shut him up. And he'll be able to play at Long Barrow now with the Doctor and Mr Gunn whenever he likes.'

———————————

Elizabeth Fancett

A film critic and freelance journalist, Elizabeth Fancett is also one of Britain's most original ghost-story writers. She has broadcast her own chilling tales on Capital Radio's *Moment of Terror* series, and has contributed to countless anthologies of the supernatural. Her imagination is wide ranging, and many of her stories, such as the one chosen here, have unusual backgrounds.

THE GHOSTS OF CALAGOU

REGUS STOOD IN THE GREY OF DAWN beneath the great tree on the edge of the empty corral.

Empty now, but not for long. Soon his horses would come and his ranch would begin.

He could not see his shadow, but he did not worry. He knew that it would reveal itself later when the sun came up. He was glad the day was ahead of him, a sunny day, when he would have the surety of his shadow.

He looked about him at his lands and blessed the wealth that had made it possible. *His* gold, though they had sought it together, he and his erstwhile partners. They had worked as hard for it, suffered for it, died for it. And by their greed they had nearly killed him too.

But he had survived, and they had hated him for it. Beyond the grave they hated him. They tried to make him think he too was dead. Had they believed such tricks could drive him to madness, to take his own life maybe—when he really would have been one of them?

He cursed the day when he had taken them on.

He had come into the little town of Calagou, the last stop on his way to the legendary mountains that towered above the intervening valleys and prairies. He knew he would need more help, more hands, strong backs, but held little hope of getting them. For as legends told—indeed, as living men still said—there was more than gold in the high and haunted hills of Calagou.

Many had gone there in the past, few had stayed more than a night there, and many more had not returned. And those who had returned—without gold, though the hills were rich with it—had told their eerie tales in the comfort of lighted cabins or the cosy warmth of saloons, and had shuddered in the telling and in the remembering of the sounds they had heard there and the things they said they had seen there. And they had recalled, with the respect that terror brings, the legendary warning that no man takes gold from Calagou and lives!

Then Regus came, himself something of a legend in this part of the West. Regus could divine gold as some could find oil or water. And Regus was bound for the hills of Calagou.

He made his choice—three young strong men, Talley, deSeegar and Carney. They were willing, they said, but had Regus heard the legends?

Yes, he had heard the tales and scorned them. Tales of disappointed men, he had told them. Excuses for their failures and their stupidity. The voices they claimed to have heard were nothing but coyotes calling from the surrounding hills, the ghosts no more than fevered imaginings of gold-greedy men—not legendary dead men jealously guarding their treasure.

Dead men there were, no doubt. Buried in the mountains, trapped by their own stupidity, their own greed, when they refused to leave before the fierce, unmerciful summer came to the hills of Calagou, when the sun scorched their backs to cinder and fried their heads to madness.

But he, Regus, would be going in the springtime and would quit before the summer came.

They had agreed to go, were eager to go, for they were strong and courageous men. But above all, they were greedy men, possessing the one essential quality to override all fear, to scorn all tales, to laugh at all legends. They had the perfect combination—guts, and the greed for gold—and this pleased and suited Regus.

Calagou was to be his final venture, and his ultimate challenge. For the mountains were enormous, cragged and sheer, the canyons deep. One false move and hell could be waiting. But the rewards were greater than the dangers for any man brave enough—or fool enough—to try.

He'd been a fool! reflected Regus grimly. A fool to trust, a fool to take them. He should have gone alone. But how was he to have known?

And they had worked so hard. They had worked cheerfully, powerfully, pouring out their young strength into the great mountains, mining the areas where he had told them to dig and find.

And they had found—time and again, and again, and again . . .

The weeks had been gruelling, packed tight with work, but they had also packed their storehouse tight with gold, harrowed out of the hills from dawn till dusk and after, and in all that time no ghostly voices called them from the heights, no spectres rose to haunt their work-filled days and they found no signs of the legendary long-since dead guarding their gold from all who dared to come to the hills of Calagou.

They had even stood on the mountaintops, Talley, deSeegar and Carney, and called in strong and mirthful voices if ghosts there be to show themselves. They had laughed about the legends in the cool nights when they rested from their labours or counted their growing sacks of gold.

But they had laughed too long! thought Regus. And they had worked too long. They should have quit when he'd said, gone when he'd decided they should leave. They had a magnificent store of gold, beyond even his wildest hopes. They should have quit when they were ahead, packed up and ridden out.

The long hot days were coming, he had warned them. The heat would be unbearable, the days unendurable, the nights unsleepable. They had not believed him. Not with the golden fire in their veins, not with the dust of gold grimed in the sweat of their calloused hands, clinging to their tattered clothing, not with the bright knowledge of the gold as yet uncovered, the riches untouched. They knew it was there, as he knew it was there. More and more and more . . .

They had enough, he had urged them. Far, far more than enough, more than any man would need in his lifetime. But for them, enough was not sufficient. They wanted more. They had stayed for more. They had stayed one day too long, one week too many, one month too late.

The sun rose higher and fiercer in the long, hot days with no shade anywhere to receive them in rest from their labours. And at night even the shelter of their cabin was an oven for their baked and sweating bodies, a furnace of heat instead of a refuge.

At night, not even the coyotes called from the high hills about them and no birds flew in the fierce, bright scorch of days above the hills of Calagou.

Regus had begged them to pull out, but they would not. Then he himself would go, he had told them. He would take his share of gold and leave the mountains. But they needed him, they had said, to find more gold, and they would kill him if he tried to go. And he knew that they would have, without qualm or hesitation, for by this time they were all not a little mad.

At night, exhausted yet unrelenting, they took it in turns to guard him, lest in the dark he should take his share of gold and pull out on them.

But the day came when they could work no more, when their scorched and blistered bodies bowed beneath the increasing burn of the day. Their young strength broke and madness came upon them. Regus had done his best for them, though his own strength too was failing, but he buried them all eventually in the gold-flecked dirt of the mountains, in the last rich vein he had just uncovered before their strength gave out and the sun had robbed them of their reason.

And in the voiceless, windless, soundless silence, when the last echo of the last clod of earth upon their graves had died away, they came and stood before him, hating him, taunting him, reviling him, cursing him because they were dead.

Assuming that madness had come upon him too, he had crawled into the cabin and lain there. And all the while they cried to him and cursed him and tried to make him think that he was one of them, willing him to die—no, not to die—telling him, *telling* him, that he was already dead, that he, like them, would never leave the golden, ghostly hills of Calagou.

But he knew that he was not dead. Sick he was, delirious without doubt, but he was alive—and he had his shadow to prove it! And when his fever abated a little he had crawled out into the hot dust, that he might see his shadow and draw comfort from it, and by it know that he still lived.

But when the hot night brought its darkness again his shadow was no longer with him. And they came with their grey, gaunt faces, their dead voices, hating him, crying out for vengeance to which he knew they had no right. He had warned them, hadn't he, he'd told them. Had he not pleaded with them to leave? It had been their own fault they had died, their fault that he was stranded here, all food and water gone, the horses and pack mules dead.

His fever left him, but they did not. They walked with him or stood about him—gaunt, grey, haggard, dead. They stood on the high peaks at sunrise and looked down upon him. They stood on the edge of the canyons at sundown and cried to him and cursed him. They walked the beds of the dried-up creeks and mocked him.

But gradually his strength had returned, enough for him to make a rough sledge from the wood of the storehouse, to load it painfully and slowly with as much of the gold as it could bear—the gold garnered by four pairs of once willing hands throughout the cool sweet springtime of the hills of Calagou.

He had spent a night loading the sledge, dragging the gold bag by bag, inch by inch, until all was stacked and ready. He used his saddle rope to pull it by and he came down from the mountains, carefully, slowly, taking a full day, lest his precious load be spilled into the clefts and chasms of the hills of Calagou. And at night he had set out on his long, slow journey across the parched prairie, dragging his burden through the hot darkness, without his shadow . . . but not alone.

For *they* came with him. Shapes in the darkness, moving mists that called to him and taunted him and screamed at him that he was dead—dead with the gold, dead though he walked, dead though he hoped, dead though he thought that he lived.

'One of us, Regus! One of us! One of the walking dead!'

He had flung their taunts back at them, giving them shout for shout, curse for curse.

'Don't waste your eternity trying to drive me mad! I know that I live! For as long as I can cast my shadow I cannot be dead! As long as my shadow lives—*I* live!'

But they had not left him, they had not ceased to cry.

'One of us, Regus! One of us! Can you see your shadow, Regus? Tell us, Regus, where is your shadow?'

But he had lived. He had won through.

When the town was in sight he had hidden the gold. They had watched him as he buried it, silently grouped around him, ghosts in the sunlight, phantoms in the bright, bright day. But his shadow was with him now, and he drew strength from it.

He wondered if they would enter the town with him, if others would see them too. He knew that if he stayed, if they talked, if they cursed him, he must be careful not to show his awareness of their presence lest the townsfolk think that he was mad.

But at the prairie's end they faded as if the cooling air of the little valley town had blown away their images.

The inhabitants had believed him readily when he told of the greed of the others, their determination to stay on, their eventual deaths, his own sickness and the loss of their animals. Yes, they had believed him. Too many in the past had died defying the sun, too many had not come back. The fact that he had walked the long, dry prairie back, they had no trouble in believing either. Big Regus, strong, indomitable Regus, could outwork and outlive many a younger man.

But most of all they believed him because he had no gold. If he had come into town, dragging his laden sledge, he knew they would not have taken his word about the others' deaths. And because he was Regus they loaned to him fresh horses and mules, the necessities of his trade, accepting his promise to repay them as soon as he hit gold.

And at night he had returned to the desert, loaded the gold and ridden away—without his shadow, alone. His ghosts had left him. And there had been no sign nor sound of them, no sight nor breath nor cry of them . . . until yesterday.

He had thought he was safe here—a two-month ride and more from Calagou. They belonged in the hills there for they were dead there, Talley, deSeegar and Carney, buried there among the gold. *That's* where their ghosts belonged. But they had come the previous sundown, when his shadow had left him, they had come in the night, calling his name. And there was more than malice in their voices, more than cursing in their callings. There was triumph . . . exultation . . .

The sun was high now, warm, bright, comforting. Regus turned his eyes to his shadow and was reassured. No man could be dead and yet not know it. That was madness, against all reason—if reason still held, if he was still *able* to reason, if madness had not yet come upon him! For how does one know if one is mad? Maybe he was, and saw ghosts where there were none, heard voices calling when none called. Maybe it had started, his madness, back there in the mountains of Calagou, when he had buried them?

Maybe.

One thing he knew—he was not dead.

Regus paced the ground and his shadow walked beside him. And they came and stood about him, waiting . . .

He looked at his shadow, his precious sentinel of hope. As long as he could see it he was safe. But his soul was weighted down with an unaccustomed dread.

Then there was the sound of hoofs pounding, of distant riders coming. Regus looked beyond the ranch gates for a glimpse of the horsemen. They rode hard, rode fast.

And still they stood there, Carney, deSeegar and Talley transparent in the sunlight, silent and waiting, watching and waiting, and through them he could see the riders beyond the gates.

As they approached, Regus looked hard at the three men in the saddles. Their faces were grey with the stubble of many nights and days, their clothes white with prairie dust. They dismounted and strode towards him.

'You Regus?' asked one.

The eyes of his questioner were hard, cold, familiar, reminding Regus of someone. He glanced at the second man, at the also familiar features, and he looked at the third man and he knew that all three must be the fathers of the three men he had buried, of the three ghosts in the sunlight, silent, watching, waiting . . .

And he knew why one of the men had a coil of stout rope in his hands as they stood before him in the sunlight, blotting out his shadow, their eyes accusing him.

He tried to deny that he was Regus, but the words would not come. And he could only shake his head.

'He's Regus sure enough!' said the second man. 'The description tallies.'

'We trailed you, Regus!' said the third man, who held the rope. 'For two months and nigh on eighteen days we trailed you, Regus!'

'Then state your business,' said Regus defiantly.

The rope twitched in the man's hand.

'If it's about the animals I borrowed,' went on Regus, 'I long since paid my debts to Calagou.'

'Not *all* your debts, Regus!' snarled the man. 'Regus the great gold hunter, Regus the robber, Regus the killer!'

Regus glanced swiftly at the three ghosts standing silent, watching. He looked at Talley, gaunt and haggard, at deSeegar, his wild eyes fever-bright, at Carney, staring evilly, and on the faces of all three—triumph, a devil's leer of victory, of a battle about to be won. And he knew that *they* had guided their fathers here, in ways known only to the ghostly heart.

'Only *you* came back, Regus! Our sons were with you—but only you came back!'

'We don't know how you worked it, Regus, how you managed to get out of those mountains on foot and with all the gold, but we're sure you found a way, Regus! You found a way!'

'We don't care about the gold, Regus. But our sons were with you—and only you came back!'

He began to protest, to tell them how it was, but the rope was uncoiled now, swung high over a branch of the great tree, and the noose was about his neck and he was up on a horse and the sunlight exploded into darkness from which the morning would never break.

The three men turned from their deed, mounted their horses and rode out past their watching phantom sons. Before the sounds of the horses' hoofs had died away, the three ghosts moved towards the tree.

'One of us, Regus! One of us!' they chorused, and with that final triumphant cry they faded in sunlight and troubled Regus no more.

In the warm, bright sunny day, on the edge of the empty corral, Regus swung beneath the great tree.

And in the last companionship of death, his shadow swung beside him.

But Regus could no longer see it.

———————————

Frederick Forsyth

b. 1938

From childhood, Frederick Forsyth, author of best-selling novels
such as *The Day of the Jackal* and *The Odessa File*, longed for
adventure and passionately wanted to learn to fly. His dream
came true when he enlisted in the RAF for his national service,
where he became the air force's youngest pilot—an experience
that provided him with the background for this ghostly tale.

THE SHEPHERD

FOR A BRIEF MOMENT, while waiting for the control tower to clear me for
takeoff, I glanced out through the Perspex cockpit canopy at the surrounding German countryside. It lay white and crisp beneath the crackling
December moon.

Behind me lay the boundary fence of the Royal Air Force base, and beyond
the fence, as I had seen while swinging my little fighter into line with the takeoff
runway, the sheet of snow covering the flat farmland stretched away to the line
of the pine trees, two miles distant in the night yet so clear I could almost see the
shapes of the trees themselves.

Ahead of me, as I waited for the voice of the controller to come through the
headphones, was the runway itself, a slick black ribbon of tarmac, flanked by
twin rows of bright-burning lights, illuminating the solid path cut earlier by the
snowploughs. Behind the lights were the humped banks of the morning's snow,
frozen hard once again where the snowplough blades had pushed them. Far
away to my right, the airfield tower stood up like a single glowing candle amid
the brilliant hangars where the muffled aircraftmen were even now closing
down the station for the night.

Inside the control tower, I knew, all was warmth and merriment, the staff
waiting only for my departure to close down also, jump into the waiting cars,
and head back to the parties in the mess. Within minutes of my going, the
lights would die out, leaving only the huddled hangars, seeming hunched
against the bitter night, the shrouded fighter planes, the sleeping fuel-bowser
trucks, and, above them all, the single flickering station light, brilliant red
above the black-and-white airfield, beating out in Morse code the name of the

station—CELLE—to an unheeding sky. For tonight there would be no wandering aviators to look down and check their bearings; tonight was Christmas Eve, in the year of grace 1957, and I was a young pilot trying to get home to Blighty for his Christmas leave.

I was in a hurry and my watch read ten fifteen by the dim blue glow of the control panel where the rows of dials quivered and danced. It was warm and snug inside the cockpit, the heating turned up full to prevent the Perspex icing up. It was like a cocoon, small and warm and safe, shielding me from the bitter cold outside, from the freezing night that can kill a man inside a minute if he is exposed to it at six hundred miles an hour.

'Charlie Delta . . .'

The controller's voice woke me from my reverie, sounding in my headphones as if he were with me in the tiny cockpit, shouting in my ear. He's had a jar or two already, I thought. Strictly against orders, but what the hell? It's Christmas Eve.

'Charlie Delta . . . Control,' I responded.

'Charlie Delta, clear takeoff,' he said.

I saw no point in responding. I simply eased the throttle forward slowly with the left hand, holding the Vampire steady down the central line with the right hand. Behind me the low whine of the Goblin engine rose and rose, passing through a cry and into a scream. The snub-nosed fighter rolled, the lights each side of the runway passed in ever quicker succession, till they were flashing in a continuous blur. She became light, the nose rose fractionally, freeing the nose-wheel from contact with the runway, and the rumble vanished instantly. Seconds later the main wheels came away and their soft drumming also stopped. I held her low above the deck, letting the speed build up till a glance at the air-speed indicator told me we were through 120 knots and heading for 150. As the end of the runway whizzed beneath my feet I pulled the Vampire into a gently climbing turn to the left, easing up the undercarriage lever as I did so.

From beneath and behind me I heard the dull clunk of the wheels entering their bays and felt the lunge forward of the jet as the drag of the undercarriage vanished. In front of me the three red lights representing three wheels extinguished themselves. I held her into the climbing turn, pressing the radio button with the left thumb.

'Charlie Delta, clear airfield, wheels up and locked,' I said into my oxygen mask.

'Charlie Delta, roger, over to Channel D,' said the controller, and then, before I could change radio channels, he added, 'Happy Christmas.'

Strictly against the rules of radio procedure, of course. I was very young then, and very conscientious. But I replied, 'Thank you, Tower, and same to you.' Then I switched channels to tune into the RAF's North Germany Air Control frequency.

Down on my right thigh was strapped the map with my course charted on it in blue ink, but I did not need it. I knew the details by heart, worked out earlier with the navigation officer in the nav. hut. Turn overhead Celle airfield onto course 265 degrees, continue climbing to 27,000 feet. On reaching height, maintain course and keep speed to 485 knots. Check in with Channel D to let them know you're in their airspace, then a straight run over the Dutch coast south of the Bevelands into the North Sea. After forty-four minutes' flying time, change to Channel F and call Lakenheath Control to give you a 'steer'. Fourteen minutes later you'll be overhead Lakenheath. After that, follow instructions and they'll bring you down on a radio-controlled descent. No problem, all routine procedures. Sixty-six minutes' flying time, with the descent and landing, and the Vampire had enough fuel for over eighty minutes in the air.

Swinging over Celle airfield at 5,000 feet, I straightened up and watched the needle on my compass settle happily down on a course of 265 degrees. The nose was pointing towards the black, freezing vault of the night sky, studded with stars so brilliant they flickered their white fire against the eyeballs. Below, the black-and-white map of north Germany was growing smaller, the dark masses of the pine forests blending into the white expanses of the fields. Here and there a village or small town glittered with lights. Down there amid the gaily lit streets the carol singers would be out, knocking on the holly-studded doors to sing 'Silent Night' and collect *Pfennigs* for charity. The Westphalian housewives would be preparing hams and geese.

Four hundred miles ahead of me the story would be the same, the carols in my own language but many of the tunes the same, and it would be turkey instead of goose. But whether you call it *Weihnacht* or Christmas, it's the same all over the Christian world, and it was good to be going home.

From Lakenheath I knew I could get a lift down to London in the liberty bus, leaving just after midnight; from London I was confident I could hitch a lift to my parents' home in Kent. By breakfast time I'd be celebrating with my own family. The altimeter read 27,000 feet. I eased the nose forward, reduced throttle setting to give me an air speed of 485 knots and held her steady on 265 degrees. Somewhere beneath me in the gloom the Dutch border would be slipping away, and I had been airborne for twenty-one minutes. No problem.

The problem started ten minutes out over the North Sea, and it started so quietly that it was several minutes before I realised I had one at all. For some time I had been unaware that the low hum coming through my headphones into my ears had ceased, to be replaced by the strange nothingness of total silence. I must have been failing to concentrate, my thoughts being of home and my waiting family. The first thing I knew was when I flicked a glance downward to check my course on the compass. Instead of being rock-steady on 265 degrees, the needle was drifting lazily round the clock, passing through east, west, south and north with total impartiality.

I swore a most unseasonal sentiment against the compass and the instrument fitter who should have checked it for 100 per cent reliability. Compass failure at night, even a brilliant moonlit night such as the one beyond the cockpit Perspex, was no fun. Still, it was not too serious: there was a standby compass—the alcohol kind. But, when I glanced at it, that one seemed to be in trouble, too. The needle was swinging wildly. Apparently something had jarred the case—which isn't uncommon. In any event, I could call up Lakenheath in a few minutes and they would give me a GCA—Ground Controlled Approach—the second-by-second instructions that a well-equipped airfield can give a pilot to bring him home in the worst of weathers, following his progress on ultraprecise radar screens, watching him descend all the way to the tarmac, tracing his position in the sky yard by yard and second by second. I glanced at my watch: thirty-four minutes airborne. I could try to raise Lakenheath now, at the outside limit of my radio range.

Before trying Lakenheath, the correct procedure would be to inform Channel D, to which I was tuned, of my little problem, so they could advise Lakenheath that I was on my way without a compass. I pressed the TRANSMIT button and called: 'Celle, Charlie Delta, Celle, Charlie Delta, calling North Beveland Control . . .'

I stopped. There was no point in going on. Instead of the lively crackle of static and the sharp sound of my own voice coming back into my own ears, there was a muffled murmur inside my oxygen mask. My own voice speaking . . . and going nowhere. I tried again. Same result. Far back across the wastes of the black and bitter North Sea, in the warm, cheery concrete complex of North Beveland Control, men sat back from their control panel, chatting and sipping their steaming coffee and cocoa. And they could not hear me. The radio was dead.

Fighting down the rising sense of panic that can kill a pilot faster than anything else, I swallowed and slowly counted to ten. Then I switched to Channel F and tried to raise Lakenheath, ahead of me amid the Suffolk countryside, lying in its forest of pine trees south of Thetford, beautifully equipped with its GCA system for bringing home lost aircraft. On Channel F the radio was as dead as ever. My own muttering into the oxygen mask was smothered by the surrounding rubber. The steady whistle of my own jet engine behind me was my only answer.

It's a very lonely place, the sky, and even more so the sky on a winter's night. And a single-seater jet fighter is a lonely home, a tiny steel box held aloft on stubby wings, hurled through the freezing emptiness by a blazing tube throwing out the strength of six thousand horses every second. But the loneliness is offset, cancelled out, by the knowledge that at the touch of a button on the throttle, the pilot can talk to other human beings, people who care about him, men and women who staff a network of stations around the world; just one touch of that button, the TRANSMIT button, and scores of them in control towers across the land that are tuned to his channel can hear him call for help. When the pilot transmits, on every one of those screens a line of light streaks from the centre of the screen to the outside rim, which is marked with figures, from one to 360. Where the streak of light hits the ring, that is where the aircraft lies in relation to the control tower listening to him. The control towers are linked, so with two cross bearings they can locate his position to within a few hundred yards. He is not lost any more. People begin working to bring him down.

The radar operators pick up the little dot he makes on their screens from all the other dots; they call him up and give him instructions. 'Begin your descent now, Charlie Delta. We have you now . . .' Warm, experienced voices, voices which control an array of electronic devices that can reach out across the winter sky, through the ice and rain, above the snow and cloud, to pluck the lost one from his deadly infinity and bring him down to the flare-lit runway that means home and life itself.

When the pilot transmits. But for that he must have a radio. Before I had finished testing Channel J, the international emergency channel, and obtained the same negative result, I knew my ten-channel radio set was as dead as the dodo.

It had taken the RAF two years to train me to fly their fighters for them, and most of that time had been spent in training precisely for emergency procedures. The important thing, they used to say in flying school, is not to know how to fly in perfect conditions; it is to fly through an emergency and stay alive. Now the training was beginning to take effect.

While I was vainly testing my radio channels, my eyes scanned the instrument panel in front of me. The instruments told their own message. It was no coincidence the compass and the radio had failed together; both worked off the aircraft's electrical circuits. Somewhere beneath my feet, amid the miles of brightly coloured wiring that make up the circuits, there had been a main fuse blowout. I reminded myself, idiotically, to forgive the instrument fitter and blame the electrician. Then I took stock of the nature of my disaster.

The first thing to do in such a case, I remembered old Flight Sergeant Norris telling us, is to reduce throttle setting from cruise speed to a slower setting, to give maximum flight endurance.

'We don't want to waste valuable fuel, do we, gentlemen? We might need it later. So we reduce the power setting from 10,000 revolutions per minute to 7,200. That way we will fly a little slower, but we will stay in the air rather longer, won't we, gentlemen?' He always referred to us all being in the same emergency at the same time, did Sergeant Norris. I eased the throttle back and watched the rev counter. It operates on its own generator and so I hadn't lost that, at least. I waited until the Goblin was turning over at about 7,200 rpm, and felt the aircraft slow down. The nose rose fractionally, so I adjusted the flight trim to keep her straight and level.

The main instruments in front of a pilot's eyes are six, including the compass. The five others are the air-speed indicator, the altimeter, the vertical-speed indicator, the bank indicator (which tells him if he's banking, i.e., turning, to left or right), and the slip indicator (which tells him if he's skidding crabwise across the sky). Two of these are electrically operated, and they had gone the same way as my compass. That left me with the three pressure-operated instruments—air-speed indicator, altimeter and vertical-speed indicator. In other words, I knew how fast I was going, how high I was and if I were diving or climbing.

It is perfectly possible to land an aircraft with only these three instruments, judging the rest by those old navigational aids, the human eyes. Possible, that is, in conditions of brilliant weather, by daylight and with no cloud in the sky. It is possible, just possible, though not advisable, to try to navigate a fast-moving jet by dead reckoning, using the eyes, looking down and identifying the curve of the coast where it makes an easily recognisable pattern, spotting a strange-shaped reservoir, the glint of a river that the map strapped to the thigh says can only be the Ouse, or the Trent, or the Thames. From lower down it is possible to differentiate Norwich Cathedral tower from Lincoln Cathedral tower, if you know the countryside intimately. By night it is not possible.

The only things that show up at night, even on a bright moonlit night, are the lights. These have patterns when seen from the sky. Manchester looks different from Birmingham; Southampton can be recognised from the shape of its massive harbour and the Solent, cut out in black (the sea shows up black) against the carpet of the city's lights. I knew Norwich very well, and if I could identify the great curving bulge of the Norfolk coastline from Lowestoft, round through Yarmouth to Cromer, I could find Norwich, the only major sprawl of lights set twenty miles inland from all points on the coast. Five miles north of Norwich, I knew, was the fighter airfield of Merriam St George, whose red indicator beacon would be blipping out its Morse identification signal into the night. There, if they only had the sense to switch on the airfield lights when they heard me screaming at low level up and down the airfield, I could land safely.

I began to let the Vampire down slowly towards the oncoming coast, my mind feverishly working out how far behind schedule I was through the reduced speed. My watch told me forty-three minutes airborne. The coast of Norfolk had to be somewhere ahead of my nose, five miles below. I glanced up at the full moon, like a searchlight in the glittering sky, and thanked her for her presence.

As the fighter slipped towards Norfolk the sense of loneliness gripped me tighter and tighter. All those things that had seemed so beautiful as I climbed away from the airfield in Lower Saxony now seemed my worst enemies. The stars were no longer impressive in their brilliance; I thought of their hostility, sparkling away there in the timeless, lost infinities of endless space. The night sky, its stratospheric temperature fixed, night and day alike, at an unchanging fifty-six degrees below zero, became in my mind a limitless prison creaking with the cold. Below me lay the worst of them all, the heavy brutality of the North Sea, waiting to swallow up me and my plane and bury us for endless eternity in a liquid black crypt where nothing moved nor would ever move again. And no one would ever know.

At 15,000 feet and still diving, I began to realise that a fresh, and for me the last, enemy had entered the field. There was no ink-black sea three miles below me, no necklace of twinkling seaside lights somewhere up ahead. Far away, to right and left, ahead and no doubt behind me, the light of the moon reflected on a flat and endless sea of white. Perhaps only a hundred, two hundred feet thick, but enough. Enough to blot out all vision, enough to kill me. The East Anglian fog had moved in.

As I had flown westward from Germany, a slight breeze, unforeseen by the weathermen, had sprung up, blowing from the North Sea towards Norfolk. During the previous day the flat, open ground of East Anglia had been frozen hard by the wind and the subzero temperatures. During the evening the wind had moved a belt of slightly warmer air off the North Sea and onto the plains of East Anglia.

There, coming in contact with the ice-cold earth, the trillions of tiny moisture particles in the sea air had vaporised, forming the kind of fog that can blot out five counties in a matter of thirty minutes. How far westward it stretched I could not tell; to the West Midlands, perhaps, nudging up against the eastern slopes of the Pennines? There was no question of trying to overfly the fog to the westward; without navigational aids or radio, I would be lost over strange, unfamiliar country. Also out of the question was to try to fly back to Holland, to land at one of the Dutch Air Force bases along the coast there; I had not the fuel. Relying only on my eyes to guide me, it was a question of landing at Merriam St George or dying amid the wreckage of the Vampire somewhere in the fog-wreathed fens of Norfolk.

At 10,000 feet I pulled out of my dive, increasing power slightly to keep myself airborne, using up more of my precious fuel. Still a creature of my training, I recalled again the instructions of Flight Sergeant Norris:

'When we are totally lost above unbroken cloud, gentlemen, we must consider the necessity of bailing out of our aircraft, must we not?'

Of course, Sergeant. Unfortunately, the Martin Baker ejector seat cannot be fitted to the single-seat Vampire, which is notorious for being almost impossible to bail out of; the only two successful candidates living lost their legs in the process. Still, there has to be a lucky one. What else, Sergeant?

'Our first move, therefore, is to turn our aircraft towards the open sea, away from all areas of intense human habitation.'

You mean towns, Sergeant. Those people down there pay for us to fly for them, not to drop a screaming monster of ten tons of steel on top of them on Christmas Eve. There are kids down there, schools, hospitals, homes. You turn your aircraft out to sea.

The procedures were all worked out. They did not mention that the chances of a pilot, bobbing about on a winter's night in the North Sea, frozen face lashed by a subzero wind, supported by a yellow life jacket, ice encrusting his lips, eyebrows, ears, his position unknown by the men sipping their Christmas punches in warm rooms three hundred miles away—that his chances were less than one in a hundred of living longer than one hour. In the training films, they showed you pictures of happy fellows who had announced by radio that they were ditching, being picked up by helicopters within minutes, and all on a bright, warm summer's day.

'One last procedure, gentlemen, to be used in extreme emergency.'

That's better, Sergeant Norris, that's what I'm in now.

'All haircraft happroaching Britain's coasts are visible on the radar scanners of our early-warning system. If, therefore, we have lost our radio and cannot transmit our emergency, we try to attract the attention of our radar scanners by adopting an odd form of behaviour. We do this by moving out to sea, then flying in small triangles, turning left, left and left again, each leg of the triangle being of a duration of two minutes' flying time. In this way we hope to attract attention. When we have been spotted, the air-traffic controller is informed and he diverts another aircraft to find us. This other aircraft, of course, has a radio. When discovered by the rescue aircraft, we formate on him and he brings us down through the cloud or fog to a safe landing.'

Yes, it was the last attempt to save one's life. I recalled the details better now. The rescue aircraft which would lead you back to a safe landing, flying wing tip to wing tip, was called the shepherd. I glanced at my watch; fifty-one minutes airborne, about thirty minutes left of fuel. Then I looked at the fuel gauge and saw that I'd lost it along with the rest when the fuse blew. I had an icy moment until I remembered the worry button—which I could press to get an approximate reading. The fuel gauge read one-third full. Knowing myself to be still short of the Norfolk coast, and flying level at 10,000 feet in the moonlight, I pulled the Vampire into a left-hand turn and began my first leg of the first triangle. After two minutes, I pulled left again. Below me, the fog reached back as far as I could see, and ahead of me, towards Norfolk, it was the same.

Ten minutes went by, nearly two complete triangles. I had not prayed, not really prayed, for many years, and the habit came hard. Lord, please get me out of this bloody mess . . . No, you mustn't talk like that to Him. 'Our Father, which art in Heaven . . .' He'd heard that a thousand times, would be hearing it another thousand times tonight. What do you say to Him when you want help? Please, God, make somebody notice me up here; please make someone see me flying in triangles and send up a shepherd to help me down to a safe landing. Please help me, and I promise—What on earth could I promise Him? He had no need of me, and I, who now had need of Him, had taken no notice of Him for so long He'd probably forgotten all about me.

When I had been airborne for seventy-two minutes, I knew no one would come. The compass still drifted aimlessly through all the points of the circle, the other electrical instruments were dead, all their needles frozen at the point where they'd stopped. My altimeter read 7,000 feet, so I had dropped 3,000 feet while turning. No matter. The fuel read between zero and a quarter full—say ten minutes' more flying time. I felt the rage of despair welling up. I began screaming into the dead microphone:

'You stupid bastards, why don't you look at your radar screens? Why can't somebody see me up here? All so damn drunk you can't do your jobs properly. Oh, God, why won't somebody listen to me?' By then the anger had subsided and I had taken to blubbering like a baby from the sheer helplessness of it all.

Five minutes later, I knew, without any doubt of it, that I was going to die that night. Strangely I wasn't even afraid any more. Just enormously sad. Sad for all the things I would never do, the places I would never see, the people I would never greet again. It's a bad thing, a sad thing, to die at twenty years of age with your life unlived, and the worst thing of all is not the fact of dying but the fact of all the things never done.

Out through the Perspex I could see that the moon was setting, hovering above the horizon of thick white fog; in another two minutes the night sky would be plunged into total darkness, and a few minutes later I would have to bail out of a dying aircraft before it flicked over on its last dive into the North Sea. An hour later I would be dead also, bobbing around in the water, a bright-yellow Mae West supporting a stiff, frozen body. I dropped the left wing of the Vampire towards the moon to bring the aircraft on to the final leg of the last triangle.

Down below the wing tip, against the sheen of the fog bank, up-moon of me, a black shadow crossed the whiteness. For a second I thought it was my own shadow, but with the moon up there, my own shadow would be behind me. It was another aircraft, low against the fog bank, keeping station with me through my turn, a mile down through the sky towards the fog.

The other aircraft being below me, I kept turning, wing down, to keep it in sight. The other aircraft also kept turning, until the two of us had done one complete circle. Only then did I realise why it was so far below me, why he did not climb to my height and take up station on my wing tip. He was flying slower than I; he could not keep up if he tried to fly beside me. Trying hard not to believe he was just another aircraft, moving on his way, about to disappear for ever into the fog bank, I eased the throttle back and began to slip down towards him. He kept turning; so did I. At 5,000 feet I knew I was still going too fast for him. I could not reduce power any more for fear of stalling the Vampire and plunging down out of control. To slow up even more, I put out the air brakes. The Vampire shuddered as the brakes swung into the slipstream, slowing the Vampire down to 280 knots.

And then he came up towards me, swinging in towards my left-hand wing tip. I could make out the black bulk of him against the dim white sheet of fog below; then he was with me, a hundred feet off my wing tip, and we straightened out together, rocking as we tried to keep formation. The moon was to my right, and my own shadow masked his shape and form; but even so, I could make out the shimmer of two propellers whirling through the sky ahead of him. Of course, he could not fly at my speed; I was in a jet fighter, he in a piston-engined aircraft of an earlier generation.

He held station alongside me for a few seconds, down-moon of me, half invisible, then banked gently to the left. I followed, keeping formation with him, for he was obviously the shepherd sent up to bring me down, and he had the compass and the radio, not I. He swung through 180 degrees, then straightened up, flying straight and level, the moon behind him. From the position of the dying moon I knew we were heading back towards the Norfolk coast, and for the first time I could see him well. To my surprise, my shepherd was a De Havilland Mosquito, a fighter-bomber of Second World War vintage.

Then I remembered that the Meteorological Squadron at Gloucester used Mosquitoes, the last ones flying, to take samples of the upper atmosphere to help in the preparation of weather forecasts. I had seen them at Battle of Britain displays, flying their Mosquitoes in the flypasts, attracting gasps from the crowd and a few nostalgic shakes of the head from the older men, such as they always reserved on September 15 for the Spitfires, Hurricanes and Lancasters.

Inside the cockpit of the Mosquito I could make out, against the light of the moon, the muffled head of its pilot and the twin circles of his goggles as he looked out the side window towards me. Carefully, he raised his right hand till I could see it in the window, fingers straight, palm downward. He jabbed the fingers forward and down, meaning, 'We are going to descend; formate on me.'

I nodded and quickly brought up my own left hand so he could see it, pointing forward to my own control panel with one forefinger, then holding up five splayed fingers. Finally, I drew my hand across my throat. By common agreement this sign means I have only five minutes' fuel left, then my engine cuts out. I saw the muffled, goggled, oxygen-masked head nod in understanding, then we were heading downward towards the sheet of fog. His speed increased and I brought the air brakes back in. The Vampire stopped trembling and plunged ahead of the Mosquito. I pulled back on the throttle, hearing the engine die to a low whistle, and the shepherd was back beside me. We were diving straight towards the shrouded land of Norfolk. I glanced at my altimeter: 2,000 feet, still diving.

He pulled out at 300 feet; the fog was still below us. Probably the fog bank was only from the ground to 100 feet up, but that was more than enough to prevent a plane from landing without a GCA. I could imagine the stream of instructions coming from the radar hut into the earphones of the man flying beside me, eighty feet away through two panes of Perspex and the windstream of icy air moving between us at 280 knots. I kept my eyes on him, formating as closely as possible, afraid of losing sight for an instant, watching for his every hand signal. Against the white fog, even as the moon sank, I had to marvel at the beauty of his aircraft; the short nose and bubble cockpit, the blister of Perspex right in the nose itself, the long, lean, underslung engine pods, each housing a Rolls-Royce Merlin engine, a masterpiece of craftsmanship, snarling through the night towards home. Two minutes later he held up his clenched left fist in the window, then opened the fist to splay all five fingers against the glass. 'Please lower your undercarriage.' I moved the lever downward and felt the dull thunk as all three wheels went down, happily powered by hydraulic pressure and not dependent on the failed electrical system.

The pilot of the shepherd aircraft pointed down again, for another descent, and as he jinked in the moonlight I caught sight of the nose of the Mosquito. It had the letters JK painted on it, large and black. Probably for call sign Jig King. Then we were descending again, more gently this time.

He levelled out just above the fog layer, so low the tendrils of candy floss were lashing at our fuselages, and we went into a steady circular turn. I managed to flick a glance at my fuel gauge; it was on zero, flickering feebly. For God's sake, hurry up, I prayed, for if my fuel failed me now, there would be no time to climb to the minimum 700 feet needed for bailing out. A jet fighter at 100 feet without an engine is a death trap with no chance for survival.

For two or three minutes he seemed content to hold his slow circular turn, while the sweat broke out behind my neck and began to run in streams down my back, gumming the light nylon flying suit to my skin. HURRY UP, MAN, HURRY.

Quite suddenly he straightened out, so fast I almost lost him by continuing to turn. I caught him a second later and saw his left hand flash the 'dive' signal to me. Then he dipped towards the fog bank; I followed, and we were in it, a shallow, flat descent, but a descent nevertheless, and from a mere hundred feet, towards nothing.

To pass out of even dimly lit sky into cloud or fog is like passing into a bath of grey cotton wool. Suddenly there is nothing but the grey, whirling strands, a million tendrils reaching out to trap and strangle you, each one touching the cockpit cover with a quick caress, then disappearing back into nothingness. The visibility was down to near zero, no shape, no size, no form, no substance. Except that off my left wing tip, now only forty feet away, was the form of a Mosquito flying with absolute certainty towards something I could not see. Only then did I realise he was flying without lights. For a second I was amazed, horrified by my discovery; then I realised the wisdom of the man. Lights in fog are treacherous, hallucinatory, mesmeric. You can get attracted to them, not knowing whether they are forty or a hundred feet away from you. The tendency is to move towards them; for two aircraft in the fog, one flying formation on the other, that could spell disaster. The man was right.

Keeping formation with him, I knew he was slowing down, for I, too, was easing back the throttle, dropping and slowing. In a fraction of a second I flashed a glance at the two instruments I needed; the altimeter was reading zero, so was the fuel gauge, and neither was even flickering. The air-speed indicator, which I had also seen, read 120 knots—and this damn coffin was going to fall out of the sky at 95.

Without warning the shepherd pointed a single forefinger at me, then forward through the windscreen. It meant, 'There you are, fly on and land.' I stared forward through the now streaming windshield. Nothing. Then, yes, something. A blur to the left, another to the right, then two, one on each side. Ringed with haze, there were lights on either side of me, in pairs, flashing past. I forced my eyes to see what lay between them. Nothing, blackness. Then a streak of paint running under my feet. The centre line. Frantically I closed down the power and held her steady, praying for the Vampire to settle.

The lights were rising now, almost at eye level, and still she would not settle. Bang. We touched, we touched the flaming deck. Bang-bang. Another touch, she was drifting again, inches above the wet black runway. Bam-bam-bam-bam-babam-rumble. She was down; the main wheels had stuck and held.

The Vampire was rolling, at over ninety miles an hour, through a sea of grey fog. I touched the brakes and the nose slammed down on to the deck also. Slow pressure now, no skidding, hold her straight against the skid, more pressure on those brakes or we'll run off the end. The lights moving past more leisurely now, slowing, slower, slower . . .

The Vampire stopped. I found both of my hands clenched round the control column, squeezing the brake lever inward. I forget now how many seconds I held them there before I would believe we were stopped. Finally, I did believe it, put on the parking brake and released the main brake. Then I went to turn off the engine, for there was no use trying to taxi in this fog; they would have to tow the fighter back with a Land-Rover. There was no need to turn off the engine; it had finally run out of fuel as the Vampire careered down the runway. I shut off the remaining systems—fuel, hydraulics, electrics and pressurisation—and slowly began to unstrap myself from the seat and parachute/dinghy pack. As I did so, a movement caught my eye. To my left, through the fog, no more than fifty feet away, low on the ground with wheels up, the Mosquito roared past me. I caught the flash of the pilot's hand in the side window, then he was gone, up into the fog, before he could see my answering wave of acknowledgment. But I'd already decided to call up RAF Gloucester and thank him personally from the officers' mess.

With the systems off, the cockpit was misting up fast, so I released the canopy and wound the hood backward by hand until it locked. Only then, as I stood up, did I realise how cold it was. Against my heated body, dressed in a light nylon flying suit, it was freezing. I expected the control tower truck to be alongside in seconds, for, with an emergency landing, even on Christmas Eve, the fire truck, ambulance and half a dozen other vehicles were always standing by. Nothing happened. At least not for ten minutes.

By the time the two headlights came groping out of the mist, I felt frozen. The lights stopped twenty feet from the motionless Vampire, dwarfed by the fighter's bulk. A voice called, 'Hello there.'

I stepped out of the cockpit, jumped from the wing to the tarmac, and ran towards the lights. They turned out to be the headlamps of a battered old Jowett Javelin. Not an Air Force identification mark in sight. At the wheel of the car was a puffed, beery face and a handlebar moustache. At least he wore an RAF officer's cap. He stared at me as I loomed out of the fog.

'That yours?' He nodded towards the dim shape of the Vampire.

'Yes,' I said. 'I just landed it.'

''Straordinary,' he said, 'quite 'straordinary. You'd better jump in. I'll run you back to the mess.'

I was grateful for the warmth of the car, even more so to be alive.

Moving in bottom gear, he began to ease the old car back round the taxi track, evidently towards the control tower and, beyond it, the mess buildings. As we moved away from the Vampire, I saw that I had stopped twenty feet short of a ploughed field at the very end of the runway.

'You were damned lucky,' he said, or rather shouted, for the engine was roaring in first gear and he seemed to be having trouble with the foot controls. Judging by the smell of whisky on his breath, that was not surprising.

'Damned lucky,' I agreed. 'I ran out of fuel just as I was landing. My radio and all the electrical systems failed nearly fifty minutes ago over the North Sea.'

He spent several minutes digesting the information carefully.

''Straordinary,' he said at length. 'No compass?'

'No compass. Flying in the approximate direction by the moon. As far as the coast, or where I judged it to be. After that . . .'

'No radio?'

'No radio,' I said. 'A dead box on all channels.'

'Then how did you find this place?' he asked.

I was losing patience. The man was evidently one of those passed-over flight lieutenants, not terribly bright and probably not a flier, despite the handlebar moustache. A ground wallah. And drunk with it. Shouldn't be on duty at all on an operational station at that hour of the night.

'I was guided in,' I explained patiently. The emergency procedures, having worked so well, now began to seem run-of-the-mill; such is the recuperation of youth. 'I flew short, left-hand triangles, as per instructions, and they sent up a shepherd aircraft to guide me down. No problem.'

He shrugged, as if to say 'If you insist.' Finally, he said: 'Damned lucky, all the same. I'm surprised the other chap managed to find the place.'

'No problem there,' I said. 'It was one of the weather aircraft from RAF Gloucester. Obviously, he had radio. So we came in here in formation, on a GCA. Then, when I saw the lights at the threshold of the runway, I landed myself.'

The man was obviously dense, as well as drunk.

''Straordinary,' he said, sucking a stray drop of moisture off his handlebar. 'We don't have GCA. We don't have any navigational equipment at all, not even a beacon.'

Now it was my turn to let the information sink in.

'This isn't RAF Merriam St George?' I asked in a small voice.

He shook his head.

'Marham? Chicksands? Lakenheath?'

'No,' he said, 'this is RAF Minton.'

'I've never heard of it,' I said at last.

'I'm not surprised. We're not an operational station. Haven't been for years. Minton's a storage depot. Excuse me.'

He stopped the car and got out. I saw we were standing a few feet from the dim shape of a control tower adjoining a long row of Nissen huts, evidently once flight rooms, navigational and briefing huts. Above the narrow door at the base of the tower through which the officer had disappeared hung a single naked bulb. By its light I could make out broken windows, padlocked doors, an air of abandonment and neglect. The man returned and climbed shakily back behind the wheel.

'Just turning the runway lights off,' he said, and belched.

My mind was whirling. This was mad, crazy, illogical. Yet there had to be a perfectly reasonable explanation. 'Why did you switch them on?' I asked.

'It was the sound of your engine,' he said. 'I was in the officers' mess having a noggin, and old Joe suggested I listen out the window for a second. There you were, circling right above us. You sounded damn low, almost as if you were going to come down in a hurry. Thought I might be of some use, remembered they never disconnected the old runway lights when they dismantled the station, so I ran down to the control tower and switched them on.'

'I see,' I said, but I didn't. But there had to be an explanation.

'That was why I was so late coming out to pick you up. I had to go back to the mess to get the car out, once I'd heard you land out there. Then I had to find you. Bloody foggy night.'

You can say that again, I thought. The mystery puzzled me for another few minutes. Then I hit on the explanation.

'Where is RAF Minton, exactly?' I asked him.

'Five miles in from the coast, inland from Cromer. That's where we are,' he said.

'And where's the nearest operational RAF station with all the radio aids, including GCA?'

He thought for a minute.

'Must be Merriam St George,' he said. 'They must have all those things. Mind you, I'm just a stores johnny.'

That was the explanation. My unknown friend in the weather plane had been leading me straight in from the coast to Merriam St George. By chance, Minton, abandoned old stores depot Minton, with its cobwebbed runway lights and drunken commanding officer, lay right along the in-flight path to Merriam's runway. Merriam's controller had asked us to circle twice while he switched on his runway lights ten miles ahead, and this old fool had switched on his lights as well. Result: Coming in on the last ten-mile stretch, I had plonked my Vampire down on to the wrong airfield. I was about to tell him not to interfere with modern procedures that he couldn't understand when I choked the words back. My fuel had run out halfway down the runway. I'd never have made Merriam, ten miles away. I'd have crashed in the fields short of touchdown. By an amazing fluke I had been, as he said, damned lucky.

By the time I had worked out the rational explanation for my presence at this nearly abandoned airfield, we had reached the officers' mess. My host parked his car in front of the door and we climbed out. Above the entrance hall a light was burning, dispelling the fog and illuminating the carved but chipped crest of the Royal Air Force above the doorway. To one side was a board screwed to the wall. It read RAF STATION MINTON. To the other side was another board, announcing OFFICERS' MESS. We walked inside.

The front hall was large and spacious, but evidently built in the prewar years when metal window frames, service issue, were in fashion. The place reeked of the expression 'It has seen better days.' It had, indeed. Only two cracked-leather club chairs occupied the anteroom, which could have taken twenty. The cloak-room to the right contained a long-empty rail for nonexistent coats. My host, who told me he was Flight Lieutenant Marks, shrugged off his sheepskin coat and threw it over a chair. He was wearing his uniform trousers but with a chunky blue pullover for a jacket. It must be miserable to spend your Christmas on duty in a dump like this.

He told me he was the second-in-command, the CO being a squadron leader now on Christmas leave. Apart from him and his CO, the station boasted a sergeant, three corporals, one of whom was on Christmas duty and presumably in the corporals' mess also on his own, and twenty stores clerks, all away on leave. When not on leave, they spent their days classifying tons of surplus clothing, parachutes, boots and other impedimenta that go to make up a fighting service.

There was no fire in the vestibule, though there was a large brick fireplace, nor any in the bar, either. Both rooms were freezing cold, and I was beginning to shiver again after recovering in the car. Marks was putting his head through the various doors leading off the hall, shouting for someone called Joe. By looking through after him, I took in at a glance the spacious but deserted dining room, also fireless and cold, and the twin passages, one leading to the officers' private rooms, the other to the staff quarters. RAF messes do not vary much in architecture; once a pattern, always a pattern.

'I'm sorry it's not very hospitable, old boy,' said Marks, having failed to find the absent Joe. 'Being only the two of us on station here, and no visitors to speak of, we've each made two bedrooms into a sort of self-contained apartment where we live. Hardly seems worth using all this space just for the two of us. You can't heat it in winter, you know; not on the fuel they allow us. And you can't get the staff.'

It seemed sensible. In his position, I'd probably have done the same.

'Not to worry,' I said, dropping my flying helmet and attached oxygen mask on to the other leather chair in the anteroom. 'Though I could do with a bath and a meal.'

'I think we can manage that,' he said, trying hard to play the genial host. 'I'll get Joe to fix up one of the spare rooms—God knows we have enough of them—and heat up the water. He'll also rustle up a meal. Not much, I'm afraid. Bacon and eggs do?'

I nodded. By this time I presumed old Joe was the mess steward.

'That will do fine. While I'm waiting, do you mind if I use your phone?'

'Certainly, certainly, of course, you'll have to check in.'

He ushered me into the mess secretary's office, through a door beside the entrance to the bar. It was small and cold, but it had a chair, an empty desk and a telephone. I dialled 100 for the local operator and, while I was waiting, Marks returned with a tumbler of whisky. Normally, I hardly touch spirits, but it was warming, so I thanked him and he went off to supervise the steward. My watch told me it was close to midnight. Hell of a way to spend Christmas, I thought. Then I recalled how, thirty minutes earlier, I had been crying to God for a bit of help, and felt ashamed.

'Little Minton,' said a drowsy voice. It took ages to get through, for I had no telephone number for Merriam St George, but the girl got it eventually. Down the line I could hear the telephone operator's family celebrating in a back room, no doubt the living quarters attached to the village post office. After a few minutes, the phone was ringing.

'RAF Merriam St George,' said a man's voice. Duty sergeant speaking from the guardroom, I thought.

'Duty Controller, Air-Traffic Control, please,' I said. There was a pause.

'I'm sorry, sir,' said the voice, 'may I ask who's calling?'

I gave him my name and rank. Speaking from RAF Minton, I told him.

'I see, sir. But I'm afraid there's no flying tonight, sir. No one on duty in Air-Traffic Control. A few of the officers up in the mess, though.'

'Then give me the Station Duty Officer, please.'

When I got through to him, he was evidently in the mess, for the sound of lively talk could be heard behind him. I explained about the emergency and the fact that his station had been alerted to receive a Vampire fighter coming in on an emergency GCA without radio. He listened attentively. Perhaps he was young and conscientious, too, for he was quite sober, as a station duty officer is supposed to be at all times, even Christmas.

'I don't know about that,' he said at length. 'I don't think we've been operational since we closed down at five this afternoon. But I'm not on Air Traffic. Would you hold on? I'll get the wing commander—flying. He's here.'

There was a pause and then an older voice came on the line.

'Where are you speaking from?' he said, after noting my name, rank and the station at which I was based.

'RAF Minton, sir. I've just made an emergency landing here. Apparently, it's nearly abandoned.'

'Yes, I know,' he drawled. 'Damn bad luck. Do you want us to send a Tilly for you?'

'No, it's not that, sir. I don't mind being here. It's just that I landed at the wrong airfield. I believe I was heading for your airfield on a ground-controlled approach.'

'Well, make up your mind. Were you or weren't you? You ought to know. According to what you say, you were flying the damn thing.'

I took a deep breath and started at the beginning.

'So you see, sir, I was intercepted by the weather plane from Gloucester and he brought me in. But in this fog it must have been on a GCA. No other way to get down. Yet when I saw the lights of Minton, I landed here, assuming it to be Merriam St George.'

'Splendid,' he said at length. 'Marvellous bit of flying by that pilot from Gloucester. 'Course, those chaps are up in all weathers. It's their job. What do you want us to do about it?'

I was getting exasperated. Wing commander he might have been, but he had had a skinful this Christmas Eve.

'I am ringing to alert you to stand down your radio and traffic-control crews, sir. They must be waiting for a Vampire that's never going to arrive. It's already arrived—here at Minton.'

'But we're closed down,' he said. 'We shut all the systems down at five o'clock. There's been no call for us to turn out.'

'But Merriam St George has a GCA,' I protested.

'I know we have,' he shouted back. 'But it hasn't been used tonight. It's been shut down since five o'clock.'

I asked the next and last question slowly and carefully.

'Do you know, sir, where is the nearest RAF station that will be manning one-twenty-one-point-five-megacycle band throughout the night, the nearest station to here that maintains twenty-four-hour emergency listening?' The international aircraft-emergency frequency is 121.5 megacycles.

'Yes,' he said equally slowly. 'To the west, RAF Marham. To the south, RAF Lakenheath. Good night to you. Happy Christmas.'

I put the phone down and sat back and breathed deeply. Marham was forty miles away on the other side of Norfolk. Lakenheath was forty miles to the south, in Suffolk. On the fuel I was carrying, not only could I not have made Merriam St George, it wasn't even open. So how could I ever have got to

Marham or Lakenheath? And I had told that Mosquito pilot that I had only five minutes' fuel left. He had acknowledged that he understood. In any case, he was flying far too low after we dived into the fog ever to fly forty miles like that. The man must have been mad.

It began to dawn on me that I didn't really owe my life to the weather pilot from Gloucester, but to Flight Lieutenant Marks, beery, bumbling old passed-over Flight Lieutenant Marks, who couldn't tell one end of an aircraft from another but who had run four hundred yards through the fog to switch on the lights of an abandoned runway because he heard a jet engine circling overhead too close to the ground. Still, the Mosquito must be back at Gloucester by now and he ought to know that, despite everything, I was alive.

'Gloucester?' said the operator. 'At this time of night?'

'Yes,' I replied firmly, 'Gloucester, at this time of night.'

One thing about weather squadrons, they're always on duty. The duty meteorologist took the call. I explained the position to him.

'I'm afraid there must be some mistake, Flying Officer,' he said. 'It could not have been one of ours.'

'This *is* RAF Gloucester, right?'

'Yes, it is. Duty Officer speaking.'

'Fine. And your unit flies Mosquitoes to take pressure and temperature readings at altitude, right?'

'Wrong,' he said. 'We used to use Mosquitoes. They went out of service three months ago. We now use Canberras.'

I sat holding the telephone, staring at it in disbelief. Then an idea came to me.

'What happened to them?' I asked. He must have been an elderly boffin of great courtesy and patience to tolerate darn-fool questions at that hour.

'They were scrapped, I think, or sent off to museums, more likely. They're getting quite rare nowadays, you know.'

'I know,' I said. 'Could one of them have been sold privately?'

'I suppose it's possible,' he said at length. 'It would depend on Air Ministry policy. But I think they went to aircraft museums.'

'Thank you. Thank you very much. And Happy Christmas.'

I put the phone down and shook my head in bewilderment. What a night, what an incredible night! First I lose my radio and all my instruments, then I get lost and short of fuel, then I am taken in tow by some moonlighting harebrain with a passion for veteran aircraft flying his own Mosquito through the night, who happens to spot me, comes within an inch of killing me, and finally a half-drunk ground-duty officer has the sense to put his runway lights on in time to save me. Luck doesn't come in much bigger slices. But one thing was certain; that amateur air ace hadn't the faintest idea what he was doing. On the other hand, where would I be without him? I asked myself. Bobbing around dead in the North Sea by now.

I raised the last of the whisky to him and his strange passion for flying privately in outdated aircraft and tossed the drink down. Flight Lieutenant Marks put his head through the doorway.

'Your room's ready,' he said. 'Number seventeen, just down the corridor. Joe's making up a fire for you. The bath water's heating. If you don't mind, I think I'll turn in. Will you be all right on your own?'

I greeted him with more friendliness than last time, which he deserved.

'Sure, I'll be fine. Many thanks for all your help.'

I took my helmet and wandered down the corridor, flanked with the numbers of the bedrooms of bachelor officers long since posted elsewhere. From the doorway of seventeen, a bar of light shone out into the passage. As I entered the room an old man rose from his knees in front of the fireplace. He gave me a start. Mess stewards are usually RAF-enlisted men. This one was near seventy and obviously a locally recruited civilian employee.

'Good evening, sir,' he said. 'I'm Joe, sir. I'm the mess steward.'

'Yes, Joe, Mr Marks told me about you. Sorry to cause you so much trouble at this hour of the night. I just dropped in, as you might say.'

'Yes, Mr Marks told me. I'll have your room ready directly. Soon as this fire burns up, it'll be quite cosy.'

The chill had not been taken off the room and I shivered in the nylon flying suit. I should have asked Marks for the loan of a sweater but had forgotten.

I elected to take my lonely evening meal in my room, and while Joe went to fetch it, I had a quick bath, for the water was by then reasonably hot. While I towelled myself down and wrapped round me the old but warm dressing gown that old Joe had brought with him, he set out a small table and placed a plate of sizzling bacon and eggs on it. By then the room was comfortably warm, the coal fire burning brightly, the curtains drawn. While I ate, which took only a few minutes, for I was ravenously hungry, the old steward stayed to talk.

'You been here long, Joe?' I asked him, more out of politeness than genuine curiosity.

'Oh, yes, sir, nigh on twenty years; since just before the war, when the station opened.'

'You've seen some changes, eh? Wasn't always like this.'

'That it wasn't, sir, that it wasn't.' And he told me of the days when the rooms were crammed with eager young pilots, the dining room noisy with the clatter of plates and cutlery, the bar roaring with bawdy songs; of months and years when the sky above the airfield crackled and snarled to the sound of piston engines driving planes to war and bringing them back again.

While he talked I emptied the remainder of the half-bottle of red wine he had brought from the bar store. A very good steward was Joe. After finishing, I rose from the table, fished a cigarette from the pocket of my flying suit, lit it and sauntered round the room. The steward began to tidy up the plates and the glass from the table. I halted before an old photograph in a frame standing alone on the mantel above the crackling fire. I stopped with my cigarette half-raised to my lips, feeling the room go suddenly cold.

The photo was old and stained, but behind its glass it was still clear enough. It showed a young man of about my own years, in his early twenties, dressed in flying gear. But not the grey suit and gleaming plastic crash helmet of today. He wore thick sheepskin-lined boots, rough serge trousers and a heavy sheepskin zip-up jacket. From his left hand dangled one of the soft-leather flying helmets they used to wear, with goggles attached, instead of the modern pilot's tinted visor. He stood with legs apart, right hand on hip, a defiant stance, but he was not smiling. He stared at the camera with grim intensity. There was something sad about the eyes.

Behind him, quite clearly visible, stood his aircraft. There was no mistaking the lean, sleek silhouette of the Mosquito fighter-bomber, nor the two low-slung pods housing the twin Merlin engines that gave it its remarkable performance. I was about to say something to Joe when I felt the gust of cold air on my back. One of the windows had blown open and the icy air was rushing in.

'I'll close it, sir,' the old man said, and made to put all the plates back down again.

'No, I'll do it.'

It took me two strides to cross to where the window swung on its steel frame. To get a better hold, I stepped inside the curtain and stared out. The fog swirled in waves round the old mess building, disturbed by the current of warm air coming from the window. Somewhere, far away in the fog, I thought I heard the snarl of engines. There were no engines out there, just a motorcycle of some farm boy, taking leave of his sweetheart across the fens. I closed the window, made sure it was secure and turned back into the room.

'Who's the pilot, Joe?'

'The pilot, sir?'

I nodded towards the lonely photograph on the mantel.

'Oh, I see, sir. That's a photo of Mr John Kavanagh. He was here during the war, sir.'

He placed the wineglass on top of the topmost plate.

'Kavanagh?' I walked back to the picture and studied it closely.

'Yes, sir. An Irish gentleman. A very fine man, if I may say so. As a matter of fact, sir, this was his room.'

'What squadron was that, Joe?' I was still peering at the aircraft in the background.

'Pathfinders, sir. Mosquitoes, they flew. Very fine pilots, all of them, sir. But I venture to say I believe Mr Johnny was the best of them all. But then I'm biased, sir. I was his batman, you see.'

There was no doubting it. The faint letters on the nose of the Mosquito behind the figure in the photo read JK. Not Jig King, but Johnny Kavanagh.

The whole thing was clear as day. Kavanagh had been a fine pilot, flying with one of the crack squadrons during the war. After the war he'd left the Air Force, probably going into secondhand car dealing, as quite a few did. So he'd made a pile of money in the booming fifties, probably bought himself a fine country house, and had enough left over to indulge his real passion—flying. Or rather re-creating the past, his days of glory. He'd bought up an old Mosquito in one of the RAF periodic auctions of obsolescent aircraft, refitted it and flew it privately whenever he wished. Not a bad way to spend your spare time, if you had the money.

So he'd been flying back from some trip to Europe, had spotted me turning in triangles above the cloud bank, realised I was stuck and taken me in tow. Pinpointing his position precisely by crossed radio beacons, knowing this stretch of the coast by heart, he'd taken a chance on finding his old airfield at Minton, even in thick fog. It was a hell of a risk. But then I had no fuel left, anyway, so it was that or bust.

I had no doubt I could trace the man, probably through the Royal Aero Club.

'He was certainly a good pilot,' I said reflectively, thinking of this evening's performance.

'The best, sir,' said old Joe from behind me. 'They reckoned he had eyes like a cat, did Mr Johnny. I remember many's the time the squadron would return from dropping marker flares over bombing targets in Germany and the rest of the young gentlemen would go into the bar and have a drink. More likely several.'

'He didn't drink?' I asked.

'Oh, yes, sir, but more often he'd have his Mosquito refuelled and take off again alone, going back over the Channel or the North Sea to see if he could find some crippled bomber making for the coast and guide it home.'

I frowned. Those big bombers had their own bases to go to.

'But some of them would have taken a lot of enemy flak fire and sometimes they had their radios knocked out. All over, they came from. Marham, Scampton, Waddington; the big four-engined ones, Halifaxes, Stirlings and Lancasters; a bit before your time, if you'll pardon my saying so, sir.'

'I've seen pictures of them,' I admitted. 'And some of them fly in air parades. And he used to guide them back?'

I could imagine them in my mind's eye, gaping holes in the body, wings and tail, creaking and swaying as the pilot sought to hold them steady for home, a wounded or dying crew and the radio shot to bits. And I knew, from too recent experience, the bitter loneliness of the winter's sky at night, with no radio, no guide for home, and the fog blotting out the land.

'That's right, sir. He used to go up for a second flight in the same night, patrolling out over the North Sea, looking for a crippled plane. Then he'd guide it home, back here to Minton, sometimes through fog so dense you couldn't see your hand. Sixth sense, they said he had—something of the Irish in him.'

I turned from the photograph and stubbed my cigarette butt into the ashtray by the bed. Joe was at the door.

'Quite a man,' I said, and I meant it. Even today, middle-aged, he was a superb flier.

'Oh, yes, sir, quite a man, Mr Johnny. I remember him saying to me once, standing right where you are, before the fire: "Joe," he said, "whenever there's one of them out there in the night, trying to get back, I'll go out and bring him home."'

I nodded gravely. The old man so obviously worshipped his wartime officer.

'Well,' I said, 'by the look of it, he's still doing it.'

Now Joe smiled.

'Oh, I hardly think so, sir. Mr Johnny went out on his last patrol Christmas Eve 1943, just fourteen years ago tonight. He never came back, sir. He went down with his plane somewhere out there in the North Sea. Good night, sir. And Happy Christmas.'

Shamus Frazer

1912–1966

James Ian Arbuthnot Frazer, being of a retiring disposition, chose
to use a pen name, Shamus Frazer, for his small output of
published fiction. Despite their rarity, the fantasy novels he wrote
in the 1930s and 1940s still enjoy a considerable reputation, and
Florinda is one of the fine horror stories that he wrote for
magazines during the early 1960s.

FLORINDA

'DID YOU AND MISS REEVE have a lovely walk, darling?' Clare asked of the
child in the tarnished depths of glass before her.

'Well, it was lovely for me but not for Miss Reeve, because she tore her
stocking on a bramble, and it bled.'

'The stocking?'

'No, that ran a beautiful ladder,' said Jane very solemnly. 'But there were two
long tears on her leg as if a cat had scratched her. We were going along by the
path by the lake when the brambles caught her. She almost fell in. She did look
funny, Mummy, hopping on the bank like a hen blackbird a cat's playing
with—and squawking.'

'*Poor* Miss Reeve! . . . Your father's going to have that path cleared soon; it's
quite overgrown.'

'Oh, I hope not soon, Mummy. I love the brambly places, and what the birds
and rabbits'll do if they're cut down I can't imagine. The thickety bushes are all
hopping and fluttering with them when you walk. And the path wriggles as if it
were living, too—so you must lift your feet high and stamp on it, the way
Florinda does . . .'

But Clare was not listening any more. She had withdrawn her glance from
Jane's grave elfin features in the shadowed recesses of the glass to fix it on her
own image, spread as elegantly upon its surface as a swan.

'And if Daddy has the bushes cut down,' Jane went on, 'what will poor
Florinda do? Where will she play? There will be no place at all for the little
traps and snares she sets; no place for her to creep and whistle in, and tinkle into
laughter when something funny happens—like Miss Reeve caught by the leg

and hopping.' This was the time, when her mother was not listening, that Jane could talk most easily about Florinda. She looked at her mother's image, wrapt in the dull mysteries of grown-up thought within the oval Chippendale glass—and thence to the rococo frame of gilded wood in whose interlacing design two birds of faded gilt, a bat with a chipped wing and flowers whose golden petals and leaves showed here and there little spots and tips of white plaster like a disease, were all caught for ever.

'That's how I met Florinda.' She was chattering quite confidently, now that she knew that it was only to herself. 'I had been down to the edge of the lake where there are no brambles—you know, the *lawn* side; and I knelt down to look at myself in the water, *and there were two of me*. That's what I thought at first—two of me. And then I saw one was someone else—it was Florinda, smiling at me; but I couldn't smile back, not for anything. There we were like you and me in the glass—one smiling and one very solemn. Then Miss Reeve called and Florinda just *went*—and my face was alone and astonished in the water. She's shy, Florinda is—and sly, too. Shy and sly—that's Florinda for you.'

The repeated named stirred Clare to a vague consciousness: she had heard it on Jane's lips before.

'Who is Florinda?' she asked.

'Mummy, I've told you. She's a doll, I think, only large, large as me. And she never talks—not with words, anyway. And her eyes can't shut even when she lies down.'

'I thought she was called Arabella.'

'That's the doll Uncle Richard gave me last Christmas. Arabella *does* close her eyes when *she* lies down, and she says "Good night, Mamma", too, because of the gramophone record inside her. But Florinda's different. She's not a house doll. She belongs outside—though I *have* asked her to come to tea on Christmas Eve.'

'Well, darling, I've lots of letters to write, so just you run along to the nursery and have a lovely tea.'

So Florinda was a doll—an ideal doll, it seemed, that Jane had invented in anticipation of Christmas. Nine in the New Year, Jane was growing perhaps a little old for dolls. A strange child, thought Clare, difficult to understand. In that she took after her mother—though in looks it was her father she resembled. With a sigh Clare slid out the drawer of the mahogany writing desk. She distributed writing paper and envelopes, the Christmas cards (reproductions of Alken prints), in neat piles over the red leather—and, opening her address book, set herself to write.

ROGER CAME IN with the early December dusk. He had been tramping round the estate with Wakefield the agent, and the cold had painted his cheeks blue and nipped his nose red so that he looked like a large, clumsy gnome. He kissed Clare on the nape, and the icy touch of his nose spread gooseflesh over her shoulders.

'You go and pour yourself some whisky,' she said, 'and thaw yourself out by the fire. I'll be with you in a minute.' She addressed two more envelopes in her large clear hand, and then, without looking round, said: 'Have we bitten off rather more than we can chew?'

'There's an awful lot to be done,' said her husband from the fire, 'so much one hardly knows where to begin. The woods are a shambles—Nissen huts, nastiness and barbed wire. One would have thought Uncle Eustace would have made some effort to clear up the mess after the Army moved out . . .'

'But, darling, he never came back to live here. He was too wise.'

'Too ill and too old—and he never gave a thought to those who'd inherit the place, I suppose.'

'He never thought we'd be foolish enough to come and live here, anyway.'

Roger's uncle had died in a nursing home in Bournemouth earlier in the year, and Roger had come into these acres of Darkshire park and woodland, and the sombre peeling house, Fowling Hall, set among them. At Clare's urging he had tried to sell the place, but there were no offers. And now Roger had the obstinate notion of settling here, and trying to make pigs and chickens pay for the upkeep of the estate. Of course, Clare knew, there was something else behind this recent interest in the country life. Nothing had been said, but she knew what Roger wanted, and she knew, too, that he would hint at it again before long—the forbidden subject. She stacked her letters on the desk and went to join him by the fire.

'There's one thing you *can* do,' she said. 'Clear that path that goes round the lake. Poor Miss Reeve tore herself quite nastily on a bramble this afternoon, walking there.'

'I'll remind Wakefield to get the men on the job tomorrow. And what was Jane doing down by the lake just now as I came in? I called her and she ran off into the bushes.'

'My dear, Jane's been up in the nursery for the last hour or more. Miss Reeve's reading to her. You know, she's not allowed out this raw weather except when the sun's up. The doctor said—'

'Well, I wondered . . . I only glimpsed her—a little girl in the dusk. She ran off when I called.'

'One of the workmen's children, I expect.'

'Perhaps . . . Strange, I didn't think of that.'

He took a gulp of whisky, and changed the subject: 'Clare, it's going to cost the earth to put this place properly in order. It would be worth it if . . . if . . .' He added with an effort, 'I mean, if one thought it was leading anywhere . . .'

So it had come out, the first hint.

'You mean if we had a son, don't you? . . . Don't you, Roger?' She spoke accusingly.

'I merely meant . . . Well, yes—though, of course—'

She didn't let him finish. 'But you know what the doctor said after Jane.

You know how delicate she is . . . You can't want—?'

'If she had a brother—' Roger began.

Clare laughed, a sudden shiver of laughter, and held her hands to the fire.

'Roger, what an open hypocrite you are! "If she had a brother", when all the time you mean "if I had a son". And how could you be certain it wouldn't be a sister? No. Roger, we've had this out a thousand times in the past. It can't be done.' She shook her head and blinked at the fire. 'It wouldn't work out.'

ROGER WENT INTO THE NURSERY, as was his too irregular custom, to say good night to Jane. She was in her pink fleecy dressing gown, slippered toes resting on the wire fender, a bowl emptied of bread and milk on her knees. Miss Reeve was reading her a story about a princess who was turned by enchantment into a fox.

'Don't let me interrupt, Miss Reeve. I'll look in again later.'

'Oh, do come in, Mr Waley. We're almost ready for bed.'

'I was sorry to hear about your accident this afternoon.'

'It was such a silly thing, really. I caught my foot in a slipnoose of bramble. It was as if somebody had set it on the path on purpose, only that would be too ridiculous for words. But it was a shock—and I tore myself painfully, trying to get free.'

There was still the ghost of that panic, Roger noticed, in Miss Reeve's pasty, pudgy features, and signalling behind the round lenses of her spectacles. 'It's not a very nice path for a walk,' she added, 'but one can't keep Jane away from the lake.'

'I'm having all the undergrowth cleared away from the banks,' said Roger; 'that should make it easier walking.'

'Oh, that'll be ever so much nicer, Mr Waley.'

'Florinda won't like it,' thought Jane, sitting stiffly in her wicker chair by the fire. 'She won't like it at all. She'll be in a wicked temper will Florinda.' But she said aloud in a voice of small protest—for what was the use of speaking about Florinda to grown-ups—'It won't be nice at all. It will be quite horribly beastly.'

THE MEN DIDN'T CARE for the work they had been set to do. It was the skeletons, they said—and they prodded suspiciously with their implements at the little lumps of bone and feather and fur that their cutting and scything had revealed. There was a killer somewhere in the woods; owls said one, stoats said another, but old Renshawe said glumly it was neither bird nor beast, that it was Something-that-walked-that-shouldn't, and this infected the others with a derisive disquiet.

All the same, fifty yards of path were cleared during the morning, which took them beyond the small Doric pavilion that once served as boathouse and was reflected by a stone twin housing the lock mechanism on the eastern side of the lake.

Miss Reeve took Jane out in the afternoon to watch the men's progress. Jane ran ahead down the cleared path; paused at the pavilion to hang over the flaking balustrade and gaze down into the water; whispered something, shook her head and ran on.

'Hello, Mr Renshawe—*alone?*' she cried, as rounding a sudden twist in the path she came upon the old man hacking at the undergrowth. Renshawe started and cut short, and the blade bit into his foot. This accident stopped work for the day.

'It wasn't right, Miss Jane, to come on me like that,' he said, as they were helping him up to the house. 'You gave me a real turn. I thought—'

'I know,' said Jane, fixing him with her serious, puzzled eyes. 'And she *was* there, too, watching all the time.'

WHATEVER THE KILLER WAS, it moved its hunting-ground that night. Two White Orpingtons were found dead beside the arks next morning, their feathers scattered like snow over the bare ground.

'And it's not an animal, neither,' said Ron, the boy who carried the mash into the runs and had discovered the kill.

'What do you mean, it's not an animal?' asked Wakefield.

'I mean that their necks is wrung, Mr Wakefield.'

'Oh, get away!' said Wakefield.

But the following morning another hen was found lying in a mess of feathers and blood, and Wakefield reported to his master:

'It can't be it's a fox, sir. That head's not been bitten off. It's been pulled off, sir . . . And there was this, sir, was found by the arks.' It was a child's bracelet of blackened silver.

THE PATH WAS CLEARED, but on the farther side of the lake the shrubberies that melted imperceptibly into the tall woods bordered it closely. Here Jane dawdled on her afternoon walk. At the bend in the path near the boathouse she waited until her governess was out of sight—and then called softly into the gloom of yew and rhododendron and laurel, 'I think you're a beast, a *beast*! And I'm not going to be your friend any more, d'you hear? And you're *not* to come on Christmas Eve, even if you're starving.'

There was movement in the shadows, and she glimpsed the staring blue eyes and pinched face and the tattered satin finery. 'And it's no use following us, so there!' Jane stuck her tongue out as a gesture of defiance, and ran away along the path.

'Are you all right?' asked Miss Reeve, who had turned back to look for her. 'I thought I heard someone crying.'

'Oh, it's only Florinda,' said Jane, 'and she can sob her eyes out now for all I care.'

'Jane,' said Miss Reeve severely, 'how many more times have I to tell you Florinda is a naughty fib, and we shouldn't tell naughty fibs even in fun?'

'It's no fun,' said Jane, so low that Miss Reeve could hardly catch a word, 'no fun at all being Florinda.'

A HARD FROST SET IN overnight. It made a moon landscape of the park and woods, and engraved on the nursery windowpanes, sharply as with a diamond, intricate traceries of silver fern. The bark of the trees was patterned with frost like chain mail, and from the gaunt branches icicle daggers glinted in the sun. Each twig of the bare shrubs had budded its teardrops of ice. The surface of the lake was wrinkled and grey like the face of an old woman. 'And Wakefield says if it keeps up we may be able to skate on it on Boxing Day . . .' But by midday the temperature rose and all out of doors was filled with a mournful pattering and dripping.

Towards evening a dirty yellow glow showed in the sky, and furry black clouds moved up over the woods, bringing snow. It snowed after that for two days, and then it was Christmas Eve.

'YOU *LOOK* LIKE THE SNOW QUEEN, but you *smell* like the Queen of Sheba. Must you go out tonight, Mummy?'

'Darling, it's a bore. We promised Lady Graves, so we have to.'

'You should have kept your fingers crossed. But you'll be back soon?'

'In time to catch Father Christmas climbing down the chimneys, I expect.'

'But earlier than that—promise . . . ?'

'Much earlier than that. Daddy wants to get back early, anyway. He and Wakefield had a tiring night sitting up with a gun to guard their precious hens . . .'

'But she . . . it never came, did it?'

'Not *last* night. And now you go to lovely sleeps, and when you wake perhaps Father Christmas will have brought you Florinda in his—'

'No,' cried the child, 'not Florinda, Mummy, *please.*'

'What a funny thing you are,' said Clare, stooping to kiss her; 'you were quite silly about her a few days ago . . .'

Jane shivered and snuggled down in the warm bed.

'I've changed,' she said. 'We're not friends any more.'

After the lights were out, Jane imagined she was walking in the snow. The snowflakes fell as lightly as kisses, and soon they had covered her with a white, soft down. Now she knew herself to be a swan, and she tucked her head under a wing and so fell asleep on the dark rocking water.

But in the next room Miss Reeve, who had gone to bed early, could not sleep because of the wind that sobbed so disquietingly around the angles of the house. At last she put out a hand to the bedside table, poured herself water, groped for the aspirin bottle and swallowed down three tablets at a gulp. It was as she rescrewed the top, she noticed that it was not the aspirin bottle she was holding. She could have sworn that the sleeping tablets had been in her dressing-table drawer. Her first thought was that someone had changed the bottles on purpose, but that, she told herself, would be too absurd. There was nothing she could do about it. The crying of the wind mounted to shrill broken fluting that sounded oddly like children's laughter.

THE FIRST THING they noticed when the car drew up, its chained tyres grinding and clanking under the dark porch, was that the front door was ajar. 'Wait here,' said Roger to the chauffeur; 'there seem to have been visitors while we were away.'

Clare switched on the drawing-room lights, and screamed at the demoniac havoc they revealed, the chairs and tables overturned, the carpet a litter of broken porcelain, feathers from the torn cushions, and melting snow. Someone had thrown the heavy silver inkwell at the wall glass, which hung askew, its surface cracked and starred, and the delicate frame broken.

'No sane person—' Roger began.

But already Clare was running up the stairs to the nursery and screaming, 'Jane! . . . Jane!' as she ran.

The nursery was wrecked, too—the sheets clawed in strips, the floor a drift of feathers from the ripped pillows. Only the doll Arabella, with a shattered head, was propped up in the empty bed. When Clare touched her she fell backwards and began to repeat, 'Good night, Mamma!' as the mechanism inside her worked.

They found Jane's footsteps in the snow, leading over the lawn in the direction of the lake. Once they thought they saw her ahead of them, but it was only the snowman Roger had helped her to build during the afternoon. There was a misty moon, and by its light they followed the small naked footprints to the edge of the lake—but their eyes could make out nothing beyond the snow-fringed ice.

Roger had sent on the chauffeur to a bend in the drive where the car head-lights could illuminate the farther bank. And now, in the sudden glare, they saw in the dark centre of ice the two small figures. Jane in her nightdress, and beside her a little girl in old-fashioned blue satin who walked oddly and jerkily, lifting her feet and stamping them on the ice.

They called together, 'Jane! . . . Jane! Come back!'

She seemed to have heard, and she turned, groping towards the light. The other caught at her arm, and the two struggled together on the black, glassy surface. Then from the stars it seemed, and into their cold hearts, fell a sound like the snapping of a giant lute-string. The two tiny interlocked figures had disappeared, and the ice moaned and tinkled at the edges of the lake.

Elizabeth Gaskell

1810–1865

Mrs Gaskell is best known for her novels *Cranford* and *North and South* and for the biography of her friend Charlotte Brontë, but she also wrote Gothic stories. Charles Dickens, who was serialising *Cranford* in his magazine *Household Words*, asked her to write a story for him; the result was *The Old Nurse's Story*, her most successful and popular tale of the macabre.

THE OLD NURSE'S STORY

Y OU KNOW, MY DEARS, that your mother was an orphan, and an only child; and I dare say you have heard that your grandfather was a clergyman up in Westmorland, where I come from. I was just a girl in the village school, when, one day, your grandmother came in to ask the mistress if there was any scholar there who would do for a nursemaid; and mighty proud I was, I can tell ye, when the mistress called me up, and spoke to my being a good girl at my needle, and a steady honest girl, and one whose parents were very respectable, though they might be poor. I thought I should like nothing better than to serve the pretty young lady, who was blushing as deep as I was, as she spoke of the coming baby, and what I should have to do with it. However, I see you don't care so much for this part of my story, as for what you think is to come, so I'll tell you at once. I was engaged and settled at the parsonage before Miss Rosamond (that was the baby, who is now your mother) was born. To be sure, I had little enough to do with her when she came, for she was never out of her mother's arms, and slept by her all night long; and proud enough was I sometimes when missis trusted her to me. There never was such a baby before or since, though you've all of you been fine enough in your turns; but for sweet, winning ways, you've none of you come up to your mother. She took after her mother, who was a real lady born; a Miss Furnivall, a granddaughter of Lord Furnivall's, in Northumberland. I believe she had neither brother nor sister, and had been brought up in my lord's family till she had married your grandfather, who was just a curate, son to a shopkeeper in Carlisle—but a clever, fine gentleman as ever was—and one who was a right-down hard worker in his parish, which was very wide, and scattered all abroad over the Westmorland Fells. When your mother, little Miss Rosamond, was about four or five years old, both her parents died in a fortnight—one after the other. Ah! that was a sad time. My pretty young mistress and me was looking for another baby, when my master came home from one of his long rides, wet, and tired, and took the fever he died of; and then she never held up her head again, but just lived to see her dead baby, and have it laid on her breast before she sighed away her life. My mistress had asked me, on her deathbed, never to leave Miss Rosamond; but if she had never spoken a word, I would have gone with the little child to the end of the world.

The next thing, and before we had well stilled our sobs, the executors and guardians came to settle the affairs. They were my poor young mistress's own cousin, Lord Furnivall, and Mr Esthwaite, my master's brother, a shopkeeper in Manchester; not so well-to-do then as he was afterwards, and with a large family rising about him. Well! I don't know if it were their settling, or because of a letter my mistress wrote on her deathbed to her cousin, my lord; but somehow it was settled that Miss Rosamond and me were to go to Furnivall Manor House, in Northumberland, and my lord spoke as if it had been her mother's wish that she should live with his family, and as if he had no objections, for that one or two more or less could make no difference in so grand a household. So though that was not the way in which I should have wished the coming of my bright and pretty pet to have been looked at—who was like a sunbeam in any family, be it never so grand—I was well pleased that all the folks in the Dale should stare and admire, when they heard I was going to be young lady's maid at my Lord Furnivall's at Furnivall Manor.

But I made a mistake in thinking we were to go and live where my lord did. It turned out that the family had left Furnivall Manor House fifty years or more. I could not hear that my poor young mistress had ever been there, though she had been brought up in the family; and I was sorry for that, for I should have liked Miss Rosamond's youth to have passed where her mother's had been.

My lord's gentleman, from whom I asked so many questions as I durst, said that the Manor House was at the foot of the Cumberland Fells, and a very grand place; that an old Miss Furnivall, a great-aunt of my lord's, lived there, with only a few servants; but that it was a very healthy place, and my lord had thought that it would suit Miss Rosamond very well for a few years, and that her being there might perhaps amuse his old aunt.

I was bidden by my lord to have Miss Rosamond's things ready by a certain day. He was a stern proud man, as they say all the Lords Furnivall were; and he never spoke a word more than was necessary. Folk did say he had loved my young mistress; but that, because she knew that his father would object, she would never listen to him, and married Mr Esthwaite; but I don't know. He never married, at any rate. But he never took much notice of Miss Rosamond;

which I thought he might have done if he had cared for her dead mother. He sent his gentleman with us to the Manor House, telling him to join him at Newcastle that same evening; so there was no great length of time for him to make us known to all the strangers before he, too, shook us off; and we were left, two lonely young things (I was not eighteen), in the great old Manor House. It seems like yesterday that we drove there. We had left our own dear parsonage very early, and we had both cried as if our hearts would break, though we were travelling in my lord's carriage, which I thought so much of once. And now it was long past noon on a September day, and we stopped to change horses for the last time at a little smoky town, all full of colliers and miners. Miss Rosamond had fallen asleep, but Mr Henry told me to waken her, that she might see the park and the Manor House as we drove up. I thought it rather a pity; but I did what he bade me, for fear he should complain of me to my lord. We had left all signs of a town, or even a village, and were then inside the gates of a large wild park—not like the parks here in the north, but with rocks, and the noise of running water, and gnarled thorn trees, and old oaks, all white and peeled with age.

The road went up about two miles, and then we saw a great and stately house, with many trees close around it, so close that in some places their branches dragged against the walls when the wind blew; and some hung broken down; for no one seemed to take much charge of the place—to lop the wood, or to keep the moss-covered carriageway in order. Only in front of the house all was clear. The great oval drive was without a weed; and neither tree nor creeper was allowed to grow over the long, many-windowed front; at both sides of which a wing projected, which were each the ends of other side fronts; for the house, although it was so desolate, was even grander than I expected. Behind it rose the Fells, which seemed unenclosed and bare enough; and on the left hand of the house, as you stood facing it, was a little, old-fashioned flower garden, as I found out afterwards. A door opened out upon it from the west front; it had been scooped out of the thick dark wood for some old Lady Furnivall; but the branches of the great forest trees had grown and overshadowed it again, and there were very few flowers that would live there at that time.

When we drove up to the great front entrance, and went into the hall I thought we should be lost—it was so large, and vast, and grand. There was a chandelier all of bronze, hung down from the middle of the ceiling; and I had never seen one before, and looked at it all in amaze. Then, at one end of the hall, was a great fireplace, as large as the sides of the houses in my country, with massy andirons and dogs to hold the wood; and by it were heavy old-fashioned sofas. At the opposite end of the hall, to the left as you went in—on the western side—was an organ built into the wall, and so large that it filled up the best part of that end. Beyond it, on the same side, was a door; and opposite, on each side of the fireplace, were also doors leading to the east front; but those I never went through as long as I stayed in the house, so I can't tell you what lay beyond.

The afternoon was closing in, and the hall, which had no fire lighted in it, looked dark and gloomy, but we did not stay there a moment. The old servant, who had opened the door for us, bowed to Mr Henry, and took us in through the door at the further side of the great organ, and led us through several smaller halls and passages into the west drawing room, where he said that Miss Furnivall was sitting. Poor little Miss Rosamond held very tight to me, as if she were scared and lost in that great place, and as for myself, I was not much better. The west drawing room was very cheerful-looking, with a warm fire in it, and plenty of good, comfortable furniture about. Miss Furnivall was an old lady not far from eighty, I should think, but I do not know. She was thin and tall, and had a face as full of fine wrinkles as if they had been drawn all over it with a needle's point. Her eyes were very watchful, to make up, I suppose, for her being so deaf as to be obliged to use a trumpet. Sitting with her, working at the same great piece of tapestry, was Mrs Stark, her maid and companion, and almost as old as she was. She had lived with Miss Furnivall ever since they were both young, and now she seemed more like a friend than a servant; she looked so cold and grey, and stony as if she had never loved or cared for anyone; and I don't suppose she did care for anyone, except her mistress; and, owing to the great deafness of the latter, Mrs Stark treated her very much as if she were a child. Mr Henry gave some message from my lord, and then he bowed goodbye to us all—taking no notice of my sweet little Miss Rosamond's outstretched hand—and left us standing there, being looked at by the two old ladies through their spectacles.

I was right glad when they rung for the old footman who had shown us in at first, and told him to take us to our rooms. So we went out of that great drawing room, and into another sitting room, and out of that, and then up a great flight of stairs, and along a broad gallery—which was something like a library, having books all down one side, and windows and writing tables all down the other—till we came to our rooms, which I was not sorry to hear were just over the kitchens; for I began to think I should be lost in that wilderness of a house. There was an old nursery that had been used for all the little lords and ladies long ago, with a pleasant fire burning in the grate, and the kettle boiling on the hob, and tea-things spread out on the table; and out of that room was the night-nursery, with a little crib for Miss Rosamond close to my bed. And old James called up Dorothy, his wife, to bid us welcome; and both he and she were so hospitable and kind, that by and by Miss Rosamond and me felt quite at home; and by the time tea was over she was sitting on Dorothy's knee, and chattering away as fast as her little tongue could go. I soon found out that Dorothy was from Westmorland, and that bound her and me together, as it were; and I would never wish to meet with kinder people than were old James and his wife. James had lived pretty nearly all his life in my lord's family, and thought there was no one so grand as they. He even looked down a little on his wife, because, till he had married her, she had never lived in any but a farmer's household. But he was very fond of her, as well he might be. They had one servant under them, to do all the rough work. Agnes they called her; and she and me, and James and

Dorothy, with Miss Furnivall and Mrs Stark, made up the family; always remembering my sweet little Miss Rosamond! I used to wonder what they had done before she came, they thought so much of her now. Kitchen and drawing room, it was all the same. The hard, sad Miss Furnivall, and the cold Mrs Stark, looked pleased when she came fluttering in like a bird, playing and pranking hither and thither, with a continual murmur, and pretty prattle of gladness. I am sure, they were sorry many a time when she flitted away into the kitchen, though they were too proud to ask her to stay with them, and were a little surprised at her taste; though to be sure, as Mrs Stark said, it was not to be wondered at, remembering what stock her father had come of. The great, old rambling house was a famous place for little Miss Rosamond. She made expeditions all over it, with me at her heels; all, except the east wing, which was never opened, and whither we never thought of going. But in the western and northern part was many a pleasant room; full of things that were curiosities to us, though they might not have been to people who had seen more. The windows were darkened by the sweeping boughs of the trees, and the ivy which had overgrown them: but, in the green gloom, we could manage to see old China jars and carved ivory boxes, and great heavy books, and, above all, the old pictures!

Once, I remember, my darling would have Dorothy go with us to tell us who they all were; for they were all portraits of some of my lord's family, though Dorothy could not tell us the names of every one. We had gone through most of the rooms, when we came to the old state drawing room over the hall, and there was a picture of Miss Furnivall; or, as she was called in those days, Miss Grace, for she was the younger sister. Such a beauty she must have been! but with such a set, proud look, and such scorn looking out of her handsome eyes, with her eyebrows just a little raised, as if she were wondering how anyone could have the impertinence to look at her; and her lip curled at us, as we stood there gazing. She had a dress on, the like of which I had never seen before, but it was all the fashion when she was young: a hat of some soft white stuff like beaver, pulled a little over her brows, and a beautiful plume of feathers sweeping round it on one side; and her gown of blue satin was open in front to a quilted white stomacher.

'Well, to be sure!' said I, when I had gazed my fill. 'Flesh is grass, they do say; but who would have thought that Miss Furnivall had been such an out-and-out beauty, to see her now?'

'Yes,' said Dorothy. 'Folks change sadly. But if what my master's father used to say was true, Miss Furnivall, the elder sister, was handsomer than Miss Grace. Her picture is here somewhere; but, if I show it you, you must never let on, even to James, that you have seen it. Can the little lady hold her tongue, think you?' asked she.

I was not so sure, for she was such a little sweet, bold, open-spoken child, so I set her to hide herself; and then I helped Dorothy to turn a great picture, that leaned with its face towards the wall, and was not hung up as the others were.

To be sure, it beat Miss Grace for beauty; and, I think, for scornful pride, too, though in that matter it might be hard to choose. I could have looked at it an hour, but Dorothy seemed half frightened at having shown it to me, and hurried it back again, and bade me run and find Miss Rosamond, for that there were some ugly places about the house, where she should like ill for the child to go. I was a brave, high-spirited girl, and thought little of what the old woman said, for I liked hide-and-seek as well as any child in the parish; so off I ran to find my little one.

As winter drew on, and the days grew shorter, I was sometimes almost certain that I heard a noise as if someone was playing on the great organ in the hall. I did not hear it every evening; but, certainly, I did very often; usually when I was sitting with Miss Rosamond, after I had put her to bed, and keeping quite still and silent in the bedroom. Then I used to hear it booming and swelling away in the distance. The first night, when I went down to my supper, I asked Dorothy who had been playing music, and James said very shortly that I was a gowk to take the wind soughing among the trees for music: but I saw Dorothy look at him very fearfully, and Bessy, the kitchen maid, said something beneath her breath, and went quite white. I saw they did not like my question, so I held my peace till I was with Dorothy alone, when I knew I could get a good deal out of her. So, the next day, I watched my time, and I coaxed and asked her who it was that played the organ: for I knew that it was the organ and not the wind well enough, for all I had kept silence before James. But Dorothy had had her lesson, I'll warrant, and never a word could I get from her. So then I tried Bessy, though I had always held my head rather above her, as I was evened to James and Dorothy, and she was little better than their servant. So she said I must never, never tell; and if I ever told, I was never to say *she* had told me; but it was a very strange noise, and she had heard it many a time, but most of all on winter nights, and before storms; and folks did say, it was the old lord playing on the great organ in the hall, just as he used to do when he was alive; but who the old lord was, or why he played, and why he played on stormy winter evenings in particular, she either could not or would not tell me. Well! I told you I had a brave heart; and I thought it was rather pleasant to have that grand music rolling about the house, let who would be the player; for now it rose above the great gusts of wind, and wailed and triumphed just like a living creature, and then it fell to a softness most complete; only it was always music and tunes, so it was nonsense to call it the wind. I thought at first that it might be Miss Furnivall who played, unknown to Bessy; but one day when I was in the hall by myself, I opened the organ and peeped all about it and around it, as I had done to the organ in Crosthwaite Church once before, and I saw it was all broken and destroyed inside, though it looked so brave and fine; and then, though it was noonday, my flesh began to creep a little, and I shut it up, and run away pretty quickly to my own bright nursery; and I did not like hearing the music for some time after that, any more than James and Dorothy did. All this time Miss Rosamond was making herself more and more beloved. The old ladies liked her to dine with them at their early dinner; James stood behind Miss Furnivall's chair, and I behind Miss Rosamond's all in state; and, after dinner, she would play about in a corner of the great drawing room, as still as any mouse, while Miss Furnivall slept, and I had my dinner in the kitchen. But she was glad enough to come to me in the nursery afterwards; for, as she said, Miss Furnivall was so sad, and Mrs Stark so dull; but she and I were merry enough; and, by and by, I got not to care for that weird rolling music, which did one no harm, if we did not know where it came from.

That winter was very cold. In the middle of October the frosts began, and lasted many, many weeks. I remember, one day at dinner, Miss Furnivall lifted up her sad, heavy eyes, and said to Mrs Stark, 'I am afraid we shall have a terrible winter,' in a strange kind of meaning way. But Mrs Stark pretended not to hear, and talked very loud of something else. My little lady and I did not care for the frost; not we! As long as it was dry we climbed up the steep brows, behind the house, and went up on the Fells, which were bleak, and bare enough, and there we ran races in the fresh, sharp air; and once we came down by a new path that took us past the two old gnarled holly trees, which grew about halfway down by the east side of the house. But the days grew shorter and shorter; and the old lord, if it was he, played more and more stormily and sadly on the great organ. One Sunday afternoon—it must have been towards the end of November—I asked Dorothy to take charge of little Missey when she came out of the drawing room, after Miss Furnivall had had her nap; for it was too cold to take her with me to church, and yet I wanted to go. And Dorothy was glad enough to promise, and was so fond of the child that all seemed well; and Bessy and I set off very briskly, though the sky hung heavy and black over the white earth, as if the night had never fully gone away; and the air, though still, was very biting and keen.

'We shall have a fall of snow,' said Bessy to me. And sure enough, even while we were in church, it came down thick, in great large flakes, so thick it almost darkened the windows. It had stopped snowing before we came out, but it lay soft, thick and deep beneath our feet, as we tramped home. Before we got to the hall the moon rose, and I think it was lighter then—what with the moon, and what with the white dazzling snow—than it had been when we went to church, between two and three o'clock. I have not told you that Miss Furnivall and Mrs Stark never went to church: they used to read the prayers together, in their quiet gloomy way; they seemed to feel the Sunday very long without their tapestry work to be busy at. So when I went to Dorothy in the kitchen, to fetch Miss Rosamond and take her upstairs with me, I did not much wonder when the old woman told me that the ladies had kept the child with them, and that she had never come to the kitchen, as I had bidden her, when she was tired of behaving pretty in the drawing room. So I took off my things and went to find her, and bring her to her supper in the nursery. But when I went into the best drawing room there sat the two old ladies, very still and quiet, dropping out a word now and then but looking as if nothing so bright and merry as Miss Rosamond had ever been near them. Still I thought she might be hiding from me; it was one of her pretty ways; and that she had persuaded them to look as if they knew nothing about her; so I went softly peeping under this sofa, and behind that chair, making believe I was sadly frightened at not finding her.

'What's the matter, Hester?' said Mrs Stark, sharply. I don't know if Miss Furnivall had seen me, for, as I told you, she was very deaf, and she sat quite still, idly staring into the fire, with her hopeless face. 'I'm only looking for my little Rosy-Posy,' replied I, still thinking that the child was there, and near me, though I could not see her.

'Miss Rosamond is not here,' said Mrs Stark. 'She went away more than an hour ago to find Dorothy.' And she too turned and went on looking into the fire.

My heart sank at this, and I began to wish I had never left my darling. I went back to Dorothy and told her. James was gone out for the day, but she and me and Bessy took lights and went up into the nursery first, and then we roamed over the great large house, calling and entreating Miss Rosamond to come out of her hiding place, and not frighten us to death in that way. But there was no answer; no sound.

'Oh!' said I at last. 'Can she have got into the east wing and hidden there?'

But Dorothy said it was not possible, for that she herself had never been there; that the doors were always locked, and my lord's steward had the keys, she believed; at any rate, neither she nor James had ever seen them: so I said I would go back, and see if, after all, she was not hidden in the drawing room, unknown to the old ladies; and if I found her there, I said, I would whip her well for the fright she had given me; but I never meant to do it. Well, I went back to the west drawing room, and I told Mrs Stark we could not find her anywhere, and asked for leave to look all about the furniture there, for I thought now that she might have fallen asleep in some warm hidden corner; but no! we looked, Miss Furnivall got up and looked, trembling all over, and she was nowhere there; then we set off again, everyone in the house, and looked in all the places we had searched before, but we could not find her. Miss Furnivall shivered and shook so much that Mrs Stark took her back into the warm drawing room; but not before they had made me promise to bring her to them when she was found. Well-a-day! I began to think she never would be found, when I bethought me to look out into the great front court, all covered with snow. I was upstairs when I looked out; but it was such clear moonlight, I could see, quite plain, two little footprints, which might be traced from the hall door, and round the corner of the east wing. I don't know how I got down, but I tugged open the great, stiff hall door; and, throwing the skirt of my gown over my head for a cloak, I ran out. I turned the east corner, and there a black shadow fell on the snow; but when I came again into the moonlight, there were the little footmarks going up—up to the Fells. It was bitter cold; so cold that the air almost took the skin off my face as I ran, but I ran on, crying to think how my poor little darling must be perished, and frightened. I was within sight of the holly trees when I saw a shepherd coming down the hill, bearing something in his arms wrapped in his maud. He shouted to me, and asked me if I had lost a bairn; and, when I could not speak for crying, he bore towards me, and I saw my wee bairnie lying still, and white, and stiff, in his arms, as if she had been dead. He told me he had been up the Fells to gather in his sheep, before the deep cold of night came on, and that under the holly trees (black marks on the hillside, where no other bush was for miles around) he had found my little lady—my lamb—my queen—my darling—stiff and cold, in the terrible sleep which is frost-begotten. Oh! the joy, and the tears of having her in my arms once again! for I would not let him carry her; but took her, maud and all, into my own arms, and held her near my own warm neck and heart, and felt the life stealing slowly back again into her little gentle limbs. But she was still insensible when we reached the hall, and I had no breath for speech. We went in by the kitchen door.

'Bring the warming pan,' said I; and I carried her upstairs and began undressing her by the nursery fire, which Bessy had kept up. I called my little lammie all the sweet and playful names I could think of—even while my eyes were blinded by my tears; and at last, oh! at length she opened her large blue eyes. Then I put her into her warm bed, and sent Dorothy down to tell Miss Furnivall that all was well; and I made up my mind to sit by my darling's bedside the livelong night. She fell away into a soft sleep as soon as her pretty head had touched the pillow, and I watched by her until morning light; when she wakened up bright and clear—or so I thought at first—and, my dears, so I think now.

She said that she had fancied that she should like to go to Dorothy, for that both the old ladies were asleep, and it was very dull in the drawing room; and that, as she was going through the west lobby, she saw the snow through the high window falling—falling—soft and steady; but she wanted to see it lying pretty and white on the ground; so she made her way into the great hall; and then, going to the window, she saw it bright and soft upon the drive; but while she stood there, she saw a little girl, not so old as she was, 'but so pretty', said my darling, 'and this little girl beckoned to me to come out; and oh, she was so pretty and so sweet, I could not choose but go.' And then this other little girl had taken her by the hand, and side by side the two had gone round the east corner.

'Now you are a naughty little girl, and telling stories,' said I. 'What would your good mamma, that is in heaven, and never told a story in her life, say to her little Rosamond, if she heard her—and I dare say she does—telling stories!'

'Indeed, Hester,' sobbed out my child, 'I'm telling you true. Indeed I am.'

'Don't tell me!' said I, very stern. 'I tracked you by your footmarks through the snow; there were only yours to be seen: and if you had had a little girl to go hand in hand with you up the hill, don't you think the footprints would have gone along with yours?'

'I can't help it, dear, dear Hester,' said she, crying, 'if they did not; I never looked at her feet, but she held my hand fast and tight in her little one, and it was very, very cold. She took me up the Fell-path, up to the holly trees; and there I saw a lady weeping and crying; but when she saw me, she hushed her weeping, and smiled very proud and grand, and took me on her knee, and began to lull me to sleep; and that's all, Hester—but that is true; and my dear mamma knows it is,' said she, crying. So I thought the child was in a fever, and pretended to believe her, as she went over her story—over and over again, and always the same. At last Dorothy knocked at the door with Miss Rosamond's breakfast; and she told me the old ladies were down in the eating parlour, and that they wanted to speak to me. They had both been into the night-nursery the evening before, but it was after Miss Rosamond was asleep; so they had only looked at her—not asked me any questions.

'I shall catch it,' thought I to myself, as I went along the north gallery. 'And yet,' I thought, taking courage, 'it was in their charge I left her; and it's they that's to blame for letting her steal away unknown and unwatched.' So I went in boldly, and told my story. I told it all to Miss Furnivall, shouting it close to her ear; but when I came to the mention of the other little girl out in the snow, coaxing and tempting her out, and willing her up to the grand and beautiful lady by the holly tree, she threw her arms up—her old and withered arms—and cried aloud, 'Oh! Heaven, forgive! Have mercy!'

Mrs Stark took hold of her; roughly enough, I thought; but she was past Mrs Stark's management, and spoke to me, in a kind of wild warning and authority.

'Hester! keep her from that child! It will lure her to her death! That evil child! Tell her it is a wicked, naughty child.' Then Mrs Stark hurried me out of the room; where, indeed, I was glad enough to go; but Miss Furnivall kept shrieking out, 'Oh! have mercy! Wilt Thou never forgive! It is many a long year ago—'

I was very uneasy in my mind after that. I durst never leave Miss Rosamond, night or day, for fear lest she might slip off again, after some fancy or other; and all the more because I thought I could make out that Miss Furnivall was crazy, from their odd ways about her; and I was afraid lest something of the same kind (which might be in the family, you know) hung over my darling. And the great frost never ceased all this time; and whenever it was a more stormy night than usual, between the gusts, and through the wind, we heard the old lord playing on the great organ. But, old lord, or not, wherever Miss Rosamond went, there I followed; for my love for her, pretty helpless orphan, was stronger than my fear for the grand and terrible sound. Besides, it rested with me to keep her cheerful and merry, as beseemed her age. So we played together, and wandered together, here and there, and everywhere; for I never dared to lose sight of her again in that large and rambling house. And so it happened, that one afternoon, not long before Christmas Day, we were playing together on the billiard table in the great hall (not that we knew the way of playing, but she liked to roll the smooth ivory balls with her pretty hands, and I liked to do whatever she did); and, by and by, without our noticing it, it grew dusk indoors, though it was still light in the open air, and I was thinking of taking her back into the nursery, when, all of a sudden, she cried out:

'Look, Hester! look! there is my poor little girl out in the snow!'

I turned towards the long narrow windows, and there, sure enough, I saw a little girl, less than my Miss Rosamond—dressed all unfit to be out-of-doors such a bitter night—crying, and beating against the windowpanes, as if she wanted to be let in. She seemed to sob and wail, till Miss Rosamond could bear it no longer, and was flying to the door to open it, when, all of a sudden, and close up upon us, the great organ pealed out so loud and thundering, it fairly made me tremble; and all the more, when I remembered me that, even in the stillness of that dead-cold weather, I had heard no sound of little battering hands upon the window glass, although the phantom child had seemed to put forth all its force; and, although I had seen it wail and cry, no faintest touch of sound had fallen upon my ears. Whether I remembered all this at the very moment, I do not know; the great organ sound had so stunned me into terror; but this I know, I caught up Miss Rosamond before she got the hall door opened, and clutched her, and carried her away, kicking and screaming, into the large bright kitchen, where Dorothy and Agnes were busy with their mince pies.

'What is the matter with my sweet one?' cried Dorothy, as I bore in Miss Rosamond, who was sobbing as if her heart would break.

'She won't let me open the door for my little girl to come in; and she'll die if she is out on the Fells all night. Cruel, naughty Hester,' she said, slapping me; but she might have struck harder, for I had seen a look of ghastly terror on Dorothy's face, which made my very blood run cold.

'Shut the back-kitchen door fast, and bolt it well,' said she to Agnes. She said no more; she gave me raisins and almonds to quiet Miss Rosamond: but she sobbed about the little girl in the snow, and would not touch any of the good things. I was thankful when she cried herself to sleep in bed. Then I stole down to the kitchen, and told Dorothy I had made up my mind. I would carry my darling back to my father's house in Applethwaite: where, if we lived humbly, we lived at peace. I said I had been frightened enough with the old lord's organ-playing; but now that I had seen for myself this little moaning child, all decked out as no child in the neighbourhood could be, beating and battering to get in, yet always without any sound or noise—with the dark wound on its right shoulder; and that Miss Rosamond had known it again for the phantom that had nearly lured her to her death (which Dorothy knew was true); I would stand it no longer.

I saw Dorothy change colour once or twice. When I had done, she told me she did not think I could take Miss Rosamond with me, for that she was my lord's ward, and I had no right over her; and she asked me, would I leave the child that I was so fond of, just for sounds and sights that could do me no harm; and that they had all had to get used to in their turns? I was all in a hot, trembling passion; and I said it was very well for her to talk, that knew what these sights and noises betokened, and that had, perhaps, had something to do with the spectre child while it was alive. And I taunted her so, that she told me all she knew, at last; and then I wished I had never been told, for it only made me afraid more than ever.

She said she had heard the tale from old neighbours, that were alive when she was first married; when folks used to come to the hall sometimes, before it had got such a bad name on the countryside: it might not be true, or it might, what she had been told.

The old lord was Miss Furnivall's father—Miss Grace as Dorothy called her, for Miss Maude was the elder, and Miss Furnivall by rights. The old lord was eaten up with pride. Such a proud man was never seen or heard of; and his daughters were like him. No one was good enough to wed them, although they had choice enough; for they were the great beauties of their day, as I had seen by their portraits, where they hung in the state drawing room. But, as the old saying is, 'Pride will have a fall'; and these two haughty beauties fell in love with the same man, and he no better than a foreign musician, whom their father had down from London to play music with him at the Manor House. For, above all things, next to his pride, the old lord loved music. He could play on nearly every instrument that ever was heard of: and it was a strange thing it did not soften him; but he was a fierce dour old man, and had broken his poor wife's heart with his cruelty, they said. He was mad after music, and would pay any money for it. So he got this foreigner to come; who made such beautiful music, that they said the very birds on the trees stopped their singing to listen. And, by degrees, this foreign gentleman got such a hold over the old lord, that nothing would serve him but that he must come every year; and it was he that had the great organ brought from Holland, and built up in the hall, where it stood now. He taught the old lord to play on it; but many and many a time, when Lord Furnivall was thinking of nothing but his fine organ, and his finer music, the dark foreigner was walking abroad in the woods with one of the young ladies; now Miss Maude, and then Miss Grace.

Miss Maude won the day and carried off the prize, such as it was; and he and she were married, all unknown to anyone; and before he made his next yearly visit, she had been confined of a little girl at a farmhouse on the Moors, while her father and Miss Grace thought she was away at Doncaster Races. But though she was a wife and a mother, she was not a bit softened, but as haughty and as passionate as ever; and perhaps more so, for she was jealous of Miss Grace, to whom her foreign husband paid a deal of court—by way of blinding her—as he told his wife. But Miss Grace triumphed over Miss Maude, and Miss Maude grew fiercer and fiercer, both with her husband and with her sister; and the former—who could easily shake off what was disagreeable, and hide himself in foreign countries—went away a month before his usual time that summer, and half-threatened that he would never come back again. Meanwhile, the little girl was left at the farmhouse, and her mother used to have her horse saddled and gallop wildly over the hills to see her once every week, at the very least—for where she loved, she loved; and where she hated, she hated. And the old lord went on playing—playing on his organ; and the servants thought the sweet music he made had soothed down his awful temper, of which (Dorothy said) some terrible tales could be told. He grew infirm too, and had to walk with a crutch; and his son—that was the present Lord Furnivall's father—was with the army in America, and the other son at sea; so Miss Maude had it pretty much her own way, and she and Miss Grace grew colder and bitterer to each other every day; till at last they hardly ever spoke, except when the old lord was by. The foreign musician came again the next summer, but it was for the last time; for they led him such a life with their jealousy and their passions, that he grew weary, and went away, and never was heard of again. And Miss Maude, who had always meant to have her marriage acknowledged when her father should be dead, was left now a deserted wife—whom nobody knew to have been married—with a child that she dared not own, although she loved it to distraction; living with a father whom she feared, and a sister whom she hated. When the next summer passed over and the dark foreigner never came, both Miss Maude and Miss Grace grew gloomy and sad; they had a haggard look about them, though they looked handsome as ever. But by and by Miss Maude brightened; for her father grew more and more infirm, and more than ever carried away by his music; and she and Miss Grace lived almost entirely apart, having separate rooms, the one on the west side, Miss Maude on the east—those very rooms which were now shut up. So she thought she might have her little girl with her, and no one need ever know except those who dared not speak about it, and were bound to believe that it was, as she said, a cottager's child she had taken a fancy to. All this, Dorothy said, was pretty well known; but what came afterwards no one knew, except Miss Grace, and Mrs Stark, who was even then her maid, and much more of a friend to her than ever her sister had been. But the servants supposed, from words that were dropped, that Miss Maude had triumphed over Miss Grace, and told her that all the time the dark foreigner had been mocking her with pretended love—he was her own husband; the colour left Miss Grace's cheek and lips that very day for ever, and she was heard to say many a time that sooner or later she would have her revenge; and Mrs Stark was forever spying about the east rooms.

One fearful night, just after the New Year had come in, when the snow was lying thick and deep, and the flakes were still falling—fast enough to blind anyone who might be out and abroad—there was a great and violent noise heard, and the old lord's voice above all, cursing and swearing awfully—and the cries of a little child—and the proud defiance of a fierce woman—and the sound of a blow—and a dead stillness—and moans and wailings dying away on the hillside! Then the old lord summoned all his servants, and told them, with terrible oaths, and words more terrible, that his daughter had disgraced herself, and that he had turned her out-of-doors—her, and her child—and that if ever they gave her help—or food—or shelter—he prayed that they might never enter Heaven. And, all the while, Miss Grace stood by him, white and still as any stone; and when he had ended she heaved a great sigh, as much as to say her work was done, and her end was accomplished. But the old lord never touched his organ again, and died within the year; and no wonder! for, on the morrow of that wild and fearful night, the shepherds, coming down the Fellside, found Miss Maude sitting, all crazy and smiling, under the holly trees, nursing a dead child—with a terrible mark on its right shoulder. 'But that was not what killed it,' said Dorothy; 'it was the frost and the cold; every wild creature was in its hole, and every beast in its fold—while the child and its mother were turned out to wander on the Fells! And now you know all! and I wonder if you are less frightened now?'

I was more frightened than ever; but I said I was not. I wished Miss Rosamond and myself well out of that dreadful house for ever; but I would not leave her, and I dared not take her away. But oh! how I watched her, and guarded her! We bolted the doors and shut the window shutters fast, an hour or more before dark, rather than leave them open five minutes too late. But my little lady still heard the weird child crying and mourning; and not all we could do or say could keep her from wanting to go to her, and let her in from the cruel wind and the snow. All this time, I kept away from Miss Furnivall and Mrs Stark, as much as ever I could; for I feared them—I knew no good could be about them, with their grey hard faces, and their dreamy eyes, looking back into the ghastly years that were gone. But, even in my fear, I had a kind of pity—for Miss Furnivall, at least. Those gone down to the pit can hardly have a more hopeless look than that which was ever on her face. At last I even got so sorry for her—who never said a word but what was quite forced from her—that I prayed for her; and I taught Miss Rosamond to pray for one who had done a deadly sin; but often when she came to those words, she would listen, and start up from her knees, and say, 'I hear my little girl plaining and crying very sad—Oh! let her in, or she will die!'

One night—just after New Year's Day had come at last, and the long winter had taken a turn, as I hoped—I heard the west drawing-room bell ring three times, which was a signal for me. I would not leave Miss Rosamond alone, for all she was asleep—for the old lord had been playing wilder than ever—and I feared lest my darling should waken to hear the spectre child; see her I knew she could not. I had fastened the windows too well for that. So I took her out of her bed and wrapped her up in such outer clothes as were most handy, and carried her down to the drawing room, where the old ladies sat at their tapestry work as usual. They looked up when I came in, and Mrs Stark asked, quite astounded, 'Why did I bring Miss Rosamond there, out of her warm bed?' I had begun to whisper, 'Because I was afraid of her being tempted out while I was away, by the wild child in the snow,' when she stopped me short (with a glance at Miss

Furnivall), and said Miss Furnivall wanted me to undo some work she had done wrong, and which neither of them could see to unpick. So I laid my pretty dear on the sofa, and sat down on a stool by them, and hardened my heart against them, as I heard the wind rising and howling.

Miss Rosamond slept on sound, for all the wind blew so; and Miss Furnivall said never a word, nor looked round when the gusts shook the windows. All at once she started up to her full height, and put up one hand, as if to bid us listen.

'I hear voices!' said she, 'I hear terrible screams—I hear my father's voice!'

Just at that moment my darling wakened with a sudden start: 'My little girl is crying, oh, how she is crying!' and she tried to get up and go to her, but she got her feet entangled in the blanket, and I caught her up; for my flesh had begun to creep at these noises, which they heard while we could catch no sound. In a minute or two the noises came, and gathered fast, and filled our ears; we, too, heard voices and screams, and no longer heard the winter's wind that raged abroad. Mrs Stark looked at me, and I at her, but we dared not speak. Suddenly Miss Furnivall went towards the door, out into the anteroom, through the west lobby, and opened the door into the great hall. Mrs Stark followed, and I durst not be left, though my heart almost stopped beating for fear. I wrapped my darling tight in my arms, and went out with them. In the hall the screams were louder than ever; they sounded to come from the east wing—nearer and nearer—close on the other side of the locked-up doors—close behind them. Then I noticed that the great bronze chandelier seemed all alight, though the hall was dim, and that a fire was blazing in the vast hearth-place, though it gave no heat; and I shuddered up with terror, and folded my darling closer to me. But as I did so, the east door shook, and she, suddenly struggling to get free from me, cried, 'Hester! I must go! My little girl is there; I hear her; she is coming! Hester, I must go!'

I held her tight with all my strength; with a set will, I held her. If I had died, my hands would have grasped her still, I was so resolved in my mind. Miss Furnivall stood listening, and paid no regard to my darling, who had got down to the ground, and whom I, upon my knees now, was holding with both my arms clasped round her neck; she still striving and crying to get free.

All at once the east door gave way with a thundering crash, as if torn open in a violent passion, and there came into that broad and mysterious light, the figure of a tall old man, with grey hair and gleaming eyes. He drove before him, with many a relentless gesture of abhorrence, a stern and beautiful woman, with a little child clinging to her dress.

'O Hester! Hester!' cried Miss Rosamond. 'It's the lady! the lady below the holly trees; and my little girl is with her. Hester! Hester! let me go to her; they are drawing me to them. I feel them—I feel them. I must go!'

Again she was almost convulsed by her efforts to get away; but I held her tighter and tighter, till I feared I should do her a hurt; but rather that than let her go towards those terrible phantoms. They passed along towards the great hall door, where the winds howled and ravened for their prey; but before they reached that, the lady turned; and I could see that she defied the old man with a fierce and proud defiance; but then she quailed—and then she threw up her arms wildly and piteously to save her child—her little child—from a blow from his uplifted crutch.

And Miss Rosamond was torn as by a power stronger than mine, and writhed in my arms, and sobbed (for by this time the poor darling was growing faint).

'They want me to go with them on to the Fells—they are drawing me to them. Oh, my little girl! I would come, but cruel, wicked Hester holds me very tight.' But when she saw the uplifted crutch she swooned away, and I thanked God for it. Just at this moment—when the tall old man, his hair streaming as in the blast of a furnace, was going to strike the little shrinking child—Miss Furnivall, the old woman by my side, cried out, 'Oh, father! father! spare the little innocent child!' But just then I saw—we all saw—another phantom shape itself, and grow clear out of the blue and misty light that filled the hall; we had not seen her till now, for it was another lady who stood by the old man, with a look of relentless hate and triumphant scorn. That figure was very beautiful to look upon, with a soft white hat drawn down over the proud brows and a red and curling lip. It was dressed in an open robe of blue satin. I had seen that figure before. It was the likeness of Miss Furnivall in her youth; and the terrible phantoms moved on, regardless of old Miss Furnivall's wild entreaty—and the uplifted crutch fell on the right shoulder of the little child, and the younger sister looked on, stony and deadly serene. But at that moment the dim lights, and the fire that gave no heat, went out of themselves, and Miss Furnivall lay at our feet stricken down by the palsy—death-stricken.

Yes! she was carried to her bed that night never to rise again. She lay with her face to the wall muttering low but muttering alway: 'Alas! alas! what is done in youth can never be undone in age! What is done in youth can never be undone in age!'

Graham Greene

1904–1991

Graham Greene began his writing career while still at school and
had published his first novel by the time he was twenty-five.
Many successful novels, plays, films and short stories were to
follow. Fellow writer William Golding has described him as
being: 'In a class by himself ... the ultimate chronicler of
twentieth-century man's consciousness and anxiety.'

A LITTLE PLACE OFF THE EDGWARE ROAD

CRAVEN CAME UP PAST the Achilles statue in the thin summer rain. It was
only just after lighting-up time, but already the cars were lined up all
the way to the Marble Arch, and the sharp acquisitive faces peered out
ready for a good time with anything possible which came along. Craven went
bitterly by with the collar of his mackintosh tight round his throat: it was one
of his bad days.

All the way up the park he was reminded of passion, but you needed money
for love. All that a poor man could get was lust. Love needed a good suit, a car,
a flat somewhere, or a good hotel. It needed to be wrapped in cellophane. He
was aware all the time of the stringy tie beneath the mackintosh, and the
frayed sleeves: he carried his body about with him like something he hated.
(There were moments of happiness in the British Museum reading room, but
the body called him back.) He bore, as his only sentiment, the memory of ugly
deeds committed on park chairs. People talked as if the body died too soon—
that wasn't the trouble, to Craven, at all. The body kept alive—and through
the glittering tinselly rain, on his way to a rostrum, he passed a little man in a
black suit carrying a banner, 'The Body shall rise again.' He remembered a
dream from which three times he had woken trembling: he had been alone in

the huge dark cavernous burying ground of all the world. Every grave was connected to another under the ground: the globe was honeycombed for the sake of the dead, and on each occasion of dreaming he had discovered anew the horrifying fact that the body doesn't decay. There are no worms and dissolution. Under the ground the world was littered with masses of dead flesh ready to rise again with their warts and boils and eruptions. He had lain in bed and remembered—as 'tidings of great joy'—that the body after all was corrupt.

He came up into the Edgware Road walking fast—the Guardsmen were out in couples, great languid elongated beasts—the bodies like worms in their tight trousers. He hated them, and hated his hatred because he knew what it was, envy. He was aware that every one of them had a better body than himself: indigestion creased his stomach: he felt sure that his breath was foul—but who could he ask? Sometimes he secretly touched himself here and there with scent: it was one of his ugliest secrets. Why should he be asked to believe in the resurrection of this body he wanted to forget? Sometimes he prayed at night (a hint of religious belief was lodged in his breast like a worm in a nut) that *his* body at any rate should never rise again.

He knew all the side streets round the Edgware Road only too well: when a mood was on, he simply walked until he tired, squinting at his own image in the windows of Salmon & Gluckstein and the ABCs. So he noticed at once the posters outside the disused theatre in Culpar Road. They were not unusual, for sometimes Barclays Bank Dramatic Society would hire the place for an evening—or an obscure film would be trade-shown there. The theatre had been built in 1920 by an optimist who thought the cheapness of the site would more than counterbalance its disadvantage of lying a mile outside the conventional theatre zone. But no play had ever succeeded, and it was soon left to gather rat-holes and spider-webs. The covering of the seats was never renewed, and all that ever happened to the place was the temporary false life of an amateur play or a trade show.

Craven stopped and read—there were still optimists it appeared, even in 1939, for nobody but the blindest optimist could hope to make money out of the place as 'The Home of the Silent Film'. The first season of 'primitives' was announced (a highbrow phrase): there would never be a second. Well, the seats were cheap, and it was perhaps worth a shilling to him, now that he was tired, to get in somewhere out of the rain. Craven bought a ticket and went in to the darkness of the stalls.

In the dead darkness a piano tinkled something monotonous recalling Mendelssohn: he sat down in a gangway seat, and could immediately feel the emptiness all round him. No, there would never be another season. On the screen a large woman in a kind of toga wrung her hands, then wobbled with curious jerky movements towards a couch. There she sat and stared out like a sheepdog distractedly through her loose and black and stringy hair. Sometimes she seemed to dissolve altogether into dots and flashes and wiggly lines. A subtitle said, 'Pompilia betrayed by her beloved Augustus seeks an end to her troubles.'

Craven began at last to see—a dim waste of stalls. There were not twenty people in the place—a few couples whispering with their heads touching, and a number of lonely men like himself, wearing the same uniform of the cheap mackintosh. They lay about at intervals like corpses—and again Craven's obsession returned: the toothache of horror. He thought miserably—I am going mad: other people don't feel like this. Even a disused theatre reminded him of those interminable caverns where the bodies were waiting for resurrection.

'A slave to his passion Augustus calls for yet more wine.'

A gross middle-aged Teutonic actor lay on an elbow with his arm round a large woman in a shift. The Spring Song tinkled ineptly on, and the screen flickered like indigestion. Somebody felt his way through the darkness, scrabbling past Craven's knees—a small man: Craven experienced the unpleasant feeling of a large beard brushing his mouth. Then there was a long sigh as the newcomer found the next chair, and on the screen events had moved with such rapidity that Pompilia had already stabbed herself—or so Craven supposed—and lay still and buxom among her weeping slaves.

A low breathless voice sighed out close to Craven's ear, 'What's happened? Is she asleep?'

'No. Dead.'

'Murdered?' the voice asked with a keen interest.

'I don't think so. Stabbed herself.'

Nobody said 'Hush': nobody was enough interested to object to a voice. They drooped among the empty chairs in attitudes of weary inattention.

The film wasn't nearly over yet: there were children somehow to be considered: was it all going on to a second generation? But the small bearded man in the next seat seemed to be interested only in Pompilia's death. The fact that he had come in at that moment apparently fascinated him. Craven heard the word 'coincidence' twice, and he went on talking to himself about it in low out-of-breath tones. 'Absurd when you come to think of it,' and then, 'no blood at all'. Craven didn't listen: he sat with his hands clasped between his knees, facing the fact as he had faced it so often before, that he was in danger of going mad. He had to pull himself up, take a holiday, see a doctor (God knew what infection moved in his veins). He became aware that his bearded neighbour had addressed him directly. 'What?' he asked impatiently, 'what did you say?'

'There would be more blood than you can imagine.'

'What are you talking about?'

When the man spoke to him, he sprayed him with damp breath. There was a little bubble in his speech like an impediment. He said, 'When you murder a man . . .'

'This was a woman,' Craven said impatiently.

'That wouldn't make any difference.'

'And it's got nothing to do with murder anyway.'

'That doesn't signify.' They seemed to have got into an absurd and meaningless wrangle in the dark.

'I know, you see,' the little bearded man said in a tone of enormous conceit.

'Know what?'

'About such things,' he said with guarded ambiguity.

Craven turned and tried to see him clearly. Was he mad? Was this a warning of what he might become—babbling incomprehensibly to strangers in cinemas? He thought, By God, no, trying to see: I'll be sane yet. I *will* be sane. He could make out nothing but a small black hump of body. The man was talking to himself again. He said, 'Talk. Such talk. They'll say it was all for fifty pounds. But that's a lie. Reasons and reasons. They always take the first reason. Never look behind. Thirty years of reasons. Such simpletons,' he added again in that tone of breathlessness and unbounded conceit. So this was madness. So long as he could realise that, he must be sane himself—relatively speaking. Not so sane perhaps as the seekers in the park or the Guardsmen in the Edgware Road, but saner than this. It was like a message of encouragement as the piano tinkled on.

Then again the little man turned and sprayed him. 'Killed herself, you say? But who's to know that? It's not a mere question of what hand holds the knife.' He laid a hand suddenly and confidingly on Craven's: it was damp and sticky: Craven said with horror as a possible meaning came to him, 'What are you talking about?'

'I know,' the little man said. 'A man in my position gets to know almost everything.'

'What is your position?' Craven asked, feeling the sticky hand on his, trying to make up his mind whether he was being hysterical or not—after all, there were a dozen explanations—it might be treacle.

'A pretty desperate one *you'd* say.' Sometimes the voice almost died in the throat altogether. Something incomprehensible had happened on the screen—take your eyes from these early pictures for a moment and the plot had proceeded on at such a pace . . . Only the actors moved slowly and jerkily. A young woman in a nightdress seemed to be weeping in the arms of a Roman centurion: Craven hadn't seen either of them before. *'I am not afraid of death, Lucius—in your arms.'*

The little man began to titter—knowingly. He was talking to himself again. It would have been easy to ignore him altogether if it had not been for those sticky hands which he now removed: he seemed to be fumbling at the seat in front of him. His head had a habit of lolling sideways—like an idiot child's. He said distinctly and irrelevantly: 'Bayswater Tragedy.'

'What was that?' Craven said. He had seen those words on a poster before he entered the park.

'What?'

'About the tragedy.'

'To think they call Cullen Mews Bayswater.' Suddenly the little man began to cough—turning his face towards Craven and coughing right at him: it was like vindictiveness. The voice said, 'Let me see. My umbrella.' He was getting up.

'You didn't have an umbrella.'

'My umbrella,' he repeated. 'My—' and seemed to lose the word altogether. He went scrabbling out past Craven's knees.

Craven let him go, but before he had reached the billowy dusty curtains of the Exit the screen went blank and bright—the film had broken, and somebody immediately turned up one dirt-choked chandelier above the circle. It shone down just enough for Craven to see the smear on his hands. This wasn't hysteria: this was a fact. He wasn't mad: he had sat next to a madman who in some mews—what was the name, Colon, Collin . . . Craven jumped up and made his own way out: the black curtain flapped in his mouth. But he was too late: the man had gone and there were three turnings to choose from. He chose instead a telephone box and dialled with a sense odd for him of sanity and decision 999.

It didn't take two minutes to get the right department. They were interested and very kind. Yes, there had been a murder in a mews—Cullen Mews. A man's neck had been cut from ear to ear with a bread knife—a horrid crime. He began to tell them how he had sat next the murderer in a cinema: it couldn't be anyone else: there was blood on his hands—and he remembered with repulsion as he spoke the damp beard. There must have been a terrible lot of blood. But the voice from the Yard interrupted him. 'Oh no,' it was saying, 'we have the murderer—no doubt of it at all. It's the body that's disappeared.'

Craven put down the receiver. He said to himself aloud, 'Why should this happen to *me*? Why to *me*?' He was back in the horror of his dream—the squalid darkening street outside was only one of the innumerable tunnels connecting grave to grave where the imperishable bodies lay. He said, 'It was a dream, a dream,' and leaning forward he saw in the mirror above the telephone his own face sprinkled by tiny drops of blood like dew from a scent-spray. He began to scream, 'I won't go mad. I won't go mad. I'm sane. I won't go mad.' Presently a little crowd began to collect, and soon a policeman came.

L. P. Hartley

1895–1972

Established as a master of the macabre by two short-story volumes
early in his career, Leslie Poles Hartley then wrote novels that
explored psychological relationships, such as *The Go-Between*. Set
in Edwardian Norfolk, the book was made into a successful film.
In that novel, as in the story offered here, it is the innocence of the
child's viewpoint that gives events their power to disturb.

SOMEONE IN THE LIFT

'THERE'S SOMEONE COMING down in the lift, Mummy!'
'No, my darling, you're wrong, there isn't.'
'But I can see him through the bars—a tall gentleman.'
'You think you can, but it's only a shadow. Now, you'll see, the lift's empty.'
And it always was.

THIS PIECE OF DIALOGUE, or variations of it, had been repeated at intervals ever
since Mr and Mrs Maldon and their son Peter had arrived at the Brompton
Court Hotel, where, owing to a domestic crisis, they were going to spend
Christmas. New to hotel life, the little boy had never seen a lift before and he
was fascinated by it. When either of his parents pressed the button to summon it
he would take up his stand some distance away to watch it coming down.

The ground floor had a high ceiling, so the lift was visible for some seconds
before it touched floor level: and it was then, at its first appearance, that Peter
saw the figure. It was always in the same place, facing him in the left-hand
corner. He couldn't see it plainly, of course, because of the double grille, the gate
of the lift and the gate of the lift shaft, both of which had to be firmly closed
before the lift would work.

He had been told not to use the lift by himself—an unnecessary warning,
because he connected the lift with the things that grown-up people did, and

unlike most small boys he wasn't overanxious to share the privileges of his elders: he was content to wonder and admire. The lift appealed to him more as magic than as mechanism. Acceptance of magic made it possible for him to believe that the lift had an occupant when he first saw it, in spite of the demonstrable fact that when it came to rest, giving its fascinating click of finality, the occupant had disappeared.

'If you don't believe me, ask Daddy,' his mother said.

Peter didn't want to do this, and for two reasons, one of which was easier to explain than the other.

'Daddy would say I was being silly,' he said.

'Oh, no, he wouldn't; he never says you're silly.'

This was not quite true. Like all well-regulated modern fathers, Mr Maldon was aware of the danger of offending a son of tender years: the psychological results might be regrettable. But Freud or no Freud, fathers are still fathers, and sometimes when Peter irritated him Mr Maldon would let fly. Although he was fond of him, Peter's private vision of his father was of someone more authoritative and awe-inspiring than a stranger, seeing them together, would have guessed.

The other reason, which Peter didn't divulge, was more fantastic. He hadn't asked his father because, when his father was with him, he couldn't see the figure in the lift.

Mrs Maldon remembered the conversation and told her husband of it. 'The lift's in a dark place,' she said, 'and I dare say he does see something, he's so much nearer to the ground than we are. The bars may cast a shadow and make a sort of pattern that we can't see. I don't know if it's frightening him, but you might have a word with him about it.'

At first Peter was more interested than frightened. Then he began to evolve a theory. If the figure only appeared in his father's absence, didn't it follow that the figure might be, could be, must be, his own father? In what region of his consciousness Peter believed this it would be hard to say; but for imaginative purposes he did believe it and the figure became for him 'Daddy in the lift'. The thought of Daddy in the lift did frighten him, and the neighbourhood of the lift shaft, in which he felt compelled to hang about, became a place of dread.

Christmas Day was drawing near and the hotel began to deck itself with evergreens. Suspended at the foot of the staircase, in front of the lift, was a bunch of mistletoe, and it was this that gave Mr Maldon his idea.

As they were standing under it, waiting for the lift, he said to Peter:

'Your mother tells me you've seen someone in the lift who isn't there.'

His voice sounded more accusing than he meant it to, and Peter shrank.

'Oh, not now,' he said, truthfully enough. 'Only sometimes.'

'Your mother told me that you always saw it,' his father said, again more sternly than he meant to. 'And do you know who I think it may be?'

Caught by a gust of terror Peter cried, 'Oh please don't tell me!'

'Why, you silly boy,' said his father reasonably. 'Don't you want to know?'

Ashamed of his cowardice, Peter said he did.

'Why, it's Father Christmas, of course!'

Relief surged through Peter.

'But doesn't Father Christmas come down the chimney?' he asked.

'That was in the old days. He doesn't now. Now he takes the lift!'

Peter thought a moment.

'Will you dress up as Father Christmas this year,' he asked, 'even though it's an hotel?'

'I might.'

'And come down in the lift?'

'Why yes, that's what it's for.'

After this Peter felt happier about the shadowy passenger behind the bars. Father Christmas couldn't hurt anyone, even if he was (as Peter now believed him to be) his own father. Peter was only six but he could remember two Christmas Eves when his father had dressed up as Santa Claus and given him a delicious thrill. He could hardly wait for this one, when the apparition in the corner would at last become a reality.

Alas, two days before Christmas Day the lift broke down. On every floor it served, and there were five (six counting the basement), the forbidding notice 'Out of Order' dangled from the door handle. Peter complained as loudly as anyone, though secretly, he couldn't have told why, he was glad that the lift no longer functioned; and he didn't mind climbing the four flights to his room, which opened out of his parents' room but had its own door too. By using the stairs he met the workmen (he never knew on which floor they would be) and from them gleaned the latest news about the lift crisis. They were working over-time, they told him, and were just as anxious as he to see the last of the job. Sometimes they even told each other to put a jerk into it. Always Peter asked them when they would be finished, and they always answered, 'Christmas Eve at latest.'

Peter didn't doubt this. To him the workmen were infallible, possessed of magic powers capable of suspending the ordinary laws that governed lifts. Look how they left the gates open, and shouted to each other up and down the awesome lift shaft, paying as little attention to the other hotel visitors as if they didn't exist! Only to Peter did they vouchsafe a word.

But Christmas Eve came, the morning passed, the afternoon passed, and still the lift didn't go. The men were working with set faces and a controlled hurry in their movements; they didn't even return Peter's 'Good night' when he passed them on his way to bed. Bed! He had begged to be allowed to stay up this once for dinner; he knew he wouldn't go to sleep, he said, till Father Christmas came. He lay awake, listening to the urgent voices of the men, wondering if each hammer stroke would be the last; and then, just as the clamour was subsiding, he dropped off.

Dreaming, he felt adrift in time. Could it be midnight? No, because his parents had after all consented to his going down to dinner. Now was the time. Averting his eyes from the forbidden lift he stole downstairs. There was a clock in the hall, but it had stopped. In the dining room there was another clock; but dared he go into the dining room alone, with no one to guide him and everybody looking at him?

He ventured in, and there, at their table, which he couldn't always pick out, he saw his mother. She saw him, too, and came towards him, threading her way between the tables as if they were just bits of furniture, not alien islands under hostile sway.

'Darling,' she said, 'I couldn't find you—nobody could, but here you are!' She led him back and they sat down. 'Daddy will be with us in a minute.' The minutes passed; suddenly there was a crash. It seemed to come from within, from the kitchen, perhaps. Smiles lit up the faces of the diners. A man at a nearby table laughed and said, 'Something's on the floor! Somebody'll be for it!' 'What is it?' whispered Peter, too excited to speak out loud. 'Is anyone hurt?' 'Oh no, darling, somebody's dropped a tray, that's all.'

To Peter it seemed an anticlimax, this paltry accident that had stolen the thunder of his father's entry, for he didn't doubt that his father would come in as Father Christmas. The suspense was unbearable. 'Can I go into the hall and wait for him?' His mother hesitated and then said yes.

The hall was deserted, even the porter was off duty. Would it be fair, Peter wondered, or would it be cheating and doing himself out of a surprise, if he waited for Father Christmas by the lift? Magic has its rules which mustn't be disobeyed. But he was there now, at his old place in front of the lift; and the lift would come down if he pressed the button.

He knew he mustn't, that it was forbidden, that his father would be angry if he did; yet he reached up and pressed it.

But nothing happened, the lift didn't come, and why? Because some careless person had forgotten to shut the gates— 'monkeying with the lift', his father called it. Perhaps the workmen had forgotten, in their hurry to get home. There was only one thing to do—find out on which floor the gates had been left open, and then shut them.

On their own floor it was, and in his dream it didn't seem strange to Peter that the lift wasn't there, blocking the black hole of the lift shaft, though he daren't look down it. The gates clicked to. Triumph possessed him, triumph lent him wings; he was back on the ground floor, with his finger on the button. A thrill of power such as he had never known ran through him when the machinery answered to his touch.

But what was this? The lift was coming up from below, not down from above, and there was something wrong with its roof—a jagged hole that let the light through. But the figure was there in its accustomed corner, and this time it hadn't disappeared, it was still there, he could see it through the mazy crisscross of the bars, a figure in a red robe with white edges, and wearing a red cowl on its head: his father, Father Christmas, Daddy in the lift. But why didn't he look at Peter, and why was his white beard streaked with red?

The two grilles folded back when Peter pushed them. Toys were lying at his father's feet, but he couldn't touch them for they too were red, red and wet as the floor of the lift, red as the jag of lightning that tore through his brain . . .

William Hope Hodgson

The ghost stories of William Hope Hodgson always contain plenty of shocks and apparitions—more than enough to keep Carnacki, his expert psychic investigator, busy. In Edwardian England, when this story was published, psychic research was very fashionable. Carnacki, with his trunk full of scientific instruments, quickly gained a wide readership for his creator.

THE GATEWAY OF THE MONSTER

IN RESPONSE TO CARNACKI's usual card of invitation to have dinner and listen to a story, I arrived promptly at Cheyne Walk, to find the three others who were always invited to these happy little times there before me. Five minutes later Carnacki, Arkwright, Jessop, Taylor and I were all engaged in the 'pleasant occupation' of dining.

'You've not been long away this time,' I remarked as I finished my soup, forgetting, momentarily, Carnacki's dislike of being asked even to skirt the borders of his story until such time as he was ready. Then he would not stint words.

'No,' he replied with brevity, and I changed the subject, remarking that I had been buying a new gun, to which piece of news he gave an intelligent nod and a smile, which I think showed a genuinely good-humoured appreciation of my intentional changing of the conversation.

Later, when dinner was finished, Carnacki snugged himself comfortably down in his big chair, along with his pipe, and began his story, with very little circumlocution:

'As Dodgson was remarking just now, I've only been away a short time, and for a very good reason too—I've only been away a short distance. The exact locality I am afraid I must not tell you; but it is less than twenty miles from here; though, except for changing a name, that won't spoil the story. And it *is* a story too! One of the most extraordinary things I have ever run against.

'I received a letter a fortnight ago from a man I will call Anderson, asking for an appointment. I arranged a time and when he turned up I found that he wished me to look into, and see whether I could not clear up, a long-standing and well authenticated case of what he termed "haunting". He gave me very full particulars and, finally, as the thing seemed to present something unique, I decided to take it up.

'Two days later I drove up to the house late in the afternoon and discovered it a very old place, standing quite alone in its own grounds.

'Anderson had left a letter with the butler, I found, pleading excuses for his absence, and leaving the whole house at my disposal for my investigations.

'The butler evidently knew the object of my visit and I questioned him pretty thoroughly during dinner, which I had in rather lonely state. He is an elderly and privileged servant, and had the history of the Grey Room exact in detail. From him I learned more particulars regarding two things that Anderson had mentioned in but a casual manner. The first was that the door of the Grey Room would be heard in the dead of night to open, and slam heavily, and this even when the butler knew it was locked and the key on the bunch in his pantry. The second was that the bedclothes would always be found torn off the bed and hurled in a heap into a corner.

'But it was the door slamming that chiefly bothered the old butler. Many and many a time, he told me, had he lain awake and just shivered with fright, listening; for a time the door would be slammed time after time, thud! thud! thud! so that sleep was impossible.

'From Anderson, I knew already that the room had a history extending back over a hundred and fifty years. Three people had been strangled in it—an ancestor of his and his wife and child. This is authentic, as I had taken very great pains to make sure, so that you can imagine it was with a feeling that I had a striking case to investigate, that I went upstairs after dinner to have a look at the Grey Room.

'Peters, the butler, was in rather a state about my going, and assured me with much solemnity that in all the twenty years of his service, no one had ever entered that room after nightfall. He begged me in quite a fatherly way to wait till the morning when there could be no danger and then he could accompany me himself.

'Of course, I told him not to bother. I explained that I should do no more than look around a bit and perhaps fix a few seals. He need not fear, I was used to that sort of thing. But he shook his head when I said that.

'"There isn't many ghosts like ours, sir," he assured me with mournful pride. And by Jove he was right, as you will see.

'I took a couple of candles and Peters followed with his bunch of keys. He unlocked the door, but would not come inside with me. He was evidently in quite a fright and renewed his request that I would put off my examination until daylight. Of course I laughed at him, and told him he could stand sentry at the door and catch anything that came out.

'"It never comes outside, sir," he said, in his funny, old solemn manner.

Somehow he managed to make me feel as if I were going to have the creeps right away. Anyway, it was one to him, you know.

'I left him there and examined the room. It is a big apartment and well furnished in the grand style, with a huge four-poster which stands with its head to the end wall. There were two candles on the mantelpiece and two on each of the three tables that were in the room. I lit the lot and after that the room felt a little less inhumanly dreary, though, mind you, it was quite fresh and well kept in every way.

'After I had taken a good look round I sealed lengths of *bebe* ribbon across the windows, along the walls, over the pictures, and over the fireplace and the wall closets. All the time, as I worked, the butler stood just without the door and I could not persuade him to enter, though I jested with him a little as I stretched the ribbons and went here and there about my work. Every now and again he would say, "You'll excuse me, I'm sure, sir; but I do wish you would come out, sir. I'm fair in a quake for you."

'I told him he need not wait, but he was loyal enough in his way to what he considered his duty. He said he could not go away and leave me all alone there. He apologised, but made it very clear that I did not realise the danger of the room; and I could see, generally, that he was getting into a really frightened state. All the same I had to make the room so that I should know if anything material entered it, so I asked him not to bother me unless he really heard something. He was beginning to fret my nerves and the "feel" of the room was bad enough already, without making things any nastier.

'For a time further, I worked, stretching ribbons across a little above the floor and sealing them so that the merest touch would break the seals, were anyone to venture into the room in the dark with the intention of playing the fool.

'All this had taken me far longer than I had anticipated and, suddenly, I heard a clock strike eleven. I had taken off my coat soon after commencing work; now however, as I had practically made an end of all that I intended to do, I walked across to the settee and picked it up. I was in the act of getting into it when the old butler's voice (he had not said a word for the last hour) came sharp and frightened: "Come out, sir, quick! There's something going to happen!" Jove! but I jumped, and then in the same moment, one of the candles on the table to the left of the bed went out. Now whether it was the wind, or what, I do not know; but just for a moment I was enough startled to make a run for the door; though I am glad to say that I pulled up before I reached it. I simply could not bunk out with the butler standing there after having, as it were, read him a sort of lesson on "bein' brave, y'know". So I just turned right round, picked up the two candles off the mantelpiece, and walked across to the table near the bed. Well, I saw nothing. I blew out the candle that was still alight; then I went to those on the two other tables and blew them out. Then, outside of the door, the old man called again: "Oh! sir, do be told! Do be told!"

'"All right, Peters," I said, and by Jove, my voice was not as steady as I should have liked! I made for the door and had a bit of work not to start running. I took some thundering long strides, though, as you can imagine. Near the entrance I had a sudden feeling that there was a cold wind in the room. It was almost as if the window had been suddenly opened a little. I got to the door and the old butler gave back a step, in a sort of instinctive way.

'"Collar the candles, Peters!" I said, pretty sharply, and shoved them into his hands. I turned and caught the handle and slammed the door shut with a crash. Somehow, do you know, as I did so I thought I felt something pull back on it, but it must have been only fancy. I turned the key in the lock, and then again, double-locking the door.

'I felt easier then and set to and sealed the door. In addition I put my card over the keyhole and sealed it there, after which I pocketed the key and went downstairs—with Peters, who was nervous and silent, leading the way. Poor old beggar! It had not struck me until that moment that he had been enduring a considerable strain during the last two or three hours.

'About midnight I went to bed. My room lay at the end of the corridor upon which opens the door of the Grey Room. I counted the doors between it and mine and found that five rooms lay between. And I am sure you can understand that I was not sorry.

'Just as I was beginning to undress an idea came to me and I took my candle and sealing wax and sealed the doors of all the five rooms. If any door slammed in the night, I should know just which one.

'I returned to my room, locked myself in and went to bed. I was waked suddenly from a deep sleep by a loud crash somewhere out in the passage. I sat up in bed and listened, but heard nothing. Then I lit my candle. I was in the very act of lighting it when there came the bang of a door being violently slammed along the corridor.

'I jumped out of bed and got my revolver. I unlocked the door and went out into the passage, holding my candle high and keeping the pistol ready. Then a queer thing happened. I could not go a step towards the Grey Room. You all know I am not really a cowardly chap. I've gone into too many cases connected with ghostly things, to be accused of that; but I tell you I funked it, simply funked it, just like any blessed kid. There was something precious unholy in the air that night. I backed into my bedroom and shut and locked the door. Then I sat on the bed all night and listened to the dismal thudding of a door up the corridor. The sound seemed to echo through all the house.

'Daylight came at last and I washed and dressed. The door had not slammed for about an hour, and I was getting back my nerve again. I felt ashamed of myself, though in some ways it was silly, for when you're meddling with that sort of thing your nerve is bound to go, sometimes. And you just have to sit quiet and call yourself a coward until the safety of the day comes. Sometimes it is more than just cowardice, I fancy. I believe at times it is Something warning you and fighting *for* you. But all the same, I always feel mean and miserable after a time like that.

'When the day came properly I opened my door and keeping my revolver handy, went quietly along the passage. I had to pass the head of the stairs on the way, and who should I see coming up but the old butler, carrying a cup of coffee. He had merely tucked his nightshirt into his trousers and he'd an old pair of carpet slippers on.

'"Hello, Peters!" I said, feeling suddenly cheerful, for I was as glad as any lost child to have a live human being close to me. "Where are you off to with the refreshments?"

'The old man gave a start and slopped some of the coffee. He stared up at me and I could see that he looked white and done-up. He came on up the stairs and held out the little tray to me.

'"I'm very thankful indeed, sir, to see you safe and well," he said. "I feared one time you might risk going into the Grey Room, sir. I've lain awake all night, with the sound of the door. And when it came light I thought I'd make you a cup of coffee. I knew you would want to look at the seals, and somehow it seems safer if there's two, sir."

'"Peters," I said, "you're a brick. This is very thoughtful of you." And I drank the coffee. "Come along," I told him, and handed him back the tray. "I'm going to have a look at what the Brutes have been up to. I simply hadn't the pluck to in the night."

'"I'm very thankful, sir," he replied. "Flesh and blood can do nothing, sir, against devils, and that's what's in the Grey Room after dark."

'I examined the seals on all the doors as I went along and found them right, but when I got to the Grey Room, the seal was broken, though the visiting card over the keyhole was untouched. I ripped it off and unlocked the door and went in, rather cautiously, as you can imagine; but the whole room was empty of anything to frighten one; and there was heaps of light. I examined all my seals, and not a single one was disturbed. The old butler had followed me in, and suddenly he said, "The bedclothes, sir!"

'I ran up to the bed and looked over, and surely, they were lying in the corner to the left of the bed. Jove! you can imagine how queer I felt. Something *had* been in the room. I stared for a while from the bed to the clothes on the floor. I had a feeling that I did not want to touch either. Old Peters, though, did not seem to be affected that way. He went over to the bed-coverings and was going to pick them up, as doubtless he had done every day these twenty years back, but I stopped him. I wanted nothing touched until I had finished my examination. This I must have spent a full hour over and then I let Peters straighten up the bed, after which we went out and I locked the door, for the room was getting on my nerves.

'I had a short walk and then breakfast, which made me feel more my own man. Then to the Grey Room again, and with Peters's help and one of the maids, I had everything taken out except the bed, even the very pictures.

'I examined the walls, floor and ceiling then with probe, hammer and magnifying glass, but found nothing unusual. I can assure you I began to realise in very truth that some incredible thing had been loose in the room during the past night.

'I sealed up everything again and went out, locking and sealing the door as before.

'After dinner that night, Peters and I unpacked some of my stuff and I fixed up my camera and flashlight opposite to the door of the Grey Room with a string from the trigger of the flashlight to the door. You see, if the door really opened, the flashlight would blare out and there would be, possibly, a very queer picture to examine in the morning.

'The last thing I did before leaving was to uncap the lens and after that I went off to my bedroom and to bed, for I intended to be up at midnight, and to ensure this, I set my little alarm to call me; also I left my candle burning.

'The clock woke me at twelve and I got up and into my dressing gown and slippers. I shoved my revolver into my right side-pocket and opened my door. Then I lit my darkroom lamp and withdrew the slide so that it would give a clear light. I carried it up the corridor about thirty feet and put it down on the floor, with the open side away from me, so that it would show me anything that might approach along the dark passage. Then I went back and sat in the door-way of my room, with my revolver handy, staring up the passage towards the place where I knew my camera stood outside the door of the Grey Room.

'I should think I had watched for about an hour and a half, when suddenly I heard a faint noise away up the corridor. I was immediately conscious of a queer prickling sensation about the back of my head and my hands began to sweat a little. The following instant the whole end of the passage flicked into sight in the abrupt glare of the flashlight. Then came the succeeding darkness and I peered nervously up the corridor, listening tensely, and trying to find what lay beyond the faint, red glow of my dark-lamp, which now seemed ridiculously dim by contrast with the tremendous blaze of the flash powder . . . And then, as I stooped forward, staring and listening, there came the crashing thud of the door of the Grey Room. The sound seemed to fill the whole of the large corridor and go echoing hollowly through the house. I tell you, I felt horrible—as if my bones were water. Simply beastly. Jove! how I did stare and how I listened. And then it came again, thud, thud, thud, and then a silence that was almost worse than the noise of the door, for I kept fancying that some brutal thing was stealing upon me along the corridor.

'Suddenly, my lamp was put out, and I could not see a yard before me. I realised all at once that I was doing a very silly thing, sitting there, and I jumped up. Even as I did so, I *thought* I heard a sound in the passage, quite near to me. I made one backward spring into my room and slammed and locked the door.

'I sat on my bed and stared at the door. I had my revolver in my hand, but it seemed an abominably useless thing. Can you understand? I felt that there was something the other side of my door. For some unknown reason, I *knew* it was pressed up against the door, and it was soft. That was just what I thought. Most extraordinary thing to imagine, when you come to think of it!

'Presently I got hold of myself a bit and marked out a pentacle hurriedly with chalk on the polished floor and there I sat in it until it was almost dawn. And all the time, away up the corridor, the door of the Grey Room thudded at solemn and horrid intervals. It was a miserable, brutal night.

'When the day began to break, the thudding of the door came gradually to an end, and at last I grabbed together my courage and went along the corridor in the half-light, to cap the lens of my camera. I can tell you, it took some doing; but if I had not gone my photograph would have been spoilt, and I was tremendously keen to save it. I got back to my room and then set to and rubbed out the five-pointed star in which I had been sitting.

'Half an hour later there was a tap at my door. It was Peters, with my coffee. When I had drunk it we both walked along to the Grey Room. As we went, I had a look at the seals on the other doors, but they were untouched. The seal on the door of the Grey Room was broken, as also was the string from the trigger of the flashlight, but the visiting card over the keyhole was still there. I ripped it off and opened the door.

'Nothing unusual was to be seen, until we came to the bed; then I saw that, as on the previous day, the bedclothes had been torn off, and hurled into the left-hand corner, exactly where I had seen them before. I felt very queer, but I did not forget to look at the seals, only to find that not one had been broken.

'Then I turned and looked at old Peters and he looked at me, nodding his head.

'"Let's get out of here!" I said. "It's no place for any living human to enter without proper protection."

'We went out then and I locked and sealed the door, again.

'After breakfast I developed the negative, but it showed only the door of the Grey Room, half opened. Then I left the house, as I wanted to get certain matters and implements that might be necessary to life, perhaps to the spirit, for I intended to spend the coming night in the Grey Room.

'I got back in a cab about half past five with my apparatus, and this Peters and I carried up to the Grey Room where I piled it carefully in the centre of the floor. When everything was in the room, including a cat which I had brought, I locked and sealed the door and went towards my bedroom, telling Peters I should not be down to dinner. He said "Yes, sir", and went downstairs, thinking that I was going to turn in, which was what I wanted him to believe, as I knew he would have worried both himself and me if he had known what I intended.

'But I merely got my camera and flashlight from my bedroom and hurried back to the Grey Room. I entered and locked and sealed myself in and set to for I had a lot to do before it got dark.

'First I cleared away all the ribbons across the floor; then I carried the cat— still fastened in its basket—over towards the far wall and left it. I returned then to the centre of the room and measured out a space twenty-one feet in diameter which I swept with a "broom of hyssop". About this I drew a circle of chalk, taking care never to step over the circle.

'Beyond this I smudged, with a bunch of garlic, a broad belt right around the chalked circle, and when this was complete I took from among my stores in the centre a small jar of a certain water. I broke away the parchment and withdrew the stopper. Then, dipping my left forefinger in the little jar I went round the circle again, making upon the floor, just within the line of chalk, the Second Sign of the Saaamaaa Ritual, and joining each Sign most carefully with the left-handed crescent. I can tell you, I felt easier when this was done and the "water-circle" complete.

'Then I unpacked some more of the stuff that I had brought and placed a lighted candle in the "valley" of each crescent. After that I drew a pentacle so that each of the five points of the defensive star touched the chalk circle. In the five points of the star I placed five portions of a certain bread, each wrapped in linen; and in the five "vales", five opened jars of the water I had used to make the "water-circle". And now I had my first protective barrier complete.

'Now anyone, except you who know something of my methods of investigation, might consider all this a piece of useless and foolish superstition; but you all remember the Black Veil case, in which I believe my life was saved by a very similar form of protection; whilst Aster, who sneered at it and would not come inside, died.

'I got the idea from the *Sigsand MS*, written, so far as I can make out, in the fourteenth century. At first, naturally, I imagined it was just an expression of the superstition of his time, and it was not until long after my first reading that it occurred to me to test his "Defence", which I did, as I've just said, in that horrible Black Veil business. You know how *that* turned out. Later I used it several times and always I came through safe, until that Noving Fur case. It was only a partial "Defence" there and I nearly died in the pentacle. After that I came across Professor Garder's "Experiments with a Medium". When they surrounded the Medium with a current of a certain number of vibrations in vacuum, he lost his position—almost as if it cut him off from the Immaterial.

'That made me think, and led eventually to the Electric Pentacle, which is a most marvellous "Defence" against certain manifestations. I used the shape of the defensive star for this protection because I have, personally, no doubt at all but that there is some extraordinary virtue in the old magic figure. Curious thing for a twentieth-century man to admit, is it not? But then, as you all know, I never did, and never will, allow myself to be blinded by a little cheap laughter. I ask questions and keep my eyes open!

'In this last case I had little doubt that I had run up against an ab-natural monster, and I meant to take every possible care, for the danger is abominable.

'I turned to now to fit the Electric Pentacle, setting it so that each of its "points" and "vales" coincided exactly with the "points" and "vales" of the drawn pentagram upon the floor. Then I connected up the battery and the next instant the pale blue glare from the intertwining vacuum tubes shone out.

'I glanced about me then, with something of a sigh of relief, and realised suddenly that the dusk was upon me, for the window was grey and unfriendly. Then I stared round at the big, empty room, over the double barrier of electric and candle light, and had an abrupt, extraordinary sense of weirdness thrust upon me—in the air, you know, it seemed; as it were a sense of something inhuman impending. The room was full of the stench of bruised garlic, a smell I hate.

'I turned now to my camera, and saw that it and the flashlight were in order. Then I tested the action of my revolver carefully, though I had little thought that it would be needed. Yet, to what extent materialisation of an ab-natural creature is possible, given favourable conditions, no one can say, and I had no idea what horrible thing I was going to see or feel the presence of. I might, in the end, have to fight with a material thing. I did not know and could only be prepared. You see, I never forgot that three people had been strangled in the bed close to me, and the fierce slamming of the door I had heard myself. I had no doubt that I was investigating a dangerous and ugly case.

'By this time the night had come (though the room was very bright with the burning candles) and I found myself glancing behind me constantly and then all round the room. It was nervy work waiting for that thing to come into the room.

'Suddenly I was aware of a little, cold wind sweeping over me, coming from behind. I gave one great nerve-thrill and a prickly feeling went all over the back of my head. Then I hove myself round with a sort of stiff jerk and stared straight against that queer wind. It seemed to come from the corner of the room to the left of the bed—the place where both times I had found the heaped and tossed bedclothes. Yet I could see nothing unusual, no opening—nothing! . . .

'Abruptly I was aware that the candles were all a-flicker in that unnatural wind . . . I believe I just squatted there and stared in a horribly frightened, wooden way for some minutes. I shall never be able to let you know how disgustingly horrible it was sitting in that vile, cold wind! And then—flick! flick! flick! all the candles round the outer barrier went out, and there was I, locked and sealed in that room and with no light beyond the weakish blue glare of the Electric Pentacle.

'A time of abominable tenseness passed and still that wind blew upon me, and then suddenly I knew that something stirred in the corner to the left of the bed. I was made conscious of it rather by some inward, unused sense, than by either sight or sound, for the pale, short-radius glare of the Pentacle gave but a very poor light for seeing by. Yet, as I stared, something began slowly to grow upon my sight—a moving shadow, a little darker than the surrounding shadows. I lost the thing amid the vagueness and for a moment or two I glanced swiftly from side to side with a fresh, new sense of impending danger. Then my attention was directed to the bed. All the coverings were being drawn steadily off, with a hateful, stealthy sort of motion. I heard the slow, dragging slither of the clothes, but I could see nothing of the thing that pulled. I was aware in a funny, subconscious, introspective fashion that the "creep" had come upon me, prickling all over my head, yet I was cooler mentally than I had been for some minutes; sufficiently so to feel that my hands were sweating coldly and to shift my revolver, half-consciously, whilst I rubbed my right hand dry upon my knee; though never for an instant taking my gaze or my attention from those moving clothes.

'The faint noises from the bed ceased once and there was a most intense silence, with only the dull thudding of the blood beating in my head. Yet immediately afterwards I heard again the slurring sound of the bedclothes being dragged off the bed. In the midst of my nervous tension I remembered the camera and reached out for it, but without looking away from the bed. And then, you know, all in a moment, the whole of the bed-coverings were torn off with extraordinary violence and I heard the flump they made as they were hurled into the corner.

'There was a time of absolute quietness then for perhaps a couple of minutes and you can imagine how horrible I felt. The bedclothes had been thrown with such savageness! And then again the abominable unnaturalness of the thing that had just been done before me!

'Suddenly, over by the door, I heard a faint noise—a sort of crickling sound and then a pitter or two upon the floor. A great nervous thrill swept over me, seeming to run up my spine and over the back of my head, for the seal that secured the door had just been broken. Something was there. I could not see the door; at least, I mean to say that it was impossible to say how much I actually saw and how much my imagination supplied. I made it out only as a continuation of the grey walls . . . And then it seemed to me that something dark and indistinct wavered there among the shadows.

'Abruptly I was aware that the door was opening and with an effort I reached again for my camera; but before I could aim it the door was slammed with a terrific crash that filled the whole room with a sort of hollow thunder. I jumped like a frightened child. There seemed such a power behind the noise, as if a vast, wanton Force were "out". Can you understand?

'The door was not touched again; but, directly afterwards I heard the basket in which the cat lay creak. I tell you, I fairly pringled all along my back. I knew that I was going to learn definitely whether what was abroad was dangerous to Life. From the cat there rose suddenly a hideous caterwaul that ceased abruptly, and then—too late—I snapped on the flashlight. In the great glare I saw that the basket had been overturned and the lid was wrenched open, with the cat lying half in and half out upon the floor. I saw nothing else, but I was full of the knowledge that I was in the presence of some Being or Thing that had power to destroy.

'During the next two or three minutes there was an odd, noticeable quietness in the room, and you must remember I was half-blinded for the time because of the flashlight, so that the whole place seemed to be pitchy dark just beyond the shine of the pentacle. I tell you it was most horrible. I just knelt there in the star and whirled round on my knees, trying to see whether anything was coming at me.

'My power of sight came gradually and I got a little hold of myself, and abruptly I saw the thing I was looking for, close to the "water-circle". It was big and indistinct and wavered curiously as though the shadow of a vast spider hung suspended in the air, just beyond the barrier. It passed swiftly round the circle and seemed to probe ever towards me, but only to draw back with extraordinary jerky movements, as might a living person who touched the hot bar of a grate.

'Round and round it moved and round and round I turned. Then just opposite to one of the "vales" in the pentacles it seemed to pause as though preliminary to a tremendous effort. It retired almost beyond the glow of the vacuum light and then came straight towards me, appearing to gather form and solidity as it came. There seemed a vast malign determination behind the movement that must succeed. I was on my knees and I jerked back, falling on to my left hand and hip, in a wild endeavour to get back from the advancing thing. With my right hand I was grabbing madly for my revolver which I had let slip. The brutal thing came with one great sweep straight over the garlic and the "water-circle", almost to the "vale" of the pentacle. I believe I yelled. Then, just as suddenly as it had swept over it seemed to be hurled back by some mighty, invisible force.

'It must have been some moments before I realised that I was safe, and then I got myself together in the middle of the pentacles, feeling horribly done and shaken and glancing round and round the barrier, but the thing had vanished. Yet I had learned something, for I knew now that the Grey Room was haunted by a monstrous hand.

'Suddenly as I crouched there I saw what had so nearly given the monster an opening through the barrier. In my movements within the pentacle I must have touched one of the jars of water, for just where the thing had made its attack the jar that guarded the "deep" of the "vale" had been moved to one side and this had left one of the "five doorways" unguarded. I put it back quickly and felt almost safe again, for I had found the cause and the "Defence" was still good. I began to hope again that I should see the morning come in. When I saw that thing so nearly succeed I'd had an awful, weak, overwhelming feeling that the "barriers" could never bring me safe through the night against such a Force. You can understand?

'For a long time I could not see the hand; but presently I thought I saw, once or twice, an odd wavering over among the shadows near the door. A little later, as though in a sudden fit of malignant rage, the dead body of the cat was picked up and beaten with dull, sickening blows against the solid floor. That made me feel rather queer.

'A minute afterwards the door was opened and slammed wide with tremendous force. The next instant the thing made one swift, vicious dart at me from out of the shadows. Instinctively I started sideways from it and so plucked my hand from upon the Electric Pentacle, where—for a wickedly careless moment—I had placed it. The monster was hurled off from the neighbourhood of the pentacles, though—owing to my inconceivable foolishness—it had been enabled for a second time to pass the outer barriers. I can tell you I shook for a time with sheer funk. I moved right to the centre of the pentacles again and knelt there, making myself as small and compact as possible.

'As I knelt, I began to have presently, a vague wonder at the two "accidents" which had so nearly allowed the brute to get at me. Was I being influenced to unconscious voluntary actions that endangered me? The thought took hold of me and I watched my every movement. Abruptly I stretched a tired leg and knocked over one of the jars of water. Some was spilled, but because of my suspicious watchfulness, I had it upright and back within the "vale" while yet some of the water remained. Even as I did so the vast, black, half-materialised hand beat up at me out of the shadows and seemed to leap almost into my face, so nearly did it approach, but for the third time it was thrown back by some altogether enormous, overmastering force. Yet, apart from the dazed fright in which it left me, I had for a moment that feeling of spiritual sickness as if some delicate, beautiful, inward grace had suffered which is felt only upon the too-near approach of the ab-human and is more dreadful in a strange way than any physical pain that can be suffered. I knew by this more of the extent and closeness of the danger, and for a long time I was simply cowed by the butt-headed brutality of that Force upon my spirit. I can put it no other way.

'I knelt again in the centre of the pentacles, watching myself with as much fear almost, as the monster, for I knew now that unless I guarded myself from every sudden impulse that came to me I might simply work my own destruction. Do you see how horrible it all was?

'I spent the rest of the night in a haze of sick fright and so tense that I could not make a single movement naturally. I was in such fear that any desire for action that came to me might be prompted by the Influence that I knew was at work on me. And outside of the barrier that ghastly thing went round and round, grabbing and grabbing in the air at me. Twice more was the body of the dead cat molested. The second time I heard every bone in its body scrunch and crack. And all the time the horrible wind was blowing upon me from the corner of the room to the left of the bed.

'Then, just as the first touch of dawn came into the sky the unnatural wind ceased in a single moment and I could see no sign of the hand. The dawn came slowly and presently the wan light filled all the room and made the pale glare of the Electric Pentacle look more unearthly. Yet it was not until the day had fully come that I made any attempt to leave the barrier, for I did not know but that there was some method abroad in the sudden stopping of that wind to entice me from the pentacles.

'At last, when the dawn was strong and bright, I took one last look round and ran for the door. I got it unlocked in a nervous, clumsy fashion; then locked it hurriedly and went to my bedroom where I lay on the bed and tried to steady my nerves. Peters came presently with the coffee and when I had drunk it I told him I meant to have a sleep, as I had been up all night. He took the tray and went out quietly, and after I had locked my door I turned in properly and at last got to sleep.

'I woke about midday and after some lunch went up to the Grey Room. I switched off the current from the Pentacle, which I had left on in my hurry; also, I removed the body of the cat. You can understand, I did not want anyone to see the poor brute.

'After that I made a very careful search of the corner where the bedclothes had been thrown. I made several holes through the woodwork and probed, but found nothing. Then it occurred to me to try with my instrument under the skirting. I did so and heard my wire ring on metal. I turned the hook end of the probe that way and fished for the thing. At the second go I got it. It was a small object and I took it to the window. I found it to be a curious ring made of some greyish metal. The curious thing about it was that it was made in the form of a pentagon; that is, the same shape as the inside of the magic pentacle, but without the "mounts" which form the points of the defensive star. It was free from all chasing or engraving.

'You will understand that I was excited when I tell you that I felt sure I held in my hand the famous Luck Ring of the Anderson family which, indeed, was of all things the most intimately connected with the history of the haunting. This ring had been handed on from father to son through generations, and always— in obedience to some ancient family tradition—each son had to promise never to wear the ring. The ring, I may say, was brought home by one of the Crusaders under very peculiar circumstances, but the story is too long to go into here.

'It appears that young Sir Hulbert, an ancestor of Anderson's, made a bet one evening, in drink, you know, that he would wear the ring that night. He did so, and in the morning his wife and child were found strangled in the bed in the very room in which I stood. Many people, it would seem, thought young Sir Hulbert was guilty of having done the thing in drunken anger and he, in an attempt to prove his innocence, slept a second night in the room. He also was strangled.

'Since then no one has spent a night in the Grey Room until I did so. The ring had been lost so long that its very existence had become almost a myth, and it was most extraordinary to stand there with the actual thing in my hand, as you can understand.

'It was whilst I stood there looking at the ring that I got an idea. Supposing that it were, in a way, a doorway—you see what I mean? A sort of gap in the world-hedge, if I may so phrase my idea. It was a queer thought, I know, and possibly was not my own, but one of those mental nudgings from the Outside.

'You see, the wind had come from that part of the room where the ring lay. I pondered the thought a lot. Then the shape—the inside of a pentacle. It had no "mounts", and without mounts, as the *Sigsand MS* has it: "Thee mownts wych are thee Five Hills of safetie. To lack is to gyve pow'r to thee daemon; and surlie to fayvor thee Evill Thynge." You see, the very shape of the ring was significant. I determined to test it.

'I unmade my pentacle, for it must be "made" afresh *and around* the one to be protected. Then I went out and locked the door, after which I left the house to get certain matters, for neither "yarbs nor fyre nor water" must be used a second time. I returned about seven thirty and as soon as the things I had brought had been carried up to the Grey Room I dismissed Peters for the night, just as I had done the evening before.

'When he had gone downstairs I let myself into the room and locked and sealed the door. I went to the place in the centre of the room where all the stuff had been packed and set to work with all my speed to construct a barrier about me and the ring.

'I do not remember whether I explained to you, but I had reasoned that if the ring were in any way a "medium of admission", and it were enclosed with me in the Electric Pentacle it would be, to express it loosely, insulated. Do you see? The Force which had visible expression as a Hand would have to stay beyond the Barrier which separates the Ab from the Normal, for the "gateway" would be removed from accessibility.

'As I was saying, I worked with all my speed to get the barrier completed about me and the ring for it was already later than I cared to be in that room "unprotected". Also, I had a feeling that there would be a last effort made that night to regain the use of the ring. For I had the strongest conviction that the ring was a necessity to materialisation. You will see whether I was right.

'I completed the barriers in about an hour and you can imagine something of the relief I felt when I saw the pale glare of the Electric Pentacle once more all about me. From then onwards, for about two hours, I sat quietly facing the corner from which the wind came.

'About eleven o'clock I had a queer knowledge that something was near to me, yet nothing happened for a whole hour after that. Then suddenly I felt the cold, queer wind begin to blow upon me. To my astonishment it seemed now to come from behind me and I whipped round with a hideous quake of fear. The wind hit me in the face. It was flowing up from the floor close to me. I stared in a sickening maze of new frights. What on earth had I done now! The ring was there, close beside me, where I had put it. Suddenly, as I stared, bewildered, I was aware that there was something queer about the ring—funny shadowy movements and convolutions. I looked at them stupidly. And then, abruptly, I knew that the wind was blowing up at me from the ring. A queer indistinct smoke became visible to me, seeming to pour upwards through the ring and mix with the moving shadows. Suddenly I realised that I was in more than any mortal danger, for the convoluting shadows about the ring were taking shape and the death-hand was forming *within* the pentacle. My goodness, do you realise it? I had brought the "gateway" into the pentacles and the brute was coming through—pouring into the material world, as gas might pour out from the mouth of a pipe.

'I should think that I knelt for a couple of moments in a sort of stunned fright. Then with a mad, awkward movement I snatched at the ring, intending to hurl it out of the pentacle. Yet, it eluded me as though some invisible, living thing jerked it hither and thither. At last I gripped it, but in the same instant it was torn from my grasp with incredible and brutal force. A great black shadow covered it and rose into the air and came at me. I saw that it was the Hand, vast and nearly perfect in form. I gave one crazy yell and jumped over the pentacle and the ring of burning candles and ran despairingly for the door. I fumbled idiotically and ineffectually with the key, and all the time I stared, with the fear that was like insanity, towards the Barriers. The Hand was plunging towards me; yet, even as it had been unable to pass into the pentacle when the ring was without; so, now that the ring was within, it had no power to pass out. The monster was chained, as surely as any beast would be, were chains riveted upon it.

'Even then, in that moment, I got a flash of this knowledge, but I was too utterly shaken with fright to reason and the instant I managed to get the key turned I sprang into the passage and slammed the door with a crash. I locked it and got to my room, somehow; for I was trembling so that I could hardly stand, as you can imagine. I locked myself in and managed to get the candle lit; then I lay down on the bed and kept quiet for an hour or two, and so I grew steadier.

'I got a little sleep later, but woke when Peters brought my coffee. When I had drunk it I felt altogether better and took the old man along with me whilst I had a look into the Grey Room. I opened the door and peeped in. The candles were still burning wan against the daylight and behind them was the pale, glowing star of the Electric Pentacle. And there in the middle was the ring—the gateway of the monster, lying demure and ordinary.

'Nothing in the room was touched and I knew that the brute had never managed to cross the pentacles. Then I went out and locked the door.

'After a further sleep of some hours I left the house. I returned in the afternoon in a cab. I had with me an oxyhydrogen jet and two cylinders, containing the gases. I carried the things to the Grey Room and there, in the centre of the Electric Pentacle, I erected the little furnace. Five minutes later the Luck Ring, once the "luck" but now the "bane" of the Anderson family, was no more than a little splash of hot metal.'

Carnacki felt in his pocket and pulled out something wrapped in tissue paper. He passed it to me. I opened it and found a small circle of greyish metal something like lead, only harder and rather brighter.

'Well,' I asked, at length, after examining it and handing it round to the others, 'did that stop the haunting?'

Carnacki nodded. 'Yes,' he said. 'I slept three nights in the Grey Room before

I left. Old Peters nearly fainted when he knew that I meant to, but by the third night he seemed to realise that the house was just safe and ordinary. And you know, I believe in his heart he hardly approved.'

Carnacki stood up and began to shake hands. 'Out you go!' he said, genially.

And, presently, we went pondering to our various homes.

Tom Hood

1835–1874

Although destined for the Church while studying at Oxford,
Tom Hood was to make his mark in life as a humorist and
caricaturist. From 1861 he edited the comic *Fun* and also
produced children's annuals. His writing had its more serious
side, however, and his novels and short stories attracted
widespread and well-deserved attention.

THE SHADOW
OF A SHADE

M Y SISTER LETTIE HAS LIVED with me ever since I had a home of my own.
She was my little housekeeper before I married. Now she is my wife's
constant companion, and the 'darling auntie' of my children, who go to
her for comfort, advice, and aid in all their little troubles and perplexities.

But, though she has a comfortable home, and loving hearts around her, she
wears a grave, melancholy look on her face, which puzzles acquaintances and
grieves friends.

A disappointment! Yes, the old story of a lost lover is the reason for Lettie's
looks. She has had good offers often; but since she lost the first love of her heart
she has never indulged in the happy dream of loving and being loved.

George Mason was a cousin of my wife's—a sailor by profession. He and
Lettie met one another at our wedding, and fell in love at first sight. George's
father had seen service before him on the great mysterious sea, and had been
especially known as a good Arctic sailor, having shared in more than one expedition in search of the North Pole and the Northwest Passage.

It was not a matter of surprise to me, therefore, when George volunteered to
go out in the *Pioneer*, which was being fitted out for a cruise in search of
Franklin and his missing expedition. There was a fascination about such an
undertaking that I felt I could not have resisted had I been in his place. Of
course, Lettie did not like the idea at all, but he silenced her by telling her that
men who volunteered for Arctic search were never lost sight of, and that he

should not make as much advance in his profession in a dozen years as he would in the year or so of this expedition. I cannot say that Lettie, even after this, was quite satisfied with the notion of his going, but, at all events, she did not argue against it any longer. But the grave look, which is now habitual with her, but was a rare thing in her young and happy days, passed over her face sometimes when she thought no one was looking.

My younger brother, Harry, was at this time an academy student. He was only a beginner then. Now he is pretty well known in the art world, and his pictures command fair prices. Like all beginners in art, he was full of fancies and theories. He would have been a Pre-Raphaelite, only Pre-Raphaelitism had not been invented then. His peculiar craze was for what he styled the Venetian School. Now, it chanced that George had a fine Italian-looking head, and Harry persuaded him to sit to him for his portrait. It was a fair likeness, but a very moderate work of art. The background was so very dark, and George's naval costume so very deep in colour, that the face came out too white and staring. It was a three-quarter picture; but only one hand showed in it, leaning on the hilt of a sword. As George said, he looked much more like the commander of a Venetian galley than a modern mate.

However, the picture pleased Lettie, who did not care much about art provided the resemblance was good. So the picture was duly framed—in a tremendously heavy frame, of Harry's ordering—and hung up in the dining room.

And now the time for George's departure was growing nearer. The *Pioneer* was nearly ready to sail, and her crew only waited orders. The officers grew acquainted with each other before sailing, which was an advantage. George took up very warmly with the surgeon, Vincent Grieve, and, with my permission, brought him to dinner once or twice.

'Poor chap, he has no friends nearer than the Highlands, and it's precious lonely work.'

'Bring him by all means, George! You know that any friends of yours will be welcome here.'

So Vincent Grieve came. I am bound to say I was not favourably impressed by him, and almost wished I had not consented to his coming. He was a tall, pale, fair young man, with a hard Scotch face and a cold, grey eye. There was something in his expression, too, that was unpleasant—something cruel or crafty, or both.

I considered that it was very bad taste for him to pay such marked attention to Lettie, coming, as he did, as the friend of her fiancé. He kept by her constantly and anticipated George in all the little attentions which a lover delights to pay. I think George was a little put out about it, though he said nothing, attributing his friend's offence to lack of breeding.

Lettie did not like it at all. She knew that she was not to have George with her much longer, and she was anxious to have him to herself as much as possible.

But as Grieve was her lover's friend she bore the infliction with the best possible patience.

The surgeon did not seem to perceive in the least that he was interfering where he had no business. He was quite self-possessed and happy, with one exception. The portrait of George seemed to annoy him. He had uttered a little impatient exclamation when he first saw it which drew my attention to him; and I noticed that he tried to avoid looking at it. At last, when dinner came, he was told to sit exactly facing the picture. He hesitated for an instant and then sat down, but almost immediately rose again.

'It's very childish and that sort of thing,' he stammered, 'but I cannot sit opposite that picture.'

'It is not high art,' I said, 'and may irritate a critical eye.'

'I know nothing about art,' he answered, 'but it is one of those unpleasant pictures whose eyes follow you about the room. I have an inherited horror of such pictures. My mother married against her father's will, and when I was born she was so ill she was hardly expected to live. When she was sufficiently recovered to speak without delirious rambling she implored them to remove a picture of my grandfather that hung in the room, and which she vowed made threatening faces at her. It's superstitious, but constitutional—I have a horror of such paintings!'

I believe George thought this was a ruse of his friend's to get a seat next to Lettie; but I felt sure it was not, for I had seen the alarmed expression on his face.

At night, when George and his friend were leaving, I took an opportunity to ask the former, half in a joke, if he should bring the surgeon to see us again. George made a very hearty assertion to the contrary, adding that he was pleasant enough company among men at an inn, or on board ship, but not where ladies were concerned.

But the mischief was done. Vincent Grieve took advantage of the introduction and did not wait to be invited again. He called the next day, and nearly every day after. He was a more frequent visitor than George now, for George was obliged to attend to his duties, and they kept him on board the *Pioneer* pretty constantly, whereas the surgeon, having seen to the supply of drugs, etc., was pretty well at liberty. Lettie avoided him as much as possible, but he generally brought, or professed to bring, some little message from George to her, so that he had an excuse for asking to see her.

On the occasion of his last visit—the day before the *Pioneer* sailed—Lettie came to me in great distress. The young cub had actually had the audacity to tell her he loved her. He knew, he said, about her engagement to George, but that did not prevent another man from loving her too. A man could no more help falling in love than he could help taking a fever. Lettie stood upon her dignity and rebuked him severely; but he told her he could see no harm in telling her of his passion, though he knew it was a hopeless one.

'A thousand things may happen,' he said at last, 'to bring your engagement with George Mason to an end. Then perhaps you will not forget that another loves you!'

I was very angry, and was forthwith going to give him my opinion on his conduct, when Lettie told me he was gone, that she had bade him go and had forbidden him the house. She only told me in order to protect herself, for she did not intend to say anything to George, for fear it should lead to a duel or some other violence.

That was the last we saw of Vincent Grieve before the *Pioneer* sailed.

George came the same evening, and was with us till daybreak, when he had to tear himself away and join his ship.

After shaking hands with him at the door, in the cold, grey, drizzly dawn, I turned back into the dining room, where poor Lettie was sobbing on the sofa.

I could not help starting when I looked at George's portrait, which hung above her. The strange light of daybreak could hardly account for the extraordinary pallor of the face. I went close to it and looked hard at it. I saw that it was covered with moisture, and imagined that that possibly made it look so pale. As for the moisture, I supposed poor Lettie had been kissing the beloved's portrait, and that the moisture was caused by her tears.

It was not till a long time after, when I was jestingly telling Harry how his picture had been caressed, that I learnt the error of my conjecture. Lettie assured me most solemnly that I was mistaken in supposing she had kissed it.

'It was the varnish blooming, I expect,' said Harry. And thus the subject was dismissed, for I said no more, though I knew well enough, in spite of my not being an artist, that the bloom of varnish was quite another sort of thing.

The *Pioneer* sailed. We received—or, rather, Lettie received—two letters from George, which he had taken the opportunity of sending by homeward-bound whalers. In the second he said it was hardly likely he should have an opportunity of sending another, as they were sailing into high latitudes—into the solitary sea, to which none but expedition ships ever penetrated. They were all in high spirits, he said, for they had encountered very little ice and hoped to find clear water further north than usual. Moreover, he added, Grieve had held a sinecure so far, for there had not been a single case of illness on board.

Then came a long silence, and a year crept away very slowly for poor Lettie. Once we heard of the expedition from the papers. They were reported as pushing on and progressing favourably by a wandering tribe of Esquimaux with whom the captain of a Russian vessel fell in. They had laid the ship up for the winter, and were taking the boats on sledges, and believed they had met with traces of the lost crews that seemed to show they were on the right track.

The winter passed again, and spring came. It was a balmy, bright spring such as we get occasionally, even in this changeable and uncertain climate of ours.

One evening we were sitting in the dining room with the window open, for, although we had long given up fires, the room was so oppressively warm that we were glad of the breath of the cool evening breeze.

Lettie was working. Poor child, though she never murmured, she was evidently pining at George's long absence. Harry was leaning out of the window, studying the evening effect on the fruit blossom, which was wonderfully early and plentiful, the season was so mild. I was sitting at the table, near the lamp, reading the paper.

Suddenly there swept into the room a chill. It was not a gust of cold wind, for the curtain by the open window did not swerve in the least. But the deathly cold pervaded the room—came, and was gone in an instant. Lettie shuddered, as I did, with the intense icy feeling.

She looked up. 'How curiously cold it has got all in a minute,' she said.

'We are having a taste of poor George's Polar weather,' I said with a smile.

At the same moment I instinctively glanced towards his portrait. What I saw struck me dumb. A rush of blood, at fever heat, dispelled the numbing influence of the chill breath that had seemed to freeze me.

I have said the lamp was lighted; but it was only that I might read with comfort, for the violet twilight was still so full of sunset that the room was not dark. But as I looked at the picture I saw it had undergone a strange change. I saw it as plainly as possible. It was no delusion, coined for the eye by the brain.

I saw, in the place of George's head, a grinning skull! I stared at it hard; but it was no trick of fancy. I could see the hollow orbits, the gleaming teeth, the fleshless cheekbones—it was the head of death!

Without saying a word, I rose from my chair and walked straight up to the painting. As I drew nearer a sort of mist seemed to pass before it; and as I stood close to it, I saw only the face of George. The spectral skull had vanished.

'Poor George!' I said unconsciously.

Lettie looked up. The tone of my voice had alarmed her, the expression of my face did not reassure her.

'What do you mean? Have you heard anything? Oh, Robert, in mercy tell me!'

She got up and came over to me and, laying her hand on my arm, looked up into my face imploringly.

'No, my dear; how should I hear? Only I could not help thinking of the privation and discomfort he must have gone through. I was reminded of it by the cold—'

'Cold!' said Harry, who had left the window by this time. 'Cold! what on earth are you talking about? Cold, such an evening as this! You must have had a touch of ague, I should think.'

'Both Lettie and I felt it bitterly cold a minute or two ago. Did not you feel it?'

'Not a bit; and as I was three parts out of the window I ought to have felt it if anyone did.'

It was curious, but that strange chill had been felt only in the room. It was not the night wind, but some supernatural breath connected with the dread apparition I had seen. It was, indeed, the chill of Polar winter—the icy shadow of the frozen North.

'What is the day of the month, Harry?' I asked.

'Today—the 23rd, I think,' he answered; then added, taking up the newspaper I had been reading: 'Yes, here you are. Tuesday, February the 23rd, if the *Daily News* tells truth, which I suppose it does. Newspapers can afford to tell the truth about dates, whatever they may do about art.' Harry had been rather roughly handled by the critic of a morning paper for one of his pictures a few days before, and he was a little angry with journalism generally.

Presently Lettie left the room, and I told Harry what I had felt and seen, and told him to take note of the date, for I feared that some mischance had befallen George.

'I'll put it down in my pocketbook, Bob. But you and Lettie must have had a touch of the cold shivers, and your stomach or fancy misled you—they're the same thing, you know. Besides, as regards the picture, there's nothing in that! There is a skull there, of course. As Tennyson says:

> *Any face, however full,*
> *Padded round with flesh and fat,*
> *Is but modelled on a skull.*

The skull's there—just as in every good figure-subject the nude is there under the costumes. You fancy that is a mere coat of paint. Nothing of the kind! Art lives, sir! That is just as much a real head as yours is with all the muscles and bones, just the same. That's what makes the difference between art and rubbish.'

This was a favourite theory of Harry's, who had not yet developed from the dreamer into the worker. As I did not care to argue with him, I allowed the subject to drop after we had written down the date in our pocketbooks. Lettie sent down word presently that she did not feel well and had gone to bed. My wife came down presently and asked what had happened. She had been up with the children and had gone in to see what was the matter with Lettie.

'I think it was very imprudent to sit with the window open, dear. I know the evenings are warm, but the night air strikes cold at times—at any rate, Lettie seems to have caught a violent cold, for she is shivering very much. I am afraid she has got a chill from the open windows.'

I did not say anything to her then, except that both Lettie and I had felt a sudden coldness; for I did not care to enter into an explanation again, for I could see Harry was inclined to laugh at me for being so superstitious.

At night, however, in our own room, I told my wife what had occurred, and what my apprehensions were. She was so upset and alarmed that I almost repented having done so.

The next morning Lettie was better again, and as we did not either of us refer to the events of the preceding night the circumstance appeared to be forgotten by us all. But from that day I was ever inwardly dreading the arrival of bad news. And at last it came, as I expected.

One morning, just as I was coming downstairs to breakfast, there came a knock at the door, and Harry made his appearance. It was a very early visit from him, for he generally used to spend his mornings at the studio, and drop in on his way home at night.

He was looking pale and agitated.

'Lettie's not down, is she, yet?' he asked; and then, before I could answer, added another question:

'What newspaper do you take?'

'The *Daily News*,' I answered. 'Why?'

'She's not down?'

'No.'

'Thank God! Look here!'

He took a paper from his pocket and gave it to me, pointing out a short paragraph at the bottom of one of the columns.

I knew what was coming the moment he spoke about Lettie.

The paragraph was headed, 'Fatal Accident to one of the Officers of the *Pioneer* Expedition Ship'. It stated that news had been received at the Admiralty stating that the expedition had failed to find the missing crews, but had come upon some traces of them. Want of stores and necessaries had compelled them to turn back without following those traces up; but the commander was anxious, as soon as the ship could be refitted, to go out and take up the trail where he left it. An unfortunate accident had deprived him of one of his most promising officers, Lieutenant Mason, who was precipitated from an iceberg and killed while out shooting with the surgeon. He was beloved by all, and his death had flung a gloom over the gallant little troop of explorers.

'It's not in the *News* today, thank goodness, Bob,' said Harry, who had been searching that paper while I was reading the one he brought, 'but you must keep a sharp lookout for some days and not let Lettie see it when it appears, as it is certain to do sooner or later.'

Then we both of us looked at each other with tears in our eyes. 'Poor George!—poor Lettie!' we sighed softly.

'But she must be told at some time or other?' I said despairingly.

'I suppose so,' said Harry; 'but it would kill her to come on it suddenly like this. Where's your wife?'

She was with the children, but I sent up for her and told her the ill tidings.

She had a hard struggle to conceal her emotion, for Lettie's sake. But the tears would flow in spite of her efforts.

'How shall I ever find courage to tell her?' she asked.

'Hush!' said Harry, suddenly grasping her arm and looking towards the door.

I turned. There stood Lettie, with her face pale as death, with her lips apart, and with a blind look about her eyes. She had come in without our hearing her. We never learnt how much of the story she had overheard; but it was enough to tell her the worst. We all sprang towards her; but she only waved us away, turned round, and went upstairs again without saying a word. My wife hastened up after her and found her on her knees by the bed, insensible.

The doctor was sent for, and restoratives were promptly administered. She came to herself again, but lay dangerously ill for some weeks from the shock.

It was about a month after she was well enough to come downstairs again that I saw in the paper an announcement of the arrival of the *Pioneer*. The news had no interest for any of us now, so I said nothing about it. The mere mention of the vessel's name would have caused the poor girl pain.

One afternoon shortly after this, as I was writing a letter, there came a loud knock at the front door. I looked up from my writing and listened; for the voice which enquired if I was in sounded strange, but yet not altogether unfamiliar. As I looked up, puzzling whose it could be, my eye rested accidentally upon poor George's portrait. Was I dreaming or awake?

I have told you that the one hand was resting on a sword. I could see now distinctly that the forefinger was raised, as if in warning. I looked at it hard, to assure myself it was no fancy, and then I perceived, standing out bright and distinct on the pale face, two large drops, as if of blood.

I walked up to it, expecting the appearance to vanish, as the skull had done. It did not vanish; but the uplifted finger resolved itself into a little white moth which had settled on the canvas. The red drops were fluid, and certainly not blood, though I was at a loss for the time to account for them.

The moth seemed to be in a torpid state, so I took it off the picture and placed it under an inverted wineglass on the mantelpiece. All this took less time to do than to describe. As I turned from the mantelpiece the servant brought in a card, saying the gentleman was waiting in the hall to know if I would see him.

On the card was the name of 'Vincent Grieve, of the exploring vessel *Pioneer*'.

'Thank Heaven, Lettie is out,' thought I; and then added aloud to the servant, 'Show him in here; and Jane, if your mistress and Miss Lettie come in before the gentleman goes, tell them I have someone with me on business and do not wish to be disturbed.'

I went to the door to meet Grieve. As he crossed the threshold, and before he could have seen the portrait, he stopped, shuddered and turned white, even to his thin lips.

'Cover that picture before I come in,' he said hurriedly, in a low voice. 'You remember the effect it had upon me. Now, with the memory of poor Mason, it would be worse than ever.'

I could understand his feelings better now than at first; for I had come to look on the picture with some awe myself. So I took the cloth off a little round table that stood under the window and hung it over the portrait.

When I had done so Grieve came in. He was greatly altered. He was thinner and paler than ever; hollow-eyed and hollow-cheeked. He had acquired a strange stoop, too, and his eyes had lost the crafty look for a look of terror, like that of a hunted beast. I noticed that he kept glancing sideways every instant, as if unconsciously. It looked as if he heard someone behind him.

I had never liked the man; but now I felt an insurmountable repugnance to him—so great a repugnance that, when I came to think of it, I felt pleased that the incident of covering the picture at his request had led to my not shaking hands with him.

I felt that I could not speak otherwise than coldly to him; indeed, I had to speak with painful plainness.

I told him that, of course, I was glad to see him back, but that I could not ask him to continue to visit us. I should be glad to hear the particulars of poor George's death, but that I could not let him see my sister, and hinted, as delicately as I could, at the impropriety of which he had been guilty when he last visited.

He took it all very quietly, only giving a long, weary sigh when I told him I must beg him not to repeat his visit. He looked so weak and ill that I was obliged to ask him to take a glass of wine—an offer which he seemed to accept with great pleasure.

I got out the sherry and biscuits and placed them on the table between us, and he took a glass and drank it off greedily.

It was not without some difficulty that I could get him to tell me of George's death. He related, with evident reluctance, how they had gone out to shoot a white bear which they had seen on an iceberg stranded along the shore. The top of the berg was ridged like the roof of a house, sloping down on one side to the edge of a tremendous overhanging precipice. They had scrambled along the ridge in order to get nearer the game, when George incautiously ventured on the sloping side.

'I called out to him,' said Grieve, 'and begged him to come back, but too late. The surface was as smooth and slippery as glass. He tried to turn back, but slipped and fell. And then began a horrible scene. Slowly, slowly, but with ever-increasing motion, he began to slide down towards the edge. There was nothing to grasp at—no irregularity or projection on the smooth face of the ice. I tore off my coat, and hastily attaching it to the stock of my gun, pushed the latter towards him; but it did not reach far enough. Before I could lengthen it, by tying my cravat to it, he had slid yet further away, and more quickly. I shouted in agony; but there was no one within hearing. He, too, saw his fate was sealed; and he could only tell me to bring his last farewell to you, and—and to her!'—Here Grieve's voice broke—'and it was all over! He clung to the edge of the precipice instinctively for one second, and was gone!'

Just as Grieve uttered the last word, his jaw fell; his eyeballs seemed ready to start from his head; he sprang to his feet, pointed at something behind me, and then flinging up his arms, fell, with a scream, as if he had been shot. He was seized with an epileptic fit.

I instinctively looked behind me as I hurried to raise him from the floor. The cloth had fallen from the picture, where the face of George, made paler than ever by the gouts of red, looked sternly down.

I rang the bell. Luckily, Harry had come in; and, when the servant told him what was the matter, he came in and assisted me in restoring Grieve to consciousness. Of course, I covered the painting up again.

When he was quite himself again, Grieve told me he was subject to fits occasionally.

He seemed very anxious to learn if he had said or done anything extraordinary while he was in the fit, and appeared reassured when I said he had not. He apologised for the trouble he had given, and said as soon as he was strong enough he would take his leave. He was leaning on the mantelpiece as he said this. The little white moth caught his eye.

'So you have had someone else from the *Pioneer* here before me?' he said, nervously.

I answered in the negative, asking what made him think so.

'Why, this little white moth is never found in such southern latitudes. It is one of the last signs of life northward. Where did you get it?'

'I caught it here, in this room,' I answered.

'That is very strange. I never heard of such a thing before. We shall hear of showers of blood soon, I should not wonder.'

'What do you mean?' I asked.

'Oh, these little fellows emit little drops of a red-looking fluid at certain seasons, and sometimes so plentifully that the superstitious think it is a shower of blood. I have seen the snow quite stained in places. Take care of it, it is a rarity in the south.'

I noticed, after he left, which he did almost immediately, that there was a drop of red fluid on the marble under the wineglass. The bloodstain on the picture was accounted for; but how came the moth here?

And there was another strange thing about the man, which I had scarcely been able to assure myself of in the room, where there were cross-lights, but about which there was no possible mistake, when I saw him walking away up the street.

'Harry, here—quick!' I called to my brother, who at once came to the window. 'You're an artist, tell me, is there anything strange about that man?'

'No; nothing that I can see,' said Harry, but then suddenly, in an altered tone, added, 'Yes, there is. By Jove, *he has a double shadow*!'

That was the explanation of his sidelong glances, of the habitual stoop. There was a something always at his side, which none could see, but which cast a shadow.

He turned, presently, and saw us at the window. Instantly, he crossed the road to the shady side of the street. I told Harry all that had passed, and we agreed that it would be as well not to say a word to Lettie.

Two days later, when I returned from a visit to Harry's studio, I found the whole house in confusion.

I learnt from Lettie that while my wife was upstairs, Grieve had called, had not waited for the servant to announce him, but had walked straight into the dining room, where Lettie was sitting. She noticed that he avoided looking at the picture, and, to make sure of not seeing it, had seated himself on the sofa just beneath it. He had then, in spite of Lettie's angry remonstrances, renewed his offer of love, strengthening it finally by assuring her that poor George with his dying breath had implored him to seek her, and watch over her, and marry her.

'I was so indignant I hardly knew how to answer him,' said Lettie. 'When, suddenly, just as he uttered the last words, there came a twang like the breaking of a guitar—and—I hardly know how to describe it—but the portrait had fallen, and the corner of the heavy frame had struck him on the head, cutting it open, and rendering him insensible.'

They had carried him upstairs, by the direction of the doctor, for whom my wife at once sent on hearing what had occurred. He was laid on the couch in my dressing room, where I went to see him. I intended to reproach him for coming to the house, despite my prohibition, but I found him delirious. The doctor said it was a queer case; for, though the blow was a severe one, it was hardly enough to account for the symptoms of brain fever. When he learnt that Grieve had but just returned in the *Pioneer* from the North, he said it was possible that the privation and hardship had told on his constitution and sown the seeds of the malady.

We sent for a nurse, who was to sit up with him, by the doctor's directions.

The rest of my story is soon told. In the middle of the night I was roused by a loud scream. I slipped on my clothes, and rushed out to find the nurse, with Lettie in her arms, in a faint. We carried her into her room, and then the nurse explained the mystery to us.

It appears that about midnight Grieve sat up in bed, and began to talk. And he said such terrible things that the nurse became alarmed. Nor was she much reassured when she became aware that the light of her single candle flung what seemed to be two shadows of the sick man on the wall.

Terrified beyond measure, she had crept into Lettie's room, and confided her fears to her; and Lettie, who was a courageous and kindly girl, dressed herself; and said she would sit with her. She, too, saw the double shadow—but what she heard was far more terrible.

Grieve was sitting up in bed, gazing at the unseen figure to which the shadow belonged. In a voice that trembled with emotion, he begged the haunting spirit to leave him, and prayed its forgiveness.

'You know the crime was not premeditated. It was a sudden temptation of the devil that made me strike the blow, and fling you over the precipice. It was the devil tempting me with the recollection of her exquisite face—of the tender love that might have been mine, but for you. But she will not listen to me. See, she turns away from me, as if she knew I was your murderer, George Mason!'

It was Lettie who repeated in a horrified whisper this awful confession.

I could see it all now! As I was about to tell Lettie of the many strange things

I had concealed from her, the nurse, who had gone to see her patient, came running back in alarm.

Vincent Grieve had disappeared. He had risen in his delirious terror, had opened the window, and leaped out. Two days later his body was found in the river.

A curtain hangs now before poor George's portrait, though it is no longer connected with any supernatural marvels; and never, since the night of Vincent Grieve's death, have we seen aught of that most mysterious haunting presence—the Shadow of a Shade.

———————

Holloway Horn

1886–?

During the 1930s, Holloway Horn was a regular contributor to magazines such as *Punch*, *Tatler* and *Good Housekeeping*, and newspapers such as the *Evening Standard*. He also wrote a number of popular novels during that time, including *Purple Claw* and *Elusive Lady*. The story that follows has been much anthologised but is a real treasure.

THE OLD MAN

MARTIN THOMPSON was not a desirable character. He possessed a clever, plausible tongue, and for years past had lived, with no little success, on his wits. He had promoted doubtful boxing competitions and still more doubtful sweepstakes. He had been a professional backer, in which capacity he had defrauded the bookies; again, a bookmaker who had swindled his 'clients'. There was more cunning than imagination in his outlook, but, within his limits, he possessed a certain distorted ability.

He was known to his intimates as Knocker Thompson, and as such had a surprisingly wide reputation. In outward appearance he was a gentleman, for long experience had taught him to avoid the flashy and distinctive in dress. Indeed, his quiet taste had often proved a valuable business asset.

Naturally, his fortunes varied, but he was usually more or less in funds. As Knocker sometimes said in his more genial moments: 'For every mug that dies, there's ten others born.'

Funds were rather low, however, on the evening when he met the old man. Knocker had spent the early part of the evening with two acquaintances in a hotel near Leicester Square. It was a business meeting, and relations had been a little strained; opinions had been freely expressed which indicated a complete lack of confidence in Knocker, and an unmistakable atmosphere had resulted. Not that he *resented* the opinions in the least, but at that juncture he *needed* the unquestioned trust of the two men.

He was not in the best of humours, therefore, as he turned into Whitcomb Street on his way to Charing Cross. The normal plainness of his features was deepened by a scowl, and the general result startled the few people who glanced at him.

But at eight o'clock in the evening, Whitcomb Street is not a crowded thorough-fare, and there was no one near them when the old man spoke to him. He was standing in a passage near the Pall Mall end, and Knocker could not see him clearly.

'Hello, Knocker!' he said.

Thompson swung round.

In the darkness he made out the dim figure, the most conspicuous feature of which was a long, white beard.

'Hello!' returned Thompson, suspiciously, for as far as he knew he did not number among his acquaintances an old man with a white beard.

'It's cold . . .' said the old man.

'What d'you want?' asked Thompson, curtly. 'Who are you?'

'I am an old man, Knocker.'

'Look here, what's the game? I don't know you . . .'

'No. But I know you.'

'If that's all you've got to say . . .' said Knocker uneasily.

'It is nearly all. Will you buy a paper? It is not an ordinary paper, I assure you.'

'How do you mean . . . not an ordinary paper?'

'It is tomorrow night's *Echo*,' said the old man calmly.

'You're loopy, old chap, that's what's wrong with you. Look here, things aren't too brisk, but here's half a dollar . . . and better luck!' For all his lack of principle, Knocker had the crude generosity of those who live precariously.

'Luck!' The old man laughed with a quietness that jarred on Knocker's nerves. In some queer way it seemed to run up and down his spine.

'Look here!' he said again, conscious of some strange, unreal quality in the old, dimly seen figure in the passage. 'What's the blinking game?'

'It is the oldest game in the world, Knocker.'

'Not so free with my name . . . if you don't mind.'

'Are you ashamed of it?'

'No,' said Knocker stoutly. 'What do you want? I've got no time to waste with the likes of you.'

'Then go . . . Knocker.'

'What do you *want*?' Knocker insisted, strangely uneasy.

'Nothing. Won't you take the paper? There is no other like it in the world. Nor will there be—for twenty-four hours.'

'I don't suppose there *are* many of tomorrow's papers on sale . . . yet,' said Knocker with a grin.

'It contains tomorrow's winners,' said the old man, in the same casual manner.

'I don't think!' retorted Knocker.

'There it is; you may read for yourself.'

From the darkness a paper was thrust at Knocker, whose unwilling fingers closed on it. A laugh came from somewhere in the recesses in the passage, and Knocker was alone.

He was suddenly and uncomfortably aware of his beating heart, but gripped himself and walked on until he came to a lighted shop front where he glanced at the paper.

'Thursday, July 29, 1926 . . .' he read.

He thought a moment.

It was Wednesday . . . he was positive it was Wednesday. He took out his diary. It was Wednesday, the twenty-eighth day of July—the last day of the Kempton Park meeting. He had no doubt on the point, none whatever.

With a strange feeling he glanced at the paper again. July 29, 1926. He turned to the back page almost instinctively—the page with the racing results.

Gatwick . . .

That day's meeting was at Kempton Park. Tomorrow was the first day of the Gatwick meeting, and there, staring at him, were the five winners. He passed his hand across his forehead; it was damp with cold perspiration.

'There's a trick somewhere,' he muttered to himself, and carefully re-examined the date of the paper. It was printed on each page . . . clear and unaltered. He scrutinised the unit figure of the year, but the 'six' had not been tampered with.

He glanced hurriedly at the front page. There was a flaring headline about the Coal Strike . . . that wasn't twenty-*five*. With professional care he examined the racing results. Inkerman had won the first race . . . Inkerman—and Knocker had made up his mind to back Paper Clip with more money than he could afford to lose. Paper Clip was merely an also-ran. He noticed that people who passed were glancing at him curiously. Hurriedly he pushed the paper into an inner pocket and walked on.

Never had Knocker so needed a drink. He entered a snug little 'pub' near Charing Cross and was thankful to find the saloon bar nearly deserted. Fortified with his drink he turned again to the paper. Inkerman had come home at 6 to 1. He made certain hurried but satisfactory calculations. Salmon House had won the second; he had expected that, but not at such a price . . . 7 to 4 on. Shallot—Shallot of all horses!—had romped away with the third, the big race. Seven lengths . . . at 100 to 8! Knocker licked his dry lips. There was no fake about the paper in his hand. He knew the horses that were running at Gatwick the following day and the results were there before him. The fourth and fifth winners were at short prices; but Inkerman and Shallot were enough . . .

It was too late to get into touch with any of the bookmakers that evening, and in any case it would not be advisable to put money on before the day of the race. The better way would be to go to Gatwick in the morning and wire the bets from the course.

He had another drink . . . and another.

Gradually, in the genial atmosphere of the saloon bar, his uneasiness left him. The affair ceased to appear uncanny and grotesque, and became a part of the casual happenings of the day. Into Knocker's slightly fuddled brain came the memory of a film he had once seen which had made a big impression on him at the time. There was an Eastern magician in the film, with a white beard, a long, white beard just like the one belonging to the old man. The magician had done the most extraordinary things . . . on the screen.

But whatever the explanation, Knocker was satisfied it was not a fake. The old chap had not asked for any money; indeed, he had not even taken the half-crown that Knocker had offered him. And as Knocker knew, you always collected the dibs—or attempted to—if you were running a fake.

He thought pleasantly of what he would do in the ring at Gatwick the following day. He was in rather low water, but he could put his hands on just about enough to make the bookies sit up. And with a second winner at 100 to 8!

He had still another drink and stood the barman one too.

'D'you know anything for tomorrow?' The man behind the bar knew Thompson quite well by sight and reputation.

Knocker hesitated.

'Yes,' he said. 'Sure thing. Salmon House in the second race. Price'll be a bit short, but it's a snip.'

'Thanks very much; I'll have a bit on meself.'

Ultimately he left the saloon bar. He was a little shaky; his doctor had warned him not to drink, but surely on such a night . . .

The following morning he went to Gatwick. It was a meeting he liked, and usually he was very lucky there. But that day it was not merely a question of luck. There was a streak of caution in his bets on the first race, but he flung caution to the wind after Inkerman had come in a comfortable winner—*and at 6 to 1.* The horse and the price! He had no doubts left. Salmon House won the second, a hot favourite at 7 to 4 on.

In the big race most of the punters left Shallot alone. The horse had little form, and there was no racing reason why anyone should back him. He was among what the bookies call 'the Rags'. But Knocker cared nothing for 'form' that day. He spread his money judiciously. Twenty here, twenty there. Not until ten minutes before the race did he wire any money to the West End offices, but some of the biggest men in the game opened their eyes when his wires came through. He was out to win a fortune. And he won.

As the horses entered the straight one of them was lengths ahead of the field. It carried the flashing yellow and blue of Shallot's owner. The groan that went up from the punters around him was satisfactory, but there was no thrill in the race for him; he had been certain that Shallot would win. There was no objection . . . and he proceeded to collect.

His pockets were bulging with notes, but his winnings were as nothing compared with the harvest he would reap from the big men in the West End. He ordered a bottle of champagne, and with a silent grin drank the health of the old man with the beard before he sent for the taxi that would take him back to the station. There was no train for half an hour, and, when at last it started, his carriage had filled with racing men, among whom were several he knew. The wiser racegoers rarely wait until the end of a meeting.

Knocker was usually very expansive after a good day, but that afternoon he took no part in the conversation, with the exception of an occasional grunt when a remark was made to him. Try as he would he could not keep his thoughts away from the old man. It was the memory of the laugh that remained with him most vividly. He could still feel that queer sensation down his spine . . .

On a sudden impulse he took out the paper, which was still in his pocket. He had no real interest in news, as such, for racing absorbed the whole of his very limited imagination. As far as he could tell from a casual inspection it was a very ordinary sort of paper. He made up his mind to get another in town and compare the two in order to see if the old man had spoken the truth. Not that it mattered very much, he assured himself.

Suddenly his incurious glance was held. A paragraph in the stop-press column had caught his eye. An exclamation burst from him.

'Death in race-train,' the paragraph was headed. Knocker's heart was pumping, but he read on mechanically: 'Mr Martin Thompson, a well-known racing man, died this afternoon as he was returning from Gatwick.'

He got no further; the paper fell from his limp fingers on to the floor of the carriage.

'Look at Knocker,' someone said. 'He's ill . . .'

He was breathing heavily and with difficulty.

'Stop . . . stop the train,' he gasped, and strove to rise and lurch towards the communication cord.

'Steady on, Knocker,' one of them said, and grasped his arm. 'You sit down, old chap . . . mustn't pull that darned thing . . .'

He sat down . . . or rather collapsed into the seat. His head fell forward.

They forced whisky between his lips, but it was of no avail.

'He's dead,' came the awe-struck voice of the man who held him.

No one noticed the paper on the floor. In the general upset it had been kicked under the seat, and it is not possible to say what became of it. Perhaps it was swept up by the cleaners at Waterloo.

Perhaps . . .

No one knows.

Elizabeth Jane Howard
b. 1923

Her first novel, *The Beautiful Visit*, won Elizabeth Jane Howard
the John Llewellyn Rhys Memorial Prize in 1950. Since then she
has written many successful novels and short stories, as well as
film and television screenplays and a biography. She was secretary
of the Inland Waterways Association for three years, and it was
during those years that she wrote this tale of a sinister canal trip.

THREE MILES UP

THERE WAS ABSOLUTELY NOTHING LIKE IT.
An unoriginal conclusion, and one that he had drawn a hundred times
during the last fortnight. Clifford would make some subtle and intelligent
comparison, but he, John, could only continue to repeat that it was quite unlike
anything else. It had been Clifford's idea, which, considering Clifford, was surprising. When you looked at him, you would not suppose him capable of it.
However, John reflected, he had been ill, some sort of breakdown these clever
people went in for, and that might account for his uncharacteristic idea of hiring
a boat and travelling on canals. On the whole, John had to admit, it was a good
idea. He had never been on a canal in his life, although he had been in almost
every kind of boat, and thought he knew a good deal about them; so much,
indeed, that he had embarked on the venture in a light-hearted, almost a patronising manner. But it was not nearly as simple as he had imagined. Clifford, of
course, knew nothing about boats; but he had admitted that almost everything
had gone wrong with a kind of devilish versatility which had almost frightened
him. However, that was all over, and John, who had learned painfully all about
the boat and her engine, felt that the former at least had run her gamut of disaster. They had run out of food, out of petrol, and out of water; had dropped their
windlass into the deepest lock, and, more humiliating, their boat hook into the
side-pond. The head had come off the hammer. They had been disturbed for
one whole night by a curious rustling in the cabin, like a rat in a paper bag, when
there was no paper, and, so far as they knew, no rat. The battery had failed and
had had to be recharged. Clifford had put his elbow through an already cracked
window in the cabin. A large piece of rope had wound itself round the propeller

with a malignant intensity which required three men and half a morning to unravel. And so on, until now there was really nothing left to go wrong, unless one of them drowned, and surely it was impossible to drown in a canal.

'I suppose one might easily drown in a lock?' he asked aloud.

'We must be careful not to fall into one,' Clifford replied.

'What?' John steered with fierce concentration, and never heard anything people said to him for the first time, almost on principle.

'I said we must be careful not to fall *into* a lock.'

'Oh. Well there aren't any more now until after the Junction. Anyway, we haven't yet, so there's really no reason why we should start now. I only wanted to know whether we'd drown if we did.'

'Sharon might.'

'What?'

'Sharon might.'

'Better warn her then. She seems agile enough.' His concentrated frown returned, and he settled down again to the wheel. John didn't mind where they went, or what happened, so long as he handled the boat, and all things considered, he handled her remarkably well. Clifford planned and John steered: and until two days ago they had both quarrelled and argued over a smoking and unusually temperamental primus. Which reminded Clifford of Sharon. Her advent and the weather were really their two unadulterated strokes of good fortune. There had been no rain, and Sharon had, as it were, dropped from the blue on to the boat, where she speedily restored domestic order, stimulated evening conversation, and touched the whole venture with her attractive being: the requisite number of miles each day was achieved, the boat behaved herself, and admirable meals were steadily and regularly prepared. She had, in fact, identified herself with the journey, without making the slightest effort to control it: a talent which many women were supposed in theory to possess, when, in fact, Clifford reflected gloomily, most of them were bored with the whole thing, or tried to dominate it.

Her advent was a remarkable, almost a miraculous, piece of luck. He had, after a particularly ill-fed day, and their failure to dine at a small hotel, desperately telephoned all the women he knew who seemed in the least suitable (and they were surprisingly few), with no success. They had spent a miserable evening, John determined to argue about everything, and he, Clifford, refusing to speak; until, both in a fine state of emotional tension, they had turned in for the night. While John snored, Clifford had lain distraught, his resentment and despair circling round John and then touching his own smallest and most random thoughts; until his mind found no refuge and he was left, divided from it, hostile and afraid, watching it in terror racing on in the dark like some malignant machine utterly out of his control.

The next day things had proved no better between them, and they had continued throughout the morning in a silence which was only occasionally and elaborately broken. They had tied up for lunch beside a wood, which hung heavy and magnificent over the canal. There was a small clearing beside which John then proposed to moor, but Clifford failed to achieve the considerable leap necessary to stop the boat; and they had drifted helplessly past it. John flung him a line, but it was not until the boat was secured, and they were safely in the cabin, that the storm had broken. John, in attempting to light the primus, spilt a quantity of paraffin on Clifford's bunk. Instantly all his despair of the previous evening had contracted. He hated John so much that he could have murdered him. They both lost their tempers, and for the ensuing hour and a half had conducted a blazing quarrel which, even at the time, secretly horrified them both in its intensity.

It had finally ended with John striding out of the cabin, there being no more to say. He had returned almost at once, however.

'I say, Clifford. Come and look at this.'

'At what?'

'Outside, on the bank.'

For some unknown reason Clifford did get up and did look. Lying face downwards quite still on the ground, with her arms clasping the trunk of a large tree, was a girl.

'How long has she been there?'

'She's asleep.'

'She can't have been asleep all the time. She must have heard some of what we said.'

'Anyway, who is she? What is she doing here?'

Clifford looked at her again. She was wearing a dark twill shirt and dark trousers, and her hair hung over her face, so that it was almost invisible. 'I don't know. I suppose she's alive?'

John jumped cautiously ashore. 'Yes, she's alive all right. Funny way to lie.'

'Well, it's none of our business anyway. Anyone can lie on a bank if they want to.'

'Yes, but she must have come in the middle of our row, and it does seem queer to stay, and then go to sleep.'

'Extraordinary,' said Clifford wearily. Nothing was really extraordinary, he felt, nothing. 'Are we moving on?'

'Let's eat first. I'll do it.'

'Oh, I'll do it.'

The girl stirred, unclasped her arms, and sat up. They had all stared at each other for a moment, the girl slowly pushing the hair from her forehead. Then she had said: 'If you will give me a meal, I'll cook it.'

Afterwards they had left her to wash up, and had walked about the wood, while Clifford suggested to John that they ask the girl to join them. 'I'm sure she'd come,' he said. 'She didn't seem at all clear about what she was doing.'

'We can't just pick somebody up out of a wood,' said John, scandalised.

'Where do you suggest we pick them up? If we don't have someone, this holiday will be a failure.'

'We don't know anything about her.'

'I can't see that that matters very much. She seems to cook well. We can at least ask her.'

'All right. Ask her then. She won't come.'

When they returned to the boat, she had finished the washing-up, and was sitting on the floor of the cockpit, with her arms stretched behind her head. Clifford asked her; and she accepted as though she had known them a long time and they were simply inviting her to tea.

'Well, but look here,' said John, thoroughly taken aback. 'What about your things?'

'My things?' she looked enquiringly and a little defensively from one to the other.

'Clothes and so on. Or haven't you got any? Are you a gypsy or something? Where do you come from?'

'I am not a gypsy,' she began patiently; when Clifford, thoroughly embarrassed and ashamed, interrupted her.

'Really, it's none of our business who you are, and there is absolutely no need for us to ask you anything. I'm very glad you will come with us, although I feel we should warn you that we are new to this life, and anything might happen.'

'No need to warn me,' she said, and smiled gratefully at him.

After that, they both felt bound to ask her nothing; John because he was afraid of being made to look foolish by Clifford, and Clifford because he had stopped John.

'Good Lord, we shall never get rid of her; and she'll fuss about condensation,' John had muttered aggressively as he started the engine. But she was very young, and did not fuss about anything. She had told them her name, and settled down, immediately and easily: gentle, assured and unselfconscious to a degree remarkable in one so young. They were never sure how much she had overheard them, for she gave no sign of having heard anything. A friendly but uncommunicative creature.

The map on the engine box started to flap, and immediately John asked, 'Where are we?'

'I haven't been watching, I'm afraid. Wait a minute.'

'We just passed under a railway bridge,' John said helpfully.

'Right. Yes. About four miles from the Junction, I think. What's the time?'

'Five thirty.'

'Which way are we going when we get to the Junction?'

'We haven't time for the big loop. I must be back in London by the fifteenth.'

'The alternative is to go up as far as the basin, and then simply turn round and come back, and who wants to do that?'

'Well, we'll know the route then. It'll be much easier coming back.'

Clifford did not reply. He was not attracted by the route being easier, and he wanted to complete his original plan.

'Let us wait till we get there.' Sharon appeared with tea and marmalade sandwiches.

'All right, let's wait.' Clifford was relieved.

'It'll be almost dark by five thirty. I think we ought to have a plan,' John said. 'Thank you, Sharon.'

'Have tea first.' She curled herself on to the floor with her back to the cabin doors and a mug in her hands.

They were passing rows of little houses with gardens that backed on to the canal. They were long narrow strips, streaked with cinder paths, and crowded with vegetables and chicken huts, fruit trees and perambulators; sometimes ending with fat white ducks, and sometimes in a tiny patch of grass with a bench on it.

'Would you rather keep ducks or sit on a bench?' asked Clifford.

'Keep ducks,' said John promptly. 'More useful. Sharon wouldn't mind which she did. Would you, Sharon?' He liked saying her name, Clifford noticed. 'You could be happy anywhere, couldn't you?' He seemed to be presenting her with the widest possible choice.

'I might *be* anywhere,' she answered after a moment's thought.

'Well you happen to be on a canal, and very nice for us.'

'In a wood, and then on a canal,' she replied contentedly, bending her smooth dark head over her mug.

'Going to be fine tomorrow,' said John. He was always a little embarrassed at any mention of how they found her and his subsequent rudeness.

'Yes. I like it when the whole sky is so red and burning and it begins to be cold.'

'*Are* you cold?' said John, wanting to worry about it: but she tucked her dark shirt into her trousers and answered composedly:

'Oh no. I am never cold.'

They drank their tea in a comfortable silence. Clifford started to read his map, and then said they were almost on to another sheet. 'New country,' he said with satisfaction. 'I've never been here before.'

'You make it sound like an exploration; doesn't he, Sharon?' said John.

'Is that a bad thing?' She collected the mugs. 'I am going to put these away. You will call me if I am wanted for anything.' And she went into the cabin again.

There was a second's pause, a minute tribute to her departure; and, lighting cigarettes, they settled down to stare at the long, silent stretch of water ahead.

John thought about Sharon. He thought rather desperately that really they still knew nothing about her, and that when they went back to London they would in all probability never see her again.

Perhaps Clifford would fall in love with her, and she would naturally reciprocate, because she was so young and Clifford was reputed to be so fascinating and intelligent, and because women were always foolish and loved the wrong man. He thought all these things with equal intensity, glanced cautiously at Clifford, and supposed he was thinking about her; then wondered what she would be like in London, clad in anything else but her dark trousers and shirt. The engine coughed; and he turned to it in relief.

Clifford was making frantic calculations of time and distance; stretching their time, and diminishing the distance, and groaning that with the utmost optimism they could not be made to fit. He was interrupted by John swearing at the engine, and then for no particular reason he remembered Sharon, and reflected with pleasure how easily she left the mind when she was not present, how she neither obsessed nor possessed one in her absence, but was charming to see.

The sun had almost set when they reached the Junction, and John slowed down to neutral while they made up their minds. To the left was the straight cut which involved the longer journey originally planned; and curving away to the right was the short arm which John advocated. The canal was fringed with rushes, and there was one small cottage with no light in it. Clifford went into the cabin to tell Sharon where they were, and then, as they drifted slowly in the middle of the Junction, John suddenly shouted:

'Clifford! What's the third turning?'

'There are only two.' Clifford reappeared. 'Sharon is busy with dinner.'

'No, look. Surely that is another cut.'

Clifford stared ahead. 'Can't see it.'

'Just to the right of the cottage. Look. It's not so dark as all that.'

Then Clifford saw it very plainly. It seemed to wind away from the cottage on a fairly steep curve, and the rushes shrouding it from anything but the closest view were taller than the rest.

'Have another look at the map. I'll reverse for a bit.'

'Found it. It's just another arm. Probably been abandoned,' said Clifford eventually.

The boat had swung round; and now they could see the continuance of the curve dully gleaming ahead, and banked by reeds.

'Well, what shall we do?'

'Getting dark. Let's go up a little way, and moor. Nice quiet mooring.'

'With some nice quiet mud banks,' said John grimly. 'Nobody uses that.'

'How do you know?'

'Well, look at it. All those rushes, and it's sure to be thick with weed.'

'Don't go up it then. But we shall go aground if we drift about like this.'

'*I* don't mind going up it,' said John doggedly. 'What about Sharon?'

'What about her?'

'Tell her about it.'

'We've found a third turning,' Clifford called above the noise of the primus through the cabin door.

'One you had not expected?'

'Yes. It looks very wild. We were thinking of going up it.'

'Didn't you say you wanted to explore?' She smiled at him.

'You are quite ready to try it? I warn you we shall probably run hard aground. Look out for bumps with the primus.'

'I am quite ready, and I am quite sure we shan't run aground,' she answered with charming confidence in their skill.

They moved slowly forward in the dusk. Why they didn't run aground, Clifford could not imagine: John really was damned good at it. The canal wound and wound, and the reeds grew not only thick on each bank, but in clumps across the canal. The light drained out of the sky into the water and slowly drowned there; the trees and the banks became heavy and black.

Clifford began to clear things away from the heavy dew which had begun to rise. After two journeys he remained in the cabin, while John crawled on, alone. Once, on a bend, John thought he saw a range of hills ahead with lights on them, but when he was round the curve and had time to look again he could see no hills: only a dark indeterminate waste of country stretched ahead.

He was beginning to consider the necessity of mooring, when they came to a bridge; and shortly after he saw a dark mass which he took to be houses. When the boat had crawled for another fifty yards or so, he stopped the engine, and drifted in absolute silence to the bank. The houses, about half a dozen of them, were much nearer than he had at first imagined, but there were no lights to be seen. Distance is always deceptive in the dark, he thought, and jumped ashore with a bowline. When, a few minutes later, he took a sounding with the boat hook, the water proved unexpectedly deep; and he concluded that by incredible good fortune they had moored at the village wharf. He made everything fast, and joined the others in the cabin with mixed feelings of pride and resentment; that he should have achieved so much under such difficult conditions, and that they (by 'they' he meant Clifford), should have contributed so little towards the achievement. He found Clifford reading *Bradshaw's Guide to the Canals and Navigable Rivers* in one corner and Sharon, with her hair pushed back behind her ears, bending over the primus with a knife. Her ears are pale, exactly the colour of her face, he thought; wanted to touch them; then felt horribly ashamed, and hated Clifford.

'Let's have a look at *Bradshaw*,' he said, as though he had not noticed Clifford reading it.

But Clifford handed him the book in the most friendly manner, remarking that he couldn't see where they were. 'In fact you have surpassed yourself with your brilliant navigation. We seem to be miles from anywhere.'

'What about your famous ordnance?'

'It's not on any sheet I have. The new one I thought we should use only covers the loop we planned. There is precisely three-quarters of a mile of this canal shown on the present sheet and then we run off the map. I suppose there must once have been trade here, but I cannot imagine what, or where.'

'I expect things change,' said Sharon. 'Here is the meal.'

'How can you see to cook?' asked John, eyeing his plate ravenously.

'There is a candle.'

'Yes, but we've selfishly appropriated that.'

'Should I need more light?' she asked, and looked troubled.

'There's no should about it. I just don't know how you do it, that's all. Chips exactly the right colour, and you never drop anything. It's marvellous.'

She smiled a little uncertainly at him and lit another candle.

'Luck, probably,' she said, and set it on the table.

They ate their meal, and John told them about the mooring. 'Some sort of village. I think we're moored at the wharf. I couldn't find any rings without the torch, so I've used the anchor.' This small shaft was intended for Clifford, who had dropped the spare torch battery in the washing-up bowl, and forgotten to buy another. But it was only a small shaft, and immediately afterwards John felt much better. His aggression slowly left him, and he felt nothing but a peaceful and well-fed affection for the other two.

'Extraordinarily cut off this is,' he remarked over coffee.

'It's very pleasant in here. Warm, and extremely full of us.'

'Yes. I know. A quiet village, though, you must admit.'

'I shall believe in your village when I see it.'

'Then you would believe it?'

'No he wouldn't, Sharon. Not if he didn't want to, and couldn't find it on the map. That map!'

The conversation turned again to their remoteness, and to how cut off one liked to be and at what point it ceased to be desirable; to boats, telephones, and, finally, canals: which, Clifford maintained, possessed the perfect proportions of urbanity and solitude.

Hours later, when they had turned in for the night, Clifford reviewed the conversation, together with others they had had, and remembered with surprise how little Sharon had actually said. She listened to everything and occasionally, when they appealed to her, made some small composed remark which was oddly at variance with their passionate interest. 'She has an elusive quality of freshness about her,' he thought, 'which is neither naive nor stupid nor dull, and she invokes no responsibility. She does not want us to know what she was, or why we found her as we did, and curiously, I, at least, do not want to know. She is what women ought to be,' he concluded with sudden pleasure; and slept.

He woke the next morning to find it very late, and stretched out his hand to wake John.

'We've all overslept. Look at the time.'

'Good Lord! Better wake Sharon.'

Sharon lay between them on the floor, which they had ceded her because, oddly enough, it was the widest and most comfortable bed. She seemed profoundly asleep, but at the mention of her name sat up immediately, and rose, almost as though she had not been asleep at all.

The morning routine, which, involving the clothing of three people and shaving of two of them, was necessarily a long and complicated business, began. Sharon boiled water, and Clifford, grumbling gently, hoisted himself out of his bunk and repaired with a steaming jug to the cockpit. He put the jug on a seat, lifted the canvas awning, and leaned out. It was absolutely grey and still; a little white mist hung over the canal, and the country stretched out desolate and unkempt on every side with no sign of a living creature. The village, he thought— suddenly: John's village—and was possessed of a perilous uncertainty and fear. I am getting worse, he thought, this holiday is doing me no good. I am mad. I imagined that he said we moored by a village wharf. For several seconds he stood gripping the gunwale, and searching desperately for anything: huts, a clump of trees, which could in the darkness have been mistaken for a village. But there was nothing near the boat except tall rank rushes which did not move at all. Then, when his suspense was becoming unbearable, John joined him with another steaming jug of water.

'We shan't get anywhere at this rate,' he began; and then . . . 'Hello! Where's my village?'

'I was wondering that,' said Clifford. He could almost have wept with relief, and quickly began to shave, deeply ashamed of his private panic.

'Can't understand it,' John was saying. It was no joke, Clifford decided, as he listened to his hearty, puzzled ruminations.

At breakfast John continued to speculate upon what he had or had not seen, and Sharon listened intently while she filled the coffeepot and cut bread. Once or twice she met Clifford's eye with a glance of discreet amusement.

'I must be mad, or else the whole place is haunted,' finished John comfortably. These two possibilities seemed to relieve him of any further anxiety in the matter, as he ate a huge breakfast and set about greasing the engine.

'Well,' said Clifford, when he was alone with Sharon. 'What do you make of that?'

'It is easy to be deceived in such matters,' she answered perfunctorily.

'Evidently. Still, John is an unlikely candidate, you must admit. Here, I'll help you dry.'

'Oh no. It is what I am here for.'

'Not entirely, I hope.'

'Not entirely.' She smiled and relinquished the cloth.

John eventually announced that they were ready to start. Clifford, who had assumed that they were to retrace their journey, was surprised, and a little alarmed, to find John intent upon continuing it. He seemed undeterred by the state of the canal, which, as Clifford immediately pointed out, rendered navigation both arduous and unrewarding. He announced that the harder it was, the more he liked it, adding very firmly, 'Anyway we must see what happens.'

'We shan't have time to do anything else.'

'Thought you wanted to explore.'

'I do, but . . . What do you think, Sharon?'

'I think John will have to be a very good navigator to manage that.' She indicated the rush- and weed-ridden reach before them. 'Do you think it's possible?'

'Of course it's possible. I'll probably need some help though.'

'I'll help you,' she said.

So on they went.

They made incredibly slow progress. John enjoys showing off his powers to her, thought Clifford, half amused, half exasperated, as he struggled for the fourth time in an hour to scrape weeds off the propeller.

Sharon eventually retired to cook lunch.

'Surprising amount of water here,' John said suddenly.

'Oh?'

'Well, I mean, with all this weed and stuff, you'd expect the canal to have silted up. I'm sure nobody uses it.'

'The whole thing is extraordinary.'

'Is it too late in the year for birds?' asked Clifford later.

'No, I don't think so. Why?'

'I haven't heard one, have you?'

'Haven't noticed, I'm afraid. There's someone anyway. First sign of life.'

An old man stood near the bank watching them. He was dressed in corduroy and wore a straw hat.

'Good morning,' shouted John, as they drew nearer.

He made no reply, but inclined his head slightly. He seemed very old. He was leaning on a scythe, and as they drew almost level with him, he turned away and began slowly cutting rushes. A pile of them lay neatly stacked beside him.

'Where does this canal go? Is there a village further on?' Clifford and John asked simultaneously. He seemed not to hear, and as they chugged steadily past, Clifford was about to suggest that they stop and ask again, when he called after them: 'Three miles up you'll find the village. Three miles up that is,' and turned away to his rushes again.

'Well now we know something, anyway,' said John.

'We don't even know what the village is called.'

'Soon find out. Only three miles.'

'Three miles!' said Clifford darkly. 'That might mean anything.'

'Do you want to turn back?'

'Oh no, not now. I want to see this village now. My curiosity is thoroughly aroused.'

'Shouldn't think there'll be anything to see. Never been in such a wild spot. Look at it.'

Clifford looked at it. Half wilderness, half marsh, dank and grey and still, with single trees bare of their leaves; clumps of hawthorn that might once have been hedge, sparse and sharp with berries; and, in the distance, hills and an occasional wood: these were all one could see, beyond the lines of rushes which edged the canal winding ahead.

They stopped for a lengthy meal, which Sharon described as lunch and tea together, it being so late; and then, appalled at how little daylight was left, continued.

'We've hardly been any distance at all,' said John forlornly. 'Good thing there were no locks. I shouldn't think they'd have worked if there were.'

'*Much* more than three miles,' he said, about two hours later. Darkness was descending and it was becoming very cold.

'Better stop,' said Clifford.

'Not yet. I'm determined to reach that village.'

'Dinner is ready,' said Sharon sadly. 'It will be cold.'

'Let's stop.'

'You have your meal. I'll call if I want you.'

Sharon looked at them, and Clifford shrugged his shoulders. 'Come on. I will. I'm tired of this.'

They shut the cabin doors. John could hear the pleasant clatter of their meal, and just as he was coming to the end of the decent interval which he felt must elapse before he gave in, they passed under a bridge, the first of the day, and, clutching at any straw, he immediately assumed that it prefaced the village. 'I think we're nearly there,' he called.

Clifford opened the door. 'The village?'

'No, a bridge. Can't be far now.'

'You're mad, John. It's pitch-dark.'

'You can see the bridge though.'

'Yes. Why not moor under it?'

'Too late. Can't turn round in this light, and she's not good at reversing. Must be nearly there. You go back, I don't need you.'

Clifford shut the door again. He was beginning to feel irritated with John behaving in this childish manner and showing off to impress Sharon. It was amusing in the morning, but really he was carrying it a bit far. Let him manage the thing himself then. When, a few minutes later, John shouted that they had reached the sought-after village, Clifford merely pulled back the little curtain over a cabin window, rubbed the condensation, and remarked that he could see nothing. 'No light at least.'

'He is happy anyhow,' said Sharon peaceably.

'Going to have a look around,' said John, slamming the cabin doors and blowing his nose.

'Surely you'll eat first?'

'If you've left anything. My God it's cold! It's *unnaturally* cold.'

'We won't be held responsible if he dies of exposure, will we?' said Clifford.

She looked at him, hesitated a moment, but did not reply, and placed a steaming plate in front of John. She doesn't want us to quarrel, Clifford thought, and with an effort at friendliness he asked: 'What does tonight's village look like?'

'Much the same. Only one or two houses, you know. But the old man called it a village.' He seemed uncommunicative; Clifford thought he was sulking. But after eating the meal, he suddenly announced, almost apologetically, 'I don't think I shall walk round. I'm absolutely worn out. You go if you like. I shall start turning in.'

'All right. I'll have a look. You've had a hard day.'

Clifford pulled on a coat and went outside. It was, as John said, incredibly cold and almost overwhelmingly silent. The clouds hung very low over the boat, and mist was rising everywhere from the ground, but he could dimly discern the black huddle of cottages lying on a little slope above the bank against which the boat was moored. He did actually set foot onshore, but his shoe sank immediately into a marshy hole. He withdrew it, and changed his mind. The prospect of groping round those dark and silent houses became suddenly distasteful, and he joined the others with the excuse that it was too cold and that he also was tired.

A little later, he lay half-conscious in a kind of restless trance, with John sleeping heavily opposite him. His mind seemed full of foreboding, fear of something unknown and intangible: he thought of them lying in warmth on the cold secret canal with desolate miles of water behind and probably beyond; the old man and the silent houses; John, cut off and asleep, and Sharon, who lay on the floor beside him. Immediately he was filled with a sudden and most violent desire for her, even to touch her for her to know that he was awake.

'Sharon,' he whispered; 'Sharon, Sharon,' and stretched down his fingers to her in the dark.

Instantly her hand was in his, each smooth and separate finger warmly clasped. She did not move or speak, but his relief was indescribable and for a long while he lay in an ecstasy of delight and peace, until his mind slipped imperceptibly with her fingers into oblivion.

When he woke he found John absent and Sharon standing over the primus. 'He's outside,' she said.

'Have I overslept again?'

'It is late. I am boiling water for you now.'

'We'd better try and get some supplies this morning.'

'There is no village,' she said, in a matter-of-fact tone.

'What?'

'John says not. But we have enough food, if you don't mind this queer milk from a tin.'

'No, I don't mind,' he replied, watching her affectionately. 'It doesn't really surprise me,' he added after a moment.

'The village?'

'No village. Yesterday I should have minded awfully. Is that you, do you think?'

'Perhaps.'

'It doesn't surprise you about the village at all, does it? Do you love me?'

She glanced at him quickly, a little shocked, and said quietly: 'Don't you know?' then added: 'It doesn't surprise me.'

John seemed very disturbed. 'I don't like it,' he kept saying as they shaved. 'Can't understand it at all. I could have sworn there were houses last night. You saw them, didn't you?'

'Yes.'

'Well, don't you think it's very odd?'

'I do.'

'Everything looks the same as yesterday morning. I don't like it.'

'It's an adventure, you must admit.'

'Yes, but I've had enough of it. I suggest we turn back.'

Sharon suddenly appeared, and, seeing her, Clifford knew that he did not want to go back. He remembered her saying: 'Didn't you say you wanted to explore?' She would think him weak-hearted if they turned back all those dreary miles with nothing to show for it. At breakfast, he exerted himself in persuading John to the same opinion. John finally agreed to one more day, but, in turn, extracted a promise that they would then go back whatever happened. Clifford agreed to this, and Sharon for some inexplicable reason laughed at them both. So that eventually they prepared to set off in an atmosphere of general good humour.

Sharon began to fill the water tank with their four-gallon can. It seemed too heavy for her, and John dropped the starter and leapt to her assistance.

She let him take the can and held the funnel for him. Together they watched the rich, even stream of water disappear.

'You shouldn't try to do that,' he said. 'You'll hurt yourself.'

'Gypsies do it,' she said.

'I'm awfully sorry about that. You know I am.'

'I shouldn't have minded if you had thought I was a gypsy.'

'I do like you,' he said, not looking at her. 'I do like you. You won't disappear altogether when this is over, will you?'

'You probably won't find I'll disappear for good,' she replied comfortingly.

'Come on,' shouted Clifford.

It's all right for *him* to talk to her, John thought, as he struggled to swing the starter. He just doesn't like me doing it; and he wished, as he had often begun to do, that Clifford was not there.

They had spasmodic engine trouble in the morning, which slowed them down; and the consequent halts, with the difficulty they experienced of mooring anywhere (the banks seemed nothing but marsh), were depressing and cold. Their good spirits evaporated: by lunch time John was plainly irritable and frightened, and Clifford had begun to hate the grey silent land on either side, with the woods and hills which remained so consistently distant. They both wanted to give it up by then, but John felt bound to stick to his promise, and Clifford was secretly sure that Sharon wished to continue.

While she was preparing another late lunch, they saw a small boy who stood on what once had been the towpath watching them. He was bareheaded, wore corduroy, and had no shoes. He held a long reed, the end of which he chewed as he stared at them.

'Ask him where we are,' said John; and Clifford asked.

He took the reed out of his mouth, but did not reply.

'Where do you live then?' asked Clifford as they drew almost level with him.

'I told you. Three miles up,' he said; and then he gave a sudden little shriek of fear, dropped the reed, and turned to run down the bank the way they had come. Once he looked back, stumbled and fell, picked himself up sobbing, and ran faster. Sharon had appeared with lunch a moment before, and together they listened to his gasping cries growing fainter and fainter, until he had run himself out of their sight.

'What on earth frightened him?' said Clifford.

'I don't know. Unless it was Sharon popping out of the cabin like that.'

'Nonsense. But he was a very frightened little boy. And, I say, do you realise . . .'

'He was a very foolish little boy,' Sharon interrupted. She was angry, Clifford noticed with surprise, really angry, white and trembling, and with a curious expression which he did not like.

'We might have got something out of him,' said John sadly.

'Too late now,' Sharon said. She had quite recovered herself.

They saw no one else. They journeyed on throughout the afternoon; it grew colder, and at the same time more and more airless and still. When the light began to fail, Sharon disappeared as usual to the cabin. The canal became more tortuous, and John asked Clifford to help him with the turns. Clifford complied unwillingly: he did not want to leave Sharon, but as it had been he who had insisted on their continuing, he could hardly refuse. The turns were nerve-racking, as the canal was very narrow and the light grew worse and worse.

'All right if we stop soon?' asked John eventually.

'Stop now if you like.'

'Well, we'll try and find a tree to tie up to. This swamp is awful. Can't think how that child ran.'

'That child . . .' began Clifford anxiously; but John, who had been equally unnerved by the incident, and did not want to think about it, interrupted. 'Is there a tree ahead anywhere?'

'Can't see one. There's a hell of a bend coming though. Almost back on itself. Better slow a bit more.'

'Can't. We're right down as it is.'

They crawled round, clinging to the outside bank, which seemed always to approach them, its rushes to rub against their bows, although the wheel was hard over. John grunted with relief, and they both stared ahead for the next turn.

They were presented with the most terrible spectacle. The canal immediately broadened, until no longer a canal but a sheet, an infinity, of water stretched ahead; oily, silent, and still, as far as the eye could see, with no country edging it, nothing but water to the low grey sky above it. John had almost immediately cut out the engine, and now he tried desperately to start it again, in order to turn round. Clifford instinctively glanced behind them. He saw no canal at all, no inlet, but grasping and close to the stern of the boat, the reeds and rushes of a marshy waste closing in behind them. He stumbled to the cabin doors and pulled them open. It was very neat and tidy in there, but empty. Only one stern door of the cabin was free of its catch, and it flapped irregularly backwards and forwards with their movements in the boat.

There was no sign of Sharon at all.

Henry James
1843–1916

Although he was born in New York, Henry James spent much of
his life in Europe, particularly Britain, and many of his novels,
such as *The Portrait of a Lady*, are based on the clash of European
and American cultures. The story included in this collection, like
James's famous novella, *The Turn of the Screw*, demonstrates the
mastery with which he creates subtle psychological tension.

THE ROMANCE
OF CERTAIN OLD
CLOTHES

TOWARDS THE MIDDLE of the eighteenth century there lived in the Province
of Massachusetts a widowed gentlewoman, the mother of three children.
Her name is of little account: I shall take the liberty of calling her Mrs
Willoughby—a name, like her own, of a highly respectable sound. She had been
left a widow after some six years of marriage, and had devoted herself to the care
of her progeny. These young persons grew up in a manner to reward her zeal
and to gratify her fondest hopes. The first-born was a son, whom she had called
Bernard, after his father. The others were daughters—born at an interval of
three years apart. Good looks were traditional in the family, and this youthful
trio were not likely to allow the tradition to perish. The boy was of that fair and
ruddy complexion and of that athletic mould which in those days (as in these)
were the sign of genuine English blood—a frank, affectionate young fellow, a
deferential son, a patronising brother, and a steadfast friend. Clever, however, he
was not; the wit of the family had been apportioned chiefly to his sisters. Mr
Willoughby had been a great reader of Shakespeare, at a time when this pursuit
implied more liberality of taste than at the present day, and in a community
where it required much courage to patronise the drama even in the closet; and
he had wished to record his admiration of the great poet by calling his daughters
out of his favourite plays. Upon the elder he had bestowed the romantic name of

Viola; and upon the younger, the more serious one of Perdita, in memory of a little girl born between them, who had lived but a few weeks.

When Bernard Willoughby came to his sixteenth year, his mother put a brave face upon it, and prepared to execute her husband's last request. This had been an earnest entreaty that, at the proper age, his son should be sent out to England, to complete his education at the University of Oxford, which had been the seat of his own studies. Mrs Willoughby fancied that the lad's equal was not to be found in the two hemispheres, but she had the antique wifely submissiveness. She swallowed her sobs, and made up her boy's trunk and his simple provincial outfit, and sent him on his way across the seas. Bernard was entered at his father's college, and spent five years in England, without great honour, indeed, but with a vast deal of pleasure and no discredit. On leaving the University he made the journey to France. In his twenty-third year he took ship for home, prepared to find poor little New England (New England was very small in those days) an utterly intolerable place of abode. But there had been changes at home, as well as in Mr Bernard's opinions. He found his mother's house quite habitable, and his sisters grown into two very charming young ladies, with all the accomplishments and graces of the young women of Britain, and a certain native-grown gentle *brusquerie* and wildness, which, if it was not an accomplishment, was certainly a grace the more. Bernard privately assured his mother that his sisters were fully a match for the most genteel young women in England; whereupon poor Mrs Willoughby, you may be sure, bade them hold up their heads. Such was Bernard's opinion, and such, in a tenfold higher degree, was the opinion of Mr Arthur Lloyd. This gentleman, I hasten to add, was a college mate of Mr Bernard, a young man of reputable family, of a good person and a handsome inheritance, which latter appurtenance he proposed to invest in trade in this country. He and Bernard were warm friends; they had crossed the ocean together, and the young American had lost no time in presenting him at his mother's house, where he had made quite as good an impression as that which he had received, and of which I have just given a hint.

The two sisters were at this time in all the freshness of their youthful bloom; each wearing, of course, this natural brilliancy in the manner that became her best. They were equally dissimilar in appearance and character. Viola, the elder—now in her twenty-second year—was tall and fair, with calm grey eyes and auburn tresses; a very faint likeness to the Viola of Shakespeare's comedy, whom I imagine as a brunette (if you will), but a slender, airy creature, full of the softest and finest emotions. Miss Willoughby, with her candid complexion, her fine arms, her majestic height, and her slow utterance, was not cut out for adventures. She would never have put on a man's jacket and hose; and, indeed, being a very plump beauty, it is perhaps as well that she would not. Perdita, too, might very well have exchanged the sweet melancholy of her name against something more in consonance with her aspect and disposition. She was a positive brunette, short of stature, light of foot, with a vivid dark brown eye. She had been from her childhood a creature of smiles and gaiety; and so far from making you wait for an answer to your speech, as her handsome sister was wont to do (while she gazed at you with her somewhat cold grey eyes), she had given you the choice of half a dozen, suggested by the successive clauses of your proposition, before you had got to the end of it.

The young girls were very glad to see their brother once more; but they found themselves quite able to maintain a reserve of goodwill for their brother's friend. Among the young men their friends and neighbours, the *belle jeunesse* of the Colony, there were many excellent fellows, several devoted swains, and some two or three who enjoyed the reputation of universal charmers and conquerors. But the home-bred arts and the somewhat boisterous gallantry of those honest young colonists were completely eclipsed by the good looks, the fine clothes, the punctilious courtesy, the perfect elegance, the immense information, of Mr Arthur Lloyd. He was in reality no paragon; he was an honest, resolute, intelligent young man rich in pounds sterling, in his health and comfortable hopes, and his little capital of uninvested affections. But he was a gentleman; he had a handsome face; he had studied and travelled; he spoke French, he played on the flute, and he read verses aloud with very great taste. There were a dozen reasons why Miss Willoughby and her sister should forthwith have been rendered fastidious in the choice of their male acquaintance. The imagination of woman is especially adapted to the various small conventions and mysteries of polite society. Mr Lloyd's talk told our little New England maidens a vast deal more of the ways and means of people of fashion in European capitals than he had any idea of doing. It was delightful to sit by and hear him and Bernard discourse upon the fine people and fine things they had seen. They would all gather round the fire after tea, in the little wainscoted parlour—quite innocent then of any intention of being picturesque or of being anything else, indeed, than economical, and saving an outlay in stamped papers and tapestries—and the two young men would remind each other, across the rug, of this, that, and the other adventure. Viola and Perdita would often have given their ears to know exactly what adventure it was, and where it happened, and who was there, and what the ladies had on; but in those days a well-bred young woman was not expected to break into the conversation of her own movement or to ask too many questions; and the poor girls used therefore to sit fluttering behind the more languid—or more discreet—curiosity of their mother.

That they were both very fine girls Arthur Lloyd was not slow to discover; but it took him some time to satisfy himself as to the apportionment of their charms. He had a strong presentiment—an emotion of a nature entirely too cheerful to be called a foreboding—that he was destined to marry one of them; yet he was unable to arrive at a preference, and for such a consummation a preference was certainly indispensable, inasmuch as Lloyd was quite too gallant a fellow to make a choice by lot and be cheated of the heavenly delight of falling in love. He resolved to take things easily, and to let his heart speak. Meanwhile, he was on a very pleasant footing. Mrs Willoughby showed a dignified indifference to his 'intentions', equally remote from a carelessness of her daughters' honour and from that odious alacrity to make him commit himself, which, in his quality of a young man of property, he had but too often encountered in the venerable dames of his native islands. As for Bernard, all that he asked was that his friend should take his sisters as his own; and as for the poor girls themselves, however each may have secretly longed for the monopoly of Mr Lloyd's attentions, they observed a very decent and modest and contented demeanour.

Towards each other, however, they were somewhat more on the offensive. They were good sisterly friends, betwixt whom it would take more than a day for the seeds of jealousy to sprout and bear fruit; but the young girls felt that the seeds had been sown on the day that Mr Lloyd came into the house. Each made up her mind that, if she should be slighted, she would bear her grief in silence, and that no one should be any the wiser; for if they had a great deal of love, they had also a great deal of pride. But each prayed in secret, nevertheless, that upon *her* the glory might fall. They had need of a vast deal of patience, of self-control, and of dissimulation. In those days a young girl of decent breeding could make no advances whatever, and barely respond, indeed, to those that were made. She was expected to sit still in her chair with her eyes on the carpet, watching the spot where the mystic handkerchief should fall. Poor Arthur Lloyd was obliged to undertake his wooing in the little wainscoted parlour, before the eyes of Mrs Willoughby, her son, and his prospective sister-in-law. But youth and love are so cunning that a hundred signs and tokens might travel to and fro, and not one of these three pair of eyes detect them in their passage. The young girls had but one chamber and one bed between them, and for long hours together they were under each other's direct inspection. That each knew that she was being watched, however, made not a grain of difference in those little offices which they mutually rendered, or in the various household tasks which they performed in common. Neither flinched nor fluttered beneath the silent batteries of her sister's eyes. The only apparent change in their habits was that they had less to say to each other. It was impossible to talk about Mr Lloyd, and it was ridiculous to talk about anything else. By tacit agreement they began to wear all their choice finery, and to devise such little implements of coquetry, in the way of ribbons and topknots and furbelows, as were sanctioned by indubitable modesty. They executed in the same inarticulate fashion an agreement of sincerity on these delicate matters. 'Is it better so?' Viola would ask, tying a bunch of ribbons on her bosom, and turning about from her glass to her sister. Perdita would look up gravely from her work and examine the decoration. 'I think you had better give it another loop,' she would say, with great solemnity, looking hard at her sister with eyes that added, 'upon my honour!' So they were forever stitching and trimming their petticoats, and pressing out their muslins, and contriving washes and ointments and cosmetics, like the ladies in the household of the Vicar of Wakefield. Some three or four months went by; it grew to be midwinter, and as yet Viola knew that if Perdita had nothing more to boast of than she, there was not much to be feared from her rivalry. But Perdita by this time, the charming Perdita, felt that her secret had grown to be tenfold more precious than her sister's.

One afternoon Miss Willoughby sat alone before her toilet glass combing out her long hair. It was getting too dark to see; she lit the two candles in their sockets on the frame of her mirror, and then went to the window to draw her curtains. It was a grey December evening; the landscape was bare and bleak, and the sky heavy with snow-clouds. At the end of the long garden into which her window looked was a wall with a little postern door, opening into a lane. The door stood ajar, as she could vaguely see in the gathering darkness, and moved slowly to and fro, as if someone were swaying it from the lane without. It was doubtless a servant-maid. But as she was about to drop her curtain, Viola saw her sister step within the garden and hurry along the path towards the house. She dropped the curtain, all save a little crevice for her eyes. As Perdita came up the path, she seemed to be examining something in her hand, holding it close to her eyes. When she reached the house she stopped a moment, looked intently at the object, and pressed it to her lips.

Poor Viola slowly came back to her chair, and sat down before her glass, where, if she had looked at it less abstractedly, she would have seen her handsome features sadly disfigured by jealousy. A moment afterwards the door opened behind her, and her sister came into the room, out of breath, and her cheeks aglow with the chilly air.

Perdita started. 'Ah,' said she, 'I thought you were with our mother.' The ladies were to go to a tea party, and on such occasions it was the habit of one of the young girls to help their mother to dress. Instead of coming in Perdita lingered at the door.

'Come in, come in,' said Viola. 'We've more than an hour yet. I should like you very much to give a few strokes to my hair.' She knew her sister wished to retreat, and that she could see in the glass all her movements in the room. 'Nay, just help me with my hair,' she said, 'and I'll go to mamma.'

Perdita came reluctantly, and took the brush. She saw her sister's eyes, in the glass, fastened hard upon her hands. She had not made three passes, when Viola clapped her own right hand upon her sister's left, and started out of her chair. 'Whose ring is that?' she cried passionately, drawing her towards the light.

On the young girl's third finger glistened a little gold ring, adorned with a couple of small rubies. Perdita felt that she need no longer keep her secret, yet that she must put a bold face on her avowal. 'It's mine,' she said proudly.

'Who gave it to you?' cried the other.

Perdita hesitated a moment. 'Mr Lloyd.'

'Mr Lloyd is generous, all of a sudden.'

'Ah no,' cried Perdita, with spirit, 'not all of a sudden. He offered it to me a month ago.'

'And you needed a month's begging to take it?' said Viola, looking at the little trinket; which indeed was not especially elegant, although it was the best that the jeweller of the Province could furnish. 'I shouldn't have taken it in less than two.'

'It isn't the ring,' said Perdita, 'it's what it means!'

'It means that you're not a modest girl,' cried Viola. 'Pray, does your mother know of your conduct? does Bernard?'

'My mother has approved my "conduct", as you call it. Mr Lloyd has asked my hand, and mamma has given it. Would you have had him apply to you, sister?'

Viola gave her sister a long look, full of passionate envy and sorrow. Then she dropped her lashes on her pale cheeks and turned away. Perdita felt that it had not been a pretty scene; but it was her sister's fault. But the elder girl rapidly called back her pride, and turned herself about again. 'You have my very best wishes,' she said, with a low curtsy. 'I wish you every happiness, and a very long life.'

Perdita gave a bitter laugh. 'Don't speak in that tone,' she cried. 'I'd rather you cursed me outright. Come, sister,' she added, 'he couldn't marry both of us.'

'I wish you very great joy,' Viola repeated mechanically, sitting down to her glass again, 'and a very long life, and plenty of children.'

There was something in the sound of these words not at all to Perdita's taste. 'Will you give me a year, at least?' she said. 'In a year I can have one little boy—or one little girl at least. If you'll give me your brush again I'll do your hair.'

'Thank you,' said Viola. 'You had better go to mamma. It isn't becoming that a young lady with a promised husband should wait on a girl with none.'

'Nay,' said Perdita, good-humouredly, 'I have Arthur to wait upon me. You need my service more than I need yours.'

But her sister motioned her away, and she left the room. When she had gone poor Viola fell on her knees before her dressing table, buried her head in her arms, and poured out a flood of tears and sobs. She felt very much better for this effusion of sorrow. When her sister came back, she insisted upon helping her to dress, and upon her wearing her prettiest things. She forced upon her acceptance a bit of lace of her own, and declared that now that she was to be married she should do her best to appear worthy of her lover's choice. She discharged these offices in stern silence; but, such as they were, they had to do duty as an apology and an atonement; she never made any other.

Now that Lloyd was received by the family as an accepted suitor, nothing remained but to fix the wedding day. It was appointed for the following April, and in the interval preparations were diligently made for the marriage. Lloyd, on his side, was busy with his commercial arrangements, and with establishing a correspondence with the great mercantile house to which he had attached himself in England. He was therefore not so frequent a visitor at Mrs Willoughby's as during the months of his diffidence and irresolution, and poor Viola had less to suffer than she had feared from the sight of the mutual endearments of the young lovers. Touching his future sister-in-law, Lloyd had a perfectly clear conscience. There had not been a particle of sentiment uttered between them, and he had not the slightest suspicion that she coveted anything more than his fraternal regard. He was quite at his ease; life promised so well, both domestically and financially. The lurid clouds of revolution were as yet twenty years beneath the horizon, and that his connubial felicity should take a tragic turn it was absurd, it was blasphemous, to apprehend. Meanwhile at Mrs Willoughby's there was a greater rustling of silks, a more rapid clicking of scissors and flying of needles, than ever. Mrs Willoughby had determined that her daughter should carry from home the most elegant outfit that her money could buy, or that the country could furnish. All the sage women in the county were convened, and their united taste was brought to bear on Perdita's wardrobe. Viola's situation, at this moment, was assuredly not to be envied. The poor girl had an inordinate love of dress, and the very best taste in the world, as her sister perfectly well knew. Viola was tall, she was stately and sweeping, she was made to carry stiff brocade and masses of heavy lace, such as belong to the toilet of a rich man's wife. But Viola sat aloof, with her beautiful arms folded and her head averted, while her mother and sister and the venerable women aforesaid worried and wondered over their materials, oppressed by the multitude of their resources. One day there came in a beautiful piece of white silk, brocaded with celestial blue and silver, sent by the bridegroom himself—it not being thought amiss in those days that the husband-elect should contribute to the bride's trousseau. Perdita was quite at loss to imagine a fashion which should do sufficient honour to the splendour of the material.

'Blue's your colour, sister, more than mine,' she said, with appealing eyes. 'It's a pity it's not for you. You'd know what to do with it.'

Viola got up from her place and looked at the great shining fabric as it lay spread over the back of a chair. Then she took it up in her hands and felt it— lovingly, as Perdita could see—and turned about towards the mirror with it. She let it roll down to her feet, and flung the other end over her shoulder, gathering it in about her waist with her white arm bare to the elbow. She threw back her head, and looked at her image, and a hanging tress of her auburn hair fell upon the gorgeous surface of the silk. It made a dazzling picture. The women standing about uttered a little 'Ah!' of admiration. 'Yes, indeed,' said Viola, quietly, 'blue is my colour.' But Perdita could see that her fancy had been stirred, and that she would now fall to work and solve all their silken riddles. And indeed she behaved very well, as Perdita, knowing her insatiable love of millinery, was quite ready to declare. Innumerable yards of lustrous silk and satin, of muslin, velvet, and lace, passed through her cunning hands, without a word of envy coming from her lips. Thanks to her industry, when the wedding day came Perdita was prepared to espouse more of the vanities of life than any fluttering young bride who had yet challenged the sacramental blessing of a New England divine.

It had been arranged that the young couple should go out and spend the first days of their wedded life at the country house of an English gentleman—a man of rank and a very kind friend to Lloyd. He was an unmarried man; he professed himself delighted to withdraw and leave them for a week to their billing and cooing. After the ceremony at church—it had been performed by an English parson—young Mrs Lloyd hastened back to her mother's house to change her wedding gear for a riding dress. Viola helped her to effect the change, in the little old room in which they had been fond sisters together. Perdita then hurried off to bid farewell to her mother, leaving Viola to follow. The parting was short; the horses were at the door and Arthur impatient to start. But Viola had not followed, and Perdita hastened back to her room, opening the door abruptly. Viola, as usual, was before the glass, but in a position which caused the other to stand still, amazed. She had dressed herself in Perdita's cast-off wedding veil and wreath, and on her neck she had hung the heavy string of pearls which the young girl had received from her husband as a wedding gift. These things had been hastily laid aside, to await their possessor's disposal on her return from the country. Bedizened in this unnatural garb, Viola stood at the mirror, plunging a long look into its depths, and reading Heaven knows what audacious visions. Perdita was horrified. It was a hideous image of their old rivalry come to life again. She made a step towards her sister, as if to pull off the veil and the flowers. But catching her eyes in the glass, she stopped.

'Farewell, Viola,' she said. 'You might at least have waited till I had got out of the house.' And she hurried away from the room.

Mr Lloyd had purchased in Boston a house which, in the taste of those days, was considered a marvel of elegance and comfort; and here he very soon established himself with his young wife. He was thus separated by a distance of twenty miles from the residence of his mother-in-law. Twenty miles, in that primitive era of roads and conveyances, were as serious a matter as a hundred at the present day, and Mrs Willoughby saw but little of her daughter during the first twelvemonth of her marriage. She suffered in no small degree from her absence; and her affliction was not diminished by the fact that Viola had fallen into terribly low spirits and was not to be roused or cheered but by change of air and circumstances. The real cause of the young girl's dejection the reader will not be slow to suspect. Mrs Willoughby and her gossips, however, deemed her complaint a purely physical one, and doubted not that she would obtain relief from the remedy just mentioned. Her mother accordingly proposed on her behalf a visit to certain relatives on the paternal side, established in New York, who had long complained that they were able to see so little of their New England cousins. Viola was dispatched to these good people, under a suitable escort, and remained with them for several months. In the interval her brother Bernard, who had begun the practice of the law, made up his mind to take a wife. Viola came home to the wedding, apparently cured of her heartache, with honest roses and lilies in her face, and a proud smile on her lips. Arthur Lloyd came over from Boston to see his brother-in-law married, but without his wife, who was expecting shortly to present him with an heir. It was nearly a year since

Viola had seen him. She was glad—she hardly knew why—that Perdita had stayed at home. Arthur looked happy, but he was more grave and solemn than before his marriage. She thought he looked 'interesting'—for although the word in its modern sense was not then invented, we may be sure that the idea was. The truth is, he was simply preoccupied with his wife's condition. Nevertheless, he by no means failed to observe Viola's beauty and splendour, and how she quite effaced the poor little bride. The allowance that Perdita had enjoyed for her dress had now been transferred to her sister, who turned it to prodigious account. On the morning after the wedding, he had a lady's saddle put on the horse of the servant who had come with him from town, and went out with the young girl for a ride. It was a keen, clear morning in January; the ground was bare and hard, and the horses in good condition—to say nothing of Viola, who was charming in her hat and plume, and her dark blue riding coat, trimmed with fur. They rode all the morning, they lost their way, and were obliged to stop for dinner at a farmhouse. The early winter dusk had fallen when they got home. Mrs Willoughby met them with a long face. A messenger had arrived at noon from Mrs Lloyd; she was beginning to be ill, and desired her husband's immediate return. The young man, at the thought that he had lost several hours, and that by hard riding he might already have been with his wife, uttered a passionate oath. He barely consented to stop for a mouthful of supper, but mounted the messenger's horse and started off at a gallop.

He reached home at midnight. His wife had been delivered of a little girl. 'Ah, why weren't you with me?' she said, as he came to her bedside.

'I was out of the house when the man came. I was with Viola,' said Lloyd, innocently.

Mrs Lloyd made a little moan, and turned about. But she continued to do very well, and for a week her improvement was uninterrupted. Finally, however, through some indiscretion in the way of diet or of exposure, it was checked, and the poor lady grew rapidly worse. Lloyd was in despair. It very soon became evident that she was breathing her last. Mrs Lloyd came to a sense of her approaching end, and declared that she was reconciled with death. On the third evening after the change took place she told her husband that she felt she would not outlast the night. She dismissed her servants, and also requested her mother to withdraw—Mrs Willoughby having arrived on the preceding day. She had had her infant placed on the bed beside her, and she lay on her side, with the child against her breast, holding her husband's hands. The night-lamp was hidden behind the heavy curtains of the bed, but the room was illumined with a red glow from the immense fire of logs on the hearth.

'It seems strange to die by such a fire as that,' the young woman said, feebly trying to smile. 'If I had but a little of such fire in my veins! But I've given it all to this little spark of mortality.' And she dropped her eyes on her child. Then raising them she looked at her husband with a long, penetrating gaze. The last feeling which lingered in her heart was one of mistrust. She had not recovered from the shock which Arthur had given her by telling her that in the hour of her agony he had been with Viola. She trusted her husband very nearly as well as she loved him; but now that she was called away for ever, she felt a cold horror of her sister. She felt in her soul that Viola had never ceased to envy her good fortune; and a year of happy security had not effaced the young girl's image, dressed in her wedding garments, and smiling with coveted triumph. Now that Arthur was to be alone, what might not Viola do? She was beautiful, she was engaging; what arts might she not use, what impression might she not make upon the young man's melancholy heart? Mrs Lloyd looked at her husband in silence. It seemed hard, after all, to doubt of his constancy. His fine eyes were filled with tears; his face was convulsed with weeping; the clasp of his hands was warm and passionate. How noble he looked, how tender, how faithful and devoted! 'Nay,' thought Perdita, 'he's not for such as Viola. He'll never forget me. Nor does Viola truly care for him; she cares only for vanities and finery and jewels.' And she dropped her eyes on her white hands, which her husband's liberality had covered with rings, and on the lace ruffles which trimmed the edge of her nightdress. 'She covets my rings and my laces more than she covets my husband.'

At this moment the thought of her sister's rapacity seemed to cast a dark shadow between her and the helpless figure of her little girl. 'Arthur,' she said, 'you must take off my rings. I shall not be buried in them. One of these days my daughter shall wear them—my rings and my laces and silks. I had them all brought out and shown me today. It's a great wardrobe—there's not such another in the Province; I can say it without vanity now that I've done with it. It will be a great inheritance for my daughter, when she grows into a young woman. There are things there that a man never buys twice, and if they're lost you'll never again see the like. So you'll watch them well. Some dozen things I've left to Viola; I've named them to my mother. I've given her that blue and silver; it was meant for her; I wore it only once, I looked ill in it. But the rest are to be sacredly kept for this little innocent. It's such a providence that she should be my colour; she can wear my gowns; she has her mother's eyes. You know the same fashions come back every twenty years. She can wear my gowns as they are. They'll lie there quietly waiting till she grows into them—wrapped in camphor and rose leaves, and keeping their colours in the sweet-scented darkness. She shall have black hair, she shall wear my carnation satin. Do you promise me, Arthur?'

'Promise you what, dearest?'

'Promise me to keep your poor little wife's old gowns.'

'Are you afraid I'll sell them?'

'No, but that they may get scattered. My mother will have them properly wrapped up, and you shall lay them away under a double lock. Do you know the great chest in the attic, with the iron bands? There's no end to what it will hold. You can lay them all there. My mother and the housekeeper will do it, and give you the key. And you'll keep the key in your secretary, and never give it to anyone but your child. Do you promise me?'

'Ah, yes, I promise you,' said Lloyd, puzzled at the intensity with which his wife appeared to cling to this idea.

'Will you swear?' repeated Perdita.

'Yes, I swear.'

'Well—I trust you—I trust you,' said the poor lady, looking into his eyes with eyes in which, if he had suspected her vague apprehensions, he might have read an appeal quite as much as an assurance.

Lloyd bore his bereavement soberly and manfully. A month after his wife's death, in the course of commerce, circumstances arose which offered him an opportunity of going to England. He embraced it as a diversion from gloomy thoughts. He was absent nearly a year, during which his little girl was tenderly nursed and cherished by her grandmother. On his return he had his house again thrown open, and announced his intention of keeping the same state as during his wife's lifetime. It very soon came to be predicted that he would marry again, and there were at least a dozen young women of whom one may say that it was by no fault of theirs that, for six months after his return, the prediction did not come true. During this interval he still left his little daughter in Mrs Willoughby's hands, the latter assuring him that a change of residence at so tender an age was perilous to her health. Finally, however, he declared that his heart longed for his daughter's presence, and that she must be brought up to town. He sent his coach and his housekeeper to fetch her home. Mrs Willoughby was in terror lest something should befall her on the road; and, in accordance with this feeling, Viola offered to ride along with her. She could return the next day. So she went up to town with her little niece, and Mr Lloyd met her on the threshold of his house, overcome with her kindness and with gratitude. Instead of returning the next day, Viola stayed out the week; and when at last she reappeared, she had only come for her clothes. Arthur would not hear of her coming home, nor would the baby. She cried and moaned if Viola left her; and at the sight of her grief Arthur lost his wits, and swore that she was going to die. In fine, nothing would suit them but that Viola should remain until the poor child had grown used to strange faces.

It took two months to bring this consummation about; for it was not until this period had elapsed that Viola took leave of her brother-in-law. Mrs Willoughby had shaken her head over her daughter's absence; she declared it was not becoming, and that it was the talk of the town. She had reconciled herself to it only because, during the young girl's visit, the household enjoyed an unwonted term of peace. Bernard Willoughby had brought his wife home to live, between whom and her sister-in-law there existed a bitter hostility. Viola was perhaps no angel; but in the daily practice of life she was a sufficiently good-natured girl, and if she quarrelled with Mrs Bernard, it was not without provocation. Quarrel, however, she did, to the great annoyance not only of her antagonist, but of the two spectators of these constant altercations. Her stay in the household of her brother-in-law, therefore, would have been delightful, if only because it removed her from contact with the object of her antipathy at home. It was doubly—it was ten times—delightful, in that it kept her near the object of her old passion. Mrs Lloyd's poignant mistrust had fallen very far short of the truth. Viola's sentiment had been a passion at first, and a passion it remained—a passion of whose radiant heat, tempered to the delicate state of his feelings, Mr Lloyd very soon felt the influence. Lloyd, as I have hinted, was not a modern Petrarch; it was not in his nature to practise an ideal constancy. He had not been many days in the house with his sister-in-law before he began to assure himself that she was, in the language of that day, a devilish fine woman. Whether Viola really practised those insidious arts that her sister had been tempted to impute to her it is needless to enquire. It is enough to say that she found means to appear to the very best advantage. She used to seat herself every morning before the great fireplace in the dining room, at work upon a piece of tapestry, with her little niece disporting herself on the carpet at her feet, or on the train of her dress, and playing with her woollen balls. Lloyd would have been a very stupid fellow if he had remained insensible to the rich suggestions of this charming picture. He was prodigiously fond of his little girl, and was never weary of taking her in his arms and tossing her up and down, and making her crow with delight. Very often, however, he would venture upon greater liberties than the young lady was yet prepared to allow, and she would suddenly vociferate her displeasure. Viola would then drop her tapestry, and put out her handsome hands with the serious smile of the young girl whose virgin fancy has revealed to her all a mother's healing arts. Lloyd would give up the child, their eyes would meet, their hands would touch, and Viola would extinguish the little girl's sobs upon the snowy folds of the kerchief that crossed her bosom. Her dignity was perfect, and nothing could be more discreet than the manner in which she accepted her brother-in-law's hospitality. It may be almost said, perhaps, that there was something harsh in her reserve. Lloyd had a provoking feeling that she was in the house, and yet that she was unapproachable. Half an hour after supper, at the very outset of the long winter evenings, she would light her candle, and make the young man a most respectful curtsy, and march off to bed. If these were arts, Viola was a great artist. But their effect was so gentle, so gradual, they were calculated to work upon the young widower's fancy with such a finely shaded *crescendo*, that, as the reader has seen, several weeks elapsed before Viola began to feel sure that her return would cover her outlay. When this became morally certain, she packed up her trunk, and returned to her mother's house. For three days she waited; on the fourth Mr Lloyd made his appearance—a respectful but ardent suitor. Viola heard him out with great humility, and accepted him with infinite modesty. It is hard to imagine that Mrs Lloyd should have forgiven her husband; but if anything might have disarmed her resentment, it would have been the ceremonious continence of this interview. Viola imposed upon her lover but a short probation. They were married, as was becoming, with great privacy—almost with secrecy—in the hope perhaps, as was waggishly remarked at the time, that the late Mrs Lloyd wouldn't hear of it.

The marriage was to all appearance a happy one, and each party obtained what each had desired—Lloyd 'a devilish fine woman', and Viola—but Viola's desires, as the reader will have observed, have remained a good deal of a mystery. There were, indeed, two blots upon their felicity, but time would, perhaps, efface them. During the first three years of her marriage Mrs Lloyd failed to become a mother, and her husband on his side suffered heavy losses of money. This latter circumstance compelled a material retrenchment in his expenditure, and Viola was perforce less of a great lady than her sister had been. She contrived, however, to sustain with unbroken consistency the part of an elegant woman, although it must be confessed that it required the exercise of more ingenuity than belongs to your real aristocratic repose. She had long since ascertained that her sister's immense wardrobe had been sequestrated for the benefit of her daughter, and that it lay languishing in thankless gloom in the dusty attic. It was a revolting thought that these exquisite fabrics should await the commands of a little girl who sat in a highchair and ate bread-and-milk with a wooden spoon. Viola had the good taste, however, to say nothing about the matter until several months had expired. Then, at last, she timidly broached it to her husband. Was it not a pity that so much finery should be lost?—for lost it would be, what with colours fading, and moths eating it up, and the change of fashions. But Lloyd gave so abrupt and peremptory a negative to her enquiry, that she saw that for the present her attempt was vain. Six months went by, however, and brought with them new needs and new fancies. Viola's thoughts hovered lovingly about her sister's relics. She went up and looked at the chest in which they lay imprisoned. There was a sullen defiance in its three great padlocks and its iron bands, which only quickened her desires. There was something exasperating in its incorruptible immobility. It was like a grim and grizzled old household servant, who locks his jaws over a family secret. And then there was a look of capacity in its vast extent, and a sound as of dense fullness, when Viola knocked its side with the toe of her little slipper, which caused her to flush with baffled longing. 'It's absurd,' she cried; 'it's improper, it's wicked'; and she forthwith resolved upon another attack upon her husband. On the following day, after dinner, when he had had his wine, she bravely began it. But he cut her short with great sternness.

'Once and for all, Viola,' said he, 'it's out of the question. I shall be gravely displeased if you return to the matter.'

'Very good,' said Viola. 'I'm glad to learn the value at which I'm held. Great Heaven!' she cried, 'I'm a happy woman. It's an agreeable thing to feel one's self sacrificed to a caprice!' And her eyes filled with tears of anger and disappointment.

Lloyd had a good-natured man's horror of a woman's sobs, and he attempted—I may say he condescended—to explain. 'It's not a caprice, dear, it's a promise,' he said, 'an oath.'

'An oath? It's a pretty matter for oaths! and to whom, pray?'

'To Perdita,' said the young man, raising his eyes for an instant, but immediately dropping them.

'Perdita—ah, Perdita!' and Viola's tears broke forth. Her bosom heaved with stormy sobs—sobs which were the long-deferred counterpart of the violent fit of weeping in which she had indulged herself on the night when she discovered her sister's betrothal. She had hoped, in her better moments, that she had done with her jealousy; but her temper, on that occasion, had taken an ineffaceable fold. 'And pray, what right,' she cried, 'had Perdita to dispose of my future? What right had she to bind you to meanness and cruelty? Ah, I occupy a dignified place, and I make a very fine figure! I'm welcome to what Perdita has left! And what has she left? I never knew till now how little! Nothing, nothing, nothing.'

This was very poor logic, but it was very good passion. Lloyd put his arm around his wife's waist and tried to kiss her, but she shook him off with magnificent scorn. Poor fellow! he had coveted a 'devilish fine woman', and he had got one. Her scorn was intolerable. He walked away with his ears tingling—irresolute, distracted. Before him was his secretary, and in it the sacred key which with his own hand he had turned in the triple lock. He marched up and opened it, and took the key from a secret drawer, wrapped in a little packet which he had sealed with his own honest bit of blazonry. *Teneo*, said the motto—'I hold.' But he was ashamed to put it back. He flung it upon the table beside his wife.

'Keep it!' she cried. 'I want it not. I hate it!'

'I wash my hands of it,' cried her husband. 'God forgive me!'

Mrs Lloyd gave an indignant shrug of her shoulders, and swept out of the room, while the young man retreated by another door. Ten minutes later Mrs Lloyd returned, and found the room occupied by her little stepdaughter and the nursery maid. The key was not on the table. She glanced at the child. The child was perched on a chair with the packet in her hands. She had broken the seal with her own little fingers. Mrs Lloyd hastily took possession of the key.

At the habitual supper hour Arthur Lloyd came back from his counting room. It was the month of June, and supper was served by daylight. The meal was placed on the table, but Mrs Lloyd failed to make her appearance. The servant whom his master sent to call her came back with the assurance that her room was empty, and that the women informed him that she had not been seen since dinner. They had in truth observed her to have been in tears, and, supposing her to be shut up in her chamber, had not disturbed her. Her husband called her name in various parts of the house, but without response. At last it occurred to him that he might find her by taking the way to the attic. The thought gave him a strange feeling of discomfort, and he bade his servants remain behind, wishing no witness in his quest. He reached the foot of the staircase leading to the topmost flat, and stood with his hand on the banisters, pronouncing his wife's name. His voice trembled. He called again, louder and more firmly. The only sound which disturbed the absolute silence was a faint echo of his own tones, repeating his question under the great eaves. He nevertheless felt irresistibly moved to ascend the staircase. It opened upon a wide hall, lined with wooden closets, and terminating in a window which looked westward, and admitted the last rays of the sun. Before the window stood the great chest. Before the chest, on her knees, the young man saw with amazement and horror the figure of his wife. In an instant he crossed the interval between them, bereft of utterance. The lid of the chest stood open, exposing, amid their perfumed napkins, its treasure of stuffs and jewels. Viola had fallen backward from a kneeling posture, with one hand supporting her on the floor and the other pressed to her heart. On her limbs was the stiffness of death, and on her face, in the fading light of the sun, the terror of something more than death. Her lips were parted in entreaty, in dismay, in agony; and on her bloodless brow and cheeks there glowed the marks of ten hideous wounds from two vengeful ghostly hands.

M. R. James

1862–1936

The publication of *Ghost Stories of an Antiquary* in 1904
established Montague Rhodes James as a writer of macabre
stories, and for the rest of his life he combined a distinguished
academic career—director of the Fitzwilliam Museum and vice-
chancellor of Cambridge University—with an impressive output
of supernatural tales, famous for their evil and malignancy.

THE ASH TREE

E VERYONE WHO HAS TRAVELLED over Eastern England knows the smaller
country houses with which it is studded—the rather dank little buildings,
usually in the Italian style, surrounded with parks of some eighty to a hundred acres. For me they have always had a very strong attraction: with the grey
paling of split oak, the noble trees, the meres with their reed beds, and the line of
distant woods. Then, I like the pillared portico—perhaps stuck on to a red-brick
Queen Anne house which has been faced with stucco to bring it into line with
the 'Grecian' taste of the end of the eighteenth century; the hall inside, going up
to the roof, which hall ought always to be provided with a gallery and a small
organ. I like the library, too, where you may find anything from a Psalter of the
thirteenth century to a Shakespeare quarto. I like the pictures, of course; and
perhaps most of all I like fancying what life in such a house was when it was first
built, and in the piping times of landlords' prosperity, and not least now, when,
if money is not so plentiful, taste is more varied and life quite as interesting. I
wish to have one of these houses, and enough money to keep it together and
entertain my friends in it modestly.

But this is a digression. I have to tell you of a curious series of events which
happened in such a house as I have tried to describe. It is Castringham Hall in
Suffolk. I think a good deal has been done to the building since the period of my
story, but the essential features I have sketched are still there—Italian portico,
square block of white house, older inside than out, park with fringe of woods,
and mere. The one feature that marked out the house from a score of others is
gone. As you looked at it from the park, you saw on the right a great old ash tree
growing within half a dozen yards of the wall, and almost or quite touching the

building with its branches. I suppose it had stood there ever since Castringham ceased to be a fortified place, and since the moat was filled in and the Elizabethan dwelling house built. At any rate, it had well-nigh attained its full dimensions in the year 1690.

In that year the district in which the Hall is situated was the scene of a number of witch trials. It will be long, I think, before we arrive at a just estimate of the amount of solid reason—if there was any—which lay at the root of the universal fear of witches in old times. Whether the persons accused of this offence really did imagine that they were possessed of unusual powers of any kind; or whether they had the will at least, if not the power, of doing mischief to their neighbours; or whether all the confessions, of which there are so many, were extorted by the mere cruelty of the witch-finders—these are questions which are not, I fancy, yet solved. And the present narrative gives me pause. I cannot altogether sweep it away as mere invention. The reader must judge for himself.

Castringham contributed a victim to the *auto-da-fé*. Mrs Mothersole was her name, and she differed from the ordinary run of village witches only in being rather better off and in a more influential position. Efforts were made to save her by several reputable farmers of the parish. They did their best to testify to her character, and showed considerable anxiety as to the verdict of the jury.

But what seems to have been fatal to the woman was the evidence of the then proprietor of Castringham Hall—Sir Matthew Fell. He deposed to having watched her on three different occasions from his window, at the full of the moon, gathering sprigs 'from the ash tree near my house'. She had climbed into the branches, clad only in her shift, and was cutting off small twigs with a peculiarly curved knife, and as she did so she seemed to be talking to herself. On each occasion Sir Matthew had done his best to capture the woman, but she had always taken alarm at some accidental noise he had made, and all he could see when he got down to the garden was a hare running across the park in the direction of the village.

On the third night he had been at the pains to follow at his best speed, and had gone straight to Mrs Mothersole's house; but he had had to wait a quarter of an hour battering at her door, and then she had come out very cross, and apparently very sleepy, as if just out of bed; and he had no good explanation to offer of his visit.

Mainly on this evidence, though there was much more of a less striking and unusual kind from other parishioners, Mrs Mothersole was found guilty and condemned to die. She was hanged a week after the trial, with five or six more unhappy creatures, at Bury St Edmunds.

Sir Matthew Fell, then Deputy Sheriff, was present at the execution. It was a damp, drizzly March morning when the cart made its way up the rough grass hill outside Northgate, where the gallows stood. The other victims were apathetic or broken down with misery; but Mrs Mothersole was, as in life so in death, of a very different temper. Her 'poysonous Rage', as a reporter of the time puts it, 'did so work upon the Bystanders—yea, even upon the Hangman—that it was constantly affirmed of all that saw her that she presented the living Aspect of a mad Divell. Yet she offer'd no Resistance to the Officers of the Law; onely she looked upon those that laid Hands upon her with so direfull and venomous an Aspect that—as one of them afterwards assured me—the meer Thought of it preyed inwardly upon his Mind for six Months after.'

However, all that she is reported to have said was the seemingly meaningless words: 'There will be guests at the Hall.' Which she repeated more than once in an undertone.

Sir Matthew Fell was not unimpressed by the bearing of the woman. He had some talk upon the matter with the Vicar of his parish, with whom he travelled home after the assize business was over. His evidence at the trial had not been very willingly given; he was not specially infected with the witch-finding mania, but he declared, then and afterwards, that he could not give any other account of the matter than that he had given, and that he could not possibly have been mistaken as to what he saw. The whole transaction had been repugnant to him, for he was a man who liked to be on pleasant terms with those about him; but he saw a duty to be done in this business, and he had done it. That seems to have been the gist of his sentiments, and the Vicar applauded it, as any reasonable man must have done.

A few weeks after, when the moon of May was at the full, Vicar and Squire met again in the park, and walked to the Hall together. Lady Fell was with her mother, who was dangerously ill, and Sir Matthew was alone at home; so the Vicar, Mr Crome, was easily persuaded to take a late supper at the Hall.

Sir Matthew was not very good company this evening. The talk ran chiefly on family and parish matters, and, as luck would have it, Sir Matthew made a memorandum in writing of certain wishes or intentions of his regarding his estates, which afterwards proved exceedingly useful.

When Mr Crome thought of starting for home, about half past nine o'clock, Sir Matthew and he took a preliminary turn on the gravelled walk at the back of the house. The only incident that struck Mr Crome was this: they were in sight of the ash tree which I described as growing near the windows of the building, when Sir Matthew stopped and said:

'What is that that runs up and down the stem of the ash? It is never a squirrel? They will all be in their nests by now.'

The Vicar looked and saw the moving creature, but he could make nothing of its colour in the moonlight. The sharp outline, however, seen for an instant, was imprinted on his brain, and he could have sworn, he said, though it sounded foolish, that, squirrel or not, it had more than four legs.

Still, not much was to be made of the momentary vision, and the two men parted. They may have met since then, but it was not for a score of years.

Next day Sir Matthew Fell was not downstairs at six in the morning, as was his custom, nor at seven, nor yet at eight. Hereupon the servants went and knocked at his chamber door. I need not prolong the description of their anxious listenings and renewed batterings on the panels. The door was opened at last from the outside, and they found their master dead and black. So much you have guessed. That there were any marks of violence did not at the moment appear; but the window was open.

One of the men went to fetch the parson, and then by his directions rode on to give notice to the coroner. Mr Crome himself went as quick as he might to the Hall, and was shown to the room where the dead man lay. He has left some notes among his papers which show how genuine a respect and sorrow was felt for Sir Matthew, and there is also this passage, which I transcribe for the sake of the light it throws upon the course of events, and also upon the common beliefs of the time:

'There was not any the least Trace of an Entrance having been forc'd to the Chamber: but the Casement stood open, as my poor Friend would always have it in this Season. He had his evening Drink of small Ale in a silver Vessel of about a pint Measure, and tonight had not drunk it out. This Drink was examined by the Physician from Bury, a Mr Hodgkins, who could not, however, as he afterwards declar'd upon his Oath, before the Coroner's Quest, discover that any Matter of a venomous Kind was present in it. For, as was natural, in the great Swelling and Blackness of the Corpse, there was Talk made among the Neighbours of Poyson. The Body was very much disorder'd as it laid in the Bed, being twisted after so extream a Sort as gave too probable Conjecture that my worthy Friend and Patron had expir'd in great Pain and Agony. And what is as yet unexplain'd, and to myself the Argument of some horrid and artfull Designe in the Perpetrators of this barbarous Murther, was this, that the Women which were entrusted with the Laying-out of the Corpse and washing it, being both sad Persons and very well respected in their mournfull Profession, came to me in a great Pain and Distress both of Mind and Body, saying, what was indeed confirmed upon the first View, that they had no sooner touch'd the Breast of the Corpse with their naked Hands than they were sensible of a more than ordinary violent Smart and Acheing in their Palms, which, with their whole Forearms, in no long time swell'd so immoderately, the Pain still continuing, that, as afterwards proved, during many Weeks they were forc'd to lay by the Exercise of their Calling; and yet no Mark seen on the Skin.

'Upon hearing this, I sent for the Physician, who was still in the House, and we made as carefull a Proof as we were able by the Help of a small Magnifying Lens of Crystal of the condition of the Skin on this Part of the Body: but could not detect with the Instrument we had any Matter of Importance beyond a couple of small Punctures or Pricks, which we then concluded were the Spotts by which the Poyson might be introduced, remembering that Ring of *Pope Borgia*, with other known Specimens of the horrid Art of the Italian Poysoners of the last Age.

'So much is to be said of the Symptoms seen on the Corpse. As to what I am to add, it is meerly my own Experiment, and to be left to Posterity to judge whether there be anything of Value therein. There was on the Table by the Beddside a Bible of the small Size, in which my Friend—punctuall as in Matters of less Moment, so in this more weighty one—used nightly, and upon his first Rising, to read a sett Portion. And I taking it up—not without a Tear duly paid to him which from the Study of this poorer Adumbration was now pass'd to the Contemplation of its great Originall—it came into my Thoughts, as at such moments of Helplessness we are prone to catch at any the least Glimmer that makes Promise of Light, to make Trial of that old and by many accounted superstitious Practice of drawing the *Sortes*: of which a principall Instance, in the case of his late Sacred Majesty the Blessed Martyr King *Charles* and my Lord *Falkland*, was now much talked of. I must needs admit that by my Trial not much Assistance was afforded me: yet, as the Cause and Origin of these dreadfull Events may hereafter be search'd out, I set down the Results, in the case it may be found that they pointed the true Quarter of the Mischief to a quicker Intelligence than my own.

'I made, then, three Trials, opening the Book and placing my Finger upon certain Words: which gave in the first these Words, from Luke xiii.7, *Cut it down*; in the second, Isaiah xiii.20, *It shall never be inhabited*; and upon the third Experiment, Job xxxix.30, *Her young ones also suck up blood*.'

This is all that need be quoted from Mr Crome's papers. Sir Matthew Fell was duly coffined and laid into the earth, and his funeral sermon, preached by Mr Crome on the following Sunday, has been printed under the title of 'The Unsearchable Way; or, England's Danger and the Malicious Dealings of Antichrist', it being the Vicar's view, as well as that most commonly held in the neighbourhood, that the Squire was the victim of a recrudescence of the Popish Plot.

His son, Sir Matthew the second, succeeded to the title and estates. And so ends the first act of the Castringham tragedy. It is to be mentioned, though the fact is not surprising, that the new Baronet did not occupy the room in which his father had died. Nor, indeed, was it slept in by anyone but an occasional visitor during the whole of his occupation. He died in 1735, and I do not find that anything particular marked his reign, save a curiously constant mortality among his cattle and livestock in general, which showed a tendency to increase slightly as time went on.

Those who are interested in the details will find a statistical account in a letter to the *Gentleman's Magazine* of 1772, which draws the facts from the Baronet's own papers. He put an end to it at last by a very simple expedient, that of shutting up all his beasts in sheds at night, and keeping no sheep in his park. For he had noticed that nothing was ever attacked that spent the night indoors. After that the disorder confined itself to wild birds, and beasts of chase. But as we have no good account of the symptoms, and as all-night watching was quite unproductive of any clue, I do not dwell on what the Suffolk farmers called the 'Castringham sickness'.

The second Sir Matthew died in 1735, as I said, and was duly succeeded by his son, Sir Richard. It was in his time that the great family pew was built out on the north side of the parish church. So large were the Squire's ideas that several of the graves on that unhallowed side of the building had to be disturbed to satisfy his requirements. Among them was that of Mrs Mothersole, the position of which was accurately known, thanks to a note on a plan of the church and yard, both made by Mr Crome.

A certain amount of interest was excited in the village when it was known that the famous witch, who was still remembered by a few, was to be exhumed. And the feeling of surprise, and indeed disquiet, was very strong when it was found that, though her coffin was fairly sound and unbroken, there was no trace whatever inside it of body, bones, or dust. Indeed, it is a curious phenomenon, for at the time of her burying no such things were dreamt of as resurrection men, and it is difficult to conceive any rational motive for stealing a body otherwise than for the uses of the dissecting room.

The incident revived for a time all the stories of witch trials and of the exploits of the witches, dormant for forty years, and Sir Richard's orders that the coffin should be burnt were thought by a good many to be rather foolhardy, though they were duly carried out.

Sir Richard was a pestilent innovator, it is certain. Before his time the Hall had been a fine block of the mellowest red brick; but Sir Richard had travelled in Italy and become infected with the Italian taste, and, having more money than his predecessors, he determined to leave an Italian palace where he had found an English house. So stucco and ashlar masked the brick; some indifferent Roman marbles were planted about in the entrance hall and gardens; a reproduction of the Sibyl's temple at Tivoli was erected on the opposite bank of the mere; and Castringham took on an entirely new, and, I must say, a less engaging, aspect. But it was much admired, and served as a model to a good many of the neighbouring gentry in after-years.

ONE MORNING (it was in 1754) Sir Richard woke after a night of discomfort. It had been windy, and his chimney had smoked persistently, and yet it was so cold that he must keep up a fire. Also something had so rattled about the window that no man could get a moment's peace. Further, there was the prospect of several guests of position arriving in the course of the day, who would expect sport of some kind, and the inroads of the distemper (which continued among his game) had been lately so serious that he was afraid for his reputation as a game-preserver. But what really touched him most nearly was the other matter of his sleepless night. He could certainly not sleep in that room again.

That was the chief subject of his meditations at breakfast, and after it he began a systematic examination of the rooms to see which would suit his notions best. It was long before he found one. This had a window with an eastern aspect and that with a northern; this door the servants would be always passing, and he did not like the bedstead in that. No, he must have a room with a western lookout, so that the sun could not wake him early, and it must be out of the way of the business of the house. The housekeeper was at the end of her resources.

'Well, Sir Richard,' she said, 'you know that there is but one room like that in the house.'

'Which may that be?' said Sir Richard.

'And that is Sir Matthew's—the West Chamber.'

'Well, put me in there, for there I'll lie tonight,' said her master. 'Which way is it? Here, to be sure'; and he hurried off.

'Oh, Sir Richard, but no one has slept there these forty years. The air has hardly been changed since Sir Matthew died there.'

Thus she spoke, and rustled after him.

'Come, open the door, Mrs Chiddock. I'll see the chamber, at least.'

So it was opened, and, indeed, the smell was very close and earthy. Sir Richard crossed to the window, and, impatiently, as was his wont, threw the shutters back, and flung open the casement. For this end of the house was one which the alterations had barely touched, grown up as it was with the great ash tree, and being otherwise concealed from view.

'Air it, Mrs Chiddock, all today, and move my bed-furniture in in the afternoon. Put the Bishop of Kilmore in my old room.'

'Pray, Sir Richard,' said a new voice, breaking in on this speech, 'might I have the favour of a moment's interview?'

Sir Richard turned round and saw a man in black in the doorway, who bowed.

'I must ask your indulgence for this intrusion, Sir Richard. You will, perhaps, hardly remember me. My name is William Crome, and my grandfather was Vicar here in your grandfather's time.'

'Well, sir,' said Sir Richard, 'the name of Crome is always a passport to Castringham. I am glad to renew a friendship of two generations' standing. In what can I serve you? for your hour of calling—and, if I do not mistake you, your bearing—shows you to be in some haste.'

'That is no more than the truth, sir. I am riding from Norwich to Bury St Edmunds with what haste I can make, and I have called in on my way to leave with you some papers which we have but just come upon in looking over what my grandfather left at his death. It is thought you may find some matters of family interest in them.'

'You are mighty obliging, Mr Crome, and, if you will be so good as to follow me to the parlour, and drink a glass of wine, we will take a first look at these same papers together. And you, Mrs Chiddock, as I said, be about airing this chamber . . . Yes, it is here my grandfather died . . . Yes, the tree, perhaps, does make the place a little dampish . . . No; I do not wish to listen to any more. Make no difficulties, I beg. You have your orders—go. Will you follow me, sir?'

They went to the study. The packet which young Mr Crome had brought—he was then just become a Fellow of Clare Hall in Cambridge, I may say, and subsequently brought out a respectable edition of Polyænus—contained among other things the notes which the old Vicar had made upon the occasion of Sir Matthew Fell's death. And for the first time Sir Richard was confronted with the enigmatical *Sortes Biblicae* which you have heard. They amused him a good deal.

'Well,' he said, 'my grandfather's Bible gave one prudent piece of advice—*Cut it down*. If that stands for the ash tree, he may rest assured I shall not neglect it. Such a nest of catarrhs and agues was never seen.'

The parlour contained the family books, which, pending the arrival of a collection which Sir Richard had made in Italy, and the building of a proper room to receive them, were not many in number.

Sir Richard looked up from the paper to the bookcase.

'I wonder,' says he, 'whether the old prophet is there yet? I fancy I see him.'

Crossing the room, he took out a dumpy Bible, which, sure enough, bore on the flyleaf the inscription: 'To Matthew Fell, from his Loving Godmother, Anne Aldous, 2 September, 1659.'

'It would be no bad plan to test him again, Mr Crome. I will wager we get a couple of names in the Chronicles. Hm! what have we here? "Thou shalt seek me in the morning, and I shall not be." Well, well! Your grandfather would have made a fine omen of that, hey? No more prophets for me! They are all in a tale. And now, Mr Crome, I am infinitely obliged to you for your packet. You will, I fear, be impatient to get on. Pray allow me—another glass.'

So with offers of hospitality, which were genuinely meant (for Sir Richard thought well of the young man's address and manner), they parted.

In the afternoon came the guests—the Bishop of Kilmore, Lady Mary Hervey, Sir William Kentfield, etc. Dinner at five, wine, cards, supper, and dispersal to bed.

Next morning Sir Richard is disinclined to take his gun with the rest. He talks with the Bishop of Kilmore. This prelate, unlike a good many of the Irish Bishops of his day, had visited his see, and, indeed, resided there for some considerable time. This morning, as the two were walking along the terrace and talking over the alterations and improvements in the house, the Bishop said, pointing to the window of the West Room:

'You could never get one of my Irish flock to occupy that room, Sir Richard.'

'Why is that, my lord? It is, in fact, my own.'

'Well, our Irish peasantry will always have it that it brings the worst of luck to sleep near an ash tree, and you have a fine growth of ash not two yards from your chamber window. Perhaps,' the Bishop went on, with a smile, 'it has given you a touch of its quality already, for you do not seem, if I may say it, so much the fresher for your night's rest as your friends would like to see you.'

'That, or something else, it is true, cost me my sleep from twelve to four, my lord. But the tree is to come down tomorrow, so I shall not hear much more from it.'

'I applaud your determination. It can hardly be wholesome to have the air you breathe strained, as it were, through all that leafage.'

'Your lordship is right there, I think. But I had not my window open last night. It was rather the noise that went on—no doubt from the twigs sweeping the glass—that kept me open-eyed.'

'I think that can hardly be, Sir Richard. Here—you see it from this point. None of these nearest branches even can touch your casement unless there were a gale, and there was none of that last night. They miss the panes by a foot.'

'No, sir, true. What, then, will it be, I wonder, that scratched and rustled so—aye, and covered the dust on my sill with lines and marks?'

At last they agreed that the rats must have come up through the ivy. That was the Bishop's idea, and Sir Richard jumped at it.

So the day passed quietly, and night came, and the party dispersed to their rooms, and wished Sir Richard a better night.

And now we are in his bedroom, with the light out and the Squire in bed. The room is over the kitchen, and the night outside still and warm, so the window stands open.

There is very little light about the bedstead, but there is a strange movement there; it seems as if Sir Richard were moving his head rapidly to and fro with only the slightest possible sound. And now you would guess, so deceptive is the half-darkness, that he had several heads, round and brownish, which move back and forward, even as low as his chest. It is a horrible illusion. Is it nothing more? There! something drops off the bed with a soft plump, like a kitten, and is out of the window in a flash; another—four—and after that there is quiet again.

'Thou shalt seek me in the morning, and I shall not be.'

As with Sir Matthew, so with Sir Richard—dead and black in his bed!

A pale and silent party of guests and servants gathered under the window when the news was known. Italian poisoners, Popish emissaries, infected air—all these and more guesses were hazarded, and the Bishop of Kilmore looked at the tree, in the fork of whose lower boughs a white tomcat was crouching, looking down the hollow which years had gnawed in the trunk. It was watching something inside the tree with great interest.

Suddenly it got up and craned over the hole. Then a bit of the edge on which it stood gave way, and it went slithering in. Everyone looked up at the noise of the fall.

It is known to most of us that a cat can cry; but few of us have heard, I hope, such a yell as came out of the trunk of the great ash. Two or three screams there were—the witnesses are not sure which—and then a slight and muffled noise of some commotion or struggling was all that came. But Lady Mary Hervey fainted outright, and the housekeeper stopped her ears and fled till she fell on the terrace.

The Bishop of Kilmore and Sir William Kentfield stayed. Yet even they were daunted, though it was only at the cry of a cat; and Sir William swallowed once or twice before he could say:

'There is something more than we know of in that tree, my lord. I am for an instant search.'

And this was agreed upon. A ladder was brought, and one of the gardeners went up, and, looking down the hollow, could detect nothing but a few dim indications of something moving. They got a lantern, and let it down by a rope.

'We must get at the bottom of this. My life upon it, my lord, but the secret of these terrible deaths is there.'

Up went the gardener again with the lantern, and let it down the hole cautiously. They saw the yellow light upon his face as he bent over, and saw his face struck with an incredulous terror and loathing before he cried out in a dreadful voice and fell back from the ladder—where, happily, he was caught by two of the men—letting the lantern fall inside the tree.

He was in a dead faint, and it was some time before any word could be got from him.

By then they had something else to look at. The lantern must have broken at the bottom, and the light in it caught upon dry leaves and rubbish that lay there, for in a few minutes a dense smoke began to come up, and then flame; and, to be short, the tree was in a blaze.

The bystanders made a ring at some yards' distance, and Sir William and the Bishop sent men to get what weapons and tools they could; for, clearly, whatever might be using the tree as its lair would be forced out by the fire.

So it was. First, at the fork, they saw a round body covered with fire—the size of a man's head—appear very suddenly, then seem to collapse and fall back. This, five or six times; then a similar ball leapt into the air and fell on the grass, where after a moment it lay still. The Bishop went as near as he dared to it, and saw—what but the remains of an enormous spider, veinous and seared! And, as the fire burned lower down, more terrible bodies like this began to break out from the trunk, and it was seen that these were covered with greyish hair.

All that day the ash burned, and until it fell to pieces the men stood about it, and from time to time killed the brutes as they darted out. At last there was a long interval when none appeared, and they cautiously closed in and examined the roots of the tree.

'They found,' says the Bishop of Kilmore, 'below it a rounded hollow place in the earth, wherein were two or three bodies of these creatures that had plainly been smothered by the smoke; and, what is to me more curious, at the side of this den, against the wall, was crouching the anatomy or skeleton of a human being, with the skin dried upon the bones, having some remains of black hair, which was pronounced by those that examined it to be undoubtedly the body of a woman, and clearly dead for a period of fifty years.'

Rudyard Kipling

1865–1936

Best known for his children's books, notably *The Jungle Books*, *Kim* and *Just So Stories*, and for poems such as *If*, Rudyard Kipling was the author of a number of chilling ghost stories. Some of these, like *The Phantom Rickshaw*, were inspired by colonial India, where he spent his youth. One of the most popular authors of his day, in 1907 he was awarded the Nobel Prize for literature.

THE PHANTOM RICKSHAW

May no ill dreams disturb my rest,
Nor Powers of Darkness me molest.

EVENING HYMN

ONE OF THE FEW advantages that India has over England is a great Knowability. After five years' service a man is directly or indirectly acquainted with the two or three hundred Civilians in his Province, all the Messes of ten or twelve Regiments and Batteries, and some fifteen hundred other people of the non-official caste. In ten years his knowledge should be doubled, and at the end of twenty he knows, or knows something about, every Englishman in the Empire, and may travel anywhere and everywhere without paying hotel bills.

Globetrotters who expect entertainment as a right, have, even within my memory, blunted this open-heartedness, but none the less today, if you belong to the Inner Circle and are neither a Bear nor a Black Sheep, all houses are open to you, and our small world is very, very kind and helpful.

Rickett of Kamartha stayed with Polder of Kumach some fifteen years ago. He meant to stay two nights, but was knocked down by rheumatic fever, and for six weeks disorganised Polder's establishment, stopped Polder's work, and nearly died in Polder's bedroom. Polder behaves as though he had been placed under eternal obligation by Rickett, and yearly sends the little Ricketts a box of presents and toys. It is the same everywhere. The men who do not take the trouble to conceal from you their opinion that you are an incompetent ass, and the women who blacken your character and misunderstand your wife's amusements, will work themselves to the bone in your behalf if you fall sick or into serious trouble.

Heatherlegh, the Doctor, kept, in addition to his regular practice, a hospital on his private account—an arrangement of loose boxes for Incurables, his friend called it—but it was really a sort of fitting-up shed for craft that had been damaged by stress of weather. The weather in India is often sultry, and since the tale of bricks is always a fixed quantity, and the only liberty allowed is permission to work overtime and get no thanks, men occasionally break down and become as mixed as the metaphors in this sentence.

Heatherlegh is the dearest doctor that ever was, and his invariable prescription to all his patients is, 'Lie low, go slow, and keep cool.' He says that more men are killed by overwork than the importance of this world justifies. He maintains that overwork slew Pansay, who died under his hands about three years ago. He has, of course, the right to speak authoritatively, and he laughs at my theory that there was a crack in Pansay's head and a little bit of the Dark World came through and pressed him to death. 'Pansay went off the handle,' says Heatherlegh, 'after the stimulus of long leave at Home. He may or he may not have behaved like a blackguard to Mrs Keith-Wessington. My notion is that the work of the Katabundi Settlement ran him off his legs, and that he took to brooding and making much of an ordinary P & O flirtation. He certainly was engaged to Miss Mannering, and she certainly broke off the engagement. Then he took a feverish chill and all that nonsense about ghosts developed. Overwork started his illness, kept it alight, and killed him, poor devil. Write him off to the System that uses one man to do the work of two and a half men.'

I do not believe this. I used to sit up with Pansay sometimes when Heatherlegh was called out to patients and I happened to be within claim. The man would make me most unhappy by describing, in a low, even voice, the procession that was always passing at the bottom of his bed. He had a sick man's command of language. When he recovered I suggested that he should write out the whole affair from beginning to end, knowing that ink might assist him to ease his mind.

He was in a high fever while he was writing, and the blood-and-thunder Magazine diction he adopted did not calm him. Two months afterwards he was reported fit for duty, but, in spite of the fact that he was urgently needed to help an undermanned Commission stagger through a deficit, he preferred to die; vowing at the last that he was hagridden. I got his manuscript before he died, and this is his version of the affair, dated 1885, exactly as he wrote it:

MY DOCTOR TELLS ME that I need rest and change of air. It is not improbable that I shall get both ere long—rest that neither the red-coated messenger nor the midday gun can break, and change of air far beyond that which any homeward-bound steamer can give me. In the meantime I am resolved to stay where I am; and, in flat defiance of my doctor's orders, to take all the world into my confidence. You shall learn for yourselves the precise nature of my malady, and shall, too, judge for yourselves whether any man born of woman on this weary earth was ever so tormented as I.

Speaking now as a condemned criminal might speak ere the drop-bolts are drawn, my story, wild and hideously improbable as it may appear, demands at least attention. That it will ever receive credence I utterly disbelieve. Two months ago I should have scouted as mad or drunk the man who had dared tell me the like. Two months ago I was the happiest man in India. Today, from Peshawar to the sea, there is no one more wretched. My doctor and I are the only two who know this. His explanation is that my brain, digestion, and eyesight are all slightly affected; giving rise to my frequent and persistent 'delusions'. Delusions, indeed! I call him a fool; but he attends me still with the same unwearied smile, the same bland professional manner, the same neatly trimmed red whiskers, till I begin to suspect that I am an ungrateful, evil-tempered invalid. But you shall judge for yourselves.

Three years ago it was my fortune—my great misfortune—to sail from Gravesend to Bombay, on return from long leave, with one Agnes Keith-Wessington, wife of an officer on the Bombay side. It does not in the least concern you to know what manner of woman she was. Be content with the knowledge that, ere the voyage had ended, both she and I were desperately and unreasoningly in love with one another. Heaven knows that I can make the admission now without one particle of vanity. In matters of this sort there is always one who gives and another who accepts. From the first day of our ill-omened attachment, I was conscious that Agnes's passion was a stronger, a more dominant, and—if I may use the expression—a purer sentiment than mine. Whether she recognised the fact then, I do not know. Afterwards it was bitterly plain to both of us.

Arrived at Bombay in the spring of the year, we went our respective ways, to meet no more for the next three or four months, when my leave and her love took us both to Simla. There we spent the season together; and there my fire of straw burnt itself out to a pitiful end with the closing year. I attempt no excuse. I make no apology. Mrs Wessington had given up much for my sake, and was prepared to give up all. From my own lips, in August 1882, she learned that I was sick of her presence, tired of her company, and weary of the sound of her voice. Ninety-nine women out of a hundred would have wearied of me as I wearied of them; seventy-five of that number would have promptly avenged themselves by active and obtrusive flirtation with other men. Mrs Wessington was the hundredth. On her neither my openly expressed aversion nor the cutting brutalities with which I garnished our interviews had the least effect.

'Jack, darling!' was her one eternal cuckoo cry: 'I'm sure it's all a mistake—a hideous mistake; and we'll be good friends again some day. *Please* forgive me, Jack, dear.'

I was the offender, and I knew it. That knowledge transformed my pity into passive endurance, and, eventually, into blind hate—the same instinct, I suppose, which prompts a man to savagely stamp on the spider he has but half killed. And with this hate in my bosom the season of 1882 came to an end.

Next year we met again at Simla—she with her monotonous face and timid attempts at reconciliation, and I with loathing of her in every fibre of my frame. Several times I could not avoid meeting her alone; and on each occasion her words were identically the same. Still the unreasoning wail that it was all a 'mistake'; and still the hope of eventually 'making friends'. I might have seen, had I cared to look, that that hope only was keeping her alive. She grew more wan and thin month by month. You will agree with me, at least, that such conduct would have driven anyone to despair. It was uncalled for; childish; unwomanly. I maintain that she was much to blame. And again, sometimes, in the black, fever-stricken night watches, I have begun to think that I might have been a little kinder to her. But that really *is* a 'delusion'. I could not have continued pretending to love her when I didn't; could I? It would have been unfair to us both.

Last year we met again—on the same terms as before. The same weary appeals, and the same curt answers from my lips. At least I would make her see how wholly wrong and hopeless were her attempts at resuming the old relationship. As the season wore on, we fell apart—that is to say, she found it difficult to meet me, for I had other and more absorbing interests to attend to. When I think it over quietly in my sickroom, the season of 1884 seems a confused nightmare wherein light and shade were fantastically intermingled: my courtship of little Kitty Mannering, my hopes, doubts, and fears; our long rides together; my trembling avowal of attachment; her reply; and now and again a vision of a white face flitting by in the rickshaw with the black and white liveries I once watched for so earnestly; the wave of Mrs Wessington's gloved hand; and, when she met me alone, which was but seldom, the irksome monotony of her appeal. I loved Kitty Mannering; honestly, heartily loved her, and with my love for her grew my hatred for Agnes. In August Kitty and I were engaged. The next day I met those accursed 'magpie' *jhampanies* at the back of Jakko, and, moved by some passing sentiment of pity, stopped to tell Mrs Wessington everything. She knew it already.

'So I hear you're engaged, Jack, dear.' Then, without a moment's pause: 'I'm sure it's all a mistake—a hideous mistake. We shall be as good friends some day, Jack, as we ever were.'

My answer might have made even a man wince. It cut the dying woman before me like the blow of a whip. 'Please forgive me, Jack; I didn't mean to make you angry; but it's true, it's true!'

And Mrs Wessington broke down completely. I turned away and left her to finish her journey in peace, feeling, but only for a moment or two, that I had been an unutterably mean hound. I looked back, and saw that she had turned her rickshaw with the idea, I suppose, of overtaking me.

The scene and its surroundings were photographed on my memory. The rain-swept sky (we were at the end of the wet weather), the sodden, dingy pines, the muddy road, and the black powder-riven cliffs formed a gloomy background against which the black and white liveries of the *jhampanies,* the yellow-panelled rickshaw, and Mrs Wessington's down-bowed golden head stood out clearly. She was holding her handkerchief in her left hand and was leaning back exhausted against the rickshaw cushions. I turned my horse up a by-path near the Sanjowlie Reservoir and literally ran away. Once I fancied I heard a faint call of 'Jack!' This may have been imagination. I never stopped to verify it. Ten minutes later I came across Kitty on horseback; and, in the delight of a long ride with her, forgot all about the interview.

A week later Mrs Wessington died, and the inexpressible burden of her existence was removed from my life. I went Plainsward perfectly happy. Before three months were over I had forgotten all about her, except that at times the discovery of some of her old letters reminded me unpleasantly of our bygone relationship. By January I had disinterred what was left of our correspondence from among my scattered belongings and had burnt it. At the beginning of April of this year, 1885, I was at Simla—semi-deserted Simla—once more, and was deep in lovers' talks and walks with Kitty. It was decided that we should be married at the end of June. You will understand, therefore, that, loving Kitty as I did, I am not saying too much when I pronounce myself to have been, at that time, the happiest man in India.

Fourteen delightful days passed almost before I noticed their flight. Then, aroused to the sense of what was proper among mortals circumstanced as we were, I pointed out to Kitty that an engagement ring was the outward and visible sign of her dignity as an engaged girl; and that she must forthwith come to Hamilton's to be measured for one. Up to that moment, I give you my word, we had completely forgotten so trivial a matter. To Hamilton's we accordingly went on the 15th of April 1885. Remember that—whatever my doctor may say to the contrary—I was then in perfect health, enjoying a well-balanced mind and an *absolutely* tranquil spirit. Kitty and I entered Hamilton's shop together, and there, regardless of the order of affairs, I measured Kitty for the ring in the presence of the amused assistant. The ring was a sapphire with two diamonds. We then rode out down the slope that leads to the Combermere Bridge and Peliti's shop.

While my Waler was cautiously feeling his way over the loose shale, and Kitty was laughing and chattering at my side—while all Simla, that is to say as much of it as had then come from the Plains, was grouped round the Reading Room and Peliti's verandah—I was aware that someone, apparently at a vast distance, was calling me by my Christian name. It struck me that I had heard the voice before, but when and where I could not at once determine. In the short space it took to cover the road between the path from Hamilton's shop and the first plank of the Combermere Bridge I had thought over half a dozen people who might have committed such a solecism, and had eventually decided that it must have been some singing in my ears. Immediately opposite Peliti's shop my eye was arrested by the sight of four *jhampanies* in 'magpie' livery, pulling a yellow-panelled, cheap, bazaar rickshaw. In a moment my mind flew back to the previous season and Mrs Wessington with a sense of irritation and disgust. Was it not enough that the woman was dead and done with, without her black and white servitors reappearing to spoil the day's happiness? Whoever employed them now I thought I would call upon, and ask as a personal favour to change her *jhampanies'* livery. I would hire the men myself, and, if necessary, buy their coats from off their backs. It is impossible to say here what a flood of undesirable memories their presence evoked.

'Kitty,' I cried, 'there are poor Mrs Wessington's *jhampanies* turned up again! I wonder who has them now?'

Kitty had known Mrs Wessington slightly last season, and had always been interested in the sickly woman.

'What? Where?' she asked. 'I can't see them anywhere.'

Even as she spoke, her horse, swerving from a laden mule, threw himself directly in front of the advancing rickshaw. I had scarcely time to utter a word of warning when, to my unutterable horror, horse and rider passed *through* men and carriage as if they had been thin air.

'What's the matter?' cried Kitty; 'what made you call out so foolishly, Jack? If I *am* engaged I don't want all creation to know about it. There was lots of space between the mule and the verandah; and, if you think I can't ride—There!'

Whereupon wilful Kitty set off, her dainty little head in the air, at a hand-gallop in the direction of the Bandstand; fully expecting, as she herself afterwards told me, that I should follow her. What was the matter? Nothing indeed. Either that I was mad or drunk, or that Simla was haunted with devils. I reined in my impatient cob, and turned round. The rickshaw had turned too, and now stood immediately facing me, near the left railing of the Combermere Bridge.

'Jack! Jack, darling!' (There was no mistake about the words this time: they rang through my brain as if they had been shouted in my ear.) 'It's some hideous mistake, I'm sure. *Please* forgive me, Jack, and let's be friends again.'

The rickshaw hood had fallen back, and inside, as I hope and pray daily for the death I dread by night, sat Mrs Keith-Wessington, handkerchief in hand, and golden head bowed on her breast.

How long I stared motionless I do not know. Finally, I was aroused by my syce taking the Waler's bridle and asking whether I was ill. From the horrible to the commonplace is but a step. I tumbled off my horse and dashed, half fainting, into Peliti's for a glass of cherry brandy. There two or three couples were gathered round the coffee tables discussing the gossip of the day. Their trivialities were more comforting to me just then than the consolations of religion could have been. I plunged into the midst of the conversation at once; chatted, laughed, and jested with a face (when I caught a glimpse of it in a mirror) as white and drawn as that of a corpse. Three or four men noticed my condition; and, evidently setting it down to the results of over-many pegs, charitably endeavoured to draw me apart from the rest of the loungers. But I refused to be led away. I wanted the company of my kind—as a child rushes into the midst of the dinner party after a fright in the dark. I must have talked for about ten minutes or so, though it seemed an eternity to me, when I heard Kitty's clear voice outside enquiring for me. In another minute she had entered the shop, prepared to upbraid me for failing so signally in my duties. Something in my face stopped her.

'Why, Jack,' she cried, 'what *have* you been doing? What *has* happened? Are you ill?' Thus driven into a direct lie, I said that the sun had been a little too much for me. It was close upon five o'clock of a cloudy April afternoon, and the sun had been hidden all day. I saw my mistake as soon as the words were out of my mouth; attempted to recover it; blundered hopelessly, and followed Kitty in a regal rage out-of-doors, amid the smiles of my acquaintances. I made some excuse (I have forgotten what) on the score of my feeling faint; and cantered away to my hotel, leaving Kitty to finish the ride by herself.

In my room I sat down and tried calmly to reason out the matter. Here was I, Theobald Jack Pansay, a well-educated Bengal Civilian in the year of grace 1885, presumably sane, certainly healthy, driven in terror from my sweetheart's side by the apparition of a woman who had been dead and buried eight months ago. These were facts that I could not blink. Nothing was farther from my thought than any memory of Mrs Wessington when Kitty and I left Hamilton's shop. Nothing was more utterly commonplace than the stretch of wall opposite Peliti's. It was broad daylight. The road was full of people; and yet here, look you, in defiance of every law of probability, in direct outrage of Nature's ordinance, there had appeared to me a face from the grave.

Kitty's Arab had gone *through* the rickshaw: so that my first hope that some woman marvellously like Mrs Wessington had hired the carriage and the coolies with their old livery was lost. Again and again I went round this treadmill of thought; and again and again gave up, baffled and in despair. The voice was as inexplicable as the apparition. I had originally some wild notion of confiding it all to Kitty; of begging her to marry me at once, and in her arms defying the ghostly occupant of the rickshaw. 'After all,' I argued, 'the presence of the rickshaw is in itself enough to prove the existence of a spectral illusion. One may see ghosts of men and women, but surely never coolies and carriages. The whole thing is absurd. Fancy the ghost of a hillman!'

Next morning I sent a penitent note to Kitty, imploring her to overlook my strange conduct of the previous afternoon. My Divinity was still very wroth, and a personal apology was necessary. I explained, with a fluency born of nightlong pondering over a falsehood, that I had been attacked with a sudden palpitation of the heart—the result of indigestion. This eminently practical solution had its effect; and Kitty and I rode out that afternoon with the shadow of my first lie dividing us.

Nothing would please her save a canter round Jakko. With my nerves still unstrung from the previous night I feebly protested against the notion, suggesting Observatory Hill, Jutogh, the Boileau-gunge road—anything rather than the Jakko round. Kitty was angry and a little hurt; so I yielded from fear of provoking further misunderstanding, and we set out together towards Chota Simla. We walked a greater part of the way, and, according to our custom, cantered from a mile or so below the Convent to the stretch of level road by the Sanjowlie Reservoir. The wretched horses appeared to fly, and my heart beat quicker and quicker as we neared the crest of the ascent. My mind had been full of Mrs Wessington all the afternoon; and every inch of the Jakko road bore witness to our old-time walks and talks. The boulders were full of it; the pines sang it aloud overhead; the rain-fed torrents giggled and chuckled unseen over the shameful story; and the wind in my ears chanted the iniquity aloud.

As a fitting climax, in the middle of the level men call the Ladies' Mile the Horror was awaiting me. No other rickshaw was in sight—only the four black and white *jhampanies*, the yellow-panelled carriage, and the golden head of the woman within—all apparently just as I had left them eight months and one fortnight ago! For an instant I fancied that Kitty *must* see what I saw—we were so marvellously sympathetic in all things. Her next words undeceived me— 'Not a soul in sight! Come along, Jack, and I'll race you to the Reservoir buildings!' Her wiry little Arab was off like a bird, my Waler following close behind, and in this order we dashed under the cliffs. Half a minute brought us within fifty yards of the rickshaw. I pulled my Waler and fell back a little. The rickshaw was directly in the middle of the road; and once more the Arab passed through it, my horse following. 'Jack! Jack dear! *Please* forgive me,' rang with a wail in my ears, and, after an interval: 'It's all a mistake, a hideous mistake!'

I spurred my horse like a man possessed. When I turned my head at the Reservoir works the black and white liveries were still waiting—patiently waiting—under the grey hillside, and the wind brought me a mocking echo of the words I had just heard. Kitty bantered me a good deal on my silence throughout the remainder of the ride. I had been talking up till then wildly and at random. To save my life I could not speak afterwards naturally, and from Sanjowlie to the Church wisely held my tongue.

I was to dine with the Mannerings that night, and had barely time to canter home to dress. On the road to Elysium Hill I overheard two men talking together in the dusk—'It's a curious thing,' said one, 'how completely all trace of it disappeared. You know my wife was insanely fond of the woman (never could see anything in her myself), and wanted me to pick up her old rickshaw and coolies if they were to be got for love or money. Morbid sort of fancy I call it; but I've got to do what the memsahib tells me. Would you believe that the man she hired it from tells me that all four of the men—they were brothers—died of cholera on the way to Hardwar, poor devils; and the rickshaw has been broken up by the man himself. 'Told me he never used a dead memsahib's rickshaw. Spoilt his luck. Queer notion, wasn't it? Fancy poor little Mrs Wessington spoiling anyone's luck except her own!' I laughed aloud at this point; and my laugh jarred on me as I uttered it. So there *were* ghosts of rickshaws after all, and ghostly employments in the other world! How much did Mrs Wessington give her men? What were their hours? Where did they go?

And for visible answer to my last question I saw the infernal Thing blocking my path in the twilight. The dead travel fast, and by short cuts unknown to ordinary coolies. I laughed aloud a second time and checked my laughter suddenly, for I was afraid I was going mad. Mad to a certain extent I must have been, for I recollect that I reined in my horse at the head of the rickshaw, and politely wished Mrs Wessington 'Good evening.' Her answer was one I knew only too well. I listened to the end; and replied that I had heard it all before, but should be delighted if she had anything further to say. Some malignant devil stronger than I must have entered into me that evening, for I have a dim recollection of talking the commonplaces of the day for five minutes to the Thing in front of me.

'Mad as a hatter, poor devil—or drunk. Max, try and get him to come home.'

Surely *that* was not Mrs Wessington's voice! The two men had overheard me speaking to the empty air, and had returned to look after me. They were very kind and considerate, and from their words evidently gathered that I was extremely drunk. I thanked them confusedly and cantered away to my hotel, there changed, and arrived at the Mannerings' ten minutes late. I pleaded the darkness of the night as an excuse; was rebuked by Kitty for my unlover-like tardiness; and sat down.

The conversation had already become general; and, under cover of it, I was addressing some tender small talk to my sweetheart when I was aware that at the farther end of the table a short, red-whiskered man was describing, with much broidery, his encounter with a mad unknown that evening.

A few sentences convinced me that he was repeating the incident of half an hour ago. In the middle of the story he looked round for applause, as professional storytellers do, caught my eye, and straightway collapsed. There was a moment's awkward silence, and the red-whiskered man muttered something to the effect that he had 'forgotten the rest', thereby sacrificing a reputation as a good storyteller which he had built up for six seasons past. I blessed him from the bottom of my heart, and—went on with my fish.

In the fullness of time that dinner came to an end; and with genuine regret I tore myself away from Kitty—as certain as I was of my own existence that It would be waiting for me outside the door. The red-whiskered man, who had been introduced to me as Dr Heatherlegh of Simla, volunteered to bear me company as far as our roads lay together. I accepted his offer with gratitude.

My instinct had not deceived me. It lay in readiness in the Mall, and, in what seemed devilish mockery of our ways, with a lighted headlamp. The red-whiskered man went to the point at once, in a manner that showed he had been thinking over it all dinner time.

'I say, Pansay, what the deuce was the matter with you this evening on the Elysium Road?' The suddenness of the question wrenched an answer from me before I was aware.

'That!' said I, pointing to It.

'*That* may be either D.T. or Eyes for aught I know. Now you don't liquor. I saw as much at dinner, so it can't be D.T. There's nothing whatever where you're pointing, though you're sweating and trembling with fright like a scared pony. Therefore, I conclude that it's Eyes. And I ought to understand all about them. Come along home with me. I'm on the Blessington lower road.'

To my intense delight the rickshaw, instead of waiting for us, kept about twenty yards ahead—and this, too, whether we walked, trotted, or cantered. In the course of that long night ride I had told my companion almost as much as I have told you here.

'Well, you've spoilt one of the best tales I've ever laid tongue to,' said he, 'but I'll forgive you for the sake of what you've gone through. Now come home and do what I tell you; and when I've cured you, young man, let this be a lesson to you to steer clear of women and indigestible food till the day of your death.'

The rickshaw kept steady in front; and my red-whiskered friend seemed to derive great pleasure from my account of its exact whereabouts.

'Eyes, Pansay—all Eyes, Brain, and Stomach. And the greatest of these three is Stomach. You've too much conceited Brain, too little Stomach, and thoroughly unhealthy Eyes. Get your Stomach straight and the rest follows. And all that's French for a liver pill. I'll take sole medical charge of you from this hour! for you're too interesting a phenomenon to be passed over.'

By this time we were deep in the shadow of the Blessington lower road, and the rickshaw came to a dead stop under a pine-clad, overhanging shale cliff. Instinctively I halted too, giving my reason. Heatherlegh rapped out an oath.

'Now, if you think I'm going to spend a cold night on the hillside for the sake of a Stomach-cum-Brain-cum-Eye illusion—Lord, ha' mercy! What's that?'

There was a muffled report, a blinding smother of dust just in front of us, a crack, the noise of rent boughs, and about ten yards of the cliff-side—pines, undergrowth, and all—slid down into the road below, completely blocking it up. The uprooted trees swayed and tottered for a moment like drunken giants in the gloom, and then fell prone among their fellows with a thunderous crash. Our two horses stood motionless and sweating with fear. As soon as the rattle of falling earth and stone had subsided, my companion muttered: 'Man, if we'd gone forward we should have been ten feet deep in our graves by now. "There are more things in heaven and earth" . . . Come home, Pansay, and thank God. I want a peg badly.'

We retraced our way over the Church Ridge, and I arrived at Dr Heatherlegh's house shortly after midnight.

His attempts towards my cure commenced almost immediately, and for a week I never left his sight. Many a time in the course of that week did I bless the good fortune which had thrown me in contact with Simla's best and kindest doctor. Day by day my spirits grew lighter and more equable. Day by day, too, I became more and more inclined to fall in with Heatherlegh's 'spectral illusion' theory, implicating eyes, brain, and stomach. I wrote to Kitty, telling her that a slight sprain caused by a fall from my horse kept me indoors for a few days; and that I should be recovered before she had time to regret my absence.

Heatherlegh's treatment was simple to a degree. It consisted of liver pills, cold-water baths, and strong exercise, taken in the dusk or at early dawn—for, as he sagely observed: 'A man with a sprained ankle doesn't walk a dozen miles a day, and your young woman might be wondering if she saw you.'

At the end of the week, after much examination of pupil and pulse, and strict injunctions as to diet and pedestrianism, Heatherlegh dismissed me as brusquely as he had taken charge of me. Here is his parting benediction: 'Man, I certify to your mental cure, and that's as much as to say I've cured most of your bodily ailments. Now, get your traps out of this as soon as you can; and be off to make love to Miss Kitty.'

I was endeavouring to express my thanks for his kindness. He cut me short.

'Don't think I did this because I like you. I gather that you've behaved like a blackguard all through. But, all the same, you're a phenomenon, and as queer a phenomenon as you are a blackguard. No!'—checking me a second time—'not a rupee, please. Go out and see if you can find the eyes-brain-and-stomach business again. I'll give you a lakh for each time you see it.'

Half an hour later I was in the Mannerings' drawing room with Kitty—drunk with the intoxication of present happiness and the foreknowledge that I should never more be troubled with Its hideous presence. Strong in the sense of my new-found security, I proposed a ride at once; and, by preference, a canter round Jakko.

Never had I felt so well, so overladen with vitality and mere animal spirits, as I did on the afternoon of the 30th of April. Kitty was delighted at the change in my appearance, and complimented me on it in her delightfully frank and out-spoken manner. We left the Mannerings' house together, laughing and talking, and cantered along the Chota Simla road as of old.

I was in haste to reach the Sanjowlie Reservoir and there make my assurance doubly sure. The horses did their best, but seemed all too slow to my impatient mind. Kitty was astonished at my boisterousness. 'Why, Jack!' she cried at last, 'you are behaving like a child. What are you doing?'

We were just below the Convent, and from sheer wantonness I was making my Waler plunge and curvet across the road as I tickled it with the loop of my riding whip.

'Doing?' I answered; 'nothing, dear. That's just it. If you'd been doing nothing for a week except lie up, you'd be as riotous as I.

> 'Singing and murmuring in your feastful mirth,
> Joying to feel yourself alive;
> Lord over Nature, Lord of the visible Earth,
> Lord of the senses five.'

My quotation was hardly out of my lips before we had rounded the corner above the Convent, and a few yards farther on could see across to Sanjowlie. In the centre of the level road stood the black and white liveries, the yellow-panelled rickshaw, and Mrs Keith-Wessington. I pulled up, looked, rubbed my eyes, and, I believe, must have said something. The next thing I knew was that I was lying face downward on the road, with Kitty kneeling above me in tears.

'Has it gone, child?' I gasped. Kitty only wept more bitterly.

'Has what gone, Jack dear? What does it all mean? There must be a mistake somewhere, Jack. A hideous mistake.' Her last words brought me to my feet—mad—raving for the time being.

'Yes, there *is* a mistake somewhere,' I repeated, 'a hideous mistake. Come and look at It.'

I have an indistinct idea that I dragged Kitty by the wrist along the road up to where It stood, and implored her for pity's sake to speak to It; to tell It that we were betrothed; that neither Death nor Hell could break the tie between us: and Kitty only knows how much more to the same effect. Now and again I appealed passionately to the Terror in the rickshaw to bear witness to all I had said, and to release me from a torture that was killing me. As I talked I suppose I must have told Kitty of my old relations with Mrs Wessington, for I saw her listen intently with white face and blazing eyes.

'Thank you, Mr Pansay,' she said, 'that's *quite* enough. *Syce ghora láo.*'

The syces, impassive as Orientals always are, had come up with the recaptured horses; and as Kitty sprang into her saddle I caught hold of her bridle, entreating her to hear me out and forgive. My answer was the cut of her riding whip across my face from mouth to eye, and a word or two of farewell that even now I cannot write down. So I judged, and judged rightly, that Kitty knew all; and I staggered back to the side of the rickshaw. My face was cut and bleeding, and the blow of the riding whip had raised a livid blue weal on it. I had no self-respect. Just then, Heatherlegh, who must have been following Kitty and me at a distance, cantered up.

'Doctor,' I said, pointing to my face, 'here's Miss Mannering's signature to my order of dismissal and—I'll thank you for that lakh as soon as convenient.'

Heatherlegh's face, even in my abject misery, moved me to laughter.

'I'll stake my professional reputation—' he began.

'Don't be a fool,' I whispered. 'I've lost my life's happiness and you'd better take me home.'

As I spoke the rickshaw was gone. Then I lost all knowledge of what was passing. The crest of Jakko seemed to heave and roll like the crest of a cloud and fall in upon me.

Seven days later (on the 7th of May, that is to say) I was aware that I was lying in Heatherlegh's room as weak as a little child. Heatherlegh was watching me intently from behind the papers on his writing table. His first words were not encouraging; but I was too far spent to be much moved by them.

'Here's Miss Kitty has sent back your letters. You corresponded a good deal, you young people. Here's a packet that looks like a ring, and a cheerful sort of a note from Mannering Papa, which I've taken the liberty of reading and burning. The old gentleman's not pleased with you.'

'And Kitty?' I asked dully.

'Rather more drawn than her father from what she says. By the same token you must have been letting out any number of queer reminiscences just before I met you. Says that a man who would have behaved to a woman as you did to Mrs Wessington ought to kill himself out of sheer pity for his kind. She's a hot-headed little virago, your mash. Will have it too that you were suffering from D.T. when that row on the Jakko road turned up. Says she'll die before she ever speaks to you again.'

I groaned and turned over on the other side.

'Now you've got your choice, my friend. This engagement has to be broken off; and the Mannerings don't want to be too hard on you. Was it broken through D.T. or epileptic fits? Sorry I can't offer you a better exchange unless you'd prefer hereditary insanity. Say the word and I'll tell 'em it's fits. All Simla knows about that scene on the Ladies' Mile. Come! I'll give you five minutes to think over it.'

During those five minutes I believe that I explored thoroughly the lowest circles of the Inferno which it is permitted man to tread on earth. And at the same time I myself was watching myself faltering through the dark labyrinths of doubt, misery, and utter despair. I wondered, as Heatherlegh in his chair might have wondered, which dreadful alternative I should adopt. Presently I heard myself answering in a voice that I hardly recognised—

'They're confoundedly particular about morality in these parts. Give 'em fits, Heatherlegh, and my love. Now let me sleep a bit longer.'

Then my two selves joined, and it was only I (half-crazed, devil-driven I) that tossed in my bed tracing step by step the history of the past month.

'But I am in Simla,' I kept repeating to myself. 'I, Jack Pansay, am in Simla, and there are no ghosts here. It's unreasonable of that woman to pretend there are. Why couldn't Agnes have left me alone? I never did her any harm. It might just as well have been me as Agnes. Only I'd never have come back on purpose to kill *her*. Why can't I be left alone—left alone and happy?'

It was high noon when I first awoke; and the sun was low in the sky before I slept—slept as the tortured criminal sleeps on his rack, too worn to feel further pain.

Next day I could not leave my bed. Heatherlegh told me in the morning that he had received an answer from Mr Mannering, and that, thanks to his (Heatherlegh's) friendly offices, the story of my affliction had travelled through the length and breadth of Simla, where I was on all sides much pitied.

'And that's rather more than you deserve,' he concluded pleasantly, 'though the Lord knows you've been going through a pretty severe mill. Never mind; we'll cure you yet, you perverse phenomenon.'

I declined firmly to be cured. 'You've been much too good to me already, old man,' said I; 'but I don't think I need trouble you further.'

In my heart I knew that nothing Heatherlegh could do would lighten the burden that had been laid upon me.

With that knowledge came also a sense of hopeless, impotent rebellion against the unreasonableness of it all. There were scores of men no better than I whose punishments had at least been reserved for another world; and I felt that it was bitterly, cruelly unfair that I alone should have been singled out for so hideous a fate. This mood would in time give place to another where it seemed that the rickshaw and I were the only realities in a world of shadows; that Kitty was a ghost; that Mannering, Heatherlegh, and all the other men and women I knew were all ghosts; and the great grey hills themselves but vain shadows devised to torture me. From mood to mood I tossed backwards and forwards for seven weary days; my body growing daily stronger and stronger, until the bedroom looking glass told me that I had returned to everyday life, and was as other men once more. Curiously enough my face showed no signs of the struggle I had gone through. It was pale indeed, but as expressionless and commonplace as ever. I had expected some permanent alteration—visible evidence of the disease that was eating me away. I found nothing.

On the 15th of May I left Heatherlegh's house at eleven o'clock in the morning; and the instinct of the bachelor drove me to the Club. There I found that every man knew my story as told by Heatherlegh, and was, in clumsy fashion, abnormally kind and attentive. Nevertheless I recognised that for the rest of my natural life I should be among but not of my fellows; and I envied very bitterly indeed the laughing coolies on the Mall below. I lunched at the Club, and at four o'clock wandered aimlessly down the Mall in the vague hope of meeting Kitty. Close to the Bandstand the black and white liveries joined me; and I heard Mrs Wessington's old appeal at my side. I had been expecting this ever since I came out, and was only surprised at her delay. The phantom rickshaw and I went side by side along the Chota Simla road in silence. Close to the bazaar, Kitty and a man on horseback overtook and passed us. For any sign she gave I might have been a dog in the road. She did not even pay me the compliment of quickening her pace, though the rainy afternoon had served for an excuse.

So Kitty and her companion, and I and my ghostly Light-o'-Love, crept round Jakko in couples. The road was streaming with water; the pines dripped like roof-pipes on the rocks below, and the air was full of fine driving rain. Two or three times I found myself saying to myself almost aloud: 'I'm Jack Pansay on leave at Simla—*at Simla*! Everyday, ordinary Simla. I mustn't forget that—I mustn't forget that.' Then I would try to recollect some of the gossip I had heard at the Club: the prices of So-and-So's horses—anything, in fact, that related to the workaday Anglo-Indian world I knew so well. I even repeated the multiplication table rapidly to myself, to make quite sure that I was not taking leave of my senses. It gave me much comfort, and must have prevented my hearing Mrs Wessington for a time.

Once more I wearily climbed the Convent slope and entered the level road. Here Kitty and the man started off at a canter, and I was left alone with Mrs Wessington. 'Agnes,' said I, 'will you put back your hood and tell me what it all means?' The hood dropped noiselessly, and I was face to face with my dead and buried mistress. She was wearing the dress in which I had last seen her alive; carried the same tiny handkerchief in her right hand, and the same card-case in her left. (A woman eight months dead with a card-case!) I had to pin myself down to the multiplication table, and to set both hands on the stone parapet of the road, to assure myself that that at least was real.

'Agnes,' I repeated, 'for pity's sake tell me what it all means.' Mrs Wessington leaned forward, with that odd, quick turn of the head I used to know so well, and spoke.

If my story had not already so madly overleaped the bounds of all human belief I should apologise to you now. As I know that no one—no, not even Kitty, for whom it is written as some sort of justification of my conduct—will believe me, I will go on. Mrs Wessington spoke, and I walked with her from the Sanjowlie road to the turning below the Commander-in-Chief's house as I might walk by the side of any living woman's rickshaw, deep in conversation. The second and most tormenting of my moods of sickness had suddenly laid hold upon me, and, like the Prince in Tennyson's poem, 'I seemed to move amid a world of ghosts.' There had been a garden party at the Commander-in-Chief's, and we two joined the crowd of homeward-bound folk. As I saw them it seemed that *they* were the shadows—impalpable fantastic shadows—that divided for Mrs Wessington's rickshaw to pass through. What we said during the course of that weird interview I cannot—indeed, I dare not—tell. Heatherlegh's comment would have been a short laugh and a remark that I had been 'mashing a brain-eye-and-stomach chimera'. It was a ghastly and yet in some indefinable way a marvellously dear experience. Could it be possible, I wondered, that I was in this life to woo a second time the woman I had killed by my own neglect and cruelty?

I met Kitty on the homeward road—a shadow among shadows.

If I were to describe all the incidents of the next fortnight in their order, my story would never come to an end, and your patience would be exhausted. Morning after morning and evening after evening the ghostly rickshaw and I used to wander through Simla together. Wherever I went there the four black and white liveries followed me and bore me company to and from my hotel. At the Theatre I found them amid the crowd of yelling *jhampanies*; outside the Club verandah, after a long evening of whist; at the Birthday Ball, waiting patiently for my reappearance; and in broad daylight when I went calling. Save that it cast no shadow, the rickshaw was in every respect as real to look upon as one of wood and iron. More than once, indeed, I have had to check myself from warning some hard-riding friend against cantering over it. More than once I have walked down the Mall deep in conversation with Mrs Wessington, to the unspeakable amazement of the passers-by.

Before I had been out and about a week I learned that the 'fit' theory had been discarded in favour of insanity. However, I made no change in my mode of life. I called, rode, and dined out as freely as ever. I had a passion for the society of my kind which I had never felt before; I hungered to be among the realities of life; and at the same time I felt vaguely unhappy when I had been separated too long from my ghostly companion. It would be almost impossible to describe my varying moods from the 15th of May up to today.

The presence of the rickshaw filled me by turns with horror, blind fear, a dim sort of pleasure, and utter despair. I dared not leave Simla; and I knew that my stay there was killing me. I knew, moreover, that it was my destiny to die slowly and a little every day. My only anxiety was to get the penance over as quietly as might be. Alternately I hungered for a sight of Kitty, and watched her outrageous flirtations with my successor—to speak more accurately, my successors—with amused interest. She was as much out of my life as I was out of hers. By day I wandered with Mrs Wessington almost content. By night I implored Heaven to let me return to the world as I used to know it. Above all these varying moods lay the sensation of dull, numbing wonder that the Seen and the Unseen should mingle so strangely on this earth to hound one poor soul to its grave.

AUGUST 27.—Heatherlegh has been indefatigable in his attendance on me; and only yesterday told me that I ought to send in an application for sick leave. An application to escape the company of a phantom! A request that the Government would graciously permit me to get rid of five ghosts and an airy rickshaw by going to England! Heatherlegh's proposition moved me to almost hysterical laughter. I told him that I should await the end quietly at Simla; and I am sure that the end is not far off. Believe me that I dread its advent more than any word can say; and I torture myself nightly with a thousand speculations as to the manner of my death.

Shall I die in my bed decently and as an English gentleman should die; or, in one last walk on the Mall, will my soul be wrenched from me to take its place for ever and ever by the side of that ghastly phantasm? Shall I return to my old lost allegiance in the next world, or shall I meet Agnes loathing her and bound to her side through all eternity? Shall we two hover over the scene of our lives till the end of Time? As the day of my death draws nearer, the intense horror that all living flesh feels towards escaped spirits from beyond the grave grows more and more powerful. It is an awful thing to go down quick among the dead with scarcely one-half of your life completed. It is a thousand times more awful to wait as I do in your midst, for I know not what unimaginable terror. Pity me, at least on the score of my 'delusion', for I know you will never believe what I have written here. Yet as surely as ever a man was done to death by the Powers of Darkness I am that man.

In justice, too, pity her. For as surely as ever woman was killed by man, I killed Mrs Wessington. And the last portion of my punishment is even now upon me.

Marghanita Laski

1915–1988

Educated at Somerville College, Oxford, Marghanita Laski
studied fashion design before taking up a career in journalism.
She published fine studies of Jane Austen and George Eliot,
several short stories and a number of acclaimed novels. She was
fascinated by the supernatural, and her most famous novel, *The
Victorian Chaise Longue*, is a classic tale of the macabre.

THE TOWER

*The road begins to rise in a series of gentle curves, passing through
pleasing groves of olives and vines. Five kilometres on the left is the fork
for Florence. To the right may be seen the Tower of Sacrifice (470 steps)
built in 1535 by Niccolo di Ferramano; superstitious fear left the tower
intact when, in 1549, the surrounding village was completely destroyed.*

TRIUMPHANTLY CAROLINE LIFTED her finger from the fine italic type. There
was nothing to mar the success of this afternoon. Not only had she taken
the car out alone for the first time, driving unerringly on the right-hand
side of the road, but what she had achieved was not a simple drive but a cultural
excursion. She had taken the Italian guidebook Neville was always urging on her
and hesitantly, haltingly, she had managed to piece out enough of the language to
choose a route that took in four well-thought-of frescoes, two universally
admired campaniles, and one wooden crucifix in a village church quite a long
way from the main road. It was not, after all, such a bad thing that a British
Council meeting had kept Neville in Florence. True, he was certain to know all
about the campaniles and the frescoes, but there was just a chance that he hadn't
discovered the crucifix, and how gratifying if she could, at last, have something of
her own to contribute to his constantly accumulating hoard of culture.

But could she add still more? There was at least another hour of daylight, and
it wouldn't take more than thirty-five minutes to get back to the flat in Florence.
Perhaps there would just be time to add this tower to her dutiful collection?
What was it called? She bent to the guidebook again, carefully tracing the text
with her finger to be sure she was translating it correctly, word by word.

But this time her moving finger stopped abruptly at the name of Niccolo di Ferramano. There had risen in her mind a picture—no, not a picture, a portrait—of a thin white face with deep-set black eyes that stared intently into hers. Why a portrait? she asked, and then she remembered.

It had been about three months ago, just after they were married, when Neville had first brought her to Florence. He himself had already lived there for two years, and during that time had been at least as concerned to accumulate Tuscan culture for himself as to disseminate English culture to the Italians. What more natural than that he should wish to share—perhaps even to show off—his discoveries to his young wife?

Caroline had come out to Italy with the idea that when she had worked through one or two galleries and made a few trips—say to Assisi and Siena—she would have done her duty as a British Council wife, and could then settle down to examining the Florentine shops, which everyone had told her were too marvellous for words. But Neville had been contemptuous of her programme. 'You can see the stuff in the galleries at any time,' he had said, 'but I'd like you to start with the pieces that the ordinary tourist doesn't see,' and of course Caroline couldn't possibly let herself be classed as an ordinary tourist. She had been proud to accompany Neville to castles and palaces privately owned, to which his work gave him entry, and there to gaze with what she hoped was pleasure on the undiscovered Raphael, the Titian that had hung on the same wall ever since it was painted, the Giotto fresco under which the family that had originally commissioned it still said their prayers.

It had been on one of these pilgrimages that she had seen the face of the young man with the black eyes. They had made a long slow drive over narrow ill-made roads and at last had come to a castle on the top of a hill. The family was, to Neville's disappointment, away, but the housekeeper remembered him and led them to a long gallery lined with five centuries of family portraits.

Though she could not have admitted it even to herself, Caroline had become almost anaesthetised to Italian art. Dutifully she had followed Neville along the gallery, listening politely while in his light well-bred voice he had told her intimate anecdotes of history, and involuntarily she had let her eyes wander round the room, glancing anywhere but at the particular portrait of Neville's immediate dissertation.

It was thus that her eye was caught by a face on the other side of the room, and forgetting what was due to politeness she caught her husband's arm and demanded, 'Neville, who's that girl over there?'

But he was pleased with her. He said, 'Ah, I'm glad you picked that one out. It's generally thought to be the best thing in the collection—a Bronzino, of course,' and they went over to look at it.

The picture was painted in rich pale colours, a green curtain, a blue dress, a young face with calm brown eyes under plaits of honey-gold hair. Caroline read out the name under the picture—*Giovanna di Ferramano, 1531–1549.* That was the year the village was destroyed, she remembered now, sitting in the car by the road-side, but then she had exclaimed, 'Neville, she was only eighteen when she died.'

'They married young in those days,' Neville commented, and Caroline said in surprise, 'Oh, was she married?' It had been the radiantly virginal character of the face that had caught at her inattention.

'Yes, she was married,' Neville answered, and added, 'Look at the portrait beside her. It's Bronzino again. What do you think of it?'

And this was when Caroline had seen the pale young man. There were no clear light colours in this picture. There was only the whiteness of the face, the blackness of the eyes, the hair, the clothes, and the glint of gold letters on the pile of books on which the young man rested his hand. Underneath this picture was written *Portrait of an Unknown Gentleman.*

'Do you mean he's her husband?' Caroline asked. 'Surely they'd know if he was, instead of calling him an Unknown Gentleman?'

'He's Niccolo di Ferramano all right,' said Neville. 'I've seen another portrait of him somewhere, and it's not a face one would forget, but—' he added reluc-tantly, because he hated to admit ignorance, 'there's apparently some queer scandal about him, and though they don't turn his picture out, they won't even mention his name. Last time I was here, the old Count himself took me through the gallery. I asked him about little Giovanna and her husband.' He laughed uneasily. 'Mind you, my Italian was far from perfect at that time, but it was hor-ribly clear that I shouldn't have asked.' 'But what did he *say?*' Caroline demanded. 'I've tried to remember,' said Neville. 'For some reason it stuck in my mind. He said either "She was lost" or "She was damned" but which word it was I can never be sure. The portrait of Niccolo he just ignored altogether.'

'What was wrong with Niccolo, I wonder?' mused Caroline, and Neville answered, 'I don't know but I can guess. Do you notice the lettering on those books up there, under his hand? It's all in Hebrew or Arabic. Undoubtedly the unmentionable Niccolo dabbled in Black Magic.'

Caroline shivered. 'I don't like him,' she said. 'Let's look at Giovanna again,' and they had moved back to the first portrait, and Neville had said casually, 'Do you know, she's rather like you.'

'I've just got time to look at the tower,' Caroline now said aloud, and she put the guidebook back in the pigeonhole under the dashboard, and drove carefully along the gentle curves until she came to the fork for Florence on the left.

On the top of a little hill to the right stood a tall round tower. There was no other building in sight. In a land where every available piece of ground is culti-vated, there was no cultivated ground around this tower. On the left was the fork for Florence: on the right a rough track led up to the top of the hill.

Caroline knew that she wanted to take the fork to the left, to Florence and home and Neville and—said an urgent voice inside her—for safety. This voice so much shocked her that she got out of the car and began to trudge up the dusty track towards the tower.

After all, I may not come this way again, she argued; it seems silly to miss the chance of seeing it when I've already got a reason for being interested. I'm only just going to have a quick look—and she glanced at the setting sun, telling herself that she would indeed have to be quick if she were to get back to Florence before dark.

And now she had climbed the hill and was standing in front of the tower. It was built of narrow red bricks, and only thin slits pierced its surface right up to the top where Caroline could see some kind of narrow platform encircling it. Before her was an arched doorway. I'm just going to have a quick look, she assured herself again, and then she walked in.

She was in an empty room with a low arched ceiling. A narrow stone staircase clung to the wall and circled round the room to disappear through a hole in the ceiling.

'There ought to be a wonderful view at the top,' said Caroline firmly to herself, and she laid her hand on the rusty rail and started to climb, and as she climbed, she counted.

'—thirty-nine, forty, forty-one,' she said, and with the forty-first step she came through the ceiling and saw over her head, far far above, the deep blue evening sky, a small circle of blue framed in a narrowing shaft round which the narrow staircase spiralled. There was no inner wall; only the rusty railing protected the climber on the inside.

'—eighty-three, eighty-four—' counted Caroline. The sky above her was losing its colour and she wondered why the narrow slit windows in the wall had all been so placed that they spiralled round the staircase too high for anyone climbing it to see through them.

'It's getting dark very quickly,' said Caroline at the hundred-and-fiftieth step. 'I know what the tower is like now. It would be much more sensible to give up and go home.'

At the two-hundred-and-sixty-ninth step, her hand, moving forward on the railing, met only empty space. For an interminable second she shivered, pressing back to the hard brick on the other side. Then hesitantly she groped forward, upwards, and at last her fingers met the rusty rail again, and again she climbed.

But now the breaks in the rail became more and more frequent. Sometimes she had to climb several steps with her left shoulder pressed tightly to the brick wall before her searching hand could find the tenuous rusty comfort again.

At the three-hundred-and-seventy-fifth step the rail, as her moving hand clutched it, crumpled away under her fingers. 'I'd better just go by the wall,' she told herself, and now her left hand traced the rough brick as she climbed up and up.

'Four-hundred-and-twenty-two, four-hundred-and-twenty-three,' counted Caroline with part of her brain. 'I really ought to go down now,' said another part, 'I wish—oh, I want to go down now—' but she could not. 'It would be so silly to give up,' she told herself, desperately trying to rationalise what drove her on. 'Just because one's afraid—' and then she had to stifle that thought too, and there was nothing left in her brain but the steadily mounting tally of the steps.

'—four-hundred-and-seventy!' said Caroline aloud with explosive relief, and then she stopped abruptly because the steps had stopped too. There was nothing ahead but a piece of broken railing barring her way, and the sky, drained now of all its colour, was still some twenty feet above her head.

'But how idiotic,' she said to the air. 'The whole thing's absolutely pointless,' and then the fingers of her left hand, exploring the wall beside her, met not brick but wood.

She turned to see what it was, and there in the wall, level with the top step, was a small wooden door. 'So it does go somewhere after all,' she said, and she fumbled with the rusty handle. The door pushed open and she stepped through.

She was on a narrow stone platform about a yard wide. It seemed to encircle the tower. The platform sloped downwards away from the tower and its stones were smooth and very shiny—and this was all she noticed before she looked beyond the stones and down.

She was immeasurably, unbelievably high and alone and the ground below was a world away. It was not credible, not possible that she should be so far from the ground. All her being was suddenly absorbed in the single impulse to hurl herself from the sloping platform. 'I cannot go down any other way,' she said, and then she heard what she said and stepped back, frenziedly clutching the soft rotten wood of the doorway with hands sodden with sweat. There is no other way, said the voice in her brain, there is no other way.

'This is vertigo,' said Caroline, 'I've only got to close my eyes and keep still for a minute and it will pass off. It's bound to pass off. I've never had it before but I know what it is and it's vertigo.' She closed her eyes and kept very still and felt the cold sweat running down her body.

'I should be all right now,' she said at last, and carefully she stepped back through the doorway on to the four-hundred-and-seventieth step and pulled the door shut before her. She looked up at the sky, swiftly darkening with night. Then, for the first time, she looked down into the shaft of the tower, down to the narrow unprotected staircase spiralling round and round and round, and disappearing into the dark. She said—she screamed—'I can't go down.'

She stood still on the top step, staring downwards, and slowly the last light faded from the tower. She could not move. It was not possible that she should dare to go down, step by step down the unprotected stairs into the dark below. It would be much easier to fall, said the voice in her head, to take one step to the left and fall and it would all be over. You cannot climb down.

She began to cry, shuddering with the pain of her sobs. It could not be true that she had brought herself to this peril, that there could be no safety for her unless she could climb down the menacing stairs. The reality *must* be that she was safe at home with Neville—but this was the reality and here were the stairs; at last she stopped crying and said, 'Now I shall go down.'

'One!' she counted and, her right hand tearing at the brick wall, she moved first one and then the other foot down to the second step. 'Two!' she counted, and then she thought of the depth below her and stood still, stupefied with terror. The stone beneath her feet, the brick against her hand were too frail protections for her exposed body. They could not save her from the voice that repeated that it would be easier to fall. Abruptly she sat down on the step.

'Two,' she counted again, and spreading both her hands tightly against the step on each side of her, she swung her body off the second step, down on to the third. 'Three,' she counted, then 'four' then 'five', pressing closer and closer into the wall, away from the empty drop on the other side.

At the twenty-first step she said, 'I think I can do it now.' She slid her right hand up the rough wall and slowly stood upright. Then with the other hand she reached for the railing it was now too dark to see, but it was not there.

For timeless time she stood there, knowing nothing but fear. 'Twenty-one,' she said, 'twenty-one' over and over again, but she could not step on to the twenty-second stair.

Something brushed her face. She knew it was a bat not a hand that touched her but still it was horror beyond conceivable horror, and it was this horror, without any sense of moving from dread to safety, that at last impelled her down the stairs.

'Twenty-three, twenty-four, twenty-five—' she counted, and around her the air was full of whispering skin-stretched wings. If one of them should touch her again, she must fall. 'Twenty-six, twenty-seven, twenty-eight—' The skin of her right hand was torn and hot with blood, for she would never lift it from the wall, only press it slowly down and force her rigid legs to move from the knowledge of each step to the peril of the next.

So Caroline came down the dark tower. She could not think. She could know nothing but fear. Only her brain remorselessly recorded the tally. 'Five-hundred-and-one,' it counted, 'five-hundred-and-two—and three—and four—'

Joseph Sheridan Le Fanu

1814–1873

Widely recognised as one of the best exponents of macabre
storytelling, Sheridan Le Fanu had a rare understanding of our
most secret fears, in particular the superstitious dread that, no
matter how much we hide from evil, somehow it will seek us out.
As well as his terrifying short stories he wrote a number of novels,
including *Uncle Silas* and *The House by the Churchyard*.

SCHALKEN THE PAINTER

YOU WILL NO DOUBT be surprised, my dear friend, at the subject of the following narrative. What had I to do with Schalken, or Schalken with me?
He had returned to his native land, and was probably dead and buried
before I was born; I never visited Holland, nor spoke with a native of that country. So much I believe you already know. I must, then, give you my authority,
and state to you frankly the ground upon which rests the credibility of the
strange story which I am about to lay before you.

I was acquainted, in my early days, with a Captain Vandael, whose father had
served King William in the Low Countries, and also in my own unhappy land
during the Irish campaigns. I know not how it happened that I liked this man's
society, spite of his politics and religion: but so it was; and it was by means of the
free intercourse to which our intimacy gives rise that I became possessed of the
curious tale which you are about to hear.

I had often been struck, while visiting Vandael, by a remarkable picture, in
which, though no connoisseur myself, I could not fail to discern some very
strong peculiarities, particularly in the distribution of light and shade, as also a
certain oddity in the design itself, which interested my curiosity. It represented
the interior of what might be a chamber in some antique religious building—
the foreground was occupied by a female figure, arrayed in a species of white
robe, part of which was arranged so as to form a veil. The dress, however, was
not strictly that of any religious order. In its hand the figure bore a lamp, by

whose light alone the form and face were illuminated; the features were marked by an arch smile, such as pretty women wear when engaged in successfully practising some roguish trick; in the background, and (excepting where the dim red light of an expiring fire serves to define the form) totally in the shade, stood the figure of a man equipped in the old fashion, with doublet and so forth, in an attitude of alarm, his hand being placed upon the hilt of his sword, which he appeared to be in the act of drawing.

'There are some pictures,' said I to my friend, 'which impress one, I know not how, with a conviction that they represent not the mere ideal shapes and combinations which have floated through the imagination of the artist, but scenes, faces and situations which have actually existed. When I look upon that picture, something assures me that I behold the representation of a reality.'

Vandael smiled, and, fixing his eyes upon the painting musingly, he said—

'Your fancy has not deceived you, my good friend, for that picture is the record, and I believe a faithful one, of a remarkable and mysterious occurrence. It was painted by Schalken, and contains, in the face of the female figure which occupies the most prominent place in the design, an accurate portrait of Rose Velderkaust, the niece of Gerard Douw, the first and, I believe, the only love of Godfrey Schalken. My father knew the painter well, and from Schalken himself he learned the story of the mysterious drama, one scene of which the picture has embodied. This painting, which is accounted a fine specimen of Schalken's style, was bequeathed to my father by the artist's will, and, as you have observed, is a very striking and interesting production.'

I had only to request Vandael to tell the story of the painting in order to be gratified; and thus it is that I am enabled to submit to you a faithful recital of what I heard myself, leaving you to reject or to allow the evidence upon which the truth of the tradition depends—with this one assurance, that Schalken was an honest, blunt Dutchman, and, I believe, wholly incapable of committing a flight of imagination; and further, that Vandael, from whom I heard the story, appeared firmly convinced of its truth.

There are few forms upon which the mantle of mystery and romance could seem to hang more ungracefully than upon that of the uncouth and clownish Schalken—the Dutch boor—the rude and dogged, but most cunning worker in oils, whose pieces delight the initiated of the present day almost as much as his manner disgusted the refined of his own; and yet this man, so rude, so dogged, so slovenly, I had almost said so savage in mien and manner, during his after successes, had been selected by the capricious goddess, in his early life, to figure as the hero of a romance by no means devoid of interest or of mystery.

Who can tell how meet he may have been in his young days to play the part of the lover or of the hero? who can say that in early life he had been the same harsh, unlicked, and rugged boor that, in his maturer age, he proved? or how far the neglected rudeness which afterwards marked his air, and garb, and manners, may not have been the growth of that reckless apathy not unfrequently produced by bitter misfortunes and disappointments in early life?

These questions can never now be answered.

We must content ourselves, then, with a plain statement of facts, leaving matters of speculation to those who like them.

When Schalken studied under the immortal Gerard Douw, he was a young man; and in spite of the phlegmatic constitution and excitable manner which he shared, we believe, with his countrymen, he was not incapable of deep and vivid impressions, for it is an established fact that the young painter looked with considerable interest upon the beautiful niece of his wealthy master.

Rose Velderkaust was very young, having, at the period of which we speak, not yet attained her seventeenth year, and if tradition speaks truth, she possessed all the soft dimpling charms of the fair, light-haired Flemish maidens. Schalken had not studied long in the school of Gerard Douw when he felt this interest deepening into something of a keener and intenser feeling than was quite consistent with the tranquillity of his honest Dutch heart; and at the same time he perceived, or thought he perceived, flattering symptoms of a reciprocal attachment, and this was quite sufficient to determine whatever indecision he might have heretofore experienced, and to lead him to devote exclusively to her every hope and feeling of his heart. In short, he was as much in love as a Dutchman could be. He was not long in making his passion known to the pretty maiden herself, and his declaration was followed by a corresponding confession upon her part.

Schalken, howbeit, was a poor man, and he possessed no counterbalancing advantages of birth or position to induce the old man to consent to a union which must involve his niece and ward in the strugglings and difficulties of a young and nearly friendless artist. He was, therefore, to wait until time had furnished him with opportunity, and accident with success; and then, if his labours were found sufficiently lucrative, it was to be hoped that his proposals might at least be listened to by her jealous guardian. Months passed away, and, cheered by the smiles of the little Rose, Schalken's labours were redoubled, and with such effect and improvement as reasonably to promise the realisation of his hopes, and no contemptible eminence in his art, before many years should have elapsed.

The even course of this cheering prosperity was, unfortunately, destined to experience a sudden and formidable interruption, and that, too, in a manner so strange and mysterious as to baffle all investigation, and throw upon the events themselves a shadow of almost supernatural horror.

Schalken had one evening remained in the master's studio considerably longer than his more volatile companions, who had gladly availed themselves of the excuse which the dusk of evening afforded to withdraw from their several tasks, in order to finish a day of labour in the jollity and conviviality of the tavern.

But Schalken worked for improvement, or rather for love. Besides, he was now engaged merely in sketching a design, an operation which, unlike that of colouring, might be continued as long as there was light sufficient to distinguish between canvas and charcoal. He had not then, nor, indeed until long after, discovered the peculiar powers of his pencil; and he was engaged in composing a group of extremely roguish-looking and grotesque imps and demons, who were inflicting various ingenious torments upon a perspiring and pot-bellied St Anthony, who reclined in the midst of them, apparently in the last stage of drunkenness.

The young artist, however, though incapable of executing, or even of appreciating, anything of true sublimity, had nevertheless discernment enough to prevent his being by any means satisfied with his work; and many were the patient erasures and corrections which the limbs and features of saint and devil underwent, yet all without producing in their new arrangement anything of improvement or increased effect.

The large, old-fashioned room was silent, and, with the exception of himself, quite deserted by its usual inmates. An hour had passed—nearly two—without any improved result. Daylight had already declined, and twilight was fast giving way to the darkness of night. The patience of the young man was exhausted, and he stood before his unfinished production, absorbed in no very pleasing ruminations, one hand buried in the folds of his long dark hair, and the other holding the piece of charcoal which had so ill executed its office, and which he now rubbed, without much regard to the sable streaks which it produced, with irritable pressure upon his ample Flemish inexpressibles.

'Pshaw!' said the young man aloud, 'would that picture, devils, saint, and all, were where they should be—in hell!'

A short, sudden laugh, uttered startlingly close to his ear, instantly responded to the ejaculation.

The artist turned sharply round, and now for the first time became aware that his labours had been overlooked by a stranger.

Within about a yard and a half, and rather behind him, there stood what was, or appeared to be, the figure of an elderly man: he wore a short cloak, and a broad-brimmed hat with a conical crown, and in his hand, which was protected with a heavy, gauntlet-shaped glove, he carried a long ebony walking stick, surmounted with what appeared, as it glittered dimly in the twilight, to be a massive head of gold; and upon his breast, through the folds of the cloak, there shone the links of a rich chain of the same metal.

The room was so obscure that nothing further of the appearance of the figure could be ascertained, and the face was altogether overshadowed by the heavy flap of the beaver which overhung it, so that no feature could be clearly discerned. A quantity of dark hair escaped from beneath this sombre hat, a circumstance which, connected with the firm, upright carriage of the intruder, proved that his years could not exceed threescore or thereabouts.

There was an air of gravity and importance about the garb of this person, and something indescribably odd—I might say awful—in the perfect, stone-like movelessness of the figure, that effectually checked the testy comment which had at once risen to the lips of the irritated artist. He therefore, as soon as he had sufficiently recovered the surprise, asked the stranger, civilly, to be seated, and desired to know if he had any message to leave for his master.

'Tell Gerard Douw,' said the unknown, without altering his attitude in the smallest degree, 'that Mynheer Vanderhausen, of Rotterdam, desires to speak with him tomorrow evening at this hour, and, if he please, in this room, upon matters of weight; that is all. Good night.'

The stranger, having finished this message, turned abruptly, and, with a quick but silent step, quitted the room before Schalken had time to say a word in reply.

The young man felt a curiosity to see in what direction the burgher of Rotterdam would turn on quitting the studio, and for that purpose he went directly to the window which commanded the door.

A lobby of considerable extent intervened between the inner door of the painter's room and the street entrance, so that Schalken occupied the post of observation before the old man could possibly have reached the street.

He watched in vain, however. There was no other mode of exit.

Had the old man vanished, or was he lurking about the recesses of the lobby for some bad purpose? This last suggestion filled the mind of Schalken with a vague horror, which was so unaccountably intense as to make him alike afraid to remain in the room alone and reluctant to pass through the lobby.

However, with an effort which appeared very disproportioned to the occasion, he summoned resolution to leave the room, and, having double-locked the door, and thrust the key in his pocket, without looking at the right or left, he traversed the passage which had so recently, perhaps still, contained the person of his mysterious visitant, scarcely venturing to breathe till he had arrived in the open street.

'Mynheer Vanderhausen,' said Gerard Douw, within himself, as the appointed hour approached; 'Mynheer Vanderhausen of Rotterdam! I never heard of the man till yesterday. What can he want of me? A portrait, perhaps, to be painted; or a younger son of a poor relation to be apprenticed; or a collection to be valued; or—pshaw! there's no one in Rotterdam to leave me a legacy. Well, whatever the business may be, we shall soon know it all.'

It was now the close of day, and every easel, except that of Schalken, was deserted. Gerard Douw was pacing the apartment with the restless step of impatient expectation, every now and then humming a passage from a piece of music which he was himself composing for, though no great proficient, he admired the art; sometimes pausing to glance over the work of one of his absent pupils, but more frequently placing himself at the window, from whence he might observe the passengers who threaded the obscure bystreet in which his studio was placed.

'Said you not, Godfrey,' exclaimed Douw, after a long and fruitless gaze from his post of observation, and turning to Schalken, 'said you not the hour of appointment was at about seven by the clock of the Stadhouse?'

'It had just told seven when I first saw him, sir,' answered the student.

'The hour is close at hand, then,' said the master, consulting a horologe as large and as round as a full-grown orange. 'Mynheer Vanderhausen, from Rotterdam—is it not so?'

'Such was the name.'

'And an elderly man, richly clad?' continued Douw.

'As well as I might see,' replied his pupil. 'He could not be young, nor yet very old neither, and his dress was rich and grave, as might become a citizen of wealth and consideration.'

At this moment the sonorous boom of the Stadhouse clock told, stroke after stroke, the hour of seven; the eyes of both master and student were directed to the door, and it was not until the last peal of the old bell had ceased to vibrate, that Douw exclaimed—

'So, so; we shall have his worship presently—that is, if he means to keep his hour; if not, thou mayst wait for him, Godfrey, if you court the acquaintance of a capricious burgomaster. As for me, I think our old Leyden contains a sufficiency of such commodities, without an importation from Rotterdam.'

Schalken laughed, as in duty bound; and, after a pause of some minutes, Douw suddenly exclaimed—

'What if it should all prove a jest, a piece of mummery got up by Vankarp, or some such worthy! I wish you had run all risks, and cudgelled the old burgomaster, stadholder, or whatever else he may be, soundly. I would wager a dozen of Rhenish, his worship would have pleaded old acquaintance before the third application.'

'Here he comes, sir,' said Schalken, in a low, admonitory tone; and instantly, upon turning towards the door, Gerard Douw observed the same figure which had, on the day before, so unexpectedly greeted the vision of his pupil Schalken.

There was something in the air and mien of the figure which at once satisfied the painter that there was no mummery in the case, and that he really stood in the presence of a man of worship; and so, without hesitation, he doffed his cap, and courteously saluting the stranger, requested him to be seated.

The visitor waved his hand slightly, as if in acknowledgment of the courtesy, but remained standing.

'I have the honour to see Mynheer Vanderhausen, of Rotterdam?' said Gerard Douw.

'The same,' was the laconic reply.

'I understood your worship desires to speak with me,' continued Douw, 'and I am here by appointment to wait your commands.'

'Is that a man of trust?' said Vanderhausen, turning towards Schalken, who stood at a little distance behind his master.

'Certainly,' replied Gerard.

'Then let him take this box and get the nearest jeweller or goldsmith to value its contents, and let him return hither with a certificate of the valuation.'

At the same time he placed a small case, about nine inches square, in the hands of Gerard Douw, who was as much amazed at its weight as at the strange abruptness with which it was handed to him.

In accordance with the wishes of the stranger, he delivered it into the hands of Schalken, and repeating his directions, dispatched him upon the mission.

Schalken disposed his precious charge securely beneath the folds of his cloak, and rapidly traversing two or three narrow streets, he stopped at a corner house, the lower part of which was then occupied by the shop of a Jewish goldsmith.

Schalken entered the shop, and calling the little Hebrew into the obscurity of its back recesses, he proceeded to lay before him Vanderhausen's packet.

On being examined by the light of a lamp, it appeared entirely cased with lead, the outer surface of which was much scraped and soiled, and nearly white with age. This was with difficulty partially removed, and disclosed beneath a box of some dark and singularly hard wood; this, too, was forced, and after the removal of two or three folds of linen, its contents proved to be a mass of golden ingots, close packed, and, as the Jew declared, of the most perfect quality.

Every ingot underwent the scrutiny of the little Jew, who seemed to feel an epicurean delight in touching and testing these morsels of the glorious metal; and each one of them was replaced in the box with the exclamation—

'*Mein Gott*, how very perfect! Not one grain of alloy—beautiful, beautiful!'

The task was at length finished, and the Jew certified under his hand that the value of the ingots submitted to his examination amounted to many thousand rix-dollars.

With the desired document in his bosom, and the rich box of gold carefully pressed under his arm, and concealed by his cloak, he retraced the way, and, entering the studio, found his master and the stranger in close conference.

Schalken had no sooner left the room, in order to execute the commission he had taken in charge, than Vanderhausen addressed Gerard Douw in the following terms: 'I may not tarry with you tonight more than a few minutes, and so I shall briefly tell you the matter upon which I come. You visited the town of Rotterdam some four months ago, and then I saw in the church of St Lawrence your niece, Rose Velderkaust. I desire to marry her, and if I satisfy you as to the fact that I am very wealthy—more wealthy than any husband you could dream of for her—I expect that you will forward my views to the utmost of your authority. If you approve my proposal, you must close with it at once, for I cannot command time enough to wait for calculations and delays.'

Gerard Douw was, perhaps, as much astonished as anyone could be by the very unexpected nature of Mynheer Vanderhausen's communication; but he did not give vent to any unseemly expression of surprise. In addition to the motives supplied by prudence and politeness, the painter experienced a kind of chill and oppressive sensation—a feeling like that which is supposed to affect a man who is placed unconsciously in immediate contact with something to which he has a natural antipathy—an undefined horror and dread—while standing in the presence of the eccentric stranger, which made him very unwilling to say anything that might reasonably prove offensive.

'I have no doubt,' said Gerard, after two or three prefatory hems, 'that the connection which you propose would prove alike advantageous and honourable to my niece; but you must be aware that she has a will of her own, and may not acquiesce in what we may design for her advantage.'

'Do not seek to deceive me, Sir Painter,' said Vanderhausen; 'you are her guardian—she is your ward. She is mine if you like to make her so.'

The man of Rotterdam moved forward a little as he spoke, and Gerard Douw, he scarce knew why, inwardly prayed for the speedy return of Schalken.

'I desire,' said the mysterious gentleman, 'to place in your hands at once an evidence of my wealth, and a security for my liberal dealing with your niece. The lad will return in a minute or two with a sum in value five times the fortune which she has a right to expect from a husband. This shall lie in your hands, together with her dowry, and you may apply the united sum as suits her interest best; it shall be all exclusively hers while she lives. Is that liberal?'

Douw assented, and inwardly thought that fortune had been extraordinarily kind to his niece. The stranger, he deemed, must be most wealthy and generous, and such an offer was not to be despised, though made by a humorist, and one of no very prepossessing presence.

Rose had no very high pretensions, for she was almost without dowry; indeed, altogether so, excepting so far as the deficiency had been supplied by the generosity of her uncle. Neither had she any right to raise any scruples against the match on the score of birth, for her own origin was by no means elevated; and as to other objections, Gerard resolved, and, indeed, by the usages of the time was warranted in resolving, not to listen to them for a moment.

'Sir,' said he, addressing the stranger, 'your offer is most liberal, and whatever hesitation I may feel in closing with it immediately, arises solely from my not having the honour of knowing anything of your family or station. Upon these points you can, of course, satisfy me without difficulty?'

'As to my respectability,' said the stranger drily, 'you must take that for granted at present; pester me with no enquiries; you can discover nothing more about me than I choose to make known. You shall have sufficient security for my respectability—my word, if you are honourable: if you are sordid, my gold.'

'A testy old gentleman,' thought Douw; 'he must have his own way. But, all things considered, I am justified in giving my niece to him. Were she my own daughter, I would do the like by her. I will not pledge myself unnecessarily, however.'

'You will not pledge yourself unnecessarily,' said Vanderhausen, strangely uttering the very words which had just floated through the mind of his companion: 'but you will do so if it is necessary, I presume; and I will show you that I consider it indispensable. If the gold I mean to leave in your hands satisfies you, and if you desire that my proposal shall not be at once withdrawn, you must, before I leave this room, write your name to this engagement.'

Having thus spoken, he placed a paper in the hands of Gerard, the contents of which expressed an engagement entered into by Gerard Douw, to give to Wilken Vanderhausen, of Rotterdam, in marriage, Rose Velderkaust, and so forth, within one week of the date hereof.

While the painter was employed in reading this covenant, Schalken, as we have stated, entered the studio, and having delivered the box and the valuation of the Jew into the hands of the stranger, he was about to retire, when Vanderhausen called him to wait; and, presenting the case and the certificate to Gerard Douw, he waited in silence until he had satisfied himself by an inspection of both as to the value of the pledge left in his hands. At length he said:

'Are you content?'

The painter said 'he would fain have another day to consider'.

'Not an hour,' said the suitor, coolly.

'Well, then,' said Douw, 'I am content; it is a bargain.'

'Then sign at once,' said Vanderhausen; ' I am weary.'

At the same time he produced a small case of writing materials, and Gerard signed the important document.

'Let this youth witness the covenant,' said the old man; and Godfrey Schalken unconsciously signed the instrument which bestowed upon another that hand which he had so long regarded as the object and reward of all his labours.

The compact being thus completed, the strange visitor folded up the paper, and stowed it safely in an inner pocket.

'I will visit you tomorrow night, at nine of the clock, at your house, Gerard Douw, and will see the subject of our contract. Farewell.' And so saying, Wilken Vanderhausen moved stiffly, but rapidly, out of the room.

Schalken, eager to resolve his doubts, had placed himself by the window in order to watch the street entrance; but the experiment served only to support his suspicions, for the old man did not issue from the door. This was very strange, very odd, very fearful. He and his master returned together, and talked but little on the way, for each had his own subjects of reflection, of anxiety, and of hope.

Schalken, however, did not know the ruin which threatened his cherished schemes.

Gerard Douw knew nothing of the attachment which had sprung up between his pupil and his niece; and even if he had, it is doubtful whether he would have regarded its existence as any serious obstruction to the wishes of Mynheer Vanderhausen.

Marriages were then and there matters of traffic and calculation; and it would have appeared as absurd in the eyes of the guardian to make a mutual attachment an essential element in a contract of marriage, as it would have been to draw up his bonds and receipts in the language of chivalrous romance.

The painter, however, did not communicate to his niece the important step which he had taken in her behalf, and his resolution arose not from any anticipation of opposition on her part, but solely from a ludicrous consciousness that if his ward were, as she very naturally might do, to ask him to describe the appearance of the bridegroom whom he destined for her, he would be forced to confess that he had not seen his face, and, if called upon, would find it impossible to identify him.

Upon the next day, Gerard Douw having dined, called his niece to him, and having scanned her person with an air of satisfaction, he took her hand, and looking upon her pretty innocent face with a smile of kindness, he said:

'Rose, my girl, that face of yours will make your fortune.' Rose blushed and smiled. 'Such faces and such tempers seldom go together, and, when they do, the compound is a love potion which few heads or hearts can resist. Trust me, thou wilt soon be a bride, girl. But this is trifling, and I am pressed for time, so make ready the large room by eight o'clock tonight, and give directions for supper at nine. I expect a friend tonight; and observe me, child, do thou trick thyself out handsomely, I would not have him think us poor or sluttish.'

With these words he left the chamber, and took his way to the room to which we have already had occasion to introduce our readers—that in which his pupils worked.

When the evening closed in, Gerard called Schalken, who was about to take his departure to his obscure and comfortable lodgings, and asked him to come home and sup with Rose and Vanderhausen.

The invitation was of course accepted, and Gerard Douw and his pupil soon found themselves in the handsome and somewhat antique-looking room which had been prepared for the reception of the stranger.

A cheerful wood fire blazed in the capacious hearth; a little at one side an old-fashioned table, with richly carved legs, was placed—destined, no doubt, to receive the supper, for which preparations were going forward; and ranged with exact regularity stood the tall-backed chairs whose ungracefulness was more than counterbalanced by their comfort.

The little party consisting of Rose, her uncle, and the artist, awaited the arrival of the expected visitor with considerable impatience.

Nine o'clock at length came, and with it a summons at the street door, which, being speedily answered, was followed by a slow and emphatic tread upon the staircase; the steps moved heavily across the lobby, the door of the room in which the party which we have described were assembled slowly opened and there entered a figure which startled, almost appalled, the phlegmatic Dutchmen, and nearly made Rose scream with affright; it was the form, and arrayed in the garb, of Mynheer Vanderhausen; the air, the gait, the height was the same, but the features had never been seen by any of the party before.

The stranger stopped at the door of the room, and displayed his form and face completely. He wore a dark-coloured cloth cloak, which was short and full, not falling quite to the knees; his legs were cased in dark purple silk stockings, and his shoes were adorned with roses of the same colour. The opening of the cloak in front showed the undersuit to consist of some very dark, perhaps sable material, and his hands were enclosed in a pair of heavy leather gloves which ran up considerably above the wrist, in the manner of a gauntlet. In one hand he carried his walking stick and his hat, which he had removed, and the other hung heavily by his side. A quantity of grizzled hair descended in long tresses from his head, and its folds rested upon the plaits of a stiff ruff, which effectually concealed his neck.

So far all was well; but the face!—all the flesh of the face was coloured with the bluish leaden hue which is sometimes produced by the operation of metallic medicines administered in excessive quantities; the eyes were enormous, and the white appeared both above and below the iris, which gave to them an expression of insanity, which was heightened by their glassy redness; the nose was well enough, but the mouth was writhed considerably to one side, where it opened in order to give egress to two long, discoloured fangs, which projected from the upper jaw, far below the lower lip; the hue of the lips themselves bore the usual relation to that of the face, and was consequently nearly black. The character of the face was malignant, even satanic, to the last degree; and, indeed, such a combination of horror could hardly be accounted for, except by supposing the corpse of some atrocious malefactor, which had long hung blackening upon the gibbet, to have at length become the habitation of a demon—the frightful sport of satanic possession.

It was remarkable that the worshipful stranger suffered as little as possible of his flesh to appear, and that during his visit he did not once remove his gloves.

Having stood for some moments at the door, Gerard Douw at length found breath and collectedness to bid him welcome, and, with a mute inclination of the head, the stranger stepped forward into the room.

There was something indescribably odd, even horrible about all his motions, something undefinable, something unnatural, unhuman—it was as if the limbs were guided and directed by a spirit unused to the management of bodily machinery.

The stranger said hardly anything during his visit, which did not exceed half an hour, and the host himself could scarcely muster courage enough to utter the few necessary salutations and courtesies: and, indeed, such was the nervous terror which the presence of Vanderhausen inspired, that very little would have made all his entertainers fly bellowing from the room.

They had not so far lost all self-possession, however, as to fail to observe two strange peculiarities of their visitor.

During his stay he did not once suffer his eyelids to close, nor even to move in the slightest degree; and further, there was death-like stillness in his whole person, owing to the total absence of the heaving motion of the chest caused by the process of respiration.

These two peculiarities, though when told they may appear trifling, produced a very striking and unpleasant effect when seen and observed. Vanderhausen at length relieved the painter of Leyden of his inauspicious presence; and with no small gratification the little party heard the street door close after him.

'Dear uncle,' said Rose, 'what a frightful man! I would not see him again for the wealth of the States!'

'Tush, foolish girl!' said Douw, whose sensations were anything but comfortable. 'A man may be as ugly as the devil, and yet if his heart and actions are good, he is worth all the pretty-faced, perfumed puppies that walk the Mall. Rose, my girl, it is very true he has not thy pretty face, but I know him to be wealthy and liberal; and were he ten times more ugly—'

'Which is inconceivable,' observed Rose.

'These two virtues would be sufficient,' continued her uncle, 'to counterbalance all his deformity; and if not of power sufficient actually to alter the shape of the features, at least of efficacy enough to prevent one thinking them amiss.'

'Do you know, uncle,' said Rose, 'when I saw him standing at the door, I could not get it out of my head that I saw the old, painted, wooden figure that used to frighten me so much in the church of St Lawrence at Rotterdam.'

Gerard laughed, though he could not help inwardly acknowledging the justness of the comparison. He was resolved, however, as far as he could, to check his niece's inclination to ridicule the ugliness of her intended bridegroom, although he was not a little pleased to observe that she appeared totally exempt from that mysterious dread of the stranger, which, he could not disguise it from himself, considerably affected him, as it also did his pupil Godfrey Schalken.

Early on the next day there arrived from various quarters of the town, rich presents of silks, velvets, jewellery, and so forth, for Rose; and also a packet directed to Gerard Douw, which, on being opened, was found to contain a contract of marriage, formally drawn up, between Wilken Vanderhausen of the Boom-quay, in Rotterdam, and Rose Velderkaust of Leyden, niece to Gerard Douw, master in the art of painting, also of the same city; and containing engagements on the part of Vanderhausen to make settlements upon his bride far more splendid than he had before led her guardian to believe likely, and which were to be secured to her use in the most unexceptionable manner possible—the money being placed in the hands of Gerard Douw himself.

I have no sentimental scenes to describe, no cruelty of guardians or magnanimity of wards, or agonies of lovers. The record I have to make is one of sordidness, levity, and interest. In less than a week after the first interview which we have just described, the contract of marriage was fulfilled, and Schalken saw the prize which he would have risked anything to secure, carried off triumphantly by his formidable rival.

For two or three days he absented himself from the school; he then returned and worked, if with less cheerfulness, with far more dogged resolution than before; the dream of love had given place to that of ambition.

Months passed away, and, contrary to his expectation, and, indeed, to the direct promise of the parties, Gerard Douw heard nothing of his niece or her worshipful spouse. The interest of the money, which was to have been demanded in quarterly sums, lay unclaimed in his hands. He began to grow extremely uneasy.

Mynheer Vanderhausen's direction in Rotterdam he was fully possessed of. After some irresolution he finally determined to journey thither—a trifling undertaking, and easily accomplished—and thus to satisfy himself of the safety and comfort of his ward, for whom he entertained an honest and strong affection.

His search was in vain, however. No one in Rotterdam had ever heard of Mynheer Vanderhausen.

Gerard Douw left not a house in the Boom-quay untried; but all in vain. No one could give him any information whatever touching the object of his enquiry, and he was obliged to return to Leyden, nothing wiser than when he had left it.

On his arrival he hastened to the establishment from which Vanderhausen had hired the lumbering, though, considering the times, most luxurious vehicle which the bridal party had employed to convey them to Rotterdam. From the driver of this machine he learned, that having proceeded by slow stages, they had late in the evening approached Rotterdam; but that before they entered the city, and while yet nearly a mile from it, a small party of men, soberly clad, and after the old fashion, with peaked beards and moustaches, standing in the centre of the road, obstructed the further progress of the carriage. The driver reined in his horses, much fearing, from the obscurity of the hour, and the loneliness of the road, that some mischief was intended.

His fears were, however, somewhat allayed by his observing that these strange men carried a large litter, of an antique shape, and which they immediately set down upon the pavement, whereupon the bridegroom, having opened the coach door from within, descended, and having assisted his bride to do likewise, led her, weeping bitterly and wringing her hands, to the litter, which they both entered. It was then raised by the men who surrounded it, and speedily carried towards the city, and before it had proceeded many yards the darkness concealed it from the view of the Dutch chariot.

In the inside of the vehicle he found a purse, whose contents more than thrice paid the hire of the carriage and man. He saw and could tell nothing more of Mynheer Vanderhausen and his beautiful lady. This mystery was a source of deep anxiety and almost of grief to Gerard Douw.

There was evidently fraud in the dealing of Vanderhausen with him, though for what purpose committed he could not imagine. He greatly doubted how far it was possible for a man possessing in his countenance so strong an evidence of the presence of the most demoniac feelings to be in reality anything but a villain; and every day that passed without his hearing from or of his niece, instead of inducing him to forget his fears, tended more and more to intensify them.

The loss of his niece's cheerful society tended also to depress his spirits; and in order to dispel this despondency, which often crept upon his mind after his daily employment was over, he was wont frequently to prevail upon Schalken to accompany him home, and by his presence to dispel, in some degree, the gloom of his otherwise solitary supper.

One evening, the painter and his pupil were sitting by the fire, having accomplished a comfortable supper. They had yielded to that silent pensiveness sometimes induced by the process of digestion, when their reflections were disturbed by a loud sound at the street door, as if occasioned by some person rushing forcibly and repeatedly against it. A domestic had run without delay to ascertain the cause of the disturbance, and they heard him twice or thrice interrogate the applicant for admission, but without producing an answer or any cessation of the sounds.

They heard him then open the hall door, and immediately there followed a light and rapid tread upon the staircase. Schalken laid his hand on his sword, and advanced towards the door. It opened before he reached it, and Rose rushed into the room. She looked wild and haggard, and pale with exhaustion and terror, but her dress surprised them as much even as her unexpected appearance. It consisted of a kind of white woollen wrapper, made close about the neck, and descending to the very ground. It was much deranged and travel-soiled. The poor creature had hardly entered the chamber when she fell senseless on the floor. With some difficulty they succeeded in reviving her, and, on recovering her senses, she instantly exclaimed in a tone of eager, terrified impatience—

'Wine, wine, quickly, or I'm lost!'

Much alarmed at the strange agitation in which the call was made, they at once administered to her wishes, and she drank some wine with a haste and eagerness which surprised them. She had hardly swallowed it, when she exclaimed with the same urgency—

'Food, food, at once, or I perish!'

A considerable fragment of a roast joint was upon the table, and Schalken immediately proceeded to cut some, but he was anticipated; for no sooner had she become aware of its presence than she darted at it with the rapacity of a vulture, and, seizing it in her hands, she tore off the flesh with her teeth and swallowed it.

When the paroxysm of hunger had been a little appeased, she appeared suddenly to become aware how strange her conduct had been, or it may have been that other more agitating thoughts recurred to her mind, for she began to weep bitterly, and to wring her hands.

'Oh! Send for a minister of God,' said she; 'I am not safe till he comes; send for him speedily.'

Gerard Douw dispatched a messenger instantly, and prevailed on his niece to allow him to surrender his bedchamber to her use; he also persuaded her to retire to it at once and to rest; her consent was extorted upon the condition that they would not leave her for a moment.

'Oh that the holy man were here!' she said; 'he can deliver me. The dead and the living can never be one—God has forbidden it.'

With these mysterious words she surrendered herself to their guidance, and they proceeded to the chamber which Gerard Douw had assigned to her use.

'Do not—do not leave me for a moment,' said she. 'I am lost for ever if you do.'

Gerard Douw's chamber was approached through a spacious apartment, which they were now about to enter. Gerard Douw and Schalken each carried a wax candle, so that sufficient degree of light was cast upon all surrounding objects. They were now entering the large chamber, which, as I have said, communicated with Douw's apartment, when Rose suddenly stopped, and, in a whisper which seemed to thrill with horror, she said—

'O God! he is here—he is here! See, see—there he goes!'

She pointed towards the door of the inner room, and Schalken thought he saw a shadowy and ill-defined form gliding into that apartment. He drew his sword, and raising the candle so as to throw its light with increased distinctness upon the objects in the room, he entered the chamber into which the figure had glided. No figure was there—nothing but the furniture which belonged to the room, and yet he could not be deceived as to the fact that something had moved before them into the chamber.

A sickening dread came upon him, and the cold perspiration broke out in heavy drops upon his forehead; nor was he more composed when he heard the increased urgency, the agony of entreaty, with which Rose implored them not to leave her for a moment.

'I saw him,' said she. 'He's here! I cannot be deceived—I know him. He's by me—he's with me—he's in the room. Then, for God's sake, as you would save me, do not stir from beside me!'

They at length prevailed upon her to lie down upon the bed, where she continued to urge them to stay by her. She frequently uttered incoherent sentences, repeating again and again, 'The dead and the living cannot be one—God has forbidden it!' and then again, 'Rest to the wakeful—sleep to the sleepwalkers.'

These and such mysterious and broken sentences she continued to utter until the clergyman arrived.

Gerard Douw began to fear, naturally enough, that the poor girl, owing to terror or ill treatment, had become deranged; and he half suspected, by the suddenness of her appearance, and the unseasonableness of the hour, and, above all, from the wildness and terror of her manner, that she had made her escape from some place of confinement for lunatics, and was in immediate fear of pursuit. He resolved to summon medical advice as soon as the mind of his niece had been in some measure set at rest by the offices of the clergyman whose attendance she had so earnestly desired; and until this object had been attained, he did not venture to put any questions to her, which might possibly, by reviving painful or horrible recollections, increase her agitation.

The clergyman soon arrived—a man of ascetic countenance—and venerable age—one whom Gerard Douw respected much, forasmuch as he was a veteran polemic, though one, perhaps, more dreaded as a combatant than beloved as a Christian—of pure morality, subtle brain, and frozen heart. He entered the chamber which communicated with that in which Rose reclined, and immediately on his arrival she requested him to pray for her, as for one who lay in the hands of Satan, and who could hope for deliverance only from Heaven.

That our readers may distinctly understand all the circumstances of the event which we are about imperfectly to describe, it is necessary to state the relative positions of the parties who were engaged in it. The old clergyman and Schalken were in the anteroom of which we have already spoken; Rose lay in the inner chamber, the door of which was open; and by the side of the bed, at her urgent desire, stood her guardian; a candle burned in the bedchamber, and three were lighted in the outer apartment.

The old man now cleared his voice, as if about to commence; but before he had time to begin, a sudden gust of air blew out the candle which served to illuminate the room in which the poor girl lay, and she with hurried alarm, exclaimed:

'Godfrey, bring in another candle; the darkness is unsafe.'

Gerard Douw, forgetting for the moment her repeated injunctions in the immediate impulse, stepped from the bedchamber into the other, in order to supply what she desired.

'O God! do not go, dear uncle!' shrieked the unhappy girl; and at the same time she sprang from the bed and darted after him, in order, by her grasp, to detain him.

But the warning came too late, for scarcely had he passed the threshold, and hardly had his niece had time to utter the startling exclamation, when the door which divided the two rooms closed violently after him, as if swung to by a strong blast of wind.

Schalken and he both rushed to the door, but their united and desperate efforts could not avail so much as to shake it.

Shriek after shriek burst from the inner chamber, with all the piercing loudness of despairing terror. Schalken and Douw applied every energy and strained every nerve to force open the door; but all in vain.

There was no sound of struggling from within, but the screams seemed to increase in loudness, and at the same time they heard the bolts of the latticed window withdrawn, and the window itself grated upon the sill as if thrown open.

One last shriek, so long and piercing and agonised as to be scarcely human, swelled from the room, and suddenly there followed a death-like silence.

A light step was heard crossing the floor, as if from the bed to the window; and almost at the same instant the door gave way, and yielding to the pressure of the external applicants, they were nearly precipitated into the room. It was empty. The window was open, and Schalken sprang to a chair and gazed out upon the street and at the canal below. He saw no form, but he beheld, or thought he beheld, the waters of the broad canal beneath settling ring after ring in heavy circular ripples, as if a moment before disturbed by the immersion of some large and heavy mass.

No trace of Rose was ever after discovered, nor was anything certain respecting her mysterious wooer detected or even suspected; no clue whereby to trace the intricacies of the labyrinth, and to arrive at a distinct conclusion was to be found. But an incident occurred, which, though it will not be received by our rational readers as at all approaching to evidence upon the matter, nevertheless produced a strong and a lasting impression upon the mind of Schalken.

Many years after the events which we have detailed, Schalken, then remotely situated, received an intimation of his father's death, and of his intended burial upon a fixed day in the church of Rotterdam. It was necessary that a very considerable journey should be performed by the funeral procession, which, as it will readily be believed, was not very numerously attended. Schalken with difficulty arrived in Rotterdam late in the day upon which the funeral was appointed to take place. The procession had not then arrived. Evening closed in, and still it did not appear.

Schalken strolled down to the church—he found it open; notice of the arrival of the funeral had been given, and the vault in which the body was to be laid had been opened. The official who corresponds to our sexton, on seeing a well-dressed gentleman, whose object was to attend the expected funeral, pacing the aisle of the church, hospitably invited him to share with him the comforts of a blazing wood fire, which as was his custom in wintertime upon such occasions, he had kindled on the hearth of a chamber which communicated by a flight of steps with the vault below.

In this chamber Schalken and his entertainer seated themselves; and the sexton, after some fruitless attempts to engage his guest in conversation, was obliged to apply himself to his tobacco pipe and can to solace his solitude.

In spite of his grief and cares, the fatigues of a rapid journey of nearly forty hours gradually overcame the mind and body of Godfrey Schalken, and he sank into a deep sleep, from which he was awakened by someone shaking him gently by the shoulder. He first thought that the old sexton had called him, but he was no longer in the room.

He roused himself, and as soon as he could clearly see what was around him, he perceived a female form, clothed in a kind of light robe of muslin, part of which was so disposed as to act as a veil, and in her hand she carried a lamp. She was moving rather away from him, and towards the flight of steps which conducted towards the vaults.

Schalken felt a vague alarm at the sight of this figure, and at the same time an irresistible impulse to follow its guidance. He followed it towards the vaults, but when it reached the head of the stairs, he paused; the figure paused also, and turning gently round, displayed, by the light of the lamp it carried, the face and features of his first love, Rose Velderkaust. There was nothing horrible, or even sad, in the countenance. On the contrary, it wore the same arch smile which used to enchant the artist long before in his happy days.

A feeling of awe and of interest, too intense to be resisted, prompted him to follow the spectre, if spectre it were. She descended the stairs—he followed; and, turning to the left through a narrow passage she led him, to his infinite surprise, into what appeared to be an old-fashioned Dutch apartment, such as the pictures of Gerard Douw have served to immortalise.

Abundance of costly antique furniture was disposed about the room, and in one corner stood a four-post bed, with heavy black cloth curtains around it. The figure frequently turned towards him with the same arch smile; and when she came to the side of the bed, she drew the curtains, and by the light of the lamp which she held towards its contents, she disclosed to the horror-stricken painter, sitting bolt upright in the bed, the livid and demoniac form of Vanderhausen. Schalken had hardly seen him when he fell senseless upon the floor, where he lay until discovered, on the next morning, by persons employed in closing the passages into the vaults. He was lying in a cell of considerable size, which had not been disturbed for a long time, and he had fallen beside a large coffin which was supported upon small stone pillars, a security against the attacks of vermin.

To his dying day Schalken was satisfied of the reality of the vision which he had witnessed, and he has left behind him a curious evidence of the impression which it wrought upon his fancy, in a painting executed shortly after the event we have narrated, and which is valuable as exhibiting not only the peculiarities · which have made Schalken's pictures sought after, but even more so as presenting a portrait, as close and faithful as one taken from memory can be, of his early love, Rose Velderkaust, whose mysterious fate must ever remain a matter of speculation.

The picture represents a chamber of antique masonry, such as might be found in most old cathedrals, and is lighted faintly by a lamp carried in the hand of a female figure, such as we have above attempted to describe; and in the background, and to the left of him who examines the painting, there stands the form of a man apparently aroused from sleep, and by his attitude, his hand being laid upon his sword, exhibiting considerable alarm; this last figure is illuminated only by the expiring glare of a wood or charcoal fire.

The whole production exhibits a beautiful specimen of that artful and singular distribution of light and shade which has rendered the name of Schalken immortal among the artists of his country. This tale is traditionary, and the reader will easily perceive, by our studiously omitting to heighten many points of the narrative, when a little additional colouring might have added effect to the recital, that we have desired to lay before him, not a figment of the brain, but a curious tradition connected with, and belonging to, the biography of a famous artist.

Penelope Lively

b. 1933

Penelope Lively has that rare talent of being equally at home
writing for children and for adults. Winner of the Carnegie
Medal for her children's book *The Ghost of Thomas Kempe*, she
won the prestigious Booker Prize in 1987 for her adult novel
Moon Tiger. As well as numerous novels and several short-story
collections, she has written scripts for radio and television.

BLACK DOG

JOHN CASE CAME HOME one summer evening to find his wife huddled in the
corner of the sofa with the sitting-room curtains drawn. She said there was a
black dog in the garden, looking at her through the window. Her husband
put his briefcase in the hall and went outside. There was no dog; a blackbird
fled shrieking across the lawn and next door someone was using a mower. He
did not see how any dog could get into the garden: the fences at either side were
five feet high and there was a wall at the far end. He returned to the house and
pointed this out to his wife, who shrugged and continued to sit hunched in the
corner of the sofa. He found her there again the next evening and at the weekend she refused to go outside and sat for much of the time watching the window.

The daughters came, big girls with jobs in insurance companies, wardrobes
full of bright clothes and twenty-thousand-pound mortgages. They stood over
Brenda Case and said she should get out more. She should go to evening
classes, they said, join a health club, do a language course, learn upholstery, go
jogging, take driving lessons. And Brenda Case sat at the kitchen table and
nodded. She quite agreed, it would be a good thing to find a new interest—
jogging, upholstery, French; yes, she said, she must pull herself together, and it
was indeed up to her in the last resort, they were quite right. When they had
gone she drew the sitting-room curtains again and sat on the sofa staring at a
magazine they had brought. The magazine was full of recipes the daughters
had said she must try; there were huge bright glossy photographs of puddings
crested with alpine peaks of cream, of dark glistening casseroles and salads
like an artist's palette. The magazine costed each recipe; a four-course dinner
for six worked out at £3.89 a head. It also had articles advising her on life

356

insurance, treatment for breast cancer and how to improve her lovemaking.

John Case became concerned about his wife. She had always been a good housekeeper; now, they began to run out of things. When one evening there was nothing but cold meat and cheese for supper he protested. She said she had not been able to shop because it had rained all day; on rainy days the dog was always outside, waiting for her.

The daughters came again and spoke severely to their mother. They talked to their father separately, in different tones, proposing an autumn holiday in Portugal or the Canaries, a new three-piece for the sitting room, a musquash coat.

John Case discussed the whole thing with his wife, reasonably. He did this one evening after he had driven the Toyota into the garage, walked over to the front door and found it locked from within. Brenda, opening it, apologised; the dog had been round at the front today, she said, sitting in the middle of the path.

He began by saying lightly that dogs have not been known to stand up on their hind legs and open doors. And in any case, he continued, there is no dog. No dog at all. The dog is something you are imagining. I have asked all the neighbours; nobody has seen a big black dog. Nobody round here owns a big black dog. There is no evidence of a dog. So you must stop going on about this dog because it does not exist. 'What is the matter?' he asked, gently. 'Something must be the matter. Would you like to go away for a holiday? Shall we have the house redecorated?'

Brenda Case listened to him. He was sitting on the sofa, with his back to the window. She sat listening carefully to him and from time to time her eyes strayed from his face to the lawn beyond, in the middle of which the dog sat, its tongue hanging out and its yellow eyes glinting. She said she would go away for a holiday if he wished, and she would be perfectly willing for the house to be redecorated. Her husband talked about travel agents and decorating firms and once he got up and walked over to the window to inspect the condition of the paintwork; the dog, Brenda saw, continued to sit there, its eyes always on her.

They went to Marrakesh for ten days. Men came and turned the kitchen from primrose to eau de nil and the hallway from magnolia to parchment. September became October and Brenda Case fetched from the attic a big gnarled walking stick that was a relic of a trip to the Tyrol many years ago; she took this with her every time she went out of the house, which nowadays was not often. Inside the house, it was always somewhere near her—its end protruding from under the sofa, or hooked over the arm of her chair.

The daughters shook their tousled heads at their mother, towering over her in their baggy fashionable trousers and their big gay jackets. It's not fair on Dad, they said, can't you see that? You've only got one life, they said sternly, and Brenda Case replied that she realised that, she did indeed. Well then . . . said the daughters, one on each side of her, bigger than her, brighter, louder, always saying what they meant, going straight to the point and no nonsense, competent with income-tax returns and contemptuous of muddle.

When she was alone, Brenda Case kept doors and windows closed at all times. Occasionally, when the dog was not there, she would open the upstairs windows to air the bedrooms and the bathroom; she would stand with the curtains blowing, taking in great gulps and draughts. Downstairs, of course, she could not risk this, because the dog was quite unpredictable; it would be absent all day, and then suddenly there it would be squatting by the fence, or leaning hard up against the patio doors, sprung from nowhere. She would draw the curtains, resigned, or move to another room and endure the knowledge of its presence on the other side of the wall, a few yards away. When it was there she would sit doing nothing, staring straight ahead of her; silent and patient. When it was gone she moved around the house, prepared meals, listened a little to the radio, and sometimes took the old photograph albums from the bottom drawer of the bureau in the sitting room. In these albums the daughters slowly mutated from swaddled bundles topped with monkey faces and spiky hair to chunky toddlers and then to spindly-limbed little girls in matching pinafores. They played on Cornish beaches or posed on the lawn, holding her hand (that same lawn on which the dog now sat on its hunkers). In the photographs, she looked down at them, smiling, and they gazed up at her or held out objects for her inspection— a flower, a seashell. Her husband was also in the photographs; a smaller man than now, it seemed, with a curiously vulnerable look, as though surprised in a moment of privacy. Looking at herself, Brenda saw a pretty young woman who seemed vaguely familiar, like some relative not encountered for many years.

John Case realised that nothing had been changed by Marrakesh and redecorating. He tried putting the walking stick back up in the attic; his wife brought it down again. If he opened the patio doors she would simply close them as soon as he had left the room. Sometimes he saw her looking over his shoulder into the garden with an expression on her face that chilled him. He asked her, one day, what she thought the dog would do if it got into the house; she was silent for a moment and then said quietly she supposed it would eat her.

He said he could not understand, he simply did not understand, what could be wrong. It was not, he said, as though they had a thing to worry about. He gently pointed out that she wanted for nothing. It's not that we have to count the pennies any more, he said, not like in the old days.

'When we were young,' said Brenda Case. 'When the girls were babies.'

'Right. It's not like that now, is it?' He indicated the twenty-four-inch colour TV set, the video, the stereo, the microwave oven, the English Rose fitted kitchen, the bathroom with separate shower. He reminded her of the BUPA membership, the index-linked pension, the shares and dividends. Brenda agreed that it was not, it most certainly was not.

The daughters came with their boyfriends, nicely spoken confident young men in very clean shirts, who talked to Brenda of their work in firms selling computers and Japanese cameras while the girls took John into the garden and discussed their mother.

'The thing is, she's becoming agoraphobic.'

'She thinks she sees this black dog,' said John Case.

'We know,' said the eldest daughter. 'But that, frankly, is neither here nor there. It's a mechanism, simply. A ploy. Like children do. One has to get to the root of it, that's the thing.'

'It's her age,' said the youngest.

'Of course it's her age,' snorted the eldest. 'But it's also her. She was always inclined to be negative, but this is ridiculous.'

'Negative?' said John Case. He tried to remember his wife—his wives who—one of whom—he could see inside the house, beyond the glass of the patio window, looking out at him from between two young men he barely knew. The reflections of his daughters, his strapping prosperous daughters, were superimposed upon their mother, so that she looked at him through the cerise and orange and yellow of their clothes.

'Negative. A worrier. Look on the bright side, *I* say, but that's not Mum, is it?'

'I wouldn't have said . . .' he began.

'She's unmotivated,' said the youngest. 'That's the real trouble. No job, no nothing. It's a generation problem, too.'

'I'm trying . . .' their father began.

'We know, Dad, we know. But the thing is, she needs help. This isn't something you can handle all on your own. She'll have to see someone.'

'No way,' said the youngest, 'will we get Mum into therapy.'

'Dad can take her to the surgery,' said the eldest. 'For starters.'

The doctor—the new doctor, there was always a new doctor—was about the same age as her daughters, Brenda Case saw. Once upon a time doctors had been older men, fatherly and reliable. This one was good-looking, in the manner of men in knitting-pattern photographs. He sat looking at her, quite kindly, and she told him how she was feeling. In so far as this was possible.

When she had finished he tapped a pencil on his desk. 'Yes,' he said. 'Yes, I see.' And then he went on, 'There doesn't seem to be any very specific trouble, does there, Mrs Case?'

She agreed.

'How do you think you would define it yourself?'

She thought. At last she said that she supposed there was nothing wrong with her that wasn't wrong with—well, everyone.

'Quite,' said the doctor busily, writing now on his pad. 'That's the sensible way to look at things. So I'm giving you this . . . Three a day . . . Come back and see me in two weeks.'

When she had come out John Case asked to see the doctor for a moment. He explained that he was worried about his wife. The doctor nodded sympathetically. John told the doctor about the black dog, apologetically, and the doctor looked reflective for a moment and then said, 'Your wife is fifty-four.'

John Case agreed. She was indeed fifty-four.

'Exactly,' said the doctor. 'So I think we can take it that with some care and understanding these difficulties will . . . disappear. I've given her something,' he said, confidently; John Case smiled back. That was that.

'It will go away,' said John Case to his wife, firmly. He was not entirely sure what he meant, but it did not do, he felt sure, to be irresolute. She looked at him without expression.

Brenda Case swallowed each day the pills that the doctor had given her. She believed in medicines and doctors, had always found that aspirin cured a headache and used to frequent the surgery with the girls when they were small. She was prepared for a miracle. For the first few days it did seem to her just possible that the dog was growing a little smaller but after a week she realised that it was not. She continued to take the pills and when at the end of a fortnight she told the doctor that there was no change he said that these things took time, one had to be patient. She looked at him, this young man in his swivel chair on the other side of a cluttered desk, and knew that whatever was to be done would not be done by him, or by cheerful yellow pills like children's sweets.

The daughters came, to inspect and admonish. She said that yes, she had seen the doctor again, and yes, she was feeling rather more . . . herself. She showed them the new sewing machine with many extra attachments that she had not used and when they left she watched them go down the front path to their cars, swinging their bags and shouting at each other, and saw the dog step aside for them, wagging its tail. When they had gone she opened the door again and stood there for a few minutes, looking at it, and the dog, five yards away, looked back, not moving.

The next day she took the shopping trolley and set off for the shops. As she opened the front gate she saw the dog come out from the shadow of the fence but she did not turn back. She continued down the street, although she could feel it behind her, keeping its distance. She spoke in a friendly way to a couple of neighbours, did her shopping and returned to the house, and all the while the dog was there, twenty paces off. As she walked to the front door she could hear the click of its claws on the pavement and had to steel herself so hard not to turn round that when she got inside she was bathed in sweat and shaking all over. When her husband came home that evening he thought her in a funny mood; she asked for a glass of sherry and later she suggested they put a record on instead of watching TV—*West Side Story* or another of those shows they went to years ago.

He was surprised at the change in her. She began to go out daily, and although in the evenings she often appeared to be exhausted, as though she had been climbing mountains instead of walking suburban streets, she was curiously calm. Admittedly, she had not appeared agitated before, but her stillness had not been natural; now, he sensed a difference. When the daughters telephoned he reported their mother's condition and listened to their complacent comments; that stuff usually did the trick, they said, all the medics were using it nowadays, they'd always known Mum would be OK soon. But when he put the telephone down and returned to his wife in the sitting room he found himself looking at her uncomfortably. There was an alertness about her that worried him; later, he thought he heard something outside and went to look. He could see nothing at either the front or the back and his wife continued to read a magazine. When he sat down again she looked across at him with a faint smile.

She had started by meeting its eyes, its yellow eyes. And thus she had learned that she could stop it, halt its patient shadowing of her, leave it sitting on the pavement or the garden path. She began to leave the front door ajar, to open the patio window. She could not say what would happen next, knew only that this was inevitable. She no longer sweated or shook; she did not glance behind her when she was outside, and within she hummed to herself as she moved from room to room.

John Case, returning home on an autumn evening, stepped out of the car and saw light streaming through the open front door. He thought he heard his wife speaking to someone in the house. When he came into the kitchen, though, she was alone. He said, 'The front door was open,' and she replied that she must have left it so by mistake. She was busy with a saucepan at the stove and in the corner of the room, her husband saw, was a large dog basket towards which her glance occasionally strayed.

He made no comment. He went back into the hall, hung up his coat and was startled suddenly by his own face, caught unawares in the mirror by the hat-stand and seeming like someone else's—that of a man both older and more burdened than he knew himself to be. He stood staring at it for a few moments and then took a step back towards the kitchen. He could hear the gentle chunk-ing sound of his wife's wooden spoon stirring something in the saucepan and then, he thought, the creak of wickerwork.

He turned sharply and went into the sitting room. He crossed to the window and looked out. He saw the lawn, blackish in the dusk, disappearing into dark-ness. He switched on the outside lights and flooded it all with an artificial glow—the grass, the little flight of steps up to the patio and the flowerbed at the top of them, from which he had tidied away the spent summer annuals at the weekend. The bare earth was marked all over, he now saw, with what appeared to be animal footprints, and as he stood gazing it seemed to him that he heard the pad of paws on the carpet behind him. He stood for a long while before at last he turned round.

Alison Lurie

b. 1926

Pulitzer Prize-winning writer Alison Lurie was for many years
Professor of American Literature at Cornell University in New
York State. Black humour pervades much of her work, and her
characters, although superficially ordinary, seldom behave as
might be expected. In this story, however, it is a thing rather than
a person that misbehaves, and in a thoroughly sinister fashion.

THE HIGHBOY

EVEN BEFORE I KNEW more about that piece of furniture I wouldn't have
wanted it in my house. For a valuable antique, it wasn't particularly attractive. With that tall stack of dark mahogany drawers, and those long
spindly bowed legs, it looked not only heavy but top-heavy. But then Clark and I
have never cared much for Chippendale; we prefer simple lines and light woods.
The carved bonnet-top of the highboy was too elaborate for my taste, and the
surface had been polished till it glistened a deep blackish brown, exactly the
colour of canned prunes.

Still, I could understand why the piece meant so much to Clark's sister-in-law,
Buffy Stockwell. It mattered to her that she had what she called 'really good
things': that her antiques were genuine and her china was Spode. She never
made a point of how superior her 'things' were to most people's, but one was
aware of it. And besides, the highboy was an heirloom; it had been in her family
for years. I could see why she was disappointed and cross when her aunt left it to
Buffy's brother.

'I don't want to sound ungrateful, Janet, honestly,' Buffy told me over lunch at
the country club. 'I realise Jack's carrying on the family name and I'm not. And
of course I was glad to have Aunt Betsy's Tiffany coffee service. I suppose it's
worth as much as the highboy actually, but it just doesn't have any past. It's got
no personality, if you know what I mean.'

Buffy giggled. My sister-in-law was given to anthropomorphising her possessions, speaking of them as if they had human traits: 'A dear little Paul Revere
sugar spoon.' 'It's lively, even kind of aggressive, for a plant-stand—but I think
it'll be really happy on the sun porch.' Whenever their washer or sit-down

mower or VCR wasn't working properly she'd say it was 'ill'. I'd found the habit endearing once, but it had begun to bore me.

'I don't understand it really,' Buffy said, digging her dessert fork into the lemon cream tart that she always ordered at the club after declaring that she shouldn't. 'After all, I'm the one who was named for Aunt Betsy, and she knew how interested I was in family history. I always thought I was her favourite. Well, live and learn.' She giggled again and took another bite, leaving a fleck of whipped cream on her short, lifted upper lip.

You mustn't get me wrong. Buffy and her husband Bobby, Clark's brother, were both dears, and as affectionate and reliable and nice as anyone could possibly be. But even Clark had to admit that they'd never quite grown up. Bobby was sixty-one and a vice-president of his company, but his life still centred around golf and tennis.

Buffy, who was nearly his age, didn't play any more because of her heart. But she still favoured yellow and shocking-pink sportswear, and kept her hair in blonde all-over curls and maintained her girlish manner. Then of course she had these bouts of childlike whimsicality: she attributed opinions to their pets, and named their automobiles. She insisted that their poodle Suzy disliked the mailman because he was a Democrat, and for years she'd driven a series of Plymouth Valiant wagons called Prince.

THE NEXT TIME the subject of the highboy came up was at a dinner party at our house about a month later, after Buffy'd been to see her brother in Connecticut. 'It wasn't all that successful a visit,' she reported. 'You know my Aunt Betsy left Jack her Newport highboy, that I was hoping would come to me. I think I told you.'

I agreed that she had.

'Well, it's in his house in Stonington now. But it's completely out of place among all that pickled-walnut imitation French-provincial furniture that Jack's new wife chose. It looked so uncomfortable.' Buffy sighed and helped herself to roast potatoes as they went round.

'It really makes me sad,' she went on. 'I could tell right away that Jack and his wife don't appreciate Aunt Betsy's highboy, the way they've shoved it slap up into the corner behind the patio door. Jack claims it's because he can't get it to stand steady, and the drawers always stick.'

'Well, perhaps they do,' I said. 'After all, the piece must be over two hundred years old.'

But Buffy wouldn't agree. Aunt Betsy had almost never had that sort of trouble, though she admitted once to Buffy that the highboy was temperamental. Usually the drawers would slide open as smoothly as butter, but now and then they seized up.

It probably had something to do with the humidity, I suggested. But according to Buffy her Aunt Betsy, who seems to have had the same sort of imagination as her niece, used to say that the highboy was sulking; someone had been rough with it, she would suggest, or it hadn't been polished lately.

'I'm sure Jack's wife doesn't know how to take proper care of good furniture either,' Buffy went on during the salad course. 'She's too busy with her high-powered executive job.

'Honestly, Janet, it's true,' she added. 'When I was there last week the finish was already beginning to look dull, almost soapy. Aunt Betsy always used to polish it once a week with beeswax, to keep the patina. I mentioned that twice, but I could see Jack's wife wasn't paying any attention. Not that she ever pays any attention to me.' Buffy gave a little short nervous giggle like a hiccup. Her brother's wife wasn't the only one of the family who thought of her as a light-weight, and she wasn't too silly to know it.

'What I suspect is, Janet, I suspect she's letting her cleaning lady spray it with that awful synthetic no-rub polish they make now,' Buffy went on, frowning across the glazed damask. 'I found a can of the stuff under her sink. Full of nasty chemicals you can't pronounce. Anyhow, I'm sure the climate in Stonington can't be good for old furniture; not with all that salt and damp in the air.'

There was a lull in the conversation then, and at the other end of the table Buffy's husband heard her and gave a kind of guffaw. 'Say, Clark,' he called to my husband. 'I wish you'd tell Buffy to forget about that old highboy.'

Well, naturally Clark was not going to do anything of the sort. But he leant towards us and listened to Buffy's story, and then he suggested that she ask her brother if he'd be willing to exchange the highboy for her aunt's coffee service.

I THOUGHT THIS WAS a good idea, and so did Buffy. She wrote off to her brother, and a few days later Jack phoned to say that was fine by him. He was sick of the highboy; no matter how he tried to prop up the legs it still wobbled.

Besides, the day before he'd gone to get out some maps for a trip they were planning and the whole thing just kind of seized up. He'd stopped trying to free the top drawer with a screwdriver, and was working on one of the lower ones, when he got a hell of a crack on the head. He must have loosened something somehow, he told Buffy, so that when he pulled on the lower drawer the upper one slid out noiselessly above him. And when he stood up, bingo.

It was Saturday, and their doctor was off call, so Jack's wife had to drive him ten miles to the Westerly emergency room; he was too dizzy and confused to drive himself. There wasn't any concussion, according to the X-rays, but he had a lump on his head the size of a plum and a headache the size of a football. He'd be happy to ship that goddamned piece of furniture to her as soon as it was con-venient, he told Buffy, and she could take her time about sending along the coffee service.

Two WEEKS LATER when I went over to Buffy's for tea her aunt's highboy had arrived. She was so pleased that I bore with her when she started talking about how it appreciated the care she was taking of it. 'When I rub in the beeswax I can almost feel it purring under my hand like a big cat,' she insisted. I glanced at the highboy again. I thought I'd never seen a less agreeable-looking piece of furniture. Its pretentious high-arched bonnet top resembled a clumsy mahogany Napoleon hat, and the ball-and-claw feet made the thing look as if it were up on tiptoe. If it was a big cat, it was a cat with bird's legs—a sort of griffin.

'I know it's grateful to be here,' Buffy told me. 'The other day I couldn't find my reading glasses anywhere; but then, when I was standing in the sitting room, at my wits' end, I heard a little creak, or maybe it was more sort of a pop. I looked round and one of the top drawers of the highboy was out about an inch. Well, I went to shut it, and there were my glasses! Now what do you make of that?'

I made nothing of it, but humoured her. 'Quite a coincidence.'

'Oh, more than that.' Buffy gave a rippling giggle. 'And it's completely steady now. Try and see.'

I put one hand on the highboy and gave the thing a little push, and she was perfectly right. It stood solid and heavy against the cream Colonial Williamsburg wallpaper, as if it had been in Buffy's house for centuries. The prune-dark mahogany was waxy to the touch and colder than I would have expected.

'And the drawers don't stick the least little bit.' Buffy slid them open and shut to demonstrate. 'I know it's going to be happy here.'

It was early spring when the highboy arrived and whether or not it was happy, it gave no trouble until that summer. Then in July we had a week of drenching thunderstorms and the drawers began to jam. I saw it happen one Sunday when Clark and I were over and Bobby tried to get out the slides of their recent trip to Quebec. He started shaking the thing and swearing, and Buffy got up and hurried over to him.

'There's nothing at all wrong with the highboy,' she whispered to me afterwards. 'Bobby just doesn't understand how to treat it. You mustn't force the drawers open like that; you have to be gentle.'

After we'd sat through the slides, Bobby went to put them away.

'Careful, darling,' Buffy warned him.

'OK, OK,' Bobby said; but it was clear he wasn't listening seriously. He yanked the drawer open without much trouble; but when he slammed it shut he let out a frightful howl: he'd shut his right thumb inside.

'Christ, will you look at that!' he shouted, holding out his broad red hand to show us a deep dented gash below the knuckle. 'I think the damn thing's broken.'

Well, Bobby's thumb wasn't broken; but it was bruised rather badly, as it turned out. His hand was swollen for over a week, so that he couldn't play in the golf tournament at the club, which meant a lot to him.

Buffy and I were sitting on the clubhouse terrace that day, and Bobby was moseying about by the first tee in a baby-blue golf shirt, with his hand still wadded up in bandages.

'Poor darling, he's so cross,' Buffy said.

'Cross?' I asked; in fact Bobby didn't look cross, only foolish and disconsolate.

'He's furious at Aunt Betsy's highboy, Janet,' she said. 'And what I've decided is, there's no point any longer in trying to persuade him to treat it right. After what happened last week, I realised it would be better to keep them apart. So I've simply moved all his things out of the drawers, and now I'm using them for my writing paper and tapestry wools.'

This time, perhaps because it was such a sticky hot day and there were too many flies on the terrace, I felt more than usually impatient with Buffy's whimsy. 'Really, dear, you mustn't let your imagination run away with you,' I said, squeezing more lemon into my iced tea. 'Your aunt's highboy doesn't have any quarrel with Bobby. It isn't a human being, it's a piece of furniture.'

'But that's just it,' Buffy insisted. 'That's why it matters so much. I mean, you and I, and everybody else'—she waved her plump freckled hand at the other people under their pink and white umbrellas, and the golfers scattered over the rolling green plush of the course—'we all know we've got to die sooner or later, no matter how careful we are. Isn't that so?'

'Well, yes,' I admitted.

'But furniture and things can be practically immortal, if they're lucky. An heirloom piece like Aunt Betsy's highboy—I really feel I've got an obligation to preserve it.'

'For the children and grandchildren, you mean.'

'Oh, that too, certainly. But they're just temporary themselves, you know.' Buffy exhaled a sigh of hot summer air. 'You see, from our point of view we own our things. But really, as far as they're concerned we're only looking after them for a while. We're just caretakers, like poor old Billy here at the club.'

'He's retiring this year, I heard,' I said, hoping to change the subject.

'Yes. But they'll hire someone else, you know, and if he's competent it won't make any difference to the place. Well, it's the same with our things, Janet. Naturally they want to do whatever they can to preserve themselves, and to find the best possible caretakers. They don't ask much: just to be polished regularly, and not to have their drawers wrenched open and slammed shut. And of course they don't want to get cold or wet or dirty, or have lighted cigarettes put down on them, or drinks or houseplants.'

'It sounds like quite a lot to ask,' I said.

'But Janet, it's so important for them!' Buffy cried. 'Of course it was naughty of the highboy to give Bobby such a bad pinch, but I think it was understandable. He was being awfully rough and it got frightened.'

'Now, Buffy,' I said, stirring my iced tea so that the cubes clinked impatiently. 'You can't possibly believe that we're all in danger of being injured by our possessions.'

'Oh no.' She gave another little rippling giggle. 'Most of them don't have the strength to do any serious damage. But I'm not worried anyhow. I have a lovely relationship with all my nice things: they know I have their best interests at heart.'

I DIDN'T SCOLD Buffy any more; it was too hot, and I realised there wasn't any point. My sister-in-law was fifty-six years old, and if she hadn't grown up by then she probably never would. Anyhow, I heard no more about the highboy until about a month later, when Buffy's grandchildren were staying with her. One hazy wet afternoon in August I drove over to the house with a basket of surplus tomatoes and zucchini. The children were building with blocks and Buffy was working on a *gros-point* cushion-cover design from the Metropolitan Museum. After a while she needed more pink wool and she asked her grandson, who was about six, to run over to the highboy and fetch it.

He got up and went at once—he's really a very nice little boy. But when he pulled on the bottom drawer it wouldn't come out and he gave the bird leg a kick. It was nothing serious, but Buffy screamed and leapt up as if she had been stung, spilling her canvas and coloured wools.

'Jamie!' Really, she was almost shrieking. 'You must never, never do that!' And she grabbed the child by the arm and dragged him away roughly.

Well naturally Jamie was shocked and upset; he cast a terrified look at Buffy and burst into tears. That brought her to her senses. She hugged him and explained that Grandma wasn't angry; but he must be very, very careful of the highboy, because it was so old and valuable.

I thought Buffy had overreacted terribly, and when she went out to the kitchen to fix two gin and tonics, and milk and peanut-butter cookies for the children, 'to settle us all down', I followed her in and told her so. Surely, I said, she cared more for her grandchildren than she did for her furniture.

Buffy gave me an odd look; then she pushed the swing door shut.

'You don't understand, Janet,' she said in a low voice, as if someone might overhear. 'Jamie really mustn't annoy the highboy. It's been rather difficult lately, you see.' She tried to open a bottle of tonic, but couldn't—I had to take it from her.

'Oh, thank you,' she said distractedly. 'It's just—Well, for instance. The other day Betsy Lee was playing house under the highboy: she'd made a kind of nest for herself with the sofa pillows, and she had some of her dolls in there. I don't know what happened exactly, but one of the claw feet gave her that nasty-looking scratch you noticed on her leg.' Buffy looked over her shoulder apprehensively and spoke even lower. 'And there've been other incidents—Oh, never mind.' She sighed, then giggled. 'I know you think it's all perfect nonsense, Janet. Would you like lime or lemon?'

I WAS DISTURBED by this conversation, and that evening I told Clark so; but he made light of it. 'Darling, I wouldn't worry. It's just the way Buffy always goes on.'

'Well, but this time she was carrying the joke too far,' I said. 'She frightened those children. Even if she was fooling, I think she cares far too much about her old furniture. Really, it made me cross.'

'I think you should feel sorry for Buffy,' Clark remarked. 'You know what we've said so often: now that she's had to give up sports, she doesn't have enough to do. I expect she's just trying to add a little interest to her life.'

I said that perhaps he was right. And then I had an idea: I'd get Buffy elected secretary of the Historical Society, to fill out the term of the woman who'd just resigned. I knew it wouldn't be easy, because she had no experience and a lot of people thought she was flighty. But I was sure she could do it; she'd always run that big house perfectly, and she knew lots about local history and genealogy and antiques.

First I had to convince the Historical Society board that they wanted her, and then I had to convince Buffy of the same thing; but I managed. I was quite proud of myself. And I was even prouder as time went on and she not only did the job beautifully, she also seemed to have forgotten all that nonsense about the highboy. That whole fall and winter she didn't mention it once.

IT WASN'T UNTIL EARLY the following spring that Buffy phoned one morning, in what was obviously rather a state, and asked me to come over. I found her waiting for me in the front hall, wearing her white quilted parka. Her fine blonde-tinted curls were all over the place, her eyes unnaturally round and bright, and the tip of her snub nose pink; she looked like a distracted rabbit.

'Don't take off your coat yet, Janet,' she told me breathlessly. 'Come out into the garden; I must show you something.'

I was surprised, because it was a cold blowy day in March. Apart from a few snowdrops and frozen-looking white crocuses scattered over the lawn, there was nothing to see. But it wasn't the garden Buffy had on her mind.

'You know that woman from New York, that Abigail Jones, who spoke on "Decorating with Antiques" yesterday at the Society?' she asked as we stood between two beds of spaded earth and sodden compost.

'Mm.'

'Well, I was talking to her after the lecture, and I invited her to come for brunch this morning and see the house.'

'Mm? And how did that go?'

'It was awful, Janet. I don't mean—' Buffy hunched her shoulders and swallowed as if she were about to sob. 'I mean, Mrs Jones was very pleasant. She admired my Hepplewhite table and chairs; and she was very nice about the canopy bed in the blue room too, though I felt I had to tell her that one of the posts wasn't original. But what she liked best was Aunt Betsy's highboy.'

'Oh yes?'

'She thought it was a really fine piece. I told her we'd always believed it was made in Newport, but Mrs Jones thought Salem was more likely. Well that naturally made me uneasy.'

'What? I mean, why?'

'Because of the witches, you know.' Buffy gave her nervous giggle. 'Then Mrs Jones said she hoped I was taking good care of the highboy. So of course I told her I was. Mrs Jones said she could see that, but what I should realise was that my piece was unique, with the carved feathering of the legs, and what looked like all the original hardware. It really ought to be in a museum, she said. I tried to stop her, because I could tell the highboy was getting upset.'

'Upset?' I laughed, because I still assumed that it was a joke. 'Why should it be upset? I should think it would be pleased to be admired by an expert.'

'But don't you see, Janet?' Buffy almost wailed. 'It didn't know about museums before. It didn't realise that there were places where it could be well taken care of and perfectly safe for, well, almost for ever. It wouldn't know about them, you see, because when pieces of furniture go to a museum they don't come back to tell the others. It's like our going to heaven, I suppose. Only now the highboy knows, that's what it will want.'

'But a piece of furniture can't force you to send it to a museum,' I protested, thinking how crazy this conversation would sound to anyone who didn't know Buffy.

'Oh, can't it.' She brushed some wispy curls out of her face. 'You don't know what it can do, Janet. None of us does. There've been things I didn't tell you about—But never mind that. Only in fairness I must say I'm beginning to have a different idea of why Aunt Betsy didn't leave the highboy to me in the first place. I don't think it was because of the family name at all. I think she was trying to protect me.' She giggled with a sound like ice cracking.

'Really, Buffy—' Wearily, warily, I played along. 'If it's as clever as you say, the highboy must know Mrs Jones was just being polite. She didn't really mean—'

'But she did, you see. She said that if I ever thought of donating the piece to a museum, where it could be really well cared for, she hoped I would let her know. I tried to change the subject, but I couldn't. She went on telling me how there was always the danger of fire or theft in a private home. She said home instead of house, that's the kind of woman she is.' Buffy giggled miserably. 'Then she started to talk about tax deductions, and said she knew of several places that would be interested. I didn't know what to do. I told her that if I did ever decide to part with the highboy I'd probably give it to our Historical Society.'

'Well, of course you could,' I suggested. 'If you felt—'

'But it doesn't matter now,' Buffy interrupted, putting a small cold hand on my wrist. 'I was weak for a moment, but I'm not going to let it push me around. I've worked out what to do to protect myself: I'm changing my will. I called Toni Stevenson already, and I'm going straight over to her office after you leave.'

'You're willing the highboy to the Historical Society?' I asked.

'Well, maybe eventually, if I have to. Not outright; heavens, no. That would be fatal. For the moment I'm going to leave it to Bobby's nephew Fred. But only in case of my accidental death.' Behind her distracted wisps of hair, Buffy gave a peculiar little smile.

'Death!' I swallowed. 'You don't really think—'

'I think that highboy is capable of absolutely anything. It has no feelings, no gratitude at all. I suppose that's because from its point of view I'm going to die so soon anyway.'

'But, Buffy—' The hard wind whisked away the rest of my words, but I doubt if she would have heard them.

'Anyhow, what I'd like you to do now, Janet, is come in with me and be a witness when I tell it what I've planned.'

I was almost sure then that Buffy had gone a bit mad; but of course I went back indoors with her.

'Oh, I wanted to tell you, Janet,' she said in an unnaturally loud, clear voice when we reached the sitting room. 'Now that I know how valuable Aunt Betsy's highboy is, I've decided to leave it to the Historical Society. I put it in my will today. That's if I die of natural causes, of course. But if it's an accidental death, then I'm giving it to my husband's nephew, Fred Turner.' She paused and took a loud breath.

'Really,' I said, feeling as if I were in some sort of absurdist play.

'I realise the highboy may feel a little out of place in Fred's house,' Buffy went on relentlessly, 'because he and his wife have all that weird modern canvas and chrome furniture. But I don't really mind about that. And of course Fred's a little careless sometimes. Once when he was here he left a cigarette burning on the cherry-pie table in the study; that's how it got that ugly scorch mark, you know. And he's rather thoughtless about wet glasses and coffee cups too.' Though Buffy was still facing me, she kept glancing over my shoulder towards the highboy.

I turned to follow her gaze, and suddenly for a moment I shared her delusion. The highboy had not moved; but now it looked heavy and sullen, and seemed to have developed a kind of vestigial face. The brass pulls of the two top drawers formed the half-shut eyes of this face, and the fluted column between them was its long thin nose; the ornamental brass keyhole of the full-length drawer below supplied a pursed, tight mouth. Under its curved mahogany tricorn hat, it had a mean, calculating expression, like some hypocritical New England Colonial merchant.

'I know exactly what you're thinking,' Buffy said, abandoning the pretence of speaking to me. 'And if you don't behave yourself, I might give you to Fred and Roo right now. They have children too. Very active children, not nice quiet ones like Jamie and Mary Lee.' Her giggle had a chilling fragmented sound now; ice shivering into shreds.

'NONE OF THAT WAS TRUE about Bobby's nephew, you know,' Buffy confided as she walked me to my car. 'They're not really careless, and neither of them smokes. I just wanted to frighten it.'

'You rather frightened me,' I told her.

Which was no lie, as I said to Clark that evening. It wasn't just the strength of Buffy's delusion, but the way I'd been infected by it. He laughed and said he'd never known she could be so convincing. Also he asked if I was sure she hadn't been teasing me.

Well, I had to admit I wasn't. But I was still worried. Didn't he think we should do something?

'Do what?' Clark said. And he pointed out that even if Buffy hadn't been teasing, he didn't imagine I'd have much luck trying to get her to a therapist; she thought psychologists were completely bogus. He said we should just wait and see what happened.

All the same, the next time I saw Buffy I couldn't help enquiring about the highboy. 'Oh, everything's fine now,' she said. 'Right after I saw you I signed the codicil. I put a copy in one of the drawers to remind it, and it's been as good as gold ever since.'

SEVERAL MONTHS PASSED, and Buffy never mentioned the subject again. When I finally asked how the highboy was, she said, 'What? Oh, fine, thanks,' in an uninterested way that suggested she'd forgotten her obsession—or tired of her joke.

The irritating thing was that now that I'd seen the unpleasant face of the highboy, it was there every time I went to the house. I would look from it to Buffy's round pink face, and wonder if she had been laughing at me all along.

Finally, though, I began to forget the whole thing. Then one day late that summer Clark and Bobby's nephew's wife, Roo, was at our house. She's a professional photographer, quite a successful one, and she'd come to take a picture of me.

Like many photographers, Roo always kept up a more or less mindless conversation with her subjects as she worked; trying to prevent them from getting stiff and self-conscious, I suppose.

'I like your house, you know, Janet,' she said. 'You have such simple, great-looking things. Could you turn slowly to the right a little? . . . Good. Hold it . . . Now over at Uncle Bobby's— Hold it . . . Their garden's great, of course, but I don't care much for their furniture. Lower your chin a little, please . . . You know that big dark old chest of drawers that Buffy's left to Fred—'

'The highboy,' I said.

'Right. Let's move those roses a bit. That's better . . . It's supposed to be so valuable, but I think it's hideous. I told Fred I didn't want it around. Hold it . . . OK.'

'And what did he say?' I asked.

'Huh? Oh, Fred feels the same as I do. He said that if he did inherit the thing he was going to give it to a museum.'

'A museum?' I have to admit that my voice rose. 'Where was Fred when he told you this?'

'Don't move, please. OK . . . What? . . . I think we were in Buffy's sitting room—but she wasn't there, of course. You don't have to worry, Janet. Fred wouldn't say anything like that in front of his aunt; he knows it would sound awfully ungrateful.'

Well, my first impulse was to pick up the phone and warn my sister-in-law as soon as Roo left. But then I thought that would sound ridiculous. It was crazy to imagine that Buffy was in danger from a chest of drawers. Especially so long after she'd gotten over the idea herself, if she'd ever really had it in the first place.

Buffy might even laugh at me, I thought; she wasn't anywhere near as whimsical as she had been. She'd become more and more involved in the Historical Society, and it looked as if she'd be re-elected automatically next year. Besides, if by chance she hadn't been kidding and I reminded her of her old delusion and seemed to share it, the delusion might come back and it would be my fault.

So I didn't do anything. I didn't even mention the incident to Clark.

Two DAYS LATER, while I was writing letters in the study, Clark burst in. I knew something awful had happened as soon as I saw his face.

Bobby had just called from the hospital, he told me. Buffy was in intensive care and the prognosis was bad. She had a broken hip and a concussion, but the real problem was the shock to her weak heart. Apparently, he said, some big piece of furniture had fallen on her.

I didn't ask what piece of furniture that was. I drove straight to the hospital with him; but by the time we got there Buffy was in a coma.

Though she was nearer plump than slim, Buffy seemed horribly small in that room, on that high flat bed—like a kind of faded child. Her head was in bandages, and there were tubes and wires all over her like mechanical snakes; her little freckled hands lay in weak fists on the white hospital sheet. You could see right away that it was all over with her, though in fact they managed to keep her alive, if you can use that word, for nearly three days more.

FRED TURNER, just as he had promised, gave the highboy to a New York museum. I went to see it there recently. Behind its maroon velvet rope it looked exactly the same: tall, glossy, top-heavy, bird-legged and claw-footed.

'You wicked, selfish, ungrateful thing,' I told it. 'I hope you get termites. I hope some madman comes in here and attacks you with an axe.'

The highboy did not answer me, of course. But under its mahogany Napoleon hat it seemed to wear a little self-satisfied smile.

W. Somerset Maugham

1874–1965

William Somerset Maugham qualified as a doctor, but then
abandoned medicine in favour of writing, and from 1897 he
produced a torrent of novels, plays and short stories. He travelled
extensively, served with the Red Cross during the First World
War, and later visited the Far East. It was these experiences that
shaped and enriched much of his writing.

THE TAIPAN

NO ONE KNEW BETTER than he that he was an important person. He was
number one in not the least important branch of the most important
English firm in China. He had worked his way up through solid ability
and he looked back with a faint smile at the callow clerk who had come out to
China thirty years before. When he remembered the modest home he had come
from, a little red house in a long row of little red houses, in Barnes, a suburb
which, aiming desperately at the genteel, achieves only a sordid melancholy, and
compared it with the magnificent stone mansion, with its wide verandahs and
spacious rooms, which was at once the office of the company and his own residence, he chuckled with satisfaction. He had come a long way since then. He
thought of the high tea to which he sat down when he came home from school
(he was at St Paul's), with his father and mother and his two sisters, a slice of cold
meat, a great deal of bread and butter and plenty of milk in his tea, everybody
helping himself, and then he thought of the state in which now he ate his
evening meal. He always dressed and whether he was alone or not he expected
the three boys to wait at table. His number-one boy knew exactly what he liked
and he never had to bother himself with the details of housekeeping; but he
always had a set dinner with soup and fish, entrée, roast, sweet and savoury, so
that if he wanted to ask anyone in at the last moment he could. He liked his food
and he did not see why when he was alone he should have less good a dinner
than when he had a guest.

He had indeed gone far. That was why he did not care to go home now, he
had not been to England for ten years, and he took his leave in Japan or
Vancouver, where he was sure of meeting old friends from the China coast. He

knew no one at home. His sisters had married in their own station, their husbands were clerks and their sons were clerks; there was nothing between him and them; they bored him. He satisfied the claims of relationship by sending them every Christmas a piece of fine silk, some elaborate embroidery, or a case of tea. He was not a mean man and as long as his mother lived he had made her an allowance. But when the time came for him to retire he had no intention of going back to England, he had seen too many men do that and he knew how often it was a failure; he meant to take a house near the racecourse in Shanghai: what with bridge and his ponies and golf he expected to get through the rest of his life very comfortably. But he had a good many years before he need think of retiring. In another five or six Higgins would be going home and then he would take charge of the head office in Shanghai. Meanwhile he was very happy where he was, he could save money, which you couldn't do in Shanghai, and have a good time into the bargain. This place had another advantage over Shanghai: he was the most prominent man in the community and what he said went. Even the consul took care to keep on the right side of him. Once a consul and he had been at loggerheads and it was not he who had gone to the wall. The taipan thrust out his jaw pugnaciously as he thought of the incident.

But he smiled, for he felt in an excellent humour. He was walking back to his office from a capital luncheon at the Hong Kong and Shanghai Bank. They did you very well there. The food was first-rate and there was plenty of liquor. He had started with a couple of cocktails, then he had some excellent Sauternes and he had finished up with two glasses of port and some fine old brandy. He felt good. And when he left he did a thing that was rare with him; he walked. His bearers with his chair kept a few paces behind him in case he felt inclined to slip into it, but he enjoyed stretching his legs. He did not get enough exercise these days. Now that he was too heavy to ride it was difficult to get exercise. But if he was too heavy to ride he could still keep ponies, and as he strolled along in the balmy air he thought of the spring meeting. He had a couple of griffins that he had hopes of and one of the lads in his office had turned out a fine jockey (he must see they didn't sneak him away; old Higgins in Shanghai would give a pot of money to get him over there) and he ought to pull off two or three races. He flattered himself that he had the finest stable in the city. He pouted his broad chest like a pigeon. It was a beautiful day, and it was good to be alive.

He paused as he came to the cemetery. It stood there, neat and orderly, as an evident sign of the community's opulence. He never passed the cemetery without a little glow of pride. He was pleased to be an Englishman. For the cemetery stood in a place, valueless when it was chosen, which with the increase of the city's affluence was now worth a great deal of money. It had been suggested that the graves should be moved to another spot and the land sold for building, but the feeling of the community was against it. It gave the taipan a sense of satisfaction to think that their dead rested on the most valuable site on the island. It showed that there were things they cared for more than money. Money be blowed! When it came to 'the things that mattered' (this was a favourite phrase with the taipan), well, one remembered that money wasn't everything.

And now he thought he would take a stroll through. He looked at the graves. They were neatly kept and the pathways were free from weeds. There was a look of prosperity. And as he sauntered along he read the names on the tombstones. Here were three side by side: the captain, the first mate and the second mate of the barque *Mary Baxter*, who had all perished together in the typhoon of 1908. He remembered it well. There was a little group of two missionaries, their wives and children, who had been massacred during the Boxer troubles. Shocking thing that had been! Not that he took much stock in missionaries; but, hang it all, one couldn't have these damned Chinese massacring them. Then he came to a cross with a name on it he knew. Good chap, Edward Mulock, but he couldn't stand his liquor, drank himself to death, poor devil, at twenty-five; the taipan had known a lot of them do that; there were several more neat crosses with a man's name on them and the age, twenty-five, twenty-six, or twenty-seven; it was always the same story: they had come out to China; they had never seen so much money before, they were good fellows and they wanted to drink with the rest: they couldn't stand it, and there they were in the cemetery. You had to have a strong head and a fine constitution to drink drink for drink on the China coast. Of course it was very sad, but the taipan could hardly help a smile when he thought how many of those young fellows he had drunk underground. And there was a death that had been useful, a fellow in his own firm, senior to him and a clever chap too: if that fellow had lived he might not have been taipan now. Truly the ways of fate were inscrutable. Ah, and here was little Mrs Turner, Violet Turner, she had been a pretty little thing, he had had quite an affair with her; he had been devilish cut up when she died. He looked at her age on the tombstone. She'd be no chicken if she were alive now. And as he thought of all those dead people a sense of satisfaction spread through him. He had beaten them all. They were dead and he was alive, and by George he'd scored them off. His eyes collected in one picture all those crowded graves and he smiled scornfully. He very nearly rubbed his hands.

'No one ever thought I was a fool,' he muttered.

He had a feeling of good-natured contempt for the gibbering dead. Then, as he strolled along, he came suddenly upon two coolies digging a grave. He was astonished, for he had not heard that anyone in the community was dead.

'Who the devil's that for?' he said aloud.

The coolies did not even look at him, they went on with their work, standing in the grave, deep down, and they shovelled up heavy clods of earth. Though he had been so long in China he knew no Chinese—in his day it was not thought necessary to learn the damned language—and he asked the coolies in English whose grave they were digging. They did not understand. They answered him in Chinese and he cursed them for ignorant fools. He knew that Mrs Broome's child was ailing and it might have died, but he would certainly have heard of it, and besides, that wasn't a child's grave, it was a man's and a big man's too. It was uncanny. He wished he hadn't gone into that cemetery; he hurried out and stepped into his chair. His good humour had all gone and there was an uneasy frown on his face. The moment he got back to his office he called to his number two:

'I say, Peters, who's dead, d'you know?'

But Peters knew nothing. The taipan was puzzled. He called one of the native clerks and sent him to the cemetery to ask the coolies. He began to sign his letters. The clerk came back and said the coolies had gone and there was no one to ask. The taipan began to feel vaguely annoyed: he did not like things to happen of which he knew nothing. His own boy would know, his boy always knew everything, and he sent for him; but the boy had heard of no death in the community.

'I knew no one was dead,' said the taipan irritably. 'But what's the grave for?'

He told the boy to go to the overseer of the cemetery and find out what the devil he had dug a grave for when no one was dead.

'Let me have a whisky and soda before you go,' he added, as the boy was leaving the room.

He did not know why the sight of the grave had made him uncomfortable. But he tried to put it out of his mind. He felt better when he had drunk the whisky, and he finished his work. He went upstairs and turned over the pages of *Punch*. In a few minutes he would go to the club and play a rubber or two of bridge before dinner. But it would ease his mind to hear what his boy had to say and he waited for his return. In a little while the boy came back and he brought the overseer with him.

'What are you having a grave dug for?' he asked the overseer point-blank. 'Nobody's dead.'

'I no dig glave,' said the man.

'What the devil do you mean by that? There were two coolies digging a grave this afternoon.'

The two Chinese looked at one another. Then the boy said they had been to the cemetery together. There was no new grave there.

The taipan only just stopped himself from speaking.

'But damn it all, I saw it myself,' were the words on the tip of his tongue.

But he did not say them. He grew very red as he choked them down. The two Chinese looked at him with their steady eyes. For a moment his breath failed him.

'All right. Get out,' he gasped.

But as soon as they were gone he shouted for the boy again, and when he came, maddeningly impassive, he told him to bring some whisky. He rubbed his sweating face with a handkerchief. His hand trembled when he lifted the glass to his lips. They could say what they liked, but he had seen the grave. Why, he could hear still the dull thud as the coolies threw the spadefuls of earth on the ground above them. What did it mean? He could feel his heart beating. He felt strangely ill at ease. But he pulled himself together. It was all nonsense. If there was no grave there it must have been an hallucination. The best thing he could do was to go to the club, and if he ran across the doctor he would ask him to give him a look over.

Everyone in the club looked just the same as ever. He did not know why he should have expected them to look different. It was a comfort. These men, living for many years with one another lives that were methodically regulated, had acquired a number of little idiosyncrasies—one of them hummed incessantly while he played bridge, another insisted on drinking beer through a straw —and these tricks which had so often irritated the taipan now gave him a sense of security. He needed it, for he could not get out of his head that strange sight he had seen; he played bridge very badly; his partner was censorious, and the taipan lost his temper. He thought the men were looking at him oddly. He wondered what they saw in him that was unaccustomed.

Suddenly he felt he could not bear to stay in the club any longer. As he went out he saw the doctor reading *The Times* in the reading room, but he could not bring himself to speak to him. He wanted to see for himself whether that grave was really there and stepping into his chair he told his bearers to take him to the cemetery. You couldn't have an hallucination twice, could you? And besides, he would take the overseer in with him and if the grave was not there he wouldn't see it, and if it was he'd give the overseer the soundest thrashing he'd ever had. But the overseer was nowhere to be found. He had gone out and taken the keys with him. When the taipan found he could not get into the cemetery he felt suddenly exhausted. He got back into his chair and told his bearers to take him home. He would lie down for half an hour before dinner. He was tired out. That was it. He had heard that people had hallucinations when they were tired. When his boy came in to put out his clothes for dinner it was only by an effort of will that he got up. He had a strong inclination not to dress that evening, but he resisted it: he made it a rule to dress, he had dressed every evening for twenty years and it would never do to break his rule. But he ordered a bottle of champagne with his dinner and that made him feel more comfortable. Afterwards he told the boy to bring him the best brandy. When he had drunk a couple of glasses of this he felt himself again. Hallucinations be damned! He went to the billiard room and practised a few difficult shots. There could not be much the matter with him when his eye was so sure. When he went to bed he sank immediately into a sound sleep.

But suddenly he awoke. He had dreamed of that open grave and the coolies digging leisurely. He was sure he had seen them. It was absurd to say it was an hallucination when he had seen them with his own eyes. Then he heard the rattle of the night watchman going his rounds. It broke upon the stillness of the night so harshly that it made him jump out of his skin. And then terror seized him. He felt a horror of the winding multitudinous streets of the Chinese city, and there was something ghastly and terrible in the convoluted roofs of the temples with their devils grimacing and tortured. He loathed the smells that assaulted his nostrils. And the people. Those myriads of blue-clad coolies, and the beggars in their filthy rags, and the merchants and the magistrates, sleek, smiling and inscrutable, in their long black gowns. They seemed to press upon him with menace. He hated the country. China. Why had he ever come? He was panic-stricken now. He must get out. He would not stay another year, another month. What did he care about Shanghai?

'Oh, my God,' he cried, 'if I were only safely back in England.'

He wanted to go home. If he had to die he wanted to die in England. He could not bear to be buried among all these yellow men, with their slanting eyes and their grinning faces. He wanted to be buried at home, not in that grave he had seen that day. He could never rest there. Never. What did it matter what people thought? Let them think what they liked. The only thing that mattered was to get away while he had the chance.

He got out of bed and wrote to the head of the firm and said he had discovered he was dangerously ill. He must be replaced. He could not stay longer than was absolutely necessary. He must go home at once.

They found the letter in the morning clenched in the taipan's hand. He had slipped down between the desk and the chair. He was stone dead.

———————————

Guy de Maupassant

1850–1893

One of France's greatest authors, Guy de Maupassant worked as a clerk until, encouraged by novelist Gustave Flaubert, he turned to writing. For much of his life he was haunted by fear of the madness that finally brought about his death in an asylum, and although his work was often light and satirical, many of his stories show a preoccupation with the darker side of life.

AN APPARITION

WE WERE SPEAKING of sequestration apropos of a recent lawsuit. It was at the close of an evening amongst friends, at an old house in the Rue de Grenelle, and each of us had a story to tell, a story alleged to be true. Then, the old Marquis de la Tour Samuel, who was eighty-two, rose, and, leaning on the mantelpiece, said, in somewhat shaky tones:

'I also know something strange, so strange that it has been an obsession all my life. It is now fifty-six years since the incident occurred, and yet not a month has passed in which I have not seen it again in a dream. The mark, the imprint of fear, if you can understand me, has remained with me ever since that day. For ten minutes I experienced such horrible fright that, ever since, a sort of constant terror is in my soul. Unexpected noises make me shudder to the bottom of my soul and objects half-seen in the gloom of night inspire me with a mad desire to take flight. In short, at night I am afraid.

'Ah, no! I would not have admitted that before having reached my present age! Now I can say anything. At eighty-two years of age, I do not feel compelled to be brave in the presence of imaginary dangers. I have never receded before real danger.

'The affair upset me so completely, and caused me such deep and mysterious and terrible distress, that I never spoke of it to anyone. I have kept it down in the depths of my being, in those depths where painful secrets are kept, the shameful secrets and all the unconfessed weaknesses of our lives. I will now tell it to you exactly as it happened, without any attempt at explanation. There is no doubt it can be explained, unless I was mad at the time. But I was not mad, and I will prove it. You may think what you like. Here are the simple facts:

'It was in 1827, in the month of July. I was stationed at Rouen. One day, as I was walking along the quay, I met a man whom I thought I recognised, without being able to recall exactly who he was. Instinctively, I made a movement to stop; the stranger perceived it, looked at me, and fell into my arms.

'He was a friend of my youth to whom I had been deeply attached. For five years I had not seen him, and he seemed to have aged half a century. His hair was quite white, and he walked with a stoop as though completely worn out. He understood my surprise, and told me his life. A misfortune had shattered it.

'Having fallen madly in love with a young girl, he had married her, but, after a year of superhuman happiness and of passionate love, she died suddenly of heart failure, of love, very probably. He had left his chateau on the very day of her burial and had come to live in his house at Rouen. There he lived, desperate and solitary, consumed by grief, and so miserable that he thought only of suicide.

'"Now that I have found you again," said he, "I will ask you to render me an important service, to go to my old home and get for me, from the desk of my bedroom—our bedroom—some papers which I greatly need. I cannot send a servant or a lawyer, as complete discretion and absolute silence are necessary. As for myself, nothing on earth would induce me to re-enter that house. I will give you the key of the room, which I myself locked on leaving, and the key of my desk—also a note to my gardener, telling him to open the chateau for you. But come and breakfast with me tomorrow, and we will arrange all that."

'I promised to do him the slight favour he asked. For that matter, it was nothing of a trip, his property being but a few miles distant from Rouen and easily reached in an hour on horseback.

'At ten o'clock the following day I was at his house, and we breakfasted alone together, but he scarcely spoke.

'He begged me to pardon him; the thought of the visit I was about to make to that room, the scene of his dead happiness, overwhelmed him, he said. He, indeed, seemed singularly agitated and preoccupied, as though some mysterious struggle were taking place in his soul.

'At last, he explained to me exactly what I had to do. It was very simple. I was to take two packages of letters and a roll of papers from the first drawer on the right of the desk, of which I had a key. He added, "I need not beg you to refrain from glancing at them."

'I was wounded at that remark, and told him so somewhat sharply. He stammered, "Forgive me, I suffer so," and he began to weep.

'I took leave of him about one o'clock to accomplish my mission.

'The weather was glorious, and I cantered over the fields, listening to the songs of the larks and the rhythmical striking of my sword against my boot. Then I entered the forest and walked my horse. Branches of trees caressed my face as I passed, and, now and then, I caught a leaf with my teeth and chewed it greedily, from that sheer joy of living which inexplicably fills one with a sense of tumultuous, impalpable happiness, a sort of intoxication of strength.

'As I approached the chateau, I looked in my pocket for the letter I had for the gardener, and was astonished at finding it sealed. I was so surprised and irritated that I was about to turn back without having fulfilled my promise, but thought that I should thereby display undue susceptibility. My friend might easily have closed the envelope without noticing that he did so, in his troubled state of mind.

'The manor seemed to have been abandoned for twenty years. The gate was open and in such a state of decay that one wondered how it stood upright; the paths were overgrown with grass, and the flowerbeds were no longer distinguishable from the lawn.

'The noise I made by tapping loudly on a shutter brought an old man from a side door, who seemed stunned with astonishment at seeing me. On receiving my letter, he read it, reread it, turned it over and over, looked me up and down, put the paper in his pocket, and finally asked:

'"Well! what is it you want?"

'I replied shortly: "You ought to know, since you have just read your master's orders. I wish to enter the chateau."

'He seemed overcome. "Then you are going into . . . into her room?"

'I began to lose patience: "See here! Do you propose to cross-examine me?"

'He stammered in confusion: "No—sir—but it is because—that is, it has not been opened since—since the—death. If you will be kind enough to wait for five minutes, I will go to—to see if—"

'I interrupted him, angrily: "Look here, what are you driving at? You cannot enter the room, since I have the key!"

'He had no more to say. "Then, sir, I will show you the way."

'"Show me the staircase and leave me. I'll find my way without you."

'"But—sir—-indeed—"

'This time I became really angry: "Now be quiet or you'll know the reason why." I pushed him aside, and went into the house.

'I first went through the kitchen; then two rooms occupied by the servant and his wife; next, by a wide hall, I reached the stairs, which I mounted, and recognised the door indicated by my friend.

'I easily opened it and entered. The apartment was so dark that, at first, I could distinguish nothing. I stopped short, my nostrils penetrated by the disagreeable, mouldy odour of unoccupied rooms, of dead rooms. Then, as my eyes slowly became accustomed to the darkness, I saw plainly enough, a large disordered bedroom, the bed without sheets, but still retaining its mattresses and pillows, on one of which was a deep impression of an elbow or a head, as though someone had recently rested there.

'The chairs all seemed out of place. I noticed that a door, doubtless that of a closet, had remained half open.

'I first went to the window, which I opened to let in the light; but the fastenings of the shutters had grown so rusty that I could not move them. I even tried to break them with my sword, but without success. As I was growing irritated over my useless efforts, and could now see fairly well in the obscurity, I renounced the idea of getting more light and went over to the writing table.

'I sat down in an armchair, let down the lid of the desk and opened the drawer that had been indicated. It was full to the top. I needed only three packages, which I knew how to recognise, and began searching for them.

'I was straining my eyes in the effort to read the superscriptions, when I seemed to hear, or rather feel, something rustle behind me. I paid no attention, believing that a draught from the window was moving some drapery. But, in a minute or so, another movement, almost imperceptible, sent a strangely disagreeable little shiver over my skin. It was so stupid to be affected, even slightly, that self-respect prevented my turning around. I had then found the second packet I needed and was about to lay my hand on the third when a long and painful sigh, uttered just over my shoulder, made me bound like a madman from my seat and land several feet away. As I jumped I had turned about, my hand on the hilt of my sword, and, truly, had I not felt it at my side, I should have taken to my heels like a coward.

'A tall woman, dressed in white, stood gazing at me from the back of the chair where I had been sitting an instant before.

'Such a shudder ran through all my limbs that I nearly fell backward. No one can understand unless he has felt it, that frightful, unreasoning terror! The mind becomes vague; the heart ceases to beat; the entire body grows as limp as a sponge, as if one's life were ebbing away.

'I do not believe in ghosts, nevertheless I completely gave way to a hideous fear of the dead; and I suffered more in those few moments than in all the rest of my life, from the irresistible anguish of supernatural fright. If she had not spoken, I should have died, perhaps! But she spoke, she spoke in a sweet, sad voice, that set my nerves vibrating. I dare not say that I became master of myself and recovered my reason. No! I was so frightened that I scarcely knew what I was doing; but a certain innate pride, a remnant of soldierly instinct, made me, almost in spite of myself, maintain a creditable countenance. I was posing to myself, I suppose, and to her, whoever she was, woman or ghost. Afterwards I realised all this, for I assure you that, at the time of the apparition, I thought of nothing. I was afraid.

'She said: "Oh! sir, you can render me a great service."

'I tried to reply, but it was impossible for me to pronounce a word. Only a vague sound came from my throat.

'She continued: "Will you? You can save me, cure me. I suffer frightfully. I suffer, oh! how I suffer!" and she slowly seated herself in my armchair.

'"Will you?" she said, looking at me.

'I replied "Yes" by a nod, my voice still being paralysed.

'Then she held out to me a tortoiseshell comb, and murmured:

'"Comb my hair, oh! comb my hair; that will cure me; it must be combed. Look at my head—how I suffer; and my hair hurts me so!"

'Her hair, unbound, very long and very black, it seemed to me, hung over the back of the chair and touched the floor.

'Why did I receive that comb with a shudder, and why did I take in my hands the long, black hair which gave to my skin a gruesome, cold sensation, as though I were handling snakes? I cannot tell.

'That sensation has remained in my fingers and I still tremble when I think of it.

'I combed her hair. I handled, I know not how, those icy locks. I twisted, knotted, and loosened them. She sighed and bowed her head, seeming to be happy. Suddenly she said: "I thank you!", snatched the comb from my hands, and fled by the door that I had noticed ajar.

'Left alone, I experienced for several seconds the frightened agitation of one who awakens from a nightmare. At length I regained my full senses; I ran to the window, and with a mighty effort burst open the shutters, letting a flood of light into the room. Immediately I sprang to the door by which she had departed. I found it closed and immovable!

'Then a mad desire to flee came on me like a panic, the panic which soldiers know in battle. I seized the three packets of letters on the open desk; ran from the room, dashed down the stairs four steps at a time, found myself outside, I know not how, and seeing my horse a few steps off, leaped into the saddle and galloped away.

'I stopped only when I reached Rouen and my own house. Throwing the bridle to my orderly, I fled to my room, where I shut myself in to think.

'For an hour I anxiously wondered whether I had not been the victim of a hallucination. Surely I had had one of those incomprehensible nervous shocks, one of those mental frights which give rise to miracles, to which the supernatural owes its power.

'I was about to believe I had seen a vision, had a hallucination, when I approached the window. My eyes fell, by chance, upon my breast. My military cape was covered with hairs; the long hairs of a woman, which had caught in the buttons! One by one, with trembling fingers, I plucked them off and threw them away.

'I then called my orderly. I was too disturbed, too upset to go and see my friend that day, and I also wished to reflect more fully upon what I ought to tell him. I sent him his letters, for which he gave the soldier a receipt. He asked after me most particularly. He was told I was ill, that I had had sunstroke or something. He seemed to be exceedingly anxious. Next morning at dawn I went to him, determined to tell him the truth. He had gone out the evening before and had not yet returned. I called again during the day; my friend was still absent. I waited for a week. He did not appear. Then I notified the authorities. A search was instituted, but not the slightest trace of his whereabouts or manner of disappearance was discovered.

'A minute inspection was made of the abandoned chateau. Nothing of a suspicious character was discovered. There was no indication that a woman had been concealed there.

'The inquiry led to nothing, and the search was stopped, and for fifty-six years I have heard nothing; I know no more than before.'

Edith Nesbit

1858–1924

Edith Nesbit began her literary career as a poet, but in 1880, when she married a hard-up socialist journalist, Hubert Bland, she started writing children's books and short stories for adults. The best known of these, *The Railway Children*, has become a much-loved classic, and her ghost stories are some of the most memorable and frightening in the genre.

MAN-SIZE IN MARBLE

ALTHOUGH EVERY WORD of this story is as true as despair, I do not expect people to believe it. Nowadays a 'rational explanation' is required before belief is possible. Let me then, at once, offer the 'rational explanation' which finds most favour among those who have heard the tale of my life's tragedy. It is held that we were 'under a delusion', Laura and I, on that 31st of October; and that this supposition places the whole matter on a satisfactory and believable basis. The reader can judge, when he, too, has heard my story, how far this is an 'explanation' and in what sense it is 'rational'. There were three who took part in this: Laura and I and another man. The other man still lives, and can speak to the truth of the least credible part of my story.

I NEVER IN MY LIFE knew what it was to have as much money as I required to supply the most ordinary needs—good colours, books, and cab fares—and when we were married we knew quite well that we should only be able to live at all by 'strict punctuality and attention to business'. I used to paint in those days, and Laura used to write, and we felt sure we could keep the pot at least simmering. Living in town was out of the question, so we went to look for a cottage in the country, which should be at once sanitary and picturesque. So rarely do these two qualities meet in one cottage that our search was for some time quite fruitless. We tried advertisements, but most of the desirable rural residences which we did look at proved to be lacking in both essentials, and when a cottage chanced to have drains it always had stucco as well and was shaped like a tea caddy. And if we found a vine or rose-covered porch, corruption invariably lurked within. Our minds got so befogged by the eloquence of house agents and the rival disadvantages of the fever-traps and outrages to beauty which we had seen and scorned, that I very much doubt whether either of us, on our wedding morning, knew the difference between a house and a haystack. But when we got away from friends and house agents, on our honeymoon, our wits grew clear again, and we knew a pretty cottage when at last we saw one. It was at Brenzett—a little village set on a hill over against the southern marshes. We had gone there, from the seaside village where we were staying, to see the church, and two fields from the church we found this cottage. It stood quite by itself, about two miles from the village. It was a long, low building, with rooms sticking out in unexpected places. There was a bit of stonework—ivy-covered and moss-grown, just two old rooms, all that was left of a big house that had once stood there—and round this stonework the house had grown up. Stripped of its roses and jasmine it would have been hideous. As it stood it was charming, and after a brief examination we took it. It was absurdly cheap. The rest of our honeymoon we spent in grubbing about in secondhand shops in the county town, picking up bits of old oak and Chippendale chairs for our furnishing. We wound up with a run up to town and a visit to Liberty's, and soon the low oak-beamed lattice-windowed rooms began to be home. There was a jolly old-fashioned garden, with grass paths, and no end of hollyhocks and sunflowers, and big lilies. From the window you could see the marsh pastures, and beyond them the blue, thin line of the sea. We were as happy as the summer was glorious, and settled down into work sooner than we ourselves expected. I was never tired of sketching the view and the wonderful cloud effects from the open lattice, and Laura would sit at the table and write verses about them, in which I mostly played the part of foreground.

We got a tall old peasant woman to do for us. Her face and figure were good, though her cooking was of the homeliest; but she understood all about gardening, and told us all the old names of the coppices and cornfields, and the stories of the smugglers and highwaymen, and, better still, of the 'things that walked', and of the 'sights' which met one in lonely glens of a starlight night. She was a great comfort to us, because Laura hated housekeeping as much as I loved folklore, and we soon came to leave all the domestic business to Mrs Dorman, and to use her legends in little magazine stories which brought in the jingling guinea.

We had three months of married happiness, and did not have a single quarrel. One October evening I had been down to smoke a pipe with the doctor—our only neighbour—a pleasant young Irishman. Laura had stayed at home to finish a comic sketch of a village episode for the *Monthly Marplot*. I left her laughing over her own jokes, and came in to find her a crumpled heap of pale muslin weeping on the window seat.

'Good heavens, my darling, what's the matter?' I cried, taking her in my arms. She leaned her little dark head against my shoulder and went on crying. I had never seen her cry before—we had always been so happy, you see—and I felt sure some frightful misfortune had happened.

'What is the matter? Do speak.'

'It's Mrs Dorman,' she sobbed.

'What has she done?' I enquired, immensely relieved.

'She says she must go before the end of the month, and she says her niece is ill; she's gone to see her now, but I don't believe that's the reason, because her niece is always ill. I believe someone has been setting her against us. Her manner was so queer—'

'Never mind, Pussy,' I said; 'whatever you do, don't cry, or I shall have to cry too, to keep you in countenance, and then you'll never respect your man again!'

She dried her eyes obediently on my handkerchief, and even smiled faintly.

'But you see,' she went on, 'it is really serious, because these village people are so sheepy, and if one won't do a thing you may be quite sure none of the others will. And I shall have to cook the dinners, and wash up the hateful greasy plates; and you'll have to carry cans of water about, and clean the boots and knives—and we shall never have any time for work, or earn any money, or anything. We shall have to work all day, and only be able to rest when we are waiting for the kettle to boil!'

I represented to her that even if we had to perform these duties, the day would still present some margin for other toils and recreations. But she refused to see the matter in any but the greyest light. She was very unreasonable, my Laura, but I could not have loved her any more if she had been as reasonable as Whately.

'I'll speak to Mrs Dorman when she comes back, and see if I can't come to terms with her,' I said. 'Perhaps she wants a rise in her screw. It will be all right. Let's walk up to the church.'

The church was a large and lonely one, and we loved to go there, especially upon bright nights. The path skirted a wood, cut through it once, and ran along the crest of the hill through two meadows, and round the churchyard wall, over which the old yews loomed in black masses of shadow. This path, which was partly paved, was called 'the bier-balk', for it had long been the way by which the corpses had been carried to burial. The churchyard was richly treed, and was shaded by great elms which stood just outside and stretched their majestic arms in benediction over the happy dead. A large, low porch let one into the building by a Norman doorway and a heavy oak door studded with iron. Inside, the arches rose into darkness, and between them the reticulated windows, which stood out white in the moonlight. In the chancel, the windows were of rich glass, which showed in faint light their noble colouring, and made the black oak of the choir pews hardly more solid than the shadows. But on each side of the altar lay a grey marble figure of a knight in full plate armour lying upon a low slab, with hands held up in everlasting prayer, and these figures, oddly enough, were always to be seen if there was any glimmer of light in the church. Their names were lost, but the peasants told of them that they had been fierce and wicked men, marauders by land and sea, who had been the scourge of their time, and had been guilty of deeds so foul that the house they had lived in—the big house, by the way, that had stood on the site of our cottage—had been stricken by lightning and the vengeance of Heaven. But for all that, the gold of their heirs had bought them a place in the church. Looking at the bad hard faces reproduced in the marble, this story was easily believed.

The church looked at its best and weirdest on that night, for the shadows of the yew trees fell through the windows upon the floor of the nave and touched the pillars with tattered shade. We sat down together without speaking, and watched the solemn beauty of the old church, with some of that awe which inspired its early builders. We walked to the chancel and looked at the sleeping warriors. Then we rested some time on the stone seat in the porch, looking out over the stretch of quiet moonlit meadows, feeling in every fibre of our being the peace of the night and of our happy love; and came away at last with a sense that even scrubbing and black-leading were but small troubles at their worst.

Mrs Dorman had come back from the village, and I at once invited her to a tête-à-tête.

'Now, Mrs Dorman,' I said, when I had got her into my painting room, 'what's all this about your not staying with us?'

'I should be glad to get away, sir, before the end of the month,' she answered, with her usual placid dignity.

'Have you any fault to find, Mrs Dorman?'

'None at all, sir; you and your lady have always been most kind, I'm sure—'

'Well, what is it? Are your wages not high enough?'

'No, sir, I gets quite enough.'

'Then why not stay?'

'I'd rather not'—with some hesitation—'my niece is ill.'

'But your niece has been ill ever since we came.'

No answer. There was a long and awkward silence. I broke it.

'Can't you stay for another month?' I asked.

'No, sir. I'm bound to go by Thursday.'

And this was Monday!

'Well, I must say, I think you might have let us know before. There's no time now to get anyone else, and your mistress is not fit to do heavy housework. Can't you stay till next week?'

'I might be able to come back next week.'

I was now convinced that all she wanted was a brief holiday, which we should have been willing enough to let her have, as soon as we could get a substitute.

'But why must you go this week?' I persisted. 'Come, out with it.'

Mrs Dorman drew the little shawl, which she always wore, tightly across her bosom, as though she were cold. Then she said, with a sort of effort—

'They say, sir, as this was a big house in Catholic times, and there was a many deeds done here.'

The nature of the 'deeds' might be vaguely inferred from the inflection of Mrs Dorman's voice—which was enough to make one's blood run cold. I was glad that Laura was not in the room. She was always nervous, as highly strung natures are, and I felt that these tales about our house, told by this old peasant woman, with her impressive manner and contagious credulity, might have made our home less dear to my wife.

'Tell me all about it, Mrs Dorman,' I said; 'you needn't mind about telling me. I'm not like the young people who make fun of such things.'

Which was partly true.

'Well, sir'—she sank her voice—'you may have seen in the church, beside the altar, two shapes.'

'You mean the effigies of the knights in armour,' I said cheerfully.

'I mean them two bodies, drawed out man-size in marble,' she returned, and I had to admit that her description was a thousand times more graphic than mine, to say nothing of a certain weird force and uncanniness about the phrase 'drawed out man-size in marble'.

'They do say, as on All Saints' Eve them two bodies sits up on their slabs, and gets off of them, and then walks down the aisle, *in their marble*'—(another good phrase, Mrs Dorman)—'and as the church clock strikes eleven they walks out of the church door, and over the graves, and along the bier-balk, and if it's a wet night there's the marks of their feet in the morning.'

'And where do they go?' I asked, rather fascinated.

'They comes back here to their home, sir, and if anyone meets them—'

'Well, what then?' I asked.

But no—not another word could I get from her, save that her niece was ill and she must go. After what I had heard I scorned to discuss the niece, and tried to get from Mrs Dorman more details of the legend. I could get nothing but warnings.

'Whatever you do, sir, lock the door early on All Saints' Eve, and make the cross sign over the doorstep and on the windows.'

'But has anyone ever seen these things?' I persisted.

'That's not for me to say. I know what I know, sir.'

'Well, who was here last year?'

'No one, sir; the lady as owned the house only stayed here in summer, and she always went to London a full month afore *the* night. And I'm sorry to inconvenience you and your lady, but my niece is ill and I must go on Thursday.'

I could have shaken her for her absurd reiteration of that obvious fiction, after she had told me her real reasons.

She was determined to go, nor could our united entreaties move her in the least.

I did not tell Laura the legend of the shapes that 'walked in their marble', partly because a legend concerning our house might perhaps trouble my wife, and partly, I think, from some more occult reason. This was not quite the same to me as any other story, and I did not want to talk about it till the day was over. I had very soon ceased to think of the legend, however. I was painting a portrait of Laura, against the lattice window, and I could not think of much else. I had got a splendid background of yellow and grey sunset, and was working away with enthusiasm at her face. On Thursday Mrs Dorman went. She relented, at parting, so far as to say—

'Don't you put yourself about too much, ma'am, and if there's any little thing I can do next week, I'm sure I shan't mind.'

From which I inferred that she wished to come back to us after Hallowe'en. Up to the last she adhered to the fiction of the niece with touching fidelity.

Thursday passed off pretty well. Laura showed marked ability in the matter of steak and potatoes, and I confess that my knives, and the plates, which I insisted upon washing, were better done than I had dared to expect.

Friday came. It is about what happened on that Friday that this is written. I wonder if I should have believed it, if anyone had told it to me. I will write the story of it as quickly and plainly as I can. Everything that happened on that day is burnt into my brain. I shall not forget anything, nor leave anything out.

I got up early, I remember, and lighted the kitchen fire, and had just achieved a smoky success, when my little wife came running down, as sunny and sweet as the clear October morning itself. We prepared breakfast together, and found it very good fun. The housework was soon done, and when brushes and brooms and pails were quiet again, the house was still indeed. It is wonderful what a difference one makes in a house. We really missed Mrs Dorman, quite apart from considerations concerning pots and pans. We spent the day in dusting our books and putting them straight, and dined gaily on cold steak and coffee. Laura was, if possible, brighter and gayer and sweeter than usual, and I began to think that a little domestic toil was really good for her. We had never been so merry since we were married, and the walk we had that afternoon was, I think, the happiest time of all my life. When we had watched the deep-scarlet clouds slowly pale into leaden grey against a pale-green sky, and saw the white mists curl up along the hedgerows in the distant marsh, we came back to the house, silently, hand in hand.

'You are sad, my darling,' I said, half-jestingly, as we sat down together in our little parlour. I expected a disclaimer, for my own silence had been the silence of complete happiness. To my surprise she said—

'Yes. I think I am sad, or rather I am uneasy. I don't think I'm very well. I have shivered three or four times since we came in and it is not cold, is it?'

'No,' I said, and hoped it was not a chill caught from the treacherous mists that roll up from the marshes in the dying light. No—she said, she did not think so. Then, after a silence, she spoke suddenly—

'Do you ever have presentiments of evil?'

'No,' I said, smiling, 'and I shouldn't believe in them if I had.'

'I do,' she went on; 'the night my father died I knew it, though he was right away in the north of Scotland.' I did not answer in words.

She sat looking at the fire for some time in silence, gently stroking my hand. At last she sprang up, came behind me, and, drawing my head back, kissed me.

'There, it's over now,' she said. 'What a baby I am! Come, light the candles, and we'll have some of these new Rubinstein duets.'

And we spent a happy hour or two at the piano.

At about half past ten I began to long for the good-night pipe, but Laura looked so white that I felt it would be brutal of me to fill our sitting room with the fumes of strong cavendish.

'I'll take my pipe outside,' I said.

'Let me come, too.'

'No, sweetheart, not tonight; you're much too tired. I shan't be long. Get to bed, or I shall have an invalid to nurse tomorrow as well as the boots to clean.'

I kissed her and was turning to go, when she flung her arms round my neck, and held me as if she would never let me go again. I stroked her hair.

'Come, Pussy, you're overtired. The housework has been too much for you.'

She loosened her clasp a little and drew a deep breath.

'No. We've been very happy today, Jack, haven't we? Don't stay out too long.'

'I won't, my dearie.'

I strolled out of the front door, leaving it unlatched. What a night it was! The jagged masses of heavy dark cloud were rolling at intervals from horizon to horizon, and thin white wreaths covered the stars. Through all the rush of the cloud river, the moon swam, breasting the waves and disappearing again in the darkness. When now and again her light reached the woodlands they seemed to be slowly and noiselessly waving in time to the swing of the clouds above them. There was a strange grey light over all the earth; the fields had that shadowy bloom over them which only comes from the marriage of dew and moonshine, or frost and starlight.

I walked up and down, drinking in the beauty of the quiet earth and the changing sky. The night was absolutely silent. Nothing seemed to be abroad. There was no scurrying of rabbits, or twitter of the half-asleep birds. And though the clouds went sailing across the sky, the wind that drove them never came low enough to rustle the dead leaves in the woodland paths. Across the meadows I could see the church tower standing out black and grey against the sky. I walked there thinking over our three months of happiness—and of my wife, her dear eyes, her loving ways. Oh, my little girl! my own little girl; what a vision came then of a long, glad life for you and me together!

I heard a bell-beat from the church. Eleven already! I turned to go in, but the night held me. I could not go back into our little warm rooms yet. I would go up to the church. I felt vaguely that it would be good to carry my love and thankfulness to the sanctuary whither so many loads of sorrow and gladness had been borne by the men and women of the dead years.

I looked in at the low window as I went by. Laura was half lying on her chair in front of the fire. I could not see her face, only her little head showed dark against the pale blue wall. She was quite still. Asleep, no doubt. My heart reached out to her, as I went on. There must be a God, I thought, and a God who was good. How otherwise could anything so sweet and dear as she have ever been imagined?

I walked slowly along the edge of the wood. A sound broke the stillness of the night, it was a rustling in the wood. I stopped and listened. The sound stopped too. I went on, and now distinctly heard another step than mine answer mine like an echo. It was a poacher or a wood-stealer, most likely, for these were not unknown in our Arcadian neighbourhood. But whoever it was, he was a fool not to step more lightly. I turned into the wood, and now the footstep seemed to come from the path I had just left. It must be an echo, I thought. The wood looked perfect in the moonlight. The large dying ferns and the brushwood showed where through thinning foliage the pale light came down. The tree trunks stood up like Gothic columns all around me. They reminded me of the church, and I turned into the bier-balk, and passed through the corpse-gate between the graves to the low porch. I paused for a moment on the stone seat where Laura and I had watched the fading landscape. Then I noticed that the door of the church was open, and I blamed myself for having left it unlatched the other night. We were the only people who ever cared to come to the church except on Sundays, and I was vexed to think that through our carelessness the damp autumn airs had had a chance of getting in and injuring the old fabric. I went in. It will seem strange, perhaps, that I should have gone halfway up the aisle before I remembered—with a sudden chill, followed by as sudden a rush of self-contempt—that this was the very day and hour when, according to tradi-tion, the 'shapes drawed out man-size in marble' began to walk.

Having thus remembered the legend, and remembered it with a shiver, of which I was ashamed, I could not do otherwise than walk up towards the altar, just to look at the figures—as I said to myself; really what I wanted was to assure myself, first, that I did not believe the legend, and, secondly, that it was not true. I was rather glad that I had come. I thought now I could tell Mrs Dorman how vain her fancies were, and how peacefully the marble figures slept on through the ghastly hour. With my hands in my pockets I passed up the aisle. In the grey dim light the eastern end of the church looked larger than usual, and the arches above the two tombs looked larger too. The moon came out and showed me the reason. I stopped short, my heart gave a leap that nearly choked me, and then sank sickeningly.

The 'bodies drawn out man-size' *were gone*, and their marble slabs lay wide and bare in the vague moonlight that slanted through the east window.

Were they really gone? or was I mad? Clenching my nerves, I stooped and passed my hand over the smooth slabs, and felt their flat unbroken surface. Had someone taken the things away? Was it some vile practical joke? I would make sure, anyway. In an instant I had made a torch of a newspaper, which happened to be in my pocket, and lighting it held it high above my head. Its yellow glare illumined the dark arches and those slabs. The figures *were* gone. And I was alone in the church; or was I alone?

And then a horror seized me, a horror indefinable and indescribable—an overwhelming certainty of supreme and accomplished calamity. I flung down the torch and tore along the aisle and out through the porch, biting my lips as I ran to keep myself from shrieking aloud. Oh, was I mad—or what was this that possessed me? I leaped the churchyard wall and took the straight cut across the fields, led by the light from our windows. Just as I got over the first stile, a dark figure seemed to spring out of the ground. Mad still with that certainty of misfortune, I made for the thing that stood in my path, shouting, 'Get out of the way, can't you!'

But my push met with a more vigorous resistance than I had expected. My arms were caught just above the elbow and held as in a vice, and the raw-boned Irish doctor actually shook me.

'Would ye?' he cried, in his own unmistakable accents—'would ye, then?'

'Let me go, you fool,' I gasped. 'The marble figures have gone from the church; I tell you they've gone.'

He broke into a ringing laugh. 'I'll have to give ye a draught tomorrow, I see. Ye've bin smoking too much and listening to old wives' tales.'

'I tell you, I've seen the bare slabs.'

'Well, come back with me. I'm going up to old Palmer's—his daughter's ill; we'll look in at the church and let me see the bare slabs.'

'You go, if you like,' I said, a little less frantic for his laughter; 'I'm going home to my wife.'

'Rubbish, man,' said he; 'd'ye think I'll permit of that? Are ye to go saying all yer life that ye've seen solid marble endowed with vitality, and me to go all me life saying ye were a coward? No, sir—ye shan't do it.'

The night air—a human voice—and I think also the physical contact with this six feet of solid common sense, brought me back a little to my ordinary self, and the word 'coward' was a mental shower-bath.

'Come on, then,' I said sullenly; 'perhaps you're right.'

He still held my arm tightly. We got over the stile and back to the church. All was still as death. The place smelt very damp and earthy. We walked up the aisle. I am not ashamed to confess that I shut my eyes: I knew the figures would not be there. I heard Kelly strike a match.

'Here they are, ye see, right enough; ye've been dreaming or drinking, asking yer pardon for the imputation.'

I opened my eyes. By Kelly's expiring vesta I saw two shapes lying 'in their marble' on their slabs. I drew a deep breath, and caught his hand.

'I'm awfully indebted to you,' I said. 'It must have been some trick of light, or

I have been working rather hard, perhaps that's it. Do you know, I was quite convinced they were gone.'

'I'm aware of that,' he answered rather grimly; 'ye'll have to be careful of that brain of yours, my friend, I assure ye.'

He was leaning over and looking at the right-hand figure, whose stony face was the most villainous and deadly in expression.

'By Jove,' he said, 'something has been afoot here—this hand is broken.'

And so it was. I was certain that it had been perfect the last time Laura and I had been there.

'Perhaps someone has *tried* to remove them,' said the young doctor.

'That won't account for my impression,' I objected.

'Too much painting and tobacco will account for that, well enough.'

'Come along,' I said, 'or my wife will be getting anxious. You'll come in and have a drop of whisky and drink confusion to ghosts and better sense to me.'

'I ought to go up to Palmer's, but it's so late now I'd best leave it till the morning,' he replied. 'I was kept late at the Union, and I've had to see a lot of people since. All right, I'll come back with ye.'

I think he fancied I needed him more than did Palmer's girl, so, discussing how such an illusion could have been possible, and deducing from this experience large generalities concerning ghostly apparitions, we walked up to our cottage. We saw, as we walked up the garden path, that bright light streamed out of the front door, and presently saw that the parlour door was open too. Had she gone out?

'Come in,' I said, and Dr Kelly followed me into the parlour. It was all ablaze with candles, not only the wax ones, but at least a dozen guttering, glaring tallow dips, stuck in vases and ornaments in unlikely places. Light, I knew, was Laura's remedy for nervousness. Poor child! Why had I left her? Brute that I was.

We glanced round the room, and at first we did not see her. The window was open, and the draught set all the candles flaring one way. Her chair was empty and her handkerchief and book lay on the floor. I turned to the window. There, in the recess of the window, I saw her. Oh my child, my love, had she gone to that window to watch for me? And what had come into the room behind her? To what had she turned with that look of frantic fear and horror? Oh, my little one, had she thought that it was I whose step she heard, and turned to meet—what?

She had fallen back across a table in the window, and her body lay half on it and half on the window seat, and her head hung down over the table, the brown hair loosened and fallen to the carpet. Her lips were drawn back, and her eyes wide, wide open. They saw nothing now. What had they seen last?

The doctor moved towards her, but I pushed him aside and sprang to her; caught her in my arms and cried—

'It's all right, Laura! I've got you safe, wifie.'

She fell into my arms in a heap. I clasped her and kissed her, and called her by all her pet names, but I think I knew all the time that she was dead. Her hands were tightly clenched. In one of them she held something fast. When I was quite sure that she was dead, and that nothing mattered at all any more, I let him open her hand to see what she held.

It was a grey marble finger.

Edgar Allan Poe

1809–1849

Edgar Allan Poe was one of America's first internationally acclaimed writers. Born in Boston, the son of theatrical folk, he earned a meagre living as a journalist before winning fame—and some notoriety—through his tortured and morbidly horrific short stories. He lived a short, dissolute life and died in abject poverty, after a prolonged drinking bout.

WILLIAM WILSON

What say of it? what say [of] CONSCIENCE grim,
That spectre in my path?

CHAMBERLAINE'S PHARONNIDA

LET ME CALL MYSELF, for the present, William Wilson. The fair page now lying before me need not be sullied with my real appellation. This has been already too much an object for the scorn—for the horror—for the detestation of my race. To the uttermost regions of the globe have not the indignant winds bruited its unparalleled infamy? Oh, outcast of all outcasts most abandoned!—to the earth art thou not forever dead? to its honours, to its flowers, to its golden aspirations?—and a cloud, dense, dismal, and limitless, does it not hang eternally between thy hopes and heaven?

I would not, if I could, here or today, embody a record of my later years of unspeakable misery, and unpardonable crime. This epoch—these later years—took unto themselves a sudden elevation in turpitude, whose origin alone it is my present purpose to assign. Men usually grow base by degrees. From me, in an instant, all virtue dropped bodily as a mantle. From comparatively trivial wickedness I passed, with the stride of a giant, into more than the enormities of an Elah-Gabalus. What chance—what one event brought this evil thing to pass, bear with me while I relate. Death approaches; and the shadow which foreruns him has thrown a softening influence over my spirit. I long, in passing through the dim valley, for the sympathy—I had nearly said for the pity—of my fellow men. I would fain have them believe that I have been, in some measure, the slave of circumstances beyond human control. I would wish them to seek out for me, in the details I am about to give, some little oasis of *fatality* amid a wilderness of error. I would have them allow—what they cannot refrain from allowing—that, although temptation may have erewhile existed as great, man was never *thus*, at least, tempted before—certainly, never thus fell. And is it therefore that he has never thus suffered? Have I not indeed been living in a dream? And am I not now dying a victim to the horror and the mystery of the wildest of all sublunary visions?

I am the descendant of a race whose imaginative and easily excitable temperament has at all times rendered them remarkable; and, in my earliest infancy, I gave evidence of having fully inherited the family character. As I advanced in years it was more strongly developed; becoming, for many reasons, a cause of serious disquietude to my friends, and of positive injury to myself. I grew self-willed, addicted to the wildest caprices, and a prey to the most ungovernable passions. Weak-minded, and beset with constitutional infirmities akin to my own, my parents could do but little to check the evil propensities which distinguished me. Some feeble and ill-directed efforts resulted in complete failure on their part, and, of course, in total triumph on mine. Thenceforward my voice was a household law; and at an age when few children have abandoned their leading strings, I was left to the guidance of my own will, and became, in all but name, the master of my own actions.

My earliest recollections of a school life are connected with a large, rambling, Elizabethan house, in a misty-looking village of England, where were a vast number of gigantic and gnarled trees, and where all the houses were excessively ancient. In truth, it was a dreamlike and spirit-soothing place, that venerable old town. At this moment, in fancy, I feel the refreshing chilliness of its deeply shadowed avenues, inhale the fragrance of its thousand shrubberies, and thrill anew with undefinable delight, at the deep hollow note of the church bell, breaking, each hour, with sullen and sudden roar, upon the stillness of the dusky atmosphere in which the fretted Gothic steeple lay embedded and asleep.

It gives me, perhaps, as much of pleasure as I can now in any manner experience, to dwell upon minute recollections of the school and its concerns. Steeped in misery as I am—misery, alas! only too real—I shall be pardoned for seeking relief, however slight and temporary, in the weakness of a few rambling details. These, moreover, utterly trivial, and even ridiculous in themselves, assume, to my fancy, adventitious importance, as connected with a period and a locality when and where I recognise the first ambiguous monitions of the destiny which afterward so fully overshadowed me. Let me then remember.

The house, I have said, was old and irregular. The grounds were extensive, and a high and solid brick wall, topped with a bed of mortar and broken glass, encompassed the whole. This prison-like rampart formed the limit of our domain; beyond it we saw but thrice a week—once every Saturday afternoon, when, attended by two ushers, we were permitted to take brief walks in a body through some of the neighbouring fields—and twice during Sunday, when we were paraded in the same formal manner to the morning and evening service in the one church of the village. Of this church the principal of our school was pastor. With how deep a spirit of wonder and perplexity was I wont to regard him from our remote pew in the gallery, as, with step solemn and slow, he ascended the pulpit! This reverend man, with countenance so demurely benign, with robes so glossy and so clerically flowing, with wig so minutely powdered, so rigid and so vast—could this be he who, of late, with sour visage, and in snuffy habiliments, administered, ferule in hand, the Draconian laws of the academy? Oh, gigantic paradox, too utterly monstrous for solution!

At an angle of the ponderous wall frowned a more ponderous gate. It was riveted and studded with iron bolts, and surmounted with jagged iron spikes. What impressions of deep awe did it inspire! It was never opened save for the three periodical egressions and ingressions already mentioned; then, in every creak of its mighty hinges, we found a plenitude of mystery—a world of matter for solemn remark, or for more solemn meditation.

The extensive enclosure was irregular in form, having many capacious recesses. Of these, three or four of the largest constituted the playground. It was level, and covered with fine hard gravel. I well remember it had no trees, nor benches, nor anything similar within it. Of course it was in the rear of the house. In front lay a small parterre, planted with box and other shrubs; but through this sacred division we passed only upon rare occasions indeed—such as a first advent to school or final departure thence, or perhaps, when a parent or friend having called for us, we joyfully took our way home for the Christmas or Midsummer holidays.

But the house!—how quaint an old building was this!—to me how veritably a palace of enchantment! There was really no end to its windings—to its incomprehensible subdivisions. It was difficult, at any given time, to say with certainty upon which of its two storeys one happened to be. From each room to every other there were sure to be found three or four steps either in ascent or descent. Then the lateral branches were innumerable—inconceivable—and so returning in upon themselves, that our most exact ideas in regard to the whole mansion were not very far different from those with which we pondered upon infinity. During the five years of my residence here, I was never able to ascertain with precision, in what remote locality lay the little sleeping apartment assigned to myself and some eighteen or twenty other scholars.

The schoolroom was the largest in the house—I could not help thinking, in the world. It was very long, narrow, and dismally low, with pointed Gothic windows and a ceiling of oak. In a remote and terror-inspiring angle was a square enclosure of eight or ten feet, comprising the sanctum, 'during hours', of our principal, the Reverend Dr Bransby. It was a solid structure, with massy door, sooner than open which in the absence of the 'Dominie', we would all have willingly perished by the *peine forte et dure*. In other angles were two other similar boxes, far less reverenced, indeed, but still greatly matters of awe. One of these was the pulpit of the 'classical' usher, one of the 'English and mathematical'. Interspersed about the room, crossing and recrossing in endless irregularity, were innumerable benches and desks, black, ancient, and time-worn, piled desperately with much-bethumbed books, and so beseamed with initial letters, names at full length, grotesque figures, and other multiplied efforts of the knife, as to have entirely lost what little of original form might have been their portion in days long departed. A huge bucket with water stood at one extremity of the room, and a clock of stupendous dimensions at the other.

Encompassed by the massy walls of this venerable academy, I passed, yet not in tedium or disgust, the years of the third lustrum of my life. The teeming brain of childhood requires no external world of incident to occupy or amuse it; and the apparently dismal monotony of a school was replete with more intense excitement than my riper youth has derived from luxury, or my full manhood from crime. Yet I must believe that my first mental development had in it much of the uncommon—even much of the *outré*. Upon mankind at large the events of very early existence rarely leave in mature age any definite impression. All is gray shadow—a weak and irregular remembrance—an indistinct regathering of feeble pleasures and phantasmagoric pains. With me this is not so. In childhood I must have felt with the energy of a man what I now find stamped upon memory in lines as vivid, as deep, and as durable as the *exergues* of the Carthaginian medals.

Yet in fact—in the fact of the world's view—how little was there to remember! The morning's awakening, the nightly summons to bed; the connings, the recitations; the periodical half-holidays, and perambulations; the playground, with its broils, its pastimes, its intrigues; these, by a mental sorcery long forgotten, were made to involve a wilderness of sensation, a world of rich incident, an universe of varied emotion, of excitement the most passionate and spirit-stirring. *'Oh, le bon temps, que ce siècle de fer!'*

In truth, the ardour, the enthusiasm, and the imperiousness of my disposition soon rendered me a marked character among my schoolmates, and, by slow but natural gradations, gave me an ascendancy over all not greatly older than myself—over all with a single exception. This exception was found in the person of a scholar, who, although no relation, bore the same Christian and surname as myself—a circumstance, in fact, little remarkable; for, notwithstanding a noble descent, mine was one of those everyday appellations which seem, by prescriptive right, to have been, time out of mind, the common property of the mob. In this narrative, I have therefore designated myself as William Wilson—a fictitious title not very dissimilar to the real. My namesake alone, of those who in school phraseology constituted 'our set', presumed to compete with me in the studies of the class—in the sports and broils of the playground—to refuse implicit belief in my assertions, and submission to my will—indeed, to interfere with my arbitrary dictation in any respect whatsoever. If there is on earth a supreme and unqualified despotism, it is the despotism of a mastermind in boyhood over the less energetic spirits of its companions.

Wilson's rebellion was to me a source of the greatest embarrassment—the more so as, in spite of the bravado with which in public I made a point of treating him and his pretensions, I secretly felt that I feared him, and could not help thinking the equality which he maintained so easily with myself a proof of his true superiority; since not to be overcome cost me a perpetual struggle. Yet this superiority—even this equality—was in truth acknowledged by no one but myself; our associates, by some unaccountable blindness, seemed not even to suspect it. Indeed, his competition, his resistance, and especially his impertinent and dogged interference with my purposes, were not more pointed than private. He appeared to be destitute alike of the ambition which urged and of the passionate energy of mind which enabled me to excel. In his rivalry he might have been supposed actuated solely by a whimsical desire to thwart, astonish, or mortify myself; although there were times when I could not help observing, with a feeling made up of wonder, abasement, and pique, that he mingled with his injuries, his insults, or his contradictions, a certain most inappropriate, and assuredly most unwelcome, *affectionateness* of manner. I could only conceive this singular behaviour to arise from a consummate self-conceit assuming the vulgar airs of patronage and protection.

Perhaps it was this latter trait in Wilson's conduct, conjoined with our identity of name, and the mere accident of our having entered the school upon the same day, which set afloat the notion that we were brothers, among the senior classes in the academy. These do not usually enquire with much strictness into the affairs of their juniors. I have before said, or should have said, that Wilson was not, in the most remote degree, connected with my family. But assuredly if we *had* been brothers we must have been twins; for, after leaving Dr Bransby's, I casually learned that my namesake was born on the nineteenth of January, 1813—and this is a somewhat remarkable coincidence; for the day is precisely that of my own nativity.

It may seem strange that in spite of the continual anxiety occasioned me by the rivalry of Wilson, and his intolerable spirit of contradiction, I could not bring myself to hate him altogether. We had, to be sure, nearly every day a quarrel in which, yielding me publicly the palm of victory, he, in some manner, contrived to make me feel that it was he who had deserved it; yet a sense of pride on my part, and a veritable dignity on his own, kept us always upon what are called 'speaking terms', while there were many points of strong congeniality in our tempers, operating to awake in me a sentiment which our position alone, perhaps, prevented from ripening into friendship. It is difficult, indeed, to define, or even to describe, my real feelings toward him. They formed a motley and heterogeneous admixture—some petulant animosity, which was not yet hatred, some esteem, more respect, much fear, with a world of uneasy curiosity. To the moralist it will be unnecessary to say, in addition, that Wilson and myself were the most inseparable of companions.

It was no doubt the anomalous state of affairs existing between us, which turned all my attacks upon him (and they were many, either open or covert) into the channel of banter or practical joke (giving pain while assuming the aspect of mere fun) rather than into a more serious and determined hostility. But my endeavours on this head were by no means uniformly successful, even when my plans were the most wittily concocted; for my namesake had much about him, in character, of that unassuming and quiet austerity which, while enjoying the poignancy of its own jokes, has no heel of Achilles in itself, and absolutely refuses to be laughed at. I could find, indeed, but one vulnerable point, and that, lying in a personal peculiarity, arising, perhaps, from constitutional disease, would have been spared by any antagonist less at his wits' end than myself—my rival had a weakness in the faucal or guttural organs, which precluded him from raising his voice at any time above a very low whisper. Of this defect I did not fail to take what poor advantage lay in my power.

Wilson's retaliations in kind were many; and there was one form of his practical wit that disturbed me beyond measure. How his sagacity first discovered at all that so petty a thing would vex me is a question I never could solve; but, having discovered, he habitually practised the annoyance. I had always felt aversion to my uncourtly patronymic, and its very common, if not plebeian praenomen. The words were venom in my ears; and when, upon the day of my arrival, a second William Wilson came also to the academy, I felt angry with him for bearing the name, and doubly disgusted with the name because a stranger bore it, who would be the cause of its twofold repetition, who would be constantly in my presence, and whose concerns, in the ordinary routine of the school business, must inevitably, on account of the detestable coincidence, be often confounded with my own.

The feeling of vexation thus engendered grew stronger with every circumstance tending to show resemblance, moral or physical, between my rival and myself. I had not then discovered the remarkable fact that we were of the same age; but I saw that we were of the same height, and I perceived that we were even singularly alike in general contour of person and outline of feature. I was galled, too, by the rumour touching a relationship, which had grown current in the upper forms. In a word, nothing could more seriously disturb me (although I scrupulously concealed such disturbance) than any allusion to a similarity of mind, person, or condition existing between us. But, in truth, I had no reason to believe that (with the exception of the matter of relationship, and in the case of Wilson himself) this similarity had ever been made a subject of comment, or even observed at all by our schoolfellows. That he observed it in all its bearings, and as fixedly as I, was apparent; but that he could discover in such circumstances so fruitful a field of annoyance can only be attributed, as I said before, to his more than ordinary penetration.

His cue, which was to perfect an imitation of myself, lay both in words and in actions; and most admirably did he play his part. My dress it was an easy matter to copy; my gait and general manner were, without difficulty, appropriated; in spite of his constitutional defect, even my voice did not escape him. My louder tones were, of course, unattempted, but then the key—it was identical; *and his singular whisper, it grew the very echo of my own.*

How greatly this most exquisite portraiture harassed me (for it could not justly be termed a caricature) I will not now venture to describe. I had but one consolation—in the fact that the imitation, apparently, was noticed by myself alone, and that I had to endure only the knowing and strangely sarcastic smiles of my namesake himself. Satisfied with having produced in my bosom the intended effect, he seemed to chuckle in secret over the sting he had inflicted, and was characteristically disregardful of the public applause which the success of his witty endeavours might have so easily elicited. That the school, indeed, did not feel his design, perceive its accomplishment, and participate in his sneer, was, for many anxious months, a riddle I could not resolve. Perhaps the *gradation* of his copy rendered it not so readily perceptible; or, more possibly, I owed my security to the masterly air of the copyist, who, disdaining the letter (which in a painting is all the obtuse can see), gave but the full spirit of his original for my individual contemplation and chagrin.

I have already more than once spoken of the disgusting air of patronage which he assumed toward me, and of his frequent officious interference with my will. This interference often took the ungracious character of advice; advice not openly given, but hinted or insinuated. I received it with a repugnance which gained strength as I grew in years. Yet, at this distant day, let me do him the simple justice to acknowledge that I can recall no occasion when the suggestions of my rival were on the side of those errors or follies so usual to his immature age and seeming inexperience; that his moral sense, at least, if not his general talents and worldly wisdom, was far keener than my own; and that I might, today, have been a better, and thus a happier man, had I less frequently rejected the counsels embodied in those meaning whispers which I then but too cordially hated and too bitterly despised.

As it was, I at length grew restive in the extreme under his distasteful supervision, and daily resented more and more openly what I considered his intolerable arrogance. I have said that, in the first years of our connection as schoolmates, my feelings in regard to him might have been easily ripened into friendship: but, in the latter months of my residence at the academy, although the intrusion of his ordinary manner had, beyond doubt, in some measure, abated, my sentiments, in nearly similar proportion, partook very much of positive hatred. Upon one occasion he saw this, I think, and afterwards avoided, or made a show of avoiding me.

It was about the same period, if I remember aright, that, in an altercation of violence with him, in which he was more than usually thrown off his guard, and spoke and acted with an openness of demeanour rather foreign to his nature, I discovered, or fancied I discovered, in his accent, his air, and general appearance, a something which first startled, and then deeply interested me, by bringing to mind dim visions of my earliest infancy—wild, confused, and thronging memories of a time when memory herself was yet unborn. I cannot better describe the sensation which oppressed me than by saying that I could with difficulty shake off the belief of my having been acquainted with the being who stood before me, at some epoch very long ago—some point of the past even infinitely remote. The delusion, however, faded rapidly as it came; and I mention it at all but to define the day of the last conversation I there held with my singular namesake.

The huge old house, with its countless subdivisions, had several large chambers communicating with each other, where slept the greater number of the students. There were, however (as must necessarily happen in a building so awkwardly planned), many little nooks or recesses, the odds and ends of the structure; and these the economic ingenuity of Dr Bransby had also fitted up as dormitories; although, being the merest closets, they were capable of accommodating but a single individual. One of these small apartments was occupied by Wilson.

One night, about the close of my fifth year at the school, and immediately after the altercation just mentioned, finding everyone wrapped in sleep, I arose from bed, and, lamp in hand, stole through a wilderness of narrow passages, from my own bedroom to that of my rival. I had long been plotting one of those ill-natured pieces of practical wit at his expense in which I had hitherto been so uniformly unsuccessful. It was my intention, now, to put my scheme in operation, and I resolved to make him feel the whole extent of the malice with which I was imbued. Having reached his closet, I noiselessly entered, leaving the lamp, with a shade over it, on the outside. I advanced a step and listened to the sound of his tranquil breathing. Assured of his being asleep, I returned, took the light, and with it again approached the bed. Close curtains were around it, which, in the prosecution of my plan, I slowly and quietly withdrew, when the bright rays fell vividly upon the sleeper, and my eyes, at the same moment, upon his countenance. I looked—and a numbness, an iciness of feeling instantly pervaded my frame. My breast heaved, my knees tottered, my whole spirit became possessed with an objectless yet intolerable horror. Gasping for breath, I lowered the lamp in still nearer proximity to the face. Were these—*these* the lineaments of William Wilson? I saw, indeed, that they were his, but I shook as if with a fit of the ague, in fancying they were not. What *was* there about them to confound me in this manner? I gazed—while my brain reeled with a multitude of incoherent thoughts. Not thus he appeared—assuredly not *thus*—in the vivacity of his waking hours. The same name! the same contour of person! the same day of arrival at the academy! And then his dogged and meaningless imitation of my gait, my voice, my habits, and my manner! Was it, in truth, within the bounds of human possibility, that *what I now saw* was the result, merely, of the habitual practice of this sarcastic imitation? Awe-stricken, and with a creeping shudder, I extinguished the lamp, passed silently from the chamber, and left, at once, the halls of that old academy, never to enter them again.

After a lapse of some months, spent at home in mere idleness, I found myself a student at Eton. The brief interval had been sufficient to enfeeble my remembrance of the events at Dr Bransby's, or at least to effect a material change in the nature of the feelings with which I remembered them. The truth—the tragedy—of the drama was no more. I could now find room to doubt the evidence of my senses; and seldom called up the subject at all but with wonder at the extent of human credulity, and a smile at the vivid force of the imagination which I hereditarily possessed. Neither was this species of scepticism likely to be diminished by the character of the life I led at Eton. The vortex of thoughtless folly into which I there so immediately and recklessly plunged, washed away all but the froth of my past hours, engulfed at once every solid or serious impression, and left to memory only the veriest levities of a former existence.

I do not wish, however, to trace the course of my miserable profligacy here—a profligacy which set at defiance the laws, while it eluded the vigilance, of the institution. Three years of folly, passed without profit, had but given me rooted habits of vice, and added, in a somewhat unusual degree, to my bodily stature, when, after a week of soulless dissipation, I invited a small party of the most dissolute students to a secret carousal in my chambers. We met at a late hour of the night; for our debaucheries were to be faithfully protracted until morning. The wine flowed freely, and there were not wanting other and perhaps more dangerous seductions; so that the gray dawn had already faintly appeared in the east while our delirious extravagance was at its height. Madly flushed with cards and intoxication, I was in the act of insisting upon a toast of more than wonted profanity, when my attention was suddenly diverted by the violent, although partial, unclosing of the door of the apartment, and by the eager voice of a servant from without. He said that some person, apparently in great haste, demanded to speak with me in the hall.

Wildly excited with wine, the unexpected interruption rather delighted than surprised me. I staggered forward at once, and a few steps brought me to the vestibule of the building. In this low and small room there hung no lamp; and now no light at all was admitted, save that of the exceedingly feeble dawn which made its way through the semicircular window. As I put my foot over the threshold, I became aware of the figure of a youth about my own height, and habited in a white kerseymere morning frock, cut in the novel fashion of the one I myself wore at the moment. This the faint light enabled me to perceive; but the features of his face I could not distinguish. Upon my entering he strode hurriedly up to me, and seizing me by the arm with a gesture of petulant impatience, whispered the words 'William Wilson!' in my ear.

I grew perfectly sober in an instant.

There was that in the manner of the stranger, and in the tremulous shake of his uplifted finger, as he held it between my eyes and the light, which filled me with unqualified amazement; but it was not this which had so violently moved me. It was the pregnancy of solemn admonition in the singular, low, hissing utterance; and, above all, it was the character, the tone, *the key,* of those few, simple, and familiar, yet *whispered* syllables, which came with a thousand thronging memories of bygone days, and struck upon my soul with the shock of a galvanic battery. Ere I could recover the use of my senses he was gone.

Although this event failed not of a vivid effect upon my disordered imagination, yet it was evanescent as vivid. For some weeks, indeed, I busied myself in earnest enquiry, or was wrapped in a cloud of morbid speculation. I did not pretend to disguise from my perception the identity of the singular individual who thus perseveringly interfered with my affairs, and harassed me with his insinuated counsel. But who and what was this Wilson?—and whence came he?—and what were his purposes? Upon neither of these points could I be satisfied—merely ascertaining, in regard to him, that a sudden accident in his family had caused his removal from Dr Bransby's academy on the afternoon of the day in which I myself had eloped. But in a brief period I ceased to think upon the subject, my attention being all absorbed in a contemplated departure for Oxford. Thither I soon went, the uncalculating vanity of my parents furnishing me with an outfit and annual establishment, which would enable me to indulge at will in the luxury already so dear to my heart—to vie in profuseness of expenditure with the haughtiest heirs of the wealthiest earldoms in Great Britain.

Excited by such appliances to vice, my constitutional temperament broke forth with redoubled ardour, and I spurned even the common restraints of decency in the mad infatuation of my revels. But it were absurd to pause in the detail of my extravagance. Let it suffice, that among spendthrifts I out-Heroded Herod, and that, giving name to a multitude of novel follies, I added no brief appendix to the long catalogue of vices then usual in the most dissolute university of Europe.

It could hardly be credited, however, that I had, even here, so utterly fallen from the gentlemanly estate, as to seek acquaintance with the vilest arts of the gambler by profession, and, having become an adept in his despicable science, to practise it habitually as a means of increasing my already enormous income at the expense of the weak-minded among my fellow collegians. Such, nevertheless, was the fact. And the very enormity of this offence against all manly and honourable sentiment proved, beyond doubt, the main if not the sole reason of the impunity with which it was committed. Who, indeed, among my most abandoned associates, would not rather have disputed the clearest evidence of his senses, than have suspected of such courses, the gay, the frank, the generous William Wilson—the noblest and most liberal commoner at Oxford—him whose follies (said his parasites) were but the follies of youth and unbridled fancy—whose errors but inimitable whim—whose darkest vice but a careless and dashing extravagance?

I had been now two years successfully busied in this way, when there came to the university a young *parvenu* nobleman, Glendinning—rich, said report, as Herodes Atticus—his riches, too, as easily acquired. I soon found him of weak intellect, and, of course, marked him as a fitting subject for my skill. I frequently engaged him in play, and contrived, with the gambler's usual art, to let him win considerable sums, the more effectually to entangle him in my snares. At length, my schemes being ripe, I met him (with the full intention that this meeting should be final and decisive) at the chambers of a fellow commoner (Mr Preston), equally intimate with both, but who, to do him justice, entertained not even a remote suspicion of my design. To give to this a better colouring, I had contrived to have assembled a party of some eight or ten, and was solicitously careful that the introduction of cards should appear accidental, and originate in the proposal of my contemplated dupe himself. To be brief upon a vile topic, none of the low finesse was omitted, so customary upon similar occasions that it is a just matter for wonder how any are still found so besotted as to fall its victims.

We had protracted our sitting far into the night, and I had at length effected the manoeuvre of getting Glendinning as my sole antagonist. The game, too, was my favourite écarté. The rest of the company, interested in the extent of our play, had abandoned their own cards, and were standing around us as spectators. The *parvenu*, who had been induced by my artifices in the early part of the evening, to drink deeply, now shuffled, dealt, or played, with a wild nervousness of manner for which his intoxication, I thought, might partially, but could not altogether, account. In a very short period he had become my debtor to a large amount, when, having taken a long draught of port, he did precisely what I had been coolly anticipating—he proposed to double our already extravagant stakes. With a well-feigned show of reluctance, and not until after my repeated refusal had seduced him into some angry words which gave a colour of pique to my compliance, did I finally comply. The result, of course, did but prove how entirely the prey was in my toils; in less than an hour he had quadrupled his debt. For some time his countenance had been losing the florid tinge lent it by the wine; but now, to my astonishment, I perceived that it had grown to a pallor truly fearful. I say, to my astonishment. Glendinning had been represented to my eager enquiries as immeasurably wealthy; and the sums which he had as yet lost, although in themselves vast, could not, I supposed, very seriously annoy, much less so violently affect him. That he was overcome by the wine just swallowed, was the idea which most readily presented itself; and, rather with a view to the preservation of my own character in the eyes of my associates, than from any less interested motive, I was about to insist, peremptorily, upon a discontinuance of the play, when some expressions at my elbow from among the company, and an ejaculation evincing utter despair on the part of Glendinning, gave me to understand that I had effected his total ruin under circumstances which, rendering him an object for the pity of all, should have protected him from the ill offices even of a fiend.

What now might have been my conduct it is difficult to say. The pitiable condition of my dupe had thrown an air of embarrassed gloom over all; and, for some moments, a profound silence was maintained, during which I could not help feeling my cheeks tingle with the many burning glances of scorn or reproach cast upon me by the less abandoned of the party. I will even own that an intolerable weight of anxiety was for a brief instant lifted from my bosom by the sudden and extraordinary interruption which ensued. The wide, heavy folding doors of the apartment were all at once thrown open, to their full extent, with a vigorous and rushing impetuosity that extinguished, as if by magic, every candle in the room. Their light, in dying, enabled us just to perceive that a stranger had entered, about my own height, and closely muffled in a cloak. The darkness, however, was now total; and we could only *feel* that he was standing in our midst. Before any one of us could recover from the extreme astonishment into which this rudeness had thrown all, we heard the voice of the intruder.

'Gentlemen,' he said, in a low, distinct, and never-to-be-forgotten *whisper* which thrilled to the very marrow of my bones, 'Gentlemen, I make no apology for this behaviour, because in thus behaving, I am but fulfilling a duty. You are, beyond doubt, uninformed of the true character of the person who has tonight won at écarté a large sum of money from Lord Glendinning. I will therefore put you upon an expeditious and decisive plan of obtaining this very necessary information. Please to examine, at your leisure, the inner linings of the cuff of his left sleeve, and the several little packages which may be found in the somewhat capacious pockets of his embroidered morning wrapper.'

While he spoke, so profound was the stillness that one might have heard a pin drop upon the floor. In ceasing, he departed at once, and as abruptly as he had entered. Can I—shall I describe my sensations? Must I say that I felt all the horrors of the damned? Most assuredly I had little time given for reflection. Many hands roughly seized me upon the spot, and lights were immediately reprocured. A search ensued. In the lining of my sleeve were found all the court cards essential in écarté, and, in the pockets of my wrapper, a number of packs, facsimiles of those used at our sittings, with the single exception that mine were of the species called, technically, *arrondées*; the honours being slightly convex at the ends, the lower cards slightly convex at the sides. In this disposition, the dupe who cuts, as customary, at the length of the pack, will invariably find that he cuts his antagonist an honour; while the gambler, cutting at the breadth, will, as certainly, cut nothing for his victim which may count in the records of the game.

Any burst of indignation upon this discovery would have affected me less than the silent contempt, or the sarcastic composure, with which it was received.

'Mr Wilson,' said our host, stooping to remove from beneath his feet an exceedingly luxurious cloak of rare furs, 'Mr Wilson, this is your property.' (The weather was cold; and, upon quitting my own room, I had thrown a cloak over my dressing wrapper, putting it off upon reaching the scene of play.) 'I presume it is supererogatory to seek here' (eyeing the folds of the garment with a bitter smile) 'for any further evidence of your skill. Indeed, we have had enough. You will see the necessity, I hope, of quitting Oxford—at all events, of quitting instantly my chambers.'

Abased, humbled to the dust as I then was, it is probable that I should have resented this galling language by immediate personal violence, had not my whole attention been at the moment arrested by a fact of the most startling character. The cloak which I had worn was of a rare description of fur; how rare, how extravagantly costly, I shall not venture to say. Its fashion, too, was of my own fantastic invention; for I was fastidious to an absurd degree of coxcombry, in matters of this frivolous nature. When, therefore, Mr Preston reached me that which he had picked up upon the floor, and near the folding doors of the apartment, it was with an astonishment nearly bordering upon terror that I perceived my own already hanging on my arm (where I had no doubt unwittingly placed it), and that the one presented me was but its exact counterpart in every, in even the minutest possible particular. The singular being who had so disastrously exposed me, had been muffled, I remembered, in a cloak; and none had been worn at all by any of the members of our party, with the exception of myself. Retaining some presence of mind, I took the one offered me by Preston; placed it, unnoticed, over my own; left the apartment with a resolute scowl of defiance; and, next morning ere dawn of day, commenced a hurried journey from Oxford to the continent, in a perfect agony of horror and of shame.

I *fled in vain*. My evil destiny pursued me as if in exultation, and proved, indeed, that the exercise of its mysterious dominion had as yet only begun. Scarcely had I set foot in Paris ere I had fresh evidence of the detestable interest taken by this Wilson in my concerns. Years flew, while I experienced no relief. Villain!—at Rome, with how untimely, yet with how spectral an officiousness, stepped he in between me and my ambition! At Vienna, too—at Berlin—and at Moscow! Where, in truth, had I *not* bitter cause to curse him within my heart? From his inscrutable tyranny did I at length flee, panic-stricken, as from a pestilence; and to the very ends of the earth I *fled in vain*.

And again, and again, in secret communion with my own spirit, would I demand the questions 'Who is he?—whence came he?—and what are his objects?' But no answer was there found. And then I scrutinised, with a minute scrutiny, the forms, and the methods, and the leading traits of his impertinent supervision. But even here there was very little upon which to base a conjecture. It was noticeable, indeed, that, in no one of the multiplied instances in which he had of late crossed my path, had he so crossed it except to frustrate those schemes, or to disturb those actions, which, if fully carried out, might have resulted in bitter mischief. Poor justification this, in truth, for an authority so imperiously assumed! Poor indemnity for natural rights of self-agency so pertinaciously, so insultingly denied!

I had also been forced to notice that my tormentor, for a very long period of time (while scrupulously and with miraculous dexterity maintaining his whim of an identity of apparel with myself), had so contrived it, in the execution of his varied interference with my will, that I saw not, at any moment, the features of his face. Be Wilson what he might, *this*, at least, was but the veriest of affectation, or of folly. Could he, for an instant, have supposed that, in my admonisher at Eton—in the destroyer of my honour at Oxford—in him who thwarted my ambition at Rome, my revenge at Paris, my passionate love at Naples, or what he falsely termed my avarice in Egypt—that in this, my archenemy and evil genius, I could fail to recognise the William Wilson of my schoolboy days—the name-sake, the companion, the rival—the hated and dreaded rival at Dr Bransby's? Impossible! But let me hasten to the last eventful scene of the drama.

Thus far I had succumbed supinely to this imperious domination. The senti-ment of deep awe with which I habitually regarded the elevated character, the majestic wisdom, the apparent omnipresence and omnipotence of Wilson, added to a feeling of even terror, with which certain other traits in his nature and assumptions inspired me, had operated, hitherto, to impress me with an idea of my own utter weakness and helplessness, and to suggest an implicit, although bitterly reluctant submission to his arbitrary will. But, of late days, I had given myself up entirely to wine; and its maddening influence upon my hereditary temper rendered me more and more impatient of control. I began to murmur—to hesitate—to resist. And was it only fancy which induced me to believe that, with the increase of my own firmness, that of my tormentor under-went a proportional diminution? Be this as it may, I now began to feel the inspiration of a burning hope, and at length nurtured in my secret thoughts a stern and desperate resolution that I would submit no longer to be enslaved.

It was at Rome, during the Carnival of 18—, that I attended a masquerade in the palazzo of the Neapolitan Duke Di Broglio. I had indulged more freely than usual in the excesses of the wine table; and now the suffocating atmos-phere of the crowded rooms irritated me beyond endurance. The difficulty, too, of forcing my way through the mazes of the company contributed not a little to the ruffling of my temper; for I was anxiously seeking (let me not say with what unworthy motive) the young, the gay, the beautiful wife of the aged and doting Di Broglio. With a too unscrupulous confidence she had previously communi-cated to me the secret of the costume in which she would be habited, and now, having caught a glimpse of her person, I was hurrying to make my way into her presence. At this moment I felt a light hand placed upon my shoulder, and that ever-remembered, low, damnable *whisper* within my ear.

In an absolute frenzy of wrath, I turned at once upon him who had thus inter-rupted me, and seized him violently by the collar. He was attired, as I had expected, in a costume altogether similar to my own; wearing a Spanish cloak of blue velvet, begirt about the waist with a crimson belt sustaining a rapier. A mask of black silk entirely covered his face.

'Scoundrel!' I said, in a voice husky with rage, while every syllable I uttered seemed as new fuel to my fury; 'scoundrel! impostor! accursed villain! you shall not—you *shall not* dog me unto death! Follow me, or I stab you where you stand!'—and I broke my way from the ballroom into a small antechamber adjoining, dragging him unresistingly with me as I went.

Upon entering, I thrust him furiously from me. He staggered against the wall, while I closed the door with an oath, and commanded him to draw. He hesitated but for an instant; then, with a slight sigh, drew in silence, and put himself upon his defence.

The contest was brief indeed. I was frantic with every species of wild excitement, and felt within my single arm the energy and power of a multitude. In a few seconds I forced him by sheer strength against the wainscoting, and thus, getting him at mercy, plunged my sword, with brute ferocity, repeatedly through and through his bosom.

At that instant some person tried the latch of the door. I hastened to prevent an intrusion, and then immediately returned to my dying antagonist. But what human language can adequately portray *that* astonishment, *that* horror which possessed me at the spectacle then presented to view? The brief moment in which I averted my eyes had been sufficient to produce, apparently, a material change in the arrangements at the upper or farther end of the room. A large mirror—so at first it seemed to me in my confusion—now stood where none had been perceptible before; and, as I stepped up to it in extremity of terror, mine own image, but with features all pale and dabbled in blood, advanced to meet me with a feeble and tottering gait.

Thus it appeared, I say, but was not. It was my antagonist—it was Wilson, who then stood before me in the agonies of his dissolution. His mask and cloak lay, where he had thrown them, upon the floor. Not a thread in all his raiment—not a line in all the marked and singular lineaments of his face which was not, even in the most absolute identity, *mine own*!

It was Wilson; but he spoke no longer in a whisper, and I could have fancied that I myself was speaking while he said:

'You have conquered, and I yield. Yet, henceforward art thou also dead—dead to the World, to Heaven and to Hope! In me didst thou exist—and, in my death, see by this image, which is thine own, how utterly thou has murdered thyself!'

Alexander Pushkin

1799–1837

A member of the Russian nobility, Alexander Pushkin entered
government service, but his liberal views soon got him into
trouble with the authorities and he was sacked. Though his life
was short—he was killed duelling with a Frenchman he
suspected of being his wife's lover—he left a magnificent legacy
of poetry, essays, verse dramas and fiction.

THE QUEEN OF SPADES

I

When bleak was the weather
They would meet together
For cards—God forgive them!
Some would win, others lost,
And they chalked up the cost
In bleak autumn weather
When they met together.

THERE WAS A CARD PARTY in the rooms of Narumov, an officer of the Horse
Guards. The long winter night had passed unnoticed and it was after
four in the morning when the company sat down to supper. Those who
had won enjoyed their food; the others sat absent-mindedly in front of empty
plates. But when the champagne appeared conversation became more lively
and general.

'How did you fare, Surin?' Narumov asked.

'Oh I lost, as usual. I must confess, I have no luck: I stick to *mirandole*, never
get excited, never lose my head, and yet I never win.'

'Do you mean to tell me you were not once tempted to back the red the
whole evening? Your self-control amazes me.'

'But look at Hermann,' exclaimed one of the party, pointing to a young officer of the Engineers. 'Never held a card in his hands, never made a bet in his life, and yet he sits up till five in the morning watching us play.'

'Cards interest me very much,' said Hermann, 'but I am not in a position to risk the necessary in the hope of acquiring the superfluous.'

'Hermann is a German: he's careful, that's what that is!' remarked Tomsky. 'But if there is one person I can't understand it is my grandmother, Countess Anna Fedotovna.'

'Why is that?' the guests cried.

'I cannot conceive how it is that my grandmother does not play.'

'But surely there is nothing surprising in an old lady in her eighties not wanting to gamble?' said Narumov.

'Then you don't know about her?'

'No, nothing, absolutely nothing!'

'Well, listen then. I must tell you that some sixty years ago my grandmother went to Paris and was quite the rage there. People would run after her to catch a glimpse of *la Vénus moscovite*; Richelieu was at her beck and call, and grandmamma maintains that he very nearly blew his brains out because of her cruelty to him. In those days ladies used to play faro. One evening at the Court she lost a very considerable sum to the Duke of Orléans. When she got home she told my grandfather of her loss while removing the beauty spots from her face and untying her farthingale, and commanded him to pay her debt. My grandfather, so far as I remember, acted as a sort of major-domo to my grandmother. He feared her like fire; however, when he heard of such a frightful gambling loss he almost went out of his mind, fetched the bills they owed and pointed out to her that in six months they had spent half a million roubles and that in Paris they had neither their Moscow nor their Saratov estates upon which to draw, and flatly refused to pay. Grandmamma gave him a box on the ear and retired to bed without him as a sign of her displeasure. The following morning she sent for her husband, hoping that the simple punishment had had its effect, but she found him as obdurate as ever. For the first time in her life she went so far as to reason with him and explain, thinking to rouse his conscience and arguing with condescension, that there were debts and debts, and that a prince was different from a coach-builder. But it was not a bit of good—grandfather just would not hear of it. "Once and for all, no!" Grandmamma did not know what to do. Among her close acquaintances was a very remarkable man. You have heard of Count Saint-Germain, about whom so many marvellous stories are told. You know that he posed as the Wandering Jew and claimed to have discovered the elixir of life and the philosopher's stone, and so on. People laughed at him as a charlatan, and Casanova in his *Memoirs* says that he was a spy. Be that as it may, Saint-Germain, in spite of the mystery that surrounded him, had a most dignified appearance and was a very amiable person in society. Grandmamma is still to this day quite devoted to his memory and gets angry if anyone speaks of him with disrespect. Grandmamma knew that Saint-Germain had plenty of money at his disposal. She decided to appeal to him, and wrote a note asking him to come and see her immediately. The eccentric old man came at once and found her in terrible distress. She described in the blackest colours her husband's inhumanity, and ended by declaring that she laid all her hopes on his friendship and kindness. Saint-Germain pondered. "I could oblige you with the sum you want," he said, "but I know that you would not be easy until you had repaid me, and I should not like to involve you in fresh trouble. There is another way out—you could win it back."

'"But, my dear count," answered grandmamma, "I tell you I have no money at all."

'"That does not matter," Saint-Germain replied. "Listen now to what I am going to tell you."

'And he revealed to her a secret which all of us would give a great deal to know . . .'

The young gamblers redoubled their attention. Tomsky lit his pipe, puffed away for a moment and continued:

'That very evening grandmamma appeared at Versailles, at the *jeu de la reine*. The Duke of Orléans kept the bank. Grandmamma lightly excused herself for not having brought the money to pay off her debt, inventing some little story by way of explanation, and began to play against him. She selected three cards and played them one after the other: all three won, and grandmamma retrieved her loss completely.'

'Luck!' said one of the party.

'A fairy tale!' remarked Hermann.

'Marked cards, perhaps,' put in a third.

'I don't think so,' replied Tomsky impressively.

'What!' said Narumov. 'You have a grandmother who knows how to hit upon three lucky cards in succession, and you haven't learned her secret yet?'

'That's the deuce of it!' Tomsky replied. 'She had four sons, one of whom was my father; all four were desperate gamblers, and yet she did not reveal her secret to a single one of them, though it would not have been a bad thing for them, or for me either. But listen to what my uncle, Count Ivan Ilyich, used to say, assuring me on his word of honour that it was true. Tchaplitsky—you know him, he died a pauper after squandering millions—as a young man once lost three hundred thousand roubles, to Zorich, if I remember rightly. He was in despair. Grandmamma was always very severe on the follies of young men, but somehow she took pity on Tchaplitsky. She gave him three cards, which he was to play one after the other, at the same time exacting from him a promise that he would never afterwards touch a card so long as he lived. Tchaplitsky went to Zorich's; they sat down to play. Tchaplitsky staked fifty thousand on his first card and won; doubled his stake and won; did the same again, won back his loss and ended up in pocket . . .

'But, I say, it's time to go to bed: it is a quarter to six already.'

And indeed dawn was breaking. The young men emptied their glasses and went home.

II

'Il paraît que monsieur est décidément pour les suivantes.'
'Que voulez-vous, madame? Elles sont plus fraîches.'

FROM A SOCIETY CONVERSATION

THE OLD COUNTESS X was seated before the looking glass in her dressing room. Three maids were standing round her. One held a pot of rouge, another a box of hairpins, and the third a tall cap with flame-coloured ribbons. The countess had not the slightest pretensions to beauty—it had faded long ago—but she still preserved all the habits of her youth, followed strictly the fashion of the seventies, and gave as much time and care to her toilette as she had sixty years before. A young girl whom she had brought up sat at an embroidery frame by the window.

'Good morning, *grand'maman*!' said a young officer, coming into the room. '*Bonjour, Mademoiselle Lise. Grand'maman*, I have a favour to ask of you.'

'What is it, Paul?'

'I want you to let me introduce to you a friend of mine and bring him to your ball on Friday.'

'Bring him straight to the ball and introduce him to me then. Were you at the princess's last night?'

'Of course I was! It was most enjoyable: we danced until five in the morning. Mademoiselle Yeletsky looked enchanting!'

'Come, my dear! What is there enchanting about her? She isn't a patch on her grandmother, Princess Daria Petrovna. By the way, I expect Princess Daria Petrovna must have aged considerably?'

'How do you mean, aged?' Tomsky replied absent-mindedly. 'She's been dead for the last seven years.'

The girl at the window raised her head and made a sign to the young man. He remembered that they concealed the deaths of her contemporaries from the old countess, and bit his lip. But the countess heard the news with the utmost indifference.

'Dead! I didn't know,' she said. 'We were maids of honour together, and as we were being presented the Empress . . .'

And for the hundredth time the countess repeated the story to her grandson.

'Well, Paul,' she said at the end; 'now help me to my feet. Lise, where is my snuffbox?'

And the countess went with her maids behind the screen to finish dressing. Tomsky was left *à deux* with the young girl.

'Who is it you want to introduce?' Lizaveta Ivanovna asked softly.

'Narumov. Do you know him?'

'No. Is he in the army?'

'Yes.'

'In the Engineers?'

'No, Horse Guards. What made you think he was in the Engineers?'

The girl laughed and made no answer.

'Paul!' the countess called from behind the screen. 'Send me a new novel to read, only pray not one of those modern ones.'

'How do you mean, *grand'maman*?'

'I want a book in which the hero does not strangle either his father or his mother, and where there are no drowned corpses. I have a horror of drowned persons.'

'There aren't any novels of that sort nowadays. Wouldn't you like something in Russian?'

'Are there any Russian novels? ... Send me something, my dear fellow, please send me something!'

'Excuse me, *grand'maman*: I must hurry . . . Goodbye, Lizaveta Ivanovna! I wonder, what made you think Narumov was in the Engineers?'

And Tomsky departed from the dressing room.

Lizaveta Ivanovna was left alone. She abandoned her work and began to look out of the window. Soon, round the corner of a house on the other side of the street, a young officer appeared. Colour flooded her cheeks; she took up her work again, bending her head over her embroidery frame. At that moment the countess came in, having finished dressing.

'Order the carriage, Lise,' she said, 'and let us go for a drive.'

Lizaveta Ivanovna rose from her embroidery frame and began putting away her work.

'What is the matter with you, my child, are you deaf?' the countess cried. 'Be quick and order the carriage.'

'I will go at once,' the young girl answered quietly, and ran into the anteroom.

A servant came in and handed the countess a parcel of books from Prince Paul Alexandrovich.

'Good! Tell him I am much obliged,' said the countess. 'Lise, Lise, where are you off to?'

'To dress.'

'There is plenty of time, my dear. Sit down here. Open the first volume and read to me.'

The girl took the book and read a few lines.

'Louder!' said the countess. 'What is the matter with you, my dear? Have you lost your voice, or what? Wait a minute ... Give me that footstool. A little closer. That will do!'

Lizaveta Ivanovna read two more pages. The countess yawned.

'Throw that book away,' she said. 'What nonsense it is! Send it back to Prince Paul with my thanks . . . What about the carriage?'

'The carriage is ready,' said Lizaveta Ivanovna, glancing out into the street.

'How is it you are not dressed?' the countess said. 'You always keep people waiting. It really is intolerable!'

Liza ran to her room. Hardly two minutes passed before the countess started ringing with all her might. Three maids rushed in at one door and a footman at the other.

'Why is it you don't come when you are called?' the countess said to them. 'Tell Lizaveta Ivanovna I am waiting.'

Lizaveta Ivanovna returned, wearing a hat and a pelisse.

'At last, my dear!' said the countess. 'Why the finery? What is it for? . . . For whose benefit? . . . And what is the weather like? Windy, isn't it?'

'No, your ladyship,' the footman answered, 'there is no wind at all.'

'You say anything that comes into your head! Open the window. Just as I thought: there is a wind, and a very cold one too! Dismiss the carriage. Lise, my child, we won't go out—you need not have dressed up after all.'

'And this is my life!' Lizaveta Ivanovna thought to herself.

Indeed, Lizaveta Ivanovna was a most unfortunate creature. 'Another's bread is bitter to the taste,' says Dante, 'and his staircase hard to climb'; and who should know the bitterness of dependence better than a poor orphan brought up by an old lady of quality? The countess was certainly not bad-hearted but she had all the caprices of a woman spoiled by society, she was stingy and coldly selfish, like all old people who have done with love and are out of touch with life around them. She took part in all the vanities of the fashionable world, dragged herself to balls, where she sat in a corner, rouged and attired after some bygone mode, like a misshapen but indispensable ornament of the ballroom. On their arrival the guests all went up to her and bowed low, as though in accordance with an old-established rite, and after that no one took any more notice of her. She received the whole town at her house, observing the strictest etiquette and not recognising the faces of any of her guests. Her numerous servants, grown fat and grey in her entrance hall and the maids' quarters, did what they liked and vied with each other in robbing the decrepit old woman. Lizaveta Ivanovna was the household martyr. She poured out tea and was reprimanded for using too much sugar; she read novels aloud to the countess and was blamed for all the author's mistakes; she accompanied the countess on her drives and was answerable for the weather and the state of the roads. She was supposed to receive a salary, which was never paid in full and yet she was expected to be as well dressed as everyone else—that is, as very few indeed. In society she played the most pitiable role. Everybody knew her and nobody gave her any thought. At balls she danced only when someone was short of a partner, and the ladies would take her by the arm each time they wanted to go to the cloakroom to rearrange some detail of their toilette. She was sensitive and felt her position keenly, and looked about impatiently for a deliverer to come; but the young men, calculating in their empty-headed frivolity, honoured her with scant attention though Lizaveta Ivanovna was a hundred times more charming than the cold, brazen-faced heiresses they ran after. Many a time she crept away from the tedious, glittering drawing room to go and weep in her humble little attic with its wallpaper screen, chest of drawers, small looking glass and painted wooden bedstead, and where a tallow candle burned dimly in a brass candlestick.

One morning, two days after the card party described at the beginning of this story and a week before the scene we have just witnessed—one morning Lizaveta Ivanovna, sitting at her embroidery frame by the window, happened to glance out into the street and see a young Engineers officer standing stock-still gazing at her window. She lowered her head and went on with her work. Five minutes afterwards she looked out again—the young officer was still on the same spot. Not being in the habit of coquetting with passing officers, she looked out no more and went on sewing for a couple of hours without raising her head. Luncheon was announced. She got up to put away her embroidery frame and, glancing casually into the street, saw the officer again. This seemed to her somewhat strange. After luncheon she went to the window with a certain feeling of uneasiness, but the officer was no longer there, and she forgot about him . . .

A day or so later, just as she was stepping into the carriage with the countess, she saw him again. He was standing right by the front door, his face hidden by his beaver collar; his dark eyes sparkled beneath his fur cap. Lizaveta Ivanovna felt alarmed, though she did not know why, and seated herself in the carriage, inexplicably agitated.

On returning home she ran to the window—the officer was standing in his accustomed place, his eyes fixed on her. She drew back, consumed with curiosity and excited by a feeling quite new to her.

Since then not a day had passed without the young man appearing at a certain hour beneath the windows of their house, and between him and her a sort of mute acquaintance was established. Sitting at her work she would sense his approach, and lifting her head she looked at him longer and longer every day. The young man seemed to be grateful to her for looking out: with the keen eyes of youth she saw the quick flush of his pale cheeks every time their glances met. By the end of a week she had smiled at him . . .

When Tomsky asked the countess's permission to introduce a friend of his the poor girl's heart beat violently. But hearing that Narumov was in the Horse Guards, not the Engineers, she regretted the indiscreet question by which she had betrayed her secret to the irresponsible Tomsky.

HERMANN WAS THE SON of a German who had settled in Russia and who left him some small capital sum. Being firmly convinced that it was essential for him to make certain of his independence, Hermann did not touch even the interest on his income but lived on his pay, denying himself the slightest extravagance. But since he was reserved and ambitious his companions rarely had any opportunity for making fun of his extreme parsimony. He had strong passions and an ardent imagination, but strength of character preserved him from the customary mistakes of youth. Thus, for instance, though a gambler at heart he never touched cards, having decided that his means did not allow him (as he put it) 'to risk the necessary in the hope of acquiring the superfluous'. And yet he spent night after night at the card tables, watching with feverish anxiety the vicissitudes of the game.

The story of the three cards had made a powerful impression upon his imagination and it haunted his mind all night. 'Supposing,' he thought to himself the following evening as he wandered about Petersburg, 'supposing the old countess were to reveal her secret to me? Or tell me the three winning cards! Why shouldn't I try my luck?. . . Get introduced to her, win her favour—become her lover, perhaps. But all that would take time, and she is eighty-seven. She might be dead next week, or the day after tomorrow even! . . . And the story itself? Is it likely? No, economy, moderation and hard work are my three winning cards. With them I can treble my capital—increase it sevenfold and obtain for myself leisure and independence!' Musing thus, he found himself in one of the main streets of Petersburg, in front of a house of old-fashioned architecture. The street was lined with carriages which followed one another up to the lighted porch. Out of the carriages stepped now the shapely little foot of a young beauty, now a military boot with clinking spur, or a diplomat's striped stockings and buckled shoes. Fur coats and cloaks passed in rapid procession before the majestic-looking concierge. Hermann stopped.

'Whose house is that?' he asked a watchman in his box at the corner.

'The Countess X's,' the man told him. It was Tomsky's grandmother.

Hermann started. The strange story of the three cards came into his mind again. He began walking up and down past the house, thinking of its owner and her wonderful secret. It was late when he returned to his humble lodgings; he could not get to sleep for a long time, and when sleep did come he dreamed of cards, a green baize table, stacks of banknotes and piles of gold. He played card after card, resolutely turning down the corners, winning all the time. He raked in the gold and stuffed his pockets with banknotes. Waking late in the morning, he sighed over the loss of his fantastic wealth, and then, sallying forth to wander about the town again, once more found himself outside the countess's house. It was as though some supernatural force drew him there. He stopped and looked up at the windows. In one of them he saw a dark head bent over a book or some needlework. The head was raised. Hermann caught sight of a rosy face and a pair of black eyes. That moment decided his fate.

III

Vous m'écrivez, mon ange, des lettres de quatre pages plus vite que je ne puis les lire.

FROM A CORRESPONDENCE

LIZAVETA IVANOVNA had scarcely taken off her hat and mantle before the countess sent for her and again ordered the carriage. They went out to take their seats. Just as the two footmen were lifting the old lady and helping her through the carriage door, Lizaveta Ivanovna saw her Engineers officer standing by the wheel. He seized her hand; before she had recovered from her alarm the young man had disappeared, leaving a letter between her fingers. She hid it in her glove, and for the rest of the drive neither saw nor heard anything. It was the countess's habit when they were out in the carriage to ask a constant stream of questions: 'Who was that we met?'—'What bridge is this?'—'What does that signboard say?' This time Lizaveta Ivanovna returned such random and irrelevant answers that the countess grew angry with her.

'What is the matter with you, my dear? Have you taken leave of your senses? Don't you hear me or understand what I say? . . . I speak distinctly enough, thank heaven, and am not in my dotage yet!'

Lizaveta Ivanovna paid no attention to her. When they returned home she ran up to her room and drew the letter out of her glove: it was unsealed. She read it. The letter contained a declaration of love: it was tender, respectful and had been copied word for word from a German novel. But Lizaveta Ivanovna did not know any German and she was delighted with it.

For all that, the letter troubled her greatly. For the first time in her life she was embarking upon secret and intimate relations with a young man. His boldness appalled her. She reproached herself for her imprudent behaviour, and did not know what to do: ought she to give up sitting at the window and by a show of indifference damp the young man's inclination to pursue her further? Should she return his letter to him? Or answer it coldly and firmly? There was nobody to whom she could turn for advice: she had neither female friend nor preceptor. Lizaveta Ivanovna decided to reply to the letter.

She sat down at her little writing table, took pen and paper—and began to ponder. Several times she made a start and then tore the paper across: what she had written seemed to her either too indulgent or too harsh. At last she succeeded in composing a few lines with which she felt satisfied.

'I am sure,' she wrote, 'that your intentions are honourable and that you had no wish to hurt me by any thoughtless conduct; but our acquaintance ought not to have begun in this manner. I return you your letter, and hope that in future I shall have no cause to complain of being shown a lack of respect which is undeserved.'

Next day, as soon as she saw Hermann approaching, Lizaveta Ivanovna got up from her embroidery frame, went into the drawing room, opened the little ventilating window and threw the letter into the street, trusting to the young officer's alertness. Hermann ran forward, picked the letter up and went into a confectioner's shop. Breaking the seal, he found his own letter and Lizaveta Ivanovna's reply. It was just what he had expected and he returned home engrossed in his plot.

Three days after this a sharp-eyed young person brought Lizaveta Ivanovna a note from a milliner's establishment. Lizaveta Ivanovna opened it uneasily, fearing it was a demand for money, and suddenly recognised Hermann's handwriting.

'You have made a mistake, my dear,' she said. 'This note is not for me.'

'Oh yes it is for you!' retorted the girl boldly, not troubling to conceal a knowing smile. 'Please read it.'

Lizaveta Ivanovna glanced at the letter. In it Hermann wanted her to meet him.

'Impossible!' she cried, alarmed at the request, at its coming so soon, and at the means employed to transmit it. 'I am sure this was not addressed to me.' And she tore the letter into fragments.

'If the letter was not for you, why did you tear it up?' said the girl. 'I would have returned it to the sender.'

'Be good enough, my dear,' said Lizaveta Ivanovna, flushing crimson at her remark, 'not to bring me any more letters. And tell the person who sent you that he ought to be ashamed . . .'

But Hermann did not give in. Every day Lizaveta Ivanovna received a letter from him by one means or another. They were no longer translated from the German. Hermann wrote them inspired by passion and in a style which was his own: they reflected both his inexorable desire and the disorder of an unbridled imagination. Lizaveta Ivanovna no longer thought of returning them: she drank them in eagerly and took to answering—and the notes she sent grew longer and more affectionate every hour. At last she threw out of the window to him the following letter:

There is a ball tonight at the Embassy. The countess will be there. We shall stay until about two o'clock. Here is an opportunity for you to see me alone. As soon as the countess is away the servants are sure to go to their quarters, leaving the concierge in the hall, but he usually retires to his lodge. Come at half past eleven. Walk straight up the stairs. If you meet anyone in the anteroom, ask if the countess is at home. They will say 'No,' but there will be no help for it—you will have to go away. But probably you will not meet anyone. The maids all sit together in the one room. Turn to the left out of the anteroom and keep straight on until you reach the countess's bedroom. In the bedroom, behind a screen, you will find two small doors: the one on the right leads into the study where the countess never goes; and the other on the left opens into a passage with a narrow winding staircase up to my room.

HERMANN WAITED FOR the appointed hour like a tiger trembling for its prey. By ten o'clock in the evening he was already standing outside the countess's house. It was a frightful night: the wind howled, wet snow fell in big flakes; the street-lamps burned dimly; the streets were deserted. From time to time a sledge drawn by a sorry-looking hack passed by, the driver on the watch for a belated fare. Hermann stood there without his greatcoat, feeling neither the wind nor the snow. At last the countess's carriage was brought round. Hermann saw the old woman wrapped in sables being lifted into the vehicle by two footmen; then Liza in a light cloak, with natural flowers in her hair, flitted by. The carriage doors banged. The vehicle rolled heavily over the wet snow. The concierge closed the street door. The lights in the windows went out. Hermann started to walk to and fro outside the deserted house; he went up to a streetlamp and glanced at his watch: it was twenty minutes past eleven. He stood still by the lamppost, his eyes fixed on the hand of the watch. Precisely at half past eleven Hermann walked up the steps of the house and entered the brightly lit vestibule. The concierge was not there. Hermann ran up the stairs, opened the door of the anteroom and saw a footman asleep in a soiled, old-fashioned armchair by the side of a lamp. With a light, firm tread Hermann passed quickly by him. The ballroom and drawing room were in darkness but the lamp in the anteroom shed a dim light into them. Hermann entered the bedroom. Ancient icons filled the icon-stand before which burned a golden lamp. Armchairs upholstered in faded damask and sofas with down cushions, the tassels of which had lost their gilt, were ranged with depressing symmetry round the walls hung with Chinese wallpaper. On one of the walls were two portraits painted in Paris by Madame Lebrun: the first of a stout, red-faced man of some forty years of age, in a light-green uniform with a star on his breast; the other—a beautiful young woman with an aquiline nose and a rose in the powdered hair drawn back over her temples. Every corner was crowded with porcelain shepherdesses, clocks made by the celebrated Leroy, little boxes, roulettes, fans and all the thousand and one playthings invented for ladies of fashion at the end of the last century together with Montgolfier's balloon and Mesmer's magnetism. Hermann stepped behind the screen. A small iron bedstead stood there; to the right was the door into the study—to the left, the other door into the passage. Hermann opened it and saw the narrow winding staircase leading to poor little Liza's room. But he turned about and went into the dark study.

The time passed slowly. Everything was quiet. The drawing-room clock struck twelve; the clocks in the other rooms chimed twelve, one after the other, and all was still again. Hermann stood leaning against the cold stove. He was quite calm: his heart beat evenly, like that of a man resolved upon a dangerous but inevitable undertaking. The clocks struck one, and then two, and he heard the distant rumble of a carriage. In spite of himself he was overcome with agitation. The carriage drove up to the house and stopped. He heard the clatter of the carriage steps being lowered. In the house all was commotion. Servants ran to and fro, there was a confusion of voices, and lights appeared everywhere. Three ancient lady's maids bustled into the bedroom, followed by the countess who, half dead with fatigue, sank into a Voltaire armchair. Hermann watched through a crack in the door. Lizaveta Ivanovna passed close by him and he heard her footsteps hurrying up the stairs to her room. For a moment something akin to remorse assailed him but he quickly hardened his heart again.

The countess began undressing before the looking glass. Her maids took off the cap trimmed with roses and lifted the powdered wig from her grey, close-cropped head. Pins showered about her. The silver-trimmed yellow dress fell at her puffy feet. Hermann witnessed the hideous mysteries of her toilet; at last the countess put on bed jacket and nightcap, and in this attire, more suited to her age, she seemed less horrible and ugly.

Like most old people the countess suffered from sleeplessness. Having undressed, she sat down in a big armchair by the window and dismissed her maids. They took away the candles, leaving only the lamp before the icons to light the room. The countess sat there, her skin sallow with age, her flabby lips twitching, her body swaying to and fro. Her dim eyes were completely vacant and looking at her one might have imagined that the dreadful old woman was rocking her body not from choice but owing to some secret galvanic mechanism.

Suddenly an inexplicable change came over the deathlike face. The lips ceased to move, the eyes brightened: before the countess stood a strange young man.

'Do not be alarmed, for heaven's sake, do not be alarmed!' he said in a low, clear voice. 'I have no intention of doing you any harm, I have come to beg a favour of you.'

The old woman stared at him in silence, as if she had not heard. Hermann thought she must be deaf and bending down to her ear he repeated what he had just said. The old woman remained silent as before.

'You can ensure the happiness of my whole life,' Hermann went on, 'and at no cost to yourself. I know that you can name three cards in succession . . .'

Hermann stopped. The countess appeared to have grasped what he wanted and to be seeking words to frame her answer.

'It was a joke,' she said at last. 'I swear to you it was a joke.'

'No, madam,' Hermann retorted angrily. 'Remember Tchaplitsky, and how you enabled him to win back his loss.'

The countess was plainly perturbed. Her face expressed profound agitation; but soon she relapsed into her former impassivity.

'Can you not tell me those three winning cards?' Hermann went on.

The countess said nothing. Hermann continued:

'For whom would you keep your secret? For your grandsons? They are rich enough already: they don't appreciate the value of money. Your three cards would not help a spendthrift. A man who does not take care of his inheritance will die a beggar though all the demons of the world were at his command. I am not a spendthrift: I know the value of money. Your three cards would not be wasted on me. Well? . . .'

He paused, feverishly waiting for her reply. She was silent. Hermann fell on his knees.

'If your heart has ever known what it is to love, if you can remember the ecstasies of love, if you have ever smiled tenderly at the cry of your newborn son, if any human feeling has ever stirred in your breast, I appeal to you as wife, beloved one, mother—I implore you by all that is holy in life not to reject my prayer: tell me your secret. Of what use is it to you? Perhaps it is bound up with some terrible sin, with the loss of eternal salvation, with some bargain with the devil . . . Reflect—you are old: you have not much longer to live, and I am ready to take your sin upon my soul. Only tell me your secret. Remember that a man's happiness is in your hands; that not only I, but my children and my children's children will bless your memory and hold it sacred . . .'

The old woman answered not a word.

Hermann rose to his feet.

'You old hag!' he said, grinding his teeth. 'Then I will make you speak . . .'

With these words he drew a pistol from his pocket. At the sight of the pistol the countess for the second time showed signs of agitation. Her head shook and she raised a hand as though to protect herself from the shot . . . Then she fell back . . . and was still.

'Come, an end to this childish nonsense!' said Hermann, seizing her by the arm. 'I ask you for the last time—will you tell me those three cards? Yes or no?'

The countess made no answer. Hermann saw that she was dead.

IV

7 mai 18—
Homme sans moeurs et sans religion!
FROM A CORRESPONDENCE

LIZAVETA IVANOVNA was sitting in her room, still in her ball dress, lost in thought. On returning home she had made haste to dismiss the sleepy maid who reluctantly offered to help her, saying that she would undress herself, and with trembling heart had gone to her own room, expecting to find Hermann and hoping that she would not find him. A glance convinced her he was not there, and she thanked fate for having prevented their meeting. She sat down without undressing and began to recall the circumstances that had led her so far in so short a time. It was not three weeks since she had first caught sight of the young man from the window—and yet she was carrying on a correspondence with him, and he had already succeeded in inducing her to agree to a nocturnal tryst! She knew his name only because he had signed some of his letters; she had never spoken to him, did not know the sound of his voice, had never heard him mentioned . . . until that evening. Strange to say, that very evening at the ball, Tomsky, piqued with the young Princess Pauline for flirting with somebody else instead of with him as she usually did, decided to revenge himself by a show of indifference. He asked Lizaveta Ivanovna to be his partner and danced the interminable mazurka with her. And all the time he kept teasing her about her partiality for officers of the Engineers, assuring her that he knew far more than she could suppose, and some of his sallies so found their mark that several times Lizaveta Ivanovna thought he must know her secret.

'Who told you all this?' she asked, laughing.

'A friend of someone you know,' Tomsky answered, 'a very remarkable person.'

'And who is this remarkable man?'

'His name is Hermann.'

Lizaveta Ivanovna said nothing; but her hands and feet turned to ice.

'This Hermann,' continued Tomsky, 'is a truly romantic figure: he has the profile of a Napoleon and the soul of a Mephistopheles. I think there must be at least three crimes on his conscience. How pale you look!'

'I have a bad headache . . . Well, and what did this Hermann—or whatever his name is—tell you?'

'Hermann is very annoyed with his friend: he says that in his place he would act quite differently . . . I suspect in fact that Hermann has designs upon you himself; at any rate he listens to his friend's ecstatic exclamations with anything but indifference.'

'But where has he seen me?'

'In church, perhaps, or when you were out walking . . . heaven only knows!— in your own room maybe, while you were asleep, for there is nothing he—'

Three ladies coming up to invite Tomsky to choose between '*oubli ou regret?*' interrupted the conversation which had become so painfully interesting to Lizaveta Ivanovna.

The lady chosen by Tomsky was the Princess Pauline herself. She succeeded in effecting a reconciliation with him while they danced an extra turn and spun round once more before she was conducted to her chair. When he returned to his place neither Hermann nor Lizaveta Ivanovna was in Tomsky's thoughts. Lizaveta Ivanovna longed to resume the interrupted conversation but the mazurka came to an end and shortly afterwards the old countess took her departure.

Tomsky's words were nothing more than the usual small talk of the ballroom; but they sank deep into the girl's romantic heart. The portrait sketched by

Tomsky resembled the picture she had herself drawn, and thanks to the novels of the day the commonplace figure both terrified and fascinated her. She sat there with her bare arms crossed and with her head, still adorned with flowers, sunk upon her naked bosom . . . Suddenly the door opened and Hermann came in . . . She shuddered.

'Where were you?' she asked in a frightened whisper.

'In the countess's bedroom,' Hermann answered. 'I have just left her. The countess is dead.'

'Merciful heavens! . . . what are you saying?'

'And I think,' added Hermann, 'that I am the cause of her death.'

Lizaveta darted a glance at him, and heard Tomsky's words echo in her soul: '. . . there must be at least three crimes on his conscience'. Hermann sat down in the window beside her and related all that had happened.

Lizaveta Ivanovna listened to him aghast. So all those passionate letters, those ardent pleas, the bold, determined pursuit had not been inspired by love! Money!—that was what his soul craved! It was not she who could satisfy his desires and make him happy! Poor child, she had been nothing but the blind tool of a thief, of the murderer of her aged benefactress! . . . She wept bitterly in a vain agony of repentance. Hermann watched in silence: he too was suffering torment; but neither the poor girl's tears nor her indescribable charm in her grief touched his hardened soul. He felt no pricking of conscience at the thought of the dead old woman. One thing only horrified him: the irreparable loss of the secret which was to have brought him wealth.

'You are a monster!' said Lizaveta Ivanovna at last.

'I did not mean her to die,' Hermann answered. 'My pistol was not loaded.'

Both were silent.

Morning came. Lizaveta Ivanovna blew out the candle which had burned down. A pale light illumined the room. She wiped her tear-stained eyes and looked up at Hermann: he was sitting on the windowsill with his arms folded, a menacing frown on his face. In this attitude he bore a remarkable likeness to the portrait of Napoleon. The likeness struck even Lizaveta Ivanovna.

'How shall I get you out of the house?' she said at last. 'I had thought of taking you down the street staircase but that means going through the bedroom, and I am afraid.'

'Tell me how to find this secret staircase—I will go alone.'

Lizaveta rose, took a key from the chest of drawers and gave it to Hermann with precise instructions. Hermann pressed her cold, unresponsive hand, kissed her bowed head and left her.

He walked down the winding stairway and entered the countess's bedroom again. The dead woman sat as though turned to stone. Her face wore a look of profound tranquillity. Hermann stood in front of her and gazed long and earnestly at her, as though trying to convince himself of the terrible truth. Then he went into the study, felt behind the tapestry for the door and began to descend the dark stairway, excited by strange emotions. 'Maybe some sixty years ago, at this very hour,' he thought, 'some happy youth—long since turned to dust—was stealing up this staircase into that very bedroom, in an embroidered tunic, his hair dressed *à l'oiseau royal,* pressing his three-cornered hat to his breast; and today the heart of his aged mistress has ceased to beat . . .'

At the bottom of the stairs Hermann saw a door which he opened with the same key, and found himself in a passage leading to the street.

V

That night the dead Baroness von W. appeared before me. She was all in white and said: 'How do you do, Mr Councillor?'

SWEDENBORG

THREE DAYS AFTER THAT FATAL NIGHT, at nine o'clock in the morning, Hermann repaired to the Convent of ——, where the last respects were to be paid to the mortal remains of the dead countess. Though he felt no remorse he could not altogether stifle the voice of conscience which kept repeating to him: 'You are the old woman's murderer!' Having very little religious faith, he was exceedingly superstitious. Believing that the dead countess might exercise a malignant influence on his life, he decided to go to her funeral to beg and obtain her forgiveness.

The church was full. Hermann had difficulty in making his way through the crowd. The coffin rested on a rich catafalque beneath a canopy of velvet. The dead woman lay with her hands crossed on her breast, in a lace cap and a white satin robe. Around the bier stood the members of her household: servants in black clothes, with armorial ribbons on their shoulders and lighted candles in their hands; relatives in deep mourning—children, grandchildren and great-grandchildren. No one wept: tears would have been *une affectation.* The countess was so old that her death could not have taken anybody by surprise, and her family had long ceased to think of her as one of the living. A famous preacher delivered the funeral oration. In simple and touching phrases he described the peaceful passing of the saintly woman whose long life had been a quiet, touching preparation for a Christian end. 'The angel of death,' he declared, 'found her vigilant in devout meditation, awaiting the midnight coming of the bridegroom.' The service was concluded in melancholy decorum. First the relations went forward to bid farewell to the corpse. They were followed by a long procession of all those who had come to render their last homage to one who had for so many years been a participator in their frivolous amusements. After them came the members of the countess's household. The last of these was an old woman retainer the same age as the deceased. Two young girls supported her by the arms. She had not strength to prostrate herself—and she was the only one to shed tears as she kissed her mistress's cold hand. Hermann decided to approach the coffin after her. He knelt down on the cold stone strewed with branches of spruce fir, and remained in that position for some minutes; at last he rose to his feet and, pale as the deceased herself, walked up the steps of the catafalque and bent over the corpse . . . At that moment it seemed to him that the dead woman darted a mocking look at him and winked her eye. Hermann drew back, missed his footing and crashed headlong to the floor. They picked him up. At the same time Lizaveta Ivanovna was carried out of the church in a swoon. This incident momentarily upset the solemnity of the mournful rite. There was a dull murmur among the congregation, and a tall thin man in the uniform of a court chamberlain, a close relative of the deceased, whispered in the ear of an Englishman who was standing near him that the young officer was the natural son of the countess, to which the Englishman coldly replied, 'Oh?'

The whole of that day Hermann was strangely troubled. Repairing to a quiet little tavern to dine, he drank a great deal of wine, contrary to his habit, in the hope of stifling his inner agitation. But the wine only served to excite his imagination. Returning home, he threw himself on his bed without undressing, and fell heavily asleep.

It was night when he woke and the moon was shining into his room. He glanced at the time: it was a quarter to three. Sleep had left him; he sat on the bed and began thinking of the old countess's funeral.

Just then someone in the street looked in at him through the window and immediately walked on. Hermann paid no attention. A moment later he heard the door of his anteroom open. Hermann thought it was his orderly, drunk as usual, returning from some nocturnal excursion, but presently he heard an unfamiliar footstep: someone was softly shuffling along the floor in slippers. The door opened and a woman in white came in. Hermann mistook her for his old nurse and wondered what could have brought her at such an hour. But the woman in white glided across the room and stood before him—and Hermann recognised the countess!

'I have come to you against my will,' she said in a firm voice: 'but I am commanded to grant your request. The three, the seven and the ace will win for you if you play them in succession, provided that you do not stake more than one card in twenty-four hours and never play again as long as you live. I forgive you my death, on condition that you marry my ward, Lizaveta Ivanovna.'

With these words she turned softly, rustled to the door in her slippers, and disappeared. Hermann heard the street door click and again saw someone peeping in at him through the window.

It was a long time before he could pull himself together and go into the next room. His orderly was asleep on the floor. Hermann had difficulty in waking him. The man was drunk as usual: there was no getting any sense out of him. The street door was locked. Hermann returned to his room and, lighting a candle, wrote down all the details of his vision.

VI

'Attendez!'
'How dare you say "Attendez!" to me?'
'Your Excellency, I said "Attendez", sir.'

TWO *IDÉES FIXES* cannot coexist in the moral world any more than two physical bodies can occupy one and the same space. 'The three, the seven, the ace' soon drove all thought of the dead woman from Hermann's mind. 'Three, seven, ace' were perpetually in his head and on his lips. If he saw a young girl he would say, 'How graceful she is! A regular three of hearts!' Asked the time, he would reply, 'Five minutes to seven.' Every stout man reminded him of the ace. 'Three, seven, ace' haunted his dreams, assuming all sorts of shapes. The three blossomed before him like a luxuriant flower, the seven took the form of a Gothic portal, and aces became gigantic spiders. His whole attention was focused on one thought: how to make use of the secret which had cost him so dear. He began to consider resigning his commission in order to go and travel abroad. In the public gambling houses in Paris he would compel fortune to give him his magical treasure. Chance spared him the trouble.

A circle of wealthy gamblers existed in Moscow, presided over by the celebrated Tchekalinsky, who had spent his life at the card table and amassed millions, accepting promissory notes when he won and paying his losses in ready money. His long experience inspired the confidence of his fellow players, while his open house, his famous chef and his gay and friendly manner secured for him the general respect of the public. He came to Petersburg. The young men of the capital flocked to his rooms, forsaking balls for cards and preferring the excitement of gambling to the seductions of flirting. Narumov brought Hermann to him.

They passed through a succession of magnificent rooms full of attentive servants. The place was crowded. Several generals and privy councillors were playing whist; young men smoking long pipes lounged about on sofas upholstered in damask. In the drawing room some twenty gamblers jostled round a long table at which the master of the house was keeping bank. Tchekalinsky was a man of about sixty years of age and most dignified appearance; he had silvery-grey hair, a full, florid face with a kindly expression, and sparkling eyes which were always smiling. Narumov introduced Hermann. Shaking hands cordially, Tchekalinsky requested him not to stand on ceremony, and went on dealing.

The game continued for some while. On the table lay more than thirty cards. Tchekalinsky paused after each round to give the players time to arrange their cards and note their losses, listened courteously to their observations and more courteously still straightened the corner of a card that some careless hand had turned down. At last the game finished. Tchekalinsky shuffled the cards and prepared to deal again.

'Will you allow me to take a card?' said Hermann, stretching out his hand from behind a stout gentleman who was punting.

Tchekalinsky smiled and bowed graciously, in silent token of consent. Narumov laughingly congratulated Hermann on breaking his long abstention from cards and wished him a lucky start.

'There!' said Hermann, chalking some figures on the back of his card.

'How much?' asked the banker, screwing up his eyes. 'Excuse me, I cannot see.'

'Forty-seven thousand,' Hermann answered.

At these words every head was turned in a flash, and all eyes were fixed on Hermann.

'He has taken leave of his senses!' thought Narumov.

'Allow me to point out to you,' said Tchekalinsky with his unfailing smile, 'that you are playing rather high: nobody here has ever staked more than two hundred and seventy-five at a time.'

'Well?' returned Hermann. 'Do you accept my card or not?'

Tchekalinsky bowed with the same air of humble acquiescence.

'I only wanted to observe,' he said, 'that, being honoured with the confidence of my friends, I can only play against ready money. For my own part, of course, I am perfectly sure that your word is sufficient but for the sake of the rules of the game and our accounts I must request you to place the money on your card.'

Hermann took a banknote from his pocket and handed it to Tchekalinsky, who after a cursory glance placed it on Hermann's card. He began to deal. On the right a nine turned up, and on the left a three.

'I win!' said Hermann, pointing to his card.

There was a murmur of astonishment among the company. Tchekalinsky frowned, but the smile quickly reappeared on his face.

'Would you like me to settle now?' he asked Hermann.

'If you please.'

Tchekalinsky took a number of banknotes out of his pocket and paid there and then. Hermann picked up his money and left the table. Narumov could not believe his eyes. Hermann drank a glass of lemonade and departed home.

The following evening he appeared at Tchekalinsky's again. The host was dealing. Hermann walked up to the table; the players immediately made room for him. Tchekalinsky bowed graciously. Hermann waited for the next deal, took a card and placed on it his original forty-seven thousand together with his winnings of the day before. Tchekalinsky began to deal. A knave turned up on the right, a seven on the left.

Hermann showed his seven.

There was a general exclamation. Tchekalinsky was obviously disconcerted. He counted out ninety-four thousand and handed them to Hermann, who pocketed them in the coolest manner and instantly withdrew.

The next evening Hermann again made his appearance at the table. Everyone was expecting him; the generals and privy councillors left their whist to watch such extraordinary play. The young officers leaped up from their sofas and all the waiters collected in the drawing room. Everyone pressed round Hermann. The other players left off punting, impatient to see what would happen. Hermann stood at the table, prepared to play alone against Tchekalinsky, who was pale but still smiling. Each broke the seal of a pack of cards. Tchekalinsky shuffled. Hermann took a card and covered it with a pile of banknotes. It was like a duel. Deep silence reigned in the room.

Tchekalinsky began dealing; his hands trembled. A queen fell on the right, an ace on the left.

'Ace wins!' said Hermann, and showed his card.

'Your queen has lost,' said Tchekalinsky gently.

Hermann started: indeed, instead of an ace there lay before him the queen of spades. He could not believe his eyes or think how he could have made such a mistake.

At that moment it seemed to him that the queen of spades opened and closed her eye, and mocked him with a smile. He was struck by the extraordinary resemblance...

'The old woman!' he cried in terror.

Tchekalinsky gathered up his winnings. Hermann stood rooted to the spot. When he left the table everyone began talking at once.

'A fine game, that!' said the players.

Tchekalinsky shuffled the cards afresh and the game resumed as usual.

CONCLUSION

HERMANN WENT OUT of his mind. He is now in room number 17 of the Obukhov Hospital. He returns no answer to questions put to him but mutters over and over again, with incredible rapidity: 'Three, seven, ace! Three, seven, queen!'

Lizaveta Ivanovna has married a very pleasant young man; he is in the civil service somewhere and has a good income. He is the son of the old countess's former steward. Lizaveta Ivanovna in her turn is bringing up a poor relative.

And Tomsky, who has been promoted to the rank of captain, has married the Princess Pauline.

Jean Rhys
1894–1979

Her stormy early years, first in the West Indies and then as the wife of a poet in 1920s Paris, gave Jean Rhys material for a collection of stories and four novels. After these met with an unenthusiastic response, she led a reclusive life, but at seventy she was finally rediscovered, when she staged a triumph with the publication of her prize-winning novel, *Wide Sargasso Sea*.

I USED TO LIVE HERE ONCE

S HE WAS STANDING by the river looking at the steppingstones and remembering each one. There was the round unsteady stone, the pointed one, the flat one in the middle—the safe stone where you could stand and look round. The next wasn't so safe for when the river was full, the water flowed over it and even when it showed dry it was slippery. But after that it was easy and soon she was standing on the other side.

The road was much wider than it used to be but the work had been done carelessly. The felled trees had not been cleared away and the bushes looked trampled. Yet it was the same road and she walked along feeling extraordinarily happy.

It was a fine day, a blue day. The only thing was that the sky had a glassy look that she didn't remember. That was the only word she could think of. Glassy. She turned the corner, saw that what had been the old *pavé* had been taken up, and there too the road was much wider, but it had the same unfinished look.

She came to the worn stone steps that led up to the house and her heart began to beat. The screw pine was gone, so was the mock summerhouse called the *ajoupa*, but the clove tree was still there and at the top of the steps the rough lawn stretched away, just as she remembered it. She stopped and looked towards the house that had been added to and painted white. It was strange to see a car standing in front of it.

There were two children under the big mango tree, a boy and a little girl, and

431

she waved to them and called 'Hello' but they didn't answer her or turn their heads. Very fair children, as Europeans born in the West Indies so often are: as if the white blood is asserting itself against all odds.

The grass was yellow in the hot sunlight as she walked towards them. When she was quite close she called again shyly: 'Hello.' Then, 'I used to live here once,' she said.

Still they didn't answer. When she said for the third time 'Hello' she was quite near them. Her arms went out instinctively with the longing to touch them.

It was the boy who turned. His grey eyes looked straight into hers. His expression didn't change. He said: 'Hasn't it gone cold all of a sudden. D'you notice? Let's go in.' 'Yes, let's,' said the girl.

Her arms fell to her sides as she watched them running across the grass to the house. That was the first time she knew.

Robert Louis Stevenson

1850–1894

Although he died at the age of only forty-four, after a long struggle against tuberculosis, Robert Louis Stevenson wrote three of the most enduringly popular books in English literature—*Treasure Island*, *Kidnapped* and *The Strange Case of Dr Jekyll and Mr Hyde*. Fascinated by evil in all its manifestations, he was also the creator of superb supernatural stories such as this grisly tale.

THE BODY-SNATCHER

EVERY NIGHT IN THE YEAR, four of us sat in the small parlour of the George at Debenham—the undertaker, and the landlord, and Fettes, and myself. Sometimes there would be more; but blow high, blow low, come rain or snow or frost, we four would be each planted in his own particular armchair. Fettes was an old drunken Scotsman, a man of education obviously, and a man of some property, since he lived in idleness. He had come to Debenham years ago, while still young, and by a mere continuance of living had grown to be an adopted townsman. His blue camlet cloak was a local antiquity, like the church spire. His place in the parlour at the George, his absence from church, his old, crapulous, disreputable vices, were all things of course in Debenham. He had some vague Radical opinions and some fleeting infidelities, which he would now and again set forth and emphasise with tottering slaps upon the table. He drank rum—five glasses regularly every evening; and for the greater portion of his nightly visit to the George sat, with his glass in his right hand, in a state of melancholy alcoholic saturation. We called him the Doctor, for he was supposed to have some special knowledge of medicine, and had been known, upon a pinch, to set a fracture or reduce a dislocation; but, beyond these slight particulars, we had no knowledge of his character and antecedents.

One dark winter night—it had struck nine some time before the landlord joined us—there was a sick man in the George, a great neighbouring proprietor suddenly struck down with apoplexy on his way to Parliament; and the great man's still greater London doctor had been telegraphed to his bedside. It was the first time that such a thing had happened in Debenham, for the railway was but newly open, and we were all proportionately moved by the occurrence.

'He's come,' said the landlord, after he had filled and lighted his pipe.

'He?' said I. 'Who?—not the doctor?'

'Himself,' replied our host.

'What is his name?'

'Dr Macfarlane,' said the landlord.

Fettes was far through his third tumbler, stupidly fuddled, now nodding over, now staring mazily around him; but at the last word he seemed to awaken, and repeated the name 'Macfarlane' twice, quietly enough the first time, but with sudden emotion at the second.

'Yes,' said the landlord, 'that's his name, Doctor Wolfe Macfarlane.'

Fettes became instantly sober: his eyes awoke, his voice became clear, loud, and steady, his language forcible and earnest. We were all startled by the transformation, as if a man had risen from the dead.

'I beg your pardon,' he said, 'I am afraid I have not been paying much attention to your talk. Who is this Wolfe Macfarlane?' And then, when he had heard the landlord out, 'It cannot be, it cannot be,' he added; 'and yet I would like well to see him face to face.'

'Do you know him, Doctor?' asked the undertaker, with a gasp.

'God forbid!' was the reply. 'And yet the name is a strange one; it were too much to fancy two. Tell me, landlord, is he old?'

'Well,' said the host, 'he's not a young man, to be sure, and his hair is white; but he looks younger than you.'

'He is older, though; years older. But,' with a slap upon the table, 'it's the rum you see in my face—rum and sin. This man, perhaps, may have an easy conscience and a good digestion. Conscience! Hear me speak. You would think I was some good, old, decent Christian, would you not? But no, not I; I never canted. Voltaire might have canted if he'd stood in my shoes; but the brains'—with a rattling fillip on his bald head—'the brains were clear and active, and I saw and made no deductions.'

'If you know this doctor,' I ventured to remark, after a somewhat awful pause, 'I should gather that you do not share the landlord's good opinion.'

Fettes paid no regard to me.

'Yes,' he said, with sudden decision, 'I must see him face to face.'

There was another pause, and then a door was closed rather sharply on the first floor, and a step was heard upon the stair.

'That's the doctor,' cried the landlord. 'Look sharp, and you can catch him.'

It was but two steps from the small parlour to the door of the old George inn; the wide oak staircase landed almost in the street; there was room for a Turkey rug and nothing more between the threshold and the last round of the descent; but this little space was every evening brilliantly lit up, not only by the light upon the stair and the great signal lamp below the sign, but by the warm radiance of the bar-room window. The George thus brightly advertised itself to passers-by in the cold street. Fettes walked steadily to the spot, and we, who were hanging behind, beheld the two men meet, as one of them had phrased it, face to face. Dr Macfarlane was alert and vigorous. His white hair set off his pale and placid, although energetic, countenance. He was richly dressed in the finest of broadcloth and the whitest of linen, with a great gold watch chain, and studs and spectacles of the same precious material. He wore a broad-folded tie, white and speckled with lilac, and he carried on his arm a comfortable driving coat of fur. There was no doubt but he became his years, breathing as he did, of wealth and consideration; and it was a surprising contrast to see our parlour sot—bald, dirty, pimpled, and robed in his old camlet cloak—confront him at the bottom of the stairs.

'Macfarlane!' he said somewhat loudly, more like a herald than a friend.

The great doctor pulled up short on the fourth step, as though the familiarity of the address surprised and somewhat shocked his dignity.

'Toddy Macfarlane!' repeated Fettes.

The London man almost staggered. He stared for the swiftest of seconds at the man before him, glanced behind him with a sort of scare, and then in a startled whisper, 'Fettes!' he said, 'you!'

'Ay,' said the other, 'me! Did you think I was dead too? We are not so easy shut of our acquaintance.'

'Hush, hush!' exclaimed the doctor. 'Hush, hush! this meeting is so unexpected—I can see you are unmanned. I hardly knew you, I confess, at first; but I am overjoyed—overjoyed to have this opportunity. For the present it must be how-d'ye-do and goodbye in one, for my fly is waiting, and I must not fail the train; but you shall—let me see—yes—you shall give me your address, and you can count on early news of me. We must do something for you, Fettes. I fear you are out at elbows; but we must see to that for auld lang syne, as once we sang at suppers.'

'Money!' cried Fettes; 'money from you! The money that I had from you is lying where I cast it in the rain.'

Dr Macfarlane had talked himself into some measure of superiority and confidence, but the uncommon energy of this refusal cast him back into his first confusion.

A horrible, ugly look came and went across his almost venerable countenance. 'My dear fellow,' he said, 'be it as you please; my last thought is to offend you. I would intrude on none. I will leave you my address, however—'

'I do not wish it—I do not wish to know the roof that shelters you,' interrupted the other. 'I heard your name; I feared it might be you; I wished to know if, after all, there were a God; I know now that there is none. Begone!'

He still stood in the middle of the rug, between the stair and the doorway; and the great London physician, in order to escape, would be forced to step to one side. It was plain that he hesitated before the thought of this humiliation. White as he was, there was a dangerous glitter in his spectacles; but while he still paused uncertain, he became aware that the driver of his fly was peering in from the street at this unusual scene and caught a glimpse at the same time of our little body from the parlour, huddled by the corner of the bar. The presence of so many witnesses decided him at once to flee. He crouched together, brushing on the wainscot, and made a dart like a serpent, striking for the door. But his tribulation was not yet entirely at an end, for even as he was passing Fettes clutched him by the arm and these words came in a whisper, and yet painfully distinct, 'Have you seen it again?'

The great rich London doctor cried out aloud with a sharp, throttling cry; he dashed his questioner across the open space, and, with his hands over his head, fled out of the door like a detected thief. Before it had occurred to one of us to make a movement, the fly was already rattling towards the station. The scene was over like a dream, but the dream had left proofs and traces of its passage. Next day the servant found the fine gold spectacles broken on the threshold, and that very night we were all standing breathless by the bar-room window, and Fettes at our side, sober, pale, and resolute in look.

'God protect us, Mr Fettes!' said the landlord, coming first into possession of his customary senses. 'What in the universe is all this? These are strange things you have been saying.'

Fettes turned towards us; he looked us each in succession in the face. 'See if you can hold your tongues,' said he. 'That man Macfarlane is not safe to cross; those that have done so already have repented it too late.'

And then, without so much as finishing his third glass, far less waiting for the other two, he bade us goodbye and went forth, under the lamp of the hotel, into the black night.

We three turned to our places in the parlour, with the big red fire and four clear candles; and as we recapitulated what had passed the first chill of our surprise soon changed into a glow of curiosity. We sat late; it was the latest session I have known in the old George. Each man, before we parted, had his theory that he was bound to prove; and none of us had any nearer business in this world than to track out the past of our condemned companion, and surprise the secret that he shared with the great London doctor. It is no great boast, but I believe I was a better hand at worming out a story than either of my fellows at the George; and perhaps there is now no other man alive who could narrate to you the following foul and unnatural events.

In his young days Fettes studied medicine in the schools of Edinburgh. He had talent of a kind, the talent that picks up swiftly what it hears and readily retails it for its own. He worked little at home; but he was civil, attentive, and intelligent in the presence of his masters. They soon picked him out as a lad who listened closely and remembered well; nay, strange as it seemed to me when I first heard it, he was in those days well favoured, and pleased by his exterior. There was, at that period, a certain extramural teacher of anatomy, whom I shall here designate by the letter K. His name was subsequently too well known. The man who bore it skulked through the streets of Edinburgh in disguise, while the mob that applauded at the execution of Burke called loudly for the blood of his employer. But Mr K— was then at the top of his vogue; he enjoyed a popularity due partly to his own talent and address, partly to the incapacity of his rival, the university professor. The students, at least, swore by his name, and Fettes believed himself, and was believed by others, to have laid the foundations of success when he had acquired the favour of this meteorically famous man. Mr K— was a bon vivant as well as an accomplished teacher; he liked a sly allusion no less than a careful preparation. In both capacities Fettes enjoyed and deserved his notice, and by the second year of his attendance he held the half-regular position of second demonstrator or sub-assistant in his class.

In this capacity, the charge of the theatre and lecture room devolved in particular upon his shoulders. He had to answer for the cleanliness of the premises and the conduct of the other students, and it was a part of his duty to supply, receive, and divide the various subjects. It was with a view to this last—at that time very delicate—affair that he was lodged by Mr K— in the same wynd, and at last in the same building, with the dissecting rooms. Here, after a night of turbulent pleasures, his hand still tottering, his sight still misty and confused, he would be called out of bed in the black hours before the winter dawn by the unclean and desperate interlopers who supplied the table. He would open the door to these men, since infamous throughout the land. He would help them with their tragic burthen, pay them their sordid price, and remain alone, when they were gone, with the unfriendly relics of humanity. From such a scene he would return to snatch another hour or two of slumber, to repair the abuses of the night, and refresh himself for the labours of the day.

Few lads could have been more insensible to the impressions of a life thus passed among the ensigns of mortality. His mind was closed against all general considerations. He was incapable of interest in the fate and fortunes of another, the slave of his own desires and low ambitions. Cold, light, and selfish in the last resort, he had that modicum of prudence, miscalled morality, which keeps a man from inconvenient drunkenness or punishable theft. He coveted, besides, a measure of consideration from his masters and his fellow pupils, and he had no desire to fail conspicuously in the external parts of life. Thus he made it his pleasure to gain some distinction in his studies, and day after day rendered unimpeachable eye-service to his employer, Mr K—. For his day of work he indemnified himself by nights of roaring, blackguardly enjoyment; and when that balance had been struck, the organ that he called his conscience declared itself content.

The supply of subjects was a continual trouble to him as well as to his master. In that large and busy class, the raw material of the anatomists kept perpetually running out; and the business thus rendered necessary was not only unpleasant in itself, but threatened dangerous consequences to all who were concerned. It was the policy of Mr K— to ask no questions in his dealings with the trade. 'They bring the body, and we pay the price,' he used to say, dwelling on the alliteration—*quid pro quo*. And, again, and somewhat profanely, 'Ask no questions,' he would tell his assistants, 'for conscience' sake.' There was no understanding that the subjects were provided by the crime of murder. Had that idea been broached to him in words, he would have recoiled in horror; but the lightness of his speech upon so grave a matter was, in itself, an offence against good manners, and a temptation to the men with whom he dealt. Fettes, for instance, had often remarked to himself upon the singular freshness of the bodies. He had been struck again and again by the hangdog, abominable looks of the ruffians who came to him before the dawn; and, putting things together clearly in his private thoughts, he perhaps attributed a meaning too immoral and too categorical to the unguarded counsels of his master. He understood his duty, in short, to have three branches: to take what was brought, to pay the price, and to avert the eye from any evidence of crime.

One November morning this policy of silence was put sharply to the test. He had been awake all night with a racking toothache—pacing his room like a caged beast or throwing himself in fury on his bed—and had fallen at last into that profound, uneasy slumber that so often follows on a night of pain, when he was awakened by the third or fourth angry repetition of the concerted signal. There was a thin, bright moonshine: it was bitter cold, windy, and frosty; the town had not yet awakened, but an indefinable stir already preluded the noise and business of the day. The ghouls had come later than usual, and they seemed more than usually eager to be gone. Fettes, sick with sleep, lighted them upstairs. He heard their grumbling Irish voices through a dream; and as they stripped the sack from their sad merchandise he leaned dozing, with his shoulder propped against the wall; he had to shake himself to find the men their money. As he did so his eyes lighted on the dead face. He started; he took two steps nearer, with the candle raised.

'God Almighty!' he cried. 'That is Jane Galbraith!'

The men answered nothing, but they shuffled nearer the door.

'I know her, I tell you,' he continued. 'She was alive and hearty yesterday. It's impossible she can be dead; it's impossible you should have got this body fairly.'

'Sure, sir, you're mistaken entirely,' said one of the men.

But the other looked Fettes darkly in the eyes, and demanded the money on the spot.

It was impossible to misconceive the threat or to exaggerate the danger. The lad's heart failed him. He stammered some excuses, counted out the sum, and saw his hateful visitors depart. No sooner were they gone than he hastened to confirm his doubts. By a dozen unquestionable marks he identified the girl he had jested with the day before. He saw, with horror, marks upon her body that might well betoken violence. A panic seized him, and he took refuge in his room. There he reflected at length over the discovery that he had made;

considered soberly the bearing of Mr K—'s instructions and the danger to himself of interference in so serious a business, and at last, in sore perplexity, determined to wait for the advice of his immediate superior, the class assistant.

This was a young doctor, Wolfe Macfarlane, a high favourite among all the reckless students, clever, dissipated, and unscrupulous to the last degree. He had travelled and studied abroad. His manners were agreeable and a little forward. He was an authority on the stage, skilful on the ice or the links with skate or golf club; he dressed with nice audacity, and, to put the finishing touch upon his glory, he kept a gig and a strong trotting horse. With Fettes he was on terms of intimacy; indeed their relative positions called for some community of life; and when subjects were scarce the pair would drive far into the country in Macfarlane's gig, visit and desecrate some lonely graveyard, and return before dawn with their booty to the door of the dissecting room.

On that particular morning Macfarlane arrived somewhat earlier than his wont. Fettes heard him, and met him on the stairs, told him his story, and showed him the cause of his alarm. Macfarlane examined the marks on her body.

'Yes,' he said with a nod, 'it looks fishy.'

'Well, what should I do?' asked Fettes.

'Do?' repeated the other. 'Do you want to do anything? Least said soonest mended, I should say.'

'Someone else might recognise her,' objected Fettes. 'She was as well known as the Castle Rock.'

'We'll hope not,' said Macfarlane, 'and if anybody does—well, you didn't, don't you see, and there's an end. The fact is, this has been going on too long. Stir up the mud, and you'll get K— into the most unholy trouble; you'll be in a shocking box yourself. So will I, if you come to that. I should like to know how any one of us would look, or what the devil we should have to say for ourselves, in any Christian witness box. For me, you know there's one thing certain—that, practically speaking, all our subjects have been murdered.'

'Macfarlane!' cried Fettes.

'Come now!' sneered the other. 'As if you hadn't suspected it yourself!'

'Suspecting is one thing—'

'And proof another. Yes, I know; and I'm as sorry as you are this should have come here,' tapping the body with his cane. 'The next best thing for me is not to recognise it; and,' he added coolly, 'I don't. You may, if you please. I don't dictate, but I think a man of the world would do as I do; and I may add, I fancy that is what K— would look for at our hands. The question is, Why did he choose us two for his assistants? And I answer, because he didn't want old wives.'

This was the tone of all others to affect the mind of a lad like Fettes. He agreed to imitate Macfarlane. The body of the unfortunate girl was duly dissected, and no one remarked or appeared to recognise her.

One afternoon, when his day's work was over, Fettes dropped into a popular tavern and found Macfarlane sitting with a stranger. This was a small man, very pale and dark, with coal-black eyes. The cut of his features gave a promise of intellect and refinement which was but feebly realised in his manners, for he proved, upon a nearer acquaintance, coarse, vulgar, and stupid. He exercised, however, a very remarkable control over Macfarlane; issued orders like the Great Bashaw; became inflamed at the least discussion or delay, and commented rudely on the servility with which he was obeyed. This most offensive person took a fancy to Fettes on the spot, plied him with drinks, and honoured him with unusual confidences on his past career. If a tenth part of what he confessed were true, he was a very loathsome rogue; and the lad's vanity was tickled by the attention of so experienced a man.

'I'm a pretty bad fellow myself,' the stranger remarked, 'but Macfarlane is the boy—Toddy Macfarlane I call him. Toddy, order your friend another glass.' Or it might be, 'Toddy, you jump up and shut the door.' 'Toddy hates me,' he said again. 'Oh, yes, Toddy, you do!'

'Don't you call me that confounded name,' growled Macfarlane.

'Hear him! Did you ever see the lads play knife? He would like to do that all over my body,' remarked the stranger.

'We medicals have a better way than that,' said Fettes. 'When we dislike a dead friend of ours, we dissect him.'

Macfarlane looked up sharply, as though this jest was scarcely to his mind.

The afternoon passed. Gray, for that was the stranger's name, invited Fettes to join them at dinner, ordered a feast so sumptuous that the tavern was thrown in commotion, and when all was done commanded Macfarlane to settle the bill. It was late before they separated; the man Gray was incapably drunk. Macfarlane, sobered by his fury, chewed the cud of the money he had been forced to squander and the slights he had been obliged to swallow. Fettes, with various liquors singing in his head, returned home with devious footsteps and a mind entirely in abeyance. Next day Macfarlane was absent from the class, and Fettes smiled to himself as he imagined him still squiring the intolerable Gray from tavern to tavern. As soon as the hour of liberty had struck he posted from place to place in quest of his last night's companions. He could find them, however, nowhere; so returned early to his rooms, went early to bed, and slept the sleep of the just.

At four in the morning he was awakened by the well-known signal. Descending to the door, he was filled with astonishment to find Macfarlane with his gig, and in the gig one of those long and ghastly packages with which he was so well acquainted.

'What?' he cried. 'Have you been out alone? How did you manage?'

But Macfarlane silenced him roughly, bidding him turn to business. When they had got the body upstairs and laid it on the table, Macfarlane made at first as if he were going away. Then he paused and seemed to hesitate; and then, 'You had better look at the face,' said he, in tones of some constraint. 'You had better,' he repeated, as Fettes only stared at him in wonder.

'But where, and how, and when did you come by it?' cried the other.

'Look at the face,' was the only answer.

Fettes was staggered; strange doubts assailed him. He looked from the young doctor to the body, and then back again. At last, with a start, he did as he was bidden. He had almost expected the sight that met his eyes, and yet the shock was cruel. To see, fixed in the rigidity of death and naked on that coarse layer of sackcloth, the man whom he had left well clad and full of meat and sin upon the threshold of a tavern, awoke, even in the thoughtless Fettes, some of the terrors of the conscience. It was a *cras tibi* which re-echoed in his soul, that two whom he had known should have come to lie upon these icy tables. Yet these were only secondary thoughts. His first concern regarded Wolfe. Unprepared for a challenge so momentous, he knew not how to look his comrade in the face. He durst not meet his eye, and he had neither words nor voice at his command.

It was Macfarlane himself who made the first advance. He came up quietly behind and laid his hand gently but firmly on the other's shoulder.

'Richardson,' said he, 'may have the head.'

Now Richardson was a student who had long been anxious for that portion of the human subject to dissect. There was no answer, and the murderer resumed: 'Talking of business, you must pay me; your accounts, you see, must tally.'

Fettes found a voice, the ghost of his own: 'Pay you!' he cried. 'Pay you for that?'

'Why, yes, of course you must. By all means and on every possible account, you must,' returned the other. 'I dare not give it for nothing, you dare not take it for nothing; it would compromise us both. This is another case like Jane Galbraith's. The more things are wrong the more we must act as if all were right. Where does old K— keep his money?'

'There,' answered Fettes hoarsely, pointing to a cupboard in the corner.

'Give me the key, then,' said the other, calmly, holding out his hand.

There was an instant's hesitation, and the die was cast. Macfarlane could not suppress a nervous twitch, the infinitesimal mark of an immense relief, as he felt the key between his fingers. He opened the cupboard, brought out pen and ink and a paper-book that stood in one compartment, and separated from the funds in a drawer a sum suitable to the occasion.

'Now, look here,' he said, 'there is the payment made—first proof of your good faith: first step to your security. You have now to clinch it by a second. Enter the payment in your book, and then you for your part may defy the devil.'

The next few seconds were for Fettes an agony of thought; but in balancing his terrors it was the most immediate that triumphed. Any future difficulty seemed almost welcome if he could avoid a present quarrel with Macfarlane. He set down the candle which he had been carrying all the time, and with a steady hand entered the date, the nature, and the amount of the transaction.

'And now,' said Macfarlane, 'it's only fair that you should pocket the lucre. I've had my share already. By the bye, when a man of the world falls into a bit of luck, has a few shillings extra in his pocket—I'm ashamed to speak of it, but there's a rule of conduct in the case. No treating, no purchase of expensive class-books, no squaring of old debts; borrow, don't lend.'

'Macfarlane,' began Fettes, still somewhat hoarsely, 'I have put my neck in a halter to oblige you.'

'To oblige me?' cried Wolfe. 'Oh, come! You did, as near as I can see the matter, what you downright had to do in self-defence. Suppose I got into trouble, where would you be? This second little matter flows clearly from the first. Mr Gray is the continuation of Miss Galbraith. You can't begin and then stop. If you begin, you must keep on beginning; that's the truth. No rest for the wicked.'

A horrible sense of blackness and the treachery of fate seized hold upon the soul of the unhappy student.

'My God!' he cried, 'but what have I done? and when did I begin? To be made a class assistant—in the name of reason, where's the harm in that? Service wanted the position; Service might have got it. Would *he* have been where *I* am now?'

'My dear fellow,' said Macfarlane, 'what a boy you are! What harm has come to you? What harm *can* come to you if you hold your tongue? Why, man, do you know what this life is? There are two squads of us—the lions and the lambs. If you're a lamb, you'll come to lie upon these tables like Gray or Jane Galbraith; if you're a lion, you'll live and drive a horse like me, like K——, like all the world with any wit or courage. You're staggered at the first. But look at K——! My dear fellow, you're clever, you have pluck. I like you, and K—— likes you. You were born to lead the hunt; and I tell you, on my honour and my experience of life, three days from now you'll laugh at all these scarecrows like a high-school boy at a farce.'

And with that Macfarlane took his departure and drove off up the wynd in his gig to get under cover before daylight. Fettes was thus left alone with his regrets. He saw the miserable peril in which he stood involved. He saw, with inexpressible dismay, that there was no limit to his weakness, and that, from concession to concession, he had fallen from the arbiter of Macfarlane's destiny to his paid and helpless accomplice. He would have given the world to have been a little braver at the time, but it did not occur to him that he might still be brave. The secret of Jane Galbraith and the cursed entry in the daybook closed his mouth.

Hours passed; the class began to arrive; the members of the unhappy Gray were dealt out to one and to another, and received without remark. Richardson was made happy with the head; and before the hour of freedom rang Fettes trembled with exultation to perceive how far they had already gone towards safety.

For two days he continued to watch, with increasing joy, the dreadful process of disguise.

On the third day Macfarlane made his appearance. He had been ill, he said;

but he made up for lost time by the energy with which he directed the students. To Richardson in particular he extended the most valuable assistance and advice, and that student, encouraged by the praise of the demonstrator, burned high with ambitious hopes, and saw the medal already in his grasp.

Before the week was out Macfarlane's prophecy had been fulfilled. Fettes had outlived his terrors and had forgotten his baseness. He began to plume himself upon his courage, and had so arranged the story in his mind that he could look back on these events with an unhealthy pride. Of his accomplice he saw but little. They met, of course, in the business of the class; they received their orders together from Mr K——. At times they had a word or two in private, and Macfarlane was from first to last particularly kind and jovial. But it was plain that he avoided any reference to their common secret; and even when Fettes whispered to him that he had cast in his lot with the lions and forsworn the lambs, he only signed to him smilingly to hold his peace.

At length an occasion arose which threw the pair once more into a closer union. Mr K—— was again short of subjects; pupils were eager, and it was a part of this teacher's pretensions to be always well supplied. At the same time there came the news of a burial in the rustic graveyard of Glencorse. Time has little changed the place in question. It stood then, as now, upon a crossroad, out of call of human habitations, and buried fathom deep in the foliage of six cedar trees. The cries of the sheep upon the neighbouring hills, the streamlets upon either hand, one loudly singing among pebbles, the other dripping furtively from pond to pond, the stir of the wind in mountainous old flowering chestnuts, and once in seven days the voice of the bell and the old tunes of the precentor, were the only sounds that disturbed the silence around the rural church. The resurrection man—to use a by-name of the period—was not to be deterred by any of the sanctities of customary piety. It was part of his trade to despise and desecrate the scrolls and trumpets of old tombs, the paths worn by the feet of worshippers and mourners, and the offerings and the inscriptions of bereaved affection. To rustic neighbourhoods, where love is more than commonly tenacious, and where some bonds of blood or fellowship unite the entire society of a parish, the body-snatcher, far from being repelled by natural respect, was attracted by the ease and safety of the task. To bodies that had been laid in earth, in joyful expectation of a far different awakening, there came that hasty, lamplit, terror-haunted resurrection of the spade and mattock. The coffin was forced, the cerements torn, and the melancholy relics, clad in sackcloth, after being rattled for hours on moonless byways, were at length exposed to uttermost indignities before a class of gaping boys.

Somewhat as two vultures may swoop upon a dying lamb, Fettes and Macfarlane were to be let loose upon a grave in that green and quiet resting place. The wife of a farmer, a woman who had lived for sixty years, and been known for nothing but good butter and a godly conversation, was to be rooted from her grave at midnight and carried, dead and naked, to that faraway city that she had always honoured with her Sunday best; the place beside her family was to be empty till the crack of doom; her innocent and almost venerable members to be exposed to that last curiosity of the anatomist.

Late one afternoon the pair set forth, well wrapped in cloaks and furnished with a formidable bottle. It rained without remission—a cold, dense, lashing rain. Now and again there blew a puff of wind, but these sheets of falling water kept it down. Bottle and all, it was a sad and silent drive as far as Penicuik, where they were to spend the evening. They stopped once, to hide their implements in a thick bush not far from the churchyard, and once again at the Fisher's Tryst, to have a toast before the kitchen fire and vary their nips of whisky with a glass of ale. When they reached their journey's end the gig was housed, the horse was fed and comforted, and the two young doctors in a private room sat down to the best dinner and the best wine the house afforded. The lights, the fire, the beating rain upon the window, the cold incongruous work that lay before them, added zest to their enjoyment of the meal. With every glass their cordiality increased. Soon Macfarlane handed a little pile of gold to his companion.

'A compliment,' he said. 'Between friends these little d—d accommodations ought to fly like pipe-lights.'

Fettes pocketed the money, and applauded the sentiment to the echo. 'You are a philosopher,' he cried. 'I was an ass till I knew you. You and K— between you, by the Lord Harry! but you'll make a man of me.'

'Of course we shall,' applauded Macfarlane. 'A man? I tell you, it required a man to back me up the other morning. There are some big, brawling, forty-year-old cowards who would have turned sick at the look of the d—d thing; but not you—you kept your head. I watched you.'

'Well, and why not?' Fettes thus vaunted himself. 'It was no affair of mine. There was nothing to gain on the one side but disturbance, and on the other I could count on your gratitude, don't you see?' And he slapped his pocket till the gold pieces rang.

Macfarlane somehow felt a certain touch of alarm at these unpleasant words. He may have regretted that he had taught his young companion so successfully, but he had no time to interfere, for the other noisily continued in this boastful strain:

'The great thing is not to be afraid. Now, between you and me, I don't want to hang—that's practical; but for all cant, Macfarlane, I was born with a contempt. Hell, God, Devil, right, wrong, sin, crime, and all the old gallery of curiosities—they may frighten boys, but men of the world, like you and me, despise them. Here's to the memory of Gray!'

It was by this time growing somewhat late. The gig, according to order, was brought round to the door with both lamps brightly shining, and the young men had to pay their bill and take the road. They announced that they were bound for Peebles, and drove in that direction till they were clear of the last houses of the town; then, extinguishing the lamps, returned upon their course, and followed a byroad towards Glencorse. There was no sound but that of their own passage, and the incessant, strident pouring of the rain. It was pitch-dark; here and there a white gate or a white stone in the wall guided them for a short space across the night; but for the most part it was at a foot pace, and almost groping, that they picked their way through that resonant blackness to their solemn and isolated destination. In the sunken woods that traverse the neighbourhood of the burying ground the last glimmer failed them, and it became necessary to kindle a match and reillumine one of the lanterns of the gig. Thus, under the dripping trees, and environed by huge and moving shadows, they reached the scene of their unhallowed labours.

They were both experienced in such affairs, and powerful with the spade; and they had scarce been twenty minutes at their task before they were rewarded by a dull rattle on the coffin lid. At the same moment Macfarlane, having hurt his hand upon a stone, flung it carelessly above his head. The grave, in which they now stood almost to the shoulders, was close to the edge of the plateau of the graveyard; and the gig lamp had been propped, the better to illuminate their labours, against a tree, and on the immediate verge of the steep bank descending to the stream. Chance had taken a sure aim with the stone. Then came a clang of broken glass; night fell upon them; sounds alternately dull and ringing announced the bounding of the lantern down the bank, and its occasional collision with the trees. A stone or two, which it had dislodged in its descent, rattled behind it into the profundities of the glen; and then silence, like night, resumed its sway; and they might bend their hearing to its utmost pitch, but naught was to be heard except the rain, now marching to the wind, now steadily falling over miles of open country.

They were so nearly at an end of their abhorred task that they judged it wisest to complete it in the dark. The coffin was exhumed and broken open; the body inserted in the dripping sack and carried between them to the gig; one mounted to keep it in its place, and the other, taking the horse by the mouth, groped along by wall and bush until they reached the wider road by the Fisher's Tryst. Here was a faint, diffused radiancy, which they hailed like daylight; by that they pushed the horse to a good pace and began to rattle along merrily in the direction of the town.

They had both been wetted to the skin during their operations, and now, as the gig jumped among the deep ruts, the thing that stood propped between them fell now upon one and now upon the other. At every repetition of the horrid contact each instinctively repelled it with greater haste; and the process, natural although it was, began to tell upon the nerves of the companions. Macfarlane made some ill-favoured jest about the farmer's wife, but it came hollowly from his lips, and was allowed to drop in silence. Still their unnatural burthen bumped from side to side; and now the head would be laid, as if in confidence, upon their shoulders, and now the drenching sackcloth would flap icily about their faces. A creeping chill began to possess the soul of Fettes. He peered at the bundle, and it seemed somehow larger than at first. All over the country-side, and from every degree of distance, the farm dogs accompanied their passage with tragic ululations; and it grew and grew upon his mind that some unnatural miracle had been accomplished, that some nameless change had befallen the dead body, and that it was in fear of their unholy burden that the dogs were howling.

'For God's sake,' said he, making a great effort to arrive at speech, 'for God's sake, let's have a light!'

Seemingly Macfarlane was affected in the same direction; for though he made no reply, he stopped the horse, passed the reins to his companion, got down, and proceeded to kindle the remaining lamp. They had by that time got no further than the crossroad down to Auchendinny. The rain still poured as though the deluge were returning, and it was no easy matter to make a light in such a world of wet and darkness. When at last the flickering blue flame had been transferred to the wick and began to expand and clarify, and shed a wide circle of misty brightness round the gig, it became possible for the two young men to see each other and the thing they had along with them. The rain had moulded the rough sacking to the outlines of the body underneath; the head was distinct from the trunk, the shoulders plainly modelled; something at once spectral and human riveted their eyes upon the ghastly comrade of their drive.

For some time Macfarlane stood motionless, holding up the lamp. A nameless dread was swathed, like a wet sheet, about the body, and tightened the white skin upon the face of Fettes; a fear that was meaningless, a horror of what could not be, kept mounting to his brain. Another beat of the watch, and he had spoken. But his comrade forestalled him.

'That is not a woman,' said Macfarlane, in a hushed voice.

'It was a woman when we put her in,' whispered Fettes.

'Hold that lamp,' said the other. 'I must see her face.'

And as Fettes took the lamp his companion untied the fastenings of the sack and drew down the cover from the head. The light fell very clear upon the dark, well-moulded features and smooth-shaven cheeks of a too familiar countenance, often beheld in dreams of both of these young men. A wild yell rang up into the night; each leaped from his own side into the roadway; the lamp fell, broke, and was extinguished; and the horse, terrified by this unusual commotion, bounded and went off towards Edinburgh at a gallop, bearing along with it, sole occupant of the gig, the body of the dead and long-dissected Gray.

Bram Stoker

1847–1912

Best known today as the author of the chilling vampire tale
Dracula, Bram Stoker wrote a number of popular novels and
supernatural short stories. Always fascinated by the theatre, he
gave up his career as a civil servant to become secretary and
touring manager to the famous actor-manager Henry Irving at
the Lyceum Theatre in London.

THE JUDGE'S HOUSE

WHEN THE TIME for his examination drew near, Malcolm Malcolmson
made up his mind to go somewhere to read by himself. He feared the
attractions of the seaside, and also he feared completely rural isolation,
for of old he knew its charms, and so he determined to find some unpretentious
little town where there would be nothing to distract him. He refrained from
asking suggestions from any of his friends, for he argued that each would recommend some place of which he had knowledge, and where he had already
acquaintances. As Malcolmson wished to avoid friends he had no wish to
encumber himself with the attention of friends' friends, and so he determined to
look out for a place for himself. He packed a portmanteau with some clothes
and all the books he required, and then took ticket for the first name on the local
timetable which he did not know.

When at the end of three hours' journey he alighted at Benchurch, he felt satisfied that he had so far obliterated his tracks as to be sure of having a peaceful
opportunity of pursuing his studies. He went straight to the one inn which the
sleepy little place contained, and put up for the night. Benchurch was a market
town, and once in three weeks was crowded to excess, but for the remainder of
the twenty-one days it was as attractive as a desert. Malcolmson looked around
the day after his arrival to try to find quarters more isolated than even so quiet an
inn as 'The Good Traveller' afforded. There was only one place which took his
fancy, and it certainly satisfied his wildest ideas regarding quiet; in fact, quiet

was not the proper word to apply to it—desolation was the only term conveying any suitable idea of its isolation. It was an old, rambling, heavy-built house of the Jacobean style, with heavy gables and windows, unusually small, and set higher than was customary in such houses, and was surrounded with a high brick wall massively built. Indeed, on examination, it looked more like a fortified house than an ordinary dwelling. But all these things pleased Malcolmson. 'Here,' he thought, 'is the very spot I have been looking for, and if I can only get opportunity of using it I shall be happy.' His joy was increased when he realised beyond doubt that it was not at present inhabited.

From the post office he got the name of the agent, who was rarely surprised at the application to rent a part of the old house. Mr Carnford, the local lawyer and agent, was a genial old gentleman, and frankly confessed his delight at anyone being willing to live in the house.

'To tell you the truth,' said he, 'I should be only too happy, on behalf of the owners, to let anyone have the house rent free for a term of years if only to accustom the people here to see it inhabited. It has been so long empty that some kind of absurd prejudice has grown up about it, and this can be best put down by its occupation—if only,' he added with a sly glance at Malcolmson, 'by a scholar like yourself, who wants its quiet for a time.'

Malcolmson thought it needless to ask the agent about the 'absurd prejudice'; he knew he would get more information, if he should require it, on that subject from other quarters. He paid his three months' rent, got a receipt, and the name of an old woman who would probably undertake to 'do' for him, and came away with the keys in his pocket. He then went to the landlady of the inn, who was a cheerful and most kindly person, and asked her advice as to such stores and provisions as he would be likely to require. She threw up her hands in amazement when he told her where he was going to settle himself.

'Not in the Judge's House!' she said, and grew pale as she spoke. He explained the locality of the house, saying that he did not know its name. When he had finished she answered:

'Aye, sure enough—sure enough the very place! It is the Judge's House sure enough.' He asked her to tell him about the place, why so called, and what there was against it. She told him that it was so called locally because it had been many years before—how long she could not say, as she was herself from another part of the country, but she thought it must have been a hundred years or more—the abode of a judge who was held in great terror on account of his harsh sentences and his hostility to prisoners at assizes. As to what there was against the house itself she could not tell. She had often asked, but no one could inform her; but there was a general feeling that there was *something*, and for her own part she would not take all the money in Drinkwater's Bank and stay in the house an hour by herself. Then she apologised to Malcolmson for her disturbing talk.

'It is too bad of me, sir, and you—and a young gentleman, too—if you will pardon me saying it, going to live there all alone. If you were my boy—and you'll excuse me for saying it—you wouldn't sleep there a night, not if I had to go there myself and pull the big alarm bell that's on the roof!' The good creature was so manifestly in earnest, and was so kindly in her intentions, that Malcolmson, although amused, was touched. He told her kindly how much he appreciated her interest in him, and added:

'But, my dear Mrs Witham, indeed you need not be concerned about me! A man who is reading for the Mathematical Tripos has too much to think of to be disturbed by any of these mysterious "somethings", and his work is of too exact and prosaic a kind to allow of his having any corner in his mind for mysteries of any kind. Harmonical Progression, Permutations and Combinations, and Elliptic Functions have sufficient mysteries for me!' Mrs Witham kindly under-took to see after his commissions, and he went himself to look for the old woman who had been recommended to him. When he returned to the Judge's House with her, after an interval of a couple of hours, he found Mrs Witham herself waiting with several men and boys carrying parcels, and an upholsterer's man with a bed in a cart, for she said, though tables and chairs might be all very well, a bed that hadn't been aired for mayhap fifty years was not proper for young bones to lie on. She was evidently curious to see the inside of the house; and though manifestly so afraid of the 'somethings' that at the slightest sound she clutched on to Malcolmson, whom she never left for a moment, went over the whole place.

After his examination of the house, Malcolmson decided to take up his abode in the great dining room, which was big enough to serve for all his require-ments; and Mrs Witham, with the aid of the charwoman, Mrs Dempster, proceeded to arrange matters. When the hampers were brought in and unpacked, Malcolmson saw that with much kind forethought she had sent from her own kitchen sufficient provisions to last for a few days. Before going she expressed all sorts of kind wishes; and at the door turned and said:

'And perhaps, sir, as the room is big and draughty it might be well to have one of those big screens put round your bed at night—though, truth to tell, I would die myself if I were to be so shut in with all kinds of—of "things", that put their heads round the sides, or over the top, and look on me!' The image which she had called up was too much for her nerves, and she fled incontinently.

Mrs Dempster sniffed in a superior manner as the landlady disappeared, and remarked that for her own part she wasn't afraid of all the bogies in the kingdom.

'I'll tell you what it is, sir,' she said; 'bogies is all kinds and sorts of things—except bogies! Rats and mice, and beetles; and creaky doors, and loose slates, and broken panes, and stiff drawer handles, that stay out when you pull them and then fall down in the middle of the night. Look at the wainscot of the room! It is old—hundreds of years old! Do you think there's no rats and beetles there! And do you imagine, sir, that you won't see none of them! Rats is bogies, I tell you, and bogies is rats; and don't you get to think anything else!'

'Mrs Dempster,' said Malcolmson gravely, making her a polite bow, 'you know more than a Senior Wrangler! And let me say, that, as a mark of esteem for your indubitable soundness of head and heart, I shall, when I go, give you possession of this house, and let you stay here by yourself for the last two months of my tenancy, for four weeks will serve my purpose.'

'Thank you kindly, sir!' she answered, 'but I couldn't sleep away from home a night. I am in Greenhow's Charity, and if I slept a night away from my rooms I should lose all I have got to live on. The rules is very strict; and there's too many watching for a vacancy for me to run any risks in the matter. Only for that, sir, I'd gladly come here and attend on you altogether during your stay.'

'My good woman,' said Malcolmson hastily, 'I have come here on purpose to obtain solitude; and believe me that I am grateful to the late Greenhow for having so organised his admirable charity—whatever it is—that I am perforce denied the opportunity of suffering from such a form of temptation! Saint Anthony himself could not be more rigid on the point!'

The old woman laughed harshly. 'Ah, you young gentlemen,' she said, 'you don't fear for naught; and belike you'll get all the solitude you want here.' She set to work with her cleaning; and by nightfall, when Malcolmson returned from his walk—he always had one of his books to study as he walked—he found the room swept and tidied, a fire burning in the old hearth, the lamp lit, and the table spread for supper with Mrs Witham's excellent fare. 'This is comfort, indeed,' he said, as he rubbed his hands.

When he had finished his supper, and lifted the tray to the other end of the great oak dining table, he got out his books again, put fresh wood on the fire, trimmed his lamp, and set himself down to a spell of real hard work. He went on without pause till about eleven o'clock, when he knocked off for a bit to fix his fire and lamp, and to make himself a cup of tea. He had always been a tea-drinker, and during his college life had sat late at work and had taken tea late. The rest was a great luxury to him, and he enjoyed it with a sense of delicious, voluptuous ease. The renewed fire leaped and sparkled, and threw quaint shadows through the great old room; and as he sipped his hot tea he revelled in the sense of isolation from his kind. Then it was that he began to notice for the first time what a noise the rats were making.

'Surely,' he thought, 'they cannot have been at it all the time I was reading. Had they been, I must have noticed it!' Presently, when the noise increased, he satisfied himself that it was really new. It was evident that at first the rats had been frightened at the presence of a stranger, and the light of fire and lamp; but that as the time went on they had grown bolder and were now disporting themselves as was their wont.

How busy they were! and hark to the strange noises! Up and down behind the old wainscot, over the ceiling and under the floor they raced, and gnawed, and scratched! Malcolmson smiled to himself as he recalled to mind the saying of Mrs Dempster, 'Bogies is rats, and rats is bogies!' The tea began to have its effect of intellectual and nervous stimulus, he saw with joy another long spell of work to be done before the night was past, and in the sense of security which it gave him, he allowed himself the luxury of a good look round the room. He took his lamp in one hand, and went all around, wondering that so quaint and beautiful an old house had been so long neglected. The carving of the oak on the panels of the wainscot was fine, and on and round the doors and windows it was beautiful and of rare merit. There were some old pictures on the walls, but they were coated so thick with dust and dirt that he could not distinguish any detail of them, though he held his lamp as high as he could over his head. Here and there as he went round he saw some crack or hole blocked for a moment by the face of a rat with its bright eyes glittering in the light, but in an instant it was gone, and a squeak and a scamper followed.

The thing that most struck him, however, was the rope of the great alarm bell on the roof, which hung down in a corner of the room on the right-hand side of the fireplace. He pulled up close to the hearth a great high-backed carved oak chair, and sat down to his last cup of tea. When this was done he made up the fire, and went back to his work, sitting at the corner of the table, having the fire to his left. For a while the rats disturbed him somewhat with their perpetual scampering, but he got accustomed to the noise as one does to the ticking of a clock or to the roar of moving water; and he became so immersed in his work that everything in the world, except the problem which he was trying to solve, passed away from him.

He suddenly looked up, his problem was still unsolved, and there was in the air that sense of the hour before the dawn, which is so dread to doubtful life. The noise of the rats had ceased. Indeed it seemed to him that it must have ceased but lately and that it was the sudden cessation which had disturbed him. The fire had fallen low, but still it threw out a deep red glow. As he looked he started in spite of his sang-froid.

There on the great high-backed carved oak chair by the right side of the fireplace sat an enormous rat, steadily glaring at him with baleful eyes. He made a motion to it as though to hunt it away, but it did not stir. Then he made the motion of throwing something. Still it did not stir, but showed its great white teeth angrily, and its cruel eyes shone in the lamplight with an added vindictiveness.

Malcolmson felt amazed, and seizing the poker from the hearth ran at it to kill it. Before, however, he could strike it, the rat, with a squeak that sounded like the concentration of hate, jumped upon the floor, and, running up the rope of the alarm bell, disappeared in the darkness beyond the range of the green-shaded lamp. Instantly, strange to say, the noisy scampering of the rats in the wainscot began again.

By this time Malcolmson's mind was quite off the problem; and as a shrill cock-crow outside told him of the approach of morning, he went to bed and to sleep.

He slept so sound that he was not even waked by Mrs Dempster coming in to make up his room. It was only when she had tidied up the place and got his breakfast ready and tapped on the screen which closed in his bed that he woke. He was a little tired still after his night's hard work, but a strong cup of tea soon freshened him up, and, taking his book, he went out for his morning walk, bringing with him a few sandwiches lest he should not care to return till dinner time. He found a quiet walk between high elms some way outside the town, and here he spent the greater part of the day studying his Laplace. On his return he looked in to see Mrs Witham and to thank her for her kindness. When she saw him coming through the diamond-paned bay window of her sanctum she came out to meet him and asked him in. She looked at him searchingly and shook her head as she said:

'You must not overdo it, sir. You are paler this morning than you should be. Too late hours and too hard work on the brain isn't good for any man! But tell me, sir, how did you pass the night? Well, I hope? But, my heart! sir, I was glad when Mrs Dempster told me this morning that you were all right and sleeping sound when she went in.'

'Oh, I was all right,' he answered, smiling, 'the "somethings" didn't worry me, as yet. Only the rats; and they had a circus, I tell you, all over the place. There was one wicked-looking old devil that sat up on my own chair by the fire, and wouldn't go till I took the poker to him, and then he ran up the rope of the alarm bell and got to somewhere up the wall or the ceiling—I couldn't see where, it was so dark.'

'Mercy on us,' said Mrs Witham, 'an old devil, and sitting on a chair by the fireside! Take care, sir! take care! There's many a true word spoken in jest.'

'How do you mean? 'Pon my word I don't understand.'

'An old devil! The old devil, perhaps. There! sir, you needn't laugh,' for Malcolmson had broken into a hearty peal. 'You young folks thinks it easy to laugh at things that makes older ones shudder. Never mind, sir! never mind! Please God, you'll laugh all the time. It's what I wish you myself!' and the good lady beamed all over in sympathy with his enjoyment, her fears gone for a moment.

'Oh, forgive me!' said Malcolmson presently. 'Don't think me rude; but the idea was too much for me—that the old devil himself was on the chair last night!' And at the thought he laughed again. Then he went home to dinner.

This evening the scampering of the rats began earlier; indeed it had been going on before his arrival, and only ceased whilst his presence by its freshness disturbed them. After dinner he sat by the fire for a while and had a smoke; and then, having cleared his table, began to work as before. Tonight the rats disturbed him more than they had done on the previous night. How they scampered up and down and under and over! How they squeaked, and scratched, and gnawed! How they, getting bolder by degrees, came to the mouths of their holes and to the chinks and cracks and crannies in the wainscoting till their eyes shone like tiny lamps as the firelight rose and fell. But to him, now doubtless accustomed to them, their eyes were not wicked; only their play-fulness touched him. Sometimes the boldest of them made sallies out on the floor or along the mouldings of the wainscot. Now and again as they disturbed him Malcolmson made a sound to frighten them, smiting the table with his hand or giving a fierce 'Hsh, hsh,' so that they fled straightway to their holes.

And so the early part of the night wore on; and despite the noise Malcolmson got more and more immersed in his work.

All at once he stopped, as on the previous night, being overcome by a sudden sense of silence. There was not the faintest sound of gnaw, or scratch, or squeak. The silence was as of the grave. He remembered the odd occurrence of the pre-vious night, and instinctively he looked at the chair standing close by the fireside. And then a very odd sensation thrilled through him.

There, on the great old high-backed carved oak chair beside the fireplace sat the same enormous rat, steadily glaring at him with baleful eyes.

Instinctively he took the nearest thing to his hand, a book of logarithms, and flung it at it. The book was badly aimed and the rat did not stir, so again the poker performance of the previous night was repeated; and again the rat, being closely pursued, fled up the rope of the alarm bell. Strangely too, the departure of this rat was instantly followed by the renewal of the noise made by the general rat community. On this occasion, as on the previous one, Malcolmson could not see at what part of the room the rat disappeared, for the green shade of his lamp left the upper part of the room in darkness, and the fire had burned low.

On looking at his watch he found it was close on midnight; and, not sorry for the *divertissement*, he made up his fire and made himself his nightly pot of tea. He had got through a good spell of work, and thought himself entitled to a ciga-rette; and so he sat on the great carved oak chair before the fire and enjoyed it. Whilst smoking he began to think that he would like to know where the rat dis-appeared to, for he had certain ideas for the morrow not entirely disconnected with a rat-trap. Accordingly he lit another lamp and placed it so that it would shine well into the right-hand corner of the wall by the fireplace. Then he got all the books he had with him, and placed them handy to throw at the vermin. Finally he lifted the rope of the alarm bell and placed the end of it on the table, fixing the extreme end under the lamp. As he handled it he could not help notic-ing how pliable it was, especially for so strong a rope, and one not in use. 'You could hang a man with it,' he thought to himself. When his preparations were made he looked around, and said complacently:

'There now, my friend, I think we shall learn something of you this time!' He began his work again, and though as before somewhat disturbed at first by the noise of the rats, soon lost himself in his propositions and problems.

Again he was called to his immediate surroundings suddenly. This time it might not have been the sudden silence only which took his attention; there was a slight movement of the rope, and the lamp moved. Without stirring, he looked to see if his pile of books was within range, and then cast his eye along the rope.

As he looked he saw the great rat drop from the rope on the oak armchair and sit there glaring at him. He raised a book in his right hand, and taking careful aim, flung it at the rat. The latter, with a quick movement, sprang aside and dodged the missile. He then took another book, and a third, and flung them one after another at the rat, but each time unsuccessfully. At last, as he stood with a book poised in his hand to throw, the rat squeaked and seemed afraid. This made Malcolmson more than ever eager to strike, and the book flew and struck the rat a resounding blow. It gave a terrified squeak, and turning on its pursuer a look of terrible malevolence, ran up the chair-back and made a great jump to the rope of the alarm bell and ran up it like lightning. The lamp rocked under the sudden strain, but it was a heavy one and did not topple over. Malcolmson kept his eyes on the rat, and saw it by the light of the second lamp leap to a moulding of the wainscot and disappear through a hole in one of the great pictures which hung on the wall, obscured and invisible through its coating of dirt and dust.

'I shall look up my friend's habitation in the morning,' said the student, as he went over to collect his books. 'The third picture from the fireplace; I shall not forget.' He picked up the books one by one, commenting on them as he lifted them. '*Conic Sections* he does not mind, nor *Cycloidal Oscillations*, nor the *Principia*, nor *Quaternions*, nor *Thermodynamics*. Now for the book that fetched him!' Malcolmson took it up and looked at it. As he did so he started, and a sudden pallor overspread his face. He looked round uneasily and shivered slightly, as he murmured to himself:

'The Bible my mother gave me! What an odd coincidence.' He sat down to work again, and the rats in the wainscot renewed their gambols. They did not disturb him, however; somehow their presence gave him a sense of companionship. But he could not attend to his work, and after striving to master the subject on which he was engaged gave it up in despair, and went to bed as the first streak of dawn stole in through the eastern window.

He slept heavily but uneasily, and dreamed much; and when Mrs Dempster woke him late in the morning he seemed ill at ease, and for a few minutes did not seem to realise exactly where he was. His first request rather surprised the servant.

'Mrs Dempster, when I am out today I wish you would get the steps and dust or wash those pictures—specially that one the third from the fireplace—I want to see what they are.'

Late in the afternoon Malcolmson worked at his books in the shaded walk, and the cheerfulness of the previous day came back to him as the day wore on, and he found that his reading was progressing well. He had worked out to a satisfactory conclusion all the problems which had as yet baffled him, and it was in a state of jubilation that he paid a visit to Mrs Witham at The Good Traveller. He found a stranger in the cosy sitting room with the landlady, who was introduced to him as Dr Thornhill. She was not quite at ease, and this, combined with the Doctor's plunging at once into a series of questions, made Malcolmson come to the conclusion that his presence was not an accident, so without preliminary he said:

'Dr Thornhill, I shall with pleasure answer you any question you may choose to ask me if you will answer me one question first.'

The Doctor seemed surprised, but he smiled and answered at once. 'Done! What is it?'

'Did Mrs Witham ask you to come here and see me and advise me?'

Dr Thornhill for a moment was taken aback, and Mrs Witham got fiery red and turned away; but the doctor was a frank and ready man, and he answered at once and openly:

'She did: but she didn't intend you to know it. I suppose it was my clumsy haste that made you suspect. She told me that she did not like the idea of your being in that house all by yourself, and that she thought you took too much strong tea. In fact, she wants me to advise you if possible to give up the tea and the very late hours. I was a keen student in my time, so I suppose I may take the liberty of a college man, and without offence, advise you not quite as a stranger.'

Malcolmson with a bright smile held out his hand. 'Shake! as they say in America,' he said. 'I must thank you for your kindness and Mrs Witham too, and your kindness deserves a return on my part. I promise to take no more strong tea—no tea at all till you let me—and I shall go to bed tonight at one o'clock at latest. Will that do?'

'Capital,' said the Doctor. 'Now tell us all that you noticed in the old house,' and so Malcolmson then and there told in minute detail all that had happened in the last two nights. He was interrupted every now and then by some exclamation from Mrs Witham, till finally when he told of the episode of the Bible the landlady's pent-up emotions found vent in a shriek; and it was not till a stiff glass of brandy and water had been administered that she grew composed again. Dr Thornhill listened with a face of growing gravity, and when the narrative was complete and Mrs Witham had been restored he asked:

'The rat always went up the rope of the alarm bell?'

'Always.'

'I suppose you know,' said the Doctor after a pause, 'what the rope is?'

'No!'

'It is,' said the Doctor slowly, 'the very rope which the hangman used for all the victims of the Judge's judicial rancour!' Here he was interrupted by another scream from Mrs Witham, and steps had to be taken for her recovery. Malcolmson having looked at his watch, and found that it was close to his dinner hour, had gone home before her complete recovery.

When Mrs Witham was herself again she almost assailed the Doctor with angry questions as to what he meant by putting such horrible ideas into the poor young man's mind. 'He has quite enough there already to upset him,' she added. Dr Thornhill replied:

'My dear madam, I had a distinct purpose in it! I wanted to draw his attention to the bell rope, and to fix it there. It may be that he is in a highly overwrought state, and has been studying too much, although I am bound to say that he seems as sound and healthy a young man, mentally and bodily, as ever I saw—but then the rats—and that suggestion of the devil.' The Doctor shook his head and went on. 'I would have offered to go and stay the first night with him but that I felt sure it would have been a cause of offence. He may get in the night some strange fright or hallucination; and if he does I want him to pull that rope. All alone as he is it will give us warning, and we may reach him in time to be of service. I shall be sitting up pretty late tonight and shall keep my ears open. Do not be alarmed if Benchurch gets a surprise before morning.'

'Oh, Doctor, what do you mean? What do you mean?'

'I mean this; that possibly—nay, more probably—we shall hear the great alarm bell from the Judge's House tonight,' and the Doctor made about as effective an exit as could be thought of.

When Malcolmson arrived home he found that it was a little after his usual time, and Mrs Dempster had gone away—the rules of Greenhow's Charity were not to be neglected. He was glad to see that the place was bright and tidy with a cheerful fire and a well-trimmed lamp. The evening was colder than might have been expected in April, and a heavy wind was blowing with such rapidly increasing strength that there was every promise of a storm during the night. For a few minutes after his entrance the noise of the rats ceased; but so soon as they became accustomed to his presence they began again. He was glad to hear them, for he felt once more the feeling of companionship in their noise, and his mind ran back to the strange fact that they only ceased to manifest themselves when that other—the great rat with the baleful eyes—came upon the scene. The reading lamp only was lit and its green shade kept the ceiling and the upper part of the room in darkness, so that the cheerful light from the hearth spreading over the floor and shining on the white cloth laid over the end of the table was warm and cheery. Malcolmson sat down to his dinner with a good appetite and a buoyant spirit. After his dinner and a cigarette he sat steadily down to work, determined not to let anything disturb him, for he remembered his promise to the Doctor, and made up his mind to make the best of the time at his disposal.

For an hour or so he worked all right, and then his thoughts began to wander from his books. The actual circumstances around him, the calls on his physical attention, and his nervous susceptibility were not to be denied. By this time the wind had become a gale, and the gale a storm. The old house, solid though it was, seemed to shake to its foundations, and the storm roared and raged through its many chimneys and its queer old gables, producing strange, unearthly sounds in the empty rooms and corridors. Even the great alarm bell on the roof must have felt the force of the wind, for the rope rose and fell slightly, as though the bell were moved a little from time to time, and the limber rope fell on the oak floor with a hard and hollow sound.

As Malcolmson listened to it he bethought himself of the Doctor's words, 'It is the rope which the hangman used for the victims of the Judge's judicial rancour,' and he went over to the corner of the fireplace and took it in his hand to look at it. There seemed a sort of deadly interest in it, and as he stood there he lost himself for a moment in speculation as to who these victims were, and the grim wish of the Judge to have such a ghastly relic ever under his eyes. As he stood there the swaying of the bell on the roof still lifted the rope now and again; but presently there came a new sensation—a sort of tremor in the rope, as though something was moving along it.

Looking up instinctively Malcolmson saw the great rat coming slowly down towards him, glaring at him steadily. He dropped the rope and started back with a muttered curse, and the rat turning ran up the rope again and disappeared, and at the same instant Malcolmson became conscious that the noise of the rats, which had ceased for a while, began again.

All this set him thinking, and it occurred to him that he had not investigated the lair of the rat or looked at the pictures, as he had intended. He lit the other lamp without the shade, and, holding it up, went and stood opposite the third picture from the fireplace on the right-hand side where he had seen the rat disappear on the previous night.

At the first glance he started back so suddenly that he almost dropped the lamp, and a deadly pallor overspread his face. His knees shook, and heavy drops of sweat came on his forehead, and he trembled like an aspen. But he was young and plucky, and pulled himself together, and after the pause of a few seconds stepped forward again, raised the lamp, and examined the picture which had been dusted and washed, and now stood out clearly.

It was of a judge dressed in his robes of scarlet and ermine. His face was strong and merciless, evil, crafty, and vindictive, with a sensual mouth, hooked nose of ruddy colour, and shaped like the beak of a bird of prey. The rest of the face was of a cadaverous colour. The eyes were of peculiar brilliance and with a terribly malignant expression. As he looked at them, Malcolmson grew cold, for he saw there the very counterpart of the eyes of the great rat. The lamp almost fell from his hand, he saw the rat with its baleful eyes peering out through the hole in the corner of the picture, and noted the sudden cessation of the noise of the other rats. However, he pulled himself together, and went on with his examination of the picture.

The Judge was seated in a great high-backed carved oak chair, on the right-hand side of a great stone fireplace where, in the corner, a rope hung down from the ceiling, its end lying coiled on the floor. With a feeling of something like horror, Malcolmson recognised the scene of the room as it stood, and gazed around him in an awe-struck manner as though he expected to find some strange presence behind him. Then he looked over to the corner of the fireplace—and with a loud cry he let the lamp fall from his hand.

There, in the Judge's armchair, with the rope hanging behind, sat the rat with the Judge's baleful eyes, now intensified and with a fiendish leer. Save for the howling of the storm without there was silence.

The fallen lamp recalled Malcolmson to himself. Fortunately it was of metal, and so the oil was not spilt. However, the practical need of attending to it settled at once his nervous apprehensions. When he had turned it out, he wiped his brow and thought for a moment.

'This will not do,' he said to himself. 'If I go on like this I shall become a crazy fool. This must stop! I promised the Doctor I would not take tea. Faith, he was pretty right! My nerves must have been getting into a queer state. Funny I did not notice it. I never felt better in my life. However, it is all right now, and I shall not be such a fool again.'

Then he mixed himself a good stiff glass of brandy and water and resolutely sat down to his work.

It was nearly an hour when he looked up from his book, disturbed by the sudden stillness. Without, the wind howled and roared louder than ever, and the rain drove in sheets against the windows, beating like hail on the glass; but within there was no sound whatever save the echo of the wind as it roared in the great chimney, and now and then a hiss as a few raindrops found their way down the chimney in a lull of the storm. The fire had fallen low and had ceased to flame, though it threw out a red glow. Malcolmson listened attentively, and presently heard a thin, squeaking noise, very faint. It came from the corner of the room where the rope hung down, and he thought it was the creaking of the rope on the floor as the swaying of the bell raised and lowered it. Looking up, however, he saw in the dim light the great rat clinging to the rope and gnawing it. The rope was already nearly gnawed through—he could see the lighter colour where the strands were laid bare. As he looked the job was completed, and the severed end of the rope fell clattering on the oaken floor, whilst for an instant the great rat remained like a knob or tassel at the end of the rope, which now began to sway to and fro. Malcolmson felt for a moment another pang of terror as he thought that now the possibility of calling the outer world to his assistance was cut off, but an intense anger took its place, and seizing the book he was reading he hurled it at the rat. The blow was well aimed, but before the missile could reach it the rat dropped off and struck the floor with a soft thud. Malcolmson instantly rushed over towards it, but it darted away and disappeared in the darkness of the shadows of the room. Malcolmson felt that his work was over for the night, and determined then and there to vary the monotony of the proceedings by a hunt for the rat, and took off the green shade of the lamp so as to ensure a wider-spreading light. As he did so the gloom of the upper part of the room was relieved, and in the new flood of light, great by comparison with the previous darkness, the pictures on the wall stood out boldly. From where he stood, Malcolmson saw right opposite to him the third picture on the wall from the right of the fireplace. He rubbed his eyes in surprise, and then a great fear began to come upon him.

In the centre of the picture was a great irregular patch of brown canvas, as fresh as when it was stretched on the frame. The background was as before, with chair and chimney corner and rope, but the figure of the Judge had disappeared.

Malcolmson, almost in a chill of horror, turned slowly round, and then he began to shake and tremble like a man in a palsy. His strength seemed to have left him, and he was incapable of action or movement, hardly even of thought. He could only see and hear.

There, on the great high-backed carved oak chair sat the Judge in his robes of scarlet and ermine, with his baleful eyes glaring vindictively, and a smile of triumph on the resolute, cruel mouth, as he lifted with his hands a *black cap*. Malcolmson felt as if the blood was running from his heart, as one does in moments of prolonged suspense. There was a singing in his ears. Without, he could hear the roar and howl of the tempest, and through it, swept on the storm, came the striking of midnight by the great chimes in the marketplace. He stood for a space of time that seemed to him endless, still as a statue and with wide-open, horror-struck eyes, breathless. As the clock struck, so the smile of triumph on the Judge's face intensified, and at the last stroke of midnight he placed the black cap on his head.

Slowly and deliberately the Judge rose from his chair and picked up the piece of the rope of the alarm bell which lay on the floor, drew it through his hands as if he enjoyed its touch, and then deliberately began to knot one end of it, fashioning it into a noose. This he tightened and tested with his foot, pulling hard at it till he was satisfied and then making a running noose of it, which he held in his hand. Then he began to move along the table on the opposite side to Malcolmson, keeping his eyes on him until he had passed him, when with a quick movement he stood in front of the door. Malcolmson then began to feel that he was trapped, and tried to think of what he should do. There was some fascination in the Judge's eyes, which he never took off him, and he had, perforce, to look. He saw the Judge approach—still keeping between him and the door—and raise the noose and throw it towards him as if to entangle him. With a great effort he made a quick movement to one side, and saw the rope fall beside him, and heard it strike the oaken floor. Again the Judge raised the noose and tried to ensnare him, ever keeping his baleful eyes fixed on him, and each time by a mighty effort the student just managed to evade it. So this went on for many times, the Judge seeming never discouraged nor discomposed at failure, but playing as a cat does with a mouse. At last in despair, which had reached its climax, Malcolmson cast a quick glance round him. The lamp seemed to have blazed up, and there was a fairly good light in the room. At the many rat-holes and in the chinks and crannies of the wainscot he saw the rats' eyes; and this aspect, that was purely physical, gave him a gleam of comfort. He looked around and saw that the rope of the great alarm bell was laden with rats. Every inch of it was covered with them, and more and more were pouring through the small circular hole in the ceiling whence it emerged, so that with their weight the bell was beginning to sway.

Hark! it had swayed till the clapper had touched the bell. The sound was but a tiny one, but the bell was only beginning to sway, and it would increase.

At the sound the Judge, who had been keeping his eyes fixed on Malcolmson, looked up, and a scowl of diabolical anger overspread his face. His eyes fairly glowed like hot coals, and he stamped his foot with a sound that seemed to make the house shake. A dreadful peal of thunder broke overhead as he raised the rope again, whilst the rats kept running up and down the rope as though working against time. This time, instead of throwing it, he drew close to his victim, and held open the noose as he approached. As he came closer there seemed something paralysing in his very presence, and Malcolmson stood rigid as a corpse. He felt the Judge's icy fingers touch his throat as he adjusted the rope. The noose tightened—tightened. Then the Judge, taking the rigid form of the student in his arms, carried him over and placed him standing in the oak chair, and stepping up beside him, put his hand up and caught the end of the swaying rope of the alarm bell. As he raised his hand the rats fled squeaking, and disappeared through the hole in the ceiling. Taking the end of the noose which was round Malcolmson's neck he tied it to the hanging bell rope, and then descending pulled away the chair.

WHEN THE ALARM BELL of the Judge's House began to sound a crowd soon assembled. Lights and torches of various kinds appeared, and soon a silent crowd was hurrying to the spot. They knocked loudly at the door, but there was no reply. Then they burst in the door and poured into the great dining room, the Doctor at the head.

There at the end of the rope of the great alarm bell hung the body of the student, and on the face of the Judge in the picture was a malignant smile.

———————————

Elizabeth Taylor

1912–1975

Elizabeth Taylor was a compulsive writer who produced novel
after novel while still at school. However, the first, *At Mrs
Lippincote's*, was not published until she was thirty-three. Its
success launched her on a widely acclaimed literary career. Many
novels and short stories followed, all demonstrating the author's
subtle and unsettling perception of character.

POOR GIRL

MISS CHASTY'S FIRST PUPIL was a flirtatious little boy. At seven years, he
was alarmingly precocious and sometimes she thought that he despised
his childhood, regarding it as a waiting time which he used only as a
rehearsal for adult life. He was already more sophisticated than his young governess and disturbed her with his air of dalliance, the mockery with which he set
about his lessons, the preposterous conversations he led her into, guiding her
skilfully away from work, confusing her with bizarre conjectures and irreverent
ideas, so that she would clasp her hands tightly under the plush tablecloth and
pray that his father would not choose such a moment to observe her teaching,
coming in abruptly as he sometimes did and signalling to her to continue her
lesson.

At those times, his son's eyes were especially lively, fixed cruelly upon his governess as he listened, smiling faintly, to her faltering voice, measuring her
timidity. He would answer her questions correctly, but significantly, as if he knew
that by his aptitude he rescued her from dismissal. There were many governesses
waiting employment, he implied—and this was so at the beginning of the century. He underlined her good fortune at having a pupil who could so easily learn,
could display the results of her teaching to such advantage for the benefit of the
rather sombre, pompous figure seated at the window. When his father, apparently satisfied, had left them without a word, the boy's manner changed. He
seemed fatigued and too absent-minded to reply to any more questions.

'Hilary!' she would say sharply. 'Are you attending to me?' Her sharpness
and her foolishness amused him, coming as he knew they did from the tension
of the last ten minutes.

'Why, my dear girl, of course.'

'You must address me by my name.'

'Certainly, dear Florence.'

'Miss Chasty.'

His lips might shape the words, which he was too weary to say.

Sometimes, when she was correcting his sums, he would come round the table to stand beside her, leaning against her heavily, looking closely at her face, not at his book, breathing steadily down his nose so that tendrils of hair wavered on her neck and against her cheeks. His stillness, his concentration on her and his too heavy leaning, worried her. She felt something experimental in his attitude, as if he were not leaning against her at all, but against someone in the future. 'He is only a baby,' she reminded herself, but she would try to shift from him, feeling a vague distaste. She would blush, as if he were a grown man, and her heart could be heard beating quickly. He was aware of this and would take up the corrected book and move back to his place.

Once he proposed to her and she had the feeling that it was a proposal rehearsal and that he was making use of her, as an actor might ask her to hear his lines.

'You must go on with your work,' she said.

'I can shade in a map and talk as well.'

'Then talk sensibly.'

'You think I am too young, I dare say; but you could wait for me to grow up. I can do that quickly enough.'

'You are far from grown-up at the moment.'

'You only say these things because you think that governesses ought to. I suppose you don't know *how* governesses go on, because you have never been one until now, and you were too poor to have one of your own when you were young.'

'That is impertinent, Hilary.'

'You once told me that your father couldn't afford one.'

'Which is a different way of putting it.'

'I shouldn't have thought they cost much.' He had a way of just making a remark, of breathing it so gently that it was scarcely said, and might conveniently be ignored.

He was a dandified little boy. His smooth hair was like a silk cap, combed straight from the crown to a level line above his topaz eyes. His sailor suits were spotless. The usual boldness changed to an agonised fussiness if his serge sleeve brushed against chalk or if he should slip on the grassy terrace and stain his clothes with green. On their afternoon walks he took no risks and Florence, who had younger brothers, urged him in vain to climb a tree or jump across puddles. At first, she thought him intimidated by his mother or nurse; but soon she realised that his mother entirely indulged him and the nurse had her thoughts all bent upon the new baby: his fussiness was just another part of his grown-upness come too soon.

The house was comfortable, although to Florence rather too sealed up and overheated after her own damp and draughty home. Her work was not hard and her loneliness only what she had expected. Cut off from the kitchen by her education, she lacked the feuds and camaraderie, gossip and cups of tea, which made life more interesting for the domestic staff. None of the maids—coming to light the lamp at dusk or laying the schoolroom table for tea—ever presumed beyond a remark or two about the weather.

One late afternoon, she and Hilary returned from their walk and found the lamps already lit. Florence went to her room to tidy herself before tea. When she came down to the schoolroom, Hilary was already there, sitting on the window seat and staring out over the park as his father did. The room was bright and warm and a maid had put a white cloth over the plush one and was beginning to lay the table.

The air was full of a heavy scent, dry and musky. To Florence, it smelt quite unlike the eau de cologne she sometimes sprinkled on her handkerchief, when she had a headache and she disapproved so much that she returned the maid's greeting coldly and bade Hilary open the window.

'Open the window, dear girl?' he said. 'We shall catch our very deaths.'

'You will do as I ask and remember in future how to address me.' She was angry with the maid—who now seemed to her an immoral creature—and angry to be humiliated before her.

'But why?' asked Hilary.

'I don't approve of my schoolroom being turned into a scented bower.' She kept her back to the room and was trembling, for she had never rebuked a servant before.

'I approve of it,' Hilary said, sniffing loudly.

'I think it's lovely,' the maid said. 'I noticed it as soon as I opened the door.'

'Is this some joke, Hilary?' Florence asked when the maid had gone.

'No. What?'

'This smell in the room?'

'No. You smell of it most, anyhow.' He put his nose to her sleeve and breathed deeply.

It seemed to Florence that this was so, that her clothes had caught the perfume among their folds. She lifted her palms to her face, then went to the window and leaned out into the air as far as she could.

'Shall I pour out the tea, dear girl?'

'Yes, please.'

She took her place at the table abstractedly, and as she drank her tea she stared about the room, frowning. When Hilary's mother looked in, as she often did at this time, Florence stood up in a startled way.

'Good evening, Mrs Wilson. Hilary, put a chair for your mamma.'

'Don't let me disturb you.'

Mrs Wilson sank into the rocking chair by the fire and gently tipped to and fro.

'Have you finished your tea, darling boy?' she asked. 'Are you going to read me a story from your book? Oh, there is Lady scratching at the door. Let her in for mamma.'

Hilary opened the door and a balding old pug-dog with bloodshot eyes waddled in.

'Come, Lady! Beautiful one. Come to mistress! What is wrong with her, poor pet lamb?'

The bitch had stopped just inside the room and lifted her head and howled. 'What has frightened her, then? Come, beauty! Coax her with a sponge cake, Hilary.'

She reached forward to the table to take the dish and doing so noticed Florence's empty teacup. On the rim was a crimson smear, like the imprint of a lip. She gave a sponge finger to Hilary, who tried to quieten the pug, then she leaned back in her chair and studied Florence again as she had studied her when she had engaged her a few weeks earlier. The girl's looks were appropriate enough, appropriate to a clergyman's daughter and a governess. Her square chin looked resolute, her green eyes innocent, her dress was modest and unbecoming. Yet Mrs Wilson could detect an excitability, even feverishness, which she had not noticed before and she wondered if she had mistaken guardedness for innocence and deceit for modesty.

She was reaching this conclusion—rocking back and forth when she saw Florence's hand stretch out and turn the cup round in its saucer so that the red stain was out of sight.

'What is wrong with Lady?' Hilary asked, for the dog would not be pacified with sponge fingers, but kept making barking advances further into the room, then growling in retreat.

'Perhaps she is crying at the new moon,' said Florence and she went to the window and drew back the curtain. As she moved, her skirts rustled. 'If she has silk underwear as well!' Mrs Wilson thought. She had clearly heard the sound of taffetas and she imagined the drab, shiny alpaca dress concealing frivolity and wantonness.

'Open the door, Hilary!' she said. 'I will take Lady away. Vernon shall give her a run in the park. I think a quiet read for Hilary and then an early bedtime, Miss Chasty. He looks pale this evening.'

'Yes, Mrs Wilson.' Florence stood respectfully by the table, hiding the cup.

'The hypocrisy!' Mrs Wilson thought and she trembled as she crossed the landing and went downstairs.

She hesitated to tell her husband of her uneasiness, knowing his susceptibilities to women whom his conscience taught him to deplore. Hidden below the apparent urbanity of their married life were old unhappinesses—little acts of treachery and disloyalty which pained her to remember, bruises upon her peace of mind and her pride: letters found, a pretty maid dismissed, an actress who had blackmailed him. As he read the Lesson in church, looking so perfectly upright and honourable a man, she sometimes thought of his escapades; but not with bitterness or cynicism, only with pain at her memories and a whisper of fear about the future. For some time she had been spared those whispers and had hoped that their marriage had at last achieved its calm. To speak of Florence as she must might both arouse his curiosity and revive the past. Nevertheless, she had her duty to her son to fulfil and her own anger to appease and she opened the library door very determinedly.

'Oliver, I am sorry to interrupt your work, but I must speak to you.'

He put down the *Strand* magazine quite happily, aware that she was not a sarcastic woman.

Oliver and his son were extraordinarily alike. 'As soon as Hilary has grown a moustache we shall not know them apart,' Mrs Wilson often said, and her husband liked this little joke which made him feel more youthful. He did not know that she added a silent prayer—'O God, please· do not let him *be* like him, though.'

'You seem troubled, Louise.' His voice was rich and authoritative. He enjoyed setting to rights her little domestic flurries and waited indulgently to hear of some tradesman's misdemeanour or servant's laziness.

'Yes, I am troubled about Miss Chasty.'

'Little Miss Mouse? I was rather troubled myself. I noticed two spelling faults in Hilary's botany essay, which she claimed to have corrected. I said nothing before the boy; but I shall acquaint her with it when the opportunity arises.'

'Do you often go to the schoolroom, then?'

'From time to time. I like to be sure that our choice was wise.'

'It was not. It was misguided *and* unwise.'

'All young people seem slipshod nowadays.'

'She is more than slipshod. I believe she should go. I think she is quite brazen. Oh, yes, I should have laughed at that myself if it had been said to me an hour ago, but I have just come from the schoolroom and it occurs to me that now she has settled down and feels more secure—since you pass over her mistakes—she is beginning to take advantage of your leniency and to show herself in her true colours. I felt a sinister atmosphere up there and I am quite upset and exhausted by it. I went up to hear Hilary's reading. They were finishing tea and the room was full of the most overpowering scent—*her* scent. It was disgusting.'

'Unpleasant?'

'No, not at all. But upsetting.'

'Disturbing?'

She would not look at him or reply, hearing no more indulgence or condescension in his voice, but the quality of warming interest.

'And then I saw her teacup and there was a mark on it—a red smear where her lips had touched it. She did not know I saw it and as soon as she noticed it herself she turned it round, away from me. She is an immoral woman and she has come into our house to teach our son.'

'I have never noticed a trace of artificiality in her looks. It seemed to me that she was rather colourless.'

'She has been sly. This evening she looked quite different, quite flushed and excitable. I know that she had rouged her lips or painted them, or whatever those women do.' Her eyes filled with tears.

'I shall observe her for a day or two,' Oliver said, trying to keep anticipation from his voice.

'I should like her to go at once.'

'Never act rashly. She is entitled to a quarter's notice unless there is definite blame. We could make ourselves very foolish if you have been mistaken. Oh, I know that you are sure; but it has been known for you to misjudge others. I shall take stock of her and decide if she is suitable. She is still Miss Mouse to me and I cannot think otherwise until I see the evidence with my own eyes.'

'There was something else as well,' Mrs Wilson said wretchedly.

'And what was that?'

'I should rather not say.' She had changed her mind about further accusations. Silk underwear would prove, she guessed, too inflammatory.

'I shall go up ostensibly to mention Hilary's spelling faults.' He could not go fast enough and stood up at once.

'But Hilary will be in bed.'

'I could not mention the spelling faults if he were not.'

'Shall I come with you?'

'My dear Louise, why should you? It would look very strange—a deputation about two spelling faults.'

'Then don't be long, will you? I hope you won't be long.'

He went to the schoolroom, but there was no one there. Hilary's storybook lay closed upon the table and Miss Chasty's sewing was folded neatly. As he was standing there looking about him and sniffing hard, a maid came in with a tray of crockery.

'Has Master Hilary gone to bed?' he asked, feeling rather foolish and confused. The only scent in the air was a distinct smell—even a haze—of cigarette smoke.

'Yes, sir.'

'And Miss Chasty—where is she?'

'She went to bed, too, sir.'

'Is she unwell?'

'She spoke of a chronic head, sir.'

The maid stacked the cups and saucers in the cupboard and went out. Nothing was wrong with the room apart from the smell of smoke and Mr Wilson went downstairs. His wife was waiting in the hall. She looked up expectantly, in some relief at seeing him so soon.

'Nothing,' he said dramatically. 'She has gone to bed with a headache. No wonder she looked feverish.'

'You noticed the scent.'

'There was none,' he said. 'No trace. Nothing. Just imagination, dear Louise. I thought that it must be so.'

He went to the library and took up his magazine again, but he was too disturbed to read and thought with impatience of the following day.

Florence could not sleep. She had gone to her room, not with a headache but to escape conversations until she had faced her predicament alone. This she was doing, lying on the honeycomb quilt which, since maids do not wait on governesses, had not been turned down.

The schoolroom this evening seemed to have been wreathed about with a strange miasma; the innocent nature of the place polluted in a way which she could not understand or have explained. Something new, it seemed, had entered the room which had not belonged to her or became a part of her—the scent had clung about her clothes; the stained cup was her cup and her handkerchief with which she had rubbed it clean was still reddened; and, finally, as she had stared in the mirror, trying to re-establish her personality, the affected little laugh which startled her had come from herself. It had driven her from the room.

'I cannot explain the inexplicable,' she thought wearily and began to prepare herself for bed. Homesickness hit her like a blow on the head. 'Whatever they do to me, I have always my home,' she promised herself. But she could not think who 'they' might be; for no one in this house had threatened her. Mrs Wilson had done no more than irritate her with her commonplace fussing over Hilary and her dog, and Florence was prepared to overcome much more than irritations. Mr Wilson's pomposity, his constant watch on her work, intimidated her, but she knew that all who must earn their living must have fears lest their work should not seem worth the payment. Hilary was easy to manage; she had quickly seen that she could always deflect him from rebelliousness by opening a new subject for conversation; any idea would be a counterattraction to naughtiness; he wanted her to sharpen his wits upon. 'And is that all that teaching is, or should be?' she had wondered. The servants had been good to her, realising that she would demand nothing of them. She had suffered great loneliness, but had foreseen it as part of her position. Now she felt fear nudging it away. 'I am not lonely any more,' she thought. 'I am not alone any more. And I have lost something.' She said her prayers; then sitting up in bed, kept the candle alight while she brushed her hair and read the Bible.

'Perhaps I have lost my reason,' she suddenly thought, resting her finger on her place in the Psalms. She lifted her head and saw her shadow stretch up the powdery, rose-sprinkled wall. 'Now can I keep *that* secret?' she wondered. 'When there is no one to help me to do it? Only those who are watching to see it happen.'

She was not afraid in her bedroom as she had been in the schoolroom, but her perplexed mind found no replies to its questions. She blew out the candle and tried to fall asleep but lay and cried for a long time, and yearned to be at home again and comforted in her mother's arms.

In the morning she met kind enquiries. Nurse was so full of solicitude that Florence felt guilty. 'I came up with a warm drink and put my head round the door but you were in the Land of Nod so I drank it myself. I should take a grey powder; or I could mix you a gargle. There are a lot of throats about.'

'I am quite better this morning,' said Florence and she felt calmer as she sat down at the schoolroom table with Hilary. 'Yet it was all true,' her reason whispered. 'The morning hasn't altered that.'

'You have been crying,' said Hilary. 'Your eyes are red.'

'Sometimes people's eyes are red from other causes—headaches and colds.' She smiled brightly.

'And sometimes from crying, as I said. I should think *usually* from crying.'

'Page fifty-one,' she said, locking her hands together in her lap.

'Very well.' He opened the book, pressed down the pages and lowered his nose to them, breathing the smell of print. 'He is utterly sensuous,' she thought. 'He extracts every pleasure, every sensation, down to the most trivial.'

They seemed imprisoned in the schoolroom, by the silence of the rest of the house and by the rain outside. Her calm began to break up into frustration and she put her hands behind her chair and pressed them against the hot mesh of the fireguard to steady herself. As she did so, she felt a curious derangement of both mind and body; of desire unsettling her once sluggish, peaceful nature, desire horribly defined, though without direction.

'I have soon finished those,' said Hilary, bringing his sums and placing them before her. She glanced at her palms which were crisscrossed deep with crimson where she had pressed them against the fireguard, then she took up her pen and dipped it into the red ink.

'Don't lean against me, Hilary,' she said.

'I love the scent so much.'

It had returned, musky, enveloping, varying as she moved. She ticked the sums quickly, thinking that she would set Hilary more work and escape for a moment to calm herself—change her clothes or cleanse herself in the rain. Hearing Mr Wilson's footsteps along the passage, she knew that her escape was cut off and raised wild-looking eyes as he came in. He mistook panic for passion, thought that by opening the door suddenly he had caught her out and laid bare her secret, her pathetic adoration.

'Good morning,' he said musically and made his way to the window seat. 'Don't let me disturb you.' He said this without irony, although he thought: 'So it is that way the wind blows! Poor creature!' He had never found it difficult to imagine that women were in love with him.

'I will hear your verbs,' Florence told Hilary, and opened the French Grammar as if she did not know them herself. Her eyes—from so much crying—were a pale and brilliant green and as the scent drifted in Oliver's direction and he turned to her, she looked fully at him.

'Ah, the still waters!' he thought and stood up suddenly. '*Ils vont,*' he corrected

Hilary and touched his shoulder as he passed. 'Are you attending to Miss Chasty?'

'Is she attending to me?' Hilary murmured. The risk was worth taking, for neither heard. His father appeared to be sleepwalking and Florence deliberately closed her eyes, as if looking down were not enough to blur the outlines of her desire.

'I find it difficult,' Oliver said to his wife, 'to reconcile your remarks about Miss Chasty with the young woman herself. I have just come from the school-room and she was engaged in nothing more immoral than teaching French verbs—that not very well, incidentally.'

'But can you *explain* what I have told you?'

'I can't do that,' he said gaily. For who can explain a jealous woman's fancies? he implied.

He began to spend more time in the schoolroom; for surveillance, he said. Miss Chasty, though not outwardly of an amorous nature, was still not what he had at first supposed. A suppressed wantonness hovered beneath her primness. She was the ideal governess in his eyes—irreproachable, yet not unapproach-able. As she was so conveniently installed, he could take his time in divining the extent of her willingness; especially as he was growing older and the game was beginning to be worth more than the triumph of winning it. To his wife, he upheld Florence, saw nothing wrong save in her scholarship, which needed to be looked into—the explanation for his more frequent visits to the schoolroom. He laughed teasingly at Louise's fancies.

The schoolroom indeed became a focal point of the house—the stronghold of Mr Wilson's desire and his wife's jealousy.

'We are never alone,' said Hilary. 'Either papa or mamma is here. Perhaps they wonder if you are good enough for me.'

'Hilary!' His father had heard the last sentence as he opened the door and the first as he hovered outside listening. 'I doubt if my ears deceived me. You will go to your room while you think of a suitable apology and I think of an ample punishment.'

'Shall I take my history book with me or shall I just waste time?'

'I have indicated how to spend your time.'

'That won't take long enough,' said Hilary beneath his breath as he closed the door.

'Meanwhile, I apologise for him,' said his father. He did not go to his custom-ary place by the window, but came to the hearth-rug where Florence stood behind her chair. 'We have indulged him too much and he has been too much with adults. Have there been other occasions?'

'No, indeed, sir.'

'You find him tractable?'

'Oh, yes.'

'And you are happy in your position?'

'Yes.'

As the dreaded, the now so familiar scent began to wreathe about the room, she stepped back from him and began to speak rapidly, as urgently as if she were dying and must make some explanation while she could. 'Perhaps, after all, Hilary is right, and you do wonder about my competence—and if I can give him all he should have. Perhaps a man would teach him more . . .'

She began to feel a curious infraction of the room and of her personality, seemed to lose the true Florence, and the room lightened as if the season had been changed.

'You are mistaken,' he was saying. 'Have I ever given you any hint that we were not satisfied?'

Her timidity had quite dissolved and he was shocked by the sudden boldness of her glance.

'No, no hint,' she said, smiling. As she moved, he heard the silken swish of her clothes.

'I should rather give you a hint of how well pleased I am.'

'Then why don't you?' she asked.

She leaned back against the chimneypiece and looped about her fingers a long necklace of glittering green beads. 'Where did these come from?' she wondered. She could not remember ever having seen them before, but she could not pursue her bewilderment, for the necklace felt familiar to her hands, much more familiar than the rest of the room.

'When shall I?' he was insisting. 'This evening, perhaps? when Hilary is in bed?'

'Then who is *he*, if Hilary is to be in bed?' she wondered. She glanced at him and smiled again. 'You are extraordinarily alike,' she said. 'You and Hilary.' 'But Hilary is a little boy,' she reminded herself. 'It is silly to confuse the two.'

'We must discuss Hilary's progress,' he said, his voice so burdened with meaning that she began to laugh at him.

'Indeed we must,' she agreed.

'Your necklace is the colour of your eyes.' He took it from her fingers and leaned forward, as if to kiss her. Hearing footsteps in the passage she moved sharply aside, the necklace broke and the beads were scattered over the floor.

'Why is Hilary in the garden at this hour?' Mrs Wilson asked. Her husband and the governess were on their knees, gathering up the beads.

'Miss Chasty's necklace broke,' her husband said. She had heard that submissive tone before: his voice lacked authority only when he was caught out in some infidelity.

'I was asking about Hilary. I have just seen him running in the shrubbery without a coat.'

'He was sent to his room for being impertinent to Miss Chasty.'

'Please fetch him at once,' Mrs Wilson told Florence. Her voice always gained in authority what her husband's lacked.

Florence hurried from the room, still holding a handful of beads. She felt badly shaken—as if she had been brought to the edge of some experience which had then retreated beyond her grasp.

'He was told to stay in his room,' Mr Wilson said feebly.

'Why did her beads break?'

'She was fidgeting with them. I think she was nervous. I was making it rather apparent to her that I regarded Hilary's insubordination as proof of too much leniency on her part.'

'I didn't know that she had such a necklace. It is the showiest trash that I have ever seen.'

'We cannot blame her for the cheapness of her trinkets. It is rather pathetic.'

'There is nothing pathetic about her. We will continue this in the morning room and *they* can continue their lessons, which are, after all, her reason for being here.'

'Oh, they are gone,' said Hilary. His cheeks were pink from the cold outside.

'Why did you not stay in your bedroom as you were told?'

'I had nothing to do. I thought of my apology before I got there. It was: "I am sorry, dear girl, that I spoke too near the point."'

'You could have spent longer and thought of a real apology.'

'Look how long papa spent and he did not even think of a punishment, which is a much easier thing.'

Several times during the evening, Mr Wilson said: 'But you cannot dismiss a girl because her beads break.'

'There have been other things and will be more,' his wife replied.

So that there should not be more that evening, he did not move from the drawing room where he sat watching her doing her wool-work. For the same reason, Florence left the schoolroom empty. She went out and walked rather nervously in the park, feeling remorseful, astonished and upset.

'Did you mend your necklace?' Hilary asked her in the morning.

'I lost the beads.'

'But, my poor girl, they must be somewhere.'

She thought: 'There is no reason to suppose that I shall get back what I never had in the first place.'

'Have you got a headache?'

'Yes. Go on with your work, Hilary.'

'Is it from losing the beads?'

'No.'

'Have you a great deal of jewellery I have not seen yet?'

She did not answer and he went on: 'You still have your brooch with your grandmother's plaited hair in it. Was it cut off her head when she was dead?'

'Your *work*, Hilary.'

'I shudder to think of chopping it off a corpse. You could have some of my hair, now, while I am living.' He fingered it with admiration, regarded a sum aloofly and jotted down its answer. 'Could I cut some of yours?' he asked, bringing his book to be corrected. He whistled softly, close to her, and the tendrils of hair round her ears were gently blown about.

'It is ungentlemanly to whistle,' she said.

'My sums are always right. It shows how I can chatter and subtract at the same time. Any governess would be annoyed by that. I suppose your brothers never whistle.'

'Never.'

'Are they to be clergymen like your father?'

'It is what we hope for one of them.'

'I am to be a famous judge. When you read about me, will you say: "And to think I might have been his wife if I had not been so self-willed"?'

'No, but I hope that I shall feel proud that once I taught you.'

'You sound doubtful.'

He took his book back to the table. 'We are having a quiet morning,' he remarked. 'No one has visited us. Poor Miss Chasty, it is a pity about the necklace,' he murmured, as he took up his pencil again.

Evenings were dangerous to her. 'He said he would come,' she told herself, 'and I allowed him to say so. On what compulsion did I?'

Fearfully, she spent her lonely hours out in the dark garden or in her cold and candlelit bedroom. He was under his wife's vigilance and Florence did not know that he dared not leave the drawing room. But the vigilance relaxed, as it does: his carelessness returned and steady rain and bitter cold drove Florence to warm her chilblains at the schoolroom fire.

Her relationship with Mrs Wilson had changed. A wary hostility took the place of meekness and when Mrs Wilson came to the schoolroom at tea times, Florence stood up defiantly and cast a look round the room as if to say: 'Find what you can. There is nothing here.' Mrs Wilson's suspicious ways increased her rebelliousness. 'I have done nothing wrong,' she told herself. But in her bedroom at night: '*I* have done nothing wrong,' she would think.

'They have quite deserted us,' Hilary said from time to time. 'They have realised you are worth your weight in gold, dear girl; or perhaps I made it clear to my father that in this room he is an interloper.'

'Hilary!'

'You want to put yourself in the right in case that door opens suddenly as it has been doing lately. There, you see! Good evening, mamma. I was just saying that I have scarcely seen you all day.' He drew forward her chair and held the cushion behind her until she leaned back.

'I have been resting.'

'Are you ill, mamma?'

'I have a headache.'

'I will stroke it for you, dear lady.'

He stood behind her chair and began to smooth her forehead. 'Or shall I read to you?' he asked, soon tiring of his task. 'Or play the musical box?'

'No, nothing more, thank you.' Mrs Wilson looked about her, at the teacups, then at Florence. Sometimes it seemed to her that her husband was right and that she was growing fanciful. The innocent appearance of the room lulled her and she closed her eyes for a while, rocking gently in her chair.

'I dozed off,' she said when she awoke. The table was cleared and Florence and Hilary sat playing chess, whispering so that they should not disturb her.

'It made a domestic scene for us,' said Hilary. 'Often Miss Chasty and I feel that we are left too much in solitary bliss.'

The two women smiled and Mrs Wilson shook her head. 'You have too old a head on your shoulders,' she said. 'What will they say of you when you go to school?'

'What shall I say of *them*?' he asked bravely, but he lowered his eyes and kept them lowered. When his mother had gone, he asked Florence: 'Did you go to school?'

'Yes.'

'Were you unhappy there?'

'No. I was homesick at first.'

'If I don't like it, there will be no point in my staying,' he said hurriedly. 'I can learn anywhere and I don't particularly want the corners knocked off, as my father once spoke of it. I shouldn't like to play cricket and all those childish games. Only to do boxing and draw blood,' he added, with sudden bravado. He laughed excitedly and clenched his fists.

'You would never be good at boxing if you lost your temper.'

'I suppose your brothers told you that. They don't sound very manly to me. They would be afraid of a good fight and the sight of blood, I dare say.'

'Yes, I dare say. It is bedtime.' He was whipped up by the excitement he had created from his fears.

'Chess is a woman's game,' he said and upset the board. He took the cushion from the rocking chair and kicked it inexpertly across the room. 'I should have thought the door would have opened then,' he said. 'But as my father doesn't appear to send me to my room, I will go there of my own accord. It wouldn't have been a punishment at bedtime in any case. When I am a judge I shall be better at punishments than he is.'

When he had gone, Florence picked up the cushion and the chessboard. 'I am no good at punishments either,' she thought. She tidied the room, made up the fire, then sat down in the rocking chair, thinking of all the lonely schoolroom evenings of her future. She bent her head over her needlework—the beaded sachet for her mother's birthday present. When she looked up she thought the lamp was smoking and she went to the table and turned down the wick. Then she noticed that the smoke was wreathing upwards from near the fireplace, forming rings which drifted towards the ceiling and were lost in a haze. She could hear a woman's voice humming softly and the floorboards creaked as if someone were treading up and down the room impatiently.

She felt in herself a sense of burning impatience and anticipation and watching the door opening found herself thinking: 'If it is not he, I cannot bear it.'

He closed the door quietly. 'She has gone to bed,' he said in a lowered voice. 'For days I dared not come. She has watched me at every moment. At last, this evening, she gave way to a headache. Were you expecting me?'

'Yes.'

'And once I called you Miss Mouse! And you are still Miss Mouse when I see you about the garden, or at luncheon.'

'In this room I can be myself. It belongs to us.'

'And not to Hilary as well—ever?' he asked her in amusement.

She gave him a quick and puzzled glance.

'Let no one intrude,' he said hastily. 'It is our room, just as you say.'

She had turned the lamp too low and it began to splutter. 'Firelight is good enough for us,' he said, putting the light out altogether.

When he kissed her, she felt an enormous sense of disappointment, almost as if he were the wrong person embracing her in the dark. His arch masterfulness merely bored her. 'A long wait for so little,' she thought.

He, however, found her entirely seductive. She responded with a sensuous languor, unruffled and at ease like the most perfect hostess.

'Where did you practise this, Miss Mouse?' he asked her. But he did not wait for the reply, fancying that he heard a step on the landing. When his wife opened the door, he was trying desperately to light a taper at the fire. His hand was trembling and when at last, in the terribly silent room, the flame crept up the spill it simply served to show up Florence's disarray which, like a sleepwalker, she had not noticed or put right.

SHE DID NOT SEE Hilary again, except as a blurred little figure at the schoolroom window—blurred because of her tear-swollen eyes.

She was driven away in the carriage, although Mrs Wilson had suggested the station fly. 'Let us keep her disgrace and her tearfulness to ourselves,' he begged, although he was exhausted by the repetitious burden of his wife's grief.

'Her disgrace!'

'My mistake, I have said, was in not taking your accusations about her seriously. I see now that I was in some way bewitched—yes, bewitched is what it was—acting against my judgment; nay, my very nature. I am astonished that anyone so seemingly meek could have cast such a spell upon me.'

Poor Florence turned her head aside as Williams, the coachman, came to fetch her little trunk and the basket-work holdall. Then she put on her cloak and prepared herself to go downstairs, fearful lest she should meet anyone on the way. Yet her thoughts were even more on her journey's end; for what, she wondered, could she tell her father and how expect him to understand what she could not understand herself?

Her head was bent as she crossed the landing and she hurried past the schoolroom door. At the turn of the staircase she pressed back against the wall to allow someone to pass. She heard laughter and then up the stairs came a young woman and a little girl. The child was clinging to the woman's arm and coaxing her, as sometimes Hilary had tried to coax Florence. 'After lessons,' the woman said firmly, but gaily. She looked ahead, smiling to herself. Her clothes were unlike anything that Florence had ever seen. Later, when she tried to describe them to her mother, she could only remember the shortness of a tunic which scarcely covered the knees, a hat like a helmet drawn down over eyes intensely green and matching the long necklace of glass beads which swung on her flat bosom. As she came up the stairs and drew near to Florence, she was humming softly against the child's pleading; silk rustled against her silken legs and all of the staircase, as Florence quickly descended, was full of fragrance.

In the darkness of the hall a man was watching the two go round the bend of the stairs. The woman must have looked back, for Florence saw him lift his hand in a secretive gesture of understanding.

'It is Hilary, not his father!' she thought. But the figure turned before she could be sure and went into the library.

Outside on the drive Williams was waiting with her luggage stowed away in the carriage. When she had settled herself, she looked up at the schoolroom window and saw Hilary standing there rather forlornly and she could almost imagine him saying: 'My poor dear girl; so you were not good enough for me, after all?'

'When does the new governess arrive?' she asked Williams in a casual voice, which hoped to conceal both pride and grief.

'There's nothing fixed as far as I have heard,' he said.

They drove out into the lane.

'When will it be *her* time?' Florence wondered. 'I am glad that I saw her before I left.'

'We are sorry to see you going, Miss.' He had heard that the maids were sorry, for she had given them no trouble.

'Thank you, Williams.'

As they went on towards the station, she leaned back and looked at the familiar places where she had walked with Hilary. 'I know what I shall tell my father now,' she thought, and she felt peaceful and meek as though beginning to be convalescent after a long illness.

———————————

H. Russell Wakefield

1888–1964

A private secretary before the First World War, and a soldier with the Royal Scots Fusiliers during that conflict, Herbert Russell Wakefield then became one of the great names in the history of the English ghost story. Like M. R. James, he had a penchant for malevolent ghosts. He, too, understood that the horror that is not precisely described is often the most disturbing.

BLIND MAN'S BUFF

'WELL, THANK HEAVENS that yokel seemed to know the place,' said Mr Cort to himself. '"First to the right, second to the left, black gates." I hope the oaf in Wendover who sent me six miles out of my way will freeze to death. It's not often like this in England—cold as the penny in a dead man's eye.' He'd barely reach the place before dusk. He let the car out over the rasping, frozen roads. '"First to the right"—must be this—"second to the left", must be this'—and there were the black gates. He got out, swung them open, and drove cautiously up a narrow, twisting drive, his headlights peering suspiciously round the bends. Those hedges wanted clipping, he thought, and this lane would have to be remetalled—full of holes. Nasty drive up on a bad night; would cost some money, though.

The car began to climb steeply and swing to the right, and presently the high hedges ended abruptly, and Mr Cort pulled up in front of Lorn Manor. He got out of the car, rubbed his hands, stamped his feet, and looked about him.

Lorn Manor was embedded halfway up a Chiltern spur and, as the agent had observed, 'commanded extensive vistas'. The place looked its age, Mr Cort decided, or rather ages, for the double Georgian brick chimneys warred with the Queen Anne left front. He could just make out the date, 1703, at the base of the nearest chimney. All that wing must have been added later. 'Big place, marvellous bargain at seven thousand, can't understand it. How those windows with their little curved eyebrows seem to frown down on one!' And then he turned and examined the 'vistas'. The trees were tinted exquisitely to an uncertain glory as the great red sinking sun flashed its rays on their crystal mantle. The vale of Aylesbury was drowsing beneath a slowly deepening shroud of mist. Above it the hills, their crests rounded and shaded by silver and rose coppices, seemed to have set in them great smoky eyes of flame where the last rays burned in them.

'It is like some dream world,' thought Mr Cort. 'It is curious how, wherever the sun strikes, it seems to make an eye, and each one fixed on me; those hills, even those windows. But, judging from that mist, I shall have a slow journey home; I'd better have a quick look inside, though I have already taken a prejudice against the place—I hardly know why. Too lonely and isolated, perhaps.' And then the eyes blinked and closed, and it was dark. He took a key from his pocket and went up three steps and thrust it into the keyhole of the massive oak door. The next moment he looked forward into absolute blackness, and the door swung to and closed behind him. This, of course, must be the 'palatial panelled hall' which the agent described. He must strike a match and find the light switch. He fumbled in his pockets without success, and then he went through them again. He thought for a moment. 'I must have left them on the seat in the car,' he decided; 'I'll go and fetch them. The door must be just behind me here.'

He turned and groped his way back, and then drew himself up sharply, for it had seemed that something had slipped past him, and then he put out his hands—to touch the back of a chair, brocaded, he judged. He moved to the left of it and walked into a wall, changed his direction, went back past the chair, and found the wall again. He went back to the chair, sat down, and went through his pockets again, more thoroughly and carefully this time. Well, there was nothing to get fussed about; he was bound to find the door sooner or later. Now, let him think. When he came in he had gone straight forward, three yards perhaps; but he couldn't have gone straight back, because he'd stumbled into this chair. The door must be a little to the left or the right of it. He'd try each in turn. He turned to the left first, and found himself going down a little narrow passage; he could feel its sides when he stretched out his hands. Well, then, he'd try the right. He did so, and walked into a wall. He groped his way along it, and again it seemed as if something slipped past him. 'I wonder if there's a bat in here?' he asked himself, and then found himself back at the chair.

How Rachel would laugh if she could see him now. Surely he had a stray match somewhere. He took off his overcoat and ran his hands round the seam of every pocket, and then he did the same to the coat and waistcoat of his suit. And then he put them on again. Well, he'd try again. He'd follow the wall along. He did so, and found himself in a little narrow passage. Suddenly he shot out his right hand, for he had the impression that something had brushed his face very lightly. 'I'm beginning to get a little bored with that bat, and with this blasted room generally,' he said to himself. 'I could imagine a more nervous person than myself getting a little fussed and panicky; but that's the one thing not to do.' Ah, here was that chair again. 'Now, I'll try the wall the other side.' Well, that seemed to go on for ever, so he retraced his steps till he found the chair, and sat down again. He whistled a little snatch resignedly. What an echo! The little tune had been flung back at him so fiercely, almost menacingly. Menacingly: that was just the feeble, panicky word a nervous person would use. Well, he'd go to the left again this time.

As he got up, a quick spurt of cold air fanned his face. 'Is anyone there?' he said. He had purposely not raised his voice—there was no need to shout. Of course, no one answered. Who could there have been to answer since the care-taker was away? Now let him think it out. When he came in he must have gone straight forward and then swerved slightly on the way back; therefore—no, he was getting confused. At that moment he heard the whistle of a train, and felt reassured. The line from Wendover to Aylesbury ran half-left from the front door, so it should be about there—he pointed with his finger, got up, groped his way forward, and found himself in a little narrow passage. Well, he must turn back and go to the right this time. He did so, and something seemed to slip just past him, and then he scratched his finger slightly on the brocade of the chair. 'Talk about a maze,' he thought to himself; 'it's nothing to this.' And then he said to himself, under his breath: 'Curse this vile, godforsaken place!' A silly, panicky thing to do, he realised—almost as bad as shouting aloud. Well, it was obviously no use trying to find the door, he *couldn't* find it—*couldn't*. He'd sit in the chair till the light came. He sat down.

How very silent it was; his hands began searching in his pockets once more. Except for that sort of whispering sound over on the left somewhere—except for that, it was absolutely silent—except for that. What could it be? The care-taker was away. He turned his head slightly and listened intently. It was almost as if there were several people whispering together. One got curious sounds in old houses. How absurd it was! The chair couldn't be more than three or four yards from the door. There was no doubt about that. It must be slightly to one side or the other. He'd try the left once more. He got up, and something lightly brushed his face. 'Is anyone there?' he said, and this time he knew he had shouted. 'Who touched me? Who's whispering? Where's the door?' What a nervous fool he was to shout like that; yet someone outside might have heard him. He went groping forward again, and touched a wall. He followed along it, touching it with his fingertips, and there was an opening.

The door, the door, it must be! And he found himself going down a little narrow passage. He turned and ran back. And then he remembered! He had put a match-booklet in his notecase! What a fool to have forgotten it, and made such an exhibition of himself. Yes, there it was; but his hands were trem-bling, and the booklet slipped through his fingers. He fell to his knees, and began searching about on the floor. 'It must be just here, it can't be far'—and then something icy-cold and damp was pressed against his forehead. He flung himself forward to seize it, but there was nothing there. And then he leapt to his feet, and with tears streaming down his face, cried: 'Who is there? Save me! Save me!' And then he began to run round and round, his arms outstretched. At last he stumbled against something, the chair—and something touched him as it slipped past. And then he ran screaming round the room; and suddenly his screams slashed back at him, for he was in a little narrow passage.

'Now, MR RUNT,' said the coroner, 'you say you heard screaming coming from the direction of the Manor. Why didn't you go to find out what was the matter?'

'None of us chaps goes to Manor after sundown,' said Mr Runt.

'Oh, I know there's some absurd superstition about the house; but you haven't answered the question. There were screams, obviously coming from someone who wanted help. Why didn't you go to see what was the matter, instead of running away?'

'None of us chaps goes to Manor after sundown,' said Mr Runt.

'Don't fence with the question. Let me remind you that the doctor said Mr Cort must have had a seizure of some kind, but that had help been quickly forthcoming, his life might have been saved. Do you mean to tell me that, even if you had known this, you would still have acted in so cowardly a way?'

Mr Runt fixed his eyes on the ground and fingered his cap.

'None of us chaps goes to Manor after sundown,' he repeated.

Elizabeth Walter

In the course of a long and distinguished career in publishing—
including over twenty years editing a popular series of crime
novels—Elizabeth Walter has found time to put together five
volumes of her own supernatural stories. The bleak and
disturbing tale featured here has been taken from her volume
Dead Woman, published in 1975.

DUAL CONTROL

'You ought to have stopped.'

'For God's sake, shut up, Freda.'

'Well, you should have. You ought to have made sure she was all right.'

'Of course she's all right.'

'How do you know? You didn't stop to find out, did you?'

'Do you want me to go back? We're late enough as it is, thanks to your fooling about getting ready, but I don't suppose the Bradys'll notice if we're late. I don't suppose they'll notice if we never turn up, though after the way you angled for that invitation . . .'

'That's right, blame it all on me. We could have left half an hour ago if you hadn't been late home from the office.'

'How often do I have to tell you that business isn't a matter of nine to five?'

'No, it's a matter of the Bradys, isn't it? You were keen enough we should get asked. Where were you anyway? Drinking with the boys? Or smooching with some floozie?'

'Please yourself. Either could be correct.'

'If you weren't driving, I'd hit you.'

'Try something unconventional for a change.'

'Why don't you try remembering I'm your wife—'

'Give me a chance to forget it!'

'—and that we're going to a party where you'll be expected to behave.'

'I'll behave all right.'

'To me as well as to other women.'

'You mean you'll let me off the leash?'

'Oh, you don't give a damn about *my* feelings!'

'Look, if it hadn't been for you, I should have stopped tonight.'

'Yes, you'd have given a pretty girl a lift if you'd been on your own. I believe you. The trouble is, she thought you were going to stop.'

'So I was. Then I saw she was very pretty, and—Christ, Freda, you know what you're like. I've only got to be polite to a woman who's younger and prettier than you are—and believe me, there are plenty of them—and you stage one of your scenes.'

'I certainly try to head off the worst of the scandals. Really, Eric, do you think people don't know?'

'If they do, do you think they don't understand why I do it? They've only got to look at you . . . That's right, cry and ruin that fancy make-up. All this because I didn't give a pretty girl a lift.'

'But she signalled. You slowed down. She thought you were going to . . .'

'She won't jump to conclusions next time.'

'She may not jump at all. Eric, I think we ought to forget the Bradys. I think we ought to go back.'

'To find Cinderella has been given a lift by Prince Charming and been spirited away to the ball?'

'She was obviously going to a party. Suppose it's to the Bradys' and she's there?'

'Don't worry, she couldn't have seen what we looked like.'

'Could she remember the car?'

'No, she didn't have time.'

'You mean she didn't have time before you hit her.'

'God damn it, Freda, what do you expect me to do when a girl steps in front of the car just as I decide—for your sake—I'm not stopping? It wasn't much more than a shove.'

'It knocked her over.'

'She was off balance. It wouldn't have taken more than a touch.'

'But she fell. I saw her go backwards. And I'm sure there was blood on her head.'

'On a dark road the light's deceptive. You saw a shadow.'

'I wish to God I thought it was.'

'Look here, Freda, pull yourself together. I'm sorry about it, of course, but it would make everything worse to go back and apologise.'

'Then what are you stopping for?'

'So that you can put your face to rights and I can make sure the car isn't damaged.'

'If it is, I suppose you'll go back.'

'You underestimate me, as usual. No, if it is I shall drive gently into that tree. It will give us an excuse for arriving late at the Bradys' and explain the damage away.'

'But the girl may be lying there injured.'

'The road isn't that lonely, you know, and her car had obviously broken down. There'll be plenty of people willing to help a damsel in distress . . . Yes, it's as I thought. The car isn't even scratched. I thought we might have a dent in the wing, but it seems luck is on our side. So now, Freda, old girl, I'll have a nip from that flask you've got in your handbag.'

'I don't know what you mean.'

'Oh yes you do. You're never without it, and it needs a refill pretty often by now.'

'I can't think what's come over you, Eric.'

'Call it delayed shock. Are you going to give it me or do I have to help myself?'

'I can't imagine—Eric, let go! You're hurting!'

'The truth does hurt at times. Do you think I didn't know you had what's called a drinking problem? You needn't pretend with me.'

'It's my money. I can spend it how I choose.'

'Of course, my love. Don't stop reminding me that I'm your pensioner, but thanks anyway for your booze.'

'I didn't mean that. Oh Eric, I get so lonely, you don't know. And even when you're home you don't take any notice of me. I can't bear it. I love you so.'

'Surely you can't have reached the maudlin stage already? What are the Bradys going to think?'

'I don't give a damn about the Bradys. I keep thinking about that girl.'

'Well, I give a damn about the Bradys. They could be important to me. And I'm not going to ruin a good contact because my wife develops sudden scruples.'

'Won't it ruin it if they know you left a girl for dead by the roadside?'

'Maybe, but they won't know.'

'They will. If you don't go back, I'll tell them.'

'That sounds very much like blackmail, and that's a game that two can play.'

'What do you mean?'

'Who was driving the car, Freda?'

'You were.'

'Can you prove that?'

'As much as you can prove that I was.'

'Ah, but it's not as simple as that. Such an accusation would oblige me to tell the police about your drinking. A lot of unpleasant things would come out. I should think manslaughter is the least you'd get away with, and that could get you five years. Because please note that apart from that swig I am stone cold sober, whereas your blood alcohol is perpetually high. In addition, you're in a state of hysteria. Who d'you think would be believed—you or I?'

'You wouldn't do that, Eric. Not to your wife. Not to me.'

'Sooner than I would to anyone, but it won't come to that, will it, my dear?'

'I've a good mind to—'

'Quite, but I should forget it.'

'Eric, don't you love me at all?'

'For God's sake, Freda, not that now, of all times. I married you, didn't I? Ten years ago you were a good-looking thirty—'

'And you were a smart young salesman on the make.'

'So?'

'You needed capital to start your own business.'

'You offered to lend it me. And I've paid you interest.'

'And borrowed more capital.'

'It's a matter of safeguarding what we've got.'

'What we've got. That's rich! You hadn't a penny. Eric, don't start the car like that. You may not be drunk but anyone would think you are, the way you're driving. No wonder you hit that girl. And it wasn't just a shove. I think you've killed her.'

'For God's sake, Freda, shut up!'

'WELL, IT WAS A GOOD PARTY, wasn't it?'

'Yes.'

'Moira Brady's a marvellous hostess.'

'Yes.'

'Jack Brady's a lucky man. We ought to ask them back some time, don't you think?'

'Yes.'

'What's got into you? Cat got your tongue? You're a fine companion. We go to a terrific party and all you can say is Yes.'

'I'm thinking about that girl.'

'She was all right, wasn't she? Except for some mud on her dress. Did she say anything about it?'

'She said she'd fallen over.'

'She was speaking the literal truth. Now I hope you're satisfied I didn't hurt her.'

'She certainly looked all right.'

'You can say that again. Life and soul of the party, and obviously popular.'

'You spent enough time with her.'

'Here we go again. Do you have to spend the whole evening watching me?'

'I didn't, but every time I looked, you were with her.'

'She seemed to enjoy my company. Some women do, you know.'

'Don't torment me, Eric. I've got a headache.'

'So have I, as a matter of fact. Shall I open a window?'

'If it isn't too draughty . . . What was the girl's name?'

'Gisela.'

'It suits her, doesn't it? How did she get to the Bradys'?'

'I didn't ask.'

'It's funny, but I never saw her go.'

'I did. She left early because she said something about her car having engine trouble. I suppose someone was giving her a lift.'

'I wonder if her car's still there?'

'It won't be. She'll have got some garage to tow it away.'

'Don't be too sure. They're not so keen on coming out at nights in the country, unless something's blocking the road.'

'I believe you're right. That's it, isn't it—drawn up on the grass verge.'

'Yes. And Eric, that's her. She's hailing us.'

'And this time, I'm really going to stop.'

'What on earth can have happened?'

'It looks like another accident. That's fresh mud on her dress.'

'And fresh blood on her head! Eric, her face is all bloody!'

'It can't be as bad as it looks. She's not unconscious. A little blood can go a very long way. Just keep calm, Freda, and maybe that flask of yours will come in handy. I'll get out and see what's up . . . It's all right, Gisela. You'll be all right. It's me, Eric Andrews. We met at the Bradys' just now. My dear girl, you're in a state. What in God's name happened? Has someone tried to murder you? Here, lean on me.'

'Eric, what's the matter? Why have you left her alone? Gisela . . .'

'Christ, Freda, shut that window! And make sure your door's locked.'

'What is it? You look as if you'd seen a ghost.'

'She *is* a ghost . . . Give me that flask . . . That's better.'

'What do you mean—a ghost?'

'There's nothing there when you go up to her. Only a coldness in the air.'

'But that's nonsense. You can't see through her. Look, she's still standing there. She's flesh and blood—blood certainly.'

'Is there blood on my hand?'

'No, but it's shaking.'

'You bet it is. So am I. I tell you, Freda, I put out my hand to touch her—I did touch her—at least, I touched where she was standing—but she's got no body to touch.'

'She had a body at the Bradys'.'

'I wonder.'

'Well, you should know. You hung round her all the evening, making a spectacle of yourself.'

'I never touched her.'

'I'll bet it wasn't for want of trying.'

'Now I think of it, nobody touched her. She always seemed to stand a little apart.'

'But she ate and drank.'

'She didn't eat. She said she wasn't hungry. I don't remember seeing a glass in her hand.'

'Rubbish, Eric. I don't believe you. For some reason you don't want to help her. Are you afraid she'll recognise the car?'

'She has recognised it. That's why she's there. We—we must have killed her on the way to the party that time when we nearly stopped.'

'You mean when *you* nearly stopped. When you hit her. Oh God, what are we going to do?'

'Drive on, I think. She can't hurt us.'

'But she could get inside the car.'

'Not if we keep the doors locked.'

'Do you think locked doors can keep her out? Oh God, I wish I'd never come with you. Oh God, get me out of this. I never did anything. I wasn't driving. Oh God, I'm not responsible for what he does.'

'Oh no, you're not responsible for anything, are you, Freda? Does it occur to you that if it hadn't been for your damned jealousy I should have stopped?'

'You've given me cause enough for jealousy since we were married.'

'A man's got to get it somewhere, hasn't he? And you were pretty useless— admit it. You couldn't even produce a child.'

'You're heartless—heartless.'

'And you're spineless. A sponge, that's all you are.'

'I need a drink to keep me going, living with a bastard like you.'

'So we have to wait while you tank up and make ourselves late for the Bradys'. Do you realise, if we'd been earlier we shouldn't have seen that girl?'

'It's my fault again, is it?'

'Every bloody thing's your fault. I could have built up the business a whole lot faster if you'd put yourself out to entertain a bit. If I'd had a wife like Moira Brady, things would be very different from what they are.'

'You mean you'd make money instead of losing it.'

'What do you mean—losing it?'

'I can read a balance sheet, you know. Well, you're not getting any more of my money. "Safeguarding our interests" I don't think! Paying your creditors is more like it.'

'Now look here, Freda, I've had enough of this.'

'So have I. But I'm not walking home so there's no point in stopping.'

'Then try getting this straight for a change—'

'Eric, there's that girl again.'

'What are you talking about? Anyone would think you'd got D.T.s.'

'Look—she's bending down to speak to you. She's trying to open your door.'

'Christ!'

'Eric, don't start the car like that. Don't drive so furiously. What are you trying to do?'

'I'm trying to outdistance her.'

'But the speed limit . . .'

'Damn the speed limit! What's the good of having a powerful car if you don't use it? . . . That's right. You hit the bottle again.'

'But the way you're driving! You ignored a halt sign. That lorry driver had to cram on his brakes.'

'What the hell! Look round and see if you can see her.'

'She's right behind us, Eric.'

'What, in her car?'

'No, she seems to be floating a little way above the ground. But she's moving fast. I can see her hair streaming out behind her.'

'Well, we're doing seventy-five ourselves.'

'But we can't go on like this for ever. Sooner or later we've got to get out.'

'Sooner or later she's got to get tired of this caper.'

'Where are we? This isn't the way home.'

'Do you want her following us home? I want to lose her. What do you take me for?'

'A bastard who's ruined my life and ended that poor girl's.'

'No one warned me you'd ruin mine. I wish they had. I might have listened. Warnings are only given to the deaf ... Look again to see if Gisela's still following.'

'She's just behind us. Oh Eric, her eyes are wide and staring. She looks horribly, horribly dead. Do you suppose she'll ever stop following us? Gisela. It's a form of Giselle. Perhaps she's like the girl in the ballet and condemned to drive motorists to death instead of dancers.'

'Your cultural pretensions are impressive. Is your geography as good?'

'What do you mean?'

'I mean where the hell are we? I swear I've never seen this road before. It doesn't look like a road in southern England. More like the North Yorkshire moors, except that even there there's some habitation. Besides, we couldn't have driven that far.'

'There's a signpost at this next crossroads if you'll slow down enough for me to read ...'

'Well?'

'I don't understand it, Eric. All four arms of the signpost are blank.'

'Vandals painted them out.'

'Vandals! In this desolate, isolated spot? Oh Eric, I don't like this. Suppose we're condemned to go on driving for ever?'

'No, Freda, the petrol would give out.'

'But the gauge has been at nought for ages. Hadn't you noticed?'

'What? So it is. But the car's going like a bird.'

'Couldn't you slow down a bit? I know you didn't for the signpost, but she— she's not so close behind us now ... Please, Eric, my head's still aching.'

'What do you think I'm trying to do?'

'But we're doing eighty ... I knew it. We'll have to go on driving till we die.'

'Don't be such an utter bloody fool. I admit we've seen a ghost—something I never believed existed. I admit I've lost control of this damn car and I don't know how she keeps running on no petrol. I also admit I don't know where we are. But for all this there's got to be a rational explanation. Some timeswitch in our minds. Some change of state.'

'That's it! Eric, what's the last landmark you can remember?'

'That blanked-out signpost.'

'Not that. I mean the last normal sign.'

'You said there was a halt sign, but I must say I never saw it.'

'You drove right through it, that's why. We shot straight in front of a lorry. I think—oh Eric, I think we're dead.'

'Dead! You must be joking. Better have another drink.'

'I can't. The flask's empty. Besides, the dead don't drink. Or eat. They're like Gisela. You can't touch them. There's nothing there.'

'Where's Gisela now?'

'A long, long way behind us. After all, she's had her revenge.'

'You're hysterical, Freda. You're raving.'

'What do you expect but weeping and wailing? We're in Hell.'

'The religious beliefs of childhood reasserting themselves.'

'Well, what do you think Hell is? Don't hurry, you've got eternity to answer in. But I know what I think it is. It's the two of us driving on alone. For ever. Just the two of us, Eric. For evermore.'

Fay Weldon

b. 1933

After serving in the Foreign Office, Fay Weldon worked in an advertising agency—where she became famous for the 'Go To Work On An Egg' campaign—before building herself a reputation as a talented novelist. *The Life and Loves of a She-Devil*, one of her best-known works, was adapted for British television and was made into a Hollywood film.

BREAKAGES

'WE BLOSSOM AND FLOURISH, like leaves on a tree. And wither and perish. But naught changeth the-e-e—' sang David's congregation in its laggardly, quavery voice. Some trick of acoustics made much of what happened in the church audible in the vicarage kitchen, where tonight, as so often, Deidre sat and darned socks and waited for Evensong to end.

The vicarage, added as a late-Victorian afterthought, leaned up against the solidity of the Norman church. The house was large, ramshackle, dark and draughty, prey to wet rot, dry rot, woodworm and beetle. Here David and Deidre lived. He was a vicar of the established church; she was his wife. He attended to the spiritual welfare of his parishioners; she presided over the Mothers' Union, the Women's Institute and ran the Amateur Dramatic Society. They had been married for twenty-one years. They had no children, which was a source of acute disappointment to them, and to Deidre's mother, and of mild disappointment to the parish. It is always pleasant, in a small, stable and increasingly elderly community, to watch other people's children grow up, and sad to be deprived of that pleasure.

'Oh no, please,' said Deidre, now, to the Coronation mug on the dresser. It was a rare piece, produced in anticipation of an event which had never occurred, the Coronation of the Duke of Windsor. It was, so far, uncracked and unchipped, and worth some £300, but had just moved to the very edge of its shelf, not smoothly and purposively, but with an uneven rocking motion which made Deidre hope that entreaty might yet calm it, and save it. And indeed, after she spoke, the mug was quiet, and lapsed into the ordinary stillness she had once always associated with inanimate objects.

'Immortal, invisible, God only wise— In light inaccessible—' Deidre joined in the hymn, singing gently and soothingly, and trying to feel happy, for the happier she felt the fewer breakages there would be and perhaps one day they would stop altogether, and David would never, ever find out; that, one by one, the ornaments and possessions he most loved and valued were leaping off shelves and shattering, to be secretly mended by Deidre, with such skills as she remembered from the early days, before marriage had interrupted her training in china restoration, and her possible future in the Victoria and Albert Museum.

Long ago and far away. Now Deidre darned. David's feet were sensitive to anything other than pure, fine wool. Not for him the tough nylon mixtures that other men wore.

DEIDRE DARNED.

The Coronation mug rocked violently.

'Stop it,' said Deidre, warningly. Sometimes to be stern worked better than to plead. The mug stayed where it was. But a fraction further and it would have fallen.

Deidre unpicked the last few stitches. She was in danger of cobbling the darn and there is nothing more uncomfortable to sensitive skin than a cobbled darn.

'You do it on purpose,' David would complain, not without reason. Deidre's faults were the ones he found most difficult to bear. She was careless, untidy and extravagant. She broke dishes, lost socks, left lids unscrewed, taps running, doors open, saucepans burning: she bought fresh bread when yesterday's at half-price would do. It was her nature, she maintained, and grieved bitterly when her husband implied that it was wilful and that she was doing it to annoy.

The Coronation mug leapt off its shelf, arced through the air and fell and broke in two pieces at Deidre's feet. She put the pieces at the very back of the drawer beneath the sink. There was no time for mending them now. Tomorrow morning would have to do, when David was out parish-visiting, in houses freshly dusted and brightened for his arrival. Fortunately, he seldom inspected the sink drawer, as he did the others in the house, looking for dirt and disorder. It smelt, when opened, of dry rot, and reminded him too forcibly of the large sums of money which ought to be spent on the repair of the house. 'We could sell something,' she would sometimes venture, but the prospect upset him. His mother had died when he was four, his father had gone bankrupt when he was eight: relatives had reared him and sent him off to boarding school where he had been sexually and emotionally abused. Possessions were his security.

She understood him, forgave him, loved him and tried not to argue. She had her own problems, with her mother.

She darned his socks. It was a larger pile than usual. Socks kept disappearing, not by the pair, but singly. They always had. David had lately discovered a pillowslip stuffed full of them pushed to the back of the wardrobe. It was his wife's deceit which worried him most, or so he said. Hiding socks! That and the sheer careless waste of it all. Losing socks! So Deidre tried tying the socks together for the wash, and thus, in pairs, the night before, spun and dried, they had neatly lain in the laundry basket. In the morning she had found them in one ugly, monstrous knot, and each sock oddly long, as if stretched and stretched by a hand too angry to know what it was doing. Rinsing had restored them, fortunately, to a proper shape, and now she darned where the ordeal had worn the wool thin.

It was always like this. David's things were attacked, as if the monstrous hand were on her side, yet it was she, Deidre, who had to repair the damage, follow its source as it moved about the house, mending what it broke, wiping tomato purée from the ceiling, toothpaste from the lavatory bowl, replanting David's seedlings, rescrewing lids, closing doors, refolding linen, turning off taps. She scarcely dared leave the house for fear of what might happen in his absence, and this David interpreted as a lack of interest in his parish. Disloyalty, to God and husband. Times were bad between them.

Deidre's finger was bleeding. She must have cut it on the sharp edge of the broken Coronation mug. She opened the table drawer, and took out the first piece of cloth which came to hand, and wrapped the finger. The cold tap started to run, but she ignored it. Blood spread out over the cloth but presently stopped.

The invisible hand swept the dresser shelf, knocking all sorts of treasures sideways but breaking nothing. It had never touched the dresser before, as if awed, as Deidre was, by the ever-increasing value of its contents—rare blue-and-white pieces, frog mugs, barbers' bowls, lustre cups, a debatedly Ming bowl.

It was getting bolder.

David did not give Deidre a housekeeping allowance. She asked for money when she needed it, but David seldom recognised that it was in fact needed. He could not see the necessity of things like washing-up liquid, sugar, toilet rolls, new scourers. Sometimes she stole money from his pocket: once she took a coin out of the offertory on Sunday morning instead of putting a coin in it.

Deceitful, dishonest; Deidre knew the sort of person she was and despised herself for it. A bad wife, a barren wife, and a poor sort of person.

David came home. The house fell quiet, as always, at his approach. Taps stopped running and china rattling. David kissed her on her forehead.

'Deidre,' said David, 'what have you wrapped around your finger?'

Deidre unwrapped the binding and found that it was a fine lace and cotton handkerchief, put in the drawer for mending, which once had belonged to David's grandmother. It was now sodden and bright, bright red.

'I cut my finger,' said Deidre, inadequately and indeed foolishly, for what if he demanded to know what had caused the wound? But he was too busy rinsing and squeezing the handkerchief under the tap to enquire. Deidre put her finger in her mouth and put up with the salt, exciting taste of her own blood.

'It's hopelessly stained,' he mourned. 'Couldn't you just for once have used something you wouldn't spoil? A tissue?'

David did not allow the purchase of tissues. There had been none in his youth: why should they be needed now, in his middle age?

'I'm sorry,' said Deidre. She was always saying she was sorry, and always providing cause for her own remorse.

He took the handkerchief upstairs to the bathroom, in search of soap and a nailbrush. 'What kind of wife are you, Deidre?' he asked as he went, desperate.

What kind, indeed? Married in a Registry Office in the days before David had taken to Holy Orders and a Heavenly Father more reliable than his earthly one. Deidre had suggested that they remarry in Church, as could be and had been done by others, but David did not want to. Hardly a wife at all.

A barren wife. A fig tree, struck by God's ill temper. David's God. In the beginning they had shared a God, who was bleak, sensible and kind. But now, increasingly, David had his own jealous and punitive God, whom he wooed with ritual and richness, incense and images, dragging a surprised congregation with him. He changed his vestments three times during services, rang little bells to announce the presence of the Lord, swept up and down aisles, and in general seemed not averse, in church as at home, to being mistaken for God.

The water pipes shrieked and groaned as David turned on the tap in the bathroom, but that was due to bad plumbing rather than unnatural causes. She surely could not be held responsible for that, too.

When the phenomena—as she thought of them—first started, or rather leapt from the scale of ordinary domestic carelessness to something less explicable and more sinister, she went to the doctor.

'Doctor,' she said, 'do mumps in adolescence make men infertile?'

'It depends,' he said, proving nothing. 'If the gonads are affected it might well. Why?'

No reason had been found for Deidre's infertility. It lay, presumably, like so much else, in her mind. She had had her tubes blown, painfully and unforgettably, to facilitate conception, but it had made no difference. For fifteen years she endured the monthly cycle of hope followed by disappointment, and bore the weight of David's sorrow, as she, his wife, deprived him of his earthly immortality, his children. 'Of course,' he said sadly, 'you are an only child. Only children are often infertile. The sins of the fathers—' David regarded fecundity as a blessing; the sign of a woman in tune with God's universe. He had married Deidre, he vaguely and hurtfully let it be known, on the rebound from a young woman who had gone on to have seven children.

David's fertility remained unquestioned and unexamined. A sperm count would surely have proved nothing. His sperm was plentiful and he had no sexual problems that he was aware of. To ejaculate into a test tube to prove a point smacked uncomfortably of onanism.

The matter of the mumps came up during the time of Deidre's menopause, a month or so after her, presumably, last period. David had been in the school sanatorium with mumps: she had heard him saying so to a distraught mother, adding 'Oh, mumps! Nothing in a boy under fourteen. Be thankful he has them now, not later.'

So, he was aware that mumps were dangerous. And Deidre knew well enough that David had lived in the world of school sanatoria after the age of fourteen, not before. Why had he never mentioned it to her? And while she wondered, and pondered, and hesitated to ask, toothpaste began to ooze from tubes, and rose trees were uprooted in the garden, and his seedlings trampled by unseen boots, and his clothes in the wardrobe tumbled in a pile to the ground, and Deidre stole money to buy mending glue, and finally went to the doctor.

'Most men,' said the doctor, 'confuse impotence with infertility and believe that mumps cause the former, not the latter.'

BACK TO SQUARE ONE. Perhaps he didn't know. 'Why have you *really* come?' asked the doctor, recently back from a course in patient-doctor relations.

Deidre offered him an account of her domestic phenomena, as she had not meant to do. He prescribed valium and asked her to come back in a week. She did.

'Any better? Does the valium help?'

'At least when I see things falling, I don't mind so much.'

'But you still see them falling?'

'Yes.'

'Does your husband see them too?'

'He's never there when they do.'

Now WHAT WAS any thinking doctor to make of that?

'We could try hormone replacement therapy,' he said.

'No,' said Deidre.

'Then what do you want me to do?'

'If I could only feel angry with my husband,' said Deidre, 'instead of forever understanding and forgiving him, I might get it to stop. As it is; I am releasing too much kinetic energy.'

There were patients waiting. They had migraines, eczema and boils. He gave her more valium, which she did not take.

Deidre, or some expression of Deidre, went home and churned up the lawn and tore the gate off its hinges. The other Deidre raked and smoothed, resuscitated and blamed a perfectly innocent child for the gate. A child. It would have taken a forty-stone giant to twist the hinges so, but no one stopped, fortunately, to think about that. The child went to bed without supper for swinging on the vicar's gate.

The wound on Deidre's finger gaped open in an unpleasant way. She thought she could see the white bone within the bloodless flesh.

Deidre went upstairs to the bathroom, where David washed his wife's blood from his grandmother's hankie. 'David,' said Deidre, 'perhaps I should have a stitch in my finger?'

David had the toothmug in his hand. His jaw was open, his eyes wide with shock. He had somehow smeared toothpaste on his black lapel. 'This mug has been broken and mended. Why was I not told? Did you do it?'

The toothmug dated from the late eighteenth century and was worn, cracked and chipped, but David loved it. It had been one of the first things to go, and Deidre had not mended it with her usual care, thinking, mistakenly, that one more crack among so many would scarcely be noticed.

'I am horrified,' said David.

'Sorry,' said Deidre.

'You always break my things, never your own.'

'I thought that when you got married,' said Deidre, with the carelessness of desperation, for surely now David would start on an inspection of his belongings and all would be discovered, 'things stopped being yours and mine and became ours.'

'Married! You and I have never been married, not in the sight of God, and I thank Him for it.'

There. He had said what had been unsaid for years, but there was no relief in it, for either of them. There came a crash of breaking china from downstairs. David ran down to the kitchen, where the noise came from, but could see no sign of damage. He moved into the living room. Deidre followed dutifully. 'You've shattered my life,' said David. 'We have nothing in common. You have been a burden since the beginning. I wanted a happy, warm, loving house. I wanted children.'

'I suppose,' said Deidre, 'you'll be saying next that my not having children is God's punishment?'

'Yes,' said David.

'Nothing to do with your mumps?'

David was silent, taken aback. Out of the corner of her eye Deidre saw the Ming vase move.

'You are a sadistic person,' said David, eventually. 'Even the pains and humiliations of long ago are not safe from you. You revive them.'

'You knew all the time,' said Deidre. 'You were infertile, not me. You made me take the blame. And it's too late for me now.'

The Ming vase rocked to the edge of the shelf: Deidre moved to push it back, but not quickly enough. It fell and broke.

David cried out in pain and rage. It was as if he himself had broken.

'You did it on purpose,' he wept. 'You hate me.'

Deidre went upstairs and packed her clothes. She would stay with her mother while she planned some kind of new life for herself. She would be happier anywhere in the world but here, sharing a house with a ghost.

David moved through the house, weeping, but for his treasures, not for his wife. He took a wicker basket and in it laid tenderly—as if they were the bodies of children—the many broken and mended vases and bowls and dishes which he found. Sometimes the joins were skilful and barely detectable to his moving forefinger: sometimes careless. But everything was spoilt. What had been perfect was now second-rate and without value. The finds in junk shops, the gifts from old ladies, the few small knick-knacks which had come to him from his dead mother—his whole past destroyed by his wife's single-minded malice and cunning.

He carried the basket to the kitchen, and sat with his head in his hands.

Deidre left without saying another word. Out of the door, through the broken garden gate, into the night, through the churchyard, for the powers of the dead disturbed her less than the powers of the living, and to the bus station.

David sat. The smell of rot from the sink drawer was powerful enough, presently, to make him lift his head.

The cold tap started to run. A faulty washer, he concluded. He moved to turn it off, but the valve was already closed. 'Deidre!' he called, 'what have you done with the kitchen tap?' He did not know why he spoke, for Deidre was gone.

The whole top of the dresser fell forward on to the ground. Porcelain shattered and earthenware powdered. He could hear the little pings of the Eucharist bell in the church next door announcing the presence of God.

He thought perhaps there was an earthquake, but the central light hung still and quiet. Upstairs heavy feet bumped to and fro, dragging, wrenching and banging. Outside the window the black trees rocked so fiercely that he thought he would be safer in than out. The gas taps of the cooker were on and he could smell gas, mixed with fumes from the coal fire where Deidre's darning had been piled up and was now smouldering. He closed his eyes.

He was not frightened. He knew that he saw and heard these things, but that they had no substance in the real world. They were a distortion of the facts, as water becomes wine in the communion service and bread becomes the flesh of the Saviour.

When next he opened his eyes the dresser was restored, the socks still lay in the mending basket, the air was quiet.

Sensory delusions, that was all, brought about by shock. But unpleasant, all the same. Deidre's fault. David went upstairs to sleep but could not open the bedroom door. He thought perhaps Deidre had locked it behind her, out of spite. He was tired. He slept in the spare room, peacefully, without the irritant of Deidre's warmth beside him.

In the morning the window cleaner arrived to do the windows which Deidre could not reach. He could not get into the bedroom through the door, so David held the ladder while he got in through the window.

'Funny sort of burglars,' the window cleaner said to the police, later. 'They'd thrown everything about, furniture, clothes, the lot, all upside down and everywhere. The wardrobe was wrong way up and blocking the door. And the carpet! Great heavy thick thing. They'd picked it right off the floor, and wrung it out as if it was a dishcloth, and wedged it between the floor and the ceiling. The Rev. and three strong men were all morning trying to untwist it but they couldn't. Now what sort of burglars can do a thing like that? If you ask me—' which they didn't, of course. They wrote the matter down on their files as U.P., or Unexplained Phenomena.

'She was a very strong woman,' said David to his new young lady organist. 'She did all that to my things and then somehow got out by the window. She wanted to frighten me, and make me believe in ghosts. That was the level of her spiritual potential, I'm afraid.'

Later they were to marry, but had no children, which as he was growing older was something of a relief though a disappointment to her, and to the parish.

Oscar Wilde

1854–1900

Oscar Wilde was an Irishman of extraordinary wit and brilliance,
as illustrated by his plays *Lady Windermere's Fan* and *The
Importance of Being Earnest*. He was the toast of London
Society until his trial and imprisonment for homosexual offences
in 1895 left him a broken man. This charming and amusing story
dates from an earlier, happier time.

THE CANTERVILLE GHOST

A Hylo-Idealistic Romance

I

WHEN MR HIRAM B. OTIS, the American Minister, bought Canterville
Chase, everyone told him he was doing a very foolish thing, as there
was no doubt at all that the place was haunted. Indeed, Lord
Canterville himself, who was a man of the most punctilious honour, had felt it
his duty to mention the fact to Mr Otis when they came to discuss terms.

'We have not cared to live in the place ourselves,' said Lord Canterville, 'since
my grand-aunt, the Dowager Duchess of Bolton, was frightened into a fit, from
which she never really recovered, by two skeleton hands being placed on her
shoulders as she was dressing for dinner, and I feel bound to tell you, Mr Otis,
that the Ghost has been seen by several living members of my family, as well as
by the rector of the parish, the Rev. Augustus Dampier, who is a Fellow of
King's College, Cambridge. After the unfortunate accident to the Duchess, none
of our younger servants would stay with us, and Lady Canterville often got very
little sleep at night, in consequence of the mysterious noises that came from the
corridor and the library.'

'My lord,' answered the Minister, 'I will take the furniture and the Ghost at a
valuation. I come from a modern country, where we have everything that
money can buy; and with all our spry young fellows painting the Old World red,

and carrying off your best actors and prima donnas, I reckon that if there were such a thing as a ghost in Europe, we'd have it at home in a very short time in one of our public museums, or on the road as a show.'

'I fear that the Ghost exists,' said Lord Canterville, smiling, 'though it may have resisted the overtures of your enterprising impresarios. It has been well known for three centuries, since 1584 in fact, and always makes its appearance before the death of any member of our family.'

'Well, so does the family doctor for that matter, Lord Canterville. But there is no such thing, sir, as a ghost, and I guess the laws of Nature are not going to be suspended for the British aristocracy.'

'You are certainly very natural in America,' answered Lord Canterville, who did not quite understand Mr Otis's last observation, 'and if you don't mind a ghost in the house, it is all right. Only you must remember I warned you.'

A few weeks after this, the purchase was concluded, and at the close of the season the Minister and his family went down to Canterville Chase. Mrs Otis, who, as Miss Lucretia R. Tappen, of West 53rd Street, had been a celebrated New York belle, was now a very handsome, middle-aged woman, with fine eyes, and a superb profile. Many American ladies on leaving their native land adopt an appearance of chronic ill health, under the impression that it is a form of European refinement, but Mrs Otis had never fallen into this error. She had a magnificent constitution, and a really wonderful amount of animal spirits. Indeed, in many respects, she was quite English, and was an excellent example of the fact that we have really everything in common with America nowadays, except, of course, language. Her eldest son, christened Washington by his parents in a moment of patriotism, which he never ceased to regret, was a fair-haired, rather good-looking young man, who had qualified himself for American diplomacy by leading the German at the Newport Casino for three successive seasons, and even in London was well known as an excellent dancer. Gardenias and the peerage were his only weaknesses. Otherwise he was extremely sensible. Miss Virginia E. Otis was a little girl of fifteen, lithe and lovely as a fawn, and with a fine freedom in her large blue eyes. She was a wonderful amazon, and had once raced old Lord Bilton on her pony twice round the park, winning by a length and a half, just in front of the Achilles statue, to the huge delight of the young Duke of Cheshire, who proposed for her on the spot, and was sent back to Eton that very night by his guardians, in floods of tears. After Virginia came the twins, who were usually called 'The Stars and Stripes', as they were always getting swished. They were delightful boys, and with the exception of the worthy Minister the only true republicans of the family.

As Canterville Chase is seven miles from Ascot, the nearest railway station, Mr Otis had telegraphed for a wagonette to meet them, and they started on their drive in high spirits. It was a lovely July evening, and the air was delicate with the scent of the pinewoods. Now and then they heard a wood pigeon brooding over its own sweet voice, or saw, deep in the rustling fern, the burnished breast of the pheasant. Little squirrels peered at them from the beech trees as they went by, and the rabbits scudded away through the brushwood and over the mossy knolls, with their white tails in the air. As they entered the avenue of Canterville Chase, however, the sky became suddenly overcast with clouds, a curious stillness seemed to hold the atmosphere, a great flight of rooks passed silently over their heads, and, before they reached the house, some big drops of rain had fallen.

Standing on the steps to receive them was an old woman, neatly dressed in black silk, with a white cap and apron. This was Mrs Umney, the housekeeper, whom Mrs Otis, at Lady Canterville's earnest request, had consented to keep on in her former position. She made them each a low curtsy as they alighted, and said in a quaint, old-fashioned manner, 'I bid you welcome to Canterville Chase.' Following her, they passed through the fine Tudor hall into the library, a long, low room, panelled in black oak, at the end of which was a large stained-glass window. Here they found tea laid out for them, and, after taking off their wraps, they sat down and began to look round, while Mrs Umney waited on them.

Suddenly Mrs Otis caught sight of a dull red stain on the floor just by the fireplace and, quite unconscious of what it really signified, said to Mrs Umney, 'I am afraid something has been spilt there.'

'Yes, madam,' replied the old housekeeper in a low voice, 'blood has been spilt on that spot.'

'How horrid,' cried Mrs Otis; 'I don't at all care for bloodstains in a sitting room. It must be removed at once.'

The old woman smiled, and answered in the same low, mysterious voice, 'It is the blood of Lady Eleanore de Canterville, who was murdered on that very spot by her own husband, Sir Simon de Canterville, in 1575. Sir Simon survived her nine years, and disappeared suddenly under very mysterious circumstances. His body has never been discovered, but his guilty spirit still haunts the Chase. The bloodstain has been much admired by tourists and others, and cannot be removed.'

'That is all nonsense,' cried Washington Otis; 'Pinkerton's Champion Stain Remover and Paragon Detergent will clean it up in no time,' and before the terrified housekeeper could interfere he had fallen upon his knees, and was rapidly scouring the floor with a small stick of what looked like a black cosmetic. In a few moments no trace of the bloodstain could be seen.

'I knew Pinkerton would do it,' he exclaimed triumphantly, as he looked round at his admiring family; but no sooner had he said these words than a terrible flash of lightning lit up the sombre room, a fearful peal of thunder made them all start to their feet, and Mrs Umney fainted.

'What a monstrous climate!' said the American Minister calmly, as he lit a long cheroot. 'I guess the old country is so overpopulated that they have not enough decent weather for everybody. I have always been of opinion that emigration is the only thing for England.'

'My dear Hiram,' cried Mrs Otis, 'what can we do with a woman who faints?'

'Charge it to her like breakages,' answered the Minister; 'she won't faint after that'; and in a few moments Mrs Umney certainly came to. There was no doubt, however, that she was extremely upset, and she sternly warned Mr Otis to beware of some trouble coming to the house.

'I have seen things with my own eyes, sir,' she said, 'that would make any Christian's hair stand on end, and many and many a night I have not closed my eyes in sleep for the awful things that are done here.' Mr Otis, however, and his wife warmly assured the honest soul that they were not afraid of ghosts, and, after invoking the blessings of Providence on her new master and mistress, and making arrangements for an increase of salary, the old housekeeper tottered off to her own room.

II

THE STORM RAGED FIERCELY all that night, but nothing of particular note occurred. The next morning, however, when they came down to breakfast, they found the terrible stain of blood once again on the floor. 'I don't think it can be the fault of the Paragon Detergent,' said Washington, 'for I have tried it with everything. It must be the Ghost.' He accordingly rubbed out the stain a second time, but the second morning it appeared again. The third morning also it was there, though the library had been locked up at night by Mr Otis himself, and the key carried upstairs. The whole family were now quite interested; Mr Otis began to suspect that he had been too dogmatic in his denial of the existence of ghosts, Mrs Otis expressed her intention of joining the Psychical Society, and Washington prepared a long letter to Messrs Myers and Podmore on the subject of the Permanence of Sanguineous Stains when connected with Crime. That night all doubts about the objective existence of phantasmata were removed for ever.

The day had been warm and sunny; and, in the cool of the evening, the whole family went out to drive. They did not return home till nine o'clock, when they had a light supper. The conversation in no way turned upon ghosts, so there were not even those primary conditions of receptive expectation which so often precede the presentation of psychical phenomena. The subjects discussed, as I have since learned from Mr Otis, were merely such as form the ordinary conversation of cultured Americans of the better class, such as the immense superiority of Miss Fanny Davenport over Sarah Bernhardt as an actress; the difficulty of obtaining green corn, buckwheat cakes, and hominy, even in the best English houses; the importance of Boston in the development of the world soul; the advantages of the baggage check system in railway travelling; and the sweetness of the New York accent as compared to the London drawl. No mention at all was made of the supernatural, nor was Sir Simon de Canterville alluded to in any way. At eleven o'clock the family retired, and by half past all the lights were out. Some time after, Mr Otis was awakened by a curious noise in the corridor, outside his room. It sounded like the clank of metal, and seemed to be coming nearer every moment. He got up at once, struck a match, and looked at the time. It was exactly one o'clock. He was quite calm, and felt his pulse, which was not at all feverish. The strange noise still continued, and with it he heard distinctly the sound of footsteps. He put on his slippers, took a small oblong phial out of his dressing case, and opened the door. Right in front of him he saw, in the wan moonlight, an old man of terrible aspect. His eyes were as red burning coals; long grey hair fell over his shoulders in matted coils; his garments, which were of antique cut, were soiled and ragged, and from his wrists and ankles hung heavy manacles and rusty gyves.

'My dear sir,' said Mr Otis, 'I really must insist on your oiling those chains, and have brought you for that purpose a small bottle of the Tammany Rising Sun Lubricator. It is said to be completely efficacious upon one application, and there are several testimonials to that effect on the wrapper from some of our most eminent native divines. I shall leave it here for you by the bedroom candles, and will be happy to supply you with more should you require it.' With these words the United States Minister laid the bottle down on a marble table, and, closing his door, retired to rest.

For a moment the Canterville Ghost stood quite motionless in natural indignation; then, dashing the bottle violently upon the polished floor, he fled down the corridor, uttering hollow groans, and emitting a ghastly green light. Just, however, as he reached the top of the great oak staircase, a door was flung open, two little white-robed figures appeared, and a large pillow whizzed past his head! There was evidently no time to be lost, so, hastily adopting the Fourth Dimension of Space as a means of escape, he vanished through the wainscoting, and the house became quite quiet.

On reaching a small secret chamber in the left wing, he leaned up against a moonbeam to recover his breath, and began to try and realise his position. Never, in a brilliant and uninterrupted career of three hundred years, had he been so grossly insulted. He thought of the Dowager Duchess, whom he had frightened into a fit as she stood before the glass in her lace and diamonds; of the four housemaids, who had gone off into hysterics when he merely grinned at them through the curtains of one of the spare bedrooms; of the rector of the parish, whose candle he had blown out as he was coming late one night from the library, and who had been under the care of Sir William Gull ever since, a perfect martyr to nervous disorders; and of old Madame de Tremouillac, who, having wakened up one morning early and seen a skeleton seated in an armchair by the fire reading her diary, had been confined to her bed for six weeks with an attack of brain fever, and, on her recovery, had become reconciled to the Church, and broken off her connection with that notorious sceptic Monsieur de Voltaire. He remembered the terrible night when the wicked Lord Canterville was found choking in his dressing room, with the knave of diamonds halfway down his throat, and confessed, just before he died, that he had cheated Charles James Fox out of £50,000 at Crockford's by means of that very card, and swore that the Ghost had made him swallow it. All his great achievements came back to him again, from the butler who had shot himself in the pantry because he had seen a green hand tapping at the windowpane, to the beautiful Lady Stutfield, who was always obliged to wear a black velvet band round her throat to hide the mark of five fingers burnt upon her white skin, and who drowned herself at last in the carp pond at the end of the King's Walk. With the enthusiastic egotism of the true artist he went over his most celebrated performances, and smiled bitterly to himself as he recalled to mind his last appearance as 'Red Reuben, or the Strangled Babe', his début as 'Gaunt Gibeon, the Blood-sucker of Bexley Moor', and the furore he had excited one lovely June evening by merely playing ninepins with his own bones upon the lawn-tennis ground. And after all this, some wretched modern Americans were to come and offer him the Rising Sun Lubricator, and throw pillows at his head! It was quite unbearable. Besides, no ghost in history had ever been treated in this manner. Accordingly, he determined to have vengeance, and remained till daylight in an attitude of deep thought.

III

THE NEXT MORNING, when the Otis family met at breakfast, they discussed the Ghost at some length. The United States Minister was naturally a little annoyed to find that his present had not been accepted. 'I have no wish,' he said, 'to do the Ghost any personal injury, and I must say that, considering the length of time he has been in the house, I don't think it is at all polite to throw pillows at him'—a very just remark, at which, I am sorry to say, the twins burst into shouts of laughter. 'Upon the other hand,' he continued, 'if he really declines to use the Rising Sun Lubricator, we shall have to take his chains from him. It would be quite impossible to sleep, with such a noise going on outside the bedrooms.'

For the rest of the week, however, they were undisturbed, the only thing that excited any attention being the continual renewal of the bloodstain on the library floor. This certainly was very strange, as the door was always locked at night by Mr Otis, and the windows kept closely barred. The chameleon-like colour, also, of the stain excited a good deal of comment. Some mornings it was a dull (almost Indian) red, then it would be vermilion, then a rich purple, and once when they came down for family prayers, according to the simple rites of the Free American Reformed Episcopalian Church, they found it a bright emerald green. These kaleidoscopic changes naturally amused the party very much, and bets on the subject were freely made every evening. The only person who did not enter into the joke was little Virginia, who, for some unexplained reason, was always a good deal distressed at the sight of the bloodstain, and very nearly cried the morning it was emerald green.

The second appearance of the Ghost was on Sunday night. Shortly after they had gone to bed they were suddenly alarmed by a fearful crash in the hall. Rushing downstairs, they found that a large suit of old armour had become detached from its stand, and had fallen on the stone floor, while, seated in a high-backed chair, was the Canterville Ghost, rubbing his knees with an expression of acute agony on his face. The twins, having brought their peashooters with them, at once discharged two pellets on him, with that accuracy of aim which can only be attained by long and careful practice on a writing master, while the United States Minister covered him with his revolver, and called upon him, in accordance with Californian etiquette, to hold up his hands! The Ghost started up with a wild shriek of rage, and swept through them like a mist, extinguishing Washington Otis's candle as he passed, and so leaving them all in total darkness. On reaching the top of the staircase he recovered himself and determined to give his celebrated peal of demoniac laughter. This he had on more than one occasion found extremely useful. It was said to have turned Lord Raker's wig grey in a single night, and had certainly made three of Lady Canterville's French governesses give warning before their month was up. He accordingly laughed his most horrible laugh, till the old vaulted roof rang and rang again, but hardly had the fearful echo died away when a door opened, and Mrs Otis came out in a light-blue dressing gown. 'I am afraid you are far from well,' she said, 'and have brought you a bottle of Dr Dobell's tincture. If it is indigestion, you will find it a most excellent remedy.' The Ghost glared at her in fury, and began at once to make preparations for turning himself into a large black dog, an accomplishment for which he was justly renowned, and to which the family doctor always attributed the permanent idiocy of Lord Canterville's uncle, the Hon. Thomas Horton. The sound of approaching footsteps, however, made him hesitate in his fell purpose, so he contented himself with becoming faintly phosphorescent, and vanished with a deep churchyard groan, just as the twins had come up to him.

On reaching his room he entirely broke down, and became a prey to the most violent agitation. The vulgarity of the twins, and the gross materialism of Mrs Otis, were naturally extremely annoying, but what really distressed him most was, that he had been unable to wear the suit of mail. He had hoped that even modern Americans would be thrilled by the sight of a Spectre In Armour, if for no more sensible reason, at least out of respect for their national poet Longfellow, over whose graceful and attractive poetry he himself had whiled away many a weary hour when the Cantervilles were up in town. Besides, it was his own suit. He had worn it with great success at the Kenilworth tournament, and had been highly complimented on it by no less a person than the Virgin Queen herself. Yet when he had put it on, he had been completely overpowered by the weight of the huge breastplate and steel casque, and had fallen heavily on the stone pavement, barking both his knees severely, and bruising the knuckles of his right hand.

For some days after this he was extremely ill, and hardly stirred out of his room at all, except to keep the bloodstain in proper repair. However, by taking great care of himself, he recovered, and resolved to make a third attempt to frighten the United States Minister and his family. He selected Friday, the 17th of August, for his appearance, and spent most of that day in looking over his wardrobe, ultimately deciding in favour of a large slouched hat with a red feather, a winding sheet frilled at the wrists and neck, and a rusty dagger. Towards evening a violent storm of rain came on, and the wind was so high that all the windows and doors in the old house shook and rattled. In fact, it was just such weather as he loved. His plan of action was this. He was to make his way quietly to Washington Otis's room, gibber at him from the foot of the bed, and stab himself three times in the throat to the sound of low music. He bore Washington a special grudge, being quite aware that it was he who was in the habit of removing the famous Canterville bloodstain, by means of Pinkerton's Paragon Detergent. Having reduced the reckless and foolhardy youth to a condition of abject terror, he was then to proceed to the room occupied by the United States Minister and his wife, and there to place a clammy hand on Mrs Otis's forehead, while he hissed into her trembling husband's ear the awful secrets of the charnel house. With regard to little Virginia, he had not quite made up his mind. She had never insulted him in any way, and was pretty and gentle. A few hollow groans from the wardrobe, he thought, would be more than sufficient, or, if that failed to wake her, he might grabble at the counterpane with palsy-twitching fingers. As for the twins, he was quite determined to teach them a lesson. The first thing to be done was, of course, to sit upon their chests, so as to produce the stifling sensation of nightmare. Then, as their beds were quite close to each other, to stand between them in the form of a green, icy-cold corpse, till they became paralysed with fear, and finally, to throw off the winding sheet, and crawl round the room, with white, bleached bones and one rolling eyeball, in the character of 'Dumb Daniel, or the Suicide's Skeleton', a role in which he had on more than one occasion produced a great effect, and which he considered quite equal to his famous part of 'Martin the Maniac, or the Masked Mystery'.

At half past ten he heard the family going to bed. For some time he was disturbed by wild shrieks of laughter from the twins, who, with the light-hearted gaiety of schoolboys, were evidently amusing themselves before they retired to rest, but at a quarter past eleven all was still, and, as midnight sounded, he sallied forth. The owl beat against the windowpanes, the raven croaked from the old yew tree, and the wind wandered moaning round the house like a lost soul; but the Otis family slept unconscious of their doom, and high above the rain and storm he could hear the steady snoring of the Minister for the United States. He stepped stealthily out of the wainscoting, with an evil smile on his cruel, wrinkled mouth, and the moon hid her face in a cloud as he stole past the great oriel window, where his own arms and those of his murdered wife were blazoned in azure and gold. On and on he glided, like an evil shadow, the very darkness seeming to loathe him as he passed. Once he thought he heard something call, and stopped; but it was only the baying of a dog from the Red Farm, and he went on, muttering strange sixteenth-century curses, and ever and anon brandishing the rusty dagger in the midnight air. Finally he reached the corner of the passage that led to luckless Washington's room. For a moment he paused there, the wind blowing his long grey locks about his head, and twisting into grotesque and fantastic folds the nameless horror of the dead man's shroud. Then the clock struck the quarter, and he felt the time was come. He chuckled to himself, and turned the corner; but no sooner had he done so, than, with a piteous wail of terror, he fell back, and hid his blanched face in his long, bony hands. Right in front of him was standing a horrible spectre, motionless as a carven image, and monstrous as a madman's dream! Its head was bald and burnished; its face round, and fat, and white; and hideous laughter seemed to have writhed its features into an eternal grin. From the eyes streamed rays of scarlet light, the mouth was a wide well of fire, and a hideous garment, like to his own, swathed with its silent snows the Titan form. On its breast was a placard with strange writing in antique characters, some scroll of shame it seemed, some record of wild sins, some awful calendar of crime, and, with its right hand, it bore aloft a falchion of gleaming steel.

Never having seen a ghost before, he naturally was terribly frightened, and, after a second hasty glance at the awful phantom, he fled back to his room, tripping up in his long winding sheet as he sped down the corridor, and finally dropping the rusty dagger into the Minister's jackboots, where it was found in the morning by the butler. Once in the privacy of his own apartment, he flung himself down on a small pallet-bed, and hid his face under the clothes. After a time, however, the brave old Canterville spirit asserted itself, and he determined to go and speak to the other ghost as soon as it was daylight. Accordingly, just as the dawn was touching the hills with silver, he returned towards the spot where he had first laid eyes on the grisly phantom, feeling that, after all, two ghosts were better than one, and that, by the aid of his new friend, he might safely grapple with the twins. On reaching the spot, however, a terrible sight met his gaze. Something had evidently happened to the spectre, for the light had entirely faded from its hollow eyes, the gleaming falchion had fallen from its hand, and it was leaning up against the wall in a strained and uncomfortable attitude. He rushed forward and seized it in his arms, when, to his horror, the head slipped off and rolled on the floor, the body assumed a recumbent posture, and he found himself clasping a white dimity bedcurtain, with a sweeping brush, a kitchen cleaver, and a hollow turnip lying at his feet! Unable to understand this curious transformation, he clutched the placard with feverish haste, and there, in the grey morning light, he read these fearful words:

> YE OTIS GHOSTE.
>
> Ye Onlie True and Originale Spook.
>
> Beware of Ye Imitationes.
>
> All others are Counterfeite.

The whole thing flashed across him. He had been tricked, foiled, and out-witted! The old Canterville look came into his eyes; he ground his toothless gums together; and, raising his withered hands high above his head, swore, according to the picturesque phraseology of the antique school, that when Chanticleer had sounded twice his merry horn, deeds of blood would be wrought, and Murder walk abroad with silent feet.

Hardly had he finished this awful oath when, from the red-tiled roof of a distant homestead, a cock crew. He laughed a long, low, bitter laugh, and waited. Hour after hour he waited, but the cock, for some strange reason, did not crow again. Finally, at half past seven, the arrival of the housemaids made him give up his fearful vigil, and he stalked back to his room, thinking of his vain oath and baffled purpose. There he consulted several books of ancient chivalry, of which he was exceedingly fond, and found that, on every occasion on which this oath had been used, Chanticleer had always crowed a second time. 'Perdition seize the naughty fowl,' he muttered, 'I have seen the day when, with my stout spear, I would have run him through the gorge, and made him crow for me an 'twere in death!' He then retired to a comfortable lead coffin, and stayed there till evening.

IV

THE NEXT DAY THE GHOST was very weak and tired. The terrible excitement of the last four weeks was beginning to have its effect. His nerves were completely shattered, and he started at the slightest noise. For five days he kept his room, and at last made up his mind to give up the point of the bloodstain on the library floor. If the Otis family did not want it, they clearly did not deserve it. They were evidently people on a low, material plane of existence, and quite incapable of appreciating the symbolic value of sensuous phenomena. The question of phan-tasmic apparitions, and the development of astral bodies, was of course quite a different matter, and really not under his control. It was his solemn duty to appear in the corridor once a week, and to gibber from the large oriel window on the first and third Wednesdays in every month, and he did not see how he could honourably escape from his obligations. It is quite true that his life had been very evil, but, upon the other hand, he was most conscientious in all things connected with the supernatural. For the next three Saturdays, accordingly, he traversed the corridor as usual between midnight and three o'clock, taking every possible precaution against being either heard or seen. He removed his boots, trod as lightly as possible on the old worm-eaten boards, wore a large black velvet cloak, and was careful to use the Rising Sun Lubricator for oiling his chains. I am bound to acknowledge that it was with a good deal of difficulty that he brought himself to adopt this last mode of protection. However, one night, while the family were at dinner, he slipped into Mr Otis's bedroom and carried off the bottle. He felt a little humiliated at first, but afterwards was sensible enough to see that there was a great deal to be said for the invention, and, to a certain degree, it served his purpose. Still, in spite of everything, he was not left unmolested. Strings were continually being stretched across the corridor, over which he tripped in the dark, and on one occasion, while dressed for the part of 'Black Isaac, or the Huntsman of Hogley Woods', he met with a severe fall, through treading on a butter-slide, which the twins had constructed from the entrance of the Tapestry Chamber to the top of the oak staircase. This last insult so enraged him, that he resolved to make one final effort to assert his dignity and social position, and determined to visit the insolent young Etonians the next night in his celebrated character of 'Reckless Rupert, or the Headless Earl'.

He had not appeared in this disguise for more than seventy years: in fact, not since he had so frightened pretty Lady Barbara Modish by means of it, that she suddenly broke off her engagement with the present Lord Canterville's grandfather, and ran away to Gretna Green with handsome Jack Castletown, declaring that nothing in the world would induce her to marry into a family that allowed such a horrible phantom to walk up and down the terrace at twilight. Poor Jack was afterwards shot in a duel by Lord Canterville on Wandsworth Common, and Lady Barbara died of a broken heart at Tunbridge Wells before the year was out, so, in every way, it had been a great success. It was, however, an extremely difficult 'make-up', if I may use such a theatrical expression in connection with one of the greatest mysteries of the supernatural, or, to employ a more scientific term, the higher natural world, and it took him fully three hours to make his preparations. At last everything was ready, and he was very pleased with his appearance. The big leather riding boots that went with the dress were just a little too large for him, and he could only find one of the two horse-pistols, but, on the whole, he was quite satisfied, and at a quarter past one he glided out of the wainscoting and crept down the corridor. On reaching the room occupied by the twins, which I should mention was called the Blue Bedchamber, on account of the colour of its hangings, he found the door just ajar. Wishing to make an effective entrance, he flung it wide open, when a heavy jug of water fell right down on him, wetting him to the skin, and just missing his left shoulder by a couple of inches. At the same moment he heard stifled shrieks of laughter proceeding from the four-post bed. The shock to his nervous system was so great that he fled back to his room as hard as he could go, and the next day he was laid up with a severe cold. The only thing that at all consoled him in the whole affair was the fact that he had not brought his head with him, for, had he done so, the consequences might have been very serious.

He now gave up all hope of ever frightening this rude American family, and contented himself, as a rule, with creeping about the passages in list slippers, with a thick red muffler round his throat for fear of draughts, and a small arquebuse, in case he should be attacked by the twins. The final blow he received occurred on the 19th of September. He had gone downstairs to the great entrance hall, feeling sure that there, at any rate, he would be quite unmolested, and was amusing himself by making satirical remarks on the large Saroni photographs of the United States Minister and his wife, which had now taken the place of the Canterville family pictures. He was simply but neatly clad in a long shroud, spotted with churchyard mould, had tied up his jaw with a strip of yellow linen, and carried a small lantern and a sexton's spade. In fact, he was dressed for the character of 'Jonas the Graveless, or the Corpse-Snatcher of Chertsey Barn', one of his most remarkable impersonations, and one which the Cantervilles had every reason to remember, as it was the real origin of their quarrel with their neighbour, Lord Rufford. It was about a quarter past two o'clock in the morning, and, as far as he could ascertain, no one was stirring. As he was strolling towards the library, however, to see if there were any traces left of the bloodstain, suddenly there leaped out on him from a dark corner two figures, who waved their arms wildly above their heads, and shrieked out 'BOO!' in his ear.

Seized with a panic, which, under the circumstances, was only natural, he rushed for the staircase, but found Washington Otis waiting for him there with the big garden syringe; and being thus hemmed in by his enemies on every side, and driven almost to bay, he vanished into the great iron stove, which, fortunately for him, was not lit, and had to make his way home through the flues and chimneys, arriving at his own room in a terrible state of dirt, disorder, and despair.

After this he was not seen again on any nocturnal expedition. The twins lay in wait for him on several occasions, and strewed the passages with nutshells every night to the great annoyance of their parents and the servants, but it was of no avail. It was quite evident that his feelings were so wounded that he would not appear. Mr Otis consequently resumed his great work on the history of the Democratic Party, on which he had been engaged for some years; Mrs Otis organised a wonderful clambake, which amazed the whole county; the boys took to lacrosse, euchre, poker, and other American national games; and Virginia rode about the lanes on her pony, accompanied by the young Duke of Cheshire, who had come to spend the last week of his holidays at Canterville Chase. It was generally assumed that the Ghost had gone away, and, in fact, Mr Otis wrote a letter to that effect to Lord Canterville, who, in reply, expressed his great pleasure at the news, and sent his best congratulations to the Minister's worthy wife.

The Otises, however, were deceived, for the Ghost was still in the house, and though now almost an invalid, was by no means ready to let matters rest, particularly as he heard that among the guests was the young Duke of Cheshire, whose grand-uncle, Lord Francis Stilton, had once bet a hundred guineas with Colonel Carbury that he would play dice with the Canterville Ghost, and was found the next morning lying on the floor of the card room in such a helpless paralytic state, that though he lived on to a great age, he was never able to say anything again but 'Double Sixes'. The story was well known at the time, though, of course, out of respect to the feelings of the two noble families, every attempt was made to hush it up; and a full account of all the circumstances connected with it will be found in the third volume of Lord Tattle's *Recollections of the Prince Regent and his Friends*. The Ghost, then, was naturally very anxious to show that he had not lost his influence over the Stiltons, with whom, indeed, he was distantly connected, his own first cousin having been married *en secondes noces* to the Sieur de Bulkeley, from whom, as everyone knows, the Dukes of Cheshire are lineally descended. Accordingly, he made arrangements for appearing to Virginia's little lover in his celebrated impersonation of 'The Vampire Monk, or, the Bloodless Benedictine', a performance so horrible that when old Lady Startup saw it, which she did on one fatal New Year's Eve, in the year 1764, she went off into the most piercing shrieks, which culminated in violent apoplexy, and died in three days, after disinheriting the Cantervilles, who were her nearest relations, and leaving all her money to her London apothecary. At the last moment, however, his terror of the twins prevented his leaving his room, and the little Duke slept in peace under the great feathered canopy in the Royal Bedchamber, and dreamed of Virginia.

V

A FEW DAYS AFTER THIS, Virginia and her curly-haired cavalier went out riding on Brockley meadows, where she tore her habit so badly in getting through a hedge, that, on their return home, she made up her mind to go up by the back staircase so as not to be seen. As she was running past the Tapestry Chamber, the door of which happened to be open, she fancied she saw someone inside, and thinking it was her mother's maid, who sometimes used to bring her work there, looked in to ask her to mend her habit. To her immense surprise, however, it was the Canterville Ghost himself! He was sitting by the window, watching the ruined gold of the yellowing trees fly through the air, and the red leaves dancing madly down the long avenue. His head was leaning on his hand, and his whole attitude was one of extreme depression. Indeed, so forlorn, and so much out of repair did he look, that little Virginia, whose first idea had been to run away and lock herself in her room, was filled with pity, and determined to try and comfort him. So light was her footfall, and so deep his melancholy, that he was not aware of her presence till she spoke to him.

'I am so sorry for you,' she said, 'but my brothers are going back to Eton tomorrow, and then, if you behave yourself, no one will annoy you.'

'It is absurd asking me to behave myself,' he answered, looking round in astonishment at the pretty little girl who had ventured to address him, 'quite absurd. I must rattle my chains, and groan through keyholes, and walk about at night, if that is what you mean. It is my only reason for existing.'

'It is no reason at all for existing, and you know you have been very wicked. Mrs Umney told us, the first day we arrived here, that you had killed your wife.'

'Well, I quite admit it,' said the Ghost petulantly, 'but it was a purely family matter, and concerned no one else.'

'It is very wrong to kill anyone,' said Virginia, who at times had a sweet Puritan gravity, caught from some old New England ancestor.

'Oh, I hate the cheap severity of abstract ethics! My wife was very plain, never had my ruffs properly starched, and knew nothing about cookery. Why, there was a buck I had shot in Hogley Woods, a magnificent pricket, and do you know how she had it sent up to table? However, it is no matter now, for it is all over, and I don't think it was very nice of her brothers to starve me to death, though I did kill her.'

'Starve you to death? Oh, Mr Ghost, I mean Sir Simon, are you hungry? I have a sandwich in my case. Would you like it?'

'No, thank you, I never eat anything now; but it is very kind of you, all the same, and you are much nicer than the rest of your horrid, rude, vulgar, dishonest family.'

'Stop!' cried Virginia, stamping her foot, 'it is you who are rude, and horrid, and vulgar, and as for dishonesty, you know you stole the paints out of my box to try and furbish up that ridiculous bloodstain in the library. First you took all my reds, including the vermilion, and I couldn't do any more sunsets, then you took the emerald green and the chrome yellow, and finally I had nothing left but indigo and Chinese white, and could only do moonlight scenes, which are always depressing to look at, and not at all easy to paint. I never told on you, though I was very much annoyed, and it was most ridiculous, the whole thing; for whoever heard of emerald-green blood?'

'Well, really,' said the Ghost, rather meekly, 'what was I to do? It is a very difficult thing to get real blood nowadays, and, as your brother began it all with his Paragon Detergent, I certainly saw no reason why I should not have your paints. As for colour, that is always a matter of taste: the Cantervilles have blue blood, for instance, the very bluest in England; but I know you Americans don't care for things of this kind.'

'You know nothing about it, and the best thing you can do is to emigrate and improve your mind. My father will be only too happy to give you a free passage, and though there is a heavy duty on spirits of every kind, there will be no

THE CANTERVILLE GHOST/Oscar Wilde

difficulty about the Custom House, as the officers are all Democrats. Once in New York, you are sure to be a great success. I know lots of people there who would give a hundred thousand dollars to have a grandfather, and much more than that to have a family ghost.'

'I don't think I should like America.'

'I suppose because we have no ruins and no curiosities,' said Virginia satirically.

'No ruins! no curiosities!' answered the Ghost; 'you have your navy and your manners.'

'Good evening; I will go and ask Papa to get the twins an extra week's holiday.'

'Please don't go, Miss Virginia,' he cried; 'I am so lonely and so unhappy, and I really don't know what to do. I want to go to sleep and I cannot.'

'That's quite absurd! You have merely to go to bed and blow out the candle. It is very difficult sometimes to keep awake, especially at church, but there is no difficulty at all about sleeping. Why, even babies know how to do that, and they are not very clever.'

'I have not slept for three hundred years,' he said sadly, and Virginia's beautiful blue eyes opened in wonder; 'for three hundred years I have not slept, and I am so tired.'

Virginia grew quite grave, and her little lips trembled like rose leaves. She came towards him, and kneeling down at his side, looked up into his old withered face.

'Poor, poor Ghost,' she murmured; 'have you no place where you can sleep?'

'Far away beyond the pinewoods,' he answered, in a low dreamy voice, 'there is a little garden. There the grass grows long and deep, there are the great white stars of the hemlock flower, there the nightingale sings all night long. All night long he sings, and the cold, crystal moon looks down, and the yew tree spreads out its giant arms over the sleepers.'

Virginia's eyes grew dim with tears, and she hid her face in her hands.

'You mean the Garden of Death,' she whispered.

'Yes, Death. Death must be so beautiful. To lie in the soft brown earth, with the grasses waving above one's head, and listen to silence. To have no yesterday, and no tomorrow. To forget time, to forgive life, to be at peace. You can help me. You can open for me the portals of Death's house, for Love is always with you, and Love is stronger than Death is.'

Virginia trembled, a cold shudder ran through her, and for a few moments there was silence. She felt as if she was in a terrible dream.

Then the Ghost spoke again, and his voice sounded like the sighing of the wind.

'Have you ever read the old prophecy on the library window?'

'Oh, often,' cried the little girl, looking up; 'I know it quite well. It is painted in curious black letters, and it is difficult to read. There are only six lines:

> *When a golden girl can win*
> *Prayer from out the lips of sin,*
> *When the barren almond bears,*
> *And a little child gives away its tears,*
> *Then shall all the house be still*
> *And peace come to Canterville.*

But I don't know what they mean.'

'They mean,' he said sadly, 'that you must weep with me for my sins, because I have no tears, and pray with me for my soul, because I have no faith, and then, if you have always been sweet, and good, and gentle, the Angel of Death will have mercy on me. You will see fearful shapes in darkness, and wicked voices will whisper in your ear, but they will not harm you, for against the purity of a little child the powers of Hell cannot prevail.'

Virginia made no answer, and the Ghost wrung his hands in wild despair as he looked down at her bowed golden head. Suddenly she stood up, very pale, and with a strange light in her eyes. 'I am not afraid,' she said firmly, 'and I will ask the Angel to have mercy on you.'

He rose from his seat with a faint cry of joy, and taking her hand bent over it with old-fashioned grace and kissed it. His fingers were as cold as ice, and his lips burned like fire, but Virginia did not falter, as he led her across the dusky room. On the faded green tapestry were broidered little huntsmen. They blew their tasselled horns and with their tiny hands waved to her to go back. 'Go back! little Virginia,' they cried, 'go back!' but the Ghost clutched her hand more tightly, and she shut her eyes against them. Horrible animals with lizard tails, and goggle eyes, blinked at her from the carven chimneypiece, and murmured 'Beware! little Virginia, beware! we may never see you again,' but the Ghost glided on more swiftly, and Virginia did not listen. When they reached the end of the room he stopped, and muttered some words she could not understand. She opened her eyes, and saw the wall slowly fading away like a mist, and a great black cavern in front of her. A bitter cold wind swept round them, and she felt something pulling at her dress. 'Quick, quick,' cried the Ghost, 'or it will be too late,' and, in a moment, the wainscoting had closed behind them, and the Tapestry Chamber was empty.

VI

ABOUT TEN MINUTES LATER, the bell rang for tea, and, as Virginia did not come down, Mrs Otis sent up one of the footmen to tell her. After a little time he returned and said that he could not find Miss Virginia anywhere. As she was in the habit of going out to the garden every evening to get flowers for the dinner table, Mrs Otis was not at all alarmed at first, but when six o'clock struck, and

Virginia did not appear, she became really agitated, and sent the boys out to look for her, while she herself and Mr Otis searched every room in the house. At half past six the boys came back and said that they could find no trace of their sister anywhere. They were all now in the greatest state of excitement, and did not know what to do, when Mr Otis suddenly remembered that, some few days before, he had given a band of gypsies permission to camp in the park. He accordingly at once set off for Blackfell Hollow, where he knew they were, accompanied by his eldest son and two of the farm servants. The little Duke of Cheshire, who was perfectly frantic with anxiety, begged hard to be allowed to go too, but Mr Otis would not allow him, as he was afraid there might be a scuffle. On arriving at the spot, however, he found that the gypsies had gone, and it was evident that their departure had been rather sudden, as the fire was still burning, and some plates were lying on the grass. Having sent off Washington and the two men to scour the district, he ran home, and despatched telegrams to all the police inspectors in the country, telling them to look out for a little girl who had been kidnapped by tramps or gypsies. He then ordered his horse to be brought round, and, after insisting on his wife and the three boys sitting down to dinner, rode off down the Ascot road with a groom. He had hardly, however, gone a couple of miles, when he heard somebody galloping after him, and, looking round, saw the little Duke coming up on his pony, with his face very flushed and no hat. 'I'm awfully sorry, Mr Otis,' gasped out the boy, 'but I can't eat any dinner as long as Virginia is lost. Please, don't be angry with me; if you had let us be engaged last year, there would never have been all this trouble. You won't send me back, will you? I can't go! I won't go!'

The Minister could not help smiling at the handsome young scapegrace, and was a good deal touched at his devotion to Virginia, so leaning down from his horse, he patted him kindly on the shoulders, and said, 'Well, Cecil, if you won't go back I suppose you must come with me, but I must get you a hat at Ascot.'

'Oh, bother my hat! I want Virginia!' cried the little Duke, laughing, and they galloped on to the railway station. There Mr Otis enquired of the stationmaster if anyone answering to the description of Virginia had been seen on the platform, but could get no news of her. The stationmaster, however, wired up and down the line, and assured him that a strict watch would be kept for her, and, after having bought a hat for the little Duke from a linen draper, who was just putting up his shutters, Mr Otis rode off to Bexley, a village about four miles away, which he was told was a well-known haunt of the gypsies, as there was a large common next to it. Here they roused up the rural policeman, but could get no information from him, and, after riding all over the common, they turned their horses' heads homewards, and reached the Chase about eleven o'clock, dead tired and almost heartbroken. They found Washington and the twins waiting for them at the gatehouse with lanterns, as the avenue was very dark. Not the slightest trace of Virginia had been discovered. The gypsies had been caught on Brockley meadows, but she was not with them, and they had explained their sudden departure by saying that they had mistaken the date of Chorton Fair, and had gone off in a hurry for fear they might be late. Indeed, they had been quite distressed at hearing of Virginia's disappearance, as they were very grateful to Mr Otis for having allowed them to camp in his park, and four of their number had stayed behind to help in the search. The carp pond had been dragged, and the whole Chase thoroughly gone over, but without any result. It was evident that, for that night at any rate, Virginia was lost to them; and it was in a state of the deepest depression that Mr Otis and the boys walked up to the house, the groom following behind with the two horses and the pony. In the hall they found a group of frightened servants, and lying on a sofa in the library was poor Mrs Otis, almost out of her mind with terror and anxiety, and having her forehead bathed with eau de cologne by the old housekeeper. Mr Otis at once insisted on her having something to eat, and ordered up supper for the whole party. It was a melancholy meal, as hardly anyone spoke, and even the twins were awe-struck and subdued, as they were very fond of their sister. When they had finished, Mr Otis, in spite of the entreaties of the little Duke, ordered them all to bed, saying that nothing more could be done that night, and that he would telegraph in the morning to Scotland Yard for some detectives to be sent down immediately. Just as they were passing out of the dining room, midnight began to boom from the clock tower, and when the last stroke sounded they heard a crash and a sudden shrill cry; a dreadful peal of thunder shook the house, a strain of unearthly music floated through the air, a panel at the top of the staircase flew back with a loud noise, and out on the landing, looking very pale and white, with a little casket in her hand, stepped Virginia. In a moment they had all rushed up to her. Mrs Otis clasped her passionately in her arms, the Duke smothered her with violent kisses, and the twins executed a wild war dance round the group.

'Good heavens! child, where have you been?' said Mr Otis, rather angrily, thinking that she had been playing some foolish trick on them. 'Cecil and I have been riding all over the country looking for you, and your mother has been frightened to death. You must never play these practical jokes any more.'

'Except on the Ghost! except on the Ghost!' shrieked the twins, as they capered about.

'My own darling, thank God you are found; you must never leave my side again,' murmured Mrs Otis, as she kissed the trembling child, and smoothed the tangled gold of her hair.

'Papa,' said Virginia quietly, 'I have been with the Ghost. He is dead, and you must come and see him. He had been very wicked, but he was really sorry for all that he had done, and he gave me this box of beautiful jewels before he died.'

The whole family gazed at her in mute amazement, but she was quite grave and serious; and, turning round, she led them through the opening in the wainscoting down a narrow secret corridor, Washington following with a lighted candle, which he had caught up from the table. Finally, they came to a great oak door, studded with rusty nails. When Virginia touched it, it swung back on its heavy hinges, and they found themselves in a little low room, with a vaulted ceiling, and one tiny grated window. Embedded in the wall was a huge iron ring, and chained to it was a gaunt skeleton, that was stretched out at full length on the stone floor, and seemed to be trying to grasp with its long fleshless fingers an old-fashioned trencher and ewer, that were placed just out of its reach. The jug had evidently been once filled with water, as it was covered inside with green mould. There was nothing on the trencher but a pile of dust. Virginia knelt down beside the skeleton, and, folding her little hands together, began to pray silently, while the rest of the party looked on in wonder at the terrible tragedy whose secret was now disclosed to them.

'Hello!' suddenly exclaimed one of the twins, who had been looking out of the window to try and discover in what wing of the house the room was situated. 'Hello! the old withered almond tree has blossomed. I can see the flowers quite plainly in the moonlight.'

'God has forgiven him,' said Virginia gravely, as she rose to her feet, and a beautiful light seemed to illumine her face.

'What an angel you are!' cried the young Duke, and he put his arm round her neck, and kissed her.

VII

FOUR DAYS AFTER THESE CURIOUS incidents a funeral started from Canterville Chase at about eleven o'clock at night. The hearse was drawn by eight black horses, each of which carried on its head a great tuft of nodding ostrich plumes, and the leaden coffin was covered by a rich purple pall, on which was embroidered in gold the Canterville coat of arms. By the side of the hearse and the coaches walked the servants with lighted torches, and the whole procession was wonderfully impressive. Lord Canterville was the chief mourner, having come up specially from Wales to attend the funeral, and sat in the first carriage along with little Virginia. Then came the United States Minister and his wife, then Washington and the three boys, and in the last carriage was Mrs Umney. It was generally felt that, as she had been frightened by the ghost for more than fifty years of her life, she had a right to see the last of him. A deep grave had been dug in the corner of the churchyard, just under the old yew tree, and the service was read in the most impressive manner by the Rev. Augustus Dampier. When the ceremony was over, the servants, according to an old custom observed in the Canterville family, extinguished their torches, and, as the coffin was being lowered into the grave, Virginia stepped forward, and laid on it a large cross made of white and pink almond blossoms. As she did so, the moon came out from behind a cloud, and flooded with its silent silver the little churchyard, and from a distant copse a nightingale began to sing. She thought of the Ghost's description of the Garden of Death, her eyes became dim with tears, and she hardly spoke a word during the drive home.

The next morning, before Lord Canterville went up to town, Mr Otis had an interview with him on the subject of the jewels the Ghost had given to Virginia. They were perfectly magnificent, especially a certain ruby necklace with old Venetian setting, which was really a superb specimen of sixteenth-century work, and their value was so great that Mr Otis felt considerable scruples about allowing his daughter to accept them.

'My lord,' he said, 'I know that in this country mortmain is held to apply to trinkets as well as to land, and it is quite clear to me that these jewels are, or should be, heirlooms in your family. I must beg you, accordingly, to take them to London with you, and to regard them simply as a portion of your property which has been restored to you under certain strange conditions. As for my daughter, she is merely a child, and has as yet, I am glad to say, but little interest in such appurtenances of idle luxury. I am also informed by Mrs Otis, who, I may say, is no mean authority upon Art—having had the privilege of spending several winters in Boston when she was a girl—that these gems are of great monetary worth, and if offered for sale would fetch a tall price. Under these circumstances, Lord Canterville, I feel sure that you will recognise how impossible it would be for me to allow them to remain in the possession of any member of my family; and, indeed, all such vain gauds and toys, however suitable or necessary to the dignity of the British aristocracy, would be completely out of place among those who have been brought up on the severe, and I believe immortal, principles of Republican simplicity. Perhaps I should mention that Virginia is very anxious that you should allow her to retain the box, as a memento of your unfortunate but misguided ancestor. As it is extremely old, and consequently a good deal out of repair, you may perhaps think fit to comply with her request. For my own part, I confess I am a good deal surprised to find a child of mine expressing sympathy with medievalism in any form, and can only account for it by the fact that Virginia was born in one of your London suburbs shortly after Mrs Otis had returned from a trip to Athens.'

Lord Canterville listened very gravely to the worthy Minister's speech, pulling his grey moustache now and then to hide an involuntary smile, and when Mr Otis had ended, he shook him cordially by the hand, and said, 'My dear sir, your charming little daughter rendered my unlucky ancestor, Sir Simon, a very important service, and I and my family are much indebted to her for her marvellous courage and pluck. The jewels are clearly hers, and, egad, I believe that if I were heartless enough to take them from her, the wicked old fellow would be out of his grave in a fortnight, leading me the devil of a life. As for their being heirlooms, nothing is an heirloom that is not so mentioned in a will or legal document, and the existence of these jewels has been quite unknown. I assure you I have no more claim on them than your butler, and when Miss Virginia grows up I dare say she will be pleased to have pretty things to wear. Besides, you forget, Mr Otis, that you took the furniture and the Ghost at a valuation, and anything that belonged to the Ghost passed at once into your possession, as, whatever activity Sir Simon may have shown in the corridor at night, in point of law he was really dead, and you acquired his property by purchase.'

Mr Otis was a good deal distressed at Lord Canterville's refusal, and begged him to reconsider his decision, but the good-natured peer was quite firm, and finally induced the Minister to allow his daughter to retain the present the Ghost had given her, and when, in the spring of 1890, the young Duchess of Cheshire was presented at the Queen's first drawing room on the occasion of her marriage, her jewels were the universal theme of admiration. For Virginia received the coronet, which is the reward of all good little American girls, and was married to her boy-lover as soon as he came of age. They were both so charming, and they loved each other so much, that everyone was delighted at the match, except the old Marchioness of Dumbleton, who had tried to catch the Duke for one of her seven unmarried daughters, and had given no less than three expensive dinner parties for that purpose, and, strange to say, Mr Otis himself. Mr Otis was extremely fond of the young Duke personally, but, theoretically, he objected to titles, and, to use his own words, 'was not without apprehension lest, amid the enervating influences of a pleasure-loving aristocracy, the true principles of Republican simplicity should be forgotten'. His objections, however, were completely overruled, and I believe that when he walked up the aisle of St George's, Hanover Square, with his daughter leaning on his arm, there was not a prouder man in the whole length and breadth of England.

The Duke and Duchess, after the honeymoon was over, went down to Canterville Chase, and on the day after their arrival they walked over in the afternoon to the lonely churchyard by the pinewoods. There had been a great deal of difficulty at first about the inscription on Sir Simon's tombstone, but finally it had been decided to engrave on it simply the initials of the old gentleman's name, and the verse from the library window. The Duchess had brought with her some lovely roses, which she strewed upon the grave, and after they had stood by it for some time they strolled into the ruined chancel of the old abbey. There the Duchess sat down on a fallen pillar, while her husband lay at her feet smoking a cigarette and looking up at her beautiful eyes. Suddenly he threw his cigarette away, took hold of her hand, and said to her, 'Virginia, a wife should have no secrets from her husband.'

'Dear Cecil! I have no secrets from you.'

'Yes, you have,' he answered, smiling, 'you have never told me what happened to you when you were locked up with the Ghost.'

'I have never told anyone, Cecil,' said Virginia gravely.

'I know that, but you might tell me.'

'Please don't ask me, Cecil, I cannot tell you. Poor Sir Simon! I owe him a great deal. Yes, don't laugh, Cecil, I really do. He made me see what Life is, and what Death signifies, and why Love is stronger than both.'

The Duke rose and kissed his wife lovingly.

'You can have your secret as long as I have your heart,' he murmured.

'You have always had that, Cecil.'

'And you will tell our children some day, won't you?'

Virginia blushed.

———————————————

Emile Zola

1840–1902

Emile Zola was a free thinker and a journalist, whose books, though very popular, were often shocking in their realism. Best known for powerful novels such as *Germinal,* the study of a poor mining community, and *Thérèse Raquin,* a darkly brooding murder, he also wrote imaginative short stories. This is one of his best.

ANGELINE, OR THE HAUNTED HOUSE

I

ALMOST TWO YEARS AGO NOW, I found myself riding on my bicycle along a deserted country lane in the region of Orgeval, just north of Poissy, when I was greatly surprised by the sudden appearance, quite close to the road, of a large house. I alighted from my machine in order that I might see it more clearly. It stood there under the grey November sky, as the cold wind swept the fallen leaves, a brick-built house of no especial character in the middle of a vast garden filled with elderly trees. But what made it unusual, what, indeed, endowed it with a wild strangeness which set one's nerves on edge, was the awful state of abandon in which it had been left. And so it was, since one of the iron gates had broken from its hinges, and since a large board announced in paint which had been faded by the rains that the property was for sale, that I entered the garden, yielding to a curiosity which was tinged with apprehension.

The house must have been uninhabited for some thirty or forty years. Through the course of many winters, bricks had worked loose from the cornices and by the window frames, allowing an invasion of moss and lichens. The walls were lined with cracks, like premature wrinkles, marking what was still a sound enough building but for which no one cared any longer. Below the front door the stone steps, broken by the frosts and guarded by nettles and brambles, seemed to present a threshold to desolation and death. But most of all, the atmosphere of melancholy emanated from those bare, glaucous windows, their curtains gone, their glass smashed by stones from passing children, which permitted a view into the sombre emptiness of the rooms, like the open eyes of a corpse whose soul has been extinguished. Around the house the vast garden was a scene of devastation. What once had been a flowerbed was now scarcely recognisable under the rampant growth of weeds, whole paths had been devoured by voracious plants, the shrubberies had reverted to the character of virgin forests: I was presented with an impression of wild vegetation such as one finds in an abandoned cemetery, and all, that day, under the damp shade of ancient trees whose last leaves were being carried off by the autumn wind crying its sad complaint.

For a long time I stood there surrounded by this wail of despair which seemed to come from all that I saw about me. My heart was heavy with a dull fear, a growing unease, yet I was held by a burning compassion, a need to know and sympathise with all I could feel around me of unhappiness and suffering. Then, having finally made my decision to leave, and having perceived beyond the way, in the fork of two roads, a sort of inn, a poor place where one could buy a drink, I went in, resolved to satisfy my curiosity by encouraging the local people to talk.

The only person I found there was an old woman, who served me a glass of beer with a great deal of complaining. She complained that she found herself here on this forgotten road, where not two cyclists a day would pass. She talked aimlessly, related the story of her life, revealed that she was known as 'mère Toussaint', that she had come from Vernon with her man in order to take over the inn, that at first things had not gone too badly, but that since she was widowed everything had gone from bad to worse. Finally, after this flood of words, when I started to ask her about the nearby house, she became suddenly more circumspect, regarding me with a suspicious eye, as if I were attempting to tear from her some awful secret.

'Oh, you mean "La Sauvagière", the haunted house, as they call it round here ... I know nothing of that, Monsieur. That goes back before my time. I shall have been here just thirty years next Easter, and that all goes back nearly forty years. When we came out here the house was already more or less in the state you see it in now. Summers pass and winters pass and no one sees anything move in there, except for the occasional falling stone.'

'But,' I asked, 'why hasn't it been sold, since it is for sale?'

'Oh, why indeed? How should I know? ... They talk about it enough ...'

In the end, I must have gained her confidence, whereupon it was clear that she was only too anxious to recount to me what it was that people talked about. First she told me how not one of the girls from the village would dare to venture into the grounds of 'La Sauvagière' after dusk, because it was rumoured that some poor soul returned there by night to haunt it. When I expressed surprise that such a story should still be found credible so near to Paris, she shrugged her shoulders, endeavouring at first to appear composed, but before long revealing her unspoken terror.

'But consider the facts, Monsieur. Why has it never been sold? I have seen prospective purchasers come and go, but they always leave more quickly than they arrived, and not one has ever come back a second time. And I can tell you one thing for sure, if any visitor dares to venture inside that house extraordinary things happen: doors slam noisily of their own accord, as if some awful wind were blowing; cries, moans, and the sound of sobbing rise from the cellars; and if anyone dares to stay longer a heart-rending voice starts to call out again and again "Angeline! Angeline! Angeline!" in such an anguished tone as to chill the very marrow of your bones ... What I am telling you are proven facts. No one will deny them.'

I assure you that my own emotions were beginning to stir, and a shiver ran down my spine.

'But who is this Angeline?'

'I can see, Monsieur, that you are determined to know the whole story, though I must tell you again that I really know nothing myself.'

Nevertheless, she proceeded eventually to tell me everything. Some forty years previously, in about 1858, just at the time when the victorious Second Empire was holding one celebration after another, Monsieur de G——, who held a post at the Tuileries Palace, lost his wife. He had by her a daughter, some ten years old, called Angeline, indescribably beautiful, and the living image of her mother. Two years later Monsieur de G—— married again, and his second wife was another renowned beauty, the widow of a general. Apparently, following this second marriage a terrible jealousy grew up between Angeline and her step-mother: the one grief-stricken to see her mother already forgotten, her place in the family so quickly usurped by this outsider; the other obsessed to distraction by the idea of having constantly before her this living portrait of a woman she feared she could never cause to be forgotten. 'La Sauvagière' belonged to the new Madame de G——, and it was there, so the story went, that one evening, on seeing the father lovingly embrace his daughter, in her jealous rage she struck the little girl such a blow that the wretched child fell to the floor dead, her neck broken. The end of the story was gruesome. The distraught father consented to bury his daughter himself in one of the cellars of the house, in order to save the murderess. The body of the child remained hidden there for years, while the story was put about that she had gone away to an aunt's. Then, one day, the howling of a dog who was found feverishly scratching at the ground caused the crime to be discovered, although the scandal of the discovery was subsequently suppressed by the Tuileries authorities. Now both Monsieur and Madame de G—— were dead, but Angeline still returned every night to answer the call of the pitiful voice which summoned her from that mysterious world beyond the darkness.

'No one will deny what I have told you,' concluded the old woman. 'It is all as true as I am standing here.'

I had listened to her account in awe, struck by its implausibility, yet captivated by the dark and violent singularity of the drama. I had heard of this Monsieur de G——. I think I had known that he had remarried and that a family tragedy had overtaken him. Was it then true? What a moving and tragic story, exposing human passion to the point of exasperated frenzy, the most awful crime of passion one could ever imagine: a little girl as beautiful as a summer's day, loved and cherished, struck down by her stepmother, and then buried by her father in the corner of a cellar! What exquisite horror! I wanted to hear more, to talk about it, but I asked myself, to what end? Why not depart with the flower of popular imagination, this terrifying tale?

As I remounted my bicycle I cast a last glance in the direction of 'La Sauvagière'. Night was falling, and the desolate house looked back at me through the lifeless eyes of its dull, empty windows, whilst the autumn wind sighed a lament among the decaying trees.

II

WHY SHOULD THAT STORY have become fixed in my mind until it became an agonising obsession? It is one of those intellectual mysteries which are difficult to account for. In vain I told myself that such myths are rife in the countryside, that this particular one could have no real interest for me personally. Despite it all, the dead child haunted my thoughts: sweet, tragic Angeline, summoned every night for forty years by a voice whimpering among the empty rooms of the abandoned house.

So, for the first two months of the winter, I set about doing some research. Obviously, if ever such a disappearance, such a dramatic happening, had been noised abroad, the newspapers of the time would surely have spoken of it. I searched through the collections in the National Library without success: there was not a line which could have been linked with such a story. Then I questioned people who might have known something at the time, employees of the Tuileries: none was able to give me a clear answer—all I obtained was contradictory information. In fact, I had all but abandoned any hope of finding out the truth, though I was still tormented by the mystery, when, one morning, fate guided me on to a new track.

Every two or three weeks, out of a feeling of comradeship, affection and admiration, it was my habit to visit the elderly poet V—, who died last April, aged seventy. For many years his legs had been paralysed, and he was restricted to an armchair in his little studio in the rue Assas, the window of which looked out on to the Luxembourg Gardens. He was coming to the end of a life of dreaming: he had lived by his imagination, and created for himself a fabulous palace, where, far from the real world, he had loved and suffered. Which of us does not recall his kind, delicate face, his white hair and childish curls, his pale blue eyes with their youthful innocence? It would be wrong to say that he never told the truth, but the fact is that he was forever inventing, with the result that one never quite knew where reality ended for him and where illusion began. He was a charming old man, who had long since ceased to be part of everyday life, but whose conversation often touched me deeply as a vague, discreet revelation of the unknown.

Thus I found myself that day chatting with him by the window in his tiny room, warmed as always by a blazing fire. Outside, there was the severest of frosts, so that the Luxembourg Gardens presented a snow-white carpet, a vast horizon of immaculate purity. For some reason, I suddenly found myself telling him of 'La Sauvagière' and the story which still preoccupied me: the father's remarriage, the stepmother's evil jealousy of the little girl who was the living portrait of her mother, the clandestine burial in the cellar. He listened to me with the same tranquil smile he wore even when he was sad. There followed a silence; his pale blue eyes gazed into the far distance, across the white expanses of the Luxembourg Gardens, and the shadow of a vision, which emanated from him, seemed to shudder vaguely around him.

'I used to know Monsieur de G— very well,' he said slowly. 'I knew his first wife, a divinely beautiful woman; I knew his second wife also, whose beauty was every bit as dazzling; and I was passionately in love with them both, although I never revealed the fact. I also knew Angeline, who was even more lovely and whom any man would have worshipped on his knees ... But things did not happen quite as you have said.'

I became very excited. Was it here, then, the unexpected truth I had despaired of ever knowing? Was I about to discover everything? At first I was only too ready to believe what he was about to tell me, and I replied, 'Oh my dear friend, what a service you will render me! at last my poor head will be eased. Tell me quickly, I must know everything.'

But he was not listening to me; he was still gazing distractedly into the distance. When at last he spoke, it was as if in a dream, as if he had created the beings and the things he evoked for me.

'Angeline, by the age of twelve years, already possessed a woman's power to love, with all its capacity to feel joy and pain. It was she who became insanely jealous of her father's new wife, whom she saw daily in his arms. She suffered at the sight of this terrible betrayal on the part of the new couple. It was no longer just her mother they were affronting, it was she herself who was being tortured, it was her heart that was wounded. Every night she heard her mother calling her from the grave; and one night, determined to be reunited with her, no longer able to stand the pain, already dying from an excess of love, this little girl of twelve years thrust a knife into her heart.'

I cried out, 'Good heavens! Can that really be?'

He went on without hearing me. 'Imagine with what terror, what horror, Monsieur and Madame de G— discovered Angeline the next morning in her bed, the knife plunged into her breast right up to the handle! They were due to leave for Italy the following day, and there was nobody left in the house other than an elderly maid who had brought up the child. In their panic that they might be accused of a crime, they had the old maid help them bury the young body; but they in fact buried it in a corner of the conservatory behind the house, at the foot of a giant orange tree. And there it was that it was found when, after the death of both parents, the old maid told her story.'

By this time some doubts had begun to enter my mind, and I looked at him anxiously, asking myself whether he was fabricating.

'But,' I asked, 'do you believe then that Angeline really could return again every night in order to answer the heart-rending cry of the mysterious voice which summons her?'

'Return again, my friend? Ah, but everyone returns again. Why shouldn't the soul of the poor child inhabit again the place in which she has both loved and suffered? If a voice is heard calling after her, then life has not yet begun again for her; but it will do, be assured of that, for everything begins again, love is never lost, nor beauty . . . Angeline! Angeline! Angeline! One day she will live again in the sun and the flowers.'

Decidedly, I was now neither convinced nor comforted. My old friend V—, the child poet, had done nothing but increase my discomposure. It was evident that he was fabricating. Yet, like all seers, perhaps he was able to divine the truth?

'You are sure that everything you have told me is the absolute truth?' I ventured to enquire with a laugh.

'Of course, it is the truth. Is not everything to do with the Infinite the truth?'

I was never to see him again, as shortly afterwards I was obliged to leave Paris. He remains in my mind, however, his pensive gaze lost on the white expanse of the Luxembourg Gardens, so calm in the certainty of his infinite dream, whereas I was still tortured by my desire to establish once and for all that elusive phenomenon, the truth.

III

A YEAR AND A HALF went by. I had been obliged to travel. My life had been affected by many joys and many sorrows on the stormy seas which bear us all away to unknown shores. But again and again I would hear, at a certain hour, first far away, then entering my conscious mind, that desperate cry: 'Angeline! Angeline! Angeline!' And it would leave me trembling, full of new doubts, tortured by the need to know. I could not forget, and there is nothing worse for me than the hell of uncertainty.

I cannot say how it came about that one glorious June evening I found myself once more on my bicycle in the deserted lane by 'La Sauvagière'. Had I consciously wished to see it again? Or was it an instinct which had directed me to turn off the main road and return to these parts? It was close on eight o'clock, but at the end of one of the longest days of the year the sky was still brilliant with a triumphantly setting sun, without a cloud, an infinity of azure and gold. And how sweet and delicate the air was, how fine the scents of the trees and the grass, what a subtle delight the immense peacefulness of the fields!

As on the first occasion when I arrived before 'La Sauvagière', astonishment caused me to jump down from my machine. For a moment I hesitated: was this the same place? A fine new gate shone in the light of the setting sun, the garden walls had been restored, and the house, which I could barely perceive behind the trees, seemed to me to have regained the joyful gaiety of youth. Was this then the promised resurrection? Had Angeline returned to life in answer to that distant voice?

I was standing transfixed in the roadway when the sound of a shuffling gait behind me caused me to start. It was 'mère Toussaint' bringing home her cow from a neighbouring field.

'So they weren't afraid?' I asked, motioning towards the house.

She recognised me and halted her animal.

'Ah, Monsieur, there are those who would trample on God Himself. The house was bought over a year ago now. It was a painter that did it, the artist B— and you know what these artists will do.'

Whereupon she moved her cow on, adding with a shake of the head, 'Well, we shall just have to wait and see what happens.'

The painter B—, that delicate, inventive artist who had portrayed so many delightful Parisiennes! I knew him slightly: we had shaken hands at the theatre, in exhibitions, places where one runs into people. Suddenly I was overcome by an irresistible desire to enter, to confess to him, to beg him to tell me what he knew of the truth about this 'Sauvagière', whose mystery obsessed me. And without further thought, without care for my dusty cyclist's attire, which custom is beginning to tolerate these days in any case, I wheeled my bicycle over to the mossy trunk of an old tree. At the clear sound of the bell, the lever of which had accidentally struck the gate, there appeared a servant to whom I gave my card and who bade me wait a moment in the garden.

My surprise increased when I looked around me. The façade of the house had been repaired: no more cracks, no dislodged bricks. The steps, garnished with roses, had become once again a threshold of joyous welcome. The living windows were now smiling, telling of the joy within, behind their white lace curtains. As for the garden, it had been cleared of its nettles and brambles, the flowerbed had reappeared like a gigantic scented bouquet, the ancient trees had acquired new youth in their peaceful old age, under the golden rain of the spring sunshine.

When the servant reappeared, he led me into a drawing room, informing me that his master had gone off to the neighbouring village but would be back before long. I was ready to wait for hours. I passed the time examining the room in which I found myself: it was luxuriously furnished with thick carpets, and cretonne curtains which matched the massive sofa and deep armchairs. These hangings were so extensive that when dusk suddenly arrived it took me by surprise. Before long it was almost completely dark. I do not know how long

I had to wait there. I had evidently been forgotten; not even a lamp was brought for me. Seated in the shadows I started to relive the whole tragic story, to lose myself in reverie. Had Angeline been murdered? Had she thrust a knife into her own heart? And I have to admit that in this haunted house, upon which darkness had fallen once again, I felt fear. What initially was not much more than a certain unease, a slight chill, proceeded to grow beyond all proportion into an irrational terror which froze my whole being.

At first it seemed to me that I could hear obscure sounds in the distance. They must be coming from the depths of the cellars: a vague moaning, stifled sobs, heavy, ghostly footsteps. Then whatever it was began to come up from below, to draw closer, until the whole house seemed in the darkness to be filled with a terrible distress. Suddenly the awful cry rang out, 'Angeline! Angeline! Angeline!', with such growing force that it seemed to me I felt a cold breath touch my face. One of the drawing-room doors opened noisily; Angeline entered, and crossed the room without seeing me. I recognised her in the dim light which had penetrated with her from the hall outside. It was indeed the dead child of twelve years, incredibly beautiful with her exquisite blonde hair upon her shoulders, dressed in white, the white of the earth from which she returned every night. She passed by in silence, abstracted, and disappeared through another door, while once again the voice called out, this time from further off, 'Angeline! Angeline! Angeline!' I was left there standing with sweat on my forehead, in a state of horror which caused every hair of my body to rise in the dreadful wind which emanated from the enigma.

Then, almost immediately, as the servant finally came in with a lamp, I was conscious that the artist B— was there, shaking my hand, and apologising for having let me wait so long. Without any attempt to preserve my self-respect, I rushed into telling him my story. As I did so, I was still trembling. At first he listened to me with no little surprise, and then with great good humour he hastened to reassure me.

'My dear fellow, you were probably unaware of the fact that I am a cousin of the second Madame de G—. The poor woman! To be accused of the murder of that child whom she loved and mourned quite as much as the father! For there is only one part of the story which is true: the poor creature did indeed die here, not by her own hand, for heaven's sake, but of a sudden fever. The shock was so great that her parents, having conceived a horror of this house, never wished to return here. Which explains why it remained uninhabited for as long as they were alive. After their deaths there followed interminable legal procedures, which prevented its sale. I wanted it, having coveted it for many years; and I can assure you that we have never yet seen any ghosts here!'

The chill returned to me as I mumbled. 'But I have just seen Angeline, here, only a moment ago . . . That frightful voice was summoning her, and she passed by here, through this very room . . .'

He looked at me, alarmed, believing perhaps that I was losing my sanity.

Then suddenly he laughed, the resounding laugh of a man who is happy.

'That was my daughter you saw just now. Her godfather was, in fact, Monsieur de G—, who gave her the name Angeline as an act of devoted memory. Having no doubt been called by her mother, she must have passed through this room.'

Thereupon he opened the door himself and called out again, 'Angeline! Angeline! Angeline!'

The child returned, now alive, now vibrant with gaiety. It was she, with her white dress, her exquisite blonde hair upon her shoulders, so beautiful, so radiant with hope, that she was like the spring itself, bearing in the form of a bud the promise of love, the lasting happiness of life.

What a charming ghost was this new child, born again from the one who had died. Death had been conquered. My old friend, the poet V—, had not lied; nothing is ever lost for ever, everything begins again, both beauty and love. Their mothers call them, these little girls of today, these lovers of tomorrow, and they live again under the sun and among the flowers. The house had been haunted by the promise of this reawakening; today the house was once more youthful and happy in the rediscovered joy of eternal life.

Acknowledgments

The Publishers would like to thank the following for kind permission to reprint copyright material:

The Estate of Robert Aickman, c/o Artellus Ltd, for RINGING THE CHANGES by Robert Aickman, © The Estate of Robert Aickman, 1964, first published in *Dark Entries* by Robert Aickman, Fontana, 1964.

The Executors of Lady Cynthia Asquith for THE CORNER SHOP by Cynthia Asquith, first published by Hutchinson, 1926.

A. L. Barker c/o Jennifer Kavanagh for THE WHIP HAND by A. L. Barker, © A. L. Barker, 1964.

A. P. Watt Ltd on behalf of Sheila Reeves for TRANSITION by Algernon Blackwood, first published in 1917.

Don Congdon Associates, Inc., for THE CROWD by Ray Bradbury, © 1943, renewed 1970 by Ray Bradbury.

The Peters Fraser & Dunlop Group Limited on behalf of Ann Bridge for THE BUICK SALOON by Ann Bridge, first published in *The Song in the House, Stories by Ann Bridge*, Chatto & Windus, 1936.

J. S. F. Burrage for SMEE by A. M. Burrage, from *Someone in the Room*, Jarrolds, 1931.

Chatto & Windus for THE JULY GHOST by A. S. Byatt, first published in *Sugar and Other Stories*, Chatto & Windus, 1987, © A. S. Byatt 1987.

Penguin Books for THE GHOST WHO VANISHED BY DEGREES by Robertson Davies, first published in *High Spirits: A Collection of Ghost Stories* by Robertson Davies, Penguin Books, 1982, © Robertson Davies 1982.

The Literary Trustees of Walter de la Mare and the Society of Authors as their representative for SEATON'S AUNT by Walter de la Mare. The text used is the definitive text reprinted from *Short Stories 1895–1926* published by Giles de la Mare Publishers Limited, 1996.

Curtis Brown Ltd, London, on behalf of the Estate of Lord Dunsany for AUTUMN CRICKET by Lord Dunsany.

Elizabeth Fancett for her story, THE GHOSTS OF CALAGOU, © Elizabeth Fancett 1991.

Hutchinson for THE SHEPHERD by Frederick Forsyth, Hutchinson 1975, © Frederick Forsyth 1975.

Mrs Joan N. Frazer for FLORINDA by Shamus Frazer, © Estate of Shamus Frazer.

David Higham Associates for A LITTLE PLACE OFF THE EDGWARE ROAD by Graham Greene, © Graham Greene 1954, first published in *Twenty-One Stories*, Heinemann, 1954.

The Society of Authors as the Literary Representative of the Estate of L. P. Hartley for SOMEONE IN THE LIFT by L. P. Hartley, first published in 1955, © Executors of the Estate of L. P. Hartley 1973.

Jonathan Cape for THREE MILES UP by Elizabeth Jane Howard, first published in *Mr Wrong* by Elizabeth Jane Howard, Cape, 1975, © Elizabeth Jane Howard 1975.

Edward Arnold Publishers Ltd for THE ASH TREE by M. R. James, © M. R. James 1931.

A. P. Watt on behalf of The National Trust for THE PHANTOM RICKSHAW by Rudyard Kipling, first published in *Wee Willie Winkie and Other Stories*, Macmillan, 1909.

David Higham Associates for THE TOWER by Marghanita Laski, from *The Third Ghost Book*, James Barrie, 1955.

David Higham Associates for BLACK DOG by Penelope Lively, first published in *Pack of Cards* by Penelope Lively, Heinemann, 1986, © Penelope Lively 1986.

Reed Books for THE HIGHBOY by Alison Lurie, first published in *She* magazine in 1990 and reprinted in *Women and Ghosts* by Alison Lurie, Heinemann, 1994, © Alison Lurie 1994.

Reed Books for THE TAIPAN by W. Somerset Maugham, from *The Complete Short Stories* by W. Somerset Maugham, published by Heinemann, 1951.

Penguin Books for the translation by Rosemary Edmonds of THE QUEEN OF SPADES by Alexander Pushkin. Translation © Rosemary Edmonds 1958, 1962, published in *The Queen of Spades and Other Stories*, Penguin Classics, 1962.

Penguin Books for I USED TO LIVE HERE ONCE by Jean Rhys from *Sleep It Off Lady: Stories by Jean Rhys*, Penguin Books, 1979, © Jean Rhys 1976.

A. M. Heath for POOR GIRL by Elizabeth Taylor,

© Estate of the late Elizabeth Taylor, from *The Third Ghost Book*, James Barrie, 1955.

Curtis Brown Group Ltd, London, for BLIND MAN'S BUFF by H. Russell Wakefield, from *Old Man's Beard* by H. Russell Wakefield, Geoffrey Bles, 1929, © H. R. Wakefield.

Elizabeth Walter for her story, DUAL CONTROL, © Elizabeth Walter 1975, from *Dead Woman*. First published by Collins Harvill Press, 1975.

Curtis Brown Group Ltd, London, for BREAKAGES by Fay Weldon, © Fay Weldon 1978, first published in *The Midnight Ghost Book* and reprinted in *Watching Me, Watching You* by Fay Weldon, Hodder & Stoughton, 1981.

Publishing details for the remaining stories are as follows:

A TOUGH TUSSLE by Ambrose Bierce was first published in a collection of stories by Ambrose Bierce, *In the Midst of Life* (Chatto & Windus, 1892).

THE TRUTH, THE WHOLE TRUTH AND NOTHING BUT THE TRUTH by Rhoda Broughton was first published in *Temple Bar* in February 1868 and reprinted in *Tales for Christmas Eve* (Bentley, 1873).

'TO LET' by B. M. Croker was first published in *London Society* (Christmas Number, 1890) and reprinted in *To Let* (Chatto & Windus, 1893).

AN APPARITION by Guy de Maupassant was first published in *Le Gaulois*, April 1883 and anthologised by Editions Monnier in 1883.

NO. 1 BRANCH LINE, THE SIGNALMAN by Charles Dickens was first published in Charles Dickens's magazine, *All the Year Round* (Christmas Number, 1866).

THE OLD NURSE'S STORY by Elizabeth Gaskell was written for the first special Christmas issue of *Household Words* (edited by Charles Dickens) in 1852.

THE GATEWAY OF THE MONSTER by William Hope Hodgson was first published in *The Idler* magazine, January 1910.

THE SHADOW OF A SHADE by Tom Hood was first published in *Frozen In, a series of stories related in a snow-storm* (*Bow Bells Annual*, Christmas, 1869).

THE OLD MAN by Holloway Horn was first published in *Great Short Stories of Detection, Mystery and Horror*, Victor Gollancz, 1931.

THE ROMANCE OF CERTAIN OLD CLOTHES by Henry James was first published in *Atlantic Monthly*, February 1868 and reprinted in *A Passionate Pilgrim and other tales* (Boston: James R. Osgood & Co., 1875).

SCHALKEN THE PAINTER by Joseph Sheridan Le Fanu was first published in *The Dublin University Magazine*, May 1839.

MAN-SIZE IN MARBLE by Edith Nesbit was first published in *Grim Tales* (Innes, 1893).

WILLIAM WILSON by Edgar Allan Poe was first published in *Burton's Gentleman's Magazine* in 1839.

THE QUEEN OF SPADES by Alexander Pushkin was first published in *The Queen of Spades and Other Stories* by Alexander Pushkin, 1834.

THE BODY-SNATCHER by Robert Louis Stevenson was first published in the *Pall Mall Magazine*, Christmas Number, 1884 and issued in book form by the Merriam Company (New York, 1895).

THE JUDGE'S HOUSE by Bram Stoker is from *Dracula's Guest* (Routledge & Sons, 1914).

THE CANTERVILLE GHOST by Oscar Wilde is from *Lord Arthur Savile's Crime and Other Stories*, 1891.

ANGELINE, OR THE HAUNTED HOUSE by Emile Zola was first published in the *London Star* in January 1899. Translation © Clive Smith 1983.

The publishers have made all possible efforts to trace copyright holders, but if any omissions have occurred please let us know.